C000072416

STAR CAT
THE FIRST TRILOGY

Star Cat: The First Trilogy

Written by Andrew Mackay

Edited by Ashley Rose Miller

Individual cover designs by Kveather

CHROMEVALLEYBOOKS.COM

ISBN: 9781791825928
Copyright © 2018 Chrome Valley Books

Chapters

Star Cat: Infinity Claws

Star Cat 2: Pink Symphony

Star Cat 3: War Mage

STAR CAT

BOOK ONE: INFINITY CLAWS

ANDREW MACKAY

STAR CAT

BOOK ONE: INFINITY CLAWS

Chapter 1

"Good morning, Tripp."

"Good morning, Manuel."

Tripp Healy sipped his cup of coffee and glanced at his reflection in the glass panel. He hadn't shaved for a couple of days. Tired and cranky, he felt twenty years older than he was, which would have made him sixty years-old. He certainly felt like a much older man today.

Personal hygiene wasn't the first thing on his mind this morning, however. He had an important call to make to his family.

The only thing stopping him from dashing to the N-Gage terminal in his quarters was the spectacular view of Earth. The two-day travel back home wouldn't be undertaken for another two months.

Tripp had been on the moon for two weeks. Fatigue and homesickness were setting in. He found his work was stressful and maddening. USARIC had made little progress since receiving what they called a "cry" from Saturn six years ago to the day.

"Patch me into N-Gage, Manuel," Tripp made his way to the seat at his terminal. "Let's get this done."

"Yes, of course."

Tripp sat in his chair and looked at the black screen. His five o'clock shadow didn't improve, no matter which reflective surface he saw himself in.

The screen fizzed and switched on.

"Would you like visual or audio interface, Tripp?"

Manuel's voice came from somewhere. The great unwashed would have sworn that they were hearing things. There were no speakers in the room. The screen itself, ultra-thin and flat, wasn't producing any audio.

"Both, please," Tripp made himself comfortable in his seat. "They're used to me looking like a dog's dinner."

"Most amusing, Tripp," came the dulcet response from thin air.

Tripp rolled his shoulders and ironed out the crick in his neck. He placed his cup of coffee on the desk and pressed his hands together, awaiting the call.

N-Gage
Healy Residence
Dialing...

A two-tone noise bubbled from the screen as a green loading panel stretched across the screen.

"Dialing now, Tripp."

"Thanks, Manuel."

Somebody answered the call and appeared on screen. A fingertip obscured a face and environs behind it.

"Tripp, sweetie?"

"Yes, it's me," he said, "Samantha? Move your finger, honey."

"Oh, sorry. The answer panel is in a weird place." She moved her finger away to reveal her face.

Much like her husband, she'd just woken up. Her hair was unwashed and the absence of makeup reminded Tripp of the girl he knew all-too-well.

"Hey."

"Hey, how's it going?"

"Wanna see something cool?"

Samantha smiled and looked off-camera for a nanosecond. "Sure."

Tripp waved his hand in front of the screen. It turned

forty-five degrees toward the window. Planet Earth loomed in the distance. A clear day back on the planet with only a smattering of clouds.

Samantha peered into the screen. The wonder of the view registered on her brow. "Wow, that's *amaziant*."

"Yes, if you look closer, you can see the outline of North America. Look."

He looked at the screen and aimed his finger along the border of Texas and Mexico.

"Oh, yes,' she said, "It's very pretty."

"Isn't it?"

"Rogan, quick," she beckoned someone from off-camera, "Come and see what Dad's showing us."

A five-year-old boy ran over to her and climbed onto her lap. "What is it?"

"Come and see the view from Daddy's bedroom on the moon."

Rogan's dropped when he realized what he was viewing. "Wow."

"*Incrediful*, isn't it?"

Tripp took the time to absorb his son's reaction. It was a face he longed to touch again. Those brilliantly blue eyes and angelic face.

"That's you, right there," Tripp held out his finger and traced the outline of land. "Wave to me."

Rogan opened his palm and waved.

His father returned the sentiment. Too far, of course, to see any detail. It was the thought that meant the world to both of them.

"You can't see me, Rogan, but I know you're there."

"When can I come with you to the moon, Daddy?"

"Maybe when you're older," Tripp traced the outline of his son's face. "I miss you and mum."

"We miss you, too. When are you coming back?"

"Soon. A couple weeks, I think."

Samantha looked over her shoulder. A black cat walked across the floor in the background.

"Hey, Spooky," Tripp said as she poked around the furniture and dug her claws into the carpet.

3

"No, don't do that," Samantha said, stomping her foot to the ground in an effort to curtail the damage the cat was doing to the carpet. "Bad girl."

Tripp chuckled to himself. "We need to get her a post or something."

'She's been behaving strangely,' Samantha returned to the screen and hugged her son. 'Ever since you left, she doesn't know what to do with herself.'

"That's very flattering," Tripp smirked. "I'm sure she'll figure something out."

"How's everything going up there?"

Tripp sighed and leaned back in his chair. He looked at his electric guitar leaning against his desk.

"Not great."

Samantha tried an encouraging smile. "You look like hell."

"I know, I've seen myself twice already today." He folded his arms and tucked his chin on his neck, feeling somewhat sorry for himself.

Tripp snapped his fingers. A holographic book, about five by eight inches big, appeared a few inches from his hand and flipped through its pages, "We're at a total loss. It's all utterly meaningless."

"Really?"

"Uh-huh. Opera Alpha is dead. Nothing, zip. Communication is completely cut off."

"Still nothing?"

"No."

"It's been two weeks, now."

Tripp looked out of the window. The planet spun slowly around, making its way out of view at the top of the window.

"The Saturn Cry transmission is ongoing."

"Saturn Cry…" The holographic tome slid through the air and nestled in Tripp's open palm.

"No, Manuel, I didn't mean—"

Manuel ignored the request and launched into its description. "—Saturn Cry is a perceived distress call from the planet of the same name—"

"—Manuel, I know what Saturn Cry is, please stop—"

"—IMS discovered the transmission in the year 2110," Manuel continued, flipping through his pages. He settled on a graphic of the ringed planet. The stars shuffled around in the background as the audio wave rumbled away. "Here is a sample of the transmission."

A hissing noise emitted, followed by what sounded like three chords of an electric guitar.

"Manuel, hush."

Samantha and Rogan couldn't make head nor tail of the noise as it played out.

"Weird, isn't it?" Tripp asked.

The noise continued. A striking 'whump' - like an excessive boom on a drum - shot through the screen.

Spooky the cat widened her eyes and shrieked. Samantha turned over her shoulder. "Bad girl."

She hissed and settled into the prone position. Ready to attack anything that came into her proximity.

"What's she doing?"

"I don't know," Samantha said, suddenly very nervous at their cat's behavior.

"Spooky," Rogan climbed off his mother's lap and walked over to the cat. "What are you doing?"

"Tilt the camera down, Samantha," Tripp said, putting two-plus-two together. "Is there anyone else there with you?"

"No," Samantha said, watching her son approach the cat. "It's just us."

"Nothing unusual happening in the room?"

"It's very unlike her,' she mused, turning back to the screen. "Rogan?"

"Yes, mummy?"

"Be careful with her."

Tripp watched the screen with great intent. Rogan approached Spooky, but felt as if he couldn't get too close. The cat was incredibly pent-up and ready to launch at someone - anyone.

"Wait, wait," Tripp looked up the ceiling and cleared his throat. "Manuel?"

"Yes, Tripp?"

"Play the message again, please."

Tripp looked at Manuel's page containing the image.

The transmission fired up again.

Static for the first two seconds.

The sound of an electric chord fired up.

And then - boom. A semi-pulsar throttle for two seconds.

Spooky shrieked once again, much to Samantha, Rogan, and Tripp's amazement.

"Her tail has gone bushy," Samantha provided a commentary as the signal continued to play. "She's upset."

"Keep an eye on her," Tripp pointed at the screen. "I'm curious to see something…"

The audio static dampened. The "chords" grew louder, followed by another thud.

Instead of shrieking, Spooky widened her eyes and let out a calm meow.

"What the…?" Samantha asked no-one in particular.

"Hey, Spooky," Rogan crouched and offered her his hand. "Give me a cuddle."

The cat turned to the hand and licked around its mouth. She thought over the opportunity for a hug for a few seconds.

The transmission static fizzed up once again, followed by a third and final "whump" - like that of a heartbeat.

Spooky jumped in the air and wailed, barely landing on her feet. The cat's violent reaction caused Rogan and his mother to yelp back in fright.

Tripp could barely believe his eyes. Spooky rolled over and returned to her feet. The poor animal was exhausted. She trundled over to her favorite area of the carpet and rolled around, quite satisfied with herself.

Rogan and Samantha turned back to the screen, not knowing what to say or think.

"My God," Tripp whispered to himself, focusing more on the family cat than his wife and son for the first time in his life, "What on Earth is going on with her?"

One Year Later…

Every major city in every country held trials to find

USARIC's one perfect feline specimen.

The United Kingdom hopped onto the opportunity much like all the other nations on planet Earth.

One such venue in northwest London's Chrome Valley was home to the company's *Star Cat* program. It wasn't the most attractive of venues. The CV Stadium was built in 2080 to house the valley's once-promising soccer team. Shortly after relegation from First Division, and with the introduction of an altered ball, CVFC was no longer sponsor-worthy.

As such, the stadium lost the majority of its funding. The knock-on effect was disastrous. The ground became decrepit and unusable. The vagrant issue was rife because it provided shelter from the intensely hot summers and deadening winters.

The CV Stadium has been home to Star Cat Trials for the past four months. Just one of six locations within London alone.

There were at least two hundred people in line, all waiting with their pet cats in carry cases.

A mother-and-son stood in line awaiting registration.

Five-year-old Jamie Anderson and his mother, Emily, approached the desk. She placed the plastic carriage on the counter.

The official looked up at Emily and smiled. 'Name?'

"Emily Anderson—"

"—No, I'm sorry, I mean the cat's name?"

"Oh," Emily said, looking through the plastic bars. An orange face poked around, wanting to be set free. "Jelly."

"Jelly?"

"Yes, Jelly Anderson."

"Okay," the official said, typing on her keyboard. She hit a button and the printer roared to life. "Jelly Anderson. Just peel off the back and attach it to the cage, if you would."

Emily took the strip of paper and examined it. The cat's name and a serial number adorned the front. She peeled the edge away and slapped the sticky end to the plastic top of the cage.

"Please go to the weigh-in, Mrs. Anderson."

"Mum?" Jamie asked as they entered a darkened causeway with many other families.

"Yes, poppet?"

"What happens if Jelly gets chosen?"

"I don't think that will happen," Emily looked at the space-themed walls, "There are so many people hoping that their cat will win."

"How many, mum?"

"I don't know. Like, maybe millions?"

"Wow, that's a lot."

"We'd stand more chance of winning the lottery than Jelly being picked."

Jamie walked alongside his pet in the cage. Due to his height - all four feet and one inch of it - he had a perfect view of Jelly rocking back and forth in her cage.

"It's okay, Jelly," Jamie smiled, "You'll be fine."

Jelly wasn't terribly happy at the prospect of being put up for selection. Of course, she was a domestic house cat. But that was the point.

A man walking in front of Emily and her son shot them a grin. "Seems really stupid, doesn't it?"

"Yeah, I know," Emily resigned herself to the fact that this whole endeavor was probably a bit silly.

"A complete waste of time. And space, probably."

Emily smiled and nodded at the man's cage. "What do you have?"

He lifted the cage and revealed his cat's face. "Abyssinian. Her name is Trixie."

"Aww, she's lovely."

"And yours?"

Jamie grabbed the cage and tried to lift it up. He barely managed it. "This is Jelly."

"Oh. Cute cat."

"Thanks," Jamie passed the cage back to his mother. "We don't think she'll win, though."

"Oh? Why not?"

"Because there are a million people all over the planet trying to win."

"It's a lot of money, though," the man said with a smile,

"And think of all the fame it will bring."

Jamie looked up at Emily. "Mum, what is fame?"

"It's when everyone knows who you are."

"Wow. So, like, if someone's cat wins, does that mean they will have lots of money and everyone will know them?"

"Yes, poppet."

The line shuffled forward.

Emily and Jamie could see the weigh-in facility a few meters in the distance. The sheer volume of participants obstructed the view.

Several giant TV screens hung on the walls. The footage of cats participating in the trials reminded everybody why they were there.

The Star Cat logo was typically futuristic, spinning around on its axis. Friendly music played over the screens as the logo disappeared. It was replaced by a bespectacled woman in a white suit standing in front of a black sky full of stars.

"Welcome to the Star Cat Trials, London Base Six. USARIC thanks you for taking the time to reach out to us and taking part in this historic event."

An illustration of a cat showed up on the screen. The woman pointed her stick at its body.

"In order to facilitate a smooth and painless process, we ask that you have your cat's documentation ready for the weigh-in. We would like to remind you of the following eligibility rules."

Emily nudged her son and pointed at the screen. "Jamie, poppet. Listen to the lady."

"Okay, mom."

"One, your cat must be female," the voice announced.

"Yes, she is," Jamie said.

"Two, she must be between three and five years of age."

"Yes," Jamie whispered to himself. "She's three-years-old."

"Three," continued the woman on the screen, "She must weigh between five and ten pounds."

Jamie jumped around, giddy with excitement. If he were playing solely by the entrance rules, Jelly would win instantly.

"Yes."

"Four. Your cat must not have any ailments, debilitations or injuries of any kind."

Emily couldn't resist smiling at her son's moment of joy. Jamie was beside himself with glee.

The overwhelming sense of victory was aided by dozens of people leaving the line with their pets.

"Imagine that," Emily muttered as she watched the disappointed men, women and families leave the venue. "Turning up and not knowing the rules? I mean, it's not as if the commercials didn't specify."

"Look at all the people leaving, mom," Jamie said.

Not everyone left, however. The line was still plenty healthy with people all desperate to get their pets into the trials proper.

Just behind the weigh-in counter a sliding door allowed the successful participants into the preparation chamber. From the tunnel, it was impossible to see what lay beyond that door.

It was like waiting in line to ride an extraordinary ghost train.

"Okay, next please," said the man by the scale pod.

Emily and Jamie stepped forward.

His little eyes lit up in full admiration of the ceramic plate. Two side vents blew the spent fur and detritus from the previous feline occupant into the air and into a nearby vacuum.

"Here she is," Emily placed the cage onto the panel and opened the gate.

"Thank you, madam," the scale man said and turned to his keyboard. "Name?"

"Jelly Anderson."

"Thank you," he punched the data into the computer. "Age?"

"Three years and one month," Emily took out a paper and handed it to the man.

"Thank you, one moment please."

Jamie stepped over to the cage and offered Jelly his hand. "Come on, Jelly. Let's get you weighed."

Jelly didn't want to come out. It wasn't until she saw her owner's smiling, cherub-like face, that she finally relented.

"Thanks, son," the scale man looked up from the terminal. "Just lead her onto the ceramic edges."

"Okay."

The man smirked, "She's very obedient. I'm sure that will help."

Jelly exited the cage and made her way onto the ceramic scales. A beautiful, dark orange house cat. Not a blemish.

Even the operator took a moment to look at Jelly's face. Her bright orange eyes were something of a wonder, and exceptionally unique.

"Cute cat," he said, double-taking and looking at Emily. "Can I have your address, telephone number, and status, please?"

As Emily gave her details, Jelly followed Jamie's hand as he moved it to the scales.

In USARIC's infinite wisdom, the two scales faced one another from opposite sides of the tunnel.

It meant that the cats on each scale had a perfect line of sight with each other. It felt combative way before the trials had even started.

A mother and father stood at the opposite scale with their young son.

The sweaty warmth in the tunnel didn't help matters much. Ventilation wasn't a top priority. The other family's cat seemed like it might not pass the weigh-in, looking as it did like a fat snowball with fur and two beady little eyes.

"Ugh, that's one ugly cat," Jamie whispered to himself and turned back to Jelly, "Hey, girl."

"Meow," she said, sitting perfectly still in the middle of the scale.

The four-digit panel above beamed to life and ran through a series of numbers as it adjusted itself to Jelly's weight.

"Okay, here we go," the scale man said, watching the numbers slow down to a crawl. The ceramic plate sunk a few millimeters and rested into position.

The panel lit up with the final score - 7.5 lbs - with a triumphant fanfare ringing around the device.

"Ta-daa," the man said, much to Emily and Jamie's excitement. "That's perfect."

A hefty buzzer sounded off from the adjacent end of the tunnel. The other family's flabby ball of fur failed its weigh-in, clocking in at nearly twice the weight of Jelly. The final result flashed in red above the scale.

"Sorry, son," the other scale operator said to the disappointed young lad who had burst into tears. "Maybe next time."

Jamie watched the boy launch into a tantrum. He stomped his foot to the ground and pointed at his furry blob of uselessness. "I hate you! I hate you! You're too fat, you stupid cat!"

"Hey," Jamie shouted from across the tunnel. "Don't call her that."

The boy turned to Jamie and scowled. "Shut up."

"Don't call your cat names. They know when you're being mean to them."

"I don't care," the boy ran off in a flood of tears, leaving his parents to persuade the fluffy ball of fur back into her cage.

Jamie turned back to Jelly to find her licking her paws as if she was the queen of the universe, "Come on, girl. Back in your little house."

Jamie ushered Jelly back into her cage. He'd seen scores of other families having to push their own cats backwards by the head.

Not with Jelly. Obediently, she gracefully obliged her owners and settled into the cage. Jamie took a moment to digest the wonder of his little feline friend.

She was a year younger than Jamie. They'd seen the world together. Grew up together. Eaten, lived, and laughed together.

The cage bolted shut.

"That's great, Mrs. Anderson," the scale operator held out his hand to the sliding screen on the far wall. "If you'd like to make your way into the preparation chamber, we can begin."

"Excuse me, sir?" Jamie asked.

"Yes, young man?"

"What happens in the preparation chamber?"

"Oh, it's nothing to worry about. It's where Jelly will get ready to participate in the events."

"Thank you," Emily picked up Jelly's cage and nodded Jamie out of the room. "Come on, poppet."

"Yes, mom."

The pair walked through the sliding doors and into the preparation chamber.

Chapter 2

"Welcome to the Preparation Chamber," came a soothing female voice as Emily and Jamie walked through the door. "Your allocated booth is marked on the slip attached to your cat's cage."

"What number are we, poppet?"

Jamie looked at the slip, "Eighteen, mom."

One hundred marked booths lined the walls in the vast space.

Quad One, to their immediate right, held booths one through twenty-four. Quad Two, twenty-five through forty-nine, and so on.

A technician dressed in a silver suit approached the pair. "Hello, there. Number?"

"Eighteen."

Jamie marveled at the set-up. The place was heaving with people of all shapes and sizes being greeted by technicians and making their way to the allocated booths.

The stench of cat was almost as tremendous as their wails for freedom.

Rattling cages.

The occasional hiss from one cat when it spotted another.

Jelly, however, remained calm and refined. It was almost as if she refused to bow down to her feline stereotype.

"Just through here, please." The technician walked the pair into the first Quadrant and put Jamie at ease. "So, exciting day today, huh?"

"Yes. My cat made it."

"What's her name?"

"Jelly."

"Oh, cool. After the movie?"

"Yes, *Star Jelly* is my favorite," Jamie said as the technician pushed a button on the wall. The door to booth eighteen slid open.

"Wow."

The individual preparation chambers measured twelve by ten feet. The bank sitting in the middle of the room contained a desk and a computer. It must have seemed vaguely threatening to the untrained eye.

It certainly caused consternation in the overactive mind of a five-year-old boy. Jamie had second thoughts about the place.

The technician clocked Jelly's name attached to her cage.

"*Jelly*?"

"Yes, mister."

"Funny name for a cat, isn't it?"

"She's named after my favorite film."

"Ah, *Star Jelly*?"

"Yes."

"Hmm," The technician pointed at the padded bank. Whatever was about to happen would at least be conducted in relative comfort for his cat.

Emily placed the cage on the surface and unclipped the plastic housing cage.

Jamie encouraged her out, "Come on, Jelly."

She wouldn't move.

"Not very obedient, is she?"

"She's a cat, mister."

"Come on, girl," Emily poked her face through the cage. "It's okay."

Jelly let out a whine, never tearing her gaze away from the computer and wires coming from the front compartment.

Emily lost her temper. "You're testing my patience, puss."

"Mom, wait. Let me try."

Jamie lowered his head and widened his eyes. Jelly tore her gaze away from the dreaded computer and stared at him.

"What's wrong, Jelly?"

Her pupils dilated and turned a stale yellow. She groaned and lowered her head.

"Jelly, girl. Gimme paw."

Jamie knew how to get the better of his feline friend. He held out the back of his hand with his fingers closed together.

It did the trick.

Jelly couldn't resist moving forward and head-butting his hand. It was enough for Jamie's hand to slide along her wonderfully silken coat and gently bring her out of the cage. "There we go."

Jelly plonked herself on the padded surface and wasted no time in checking out her surroundings.

Not much to see upon initial viewing; four walls, a bright fluorescent bulb on the ceiling and three humans smiling back at her.

The technician hit a button on the console. The screen jumped to life which, in turn, made Jelly jump back.

Three rows appeared on screen, each of them waiting for a connection to their subject.

The technician slid his hand under Jelly's stomach and brought her over to the wires, "We'll get her hooked up and see what's doing."

"Paw," Jamie held out his hand. Jelly looked at his palm and sniffed around.

She did as instructed. It was enough for the technician to attach the connected band around her wrist.

"Can you hold her for me, please?" the technician asked.

"Sure."

Jelly trundled into his Jamie's arms. The second she relaxed, she knew something was amiss.

"Meow," Jelly said, her body starting to vibrate.

The first row pinged to life, measuring her heart-rate.

Bip… bip… bip…

"Steady, steady," the technician looked at his transparent tablet and made a note on the screen. "That's good, a constant fifty-five BPM."

"What are you doing, mister?" Jamie asked, keeping Jelly pinned to the surface.

"We need to make sure Jelly, here, is fit for the trials. The good news is that her heartbeat is regular. I see she weighs seven and a half pounds, which is what we want."

A commotion came from outside the room.

Jamie, Emily, and the technician turned to look through the window in the door. They saw a man pacing around, running his hands through his hair. "Oh, no!"

"I'm sorry, sir," a female technician approached him, carrying an unconscious cat in her arms. "I can assure you, she'll be fine."

"What did you do?"

"She's allergic to the computer. I'm afraid we'll have to send her to the recovery room."

The technician followed the man away from the door to a crowd of petrified onlookers.

"Oh no," Jamie said. "What happened?"

"Allergies," the technician said, "Some participants have undiscovered allergies picked up by the computer. Some are allergic to the chip we need to install, so it's better we know now before we commit."

"I don't know what that means? A chip?"

"Look," the technician pointed to Jelly, who had a synthetic cap stretched around the top of her head. "See this?"

"Yes."

"Look at the screen."

An imprint of Jelly's brain glowed on screen in various colors. "This is Jelly's brain. No sign of any damage, which is good."

He pointed at the top of the image, "This is the frontal lobe, the part of the brain that acts as a sonar. Over here in the middle is the sleep center, which is slightly smaller than usual. The back of the brain is very active."

"What does that do?"

"Is Jelly protective of you and your house?"

"Yes, but we don't live in a house. We live in an apartment. She's always looking for things to fight with."

"Makes sense. This is the area of the brain that lets her fight and mark her territory."

The technician looked at Jelly. She screwed her face back at him, unhappy with the intrusion on her privacy.

"Well done, Jelly." The technician reached under the console and hit a button.

The screen went dead and slid up, revealing a metal cage. He pulled it forward and opened the door.

"What happens now?" Emily asked.

"Well, she's fit to take part in the trials."

The technician removed Jelly's cap and wristband. He covered her face with his palm and pushed her backwards.

"Hey," Jamie got defensive. "Don't do that."

"I need to get her into the box."

Jelly clawed back at the technician, having no choice but to walk backwards. "That's right, Jelly. In you go."

"Stop that," Jamie grabbed the man's arm, "She'll go in herself."

"Sorry, no. We can't take the risk," the technician placed his hand on the box to to prevent it from sliding back. "Look at her, she's already putting up a fight."

"That's because you're forcing her."

"Poppet, let the man do his thing."

"But—"

Jelly whined. A final attempt to claw the technician's hand as it left her face was thwarted when he shut the door.

A whirring noise from behind the screen started up. Behind it, a mini conveyor belt traveled backwards, much like a baggage delivery system at an airport.

"Bon voyage, and good luck," the technician said, waving at Jelly.

Jelly's disillusionment was matched by Jamie's.

She placed her paw on the glass door, begging for Jamie to reach out.

"Jelly…"

"Poppet, it's okay. She's perfectly safe."

"But, but…"

Jelly meowed as her cage rolled backwards along the belt and into the darkness.

"It's okay, Jamie," the technician said, "You'll see her out in the arena in about half an hour. She's perfectly safe, I can assure you."

Jamie wasn't convinced. For the first time in his young

life, his best friend had abandoned him.

Emily wasn't much consolation either, no matter how hard she rubbed her son's shoulder.

The technician took pity on the mother and son as the belt delivered Jelly to her destination and out of sight. "It's never a nice feeling. But I promise, Jamie, it will all be worth it."

The Manuel
Page 200, 456 - "Saturn Cry"

Let's look at a live feed of Saturn, our solar system's sixth planet, and its second-largest.

The images you can see are provided by something called a Star Drone. *It was sent to the ringed planet three years ago to discover what happened to a vessel named* Space Opera Alpha.

In the year 2110 the International Moon Station, *known in common parlance as* IMS, *received what could be readily described as a distress call from the ringed planet.*

The message itself reached the primary radio situated on the space station in just under an hour and a half.

The world's foremost linguisticians and authorities on communication could not make head nor tail, if you'll forgive the pun, of the message.

The communication itself lasted only thirty seconds. A mixture of sounds that the common human being would recognize as static, more often than not punctuated by the sound of three chords from an electric guitar.

One of Earth's most intelligent scientific minds, Pascal D'Souza *(2056 - 2111), studied the waveform.*

He spent three months listening to the recording on virtual repeat and came up with nothing.

Absolutely nothing.

The intense diet of listening to nothing other than Saturn Cry *affected his health in general. Whenever he spoke to his wife or child, a strange hum would fall out of his mouth instead of the words he intended to use.*

For example, saying 'Hello, honey. How was your day?' came out as the sound of a yet-to-be-opened bottle of soda releasing its gas, followed by a hiccup.

His wife grew increasingly fed up with her husband's insistence on listening to Saturn Cry. *Especially over and above sundry conversations about paying bills, securing a place at a top school for their child and how often she thought they should indulge in congress.*

One sunny day as (she prepared to wash the dishes) Pascal asked what was for dinner. At least, that's what he thought he had asked. In actuality, all he had done was clear his throat and say the word 'frog' in a sarcastic manner.

She turned around and thumped him across the head with her fist in frustration.

The result of this action caused the playback in Pascal's memory bank to slow down quite accidentally. It was at this time that D'Souza made what was to become a very important discovery.

Three distinct 'boom' sounds occurred throughout the message.

When played at regular speed, the 'booms' were indistinct. Slowed down by approximately fifteen percent, however, they became very noticeable indeed.

The discovery of the three 'bumps' was a revolutionary moment in humanity's comprehension of Saturn Cry.

Due to the marital upset the dishes were never washed that night…

USARIC

United States and Russian Intergalactic Confederation
Location: IMS International Moon Station
Date: 13th January, 2117
Committee Meeting #1029 / 12

The boardroom.

A cone-shaped table with twelve chairs surrounding it. In each chair, a man in a suit engaged in conversation with their neighbor.

USARIC's logo hologram spun around on the surface of the conference table.

"People, may I have your undivided attention, please?" asked the hologram. "Thank you."

The logo fizzed away to nothing as the men adjusted themselves in their seats.

One of them rose from his chair at the head of the table.

The deputy chief of USARIC stood awkwardly on account of his unsound leg. In his sixties, he spoke with a Russian-cum-Texan drawl.

His name appeared on the holographic console; Dimitri Vasilov.

Tripp Healy sat in the eighth chair dressed in his American Star Fleet uniform.

Dimitri cleared his throat and looked at Tripp.

"As you know, the Select Committee has concluded its deliberations. I've asked Commander Tripp Healy from the American Star Fleet here today to deliver their update on Opera Alpha. Tripp?"

"Thank you, Dimitri."

Tripp stood up and yanked on the sleeves of his combat jacket, "Can we call up Opera Alpha, please?"

"Yes, Commander."

A holoprint of Space Opera Alpha appeared several inches above the surface of the console. It spun around on its central axis very slowly, offering the board members every conceivable angle of its body.

"Forgive me for the summary, but I feel it's important to establish the findings of the select committee. As you know, in 2113, USARIC sent Opera Alpha to Saturn to try to discern the source of Saturn Cry."

A picture of a Japanese woman in her twenties appeared above the rotating ship.

"On board was captain Zillah Chin-Dunne and a manned crew of five. Also on board was a series two Androgyne unit, along with the autopilot computer, Manuel."

The holoprint of Zillah vanished. Tripp waved his hand to the left, enlarging the image of the vessel.

"A year later, Opera Alpha confirmed with USARIC Base that they'd reached Saturn's vicinity. Specifically, one of its moons named Enceladus. It was established that Enceladus was the source of the transmission. Approximately five days later, all communications were cut. Three years later, we are still without communicable channels to Opera Alpha. Saturn, or, more precisely, Enceladus, continues to "cry" and our primary radio satellites continue to receive the message."

Tripp splayed his fingers and enlarged the Enceladus holoprint.

"Excuse me, Tripp?" asked a board member.

"Yes?"

"What of Space Opera Alpha?"

"We don't know," Tripp snapped his fingers and called up a recorded video, "Since 2110 we've been at a loss in trying to decode the message. Space Opera Beta is in its tertiary phase and will launch next year."

Tripp pressed the play button on the holovideo. A picture of his son and wife appeared on the screen.

"Three weeks ago, however, I made something of a discovery. Before you watch it, I'd like you to bear in mind that USARIC's select committee has green-lit the proposal I am about to put forward to you."

Tripp lifted his palm, raising the sound.

The recorded video displayed Spooky, The Healy family's cat, sitting on Samantha's lap. Tripp's voice spoke to her from behind the camera.

"Honey, I'll play the message again."

"Okay," Samantha pressed her cheek on top of Spooky's head. "Shh, don't worry."

"Meow," Spooky licked her paw, enjoying her owner's warmth.

"Okay, do it."

A button click, launching the recording of Saturn Cry.

A hiss started, followed by an electric guitar chord.

Spooky turned to the monitor, trying to ascertain the source of the noise.

And then - *whump*.

Spooky launched out of Samantha's arms and landed on her lap, terrified. She let out a death-defying growl.

"Keep her still, honey," Tripp's voice came from behind the lens.

"I'm trying, Tripp," she grumbled, struggling to clutch the cat. "She's really hassled, right now. She wants me to let her go—"

"—No, don't let her go. Let the sound keep playing."

As the hiss died down and the "strumming" of the guitar loudened, a dog trundled into shot, wondering what was going on.

Whump. The second jolt within the message flew through the screen. Spooky meowed loudly and curled up in Samantha's arms.

"How is she now?" Tripp asked.

"She's purring."

"My God," Dimitri leaned into the recording, "Are you trying to tell us that the *cat* is responding to Saturn Cry?"

Tripp slammed his palm into the holographic recording, pausing it. A freeze-frame of the dog showed its silly face all confused.

"That's right. Interestingly, Sparky, our dog, isn't responding at all."

Dimitri turned to his superior, Maar Sheck, the CEO of USARIC.

"Tripp?" Maar placed his hands onto the edge of the console, "Are you trying to tell me that your cat can *read* the message?"

"No. I'm not saying that."

"So you're saying…" Maar tried before resigning to confusion, "What are you saying?"

"I'm saying the message is eliciting a response from my cat, and not my dog."

Maar folded his arms and shook his head, "Explain it to me like I'm a five-year-old."

"Keep watching."

Tripp resumed the video. The static crept over the guitar's strings and provided the final *boom* as the recording closed. Spooky's eyes bulged. She let out a long wail.

Tripp paused the video, "There are three distinct bumps in the audio. The first occurs at twelve seconds. It angers the cat. The second bump happens at exactly twenty seconds, which appears to makes her comfortable."

"And the third bump?" Maar asked.

"As you saw, it made her howl like a dog. It happens at the twenty-six second mark."

Maar pointed at the paused Sparky, "And the dog?"

24

"He didn't respond at all," Tripp shrugged his shoulders, "He may as well have been listening to Strauss. No reaction whatsoever."

"Have we tried other animals?" Dimitri asked.

"I'm glad you asked that because that was my first thought. Here's a selection of other animals we played the track to."

Up first, a recording of a parrot in a cage. The woman on screen angled the video to its cage.

"Who's a pretty boy, then?" said the parrot.

"Clarkey," the woman's voice came from behind the camera, "Listen carefully. My friend is going to play you a song."

"Play-a-song, play-a-song," Clarkey squawked.

The message began to play - *hisssss*.

Electric guitar chords.

WHUMP - twelfth second.

Clarkey bopped his head back and forth, largely unperturbed by the message.

"Clarkey?" the woman asked, "Do you like this song?"

"It's terrible-terrible-terrible."

A bearded man with spectacles looked into the lens and turned his device to the left.

Round two: A recording of a tank of exotic fish. A babbling brook coughed out bubbles around the dozens of goldfish swimming around it.

"Okay, is that good?" asked the man.

"Yeah," Tripp's voice came from behind the lens, "Make sure the speaker is right up against the glass."

"You got it."

"Okay, in three, two, one…"

Hisssss… the message fired up.

"Nothing's happening," the man peered into the fish tank, "They're just sort of swimming around."

"Of course they're swimming around," Tripp snapped. "They're fish. Be quiet a moment and let me listen."

The twelfth second struck - *boom*.

The sound wave hit the glass and sent a riptide across the water. The fish swam against the current, failing to react to the noise. They couldn't have been less interested.

The man looked into the camera. "Tripp, did you get what you need?"

"Ugh, forget it."

The third and final video.

Dimly-lit sneakers scurried along a gravel path.

"I could get in serious trouble for this, you know," a woman's voice whispered above the frantic movement into the tiger enclosure.

"Thanks for doing this, Shannon," Tripp's voice came from behind the lens.

She lifted the camera. A tiger enclosure bleached into view.

"A zoo?" Maar looked up from the screen, "You've got too much time on your hands, Tripp."

"You call process of elimination a waste of time?" Tripp asked, before realizing who he was dealing with. "Oh, of course. You're just the money man, you're not a scientist."

"Don't get insolent, Healy."

Tripp ignored his superior's remark and placed his index finger against his lips. "Shh. Watch."

"Don't shush me, Healy."

"Look," Tripp interjected, "If it didn't work with a dog or a fish or a bird, then the last natural course of action was to try it with a bigger cat."

"Oh, my," Dimitri opened his mouth in wonder as the recording played out..

Shannon focused her lens on the sleeping tiger. "Tripp?"

"Yes?"

"I'm not going in. I'm setting the player down behind the cage. It'll be plenty loud enough for her to hear it."

"And it's definitely a female?"

Shannon set the camera down on the stone ledge and focused the lens on the beast.

"Yes, this is Daisy. She's relatively sedentary, as you can see. Perfectly harmless."

"Okay, play the message when you're ready."

"Hang on," Shannon reached into her belt and pulled out a tiny black device. She flicked the switch, enabling an array of blue lasers to shoot out and form an audio wave in thin air. "I can't believe I'm doing this for you. I could lose my job."

"You always were one for adventure," Tripp joked.

She shot the lens a look of incredulity, "Oh, *har-har*. Remind me to wipe out all those dates we had before you joined NASA and ran off and married my sister."

"Shh. Keep your voice down and play the track."

Shannon giggled and hit the play button, "Okay, okay. Here we go."

The waveform sprang to life, rifling through the lines of the hiss.

Daisy didn't budge.

"Nothing's happening."

"I know," Tripp said, "Give it five more seconds."

Guitar chord…. Nine, ten, eleven, and…

Whump.

Daisy continued to sleep. No reaction whatsoever.

"Shannon?"

"Yes?"

"Can we wake her up? She might not be able to hear."

"She's alert, even when she's asleep."

The twentieth second rolled round in time for the second *boom.*

Still nothing.

The audio wave's visual *bump* representation slid off to the left and out of their lives forever.

The holovideo paused on Daisy the tiger.

The board members - and Dimitri and Maar - turned to Tripp for an explanation.

"So, this is the result. The message only gets a response from cats. Specifically, domesticated female house cats. We played the message to males and they didn't respond."

"Did you try any other lifeforms?" Maar asked.

"The investigation was, and still is, under embargo as per the Infinity Clause. Subsection twelve-point-eight, subsection three. If it wasn't for that, I could have outsourced."

"I've heard enough, Tripp," Maar walked around the console and waved his hand across the image.

It rolled several thousand frames back to the start of the video, ending with a freeze-frame of Spooky's confused face.

Maar addressed the board members, none-too-happy about the decision he was about to make.

"People of the board. USARIC finds itself in a rather invidious position. At once, we have a missing vessel with five of USARIC's souls on board. Their whereabouts and state of wellbeing is unknown. We must presume they have expired. Dimitri?"

The board members looked to Dimitri in solemnity. He stood up and address the members around the cone-shaped spacecraft above the table.

"It strikes me that Tripp, here, has made a worthwhile discovery. The 2085 Bering Treaty stipulates that major advances be kept under embargo until such time as they are established as fact. Since we cannot establish any facts - about the well-being of Space Opera Alpha, the nature of the Saturn Cry or, indeed, if this cat *revelation* is a hoax - it must remain embargoed."

Tripp pressed his hands together, hoping to convince his superiors, "Am I right in thinking if the board votes unanimously twelve-to-one in favor of a decision, it will pass?"

"Correct."

Tripp turned to the twelve board members, "People, you have seen the evidence presented before you. It sounds as laughable as it is silly, I grant you, but the *fact* remains that USARIC and its scientists and crew are stuck. Opera Beta is due to launch next year, 2118."

Tripp clicked his fingers.

An imprint of Opera Beta appeared above the table. A brilliant-white, cone-shaped space vessel with a revolving cylindrical midsection.

"I am the commander for this upcoming mission to Enceladus. We need answers. Not only to what happened to Opera Alpha, but also to the meaning of Saturn Cry. The question is, can you, in good conscience, send me and my crew up there *knowing* that we failed to thoroughly scrutinize the opportunities present in my findings?"

The board muttered amongst themselves. Maar stepped forward with a great deal of sincerity.

"Be careful what you wish for, Tripp."

"I know what I'm doing."

The board members reached a conclusion quicker than Tripp was able to ask.

"Board members, I ask your permission for a temporary lift of Infinity Clause twelve-point-eight, subsection three. Ergo, you afford USARIC the opportunity to pursue this feline line of inquiry with regard to Saturn Cry. To make it public and, if the research should produce results, find the most suitable subject to join the Opera Beta crew and assist them in deciphering the code."

All twelve board members raised their hands, much to Dimitri and Maar's astonishment.

Tripp breathed a sigh of relief. The board voted unanimously to kick-start the search for the first cat in space. A historic moment.

"Quite amaziant, Healy," Dimitri chuckled, "You're good."

"I know."

Chapter 3

Do you own a cat?

If so, USARIC needs your help.

We are on the hunt to find the most suitable domesticated feline for the first ever cross-species manned flight into space.

Hundreds of thousands of participants are signing up their pets to USARIC's Star Cat Project.

The selected candidate will receive a lifetime of fully comprehensive insurance. Her owners will be awarded two-hundred-and-fifty-thousand dollars.

The entry criteria is simple and subject to official verification:

1: Your cat must be female.

2: She must be unsterilized and free from ailments.

3: Aged between three and five years.

4: Weigh between five and ten pounds.

Could your cat be the first in space? If she conforms to the entry criteria, and you wish to take part in this ground-breaking advancement in space exploration, please visit StarCatProject on all Individimedia channels and enter your pet today.

USARIC. The prowl is on.

CV Stadium (United Kingdom) - Presently...

Jamie watched the commercial on the one-thousand-foot screen that hung on the north-side of the arena. It resembled a proper sports stadium; about the size of a regular football pitch.

The logo for the Star Cat Project contained a furry paw with shiny metal claws encased on a titanium circle. The image revolved to cheers from at least fifty-thousand audience members.

Jamie and Emily sat in the participant gallery, surface level to the events that were about to play out on the pitch.

The commotion from the audience forced Jamie to raise his voice.

"Mom?"

"Yes, poppet?"

"What happens now?"

Emily pointed to a bank of metal cages being hauled to the west side of the arena.

"See that?"

"Yes. What is it?"

"The numbers go from one to fifty. Jelly is in paddock eighteen. They're going to race."

Jamie leaned forward onto the back of a little girl's chair. Her blonde hair folded over the back and got trapped under his arm.

"Hey!"

"Oh, sorry," Jamie lifted his arms, "I didn't mean to do that."

She brushed her shoulder and smiled at him, "That's okay."

Jamie screwed his face and mustered up the courage to break the ice, "Is your cat taking part?"

"Yes."

"What's her name?"

"Cindee," the girl said. "She's number forty-four."

"My name is Jamie. What's your name?"

"Fiorina. Nice to meet you, Jamie," she took his hand and yanked it up and down. Clearly, Jamie had never shaken anyone's hand until now. In fact, neither had she. Both had seen adults do it a lot, recently, and it made them feel like a bit older than they were.

Fiorina's mother smiled at Jamie. He returned the sentiment and leaned back in his chair.

"My cat's name is Jelly, and she's going to win."

"Oh yeah?" Fiorina asked. "Like Star Jelly?"

"Yeah," Jamie revealed, confidently, "She's always running up trees and stuff."

"Cindee does that, too," Fiorina chuckled to herself, "We'll see who wins."

Dramatic music rocketed out of the arena speakers as the lights dipped down. The commotion from the audience died down with it.

The arena's mega-screen flickered, propelling a holographic title into the middle of the grounds.

"Welcome, people, to the Chrome Valley CV Arena. Please remain seated and ensure all Individimedia and Outernet devices are switched off."

Emily looked at Jamie, "Show me your arm, poppet—"

"—but, Mom, I switched it off, already."

"Just do it, please."

Jamie rolled up his shirt sleeve and presented his wrist to his mother. The black imprint stretched across his skin like a moving Rorschach inkblot. The square closed in on itself and formed a straight line from his wrist to the crook of his elbow.

"See?"

"Good. The last thing we want is to get disqualified because you didn't turn it off."

"I know, Mom."

A spotlight shone on the banks of paddocks on the stage. Seconds later, fifty white lines shot up the width of the arena from the paddock gates to the east wall.

Another light snapped on to the end-point. Each end of the fifty rows illuminated to reveal a five-inch-high bank containing five holes. That was about all the audience could see from this distance.

"Attention people," the female voice announced from behind the mega screen, "USARIC is committed to the safety and the wellbeing of all the contenders. We ask that you remain seated at all times during the trials. Any attempts to interact with the contenders will result in immediate disqualification."

A soundtrack began to play as the white running lines lit up. "People, welcome to the Star Cat Project, and the Star Cat Trials, London. Now, please welcome your host... Gunnar

Kane."

The audience erupted with excitement as Gunnar, a smartly dressed man with bright white teeth, sprinted in front of the track and held out his arms. He gripped his headset and pointed and winked at random people in the audience.

"Wow, thank you for that wonderful app-paws!" he said in his thick, southern-American accent.

The crowd laughed at the joke as Gunnar stepped back and pointed at the paddocks.

"We truly have the cream of the crop with us today. Fifty of London's premiere contenders. Give it up for the felines, would you?"

The crowd burst into applause once again.

The cats in the paddocks rattled the bars. Some with their paws, others with their noses. They didn't look especially happy to be cooped up in the cages.

Jelly didn't move very much. She dug her claws into the fabric surface and licked her lips, itching for the bars to open up.

"Let's begin." Gunnar joined a panel of three judges at a desk near the participants' seating block. "Round one…"

Round One
- Agility -

The title of the activity appeared on the mega-screen showing various clips of cats running and jumping around.

"Agility. In this first round, whichever contender reaches the end of the one-hundred meter track and hits the button on the floor wins. The first three will then proceed to the next round."

"Mom, look," Jamie pointed at the eighteenth paddock, "There she is."

Jelly pressed her nose through the bars and sniffed around. Jamie and Emily could just about make her out from their seats.

"This will be interesting," Emily said. "Come on, Jelly. Don't screw this up."

Jamie shuffled in his seat and pressed his palms together.

"Come on, Jelly."

"Here we go," Gunnar announced through his headset, "In three... two... one..."

The music ground to a halt as the audience held their breath in anticipation. Gunnar waved his hand down, signaling the start of the activity.

"Go!"

The paddock cages flew open and released the animals.

Ten of the cats, including Jelly, jumped out.

The others whined and either nestled down for comfort or tried to attack the opened bars.

"Okay, that's ten, eleven, fifteen and eighteen out of the paddock, followed by twenty-two, twenty-five and forty-two and forty-four," Gunnar commentated over the proceedings, "Not much in it between them as they wander around."

Jelly stepped forward and poked around the white line. A spark ignited, forcing her back into her lane.

"No, they're hurting her!" Jamie jumped to his feet, "There's electricity keeping them in line."

"What?"

Jelly shook her head and turned to the east side. The white lines flickered and trailed along the width of her path, promising salvation one hundred meters away.

"Go on, Jelly!" Jamie shouted over the crowd as he watched his cat trundle along the path, "Yes, yes."

Fiorina climbed to her feet and threw her arms in the air, "Come on, Cindee. Run."

The white cat in lane forty-four made eyes at Jelly in lane eighteen and hissed.

Jelly stood her ground and flicked her tail, "Meow."

"I think our contestants need a little encouragement, guys," Gunnar said to the audience, "How about it?"

The crowd cheered with excitement.

Just then, the cat in lane twenty-two, a slinky silver-furred beast, figured out what she was supposed to be doing. She leaned back on her haunches and propelled forward.

"Jelly," Jamie screamed at Jelly, "Run, run."

Gunnar hit a button on the console. A holograph of a mouse snapped into each of the fifty lanes. The image shot along the path and caught the cats' attention.

Jelly meowed and bolted after the rodent.

"Yes, go. Go," Jamie clapped his hands, keeping an eye on lane forty-four.

Cindee chased after her holographic mouse, keeping up with Jelly's speed.

The silver pet in lane twenty-two gained on Cindee and Jelly as they raced forward.

"Here we go," Gunnar said. "It seems it's between eighteen, twenty-two, and forty-four."

The holographic mouse whizzed toward the east end of the arena, with Jelly, Cindee and the nameless silver cat in hot pursuit.

"Cindee's going to win," Fiorina jumped in her shoes with astonishment, "Go, Cindee."

"No, she's not," Jamie barked at his new friend, "Jelly's gonna smash her."

The mega-screen displayed a top-down view of the racing track. Cindee's paws pushed out a few inches in front of Jelly.

The silver cat shot in between the pair and launched into the air, trying to take a swipe at the mouse.

It was enough to catapult the shiny ball of fluff through the holograph and ahead by several lengths.

Jelly sped up and ran through her holographic mouse. Her fur sparked and stood on end, "Meeoow."

"Eighteen is leading by a nose to twenty-two in second and, finally, forty-four in third," Gunnar announced to the audience. "Only twenty meters to go."

Cindee gained on the pair and deliberately jumped to the left, knowing that the white line might zap her and send her to the head of the pack.

It did.

Cindee's shoulder connected with the invisible barrier and spun her around in mid-air, throwing her to her paws, aiding her travel.

She blasted through her holographic mouse, sending a shower of orange sparks forward as she passed the finish line.

She slammed her paws on the button surface and tumbled

over three times.

A giant gong sounded off as the mega screen burst to life, revealing that lane forty-four had won.

"We have a winner," Gunnar watched the silver cat storm into second position.

Jelly screeched to a halt in third place and tumbled over the button on the ground...

Round One

Agility Results
1st place: Cindee (The Family Beamish)
2nd Place: Bullet (The Family Cotter)
3rd Place: Jelly (The Family Anderson)

Three cat handlers approached the winners of the race and ushered each of them into a mobile cage.

"Aww, man," Jamie stomped on the ground and folded his arms in a huff.

"Calm down, poppet," Emily pushed him back to his seat, "Cindee won that one, fair and square."

"It's not fair."

Fiorina clapped her hands together amid the onslaught of adulation from the crowd behind them, "Yes, yes, yes..."

"That's not fair," Jamie thumped the girl on her shoulder, "Your cat cheated."

"She did not."

"Yes, she did. She used the electric barrier to speed her up."

"So? That's allowed, you know," the girl spun around and threatened to smack Jamie, "Your stupid orange cat is just too fat and slow."

"Don't say that about Jelly."

"Hey, hey. Stop this *lessense*, please," Fiorina's mother broke the two children apart with her hands, "Play nice, or don't play at all."

"She was the one talking *lessense*," Jamie said with complete superiority, "Silly cheater."

"I never cheated. You're just a bad loser."

"I'm sorry about this, Mrs Beamish," Emily clutched her

son's arm and forced him back to his seat. "Jamie's just a bit upset about the result."

"That's fine, but I'd appreciate it if your son wouldn't hit my daughter."

Fiorina scowled at Jamie. She stuck her tongue out at the boy and sat back into her seat.

"Idiot," Jamie muttered a little too loudly.

"Shut up, ugly."

Round Two
- *Prowess* -

"And then there were three," Gunnar stepped back. The white panels slid across to the middle of the arena.

"Round two will measure our three contenders ability to think, consider and operate to the best of their intelligence. Welcome to... Prowess."

The title of the game fizzed to life on the mega-screen. It displayed footage of a variety of pets pushing objects around a gleaming surface.

A female voice provided a narration to the game, "It could be pure intelligence. Of course, it could be luck. Prowess contains four holes on the white panel. It's just a matter of who completes the activity first."

Four shapes lined the panels.

1 - Square

2 - Circle

3 - Star

4 - Crescent

The plastic blocks lay several inches ahead of the slots. Their arrangement, however, did not naturally correspond to the correct hole.

"Which of the three finalists can conquer Prowess first - and quickest?" asked the female announcer as the footage faded to black.

Gunnar stepped forward and held out his palm to the activity center in the middle of the arena.

The mega-screen displayed the three finalists in their cages, ready to hop out and do... something, at least.

"Here we go," he said. "Handlers, please release our contestants."

The handlers popped open the cages and offered the three cats out and onto the podium in front of the activity.

Jelly trundled out, quite the happy cat. Obediently, she sat on the padded surface, somewhat distracted by the four toys in front of her.

After some coaxing, Cindee exited the cage and followed her tail around three times before settling down.

Still to come out of her cage was Bullet.

"Come on," her handler said. "Bullet, let's go."

"She's not very quick, is she?" Fiorina grew impatient and crossed her legs on her seat, "Whose cat is that, anyway?"

"I don't know," Jamie looked around for the owner, "They must be here, someplace."

"She's my cat," said a bearded, pasty-faced man his fifties. Jamie looked to his right to find he the man sitting all on his own.

"Her name is Bullet?"

"Yes."

"Not very quick, is she?"

"She's usually pretty good at obeying orders," he said, worried at Bullet's refusal to exit the cage.

"Are you here all on your own, mister?"

The man looked down and rubbed his knees through his jeans. "Yes. It's just me and her."

"Why did you put Bullet in the contest?"

"Poppet, leave the man alone."

He turned to Emily and tried for a smile, "No, it's okay. It's quite simple, really. I need the money."

"Yeah," Emily giggled, "Don't we all?"

"But what if Bullet wins the trials?" Jamie asked, quite forthrightly. "You would be all on your own?"

"I could get a new cat with the money, though," the man said.

A curious response for a five-year-old to fully comprehend. Jamie thought the man's response over for what felt like an eternity.

The idea of selling your best friend to make a quick buck

gave Jamie the chills, "How could you do that?"

"Quite easily," the man said. "It's not as if I'd never see her again. Life would be better for both of us if she won. And you know something, young man?"

"No, what?"

"She will win," he chuckled and punched his knuckles together.

"No, she won't. She's no match for Jelly."

"We'll see about that."

Bullet's handler had little choice but to hoist her forward under the arms. He plonked the silver cat onto her podium and shut the cage door.

"Oh dear," Gunnar said, his image displayed on the megascreen, "I think the judges may knock off a few points for Bullet's refusal to take part."

The audience booed and rumbled the ground with their feet. Bullet's owner folded his arms and sat back into his seat, "Okay, now that is unfair."

Jelly appeared on the giant screen, looking directly at the audience, "Mom, look."

"Yes, it's her," Emily looked at her cat's face and smiled, "Isn't she gorgeous?"

"You can do this, Jelly," Jamie whispered. "Just put the right block in the hole."

The stadium spotlights twisted around and shone onto the three feline participants, causing the audience to tense up.

"Okay, here we go…" Gunnar announced. "In… three… two… one…"

"Come on, Cindee!" Fiorina muttered loudly enough for Jamie to hear.

"… and, go," Gunnar finished.

Jelly sniffed around the first star-shaped plastic block hoping it wouldn't pounce back.

Satisfied that the block wasn't the enemy, she rubbed the side of her face along its top and knocked it onto its side.

"No, Jelly," Jamie gasped. "What are you doing? Don't play with it, you silly girl."

Cindee extended her paw at the square block and tapped it three times in a row. She growled and flicked it onto its side.

"Yes," Fiorina beamed with glee, "Do it."

Cindee knocked the square into the correct hole, enabling a buzzer to sound off around the arena. The square hole lit up, indicating that it had been solved.

A strange, continual hissing noise played through the speakers. The three cats looked up in confusion.

"That was just lucky," Jamie said to Fiorina, keeping an eye on Jelly.

Bullet, on the other hand, found the crescent shape utterly fascinating. She pawed the top, forcing it to rock back and forth along its curve.

Cindee turned to Bullet and hissed at her. Bullet hissed back and smashed the crescent with her left paw as hard as she could.

The plastic toy rolled off the deck and hit the floor a few feet below them.

Another buzzer sounded off, followed by a red spotlight shining over Bullet's crescent-shaped hole.

"Oh, the judges won't like that," Gunnar narrated

Jelly scanned the four pieces of plastic and then looked down at the four holes, "Meow."

Jamie shuffled in his seat, trying to transmit good vibes. "Come on, Jelly. Do it."

She lifted her paw and felt around the circular hole and sniffed around at it.

"Don't just sit there being stupid," Jamie said. "Put the thing in the thing."

Cindee turned to Jelly and murmured. Jelly ignored her and flicked her tail around. She reached forward with both paws, grabbed the circular piece of plastic and threw it into the hole.

Another buzzer shot around the arena, followed by a white spotlight on the completed unit.

"Ooo, now we're neck-and-neck," Gunnar said. "It's amaziant. An intense test of paw-eye coordination."

The hiss through the speakers grew louder and louder, putting the three cats off their game.

And then, twelve seconds into the noise, the whump sound occurred.

Jelly, Cindee, and Bullet jumped into the air, startled.

The crowd let out a collective "Oooooh" as the cats returned to their podium, full of anxiety.

"What was that noise, Mom?"

"I don't know, poppet."

Judging by the look on Gunnar's face, he knew precisely what was going on.

The great unwashed public knew nothing of Saturn Cry. The heats would be a test of the unwashed and their response to it.

Typically, the humans just found it confusing. Perhaps a glitch in the arena's sound system?

The three cats, however, felt that something antagonistic was abound.

Pent-up with anxiety, Bullet accidentally knocked the square off the activity desk, sending it crashing to the ground below. She let out an angry whine and bristled her tail, ready to attack something.

"Bullet, no," the man next to Jamie said. "Don't do it."

"Shh," Fiorina said over her shoulder as she turned back to watch the event.

Bullet dug her claws into the fabric of the podium seat, and poised to move.

"What's she doing?" Fiorina asked herself, watching Bullet turn forty-five degrees to face Cindee, "She's not playing."

Cindee knocked the next shape into the correct hole and reward herself by laying down and licking her paws. It afforded her a perfect view of Bullet, who prepared to launch at her.

The two cats snarled at each other.

Cindee hopped back to her feet and crouched down, her internal alarm sounding off.

Bullet sprang from her podium and pounced onto Cindee, paws-first.

Cindee wailed and smacked Bullet across the face with her claws.

"Hey, wait, wait," Gunnar said. "This isn't on."

Bullet fought back and dug her claws into Cindee's stomach, pushing her onto her back.

The two tussled and tried to tear into each other.

Jelly watched the tussle between her two rivals and accidentally knocked her circular plastic toy into the correct hole. The action took her by surprise.

Cindee and Bullet went at it, screeching and wailing, tumbling back and forth. The remainder of Cindee's blocks flew off the activity bench.

"Someone stop them!" Emily stood up and shouted at the arena floor, "This is crazy."

The handlers moved forward very cautiously, not wanting to alert the two feuding cats.

Then, twenty-seconds into the hissing, another whump blasted through the speakers.

Cindy and Bullet rolled away from each other and began to purr.

Jelly did the same and returned to sniff her blocks.

Bullet rolled around and stood upright, rubbing Cindee's face with hers.

"Why are they behaving like this?" She scanned the ceiling of the arena, "And what's that stupid noise?"

"I don't know." Jamie saw Cindee poke her nose around Bullet's behind. She leapt from Cindee's podium and back to her own.

Jelly knocked her fourth and final piece, the crescent, into the slot by accident.

The entire console lit up, followed by a shower of orange sparks.

"I think we have a winner," Gunnar pointed at the first podium, "Jelly Anderson."

The crowd cheered as they watched Jelly's face appear on the mega-screen.

"Wow!" Jamie said and clutched Emily's arm, "Mom, Jelly won."

"I know." Emily wasn't as over-the-moon as her son, though. The hissing noise swam around the arena walls, making her uneasy. "I don't quite believe it."

Jelly walked around the podium and displayed her tail to the audience. It was as if she knew she'd won something.

Twenty-six seconds into the noise, another whump sounded off. Jelly looked up and screamed at the ceiling.

Cindee and Bullet turned to each other, angrily, ready for war once again.

"No, no, no," Gunnar said to the two cats, "Not again."

Cindee and Bullet propelled themselves forward and jumped into the air.

Their bodies collided in mid-air. They squealed as they swiped at each other and landed onto Jelly's activity desk.

Jelly backed up and watched the two tear themselves apart.

"No. Cindee!" Fiorina stood up and begged the handlers to intervene. They were too far away to hear her, "Please make them stop!"

Jelly trundled around the fighting duo and analyzed the situation. She waited for an opportune moment to strike.

She sat up straight and meowed at the top of her lungs. Cindee and Bullet turned to the side and shot Jelly a look of confusion.

Jelly ran her tongue over her teeth and let out a very low howl.

Bullet pushed Cindee away and jumped back to her feet. Cindee rolled around and sat on the corner of the console.

Jelly growled once again, telling the pair off. At least, that's what it looked like on the giant screen. Two disobedient and unruly pets brought to task by their victor.

"The judges' decision is in," Gunnar said to the audience, "The winner is… Jelly Anderson."

The crowd exploded with delight.

Fiorina burst into tears.

"That's not fair," she turned to Bullet's owner sitting in the row behind her. "Your cat ruined Cindee's chances."

"It wasn't my fault," the man tried not to get upset at

Bullet's strange behavior.

"Hey, stop it," Jamie said to the pair. He turned his attention to the inconsolable girl in front of him, "Please don't cry."

"Cindee lost," she snorted through her tears and pointed at the screen, "Jelly won. It's not fair."

"Yeah." Jamie looked at Jelly's face on the screen. She had won, and there was no doubt that she knew.

Her vital statistics appeared on the screen.

Gunnar approached Jelly and lifted her into his arms, "Jelly Anderson, you're through to the finals. Next month, at Cape Claudius."

Jamie and Emily should have joined the elation coming from the audience in the arena, but they were more concerned about Jelly's response to the fight.

And what the future now held for her.

Chapter 4

Emily and Jamie sat in first class on their transatlantic flight. It was an experience neither of them could have foreseen happening in their lifetimes.

Citizens of the United Kingdom rarely, if ever, were in receipt of such luxuries. Much like the rest of the confederate states of Europe.

Jamie remembered his father telling him about their ancestors being able to travel freely from country to country. Many made it a hobby. Jamie's great-great-grandfather boasted about his conquests at the turn of the twenty-first century. He'd managed to travel the world with relative freedom and blow all his wealth on alcohol and women.

And it was just as well, too.

If he hadn't have been so reckless with money, he wouldn't have met his future wife who would go on to give birth to Jamie's grandfather.

Now, with much of planet Earth's natural resources close to nothing, and with the weather's increasingly erratic temperament, commercial airliners operated one or two flights a week.

Oh, how wonderful it must have been to be alive at the turn of the twenty-first century, Jamie wondered. But this lucky little boy would be the only one among his friends to have ever flown amongst the clouds and visit another country outside of what used to be known as Europe.

Sure, he'd seen America before in virtual reality. But nothing could compare to actually going there.

Jelly Anderson had won the UK heats in the Star Cat Trials. They were on their way to Cape Claudius in South

Texas for the international finals in two days' time.

Jelly wasn't able to enjoy the flight's first class luxuries that USARIC had laid on for her owners. She was ensconced in the fuselage along with all the other animals.

The standard six month quarantine had been expedited to just six days for Jelly Anderson.

"Mom?"

"Yes, poppet?" Emily asked, enjoying the comfort of her reclining first class seat and took a sip from her umpteenth flute of champagne.

"What happens if Jelly wins?"

"Wins the Star Cat Trials?"

"Yes."

"They'll send her into space."

"But, why?"

"They won't tell us why. I think USARIC just want to be the first to put a cat in space."

Jamie mulled over his mother's response, "But why would you want to be a cat in space, mom?"

"I really don't know, poppet. But they pay a lot of money," Emily took a mouthful of champagne and swished it around her mouth, "And, anyway, Jelly will be perfectly safe. They've been sending people to the moon and other planets for over a hundred years, now."

"Yes, but they are all human people."

"Exactly. So a little cat shouldn't be too much of a problem, right?"

"Hmm."

Jamie turned to his right and looked out of his window. The clouds drifted slowly under the curvature of what seemed like the end of the planet. Looking up, he could make out the edge of the dark, bleakness of space that hung above.

"Mom?"

Emily sighed and pressed the side of her face against her headrest, trying to relax. She closed her eyes, "Yes, poppet. What is it?"

"Space is really high in the sky, isn't it?"

Jamie looked past his reflection in the window and

pressed his nose against the glass. His mother didn't answer.

"It's like, *really* high…"

He turned around for a response, only to find his mother had fallen asleep in something of a drunken stupor…

USARIC's *The One* Arena
Cape Claudius
South Texas: South-eastern Peninsula
(One hundred miles north of Corpus Christi)

"You join us here at Cape Claudius on a bright and sunny day for what should prove to be the mother of all finals…"

The news reporter, a feisty young lady named Dreenagh Remix, stood in front of thousands of people lined up at the entrance to *The One* arena.

A road split the crowd in two sections, barricaded by signage advertising the Star Cat Trials - a black canvas with a silhouette of a cat looking up at the stars.

Heavily armed guards adorned the entrance to the arena. Flashing lights from various personal handsets took pictures.

Fans of the show took selfies. They tried to catch Dreenagh's attention as she reported to the floating camera drone in front of her.

"As you can see, the event has drawn quite an impressive crowd. Indivimedia has gone off the charts," Dreenagh inspected her forearm. The black ink-like substance showed on screen, spinning numbers around at a furious rate, "It seems half the planet's population is tuning in to see just who will win today's spectacular event. Over to the data-glaze now for the odds-on favorites here, today, at Cape Claudius."

The screen flashed and buzzed, revealing the betting odds for the finalists.

Soozie Q-Two (USA) - 20/1
J. Anderson (UK) - 12/1
Bisoubisou (Russia) - 6/1
(all other contestants 25/1 bar)

A black limousine pulled up along the road to a deafening

chorus of approval from the insatiable crowd.

Dreenagh approached a little girl cheering behind the railings. She held her wrist to the girl's face, "Hey, there, do you mind if I ask you a few questions?"

"Yes, it's okay," the girl said, keeping her attention on the limousine.

"Who's your favorite to win the finals today?" Dreenagh asked over the roars from the crowd.

"I like Bisoubisou, the Russian Blue cat," the girl said, pulling out her personal handset. She enlarged a picture of a particularly striking gray face and whiskers. The cat's yellow eyes perfected the determined look, "She's got the agility and fight in her. I think she'll beat everyone else."

The limousine crept to a halt.

Two security guards opened the back passenger door and allowed the couple out.

A woman in her forties stepped out from the passenger side, dressed in an expensive dress and shade-wear. The crowd whistled and whooped as she posed for several hovering drones, all hungry for her image.

The woman kept the door open for her five-year-old son. He clutched a medium-sized cage in his hands and waved at the crowd as the car door shut behind him. Like his mother, he sported expensive shade-wear. He removed them so the crowd could get a decent look at his smug, over-confident face.

"Look, there he is. Remy Gagarin," the little girl squealed, unable to contain her excitement, "Remy! I love you!"

Remy couldn't hear his fan's screams of adulation. He walked along the carpet with his mother, who threatened to steal the thunder with her incredible beauty.

"One has to wonder," Dreenagh commented over the scene, "If Remy Gagarin's mother, Elena, isn't trying to vie for some commercial work. She looks absolutely stunning as she makes her way with her son over to the arena."

The Manuel
Individimedia and the future of communication
Pg 301,133

(exposition dump #109/3b)

Those of you who were born in the middle of the last century may remember something called Social Media. *A concept noble in intent and, for a short while, rather successful.*

It began in earnest at the turn of the twenty-first century. Several "websites" (i.e. pages on the internet connected by computers and "modems") were set up. Some failed, and others succeeded. The intention of social media was to connect people together.

And connect, it did.

Family, friends, acquaintances, and strangers-in-law.

What the investors of Social Media *could not have foreseen was the temerity of the people who used their service. In order for it to be free they had to give up their privacy.*

Around twenty years after its inception, people realized quite quickly that other people "sucked" (an outmoded term for "not being much use.")

The irony of social media *was that, in trying to get users to socialize, it had the complete opposite effect. So used to utilizing these platforms were the users that they forgot how to operate as human beings. Particularly when it came to interpersonal relations.*

Marriages broke up.

Some humans forgot how to speak.

Interaction with others grew into an art form.

ADD (Attention Deficit Disorders, and it's High Definition variant, ADHD) became common place.

The Social Media *war lasted ten days. It claimed over twenty million casualties - all over one idiotic comment a user left on someone's video of their dog jumping from a roof into a paddling pool.*

In 2068, Social Media *was outlawed in a desperate bid to reverse the damage.*

Popular "video" streaming sites were closed down.

People were forced to physically interact once again.

It was absolute chaos.

The events that followed the prohibition of Social Media *gave rise to the vastly superior concept of* Individimedia.

Harnessing the same connectivity, Individimedia *was an altogether different beast. Some experts argue that it went right where its predecessor went wrong.*

Individmedia, *simply put, espoused the virtues of individual broadcast and fame. It did not include the ability to comment or interact via those channels.*

The result was a return to physical interaction. Today, Individimedia *is installed on the left forearm of all human beings born after the year 2070.*

It's powered by micro pulses from the user's brain. No need for batteries.

A simple tap on your skin, and the universe's database of knowledge is at your disposal.

You can also broadcast yourself to others.

In the early part of the twenty-first century, the same people would have owned ridiculous devices such as "smart" phones (#irony, as the same imbeciles might have joked at the time - "smart") and ghastly contraptions called tablets. Rectangular pieces of junk that rarely operated properly, if ever.

Thankfully, the only "tablets" users have today are the ones needed to quell their anxiety. We have to thank for Large Pharma for that.

God bless Large Pharma.

And God bless Individimedia.

***

Jamie and Emily sat in the back of their limousine as it made its way to the arena.

The back passenger window displayed a news reporter; a smartly-dressed man with a powerful voice named Santiago Sibald, in the middle of an Individimedia newscast.

"Tensions between the United States and Russia escalated earlier today when foreign diplomat minister, Viktor Rabinovich, was rushed to hospital after taking ill in a restaurant in Minneapolis Two."

Shaky camera footage showed medicians operating a stretcher drone into the back of an air ambulance. Viktor lay unconscious on it with breathing apparatus over his face. The medicians slid their patient into the helicopter and flew away from the concerned onlookers.

"Unconfirmed reports speculate that Rabinovich had been poisoned with a toxic nerve agent," Santiago continued as the footage wiped away to reveal his face, "If these assertions prove to be true, it could spell disaster for diplomacy between the United States and Russia, and unravel all attempts at peace. For more on this story, make sure you link up to my Individimedia channel. This is Santiago Sibald."

"Poppet,' Emily swiped the screen off, "Pay attention. We're nearly here."

Jelly sat in her cage and toyed with the bars.

"Mom, look," Jamie pointed at the windshield. The arena, and surrounding fuss, crept into view. "There it is."

"Oh, wow," Emily leaned forward and suddenly felt the enormity of the ordeal thunder through her body, "There are thousands of them."

Remy and his mother reached the doors to the arena and turned around for a final wave.

"Bisoubisou, Bisoubisou," the crowd chanted the clear favorite contender of the day.

Remy held up the cage for the crowd. Most couldn't see what lay behind the bars. Only those in the first few rows caught a glimpse of the gray, petrified cat wanting to be whisked away from the commotion.

"Hey," a blue-haired man shouted from the railings, "Cease this cruelty right now."

"Oh my," Dreenagh said to her camera-drone, "What's going on here? Looks like someone is making a go for Remy."

The blue-haired man ushered his gang through the crowd and hopped over the railings, waving his placard at them.

"Is that who I think it is?" Dreenagh asked. "It looks like Handax Skill. We're in trouble, now."

"Bring that animal back here," Handax threatened Remy.

"No," the kid shouted in his thick Russian accent, "Leave us alone."

The crowd went silent as the man held up his placard. The sign on the front contained a picture of the USARIC logo with a red strike through it. Underneath it in big, bold letters read:

P.A.A.C.
People Against Animal Cruelty

The crowd choked with silence as the man reached into his jacket.

"This is an outrage," Handax shot Dreenagh a look of evil and turned to his gang, "We will not lie down until USARIC reverses its decision to use animals for space exploration."

"Death to human scum who practice inhumane treatment of animals," screamed a female PAAC member.

She threw her placard to the ground and removed her denim jacket, revealing a vest stuffed with dynamite and wires tightened around her waist, "Good people, we cannot allow this corporate *terriful* practice to affect animals. Free the animals."

The audience froze still, afraid to move. The armed security detail pointed their weapons at them. "Person! Raise your arms in the air and slowly lower yourself to your knees."

"No," the girl gripped her utility chain and threatened to yank it, "We demand satisfaction. Remy Gagarin, you have the facility and audience to do the right thing. In front of all Indivimedia, open the cage and let your pet free. Do the right thing."

Remy, not knowing how to react, turned to his mother for a response. She spat at the floor and lowered her shade-wear down the bridge of her nose.

"Remy, do not listen to them. They are imbeciles."

Contrary to his mother's command, Remy set the cage to the floor. He didn't want to die in a terrorist attack.

"That's right," the girl said with a smile, "Now open the cage—"

"—Person," the main security guard roared, "I repeat, release the chain and put your arms in the air."

Dreenagh's drone zoomed over to the commotion and joined dozens of others.

Jamie slid his thumb across the back passenger window, activating it.

"Individimedia Zero-Five," Jamie said.

The sheen on the glass sparked and displayed a live feed from the drone. The ticker-tape underneath read "Live From The One Arena, Cape Claudius. Terrorist Siege Underway."

"Mom, look!" Jamie pointed at the screen, sending his mother into a fit of anxiety, "It's that man with the blue hair who gave us Jelly."

"Driver?" Emily asked.

"Yes?"

"Look at your feed."

"Oh, no. Not *them* again." The driver slammed on the brakes and caught the live feed in the corner of his rear view mirror, "They're always causing trouble."

"What if they find out we entered Jelly in the Star Cat Trials, mom?"

The driver reversed from the road and threw the stick shift into first gear, "What's your son talking about?"

"We got Jelly from PAAC," Emily asked. "I know that man with the blue hair. Does this happen often?"

"Yes, all the time," he chuckled and floored the gas pedal.

"What are you doing? You're not taking us closer to them, are you?"

"Nothing to be worried about."

The female animal rights terrorist knew that Remy would never open his pet's cage. Handax pulled out a pistol, scaring the crowd back a few feet.

"In the name of science and humanity, if you choose not to let animals live in peace, then we want no part of the planet."

He placed the barrel of the gun to his head and threatened to shoot himself.

"Person, please," the security guard said. "We'll save you the bother. Lower your gun."

"The statement needs to be made." The female activist turned to the crowd and then up at the drones. They buzzed around, trying to get a good view of the stand-off. "Do you hear us, USARIC? *You're* responsible for *this…*"

The female protester snarled at the camera and yanked the chain away from her vest.

"Everybody down."

The security guards hit the deck. The crowd did the same, trampling over one another, causing some serious injuries - which wasn't PAAC's intention.

KA-SNAP-PAP!

Instead of detonating, several party poppers and harmless incendiaries exploded into the sky, in and out of the hovering drones.

The girl laughed as loud as she could and dropped to her knees.

The fake sticks of dynamite released a pretty array of fireworks into the sky.

The security guards made a beeline for her and scooped her up from the floor. They escorted Handax off the premises to a wave of whoops and hollers of approval from the crowd.

Dreenagh looked at her camera-drone and breathed a sigh of relief, "Well, you saw it here first."

"You haven't heard the last from us,' Handax yelled as the guards marched him away from the crowd, "Freedom for the animals!"

Jamie and Emily's limousine rolled up to the red carpet at the front of the arena.

The crowd bent over the railings trying to catch a glimpse of the people inside the car.

"Mom, I'm scared," Jamie shot her a look and grabbed Jelly's cage handle.

"Me too, poppet," she said over Jelly's whining from within the cage, "But we have to go, right? We can't very well have the driver turn around and take us back to the hotel, can we?"

Jamie shook his head enthusiastically, "We're here to win. We're going to win, aren't we?"

Emily smiled. She knew she had to fabricate the truth and keep her son's spirit up.

"Brits? Second to a Russian? We already had one cold war," Emily snorted and kicked the back door open. "And I'm all for doing it again if they want to mess around with us."

"Wait," Jamie called after her as the crowd whistled at her, "What's a cold war?"

"Doesn't matter, poppet," Emily pointed at the crowd behind her, "Bring Jelly out. Let's show these Americans that victory always begins at *home*."

Jamie didn't know what his mother had meant by that, but he trusted her enough to jump out of the car to an adoring crowd.

"We love you, Jamie," screamed a bunch of similarly-aged American girls from behind the railings.

"Jelly! Jelly! Jelly!"

Dreenagh clapped and whistled along with the crowd, "There she is, little Jelly Anderson all the way from the United Kingdom."

Jamie marveled at the sheer enormity of the crowd. A first taste of super-stardom which overwhelmed him to the point of hysteria.

"Hello, everybody," Jamie waved as he and his mother walked along the carpet.

This time, security came running over to greet and escort them. "Mrs Anderson?"

"Ms Anderson, thank you very much," Emily said, walking alongside them toward the arena doors. "Take us inside, please."

"Yes, of course," the security guard walked with her, trying to remember the name of her contestant. "As soon as you're in, we need to take, uh…"

"—Jelly, mister?" Jamie corrected him.

"Yes, Jelly," The guard turned to Emily and ushered her forward. "As soon as we're through the doors, we'll get you and your son in makeup. An official will take Jelly to the prep room. And please don't call me *mister*."

***

A teenage Star Cat Trials official named Lindsey ushered Jamie through a tunnel. He'd been separated from his mother.

"Where are we going?" Jamie asked, suddenly aware that he was on his own.

"We're going to the main stage. You'll get to meet the finalists. Won't that be fun?"

"Why are you talking to me like I'm a child?"

"You *are* a child, aren't you?" Lindsey spat, looking up the length of the corridor.

"Yes, but I'm not stupid," Jamie raced forward, catching up with Lindsay.

"No, of course you're not."

The audience hubbub came from behind the walls. It felt like there were at least a million people in attendance.

Anxiety rushed through Jamie's body, "I want my mom."

"No, sweetie. She'll be in the audience. You'll see her in the family and friends section," Lindsey clicked a button on her headset, "Approaching door B-Two, now. Are the others ready?"

"Yes, they're waiting for you, now," came the response. "Five minutes till show time."

The stage music and audience commotion grew louder and louder as the pair approached a set of double doors.

Lindsey reached the door handle and grabbed it, shooting him a smile. "Ready?"

"No."

"Honestly, there's nothing to worry about," Lindsey chuckled. She developed a soft spot for the kid right there and then, "We'll walk in and Gunnar will introduce you all. Just do as he says."

"Okay."

The stage doors flew open.

Lindsey and Jamie approached the arena's central stage to overwhelming applause. Music played amid an array of fireworks.

Jamie looked up and saw his name and nationality on the mega-screen. He looked at the audience. Most were in pitch darkness due to the colossal stage lamps shining in his eyes from the gods.

"And finally," Gunnar said from under the spotlight, "All

the way from the United Kingdom… Jamie Anderson and his contender, *Jelly*."

Another spotlight shone down on Jelly, who sat patiently at the right of the stage. Next to her was Bisoubisou, the Russian Blue. Next to her sat a white American bobtail. Each had a plastic tie around their necks which shackled them to the wall. They were very unhappy about the restriction.

The audience continued their adoration as Jamie made his way to a marked-out area in front of a grid of twenty-four panels, measuring five-by-five feet.

"So, we're down to three. The cream of the crop," Gunnar said over the music as Jamie, Remy and a girl each took their respective grids, "Just two more rounds in the finals of the Star Cat Trials. Here we go…"

The music thundered across the arena as the lights dimmed down, forcing everyone to focus on the mega-screen.

Three handlers unfastened the plastic shackles on each cat and carried them over to their respective grids.

The Finals

Round One
- Obedience -

A female voice narrated the event as the three kids and their cats prepared to begin the event.

"Each contestant has a grid of twenty-four panels that light up. The owner will use their gears to light up one panel at a time. Each time their cat hits the corresponding panel, they will score one point. Will their pet obey their instruction? Welcome… to *Obedience*…"

Jamie looked at a panel of gears on a machine deck in front of him. He made a face at Remy, who fiddled with his controls in the middle of the three contestant line-up.

"Hey, I'm Jamie."

"I know," Remy said in his Russian accent, trying to ignore the kid, "I saw your name on the screen. Do not talk to me."

"What's your name?"

"Remy."

"Remy, it's very nice to meet—"

"—Do not talk to me. *English*."

Jamie mocked the boy with a bad attempt at a Russian accent, "Do not look at me."

He looked over at the girl, who sat to Remy's right. "Who's she?"

"That is Leesa. I said do not speak to me, English. You must concentrate," Remy nodded at his Bisoubisou. She lifted her paw and waved back, as if on cue. "You ready, Bisoubisou?"

"Meow," she responded, frightened by the impressive arena lights.

Jamie decided to enact the same action with Jelly, "Hey, girl. You ready?"

Jelly didn't say anything as her handler plonked her on the starting grid. No lift of the paw. Jamie felt immediately inferior and wondered why Jelly didn't wave back like Bisoubisou had done with Remy.

Of course, they didn't have *that* kind of relationship. Remy had clearly done his homework. It pleased the Russian kid no end that the stupid Brit hadn't taken the time to train his own pet.

"Useless, English."

"Shut up," came Jamie's provocative retort.

Gunnar waved his hands and held the microphone to his mouth, "Okay, I think the contenders are ready."

A dramatic game show-like synthesizer replaced the music.

Jamie, Remy, and Leesa's gears lit up.

"And… go!" Gunnar said.

Jamie looked at his controls without the faintest idea what to do. "What do I do?"

Remy looked over and smirked. "Make it up, English."

"Okay, *Russian*," Jamie muttered sarcastically as he hit the first panel on his deck. It lit up and seemed to growl. He lifted his head and nodded at Jelly, "Go on, girl."

She trundled forward and sat in the middle of the grid on the lit panel. It sunk in a few inches and made a 'ping' noise, indicating that she'd selected the right one.

The tile turned white under her paws. "Meow," she yelped and jumped into the air.

"Good girl," Jamie said to a wave of applause from the audience behind him.

Remy hit the third panel. Bisoubisou wouldn't move. "Come on, you insolent feline. Move," he instructed her, tapping the button over and over again.

Instead of obliging she rolled onto her side and licked her paw.

"Ugh, you idiot."

Leesa hit the fifth panel button and looked at Remy.

The boy made a face at her. "What are you looking at?"

"I don't know," she said. "Maybe an idiot?"

Ping.

Suzie Q-Two jumped forward and hit the fifth panel with her paws.

It lit up, scaring the life out of her, "Meow!"

"Whoa," Gunnar chuckled into the microphone, "Okay, it's between Jelly and Suzie Q-Two. One for one for those two, and Bisoubisou is looking a bit out of her league."

"No she does not," Remy thumped the controls and kicked the deck. "This is unfair."

The crowd erupted in waves of laughter as they watched Bisoubisou lick her paws, completely ignoring her master's instruction.

"Let's mix this up a bit," Gunnar said to the crowd.

"What?" Jamie looked down at his controls. The gears and buttons powered down.

Daft Punk's *Harder Better Faster Stronger* kicked off through the arena speakers.

"It's a dance-off!" Gunnar turned and pointed at the grids, "A classic track all the way from the early twentieth century. Here we go."

Jelly's head jumped from left to right and up and down as she observed the panels come to life against the beat of the tune.

Bisoubisou jumped to her feet and growled.

Suzie Q-Two did the same and hopped to the first panel, pressing it down.

The buzzer went off, awarding a point to the white bobtail.

"Yes, yes, yes," Leesa jumped in her seat and applauded her cat. The tiny ball of fluff hopped to the next panel and racked up some more points in tune to the beat, "You go, girl."

Remy looked at Bisoubisou and clenched his fists, "Commence dancing, you stupid cat."

Bisousbisou jumped to her feet and raced into the middle of her twenty-four panels. They lit up, one-by-one, in time to the beat. She twisted around and followed the lit panels with her head, whining to herself.

Jamie stood out of his chair and clapped along with the music,"Go, go, go." Jelly hopped from one panel to the other, racking up some points.

The timing of the music intensified. The grid panels flashed faster.

"Wow," Jamie marveled at Jelly as she jumped from one to the other. She wasn't doing a perfect job, however. One particularly difficult jump sent her onto her hind legs and tumbling over onto a grayed-out panel.

Bzzz.

"Oh. That's an error, right there," Gunnar said into his microphone, "Anderson may lose points for that."

"No!" Jamie yelled from his seat, "It's going too fast. That rubbish olden days music is too quick."

Jelly scrambled to her feet and squealed. Her pupils dilated as she tried to keep up the attack on the flashing panels.

Suzie Q-Two caught up with each panel and totaled over thirty points which displayed on the mega-screen.

"Suzie Q-Two is winning," Gunnar commentated, "But can she keep this up?"

Bisoubisou finally got involved in the event. She jumped from one lit panel to the other with extraordinary grace and ability.

"And we're back in the game," Gunnar said, watching Bisoubisou trashing her opponents.

Suzie Q-Two had a hard time keeping up with her rivals. The panels blinked away even faster against the thrust of the music. Her eyes turned a urine-stained yellow.

"No, Suzie Q-Two!" Leesa screamed, "Don't do that now!"

Her cat shrieked and bushed out her tail. She launched into a flying hissy fit and attacked her grid at random, flying into the air. Her tail got in the way.

Bzzz-Bzzz-Bzzz...

The mega-screen showed Suzie Q-Two's points drain away to zero as she hit the wrong panels.

"No, no, no," Leesa started to sob as her cat jumped from her own grid and raced across Bisousbisou's, pushing her out of the way.

"Whoooaaaaa," the crowd roared as they watched Suzie Q-Two hop into Jelly's grid and threaten to attack her as she danced.

Bzzz.

Jelly flipped in the air and clipped Suzie Q-Two around the face with her paw.

The music track crashed to a halt, leaving a flummoxed Jelly catching her breath. Suzie Q-Two rolled around on her belly and licked her paws.

"I think we'd regard that as a disqualification," Gunnar said.

The panels buzzed out. The lights on her grid flipped off.

Leesa burst into tears, lamenting her cat's disobedience.

A bunch of audience members scrunched up their betting slips and threw them to the ground.

"Ugh, absolutely useless," one of them said to his friend.

Leesa looked over her shoulder at her mother and father. They didn't know how to respond.

"Sorry, honey."

"It's not fair," she bawled back at them.

The three cat handlers ran onto the three grids. Lindsey

lifted Jelly into her arms as the crowd made a fuss over her.

"Jelly, Jelly, Jelly," they chanted.

It hadn't gone unnoticed by Jamie that the largely American crowd were not in favor of the Russiant winning over-and-above its British contender.

Remy was riled up by this fact.

"Let's look at the final scores, please," Gunnar held his hand up to the mega screen.

The numbers whizzed around and settled on the final result.

Obedience - Final Scores
J. Anderson = 42 pts
B. Gagarin = 40 pts

Remy face-palmed himself and sat into his chair in utter disbelief, "Nooooo."

"Yes," Jamie punched the air and waved at Jelly as Lindsey carried her back to her box, "Way to go, Jelly."

Emily whistled from the family and friends audience section, catching her son's attention.

"Mom, we're winning!"

"I know, poppet," Emily giggled, excitedly, "Just one more round to go."

Gunnar stepped forward as the tiled grids spun around on their axis and sank into the floor.

"Could the contenders please visit their pets one final time and prepare for the final round."

Remy and Jamie jumped out of their seats and raced each other to the two cages at the right of the stage.

Lindsey held out her arms in an attempt to prevent the boys from getting too close, "Wait a second, please."

Jamie watched as a technician lifted Jelly out of her cage and slipped a device onto Jelly's right paw.

Bisoubisou received the same treatment from another technician.

Both cats had a lightweight glove clamped to their right paw.

"What's going on?" Jamie asked.

Lindsey explained over the commotion coming from the restless crowd, "It's a special device they need for the final round."

Remy approached the deck and eyed the device attached to his cat's right paw, "What is it?"

"Watch, up there."

Jamie and Remy turned around and looked up at the screen.

The lights died down, focusing the audience's attention on the screen.

Footage of a cat's paw flashed up. A human hand slipped on a set of metal ridges that ran over the cat's own claws.

"The final round," the female narration played out. "Infinity Claws. The ultimate test of strength, character and... *combat.*"

The screen displayed record footage of several cats in a one-on-one, swiping at each other with their infinity claw gloves.

"No, no," Remy moved forward trying to stop the proceedings, "They're sharp. It will hurt them."

"Oh no," Lindsey whispered to the boys under the loud music playing on the footage, "It's perfectly safe. These claws are designed to *not* cause injury. If they were using their real claws, it would."

"So they're like Jitsaku gloves?" Jamie asked.

"Yes, they're a bit like boxing gloves," Lindsey turned to Jelly and Bisoubisou. The latter sank her teeth into the contraption and tried to tear it off her paw - to little success.

"I do not like this," Remy said. "Look, it upsets her."

Jamie agreed, although Jelly didn't seem to mind her new toy as much as her opponent. She sniffed around as she operated her new 'claws', winding them in and out.

Jamie clapped his hands, attracting Jelly's attention. She looked back at him, failing to emote. Her face displayed a steely, determined expression. At least that's what it looked like to Jamie.

He walked over to her and ran his hand across the top of her head. She head-butted him back and purred.

"We're going to win. Aren't we, girl?"

Jelly rubbed the side of her face along his palm and purred. She may as well have just said "Hell, yeah," judging by her response.

Bisoubisou, on the other hand, found her new glove very uncomfortable.

Remy folded his arms and stared at her, "Bisoubisou?"

She stopped fussing and looked right at her owner.

"Do not ruin this for me, you understand?"

As Remy finished his sentence, the combat zone lit up behind him to a ravenous audience. He and Jamie turned to face the arena.

The zone measured ten by ten feet. The left half lit up red, the right in blue.

A ten foot cage surrounded all four walls.

"Oh, wow…" Jamie gasped. "That's insane."

Lindsey smirked, "Okay, guys. Let's get ready…"

Chapter 5

Final Round
- Combat -

Lindsey carried Jelly in her arms to the hole in the caged combat zone. She pushed her through and wiped her palms down on her pants.

Jelly couldn't get out. She raced up to the western side of the metal railings in an attempt to approach Jamie.

The railing sparked, threatening to zap her if she touched it. An electrified fence. She couldn't get out.

Jelly whined and ducked her head, deeply unimpressed.

"Not now, girl," he whispered, "Look. All these people watching. You made it to the finals."

Jelly spun around and whipped her tail around, purposely showing him her behind.

"That's not nice. How would you like it if I did that to you?"

Jelly lifted her right paw and attempted to claw at the cage, teasing the electricity out.

"No, don't do that—"

Zap.

"—Meow," Jelly yelped and jumped back. A whiff of singed fur wafted around Jamie's immediate vicinity.

An angry growl from Bisoubisou in the blue half forced her to turn around.

The house lights in the arena drew to a close. Two flood lamps illuminated the combat zone.

Blue streaks of electricity shot across the metal railings. The ground began to rumble as a high-pitched whine flew across the stage.

"Good people," announced the female voice, "Welcome to the final of the Star Cat Trials. In the red left corner, representing the United Kingdom... Jelly Anderson."

A shower of fireworks burst around the western red half of the combat zone, scaring Jelly into a huddle of tense nervousness.

The crowd cheered and chanted, "Jell-ee! Jell-ee!"

Remy folded his arms in a huff, trying block out the audience's love for his opponent.

Bisoubisou tumbled around, clawing at her metal 'glove' in a frantic bid to remove it.

"And her opponent in the blue corner, hailing from Russia, Bisoubisou."

The crowd were less than enthusiastic about the Russian Blue currently occupying the blue half. Angered, Remy held up his middle finger to the crowd, which only made them eager for his team to lose.

"*Combat* combines the disciplines of Jujitsu and Kung Fu," Gunnar said into the drone camera at the edge of the stage, "Jitsaku is the name of the game in *Combat*. In just a few minute's time, we'll have a winner, won't we?"

Aggressive music started up, suggesting that the action wasn't far away.

Gunnar raised his hand, "Let's begin," he walked over to his podium and pushed a lever forward, "Zero gravity, ready."

The crowd fell silent as the combat railings vibrated, jolting hundreds of thousands of volts through the metal girders.

Jelly's paws lifted slowly from the ground as weightlessness set in. Scared, she revolved in the air, trying to hold on to something to stop her from levitating.

She nearly hit the railing but remembered the electric shock that would occur if she did. Her claws retracted and, instead, pushed forward, tossing her around in mid-air.

Bisousbisou went wild with fear. She tried to catch her tail as it drifted in front of her eyes.

"No, girl," Remy screamed, "Get upright and get ready to fight."

Bisoubisou squealed in terror, wondering just what the heck was going on.

An audience member turned to his friend, munching on a bucket of popcorn, "Cats doing Jitsaku?"

"Yeah, really," his friend snorted.

"That's a bit stupid, isn't it?"

"Nah, they're dressing it up as Jitsaku," another man sitting near them interrupted, "They're probably gonna just scrap like they usually do."

"Welcome to Combat," announced the female voice, "One strike equals one point. There is only one round. There will only be *one* winner... who will become USARIC's *Star Cat?*"

The music crashed to a halt.

Jelly and Bisoubisou floated in the air, ready to attack each other. It wasn't because they had to fight but because they felt the desire to kill.

They developed that desire from being holed up in an electrified cage. Everyone knew it. Only the Anderson and Gagarin family seemed to care.

Jamie knew that the setting was designed to provoke the animals. It was the first time in his life that he took exception to something that didn't directly involve him. Sure, he'd been hurt before - and experienced injury - but this particular event felt incredibly unethical. He didn't even know what "unethical" meant, but was sure that a decent example of it stood before him.

"Here we go, guys," Gunnar said. "Let's *Combat!*"

A buzzer sounded off. The central section of the cage shot down, allowing the two cats to go at each other.

Bisoubisou wasted no time.

She threw her gloved paw forward, hurtling the rest of her body through the air.

Bisoubisou took a swipe at Jelly's face and narrowly missed. She tumbled back-first against the electrified railing and felt a wave of electricity shudder down her spine.

"Meeooooww," Jelly floated back. Her hind legs hit the floor, providing her with an opportunity to push herself toward her rival.

Jelly threw her claws forward and latched onto the spinning Bisoubisou. The two tussled in mid-air, gnawing and gnashing away at each other.

Jelly sank her fangs into Bisoubisou's neck and tore out a clump of fur. A final smack to the head put the Russian Blue out of action for a few moments.

Zaapp-pp.

Bisousbisou's head caught in the railing, jolted by a split-second's worth of electricity, "Raooowwaar!"

Jelly realized what she had done. She ducked her head and turned herself upside down as Bisoubisou kicked away from the cage.

The lightning bolt rumbled through Bisoubisou's hind legs causing her fur to stand on end as she rocketed toward Jelly.

"No, no!" Jamie threw his hands into the air and looked at Gunnar, "You're hurting them. Please, stop it."

"They're not hurt, kid," Gunnar giggled. "It's just a bit of a nudge to get them to engage. If they can't handle the action on Earth, how are they going to cope in space if they meet aliens?"

"Aliens?" Jamie asked himself.

Remy punched the air, furious on Bisoubisou's behalf. "Go on, smash her. Kick that orange lump of fur."

Bisoubisou swiped her claw and caught Jelly on the shoulder. The metal hanging over her claws dug into Jelly's fur, causing her to screech out loud.

The exhilaration coming from the audience was palpable. Ordinarily they'd be cheering but the violent action taking place caused them to choke. The combat was far more furious - and dangerous - than expected.

"My God," an audience member stood up and screamed, "This is horrible. Make them stop."

"No, no," Jamie whispered under his breath, looking at Jelly, "Don't stop. Defend yourself, girl."

Swish-swipe.

"Twenty seconds remaining," announced the female voice.

Jelly gave it her best shot. She lifted her hind legs and kicked Bisoubisou in the stomach, pushing her back. "Grrrrr."

Jelly looked at her hind paws and deliberately pressed them against the railings, knowing she'd receive a nasty nip of a shock.

A jolt of electricity blasted through her body.

"Whoa, that's gotta hurt!" Gunnar laughed into the microphone. He looked at the screen, "Jelly's on eight points. Bisoubisou is on seven."

Jelly's hind paws hit the railing. She screamed in pain and saw the bolt of electric blue run up her legs. She pushed forward and revolved around in the air, ready to knock ten shades of hell out of her opponent.

Unfortunately for her, Bisoubisou was ready. Like Jelly, she utilized the anger-inducing electric shock with her glove. She pushed back, purposely zapping herself.

Bisoubisou and Jelly stormed head-to-head through the air, ready to obliterate each other.

"This is it," Gunnar yelled into the microphone, "Ten seconds left."

Jelly meowed at the top of her lungs, raising her infinity claws above her head and ready to smack the hell out of her rival.

Bisoubisou did the same, revealing her sharp, white fangs.

"Six... five... four..." announced the female voice.

Everything seemed to crash into slow motion for Jamie and Remy. They briefly caught each other's eyes as they turned to their pets.

Jelly threw the first punch and grabbed Bisoubisou's face in her claws. She yanked her opponent around as their bodies tumbled over and over together.

Bisoubisou's face tore open as one of Jelly's infinity claws pulled away. It proved to be just the pain that Bisoubisou needed to develop an incandescent rage.

She reached up and socked Jelly in her stomach, sending her tumbling against the metal railing.

"Woooooooh!" the audience finally exhaled.

Electric sparks blistered out from behind Jelly as her

shoulder blades hit the railings. "Mwaahhh."

"… two… one… and, game over."

Bzzz. The combat cage collapsed out and folded over itself, sinking into the floor.

Bisousbiou and Jelly were no longer the subject of zero gravity. They shot down to the floor and landed on their paws.

The mega-screen played some of the highlights of both rounds as the totals calculated.

Gunnar and the crowd cheered the two cats as their respective handlers lifted them out of the cage.

Lindsey ran her hand over Jelly's head and examined her face, "Hey, Jelly. How are you?"

She lashed out at the woman and tried to claw her face. Clumps of her fur had burned away. She was injured and extremely upset.

Remy watched Bisoubisou in his handler's arms, "Give me her."

"No," the handler held the cat in the air for the audience to see, "We need to do this."

"Give me my cat back," Remy stomped his foot on the ground, "You hurt her."

"Okay, everybody," Gunnar stepped forward and pressed his index finger to his lips, "The results are in. The points have been tallied up. It seems we have a winner."

The crowd fell silent, as did Jamie and Remy. Everyone turned to the mega screen for the payoff.

"And here are the results…" announced the female voice. "In second place…"

Jamie turned to his mother and bit his lip. She looked at the big screen.

"… Jelly Anderson, from the United Kingdom. With a total of fifty-two points."

"Huh?" Jamie asked himself, confused. "So if Jelly came in second, then that means—"

"—Yes," Remy jumped in with extreme excitement, "Yes. We won."

"What?" Jamie stomped his foot to the floor. "That's not

right, Jelly won that!"

Gunnar took Bisoubisou from the handler and held her up, "Attention, people. The winner of USARIC's Star Cat Project... from the Russian Federation, I give you... Bisoubisou Gagarin!"

The crowd cheered politely but were undoubtedly disappointed.

A thousand lights shone on Bisoubisou and Remy as the celebrations took place.

Deflated and exhausted, Jamie slumped to his knees and accepted the noise of failure in his head. After a few seconds, the adulation for his opponent dampened in his ears and left a permanent scar on his brain.

The crowd escaped from the gantry and flooded the stage, all vying to be the first to pet and congratulate the winner.

Emily jumped onto the stage and made a beeline for Jamie, "Oh, poppet. Come here."

She scooped him up in her arms and hugged him. He went limp and buried his crying face on her shoulder, "It's not fair, they tried to hurt them."

"I know, poppet," she whispered, "If I had known, I would never have let her take part."

"I want Jelly," he sobbed, looking up at Jelly in Lindsey's arms.

"Not yet, Jamie," Lindsey said. "We need to make sure she's okay and we'll get her back to you."

Jamie looked at the crowds surrounding the winner. Remy looked very happy with himself as Dreenagh pushed her wrist into his face and asked him some questions.

His parents looked even happier, proud of their son and his cat.

Of course, Bisoubisou was the center of attention.

A tear rolled down Jamie's cheek. A rousing experience of failure, and one he'd likely never forget till the day he died.

"I want to go home," Jamie cried into his mother's comforting arms, "I don't like it here—"

"Meoowwwwwwww."

Jamie was interrupted by Bisoubisou lashing out at the

crowd from out of nowhere.

Everyone turned to the cat and gasped.

Bisoubisou threw her paws out and chewed at the infinity claw on her right paw, whining and growling.

"Oh, god," her handler looked at her paw and turned to Gunnar. "She's bleeding. We need to get her to medical, right now."

Confused, the crowd stepped back. The cameras pointed at Bisoubisou, showing her turmoil and sheer agony on the mega-screen.

"Everybody get back. Now," Gunnar waved the crowd away. The place fell silent.

Bisoubisou wailed in horror as her fangs dug into the metal, trying to wrench the godforsaken infinity claws away from her paws.

Her handler darted off toward the back of the stage, leaving a worried crowd wondering what had happened. Spots of blood lined the stage floor as she carried the injured cat away.

Jamie saw the frantic handler kicked through the stage door, screaming for help…

***

The handler barged through another door leading to a backstage medical room.

"Where's Wool? We need her, fast."

Wool ar-Ban, an Iranian lady dressed in a lab coat and glasses, jumped out from behind her desk and joined the handler.

"I'm here, what's wrong?"

She took a look at the ailing gray cat in the handler's arms.

"Oh, no. Quick, over here. Lay her on the bed," Wool said, pressing her finger into her ear, "I need surgery down here, stat. Medicians on standby please attend."

The handler lay her down on her side and burst into tears, "She's going to be okay, isn't she?"

"Please, move out of the way. We need some space," Wool held up Bisoubisou's right arm and nearly lost her

76

temper. "Don't tell me. That stupid combat stuff?"

The handler folded her arms and hugged herself in floods of tears. "Yes."

"Honestly, I *told* them not to infuriate the cats. But would they listen? No."

She reached into her inner pocket and pulled out a small syringe.

Two medicians ran through the door and sprung into actions. One of them pushed an ECG monitor on a trolley over to the bed. She unpacked two pads and fired up the machine.

"Her heart's climbing out of her throat," the other medician said, "Checking pulse."

"One-fifty over one," said the first medician as Wool injected the cat with her syringe, "One fifty-two, one fifty-three…"

"Three emm-gee," Wool tried to keep her composure as she watched Bisoubisou's monitor. Her heart was near exploding. She turned to the battered infinity claw and prised it away with her fingers as carefully as she could. It unfastened in Wool's hand.

"Ugh, got it."

She passed the infinity claw to Bisoubisou's handler. "Please, Wool. Tell me she's going to be okay?"

"Stop talking, you stupid woman," Wool fanned the cat's claws apart. "She's lost a lot of blood. Please, let us work."

Bisoubisou's head hit the side of the bed's surface. A rope of saliva collected out and bled along her cheek.

"God, no," Wool said. "She's going into septic shock."

The heart rate sped up on the screen.

"Laceration at oh-one-five," Wool prodded Bisoubisou's stomach and felt along her chest, keeping an eye on the screen. The cat's tongue slipped out from her mouth and hung down her face.

"God, no, no," the first medician said, "She's gone into shock."

"Another at oh-two-six, and five-oh-three."

"Morphine, Doctor?" asked one of the medicians as Wool rubbed her face in a frantic attempt to save the cat's life.

"No," Wool said, "She's had enough—"

Bisoubisou croaked and let out a fountain of vomit. Her right paw had swelled up beyond recognition. Her rightmost claw lilted and threatened to come free.

Her breathing gradually slowed down to nothing.

A clump of fur fell off her chest as she exhaled for the final time.

"It's the claws," Wool thumped the table and held her fist to her mouth, trying not to emote, "Nu-huh, no."

Bisoubisou flatlined.

Wool closed her eyes and took a deep breath, suppressing the urge to cry. She wanted to kill someone for what had happened to the beautiful Russian Blue cat laying before her.

The constant beep signaling the cat's death was the only thing anyone could hear.

"You call it," Wool looked away.

"Four-fifteen," the first medician set Bisoubisou's lifeless paw on the bed, "Wool?"

She didn't respond. Instead, she kept looking away, silently cursing the day she signed on to the project.

"Wool?" the first medician asked. "Would you like me to notify the bereaved?"

"No, it's okay." She looked at her colleague and blinked, "I'll do it. This is all my damn fault anyway."

"But didn't she pass the assessment?" the first medician asked.

"Doesn't matter if she did or didn't," the second medician said, "It doesn't test for allergies to company product."

The handler cried in the corner regretting her involvement in the proceedings.

"Oh, stop crying," Wool thumped her desk and took no pity on the woman, "You're just the lackey. You didn't do anything wrong, so shut up and stop crying. Go back out on stage and look pretty."

Jamie and Emily sat in the back of the limousine en route to their hotel.

Jelly rested in her carry case between them taking a well-earned nap. She'd survived the day very well. Much like the limousine's engine, her purring rumbled away from within now that she was on her way home.

Jamie stared out of the window.

The beach front at Cape Claudius whizzed by. Children and their families enjoyed the sun and ocean, offering him a glimpse of what life might have been like had he been born in South Texas.

A giant rig loomed in the background. It would house the spacecraft someday soon and launch it into the stars.

Alas, the Anderson family would never be involved. Jamie bit his lip and sat back in his seat.

"I'm glad we're going home, mom."

"Yes, poppet," Emily looked at Jelly through the bars of the cage, "Perhaps it's better this way—"

The driver's forearm started ringing. He lifted it to his face and took the call as quietly as possible.

"She did well, though, didn't she?"

Emily didn't say anything. She felt sorry for her son, but they'd achieved more in the past few months than most ever did in their entire lifetimes.

"Yes, poppet," she whispered. "Jelly did very—"

The car screeched to a halt, kicking dust into the air. The traffic from behind slammed their brakes and blared their horns.

Jelly's cage slipped forward. Jamie caught it in his hands before it fell to the foot well.

"What are you doing?"

Emily held her hands out and pressed the back of the driver's seat, shielding herself from colliding with it. "What's going on?"

The driver looked over his chair and threw the stick in reverse.

"I've just had an update," he said. "We're heading back to the arena…"

"What?" Jamie asked. "Why?"

"Actually, we're heading to USARIC, not the arena."

"What?" Emily asked. Why?"

"Something has happened," the driver performed a hasty three-point turn in the middle of the road, angering a lot of the oncoming drivers, "USARIC want to talk to you very urgently."

***

Emily, Jamie, and the caged Jelly found themselves in USARIC's main conference room.

They'd been hurried into the building via the back entrance to avoid the crowds milling around the front.

The Gagarin family had won the trials. As far as they were concerned, Bisoubisou was recuperating with Wool ar-Ban and her team.

Emily caught sight of the attention Remy and his family received as they drove past. No one was any the wiser to the clandestine meeting that took place between USARIC and the Anderson family.

Maar Sheck and Dimitri Vasilov were in attendance, along with Tripp Healy and Wool ar-Ban.

They updated Emily on the events that had taken place after the finals were finished. The news came as a complete shock and didn't go down well with either her or her son.

"How did it happen?" Emily asked.

Wool sat up in her chair with a degree of solemnity, "A combination of her injuries and a reaction to the utility that was strapped to her paw. Essentially, it culminated in progressive organ failure and she went into cardiac arrest. She wouldn't have felt anything. It all happened so fast."

Emily exhaled and looked at her lap. She felt disgusted with herself, "It was Jelly's fault, wasn't it?"

"Oh no, no," Wool said, "Jelly had nothing to do with—"

"—we saw it with our own eyes," Emily interrupted. "You made them fight. We saw Jelly injure her. She can't have helped."

"No," Wool said. "I can't argue with that. She can't have helped."

"So, how much trouble are we in?" Emily rubbed Jamie's knee, signaling that she had everything under control, "Just so you know, we intend to get representation in court. We can't be held responsible—"

"—in court?" Maar asked, confused. "Why would you need a lawyer?"

"Well, because of all this. You're suing us, aren't you?"

Maar and Dimitri looked at each other, realizing that the woman had gotten the wrong end of the stick. Maar spoke slowly, intending to correct her.

"Uh, no... we're not planning to sue you."

"No?"

"No. Actually, we want to use Jelly. We consider her to be the winner in all this."

"I beg your pardon?"

Jamie's ears pricked up. He felt an internal whirl of delight, "You mean Jelly won?"

"In a manner of speaking, yes."

Tripp looked at Emily and threw her a smile. "Bisoubisou can't go. But Jelly can, if you allow it."

Emily shook her head instinctively. She didn't want to hear another word.

"No, no, no, you don't get to do this to us. To Jelly. No, a thousand times no."

"How about two-hundred-and-fifty-thousand times *yes*?" Dimitri tried.

"You can't seriously be suggesting that Jelly take Bisoubisou's place?"

"That *is* what we're suggesting," Dimitri glanced at his colleagues, "Jelly, here, proved a number of things. One, she's the best candidate for the task. Two, she technically *beat* her competitor. It's just a shame that the results were announced before—"

Emily slammed the table. Her emotions get the better of her. Jelly growled in her cage as she felt the impact.

"You *forced* our cat to attack her. She had no choice. Jelly was defending herself. How *dare* you suggest she's a killer."

"We didn't say she was a killer," Maar said. "All we're saying is that, technically, she won."

"I've heard enough," Emily grabbed her son's hand and clutched Jelly's carry case, "We're leaving. Let us out."

She marched Jamie toward the door, leaving a thoroughly disappointed USARIC team behind her.

Just one, last baiting technique was left to be dealt by Maar, "As I say, if Jelly won, which she did, then that also means her family won the prize money."

Emily stopped before the door and closed her eyes. "What?"

Maar rose from his seat. "Perhaps my colleague wasn't clear enough a moment ago. The two-hundred-and-fifty-thousand dollar final prize," he grinned behind her back, much to Dimitri's amusement, "It's all yours. You won."

Emily paused for a second longer and thoroughly digested this new dilemma. She had two options available to her.

1: Uphold her and her family's dignity and walk away. Sure, they'd be broke. Jamie wouldn't get out of Chrome Valley and lead a life worth living. Back to a life of obscurity. Or...

2: She could accept. The money would at least go some way to dampen the effect of the issues raised on point one. It might afford them opportunities in life.

Of course, Emily settled on the latter of the two options. But some caveats she'd yet to think of would need to be put in place.

Emily turned around and made sure they saw her displeased reaction, "The money?"

"That's right, *Emily*," Maar said. "It's yours."

"Right."

She walked back to the conference desk with Jamie.

"Mom, what are we doing?"

"Be quiet, poppet," she returned into the seat and pressed her hands together, "I will allow Jelly to take part on two conditions."

"We are all ears," Dimitri said, suppressing the urge to smile at USARIC's impending victory.

"The money. Half of it is to be transferred directly into a secure fund for my son when he reaches eighteen."

"Mom?"

"Hush, poppet," she turned to Maar and Dimitri for an answer.

"Of course, as you wish."

"Okay," Emily continued, "Two. You go out there right

now and tell that poor family what happened to their pet."

This was a condition USARIC did *not* want to entertain. Maar leaned forward and pleaded with her, "The Gagarin family are under the impression Bisoubisou is alive and well and a part of the Opera Beta mission."

"I don't care. Do you understand?" Emily said, defiantly, "If you want Jelly, you will go out there and tell that little Russian boy that his cat died because of you… *and* us."

"Are you out of your tiny English mind?" Dimitri yelped. "Emily, I beg you to reconsider."

"And stop calling me *Emily*," she fumed, wondering why the men in the room weren't using formal address, "You don't know me. We're not on first-name terms."

"I'm sorry if I offended you, but—"

"—Stop talking. I don't want your apologies."

Emily took a moment to catch her breath and calm down, much to the consternation of those in the room.

"That's the offer," she said. "I want proof of them having been told. I can be there with you if you like, but I need to know you did it."

"One moment, please," Maar said.

He and Dimitri whispered to each other, holding their hands over their mouths.

Emily tried to catch on to what they were saying but their conversation was surreptitious to a fault.

Wool and Tripp looked away from Emily and, instead, smiled at Jamie.

"Looking at my son won't do any good, mate," she said to Tripp. "This condition isn't up for negotiation."

Wool tried for a smile, "You do know that if Jelly joins us on the mission to Saturn, she'll be an instrumental part in deciphering the first extra-terrestrial message we've ever received. It could be a life changing event."

"Saturn?" Jamie blurted. "She's going to Saturn?"

"I'm sure it will be a life-changing event," Emily smiled back at her, angrily, "Let's hope your bosses make the right decision."

Maar and Dimitri adjusted their ties and cleared their throats, "We have decided on a compromise."

"It'd better be good."

"We *will* inform Remy and his family of what happened to his cat. But we would rather keep this update hidden from the public."

"Fine by me. I don't care about the public," Emily said, somewhat satisfied, "All I care about is them being told."

"Relations right now between our two countries are not exactly strong, despite our confederacy," Dimitri said. "We are trying to strengthen our relationship and abide by the 2085 Bering Treaty. If word gets out that a Russian citizen died during this process, it could start a second cold war."

"So, you'll tell them?"

"Yes," Maar said. "And as far as everyone is concerned, Bisoubisou is alive and well and a member of the crew of Space Opera Beta. No one will know that Jelly took her place. We pay the Gagarin family for their silence, and pay you for your participation—"

"—and everybody is happy," Dimitri finished.

A sense of satisfaction settled across the table.

Emily looked through the bars of Jelly's carry case. The cat looked back at her and licked her mouth.

"I suppose that suits us," Emily took a final glance at the team, "It looks like you've got yourselves your first cat in space."

"I guess that's excellent," Maar said. "Pleasure doing business with you."

Everyone stood up from their chairs and tucked them under the table. Business had been conducted, and USARIC and the Anderson family were happy.

"Mom?"

"What, poppet?"

"Does this mean Jelly is going, after all?"

"Yes," she whispered.

"So, here's what will happen next," Tripp said. "We'll take delivery of Jelly tomorrow morning. We'll message the papers to your hotel so you can peruse them and return them to us tomorrow, all signed and sealed. Sound good?"

"Sounds good," Emily said.

Tripp walked over to Jamie and squatted in front of him,

"And tomorrow, we can give you a little tour of Space Opera Beta. Show you where Jelly's going to spend the next few years."

"Oh, wow," Jamie jumped on the spot, "Really?"

"Yes, really. It's the least we can do," Tripp said. "Look, I promise you, Jamie. Jelly is going to be fine. And I'd like to introduce you to every one who'll be working with her."

Tripp did a great job of reassuring Jamie. It meant the world to his mother.

Chapter 6

USARIC Headquarters
Cape Claudius

"Welcome to the United States and Russian Intergalactic Confederation."

The USARIC logo, a dead-mix of fifty-two stars and a hammer, spun around on its axis in the middle of the room. Random footage of planets orbiting the solar system, happy families, and astronauts working on IMS zipped around it.

"For the past quarter-century, USARIC has been searching the outer reaches of our galaxy. Exploring the depths of civilization and strengthening the lives of all its citizens. We hope you enjoy your visit. May your day be productive and full of vigor."

Jamie admired at the screen as he held Jelly in her carry case, "I can't believe we're actually here."

Emily tugged his sleeve and nodded at the double doors, "I think that's them."

"Ah, hello. Emily," Tripp held out his hand to shake.

She smiled, finding it hard to ignore his pulchritude. The man was good-looking, to be sure, but this was pure business. She remained as professional as she could.

"Good after-morning, captain."

"Oh, I'm not the captain," Tripp explained, "I'm second-in-charge, Commander Healy."

"I see," Emily finally looked him up and down, "I have to ask, what does your wife think about you spending years away from home?"

"She's used to the idea. It's part and parcel of the business, I'm afraid," Tripp smiled and threw Jamie a sly wink, "S'up, champ?"

"Hello, sir."

"Jamie, right?"

"Yes."

"Well, Jamie, here in the United States we no longer use gender-specific titles."

"What is that?"

"You know. Titles? You're too young to remember when everyone called people mister and missus and things like that, right?"

'No," Jamie said. "We do that all the time. It's polite."

'Well, it's the law here now. It's very rude to assume people's genders when we—"

Tripp stopped talking when he saw Jelly's carry case. She revealed her teeth and showed him her behind.

"Huh. Charming," Tripp stood back up and addressed Jamie. "In our country we use people's first names so we don't offend people."

"That's weird," Jamie said in his naivety.

"That's fine. You Brits talk weird, anyway," Tripp rubbed his hands together and clocked Jamie and Emily's visitor badges. "Okay, you're all signed in?"

"Yes," Emily fought back the desire to pick up Tripp's blatantly xenophobic remark, "We're ready."

"Good stuff," Tripp turned around and nodded at the receptionist, who hit a button and opened the entrance gates. "Let's go see the spaceship!"

"Yay," Jamie skipped forward alongside Tripp.

"*Brits?*" Emily muttered, shook her head and followed behind them, "Pfft. Cheeky git."

Space Opera Beta

It was the mother of all space crafts. Beautiful and elegant, almost prestigious-looking. The cone-shaped vessel stood upright on its thrusters, pointing at the sky. There was no denying its profound uniqueness in relation to its sister space crafts.

The sheer size of its structure impressed Jamie as he, Tripp, and Emily walked along the airstrip to the scaffolding keeping the ship in place.

A couple of fighter jets, military personnel and technicians littered the runway. The latter performed checks on various vehicles.

The back of Jamie's head hit his neck, so tall was the structure of the cone-shaped craft. "Wow, is that the spaceship?"

"Yes, this is Space Opera Beta," Tripp said. "How tall do you reckon it is?"

"It's massive. It's like a skyscraper but, like, an ice cream cone skyscraper."

"Ha, very true. It's nearly one thousand feet, end to end. About the length of the Eiffel Tower. Do you know what that is?"

Jamie shook his head as they kept walking.

"It's that triangle-shape building in Paris, France. It's really big. It's sort of the same shape, really?"

"Yes, but it looks like a white, upside-down ice-cream cone."

"Yes, that's true," Tripp wondered aloud, finally able to see the ship through the eyes of a child, "You're quite right."

Emily was impressed, also, but tried not to display her wonder, "It's pretty good, I suppose."

"You *suppose?*" Tripp approached the landing gantry that led to the opening at the base of the spaceship, "Suppose nothing. This is absolutely amaziant. Wait until you see inside."

The view from Jelly's cage was less impressive. She saw the ship through several plastic bars. The edges of her cage meant she couldn't grasp the enormity of the vessel. Then again, she was only a cat, and it didn't matter as much as it did to Tripp.

Jamie felt the need to hold her up so she could get a better view of her new home for the foreseeable future..

"Look, girl. This is all for you."

Jamie and Emily entered the spacecraft. Tripp jumped up and down on the grille on the floor, trying to prove a point.

"Know what's underneath here?"

"No," Jamie said, "What is?"

"The thrusters. The back of the cone is effectively one huge blaster that makes the spaceship go forwards and backwards."

"Like a big fire?" Jamie asked.

"Sure."

A slightly overweight man with glasses, Captain Daryl Katz, approached the trio. In his fifties, he sported a withered face that had seen many a flight in his time.

"Well, here's the captain," Tripp said. "Why not ask him?"

"And who do we have here, Commander Healy?" Katz asked in his thick Texan accent. He shook Emily's hand.

"This is Jamie Anderson and his mother, Emily. And their cat, Jelly."

Katz pressed his hands to his knees and took a good look at her through cage's bar, "Cute little thing, ain't she? Coochie-coo, oh, you're cute, aren't you? Yes, yes... *yeeeeees...* you *are*."

The others sniggered as Katz spoke to her in a silly voice.

"Mister?"

"You can call me captain, champ," Katz adjusted his spectacles.

Jamie looked at the strange object on his face. They had no lenses in them.

"What's that thing covering your eyes, Captain?"

"Oh these," Katz slid them off his face and showed them to the boy, "They're called glasses. People used to wear them decades ago."

"Why?" Jamie took them and put them over his face. "They look silly."

"Well, in the old days folk were born with eyes that didn't see so good. So they needed to wear these to help them see better."

"Weird," Jamie decided he didn't like the antiquated gadget and handed them back.

Katz admired the unusual device for a moment and thought about his past. "Ah, they're more for decoration, really. They remind me of my grandfather. He used to wear them."

Tripp chuckled to himself, "I was just about to explain to young Jamie, here, how the thrusters work."

"Ah, the thrusters," Katz put his glasses back on and looked at the fat-end of the ship, "Gaseous core nuclear engines. Powerful stuff, but the ol' girl gets the job done, don't it?"

"What is *gassy binocular*?" Jamie asked, unsure if he'd heard the man correctly.

"Nuclear engines, Jamie," Katz banged the side of the vessel, "Kinda like tiny nuclear bombs that get thrown out the back and blast the spaceship to where it needs to go."

"Wow," Jamie blinked at the captain. "Sounds powerful."

"It sure is," Katz walked along the corridor and waved his hands, "The bombs create a ripple in the fabric of space and Opera Beta can surf on them to get where it needs to go much faster."

"Yeah," Jamie nodded. "Surfing is cool."

"Cool? It's positively *chilling*, young man," Katz chuckled at the child's wonder at the information. "Speaking of which, the whole outside of the ship is made of ceramic. The heat shields are made of it, too, to protect the crew."

"What is that?" Jamie asked, "Ceramic?"

"It's kinda like what your dinner plates are made from. You know when you take your dinner out of the microwave, and the plate isn't as hot as the food?"

"Oh yeah?"

"Yeah, like that. All the older spaceships didn't have it, and the people inside got very hot. But the clever scientists at USARIC figured out a way to modify its structure. It's lightweight and heat retardant, and works well."

Jamie sniggered to himself, hoping not to get caught.

"What's so funny, young man?"

"Nothing," Jamie wiped his mouth and tried to stop laughing.

"Naw, c'mon," Katz said. "Spit it out?"

"You said *retard*."

"Eh?"

Katz looked at Tripp for answer. All he got was an "I dunno" shrug of the shoulders.

"Did I say that?"

Tripp pushed through to the next point of interest.

"Aww, no," Katz finally caught on, "I said retardant, not *retard*. Though, I guess they mean the same thing…"

The door to the armory slid open.

Jaycee, dressed in his threatening exo-suit, inspected a variety of weapons.

"Ah, Jaycee," Katz said. "We have guests. Thought you'd like to meet them?"

Jaycee stood up from the bench and lowered the machine gun in his hands. As he stepped forward, the room rumbled back and forth under his heavy mechanical suit and footwear.

He saluted Jamie and smiled at his mother. "Yes."

"Jamie, this is Jaycee Nayall," Katz tapped Tripp on the back, "He's in charge of the armory on the spaceship. I'm afraid I have to go and run some last-minute checks. I'll leave you in the company of my second-in-command."

"Bye, Captain."

Katz winked at him and pointed at Jelly's cage on the way out. "Cute cat, by the way. Looking forward to working with her."

Tripp looked up at Jaycee and made some small talk. "Jaycee? Wanna tell the kid about yourself?"

"Sure," Jaycee slung the machine gun over his shoulder and pulled out a pistol. "This here is the Rez-9." He dropped the clip into his palm, satisfied that the chamber was empty.

"Here, wanna hold it?"

"Okay."

Emily watched her son take the gun in his hand and aim it at the lockers on the wall.

"Careful where you point that thing, Poppet," Emily turned to Jaycee. "Sorry, we don't have guns back home."

"I know," Jaycee sniggered, "And look where that's gotten you."

Emily ignored his pithy remark and turned her head.

"Bang," Jamie pretended to shoot the locker door, having the time of his life. "Wow, I love this. Can I keep it?"

"Oh, no, no," Jaycee grabbed the gun from out of his hands and slipped it back into his belt. "It's not a toy, it's very dangerous. It'll disintegrate every molecule in your body if you're not careful."

Tripp snapped out of his daydream and saw that Emily wasn't impressed with the armory.

"Hey, thanks, Jaycee," he said. "I think we'll move on, now. Time is of the essence."

"Any time."

"Follow me," Tripp pressed his palm against the panel on the wall. The door slid open, allowing him and Emily through.

Jamie approached the door and turned back to look at Jaycee. He placed his left boot on the workbench and tied his shoelaces.

"He looks really sad," Jamie muttered.

"So, this is the main passageway that connects all the different areas of the ship. We call it the hub."

Tripp pointed at various protrusions coming from the corridor walls.

Pipework.

Fuse boxes.

Connected strip lights shot into the foreground, illuminating the shiny linoleum-esque flooring.

"What is a hub?" Jamie asked.

"It's like a central point for people to meet. No point showing you that as it's just a big meeting room. Pretty boring."

Tripp turned a corner and made his way to the medical facility.

"Okay, this one is cool," Tripp approached the door. "This is Wool's office. You remember her, right?"

"Yes, the brown lady?"

"Yeah," Tripp spat. "The *brown* lady. Jelly's new carer."

The three of them made their way into the area.

"It's like a hospital in here," Emily said, sniffing around.

"Welcome to Medix," Tripp looked around the tables and beds for his colleague. "USARIC has some of the highest-trained medicians on the planet. Wool is the best one we have."

He moved forward and looked over at her computer desk, "Wool, are you here?"

Jamie was fascinated by the beds. One in particular, a much smaller structure, sat at the far end of the room. A drip lay next to it along with a small monitor on a metal tray.

"This looks like an animal bed?" Jamie said. "It's too small for a person."

"Yes," a familiar voice came from behind Jamie. "It's exclusively for Jelly."

Wool ar-Ban approached the trio with a great big smile.

"Hi, Wool," Jamie said.

"Hey, Jamie," she turned to Emily, "You must be his mother?"

"Yes. Hi."

"Before we go on, I'd like to apologize for what happened yesterday," Wool shook Emily's hand, "It was very unfortunate, but I can assure you that it's not symptomatic of USARIC's usual handling of things."

"That's okay," Emily said. "It's not for my benefit. It's for my son. He loves space and spaceships and stuff like that."

"Yes, so I hear," Wool smiled at Jamie and held out her hands. "So, this is my area of the ship."

Jamie looked around, impressed, "You're a doctor?"

"No, I'm a *medician*."

"You do magic tricks and stuff?"

"No, not a magician. Medician."

"What is that?"

"I'm a veterinarian and general practitioner for human beings."

"Why are you brown?" Jamie asked in his infinite naivety. "Are you Indian?"

Wool burst out laughing and shook her head. "Gosh, no. Whatever makes you think that?"

"You've got brown skin like an Indian."

"No, I'm half Iranian," Wool said in her perfect American accent. "My father was Iranian and my mother was American. And you're English, right?"

"Yes."

"And where's your father?"

Jamie shrugged his shoulders and lifted Jelly's case into the air. "He's in heaven, now."

Emily looked away from Wool and bit her lip. Her son's somewhat emotionless remark hit her right in the gut. It wasn't the woman's fault she's asked such an unfortunate question.

Wool caught on immediately and turned the emotional tables around. "I've heard her name is Jelly?"

"Yeah. Wanna meet her?" Jamie asked.

"Sure. Put her on her bed and we'll take a look."

Jamie plonked the cat's carry case on the little hospital bed and unclipped the locks.

The cage sprung out, inviting Jelly to freedom. She wouldn't come out of the case. Wool ducked her head down and looked the cat in eyes. "Hey, girl."

Jelly ducked her head and looked at her paws.

"C'mon, let's get you out of there," Wool reached in and grabbed Jelly under the arms. The cat fought back at first. Once she was in the arms of her new carer, she purred and rather enjoyed the comfort.

"I think she likes me," Wool said, cradling Jelly in her arms. "Who's a *good* girl, then? My little honey."

"She likes you, Wool."

"Yes," she said and stroked the cat's chin with her knuckle, "She looks very happy. Evidently feels safe with her little engine running."

"Great stuff," Tripp approached his colleague and held her shoulder. "We don't have much time, and I'd like Jamie to meet everyone."

"Oh, sure," Wool offered Tripp Jelly to carry. "You want to take her, Commander?"

"Sure, hand her over."

Tripp took Jelly into his arms and observed her face. "Wow, she really is special, isn't she?"

"She's one in a million. Quite literally." Wool winked at Jamie, who grinned back at her. "Jamie, don't worry. She's in safe hands. My job is to look after her, and I intend to do just that."

"Will you feed her and make sure she gets lots of exercise?"

"Of course, Jamie," Wool walked back to her computer desk. "Have fun checking out the ship. I'll make sure you get some screen time with Jelly once we're out of hyper-sleep, okay?"

"Okay."

Tripp, Jamie and Emily made their way to the other end of the corridor. A silver screen door lay at the very end.

Tripp crouched down and allowed Jelly out from his arms. "Go on, girl."

"Wait. Is it safe?" Jamie asked.

"She can only go forwards or backwards. She'll probably reach the next room before us, anyway. It's good for her to have a bit of a run around. Get her used to the ship."

Jelly reached the door to an area named *Botanix*. She scratched at the glass, excited at the playground that lay behind it.

"Where are we going now?" Jamie asked.

"Botanix," Tripp explained. "It's the part of the ship that provides us with oxygen and fresh water."

"How does it do that?"

"You'll see."

They reached Jelly, who butted her head against the door. He placed his palm onto the panel on the wall. "Open up."

It slid open and offered a full view of what Jelly had seen moments ago.

Rows and rows of plants, too varied and numerous to mention. Two powerful lamps shone over them. Silver foil lined the soil as far as the eye could see.

Jamie and his mother were taken aback by just how clean the air was. As expected, Jelly ran up the rows and explored the place for all it was worth.

"Haloo?"

"Hello?" Jamie asked. "What?"

"No, Haloo," he said, "My colleague."

A young woman hosed the second row of plants and spotted her new visitors entering the room. She saw the cat weaving in and out of the plants.

"Hey, guys. Is that our winner poking around my geraniums?" Haloo asked.

"Yes, that's Jelly."

"Huh," Haloo watched her rummage away at the soil. "Gonna have to keep an eye on her, then."

"My name is Jamie Anderson. I'm Jelly's *human*," he said, offering his hand.

Haloo smirked and took the kid's hand in hers. "Nice to meet you. I'm Haloo Ess, Opera Beta's botanist."

"Botanist?"

"Yes, I look after the plants."

"Cool," Jamie threw her hand away and ran after Jelly. "Hey, girl, come back here."

Emily and Tripp chuckled as they watched Jelly sneak around the plants trying to hide from her master.

"Hey, Tripp. Did we get those new purifiers I ordered?"

"I'm not sure. I'm about to have Baldron, our new engineer, and the other new guy check it. I forget his name."

"Tor, I think."

"Right, that's him," Haloo smiled at Emily. "Hey, congratulations on winning, by the way. A real honor to be working with your... *cat*. Jelly?"

"Yes, Jelly," Emily said. "Is she really going to be *the first*?"

"Yes, she is. Is there anything you'd like to ask while you're here? You can ask anything."

Emily looked around and took in the sheer height of the room. At least thirty-feet tall. "This is really impressive. So, all this provides all the oxygen you need?"

"Yes, it's a cyclical process. As long as us humans, and, uh, *felines*, keep on producing carbon dioxide, the plants continue to generate oxygen and provide fresh water."

Haloo nodded over at the far end of room. "The room is hermetically sealed when not in use, so CO_2 levels remain constant. God forbid we ever have a fire in here."

"Why?"

"The place would go up in an instant, so the entire place is fireproof. Bombproof, actually."

"Well, that is reassuring," Emily looked over at Jamie and Jelly playing around in the plants. "Hey, guys. C'mon, don't disrupt the lady's work area."

"Oh, they're fine."

Jamie scooped Jelly up in his arms and scrambled over to his mother. "I think she likes this room."

"I'm not surprised," Emily said, "Loads of opportunity to hide and trash the place."

The statement received a knowing chuckle from Tripp and Haloo.

"Okay, I better get back to work," Haloo said. "The tank needs refilling."

"Okay."

Haloo returned to her hose amongst the plants. "Please check on those filters, Tripp."

***

"This spaceship is so big," Jamie said to Tripp as they made their way to the front of the vessel.

Emily clutched the handle on Jelly's carry case. She looked through the bars to see that her pet was unhappy. The cat clawed at the bars and whined.

"Hush, Jelly," Emily said.

"We're going to meet a very special person," Tripp walked into the Fit Room.

"Wow," Jamie took a look around.

Treadmills.

Exercise bicycles.

Rowing machines.

In the corner, a young woman with brunette hair held her fists up at a mannequin. She bounced around on the spot, ready to attack it.

A holograph of a man's face appeared on the silver head of the mannequin. The woman squinted at it and clenched her right fist.

"Stop looking at me," she screamed at the mannequin's face. Her body lifted into the air and roundhouse-kicked the mannequins head. The piece of plastic exploded and bounced off the wall, leaving fine debris remnants to float to the ground.

"Bonnie?" Tripp shouted across the room. "Are you fit?"

She lowered her head and slowed her breathing. "I'm fine," she said, socking the headless mannequin in the gut with anger.

"Whoa," Jamie stopped in his tracks, afraid to go anywhere near her. "Who's she?"

Bonnie twisted her head to the young boy and flicked her hair over her shoulder. "Who are you?"

"This is Jamie Anderson and his mother, Emily," Tripp said.

'Hi,' Jamie offered, innocently.

Bonnie took a towel from the wall holder and wiped the sweat from her brow. "So?"

"Their cat won the Star Cat Project." Tripp took the carry case from Emily and presented it to Bonnie. "Here she is. Jelly."

Bonnie looked through the bars with a blatant nonchalance. "Oh, cool."

Jelly meowed at her from inside the case. Bonnie's demeanor changed the moment she clapped eyes on the animal.

"Can I hold her?" she asked.

"Sure."

Bonnie opened the cage. Jelly relished the opportunity to jump out into her hands. She nestled quite comfortably in her arms and clawed at the woman's fingers. "Cute cat. What's her name?"

"Jelly," Jamie said. "I'm her *human*."

"Cool."

Jelly's purring was so loud that it could be heard from the other end of the room.

"I'm Dr. Bonnie Whitaker," she smiled. "Opera Beta's physicist."

"Why were you punching that plastic thing?" Jamie asked,

to the amusement of Tripp and Bonnie.

"Oh, just getting some exercise. Do you know Jitsaku?"

"No? What is it?"

"It's a fusion of Jujitsu and Kung Fu. You use your enemy's power against them." She looked for a reaction from Tripp. "We have to stay fit and exercise otherwise we'll slow down. Shame we can't do the same for our mental state, isn't it?"

Tripp grinned at Jamie. "Bonnie, why don't you show young Jamie, here, your special feature?"

"Sure."

She passed Jelly to Jamie and unbuckled her inner-suit pants. Emily widened her eyes, expecting the worst.

"Actually, it's better if you don't—"

"—No, it's not what you think."

Bonnie stepped out of her pants. Metal bolts and wires adorned her right leg. She lifted her thigh and showed off the unusual amalgam of joints and connectors.

"Oh wow," Jamie said with awe, "What happened to you?"

"I don't remember, exactly. When I was a girl I got an infection. It started in my foot and spread to my joints, here." She pointed at her hip.

Her left leg was perfectly fine, and perfectly formed. Jamie's attention was drawn to what lay between them behind her underwear.

"Hey, kid. Look at my leg, not my crotch."

"Sorry."

"I think you may have a new admirer, Bonnie,' Tripp joked and threw her a wink.

"Shut up.' Bonnie lifted her right knee and wiggled it around. The mechanics whirred away under her fingertip. "Jamie, you see that?"

"Yes?"

She removed the lower half of her false leg. "I can take it off and replace it with various things. It's made of titanium, a bit like the claws we'll be putting on Jelly, here."

"What?"

"Ah," Tripp tried to hush his colleague, "Yes, we haven't

quite gotten around to discussing that just yet."

"I'm sorry," Emily butted in, full of confusion. "Did you say you're going to be putting Titanium on Jelly?"

"Oh," Bonnie reattached her leg and pulled up her pants. "Do they not know?"

"They do *now*," Tripp shook his head, angry at having been put on the spot.

"What's this about?" Emily took Jelly from Jamie's arms and cradled her, "You're not going to interfere with her, are you?"

"It's a small procedure, but a necessary one," Tripp explained. "When we've reached our destination, Wool will perform what's known as a *cuticle restructure*."

"What's that?"

Bonnie buckled her belt and pressed a button on the wall. "Her claws will be removed and replaced with a set of Titanium ones, along with a *thumb* attachment."

Jelly looked at the humans in the room, understanding very little of the surgical proposition.

"What?" Emily grew nervous. "No, I don't think so."

"It's a perfectly straightforward operation. Of course, it'll be reversed when she returns to Earth."

"No," Emily turned around and made for the door. "Come on, Jamie. We're leaving. I knew this was too good to be true."

"I'm afraid you've already agreed to it," Tripp said. "In the contract, the stipulation under enhanced modification."

Emily had heard enough. "No, I'm afraid not. We're going. Come on, Jamie."

"But, mom—"

"—No buts." Emily stormed out of the Fit Room, looking for the ship's exit. "This is *terriful*. No way to treat a cat. They should be locked up."

Jamie chased after his mother as she left the room, leaving Bonnie looking a little worse for wear.

"Sorry."

"*Great*," Tripp said, sarcastically. "Thanks for that, Bonnie. If it weren't for your big mouth, they'd have never known."

"I'm sorry," Bonnie said. "I forgot."

Tripp ran after the Andersons with his voice lowered. "Yeah, that's your whole problem."

"Excuse me," Emily asked a technician in the hub corridor. "Where is the way out, please?"

He pointed at the far end of the walkway. "About a quarter of a mile down there, to section Z."

"Thanks."

She grabbed Jamie's hand and sprinted down the corridor with Tripp in pursuit.

"Emily, listen—"

"—No, leave us alone. The whole thing is off."

"No, you don't understand," Tripp pushed past the technician. "Please, stop. Let me set your mind at rest."

Emily halted in her tracks, intending to make a point in full view of the technicians. "No. Let me set *your* mind at rest, okay?"

Tripp slowed down and nodded, "Okay?"

"There is no way on Earth I am going to allow you to interfere with or *modify* my cat."

"It won't happen *on Earth*, in fact," Tripp hoped his clever joke might change her mind.

It didn't. It had the very opposite effect.

"Are you taking me seriously?"

"Of course," Tripp said. "It's a procedure we must put in place. Please allow me to explain."

"You've got thirty seconds."

A crowd of technicians couldn't help but listen in as they pretended to work.

"Jelly is the first cat on a manned mission to Saturn. She can't defend herself or perform basic procedural commands as she is. The infinity claws are a basic insurance policy for us and for her."

"What utter *lessense*—"

"—No, Emily, please. Stop talking and listen to me to me very carefully. We take Jelly's safety and well-being extremely seriously. I know it sounds strange. Bizarre, even. The whole removal of her claws sounds painful. I can assure you it isn't."

"You guys are sick."

Tripp sighed, nevertheless determined to make his point. "You saw what happened to Bisoubisou, yesterday? An allergic reaction?"

"Yes, it was *terriful*."

"Exactly. The primary reason why we couldn't take her on. Jelly responded well to the temporary set yesterday during the finals. There's no danger. She'll be absolutely fine."

"Mom?" Jamie looked up at her, "She'll be okay."

Emily considered her position on the matter. The look in her little boy's eye was reassuring - to a point. There was simply no way Jamie would agree to the whole venture if he thought Jelly would come to any harm.

Then again, he was only five-years-old.

Emily looked Tripp dead in the eyes, wanting her arm twisted once and for all.

"No pain?" she reaffirmed.

"No. None whatsoever. I can have Wool walk you through the procedure—"

"—And she returns to normal once she's back, right?"

"That's right."

Emily huffed and took a final look at Jelly. In a strangely ironic twist she dug her claws into Emily's arm, offering her approval.

Chapter 7

"Welcome to the Control Deck," Tripp said. "This is where we operate Opera Beta. All the communications are conducted from this area, here."

Tripp walked Jamie over to a huge bank of screens and buttons. An impressive sight for such young eyes. It resembled a video game console with ample opportunity for fun.

"Wow, can I sit in the seat?" Jamie ran over to the swivel chair parked in the middle of the unit.

"Sure. Please don't touch anything, though."

Tripp offered Emily a smile of contrition. He hoped that the debate they'd had in the corridor hadn't shown USARIC in too bad a light.

His attention was drawn to the flight deck. Dimitri Vasilov talked to two men Tripp didn't recognize.

"Jamie?"

"Yes, Tripp?"

"Over there, where those three men are. That's the flight deck."

"Wow."

Jamie stood up and jumped on the spot. "That's where you fly the spaceship?"

"Yes," Tripp whistled at the three men. "Hey, Dimitri."

The elderly man turned around, surprised to see that he and his colleagues had company. "Oh, yes. Of course. Hello, Tripp."

Dimitri walked with the two men over to the communications deck. "Tripp, your timing is impeccable. I'd like you to meet our new intake. Communications Officer Tor Klyce and Engineer Baldron Landaker."

"Ah, yes," Tripp shook their hands in turn. "I thought you were due to arrive tomorrow?"

"Good to meet you, finally." Tor Klyce, a thin man in his early thirties, spoke with a clear mid-western American accent. "Yes, we left Minneapolis Two a day early to run a few diagnostics on The Manuel."

"You know what USARIC is like. Always ahead of schedule," Baldron clocked Jamie and his mother - and the cat in the carry case. He seemed perturbed by their presence. "What's this? Are we allowing civilians aboard our vessels, now?"

"Oh, no. Not quite," Tripp explained. "Jamie and Emily are the owners of Jelly, here. The winner of the Star Cat Project."

"Okay," Baldron made eyes at the cat as it sniffed around the plastic bars. "One in a million, right?"

"Something like that," Tripp smiled. "She's a very special addition to Opera Beta."

"It's ridiculous," Baldron cleared his throat and looked at Dimitri. "Sending a cat into space. I'm sorry, Jamie, but it's ridiculous. Please excuse me."

Baldron walked off, leaving Tripp, Jamie, Emily, and Tor lost for words, "I'll be with Wool if you need me."

"I'm sorry about my colleague," Tor walked over to the communications deck, "He's a bit jet-lagged from the flight. He's very concerned about the logistics of the whole *cat* thing."

"How's Manuel doing? Retained all his faculties?"

"He's fine," Tor punched a few buttons on the panel, "Fifteen brontobytes of data need to be reconciled. He booted up about an hour and seems bright and perky, which is a good sign. You want to meet him?"

"What is a... *man-well?*" Jamie asked.

"The autopilot. A veritable data bank of knowledge," Tor explained, pointing at the screen in front of him. "To activate him, all you need to do is click your fingers and say his name."

"Okay."

"Did you ever see Fawlty Towers?" Tripp smirked. "That old TV show from the twentieth century?"

"What is a TV show?" Jamie asked. "Is it like a screen?"

"Never mind," Tor chuckled. "Just click your fingers and say his name."

Jamie held up his hand and snapped his fingers. "Manuel?"

Snap.

A holograph of a book appeared in the middle of the room, floating on the spot, flapping its pages from end to end. "Good pre-afternoon. How may I assist you?"

Jamie blinked at the transparent object floating in the air. "What do I—"

"—Ask it anything you like. It has all the answers."

Jamie looked around, taking the sheer wonder of the deck into his mind. He drew a blank for the first time in his inquisitive, young life.

"Uh, why are you called Manuel?"

Manuel sped over to Jamie and opened up its pages, displaying a black and white image of Pascal D'Souza.

"My full name is The Manuel. I was put together by my creator, the late Pascal D'Souza. Originally, I was referred to as The Manual, however, when they loaded me into USARIC's mainframe the first time, an error was made. As you can see."

The picture of Pascal D'Souza moved like a recorded video. He bopped his fellow scientist on the back in anger.

"Why isn't The Manual responding to my commands?"

His colleague hit a button on his computer and pointed to the erroneous letter in the manual's name. "There's been a slip up. Someone must have pressed E when they meant to press A."

Pascal shook his head in incredulity. "So we've christened our hyper-intelligent autopilot and data bank as… *The Manuel*? What is this, some kind of joke?"

"I'm sorry, Dr D'Souza—"

The image paused, allowing Manuel the flip over by one page.

Manuel's holograph turned to Jamie. "I am able to process close to one billion commands at any given time."

"Wow, that's a lot."

Tor chuckled to himself. "We were just completing Manuel's assessment. Would you like to see it?"

"Yes, please," Jamie said.

"Manuel?" Tor asked. "What does USARIC stand for?"

"It won't stand for anything," Manuel said. "They are a very stern company."

Emily and Tripp smirked at the crude joke.

"That's not that I meant and you know it," Tor said. "Please, give me the correct answer."

"It was just a joke."

"I know, give me the correct answer."

"USARIC stands for the United States and Russian Intergalactic Confederation."

"Correct," Tor pressed a button on the communications panel. Manuel's holograph lit up. "Tell me the genesis of the company, please?"

"Certainly. USARIC was formed in the year 2100, shortly after the disbanding of NASA."

"Correct." Tor winked at Jamie. "Good, isn't he?

"Yes. I want one when we get back home."

"Ha," Tor punched in some data on the comms panel. "Manuel?"

"Yes, Tor?"

"Can you explain to our guest why USARIC was formed?"

"Certainly," Manuel opened his pages and whizzed to the end of his book. Footage of a space shuttle launching from its pad played out.

The Manuel
A Brief History Of USARIC
Pg 808,107
(exposition dump #157/b)

The United States and Russian Intergalactic Confederation (USARIC) *is the result of a convergence of two states - the US state of Alaska, and the north-eastern territory of Chukotka in Russia. The Bering Strait lies in the middle, separating the two nations, which lent its name to the treaty drawn between the two nations.*

The two states amalgamated to form Chukaska, across the start and end point of the international time zone.

In order to allay a second cold war, the presidents of both countries agreed that the two states merge jurisdictions, thereby forming an alliance.

The switch took place in 2087, two years after the Bering Treaty was formed. In 2088, it was decided that the two nations conform to a confederacy.

The result was the free movement of people from both the US and Russia into both jurisdictions.

In five years, both economies saw a surge in productivity. As a result, wages kept in line with inflation. Companies set up shop globally, at various points in both countries to quell the cost of distribution.

The most remarkable effect was the formation of USARIC. NASA was summarily disbanded. Its protocols and legislature was reconfigured to merge both the US and Russia's efforts to explore outer space as one entity. In effect, any discoveries that were made would be shared equally. A combined space race, with certain caveats, if you will.

Two months after this formation, tragedy struck. Cape Canaveral in Florida disappeared, along with the rest of the state due to The Great Southern Flood of 2092. Four million people lost their lives and the nation lost its sunshine state. It proved to be an avoidable event. For the previous one hundred years, scientists had speculated that global warming would have this effect. The government chose not to listen.

Floridians fled to Texas, contributing to the density of that state's populace.

On the recommendation of the governor at the time, the United States opted to split the state into North and South.

Despite the loss of Florida, The United States gained three states in the amalgamation of Chukaska and the division of Texas. Of course, the flag was redesigned to represent the fifty-two states and its convergence with Russia, hence the addition of the hammer (but not the familiar sickle, as it was deemed to be an outmoded tool.)

USARIC relocated their base to Cape Claudius in the state of South Texas.

Located on the southeast peninsula, it is the closest point to the equator that can launch vessels into space. One of the protocols in the Infinity Clause stipulates that no Russians may take part in any manned exploration. It was a stipend that caused no end of frustration to that particular nation—

"—Okay, that's enough, Manuel," Tor clicked his fingers. "We don't want to bore the poor boy, do we?"

Jamie blinked rapidly, his little mind going into overdrive. "Wow."

"Funny you should mention that, Tor," Manuel flipped his pages and landed toward the middle of the book. "In conjunction with Pure Genius, I have been conducting research on evolution since my reboot. My findings have been quite curious. Would you like to see them?"

"Uh, okay?" Jamie pretended to understand. He knew it sounded scientific and serious, and that was enough for him.

"With your permission, I'd like to explain to you a concept I have named *The Natural Order of Life.*"

"Go ahead, Manuel," Tor said. "But make it quick, we can't stand around chatting all day."

"Certainly," Manuel rose into the air and beamed an image onto the floor. "Observe. The Natural Order of Things has long-since been a quandary for humankind. Life, hence, any living and breathing organism."

A recorded holograph of a cat pouncing on a rat played out across the floor. Jamie waved his hand right through it in amazement.

"Thus, we can reasonably ascertain the following. Every predator has a prey, as exemplified in my findings.

For every name that appeared, a corresponding image floated next to it.

"Where the greater-than symbol is present denotes *is afraid of.* Broadly-speaking, the chain is as follows…"

Insect > Mouse

Mouse > Cat

Cat > Dog

Dog > Man

Man > Woman

Tripp and Tor took in the information with great expediency.

Jamie just sat there, stunned. "What does that mean?"

"The Natural Order of Life," Manuel explained. "However, the discovery was the reconciliation of the loop. Thus..."

Woman > Insect

"That's quite the discovery, Manuel," Tor rolled his eyes at Tripp. He lowered his voice enough for Manuel not to hear him. "He may need a bit more calibrating before we actually take off, by the way."

"Yes, it's good to see he hasn't lost his sense of humor," Tor chuckled and rubbed his hands, eager to leave. He looked at Jelly and raised his eyebrows. "I'll be back soon. We just have a small matter of the acquisition of our new colleague to deal with…"

USARIC Headquarters
Conference Chamber

Dimitri Vasilov and Maar Sheck sat at the far end of the conference table chatting to themselves.

Jamie stroked Jelly as she lay on the other end of the table. She was sedentary for the time being, enjoying the final few moments she had with her owner.

Tripp sat with Emily, going through the final particulars of the contract. He flipped over to the last summary sheet.

"Just need your signature in triplet. Here, here, and here," Tripp pointed at the three sets of dotted lines.

"Okay," Emily hesitated for a second and looked at her son as he tickled Jelly's stomach.

"Meow."

"Are you quite sure she's going to be all right?" Emily asked Tripp. She wondered why the two stern-looking men were at the other end of the table and disassociating themselves so blatantly.

"Yes, of course," Tripp said, watching her sign the documents. "I will make sure of that, personally. You have my word."

"I hope so."

"You know, Emily," Tripp tried to reassure her. "I have a son your boy's age. I know how much Jelly means to him."

Emily scribbled her signature as quick as she could and pushed the paper away from her chest.

"A very antiquated way of conducting business. Pen and paper?" She passed the pen back to him and watched the ink dry on the paper.

"It's the way we like to do things. *Some* of us at USARIC haven't quite shaken off the analog stuff just yet."

Maar broke away from his conversation with Dimitri. "All good?"

"Yes, I think so," Tripp lifted the papers in his hand and showed them to his superiors.

"Good," Dimitri said. "So, I think we're all done here."

"It seems so," Tripp added.

"Are there any final questions or queries you have for us?" Maar asked.

"You can't tell me what the mission is? Where, exactly, she's going?"

"I'm afraid not," Maar said. "If anything goes wrong it would be bad news."

"What if something does go wrong?"

"It won't."

"Right," Emily said, not terribly convinced.

"But if it does, it's better that you don't know the details. Trust us, everything will be fine."

Jamie stroked Jelly's face. She loved every second of it. He looked up and tried his luck. "When does Opera Beta leave?"

"Two weeks from now, young man," Maar said. "She's due to return in at the end of 2120. How old will you be then?"

"Eight."

The door to the conference room opened and Wool walked in with a silver plastic cage under her arm. "Hello, everyone. Hi, Jamie."

"Hi, Wool."

She offered the boy a smile and sat the cage onto the conference desk. "Is she ready?"

Jelly rolled over and stretched her hind legs out. Her tail flapped around. Jamie took a moment to watch her in action. A small, quiet movement he decided to commit to memory before she jumped to her feet and demanded one, last hug.

"Meow."

Jamie held out his hand and pressed his fingers together. Jelly ran her face along his hand, making a fuss of the connection. He held her head in both hands and looked her in the eyes. She had no clue what was about to happen.

"We'll see each other again, girl," Jamie whispered. The reality set in the moment the words escaped his lips. He began to tear up. Jelly wanted to know why he was so sad.

"Take her," he said through his tears.

Jelly tilted her face, wondering why her friend was so upset. The drama set Emily off, too. "Oh God, please. Just do it."

"Yes, of course," Wool clapped her hands together and showed Jelly to the cage. "In you go, honey."

"Meow," Jelly looked at it and decided not to go. She approached the end of the table and tried to get Jamie's attention.

"No, no," Wool cupped Jelly's face in her hand with deft expertise. She slid the cage up to her behind and pushed her back.

The cage door slammed shut, imprisoning Jelly. She clawed at the cage, trying to push it open.

Wool lifted the cage and made her way to the conference room door.

Jamie took a final glance at his cat being escorted out of his life. She had a look of disappointment on her face. How could my best friend do this to me? The look seemed to say it. It was hard for Jamie to shake off.

Then, he slammed the conference desk and stood up, barely able to peer over it. Tripp, Maar, Dimitri, and his mother turned to him in shock.

"Take me with you," Jamie pleaded.

"What?" Tripp asked.

"Take me with you. I know how space works and I can help you on your mission."

"But, Jamie, it doesn't work like that."

"Poppet, no," Emily held her son back. The same couldn't be said for his floods of tears. "Jamie, listen—"

"—Mr. Healy, you're an astronaut. I'm going to be an astronaut one day, too. Let me go with you."

"Jamie," Tripp tried, calmly, "It takes years of training. And we can't allow children on—"

"—But you're taking a cat,' Jamie interrupted and pointed at the cage. "You can take a cat but you can't take me?"

"Poppet, please."

Tripp held out his hands. He felt useless. "I, uh, don't know what to say?"

"Then say *yes*." Jamie released himself from his mother's clutches and clambered toward the cage in Wool's hand. "I want to go with her."

Emily caught his jacket and pulled him back. "No. It's done."

Tripp felt sorry for the poor little boy. "I'm sorry, Jamie.'

"We should get going," Wool turned to do the door, trying to avoid the unfolding grief in the room. "Goodbye, Jamie."

"But, mom," Jamie struggled to free himself, choking with regret through his vocal chords. "I d-don't want her to g-go—"

"—Jamie, no. It's done," Emily whispered.

The door shut on Jelly's face.

His cat was gone forever, as far as Jamie was concerned.

Little consolation for the boy who broke down on the table in a heap of turmoil, crying his eyes out.

A day he'd never forget.

A decision he'd never forgive himself for making.

He'd allowed his friend go off into the great unknown. If only he could take it all back.

The USARIC logo spun around above his head, triumphantly. The company had won.

A five-year-old's loss wasn't enough to stop the company's endeavor…

Chapter 8

USARIC Data Point
Space Opera Beta
Year: 2119
Days traveled: 551
Distance to Enceladus: 203,140 miles

The hyper sleep arena contained nine chambers, the first and sixth of which had been opened.

Tripp Healy lay asleep in the second pod. He'd grown an impressive amount of facial hair during the journey.

Captain Daryl Katz surveyed the chamber, enjoying what was about to be the last moment of pure solitude.

"Manuel?" Katz asked.

"Yes, Daryl?"

"We'll start with chamber two and Tripp Healy. Once he's oriented we'll move on to the others. Can you prepare the debrief in the meantime, please."

"Certainly, Daryl," Manuel said, "Do you wish to notify Tripp about what we've found?"

"Not yet. I'll update him myself when he's oriented."

"Understood. Releasing chamber two, now."

Katz approached Tripp's chamber and pressed his palm to the wall. "Okay, Tripp..."

The Perspex on the second chamber unbolted and lifted down. Tripp remained asleep for a few moments. His eyelids fluttered against the vibrations of his unit.

"Tripp?" Katz asked, softly. "Wakey-wakey."

He opened his eyes very slowly, adjusting his retinas to the light shining down on him.

He reached up and wiped his mouth.

"Ugh," Tripp inspected the thin layer of black film that had wiped off on his finger. "Are we here?"

"Yes," Katz said, making his way to the computer console. "Be careful with your first few steps. I'll fix you a drink."

"Thanks."

Tripp stepped out of the chamber and temporarily lost his balance. He looked down the length of his body, analyzing his underwear and paper footwear.

"My legs feel like concrete logs."

"You're acting like you've never been in space before."

"I know, I know," Tripp pushed himself away from the wall and ground his right heel into the ground. "I've been asleep for over a year. Somehow, it doesn't feel that long."

Tripp looked at the remaining chambers that housed the rest of the crew. He clocked the opened sixth chamber. "Haloo is awake, as well?"

"Yes. You, me, her, and Manuel," Katz offered Tripp a cup of coffee and a small, white pill, "Get some caffeine in you, and take this."

"Thanks," Tripp tossed the pill in his mouth and knocked it back with a swig of coffee.

Katz eyed him, trying to see if his colleague managed to retain his faculties after a year of deep sleep.

"All good?"

"Yeah, I'm fine," Tripp rolled his shoulders and tilted his neck. "So, what's the news? When did you wake up?"

"This time yesterday," Katz moved to the console and hit a button. A spectral image of Space Opera Alpha hovered over the desk and spun on its axis. "Look at this."

"Opera Alpha?"

"Yes."

"Why are you showing me Alpha?"

Katz looked at Tripp and performed a last-minute check to see if anyone was eavesdropping. "Manuel discovered it en route to Enceladus about two months ago. Alpha never disappeared."

"What? Where is it now?"

"It's orbiting the dark side of Enceladus, about two hundred thousand miles away.

"That's ridiculous," Tripp shook his head, thinking he was still dreaming. "That moon doesn't have enough pull for orbit."

"It's not gravitational, Tripp," Katz pointed at the thrusters on the back of the holoprint. "The vessel is active, still running. Traveling alongside it. Our star drones never picked it up. It's been sheltered in darkness."

"Have we tried making contact with Opera Alpha?"

"Yes."

"And?"

"Nothing. It's not responding," Katz enlarged the image and kept his voice quiet. "It's been missing for four years, all communication lost. Until now."

"Do the others know?"

"Of course they don't, they're all asleep."

"No, I don't mean *them*," Tripp waved his hand at the hyper sleep chambers. "I mean back home. Does USARIC know?"

"Not yet. I've waited to inform you before proceeding. I've talked it over with Manuel."

"What did he suggest?"

"That we wake everyone up and inform them, then report to USARIC with a unanimous decision to divert our course."

Tripp found the revelation compelling. "What are we going to tell them?"

"The truth, of course."

Botanix

Tripp pressed the creases out from his inner suit as he walked along the concourse. He reached the single door and pressed his palm against the panel on the wall.

"Level Three. Botanix," a female voice announced. "Please ensure all incendiaries are secure."

"The door beeped and slid open, allowing Tripp into the area.

Six rows of plants covered in silver foil lined the room. Tripp glanced at the newly-installed fresh water filter in the middle of the room.

"Haloo? Are you here?"

"Tripp?" She poked her head out from around the fountain and lifted the watering hose. "You're awake?"

"Yes, came out about an hour ago."

Tripp walked along the plant life and took the opportunity to get a lungful of the freshest air aboard the vessel. "Remind me to spend more time in here when I'm resting."

Haloo returned to watering a row of flowers by her feet. "Have you come to recuperate, or do you need something?"

"Just saying hello before everyone else wakes up."

Haloo didn't seem impressed. "Why do I get the feeling that you're here to ask a favor?"

Tripp watched Haloo hose down the soil, wondering how on Earth - or space - she knew his real intentions.

"What makes you say that?"

"Your posture," she said. "The way you entered the room."

"That's creepy."

"Also, you gave me an answer to a question I never asked."

"You asked if I was awake?"

Haloo spun the dial on the hose, shutting off the water. She arched her back and smiled at him. "I didn't ask anything. I made an observation."

Tripp chuckled. "Are you always like this?"

"You want me to soak you?" Haloo lifted the nozzle in Tripp's direction.

"No."

"Explain this for me," Haloo retrieved a black capsule from her inner thigh pocket. "Is this what I think it is?"

"Yes. Standard issue for all galactic exploration."

"I don't like it. We're not in the KGB. We can't be expected to commit suicide if it all goes wrong.

"You may find you'd reassess that decision if you found yourself in serious trouble. It's just an insurance policy. Everyone has one."

A spurious silence fell between the two. She slipped the black capsule back into her pocket with displeasure. "Anything else?"

"We've found Opera Alpha."

"Katz has told you, then?" Haloo and Tripp stared at each other for two seconds longer than comfort allowed. She finally looked away and rolled up the hose. "Of course I knew. What do you think Katz and I have been doing while you guys have been asleep?"

"Do we know if Botanix on Alpha is operational?"

"We don't know anything, yet."

"Because if it is, there's a good chance Zillah and her crew might still be alive."

Haloo stopped and turned around, upset. "Don't you think we already thought of that?"

"You're right. I'm sorry."

She made her way to the door, "We need to investigate Alpha. Make sure that they're actually *dead...*"

The Crew Hub
Six Hours Later...

The hub served as the crew meeting point in the nucleus of Space Opera Beta.

The screen on the wall provided a beautiful view of space and Saturn revolving some hundreds of thousands of miles in the distance.

It had taken the best part of the day to ensure everyone disembarked their hyper-sleep pods successfully.

Captain Katz stood by the window and caught everyone's attention. "Beta team, I think we're ready. We're just waiting for Wool."

Haloo and Tripp sat next to each other at the conference table.

Opposite them, Tor Klyce and Baldron Landaker downed their fifth cup of coffee.

Jaycee, decked out in his armor exo-suit, sat with Bonnie at the foot of the table.

The door to the hub slid opened.

Wool ar-Ban walked in and rubbed her hands together. "Sorry I'm late, Daryl."

"Wool, during debrief I am *Captain*, if you please."

"I'm sorry," Wool took her seat next in between Jaycee and Bonnie.

"It's nothing personal. It's more for the minute-taking and data points."

"Yes, Captain."

"Okay," Katz snapped his fingers, beckoning Manuel over. "Manuel?"

"Yes, Captain," the holographic book flew over and flipped through its pages. A blank sheet appeared, followed by a hovering transparent pen. "Ready when you are."

"Don't minute this part, Manuel." Katz approached the conference table and pressed his finger on the glass surface. A diagram of Space Opera Alpha appeared in front of the crew.

Manuel's pen clicked off. The pages flipped shut as he sidled over to the captain.

"Until twenty-four hours ago, we thought Saturn Cry was transmitting from Enceladus. It wasn't."

"No?" Tor took a keen interest in the revelation. "So where is it coming from?"

"Here." Katz pointed at the radio transmitter on the bridge of Space Opera Alpha. "It seems like Enceladus is using Opera Alpha as a beacon to send the message."

"Alpha is present?" Bonnie asked.

"Yes, Dr Whitaker. She's orbiting the dark side of Enceladus."

"Do we know if the crew are alive?" Baldron asked.

"We don't know anything, yet. We've tried to communicate with Alpha's Manuel, but to no avail."

"What are you suggesting, Captain?" Tripp asked, knowing the answer already.

"I am recommending a change of course. We dock with them, establish contact and rescue any souls on board."

"What if no-one survived?" Haloo asked.

"Then there's nobody to rescue. We continue our trajectory to Enceladus and conduct our inquiries."

Tripp stood up and pointed at the holograph of the ship. "It makes sense to investigate. Enceladus itself can't possibly be sending the signal. It's just gas and ice. It's using Opera Alpha's comms to transmit the signal, that much we do know."

"Hold on a second," Bonnie stood up, giving as good as the crew were getting. "Alpha goes off-radar for five years. Missing."

"Yes."

"And now it's suddenly reappeared?"

"Well, I'm not sure if—"

"—And you want us to go and check it out?"

Tripp interrupted the feisty woman. "Let's review our situation, Dr. Whitaker. Our mission to Enceladus is to investigate the source of Saturn Cry."

"Right."

"And we *know* it's using Alpha to transmit that signal. I mean, that's just plain fact, now."

"How do we know?"

Tripp pressed his finger to the glass. "Manuel?"

The book floated over to the screen and opened up. "Yes, Commander?"

"Configure point A on Opera Alpha radar and broadcast, please."

"Configuring now."

Manuel beeped three times and tuned himself into the holograph on the screen. The radio transmitter flashed red, and threw its connection to the speaker on the book.

A hissing noise fired up, followed by three strings of an electric guitar.

"Ugh, we're fed up with hearing this thing, already," Tor shook his head and nudged Baldron in the ribs. "We'd rather go back to sleep."

"Don't be funny, Tor," Tripp said, encouraging the crew to listen to the message play out.

Whump-whump-whump… hiss…

"Sounds different?"

"Twelve seconds in," Tripp held up his hand to halt the chatter, "Shh."

A warbled thud followed by a high-pitch squeal, like that of an injured lion, streaked across the audio.

"You hear that?"

"Yes," Jaycee said, "Sounds different to the one we're used to hearing."

"We're closer to the signal so the quality is better. Pause playback, Manuel."

"Yes, commander."

The hissing stopped. Everyone's attention turned to the diagram of Space Opera Alpha.

Katz walked up to Tripp and addressed the crew. "As far as Commander Healy and I can see, we have two options. One, we establish a Task and Finish protocol to rescue whatever we can of Alpha."

"What's the second option?" Bonnie asked.

"We ignore Alpha entirely and continue our course to Enceladus proper."

"In other words, we do what we're supposed to?"

Katz sighed. "I need to report back to USARIC and notify them of our unanimous decision to investigate Alpha. For that, we need consent from every soul on board this ship, as per The Infinity Clause."

Tripp looked at each crew member. Most seemed to be on board with the rescue attempt - all except Bonnie.

"Can we, in good conscience, ignore Alpha? Can we continue our mission to Enceladus *knowing* that we ignored our colleagues and left them for dead?"

Katz interjected. "Dr. Whitaker, can I ask you what the problem is?"

Everyone turned to her for a response.

"Sure," she said. "We don't know what state the ship is in. We don't know what happened to Alpha. What if they're all dead? Or something has happened to them? We could suffer the same fate."

"The fate of being hidden on the dark side of Saturn's sixth moon?" Tor suggested, somewhat sarcastically, "That we were okay all along and went missing, only for our friends to come poking around and ignore our cry for help?"

"That's the point, Tor,' Bonnie interjected, 'Alpha isn't

crying for help. It's just *there*. You seem very keen for us to board and investigate," Bonnie turned to the holograph of Space Opera Alpha, "Opera Alpha isn't reaching out to us. If they were alive they'd be yelling at us to rescue them."

Tor ducked his head and folded his arms. He didn't have a response.

"What if they're unable to reach out for help, Dr. Whitaker?" Katz attempted to balance the odds, "If, somehow, they're unable to communicate for whatever reason?"

"Then that's a bunch of souls aboard a spaceship I don't want to go anywhere near."

"So you're saying *no*, Dr. Whitaker?" Katz asked, disappointed. "We discover that Alpha is there and *don't* investigate?"

"I'm not saying *no*," Bonnie scanned her crew mates the table, "Oh, *come on*. Am I the only one here who's concerned about this change of course?"

Tor and Baldron looked away.

Jaycee couldn't look Bonnie in the eyes.

Haloo, Tripp, and Katz, on the other hand, had no compunction in demonstrating their desire to rescue the ship.

"What's the first rule?" Bonnie asked. "Be skeptical. Question *everything*. My question is this. Why did Alpha go missing? Why is it back? Why is it being used by a *moon* to transmit a message."

"We don't know, Dr. Whitaker," Tripp said, "Are you saying you don't want to find out?"

She shot him a look of disdain, knowing full well that her superior was correct.

"Ugh."

"Okay, all those in favor of diverting course to check out Alpha raise your hand. Ayes?"

Everyone's hand rose into the air. Everyone, that is, except Bonnie's.

Tripp gave her a smile, keeping his hand up. "Dr. Whitaker?"

"Fine," she caved in and raising her hand, "But I want it on record that I'm not happy with this."

"Looks like the ayes have it. Unanimous," Katz made his way out of the hub, "We are less than twenty hours from Opera Alpha. I suggest you all orient yourself as you see fit and prepare for contact."

Katz reached the door and turned around to Wool ar-Ban. "Can you wake up our feline guest, please?"

"Yes, Captain," Wool joined Katz and walked out of the hub.

Tor turned to the others and shook his head. "I keep forgetting that stupid cat is on board."

"Don't call her stupid," Tripp said. "She might just be the key to what we're looking for."

"Yeah, right," Tor said, kicking his chair away from the console in defiance. "She's more trouble than she's worth. Landaker, can I have a word, please?"

"Yes."

The pair walked out of the hub talking to themselves, leaving Bonnie, Tripp, Haloo, and Jaycee to chat amongst themselves.

***

Wool leaned over Jelly's hyper-sleep pod and hovered her finger over the release switch. A smile crept across her face as she took a moment to absorb the beauty of the creature.

"Look at you, honey," she whispered, "You look so peaceful. So perfect."

Jelly looked as comfortable as could be, resting face-up toward the glass.

"There's a lot to play with up here. I think you're going to like it."

Wool hit the button.

The glass retracted along the length of Jelly's body. A few strands of fur lifted into the air as she shuffled around, still unconscious.

Wool put on a pair of plastic gloves and reached into the pod. She stroked Jelly's stomach with her knuckle. The monitor attached to the unit began to beep, indicating that Jelly was about to wake up.

"Jelly?"

The cat opened her eyes and lifted her paws to her face. She wiped her brow and spun onto her side.

"There we go," Wool reached in and lifted Jelly under her arms.

"Meow," Jelly grunted, exercising her vocal chords for the first time in over a year.

"Good girl," Wool whispered and cradled Jelly in her arms. "Take your time, honey."

Jelly shuffled around and kicked her hind legs forward, stretching every muscle in her body. She licked her lips and dug her paws into Wool's inner-skin suit.

"Hey, gorgeous. How are you?"

Jelly licked her lips again and clung to Wool's arm. She let out a whine, fascinated by her surroundings.

An infinite playground surrounded her.

Desks, monitors, and chairs - ample opportunity to mess around, discover things and hide.

"Meow."

"Yes, Jelly," Wool walked over to the lab's bench in the middle of the room. "This is your new home."

Wool set her on the bench. Jelly jumped from her arms and immediately made for the edge. A five-foot drop to the floor didn't seem like much of a task.

"Oh no, no, no," Wool grabbed Jelly and slid her back along the bench. "Not yet you don't, honey. I need to inspect you."

"Meow." Jelly struggled to release herself from Wool's clutches.

"Hold on, girl."

"Look at me, Anderson," Wool took out a mini flashlight and shone it in Jelly's face, "Left eye, please."

Jelly's orange pupil focused on Wool's face.

"Seems good. Right eye, please."

The light zipped over to Jelly's other eye. Wool look around for signs of anything that may be untoward.

"Yep. Looking good."

"Meow."

"All set. A bit dilated, but nothing to worry about.," Wool

ran her hand along Jelly's back smoothing out her fur. "Hungry?"

Jelly ran the side of her head along Wool's hand and purred.

"Very good, Jelly. Very good."

Wool ran her thumb over Jelly's right shoulder and observed the scar where the chip had been implanted. "Manuel?"

"Yes, Wool?"

"Can we synchronize our guest with your coordinates, please?"

"Of course."

The holographic book appeared from out of thin air and flashed a green locater against a map of the ship. "J. Anderson is currently in the hyper-sleep quarters."

"Yes, I know she is. She's right here."

"Meow." Jelly launched into the air and tried to claw at the holographic book. It flew backwards in an attempt to evade capture.

The book fluttered to the other side of the bench. Jelly turned around and made for it once again.

"Ha. Jelly, it's no use, honey. You can't touch Manuel."

"Meow."

Jelly swiped at Manuel but missed as he hovered several feet into the air.

"I know she can't touch me," Manuel said, "But she scares me."

"She's just a cat, Manuel."

"I realize that. I think I'll just stay up here for a moment."

Wool chuckled and lifted Jelly under her arms, "Come here, honey."

"Meow."

Jelly threw her arms over Wool's shoulder and kept looking around as they made their way out of the hyper-sleep quarters.

Wool carried Jelly through the hyper-sleep concourse - a long corridor with boxes and attached units on either side of the wall.

"Now, if I let you down do you promise not to run off?"

"Meow."

"I'll take that as a yes."

Wool squatted and released Jelly onto the ground. "Enjoy yourself while you can."

The cat wasted no time exploring the concourse. She bolted to the far end as fast as her legs could carry her.

"Whoa. Calm down, honey," Wool yelled.

Jelly reached the far door and found that it wouldn't open. She whined and knocked it with her head.

Then, the door slid open, startling her. "Meow."

She looked up the legs of the man standing in front of her. Tripp looked down and smiled.

"Ah, she's awake."

"Yes, Tripp," Wool said, hopping after Jelly. "Just stretching her legs."

"I can see that," Tripp looked at the mischievous cat. "Wearing yourself out, are you?"

"Meow."

"Such a good girl," Tripp crouched down and offered her his hand. She ran her face along his fingers. "How long till we suit her up?"

Wool scooped Jelly into her hands and looked at her face. "We'll get her fed and let her get her energy up. Shouldn't take more than a couple of hours to suit her up."

"Very good," Tripp began to walk away.

"Tripp?"

"Yes?"

"We're going to be okay, aren't we?"

"Of course we are."

"What with the change of course and everything?"

"Yes, of course. Why wouldn't we be?"

Wool placed her face on top of Jelly's head and breathed in. "If something happened to Jelly, I'd never forgive myself."

"Wool, look," Tripp walked back and offered her some reassurance. "We'll be fine. Androgyne will check Opera Alpha out first and let us know what's happening. There's absolutely nothing to be afraid of."

"I know," Wool muttered. "That's what's scaring me."

"What, you're scared because there's nothing to be scared about?"

"Yes," Wool half-chuckled at her own revelation. "Something doesn't seem right."

"Exactly," Tripp smiled. "That's what we're here to fix."

Chapter 9

Daryl entered the control deck at the front of the ship and made his way to the pilot's seat.

Tor Klyce busily tapped away on the board on his communication panel.

"Tor, any response from Opera Alpha?"

"I'm patching into their network now, Captain."

"We're off record, Tor. You can call me Daryl for the time being," Katz strapped himself into his chair. He flipped two red switches which created a polymorphic grid on the screen overlooking Saturn. "Hit the radio on frequency zero-five-four-niner."

"Understood."

Tor unhooked the comms device and squeezed it in his hand. "This is USARIC vessel Space Opera Beta, communicating on a frequency of zero-five-four-niner. Do we have contact?"

Nothing but a short burst of static came from the speaker. Tor held the button down again.

"I repeat, USARIC vessel Space Opera Beta, communicating on—"

A short burst of warbled static shot through the speaker, cutting Tor's announcement.

"What was that?"

Katz turned to him in haste, "Try again."

"Space Opera Alpha, do you read us?"

The warbled sound dampened down into a familiar hiss.

"I'm not sure what that interruption was."

"—Everything okay, here?" Baldron Landaker walked into the control deck and adjusted his inner-suit sleeves, "Do we have contact with Opera Alpha?"

"Not as such, no," Tor turned a dial on his control bank, "Just a weird static. Erratic at best, and we can't do anything about it."

Baldron punched his mechanical fists together and looked over at Katz. "We still on with them?"

"Yes we are, Baldron," Katz returned to his controls. "Just making up our revised route to the docking bay, now. Is Androgyne prepped?"

"Jaycee and Tripp are with her now," Baldron slowed his speech. The enormity of Saturn and her rings overwhelmed him for the first time since waking up. "My God, would you look at that. She's a beast, right?"

"Yes she is," Katz said as he punched the data into his computer, "Alas, she's not where we're headed. See that tiny white dot, top-left?"

"Yes," Baldron walked over to the flight deck. He stood next to Katz and took in the view.

"That, there, is Opera Alpha," Katz said. "We're just a few hours away…"

N-Vigorate Chamber
Level Three

Tripp and Bonnie entered the smallest compartment aboard the spaceship.

A circular hub with a diameter of exactly fifty feet.

Tripp made a beeline for a silver-coated 'woman' resting on an electric chair at the opposite end of the room.

"You think she's up for the job?" Bonnie asked, following behind Tripp.

"With a one hundred percent success rate?" Tripp asked, "I'm surprised we haven't been replaced by the Androgyne series altogether."

"Yeah," Bonnie shot the sleeping droid a stern look, "Look at her. A useless piece of junk."

"Until we boot her up, that is," Tripp felt the side of

Androgyne's neck. The droid was extremely lifelike. He pushed her earlobe out with his knuckle, revealing a small tattoo on her neck which read *Manning/Synapse.*

Tripp nodded over to the gears on the desk beside Androgyne's chair. "Bonnie, hit the juice."

"My pleasure."

She walked over to the lever and yanked it back.

The droid's chair lit up and vibrated.

"Activating Androgyne," announced a female voice.

Tripp took a step back, allowing the droid some space. "Moment of truth."

Bonnie smirked and scratched the side of her leg. "She's such a show-off."

Androgyne's eyelids lifted to reveal her crystal blue eyes. She blinked a couple of times, emotionless and peaceful. A faint sound of the mechanics operating her joints could be heard.

Finally, she performed a smile. To say it was anything other than lifelike would be a gross understatement.

"Oh, my. I am awake," Androgyne said, lifting her head forward slightly. "Good after-morning, Tripp Healy. Dr Whitaker."

"It's actually evening by our watches," Tripp smiled at her. "But we forgive you. It is dark outside after all."

"Is it not always dark in space, commander?" Androgyne blinked twice and tilted her head left and right.

"How are you, Androgyne?" Bonnie asked.

She turned her head to Bonnie and went to stand out of her chair. "I need to calibrate, could you please—"

A thick cable attached to the back of her head yanked back, throwing her bottom to the seat once again.

"Whoa. Easy, tiger," Tripp moved forward and held Androgyne by the sides of her face. "You're still plugged in. Don't move."

"Plugged in?"

"Yes, uh, give me a second…"

Tripp reached around the back of her head and lifted her hair up. The cable came free as he twisted it away from the top of her neck. "There, you're free now."

"What was the problem?" Androgyne asked. "Was there something on my head?"

"Uh, no," Tripp shot Bonnie a threatening stare. She tried not to laugh.

The Manuel
Pg 11,256

The Androgyne series first came to fruition in the year 2075. It was designed to replace canaries on space missions, to use the laymen vernacular.

Official estimates are unclear but, since records began in the early twentieth century, an estimated three hundred birds had been used on missions and all but two of them died on their expeditions.

They were used to test the atmosphere and oxygen levels of planets, in much the same way miners did when scavenging the depths of the Earth.

Due to the extreme upheaval caused by PAAC, People Against Animal Cruelty, the decision to abandon guinea pigs with wings (the nomenclature associated with canaries in such conditions) was enacted. They were replaced by androids with a human brain and organs.

The Androgyne series is commonly referred to as a simple machine. *It operates much like a human: it requires oxygen to breathe. It desires attention and a sense of belonging and purpose.*

Unlike a human being, however, the Androgyne does not know that it is not human. It is therefore essential that any and all crew members oblige the android accordingly.

On the 21st October, 2102, USARIC, together with the Androgyne series company, Manning/Synapse, *conducted an experiment.*

Under controlled conditions, they hooked up an early series droid to an E-MRI scan and attached its wrists and ankles to a rejuvenation console. In other words, it had its power cable attached to the back of its neck.

The lab technician entered the room and proceeded to tell the droid that it had been remanded in custody. That 'she' was under suspicion of attacking a crew member.

It was absolute lessense.

The series 1.0 Androgyne had committed no such crime. Naturally, she questioned the veracity of the claim. The E-MRI reported that the droid was capable of feeling confused and angered. That particular aspect was checked off the lab technician's list.

Also 'checked off' the lab technician's list was the ability to breathe properly when Androgyne strangled him a few moments later.

He had told her that she was not human - that her ability to recall basic prior events was not a function built into her programming.

The technician was not lying.

All of these things were true. Once powered off for energizing, the Androgyne system underwent a "crypt-wipe' - ergo, it forgot everything it ever knew in an instant.

When Androgyne 1.0 learned of her non-human status, she flipped out and attacked the technician. It took fifteen of his colleagues around three minutes, which is a very long time by anyone's measurements, to pull the droid off the man and power her down.

The off switch was relocated in the recent 2.0 upgrade - from inside the left thigh, to the forearm, complete with protective casing.

It was a commonly held misconception that Androgyne would be readily available for home use by the year 2110. Due to its violent and erratic nature, it was sold to USARIC by Manning/Synapse for $10 bn for exclusive space exploration use.

The lab technician continues to eat his meals through a straw some sixteen years later...

***

Wool ar-Ban spent a good hour or so chasing Jelly around the mid-section of the vessel. The cat had had a good work out and felt fatigue start to set in.

Jelly accidentally found her way to Botanix. She clawed at the glass door, wanting to get into the vast green playground that tempted her from the other side of the screen door. It was an area she remembered well from the tour of the ship.

A place to play.

Wool stepped after her and placed her hands on her hips. "You want to go in and see the plants?"

"Meow."

Jelly ran her claws along the glass a second time, demanding satisfaction.

The door slid open before Wool had a chance to explain

137

to her new feline friend that it might not be a good idea.

"Jelly," Haloo emerged from behind her computer terminal and chuckled as Jelly darted through the first row of plants. "Oh, my. She's a curious one, isn't she?"

"Thanks for opening the door," Wool said, sarcastically. "We'll never catch her, now."

"Ah, she'll be fine," Haloo watched Jelly rummage around the soil, looking for something to kill. "The door is closed. She can't get lost in here."

"How is everything?" Wool asked.

"Still turning carbon dioxide into oxygen if that's what you mean."

Wool took in the impressive view of various plant life. The rows were illuminated by a set of powerful lamps hanging from the ceiling.

"Would you like some fresh H2O?"

"Yes," Wool followed Haloo over to a unit in the corner of the room. "Jelly's tiring herself out. She's already had a go on my inner-suit."

"Got some sharp claws on her, huh?"

"You could say that," Wool inspected her sleeve and tugged a string of fabric away. "She must be thirsty."

"Call her over. I'll fix a saucer for her."

Haloo pressed a button on the machine and held a paper cup under the nozzle. The unit hummed to life and released a jet of ice-cold water.

"Here, get your lips around this."

"Thanks.

Wool took a sip and felt a shiver roll down her spine. "Mmm. That's crazy good."

"I know, right?"

Jelly snaked in and out of the bamboo plants. She bent over and patted her knees "Jelly? Come here, girl."

"Meow."

Jelly was too preoccupied with her new playground to obey any orders.

Haloo shook her head and giggled, "How on Earth did she pass the obedience test?"

"No idea."

"This is silly," Haloo stood up straight and removed a paper cone from the holder. She slid her fingernail under the glue and bent the edges out, "Maybe she'll respond to this."

Haloo held the makeshift paper saucer under the water nozzle and filled it half way.

"Ooh, you're good," Wool chuckled. "I'll have a refill after you're done with her."

"Sure," Haloo set the half-full paper saucer onto the floor and squatted in front of it. She clapped her hands together and whistled. "Jelly? Come, get some *fresh*."

"Meow."

Jelly knew exactly what was on offer and ran out from the plants. She screeched to a halt on her paws and helped herself to the water.

"Good girl," Haloo aided Jelly's drinking session by rubbing her back, "You're such a cute little thing, aren't you?"

"Don't let her charming exterior fool you, Haloo," Wool laughed and refilled her paper cone. "She's a vicious little thing when she wants to be.'

"Yes, but she's *our* vicious little thing," Haloo giggled and ran her palm over Jelly's head as she drank from the saucer. "When is she due for installation?"

"The Infinity Claws operation only takes twenty minutes, but she'll need an hour of R and R after we're done."

"How's her paw-eye coordination?"

"Did you see her entrance a few minutes ago?" Wool licked her lips with excitement, "It's on point."

"Aww."

Haloo couldn't resist Jelly's adorableness. "Such a *good* little girl, aren't you? Yes. Yes, you are."

Jelly purred loudly as she sucked down the last drop of water.

"Come here," Haloo scooped Jelly under her stomach and cradled her in her arms. She looked at the cute face staring up at her.

The light from the lamps reflected across Jelly's eyes. Haloo brushed her thumb over the cat's face, feeling the soft, voluminous fur.

"Beautiful creature, you are. So healthy. So *alive*."

Wool smiled and tossed the paper cone in the recycle bin next to the dispenser. "She's the most perfect cat I've ever met in that respect. Not a blemish. Absolutely nothing wrong with her. A truly unique specimen."

"That little boy back home must be missing her," Haloo said, finding it difficult to tear her eyes away from Jelly's face. "I feel sorry for him. What was his name?"

"Jamie."

"Yeah, I remember now. Jamie."

"He knows she's in good hands. We'll look after her."

"Yes, we will," Hallo moved her nose onto Jelly's and kissed her on the head.

"Meow." Jelly rubbed her face on Haloo's and licked the ends of her hair.

"Oh. She doesn't do that with me," Wool said, pretending to take offense. "Well, well, well… talk about allegiance."

"Ha," Haloo chuckled, pulling Jelly's mouth away from her face, "Well, it could be because I have cleaner hair than you."

"Dry shampoo?" Wool snorted held out her hands, "I doubt that. Pass her over."

"Sure."

Haloo passed Jelly back to her. The cat licked her lips and got comfy in Wool's arms.

"Swing by Medix when you have time. Don't be a stranger."

"I will," Haloo smiled and waved at Jelly, "Bye-bye, sweetie. Have a good operation."

"Meow."

USARIC Weapons & Armory
Space Opera Beta - Level Four

A metal boot slammed to the floor.

The laces tightened across the tongue of the boot and squeezed shut. The foot stomped onto the ground three times.

"Pure Titanium, that is," Jaycee said, looking down at his leg, "Absolutely impenetrable."

Baldron Landaker stood beside him, impressed with his colleague's footwear. "What's that got to do with weapons?"

"This." Two barrels swung out from the sides of the boot and armed themselves. "Stand back."

"Okay."

Jaycee lifted his knee and aimed it down the shooting gantry.

BLAM-BLAM-BLAM-BLAM!

Two bullets fired from each cylinder and hit the silhouetted mannequin target. Bits of plastic flew in all directions. Even at a clear fifty-foot distance, the boots provided a remarkably accurate shot.

Baldron waved the smoky residue from his face and pulled the creases out from his inner-suit. "So, if we come across any tangos, we just shoot them with our feet?"

"No, the footwear is for me. I just want you to know I have them."

"Understood."

"Katz wanted me to show you the firepower, so here it is," Jaycee snapped his fingers. "Manuel?"

The holographic book appeared in the air and hovered around, awaiting instructions. "Yes, Jaycee?"

"Captain Katz has asked me to acclimatize Mr Landaker here with our arsenal. Can you avail Armory One, please?"

"Certainly."

The book flickered into nothingness as Jaycee marched away from the shooting range and into the armory proper. Four bays stood before them, ensconced in the wall.

"Opening bay one..." Manuel's voice advised.

"Wait till you see this," Jaycee smirked as the bay doors slid open.

Baldron watched in wonder as an infinite assortment of weapons revealed themselves.

"What kinda guy are you?" Jaycee asked, approaching the first bay.

"Eh?" Baldron double-took, snapping out of his mire. "What kinda guy am I?"

"Yeah, you know, slow and measured? Or run-in-and-flank-on-a-whim-and-a-prayer type of guy?"

"Oh," Baldron said, "I've flanked a few back in my service days."

"And they thought you were the best for Opera Beta?"

"I guess so."

"You don't convince me. I can see I'll have to test you."

Jaycee unhooked a particularly vicious-looking shotgun from within the first bay. He threw the side lever down and cocked the barrel.

"Do you know what this is?"

"A gun?" Baldron tried.

"Very funny," Jaycee flipped the catch down and slammed the under-barrel into his left palm. His right hand squeezed the grip, forcing his index finger around the trigger. "This here is the K-SPARK. Flick the switch down for semi-auto, flip it center for the single-most devastating proton blast the galaxy has ever seen. Don't point it at anything you *don't* want destroyed. Here."

He passed the behemoth to Baldron, who buckled slightly under its sheer weight. "Whoa, this is heavy."

"Yeah, it's not exactly user-friendly. You should be used to the weight, right? Being an engineer?"

"Definitely. It's not *that* heavy."

"Good. It's not my weapon of choice for mobility, but when this baby is ground mounted it'll fend off swathes of bad guys."

Jaycee watched on as Baldron tried to wrap his finger around the trigger. "Be careful with that, pal."

"Why?"

Jaycee flicked the side switch up, locking the trigger down. "I have a feeling if you fire this baby, it'll jump out of your hands."

"Yeah," Baldron passed the gun back to Jaycee and took note of his huge frame in the process, "Well, not all of us are seven foot tall and built like a brick house."

"And don't forget it," Jaycee moved to the second bay and grabbed a cylindrical device from the shelf. "Do you know what the difference is between a smart bomb and a dumb bomb?"

He pushed the black grenade into Baldron's chest. "Uh,

no?"

"A smart bomb can be deactivated once the pin is pulled."

Baldron inspected the black grenade. "And a dumb bomb can't?"

"Correct."

Jaycee pulled the pin out of the grenade, causing Baldron to soil himself. "Guess which one you're holding?"

"Uh, the d-dumb bomb?"

"Nope," Jaycee slammed the pin back into the grenade and snatch it out of his trainee's hand. "That would've been a dumb move. Smart bombs are black. Dumb bombs are red. Remember that."

"Okay."

"Right, firearms. Ones that won't slow you down," Jaycee returned his K-SPARK onto its holster. "We have to start you somewhere. I tell you what. We'll KISS it."

"Kiss it?"

"KISS. Keep it Simple, Stupid,"

Jaycee reached for a mini hand gun in the third bay and threw it into his right hand.

"The Rez-9. The lightest firearm we have. Standard release mechanism. One hundred per magazine. Once you're used to it it'll take three seconds to reload."

Jaycee slid the catch back and tilted his head at the sight on the weapon. "Two spare mags sit in the housing for easy refill. See what you think of this."

He tossed it to Baldron, who caught it clumsily in his hands.

"Be careful you don't blow your thighs open, there."

"Sorry." Baldron held the gun in his hand and pointed it at Jaycee. "Put your hands up, sucker."

Jaycee chuckled to himself and held up his hands. "Oh no, you caught me. What did I do wrong, officer?"

"Ha."

Without warning nor notice, Jaycee swiped the barrel out of Baldron's hands, locked his arm around his back and buried the barrel of the gun into his temple.

"Agh, help. Help."

"Don't you ever, *ever*, point a weapon at people you work

with. Do you understand me?"

"Yes, yes," Baldron squirmed in Jaycee's clutches. "I u-understand. Please let me g-go——"

Jaycee yanked his arm up his back and cocked the gun, threatening to blow Baldron's brains out.

"——What's your role on this vessel?"

"I'm... I'm Beta's engineer, sir."

"First Lieutenant, Mr Landaker," Jaycee shouted in his ear, angrily, "I'm not a sir. What's the first rule of USARIC's Infinity Claws, one point one?"

"What?" Baldron asked, about to soil himself. Death was a hair trigger away.

"I said what is the first point in USARIC's Infinity Claws?"

"That all v-ventures be manned appropriately with just cause and for the benefit of mankind."

"That's right. Good work," Jaycee released the man and returned the Rez-9 firearm to the first bay.

Jaycee patted Baldron on the back, trying to coax him out of his impending coronary. "I like you, you're funny."

"I think you broke my arm."

"That's okay, you know how to replace a damaged limb, don't you?," Jaycee pushed Baldron in the chest with his huge fist. "Just remember what I said. No funny business."

"Okay, okay," Baldron squirmed. "I'd have to be out of my mind picking a fight with you."

"That's the second thing you've got right. Never forget it," Jaycee stormed away from the armory. "I'll show you the rest of the arsenal later. Let's get you strapped up and see how good your aim is."

Jaycee stormed out of the room, leaving a petrified Baldron quaking himself in his shoes. He looked down at his hand, thankful that Jaycee hadn't seen him swipe a red dumb bomb from the cabinet.

He tucked it in his inner-suit pocket and walked after him.

Chapter 10

Medix
Space Opera Beta - Level three

"Jelly? Can you hear me?"

It was pitch dark. All the cat could hear was Wool's voice.

A sound of whirring emitted from her claws. Something felt weird.

"Jelly, honey? Open your eyes."

A thin sliver of light crept into her retinas. A pair of blurred paws came into view.

"Meow."

The claws were not a dull gray as she'd expected. Now, they were a unique kind of silver. She pulled her claws in and back out.

An additional side-claw had been clamped to both paws. She moved the tendons back and forth on all four cuticles. A mechanical whirring occurred with each swift action.

Wool peered into view and smiled. "How are you feeling?"

Jelly rolled onto her side and caught sight of her inner-skin suit. The name *J. Anderson* adorned the side.

A specially-designed scratch post had been installed at the foot of her surgery bed.

"Meow," Jelly tried to take off her new claws. She needed to use the set on her other paw to do it, but it was no use. She gave up, made her way to the wiry scratch post and dug her shiny new claws right in, stretching them away from her paw.

It felt better.

But those dastardly metallic and sharp additions confused her.

"Opposable thumbs," Wool ran her finger underneath them. She turned the other way to grab something from the surgery bench.

Jelly looked up and managed to make her 'thumbs' move, but didn't have a clue what to do with them.

Wool produced a squishy rubber ball. She pinched it between her thumb and forefinger. "See?"

"Meow," Jelly tilted her head and observed Wool squeezing the ball in her hand.

"Catch," Wool dropped it on the bed. Instead of catching it in her paw, she accidentally batted it away.

"No, no," Wool caught it as it rolled off the edge of the bench, "Try again. Here…"

Wool rolled the ball gently toward Jelly. She pressed her stomach to the surface of the bed and eyed it with intent.

Jelly waiting for the right moment to pounce.

Then, she launched forward and grabbed the ball with both paws. Her thumb cuticles were wasted on the endeavor.

The pads on her paws kept the ball in place as Jelly sniffed around, ensuring it wouldn't strike back.

"This is going to take some time to get used to, isn't it?"

"Meow," Jelly opened her mouth and sunk her fangs into the ball, playing with it.

Katz's voice appeared in Wool's ear, "Wool, are we ready, yet?"

"Yes," she held her finger to her ear, "She's awake and relatively sedentary."

"Glad to hear it. Can we proceed?"

"I think so," Wool held out her hand for the ball. Jelly played with it, reticent to let it go so soon, "Give me the ball, Jelly."

The cat whined and covered it with her paw. She wasn't done with it yet.

"Jelly, don't make me ask twice."

"Wool?" Katz asked, "What are you doing? Are you talking to Anderson?"

"I'm waiting for her to stop playing the fool," Wool shot Jelly a stern look and clicked her fingers, "Now, please."

"Meow," Jelly scanned the ball and decided to let it go. Quite by accident, she clutched the ball using her new thumbs and rolled it back to Wool.

"Good girl," Wool pocketed it and held out her arms, beckoning Jelly into them. "Let's go and do some work."

The Manuel
The Speed of Thought
Pg 773,313
(exposition dump #779/7a)

Pure Genius *is a super-computer. Invented by USARIC, it became a revolutionary communication device which changed the course of the future and, in some cases, even the past.*

Shortly before his death, Pascal D'Souza worked with USARIC to develop a logical system of interpretation. The result was Pure Genius, *a room that harnessed every emotion, physicality and attribute of the user inside it.*

First to use Pure Genius *was D'souza himself. He and his team invented the Genius Drive that harnessed one of the twenty-first century's greatest findings -* The Speed of Thought *- a speed several times faster than the commonly regarded* Speed of Light.

The Speed of Thought*'s speed is approximately 788,501,118 miles per second.*

Until October of 2110, humans believed that nothing could travel faster than light. Saturn Cry changed all this when it was decoded by D'Souza. Light, being a physical utility was limited because of its tangibility. The first clue that 'things' could travel faster than the speed of light was discovered by USARIC.

To understand this concept better, it is useful to conduct the following experiment:

1: Imagine a picture of a black cat. Do you see it?

2: The image you thought of took approximately 0.2478 seconds to appear, which is ten times faster than the speed of light.

3: The ability to transmit said image to another location is just as fast.

The intangible - electronic messages, for example - and hyper-

connectivity with the Outernet were sent at a rate way faster than 186, 282 miles per second; the approximate speed of light. The ability to transmit data through space and time became the exemplar for The Speed of Thought.

The discovery was the backbone of Pure Genius *during its conception. It devised the concept of travel along ripples through the fabric of space and time. A wholly remarkable discovery, and one that would set a precedent for scientific discovery hence.*

It was little surprise that USARIC, under the guidance of D'Souza, named this facility Pure Genius.

Not only did it change space exploration, it also improved commercial flights and communication in general. The International Moon Station was able to detect Saturn Cry because of it...

Pure Genius
Space Opera Beta - Level Five

Wool carried Jelly into Pure Genius. A cylinder-shaped room with several fluorescent tiles lit up on the floor, walls, and ceiling.

Apart from an almost indecipherable low-emission hum, the place was immaculate and completely devoid of sound.

In truth, it was a little eerie.

Wool stood in the middle and looked around, trying to figure out where the door she had walked through was. The tiles seemed to blend into each other. It was quite typical for a person entering Pure Genius to become quickly disoriented.

The chilling effect of the light and pure silence disturbed Jelly. It was possibly the first time either she, or Wool, had been in such a place of sheer tranquility.

"Tor?" Wool scanned the surrounding tiles. "We're here."

One of the tiles on the ceiling slid open, releasing the hum of Space Opera Beta into the room for a short time.

"Yes, I know. I'm here, too."

"Where are you? This place is freaking me out. I don't want to be in here any longer than necessary."

"I'm up here," Tor climbed into the cylinder from the open tile in the ceiling. "Whatever you do, don't jump. Stay out of dead-center or you'll get pulled apart."

"I don't intend to move, Tor."

Gravity didn't behave in the way people are accustomed to within Pure Genius. Each surface had its own pull, which exacerbated the feeling of unease.

Tor walked down the curvature of the wall and stepped onto what Wool knew to be the ground.

"Glad you could make it," Tor took out a screen and stretched it from his hand. "We're going to have to leave Jelly in here by herself while we conduct the decoding.

"Okay."

"Can you set her down, please?"

Wool squatted to the ten by ten floor tile and released Jelly onto it. She looked at her tail and followed it around for a few seconds, trying to attack it with her infinity claws.

Tor chuckled as he looked at his screen. "How's she getting on with her new toy?"

"She's taken to Infinity Claws remarkably well. No allergies, no reactions."

"Did she figure out how to use her thumbs, yet?"

"Not yet," Wool puckered her lips at Jelly as she trailed around, meowing at her own behind.

"Okay, let's start," Tor looked up at the ceiling and barked out a command. "Pure Genius. Cuboid, twelve-eight-six."

Jelly sat on her hind legs and licked her paws.

"Right, let's go," Tor clutched his screen and planted his foot on the curve of the wall. "It's okay, follow me. It's perfectly safe."

"I trust you," Wool smiled and stepped onto the wall, following behind Tor as he walked to the open tile in the ceiling.

He stepped through and offered Wool a helping hand. "Just through here."

"Will Jelly be okay?"

"She's perfectly fine," Tor said, "Take my hand, and prepare for a little disorientation."

He pulled her through and allowed the tile to slide shut behind them.

Jelly looked around at the brightly lit tiles and squinted.

One of them began to change shape.

All the others changed, too. Very slowly.

The cylinder flattened out and folded onto itself, startling Jelly. "Meoowww..."

The corners of the flat surface branched out and locked together, forming a cuboid structure all around her from every angle.

The silence was completely deafening.

For Jelly, it wasn't a matter of escape. If she wanted to run away, she wouldn't be too sure she'd run back to the same place.

So, she did what any cat would have done under the circumstances and made for what she thought was the door. One of many of perfectly-squared tiles measuring ten by ten feet.

She hopped onto it, surprised that it had its own gravity. The *door* had become the floor.

Jelly whined and looked around. Six walls, a ceiling and a floor, all containing twenty-four tiles.

"Jelly?" Tor's voice buzzed into the room. She shrieked and jumped into the air, wondering where the voice came from. "Shh, it's okay, girl. Calm down."

Tor sat at the Pure Genius deck with an audience watching the screen from behind.

Bonnie, Wool, Jaycee, Haloo, Baldron, and Katz were captivated by the visual of Jelly in the cuboid on the large screen.

"Activating Saturn Cry," Tor pressed a button on the console. The familiar static-hiss started to play.

"What's going on?" Bonnie asked. "Can she hear it?"

"Yes, the message is coming at her from all directions," Tor said. "We're closer to the source of the signal, so she's in a position to respond due to the strength and quality."

A twang of an electric guitar shot through the room.

Jelly jumped into the air as visual audio waves from the guitar twang flew around her. She landed on the adjacent tile, somewhat disappointed that she hadn't caught the waveform.

"Nine... ten," Tor said, analyzing his controls, "Eleven... and..."

WHUMP.

A blast of pink audio illuminated the cube. Jelly tossed herself into the air and tried to claw at it. She shrieked at the top of her lungs and landed onto what she knew to be the ceiling.

Her paws hit the tile, pressing it like a button. It turned pink and displayed a readout in the middle of the cuboid.

"Amaziant. Someone take a note of that," Tor looked at Baldron, who unfolded his screen and scribbled down the set of numbers:

1691411

"Coordinates?"

"Could be," Tor raised the volume of the audio message. "Hang on. Fifteen... sixteen..."

"We're waiting for the twentieth second?" Tripp asked. "The second bump?

"Yes, shh."

The guitar sound crept into the hiss and struck three successive chords.

The second *whump* blasted around the cuboid, scaring Jelly across the middle of the structure.

Another blast of pink light zipped from her previous tile to the one directly opposite. She tried to catch it but it was far too fast for her.

The pink waveform splashed against the tile, moving out for Jelly to land against it.

The tile lit up and produced another number.

"Meow," Jelly dug her hind legs into the tile and rolled over, angry with herself.

"Baldron," Tor said, "Capture the result, please."

"Got it," he said, writing it down. "One, niner, two, five, one, three, one, six."

"Nineteen and thirteen are prime numbers," Haloo said. "But the others aren't."

"We're clearly not dealing with an intelligent life form,

whatever it is," Tripp said. "What do we know of these coordinates?"

"We don't know yet till we reach the twenty-sixth second," Baldron looked at the screen and poised himself, ready to capture the next set of numbers.

The hiss died down. Four successive chords from the sound that resembled an electric guitar played out.

"Twenty-four. Twenty-five…" Tor muttered, "And…"

Whump.

Jelly didn't know where to turn. The cuboid room seemed to revolve on its axis, tipping her away from her tile.

She shrieked and dug her thumb claw into the side of the tile, clinging on for dear life.

A third and final pink image screeched around the center of Pure Genius, toying with Jelly.

She propelled herself from the tile and flew toward the haze of warbled pink sound, intending to ravage it.

"What is that, it sounds familiar?" Bonnie asked.

"Da-da-da-dum," Wool hummed to herself. "Like Beethoven's fifth?"

"No, that's impossible—" Katz said.

"—Anything is possible," Tor kept his eye on the screen, "Keep watching."

Jelly burst through the pink cloud and purred, suspended in the center of the room. Her metal whiskers buzzed to life, causing an electrical spark. Her face pushed back under her hind legs.

"What's happening to her?"

"That third and final bump," Tor pointed at the screen. "Look, it's disappeared."

Jelly hit the ceiling and meowed as loud as she could. The tile flashed under her feet, upsetting her.

"That's enough. Get her out of that room," Wool went to walk away, only for Baldron to keep her back.

"No, it's over. We're done. Anderson's safe."

"That stupid room is scaring her."

"Be quiet, Wool," Tor punched the data from the three lit-up tiles into the computer, "Here we go. Panels twelve, twenty… and twenty-six."

Everyone held their breath. Katz leaned into the screen and watched Jelly licking her paws, quite happy with herself.

"Twelve, twenty, twenty-six?" he said.

"Yep," Tor smiled. "The exact points in the message where those bumps happen.

"But what does that—"

The final set up of numbers appeared in the middle of the room.

8151425

"Got that, Baldron?" Tor asked.

"Yep, the entire string is complete."

"Get her out of there," Tor looked at Wool, "Make sure you grab her once she's out. She's likely to be upset. Bring her down slowly."

"Right," Wool marched off toward the door, "Open it up."

"Okay, all we have to do is feed the coordinates into Pure Genius and see what the result is. Should take about an hour."

"An hour?" Tripp asked. "Why so long?"

"We're expecting over a trillion permutations. It could be less. Either way, we need to give it time to analyze the data."

The door to Pure Genius slid open, revealing Jelly sitting on the ceiling.

"Meow."

Wool looked up and held out her arms. "Hey, Jelly. Come to me."

She purred and remained seated, licking at her right paw.

"Don't play the fool, Jelly. You can't stay in there all day," Wool snapped her fingers. "Let's go, come on."

Wool returned to the crew with Jelly in her arms. Everyone applauded and cheered.

"Well done, Anderson," Katz said. "Not just a pretty face, huh?"

Tor and Baldron high-fived each other and watched Jelly snake around the ankles of her new friends.

"She did well," Tor said.

Jelly didn't seem particularly happy with him. She crouched back and snarled with a furious bushy tail.

"Whoa," Tor stepped back and held out his hands. "Don't take it so personally, Anderson."

She snarled and threatened to pounce on him. Wool lifted her up by her stomach before she could act.

"Meow."

"Hey, honey," Wool cradled her and rubbed her nose against Jelly's head. "Let's get you your medicine, yes? Let you run around for a while."

***

Jelly sat upright on her bed looking at Wool. She inspected the cat's face and pressed her thumbs down under her eyes.

"You seem okay," Wool whispered, "It must have been weird being in that nasty room, right?"

"Meow," Jelly rubbed her face on Wool's wrist.

"I know, sweetie. You did well."

"So, you're going to take this," Wool produced a white pill and held it flat in her palm, "It'll help with your digestion."

"Meow," Jelly sniffed around at the pill but decided not to slurp it up.

"Come on," Wool grabbed Jelly's chin. "It's for your own good."

She opened the cat's mouth and plonked the pill inside. "Good girl, swallow."

She ran her knuckle up and down Jelly's neck, forcing her to gulp it down.

Observation Deck
One hour later…

Tripp enjoyed a cup of coffee as he looked through the giant, transparent dome.

Saturn hung in the array of stars, surrounded by its many moons. Enceladus stood out among them; indicated by a red digital reticule stretched over the transparent window.

Tripp made out the cone-shaped Space Opera Alpha

traveling alongside it.

He took a sip of coffee, lost in his own thoughts. A picture of his son and wife appeared on the screen.

"No, thanks, Manuel."

"I thought you may want a reminder," Manuel's voice suggested.

"No, sometimes it's just better without visual aids."

"Very well. You know where I am if you need me."

"Yes. Thanks."

The image of his family vanished, pulling Saturn's vastness into view.

"Meow."

Tripp turned around and watched Jelly saunter into the observation deck, "Oh, hey girl. What are you doing here?"

She ran the side of her face along his shin, wanting attention.

"You want a hug?" Tripp chuckled and set his coffee down. "Yeah. I know the feeling."

He lifted Jelly into his arms and caught a glimpse of Wool by the door. "Hey."

"Hey."

"You okay, Wool?"

"I'm fine. Jelly seems to be curious about the observation deck."

"So you caved in and let her visit?"

"Something like that," Wool chuckled to herself, "Need a bit of time to myself. Can she stay here with you for a little while?"

"Sure."

Wool smiled and moved off, leaving Jelly in Tripp's capable hands. It wasn't long before he felt the urge to talk to her.

"See that up there?" Tripp asked Jelly, "That's Saturn. Those are her rings, look. Big and beautiful. A bit like you."

Jelly snuggled into his arms and lifted her head. Her internal engine fired up, emitting a healthy purr.

She watched as Tripp grabbed the lever. He pressed his thumb on the handle and shifted the observation dome a few clicks to the right.

Space Opera Alpha came into view in the distance.

"That little white dot is our friends. They got lost, so we're going to help them. You're very good at helping our friends aren't you?"

Jelly traced her tongue up the side of her new Titanium thumb.

"Yes, you are."

She began to feel restless and pawed at his sleeves.

"You want down?" Tripp asked. "Okay, I have a seat here just for you."

Manuel's holograph appeared, startling Jelly out of Tripp's arms. She landed on the recliner and looked up at the stars.

"Tripp, Daryl would like you and the crew to meet him at the hub."

"What, now?"

"Yes, right now. They have the results and wish to share their findings with you."

"Wow, that was fast."

He was about to collect Jelly but had second thoughts. It seemed she was having a private moment. She was safe in the observation deck. What harm could a little isolation do while he visited the hub?

"I'll leave you in peace, Jelly. Enjoy it while it lasts."

Jelly never looked back. She turned her head, taking in the incredible view, "Meow."

"Good girl. I'll be back in a moment."

Tripp opened the door and exited the observation deck.

Jelly scrunched her nose as she took in the bright stars scattered across the unending chasm of space. She couldn't find what she was looking for, however.

In front of her stood the observation deck controls. A yellow joystick the size of a human fist begged to be played with.

"Meow," Jelly tried to talk to it, but it didn't move.

Perhaps a little tap might make it do something?

Jelly pressed the paw to the side, knocking the stick left. The observation deck swiveled for a second, shifting the view of Saturn over to the right.

Jelly considered what had happened. If she hit the stick, Saturn would move again.

It did.

She pressed her paw against the side, this time keeping it held down longer.

The stars struck out like a sloppy string of ink across the black canvas. The giant Jupiter moved across.

Jelly released the stick and raised her ears. "Meow."

Curious, she pressed the stick to the left once again. A tiny blue star caught her attention. It seemed so far away.

"Meow."

Little did Jelly know that the tiny reflection in her eyeballs was that of Earth. Nearly a billion miles away. Her mouth opened, the sense of awe hitting her deep inside.

Nevertheless, home was home. Of course, her homing instincts were far beyond her ability to get home all by herself. But that small dot that glimmered in the distance was where she knew she should be.

Not stuck in a cone-shaped vessel made of advanced ceramic hundreds of thousands of miles away from its final destination...

Back on Earth...

Jamie sat on the tiny brick wall in his back garden, holding his mini-telescope in his hands.

He extended it and held the small end to his eye, "There's the moon."

Jamie adjusted the lens and a series of craters, came into focus. "The man on the moon."

"Jamie, poppet," his mother's voice drifted from the kitchen door. "Come in for your dinner."

"Yes, mom."

"And can you collect your sister's bottle from the counter, please?"

"Okay, mom," Jamie tapped the thick end of the telescope in his hand, "You'll be at Saturn by now, Jelly."

He moved the small end of the device to his eye and settled on a shimmering white dot to the left of the moon, "I have a new daddy, now. Just like you."

Jamie removed the telescope and held it between his legs. He pursed his lips and considered the events of the past twelve months.

"I'll wait for you, Jelly." He stood up and took one final look at the starry sky. A lump formed in his throat, "I should never have let you go. I miss you…"

Chapter 11

The entire crew took their seats around the table.

"We have the results from Pure Genius," Tor said.

"So, what's the skinny?" Bonnie asked.

Tor waved his hand. A string of numbers displayed over the conference table.

Androgyne was the last crew member to enter the room, dressed in her USARIC outer-skin, "Captain Katz?"

"Yes, Androgyne?"

"I am ready to board Opera Alpha."

"So I see," Katz turned to Tor, who waited for the chance to present his findings, "We have an update. Please listen carefully."

Tripp took Jelly from Wool and cradled her in his arms, "What did we find?"

"Take a look at these numbers," Tor said.

$$1691411192513168151425$$

"Okay?" Wool said. "What of them?"

"This is what we flushed into Pure Genius. Along with Manuel, she scanned for every known linguistic permutation we are aware of. It took Pure Genius less than ten minutes to arrive at the answer."

"Why?" Katz asked.

"Because it was staring us in the face all along. Unusually simple, which may or may not reflect the intelligence of whatever we're dealing with."

Tor pushed the tops of his hands together and spread the numbers out.

16 9 14 11 19 25 13 16 8 15 14 25

"Twelve individual numbers," Tor explained. "Can anyone see the pattern, here?"

The crew looked along the string. It didn't take Androgyne very long to figure out what it meant, "Oh, yes. It is simple."

"Exactly," Tor smiled. "Anyone else?"

"Eleven," Haloo smiled and picked out the relevant numbers, "Nineteen and thirteen. Primary numbers?"

"True, but that's not the point," Tor said, "But you're looking in the wrong place. Take a step back and look at them again."

"I don't understand?" Haloo said, dismayed by her lack of comprehension, "Step back?"

"Androgyne?" Tor turned to her and pointed at the numbers. "Would you like to explain?"

"Certainly."

She walked over to the table and pointed at the first two-digit number, "The sixteenth letter of the alphabet. P."

"Oh," Bonnie now understood the answer. "What's the ninth letter?"

"I," said Tripp. "Which means fourteen is N."

"And there you have it," Tor clicked his fingers. Each number spun around revealing their corresponding letter.

PINK SYMPHONY

Baldron joined Tor and snapped his fingers, "Pink Symphony. It explains the color of the waveform we saw while Jelly was in Pure Genius extracting the data."

"Yes, it was pink," Katz said.

"What does Pink Symphony mean?" Jaycee asked.

"We don't know."

"So what use is it to us?"

Tor made eyes at Baldron, "I'll let my colleague explain."

Baldron pushed the test aside and brought up a live visual feed of Enceladus. A live visual feed of Enceladus appeared in an inset in at the top of the screen, "How long till we reach Alpha, Katz?"

"A little under an hour."

"Okay," Baldron pointed at the live feed of Enceladus, "Here, one of USARIC's Star Drones currently orbiting Enceladus. This image is live but on a two-minute delay. If you look closely at the dark side you may see something occurring right in the middle."

Baldron enlarged the image, revealing a small pink dot. It appeared to breathe in and out from within the darkness.

"It's pink," Tripp dropped Jelly to the conference table, "Is that something to do with the deciphering of the message?"

"Again, we don't know," Baldron offered.

Bonnie felt her patience reach an end. "Well, what *do* you know?"

A vector image of Enceladus appeared next to the visual representation of Alpha. A dotted line shot out from the center of the moon and marched its way to the transmitter on Opera Alpha.

"We know that Enceladus is using Alpha as a transmitter," Baldron explained. "Somewhere deep in her core. It's sending the source signal to Alpha and using her as a sort of repeater to strengthen its message."

Tor stepped forward and pointed at the vector of Enceladus, "Before Alpha went to investigate Enceladus, the message received by IMS and Corpus Claudius was just a bunch of noise. Now, with the Saturn Cry going through Alpha, the signal is stronger and filtered."

"Let me see if I have this correct," Katz tried to make sense of what he was hearing. "The original message was designed to get Alpha to go to Enceladus. To figure out what was going on?"

"Yes," Baldron said.

"With the express purpose of using Alpha as a transmitter to send a strengthened signal?"

"It seems so."

"Why would it do that?" Katz asked.

"Who knows," Tor said. "What we do know is that we got a response. A response that enabled us to get Anderson up here to make sense of the message. And it worked."

Androgyne considered the revelation, "Whatever, or whoever, is sending that message clearly knows English. Numbers."

"And music," Wool added. "Could we have found life out here?"

"The probability of life out here is beyond calculation," Androgyne said. "Even in this vicinity. Extended to neighboring galaxies. It's not possible. And even if it were true, they wouldn't know English."

The team were perplexed. Faced with the daunting fact that Saturn Cry originated from a place where numbers and, more bizarrely, the English language were a known quantity.

"It's futile to speculate any further," Baldron said. "We're due to dock with Alpha shortly. We'll ask questions when we get there. The most likely explanation is that whoever, or whatever, is using Alpha to transmit their message has done so from what they've learned about her."

"It explains why the code was so simple and easy to decrypt," Tor rubbed his chin, thinking over his answer. "Yes, it makes sense. What we have here, Pink Symphony, is an answer to a question we do not know."

"It is remarkable just how simple it was to decipher," Baldron said as the rest of the crew turned to Jelly. She licked her private parts in full view of them with nary a care in the world.

Or the galaxy.

"I'm sure one of us would have figured out given enough time," Wool said. "It wouldn't have taken a genius."

Tor and Baldron looked at Jelly, who stopped licking herself and looked up at them.

"It didn't," Tor quipped.

Rest & Recuperation
Space Opera Beta - Level Two

Space Opera Beta's mess hall was large enough to house a few beds and a kitchen counter set-up. A place for the crew to relax and maybe read a book or watch a movie.

Its primary function was to serve hot meals. Long gone were the days of having to drink through straws and eat from packets.

The kitchen contained all the essentials one could possibly want.

A kettle.

A microwave.

A wash basin.

An electric cooker.

A coffee machine capable of making fancy hot drinks.

The rectangular table in the middle of the room contained assorted snacks. Three bowls of fruit hung from the ceiling, a few inches from the table top.

In the corner of the room, unofficially referred to as "hind quarters', was where Jelly went to the bathroom. In many ways, she was spoiled aboard the Space Opera Beta.

She had a larger-than-necessary sleeping area with a mattress and sheets. A water dispenser released pure H2O into a bowl on the hour, every hour.

Jelly lapped away at the water, washing down the contents of her lunch - a chicken medley. Her favorite.

Baldron waited for the coffee machine to reach its boil and took out two mugs from the cabinet.

"It's *amaziant*, really, when you think about. How much you miss the little things."

Katz turned to look at Jelly drinking from her bowl, "This time, we *do* have a little thing with us."

"Ha," Baldron reached inside his pocket and took out a bunch of napkins, "That's not quite what I meant."

"I know," Katz chuckled. "Hey, Jelly. How you doing?"

She looked up from her bowl and meowed.

Katz, much like the majority of the crew, couldn't resist the urge to talk cutesy at her, "You're a good girl, aren't you?"

"You take milk?" Baldron poured some of the white stuff into his mug.

"Yes, please. One sugar," Katz cautiously approached Jelly and held out his arms, "Water's good, huh?"

"One sugar," Baldron whispered to himself as he fanned out the napkin. His black cyanide capsule lay in the middle. A quick check over his shoulder to ensure the captain couldn't see him was all he needed, "Coming right up."

Jelly's ears pricked up. She watched as Baldron break the two plastic ends and drop the yellowy dust into the second USARIC-themed mug. He poured the hot coffee into it and watched the froth race up the sides of the ceramic and spread across the surface.

Katz scooped Jelly up under her belly, "Ooh, gotta be careful. You've just eaten."

"Meow."

Baldron poured the coffee into his blue mug and replaced the coffee filter into its housing.

"I have to say, Daryl, that we're very appreciative of everything you've done for us. You've been a real inspiration for the crew of Opera Beta."

Katz, having seen nothing of Baldron's sneaky move, approached the middle table and eyed his coffee. Jelly purred in his arms as he made a fuss over her.

"It's not often you get to hear that from your own team. But thanks for saying that. It means a lot."

Baldron smiled and nodded at the cat, "Anderson's something else, isn't she?"

"Oh, you can say that again."

Jelly looked up at Baldron and showed him her fangs. She lifted her paws away from Katz in an attempt to free herself. Obligingly, he dropped her to the table.

"There you go, puss."

Baldron made conversation, trying not to look at the two mugs, "So, not long to go now till we board Alpha?"

"Nope," Katz eyed the two coffee mugs. He reached out for the handle on the red one nearest to him. Baldron suppressed his desire to celebrate his plan coming to fruition.

Jelly walked around the two mugs, sniffing the rim on

each one. She whined and blinked up at Baldron.

"What are you looking at, Anderson?"

"Meow," she ran her face along the side of the piping hot red mug. The heat made her tear her face away and rub it with her paw, "Meeooowww."

"What's the matter, girl?" Katz hooked his finger around the cyanide-laced mug of coffee, "You can't drink this. It's not good for you, pet."

"Meow."

Baldron lifted his mug and offered to clink it against Katz's, "We have what we need, now. We solved the puzzle. Cheers."

"Yes, of course," Katz lifted the red mug and clinked it against Baldron's, "To Jelly Anderson."

"Yes, to Jelly Anderson."

As Baldron lifted the mug to his mouth, Jelly launched at him and scratched his forearm.

"Oww."

Baldron's mug tilted and spilled a few drops of coffee over the floor. Katz put the red mug down and accosted Jelly, who looked up at him with widened eyes.

"Bad cat," Katz snatched the blue mug from Baldron's hand. Jelly hissed back at him.

"That damn creature is more trouble than she's worth," Baldron inspected his torn inner-suit sleeve, "Ugh, can't we just have her dealt with?"

He reached over the kitchen counter, tore off a sheet of paper from its holder and mopped his arm down.

"Dealt with?" Katz asked.

Baldron scrunched the paper and threw it into the basin, "Yes. *Dealt with*. We have everything we need from her. She's only getting in the way, now."

"Meow," Jelly definitely *knew* who the bad guy was in all of this.

Katz picked up the red mug. He watched Jelly's face following the rim, "Here, take your drink back.."

"Thanks," Baldron took the red mug failing to realize that Katz had swapped them around.

Katz picked up the blue mug and lifted it to his lips. His

mood flipped on a dime, "We'll deal with her when we return to Earth, I think."

"Fine," Baldron huffed and watched the tip of the blue mug rise as Katz sipped away at it, "But, but…"

"What's wrong, Baldron?" Katz said with a smile. "Not going to drink?"

"No, I—"

"Meow," Jelly shifted along the counter and yawned at Baldron as if to say "Hey, drink it."

Katz gulped down the contents of the blue mug and slammed it to the counter, "Ahh, that's better." He reached into his inner-skin suit flap with his right hand and watched Baldron with his red mug, "You must be parched, fella."

"I, uh, suddenly don't feel too well."

"Oh," Katz feigned sympathy, "Well, a bit of caffeine might perk you up a bit, right?"

Baldron didn't know what to do. If he drank the coffee, he was dead. If he didn't, he was busted.

Katz clenched his fist within his inner-suit, losing his patience. Jelly completed the double-act by growling louder than before. They both wanted Baldron to drink whatever was in the red mug.

"Come on, drink up."

Baldron closed his eyes and double-over himself, pretending to feel sick, "Ugh, must be something I ate. My stomach—"

He released the red mug from his hands.

It shattered across the floor, spreading the fizzing, deadly contents around their shoes.

Katz took out his Rez-9 firearm and pointed it at Baldron.

Jelly squealed in the man's face, backing her captain up.

"*Cyanide*?" Katz flicked the side catch on his Rez-9 down, arming it, "You try to kill me on *my* ship?"

"I'm s-sorry, please don't shoot me—"

"—Don't say another word, Landaker," Katz shifted the barrel of the gun to his face. Baldron put his hands in the air as Katz snapped his fingers with his free hand.

"Manuel."

The holographic book appeared out of thin air and

hovered around the kitchen counter, "Yes, Captain?"

"Call Jaycee to R&R," Katz said, "We have a problem here that needs to be *dealt with*."

Baldron trembled with fear, "No, please, don't tell the others—"

"—I swear, Landaker. You say one more thing and I'll blow your god damn head off. Don't you make a move or say another word."

Baldron hung his head in shame. The cyanide-infused coffee spat and sizzled around their feet, burning into the ground. Katz turned to Jelly, "Stay there, pet."

"Meow," Jelly snarled at Baldron.

***

Jaycee pushed Baldron down the vessel carriageway by the back of his shoulders.

"Hey!"

"Shut up, killer," Jaycee's sheer size, made even larger on account of his exo-suit, somehow felt more threatening than ever before. He hulked his K-SPARK shot gun in his arms, enjoying tormenting his prisoner, "Get off the floor and walk."

Baldron scrambled to his feet and walked backwards along the corridor, "I swear, it was a mistake."

"The only mistake that was made was letting you on board, traitor," Jaycee lifted his behemoth of a gun to the man's head, "Right between the eyes, if I had my way."

"Wh-where are you taking me?"

"Keep walking," Jaycee stormed forward and threaten to pulverize his new captive, "If I had my way I'd put a proton charge right between your eyes. Then I'd take you to the airlock and flush you out of this ship along with all the other human waste."

"P-Please, d-don't kill me," Baldron pleaded for his life. At the far end of the corridor was the ship's prison - N-Carcerate.

"Crew of Opera Beta, may I have your attention, please?" Katz's voice came through the speakers in the corridor and vessel at large, "I regret to inform you that we have uncovered a traitor among us. Do not be concerned. Jaycee is dealing with him as we speak...."

Jaycee booted Baldron in the chest, sending him tumbling down the corridor, closer to N-Carcerate, "Congratulations, big man. You're famous."

Katz held the communication device in his hand. He kept on speaking as Tor watched on, utterly dumbfounded by the revelation.

Androgyne entered the room and scanned the control deck's walls.

"... communications second officer Baldron Landaker has been placed under arrest for attempted murder. He will be housed in N-Carcerate until we return home, where USARIC will deal with him. Please do not approach or attempt to communicate with him. Failure to comply with this order will be seen as a contravention of Infinity Clause twenty-five-point-five. Thank you. Katz, over and out."

Tor shook his head and felt like crying, "Baldron?"

"Yeah," Katz hooked the communicator to the flight deck, "Baldron Landaker. Tried to kill me."

"How?"

"Dropped his cyanide capsule into my drink. If it weren't for Jelly acting up you'd be speaking to a corpse right now. Under commander Healy's directions."

"Unbelievable," Tor sat into his chair and looked at Androgyne, "Uh, what will happen to him now?"

"He'll spend the next eighteen months in N-Carcerate, twelve of them in hyper-sleep. When we get back, USARIC will try him on the evidence. Pretty compelling stuff. I wouldn't be surprised if they execute him."

"Wow," Tor shook his head once again, "Did he say why he did it?"

"No."

"Did you upset him?"

"No."

"Why do you think he did it?"

"I don't know."

"Did he say why he did it?"

"What do you think, Tor? I don't know." Katz let out a violent exasperation, "Yeah, the second I asked nicely, he was all like "Oh, Daryl, I really love you, but you're married, and if I can't have you, no one can!" Idiot."

"I'm sorry, Daryl," Tor cleared his throat. He hadn't seen this Katz's wrath of venom before now, "I didn't mean to—"

"—No, you didn't *meant to*, whatever that means. No one ever *means to*," Katz took a deep breath and felt sorry for his first comms officer. He was only trying to help, after all, "I'm sorry, Tor. I shouldn't take it out on you. I'm a bit on edge."

"Captain Katz?" Androgyne stood in her outer-suit, prepared for action. The helmet sat around her shoulders with the visor opened, "Should I proceed to the primary airlock?"

Katz took a deep breath and tried to acclimatize himself to his work environment, "Yes. Good idea. I'll have Bonnie accompany you to disembarkation."

"Thank you, Captain."

Androgyne turned around and made her way out of the control deck.

"Oh, and… Androgyne?"

"Yes, captain?"

"Watch your six," Katz returned to the control deck, "You never know where danger is going to spring from."

Chapter 12

Primary Airlock
Space Opera Beta - Level One

Androgyne and Bonnie reached the primary airlock. The latter pressed her finger to her ear, "Okay, we're all set."

"Understood," Katz voice came through her headset, "When Androgyne reaches Alpha's dock all she has to do is press her glove to the outer plate and it should open. Standby for bridge connection."

Bonnie patted down Androgyne's outer-skin; a thin, silver spacesuit that clung to her skin like a pair of leggings. Androgyne's helmet was more traditional - resembling a small goldfish bowl.

"You ready?"

"I'm scared, Dr. Whitaker."

"Don't be. We're right behind you. Check your comms," Bonnie nodded at her ear, "Say something."

Androgyne flipped down her visor. It locked to the rim of the helmet. An ear piece automatically folded around her mouth, "Can you hear me?"

Bonnie turned away to make sure she could hear her voice, "Loud and clear. You read me?"

"Yes," Androgyne looked around inside her helmet, "You're coming through crystal clear."

The ship began to rumble.

Bonnie looked through the first door to the airlock.

Through the second window, the pair could see the bridge extend away from the ship and head for the airlock on Space Opera Alpha.

"We don't know what you'll find in there."

"Bonnie," Katz interrupted through the headset, "Don't intimidate the poor girl. Androgyne, can you read me?"

"Yes, Captain."

Androgyne took in the enormity of what was about to happen, "When you board Alpha, we need to establish three things. One, that the ship is habitable for human life. Two, that Alpha's on board Manuel is operational. He's an older generation, so if he's operational, you should expect some differences to our own."

"Yes, Captain."

"Three, we need to know who survived. It's that simple."

"Understood, Captain."

"Once we've established those three facts we'll join you and see what we can salvage and rescue."

"I understand," she stared through the airlock window and feared for her life.

"There's nothing to be worried about, Androgyne," Katz said. "I want you to provide a running commentary at all times. If there's a period of more than ten seconds of radio silence, we'll assume something is wrong and act accordingly. You're in safe hands."

The primary airlock door slid to the side and offered Androgyne into the compression chamber.

"The bridge is ready," Katz said. "Prepare to disembark."

Bonnie held Androgyne's shoulder and reassured her, "Good luck. Remember, keep in constant contact."

"Yes."

Androgyne took a deep breath and stepped into the airlock. The door slid behind her as she stood perfectly still, "I'm ready, Captain."

"Good."

Bonnie waved at her as the outer door opened onto the white, ceramic bridge that presented a thirty second walk to Space Opera Alpha's airlock, "Good luck."

"Thanks, Bonnie."

Androgyne stepped onto the bridge and took her first few weightless steps. She held the bridge railing for dear life.

She took in the view of Saturn and her rings looming above her head, spinning very, very slowly, "Wow."

"What's up, Androgyne?" Katz asked.

"It's *amazient*. It's so big."

"Try not to look up, keep focused," Bonnie's voice beamed around her head, "Admiring the view will only slow you down."

Androgyne twisted her head to the left. Enceladus shone brightly, illuminating her visor. She felt a hum rattle through her outer skin and numb her limbs.

Her feet lifted away from the bridge floor as she moved forward. She grabbed the railing and yanked herself toward the spaceship, her toes barely trailing along the surface.

"Another fifteen seconds, and I'll be there."

"Keep on the bridge. Don't let go," Katz advised. "That's what the rails are for. Use them."

Androgyne reached the edge of the bridge and pressed her palms against Alpha's airlock door. She scanned the ridges for the plate that would open it.

"I'm here."

"The plate should be shoulder-high to you on the right of Alpha's airlock," Bonnie said.

"Understood."

The plate was exactly where Bonnie said it would be. Androgyne slapped her palm against the surface, "Opening now."

"Understood. You might want to take a step back so the bridge can connect."

She did as instructed.

Alpha's airlock door flew up and released a burst of pressurized air. The edge of the bridge snapped to the metal rim, locking into place.

"Get in," Katz said.

"Yes."

She yanked herself forward and floated into the airlock, looking down at the bridge completing its connection. Opera

Alpha and Opera Beta joined together by the bridge.

"Releasing thrusters, now," Katz advised. "Confirm connection, please, Androgyne."

"Connection confirmed," She slammed a red button on the wall of the airlock with her fist, "Closing outer airlock hatch, now."

The room whirred, preparing to shut the door.

"Understood," Katz said.

The door slid down and closed off the exit as Androgyne looked around. An alarm sounded off, followed by a flashing red light.

"What's that?" she blurted, thinking she was about to die.

"It's just the airlock hatch closing. Nothing to be scared about."

"Okay."

The door slid down its housing, locking her into place, "I think I'm decompressing."

"Standby. The inner airlock door will open in a few seconds."

Katz stood up from his flight deck console and angled his screen to the control deck.

Tor looked over at the screen and held his headset in place, "Visual?"

"Yep, this is what she's seeing," Katz pointed at his screen.

It offered a live feed from Androgyne's visor. The pair watched as she moved through the inner airlock door and into the ship.

"Androgyne, we have POV visual. We can see what you can see."

"Okay," her voice came through the screen, "It's dark. I can't see anything."

Katz folded his arms and watched the monitor, "Give Manuel a command."

"What should I tell him?"

"Maybe turn the lights on?"

The screen went pitch black as Androgyne stepped into the darkness and looked around, "On-board computer,

Manuel. Do you read me?"

No response.

"Manuel?" Androgyne was close to giving up, "Nothing is happening."

"The live feed is a bit patchy, can you see anything?" Katz asked and turned to Tor for a reaction, "Alpha's power must be down."

Tor didn't know how to respond, "It could have gone into stasis. Knock it out of sleep mode."

"Androgyne," Katz said. "Try the following command. A-W-A-K-E-4-5-7."

"Affirmative. A-W-A-K-E-4-5-7."

The moment she finished repeating the command, the lights flickered. The interior of Space Opera Alpha sprang to life.

It felt like she was breathing once again.

She was faced with a dusty, corridor leading to the control center, "Should I unmask, now?"

"Yes, take an atmosphere reading," Katz bit his lip in the hope that the exposure wouldn't fry her circuits, "Report on atmosphere levels, please."

Androgyne closed her eyes and flicked a switch on her visor. The front panel lifted up.

She was convinced she'd suffocate. Once her lungs filled with oxygen her mind was put at rest.

"I can breathe," she took out a thin black panel out of her pocket, "Taking a reading now."

Classical music played in the distance. A familiar tune to anyone who could hear it.

The panel beamed to life. Its numbers spun around as she waved it around. The result appeared on the screen: 81mm Hg.

"Did you get the reading?"

"Yes, just patching it through now," Katz looked at the number appear in the top-right of the screen. "Eighty-one milligrams? Seems perfectly reasonable. Botanix must still be in operation."

"Manuel?" Androgyne asked. "Can anyone read me?"

"Still nothing?" Katz asked.

"No. I'm making my way to the control deck," she said, walking toward the door.

Several clanging noises waded through the ship's vibration as she made her way to the door, "Centrifuge is normal."

"Understood. So it's just Manuel we're having issues with?"

"It seems so."

Androgyne reached the door to the control desk and hit the button on the wall.

It slid open to reveal an exact replica of Space Opera Beta's deck.

A front panel with exactly the same ship controls - and an empty chair. To her left, the comms panel, and an empty chair. *Beethoven's 5th Symphony in C Minor* played from the communications panel.

"Can you hear the music?"

"Yes," Katz voice came through the headset.

"Captain? Can you see what I'm seeing?"

"Yes. How's the flight deck? Is it operational?"

"The controls are on but there's nobody here."

Back on Opera Beta, Manuel appeared beside Katz's face and flapped its pages, "Captain, may I suggest something?"

"Yes, Manuel?"

"Perhaps if I board the vessel I can infiltrate the main unit and start investigating?"

"Let's wait a moment and see what we find," Katz returned to the live feed, "Androgyne? Can you read me?"

"Yes, Captain."

"Atmosphere levels confirmed, but no sign of life."

"That is correct."

Tor placed his hand on the screen, "Androgyne, this is Tor. Can you patch into Alpha's mainframe on the comms panel, please?"

Katz looked at him, quizzically, "What are you doing?"

"I want to know the status of communication. I think you'd want to know too, right?"

"Sure, go ahead."

Tor raced over to the comms panel, sat into his chair and began typing.

Androgyne did the same on Opera Alpha, "Okay, I'm here."

"Try this. I'm sending you the coordinates," Tor said. "If Alpha is operational it should respond to the following code."

"Okay."

"USARIC, hyphen, S, O, A, hyphen, one, one, eight.."

"Understood," Androgyne typed the command into the comms deck, "Done."

"We're looking for captain Zillah Chin-Dunne," Tor said. "OSR. One, One Eight."

Androgyne typed O-S-R-1-1-8 onto the keyboard, "Okay, done."

The mainframe beeped and sprung to life. The screen displayed a colossal amount of static which took Androgyne by surprise, "What's happening?"

A voice from behind her, "What are you doing?"

Androgyne spun around on her chair and gulped back the urge to scream. She froze solid and stared at the vision in front of her.

"Z-Zillah?"

"My God," Katz looked at the screen with bewilderment, "Tor, look at this."

"What?"

Tor joined Katz to observe the woman in Androgyne's POV feed, "Is that her?"

Katz interrupted him, "Androgyne?"

Zillah Chin-Dunne, the Japanese captain of Space Opera Alpha, stood a few feet away from Androgyne. Apart from her unhappy demeanor she seemed to be a picture of health.

Zillah shut the music off, catching Androgyne's attention, "What are you doing here?"

"I, uh, don't know what to say—"

"—I put you back in N-Vigorate for your own safety. How did you get out?"

Zillah made her way to the communications panel and

shut it down. Androgyne couldn't help but stare at her, utterly confused.

"Androgyne," Katz whispered, "This is Zillah, the captain of Opera Alpha. Judging by the way she's talking, she thinks you're Alpha's Androgyne unit. Just play along with it."

"Honestly," Zillah flicked the levers off one-by-one on the communications unit, "What are you doing here? Why are you fiddling around with things that don't involve you?"

"She thinks I'm a droid?" Androgyne whispered a bit too loud.

"No, don't say—" Katz's voice cut off.

"Huh?" Zillah shot Androgyne a look of suspicion. "Who are you talking to?"

"Umm, no-one. Captain."

"Who woke you?" Zillah planted her hands on Androgyne's shoulders and inspected her face, "You can't wake yourself up, so someone must have done it. Who was it?"

"I, uh, do not know how to respond."

"Oh…" Zillah finally put two and two together, "You're not *my* Androgyne, are you?"

"Yes, I am," she said, afraid to reveal the truth.

"What *lessense*," Zillah pushed her away, "Manuel?"

The Alpha's Manuel appeared beside Zillah and hovered around her, "Yes, Captain?"

"Who is this impostor?"

The holographic book fluttered over to Androgyne and inspected her, "She's not one of ours, Captain. She's from the ship that has just connected to us."

Zillah couldn't believe what she was hearing, "What ship?"

"I'm getting a reading that another ship has docked with us."

Androgyne held her breath, waiting for Zillah's response. Hopefully it would be one in which she didn't end up killing her.

"We've been rescued?" A smile crept along Zillah's face, "The rescue vessel responded? They got our message?"

Manuel floated back to her, "It seems so, Captain."

"Oh, goodie!" Zillah danced a happy dance and clapped her hands together, "My God, I thought we were doomed."

"I, uh," Androgyne stepped out of the chair and ran an array of excuses through her mind, "I'm not sure—"

"—USARIC got our message and have come to save us!" Overjoyed, Zillah became very emotional. She held out her hand for Androgyne to shake, "Thank you so much for coming. Can I speak to your Captain, please?"

"Umm, yes. Okay," she said. "Captain Katz?"

"Yes?"

"Captain Chin-Dunne would like to speak to you."

A few moments later, Zillah patched her headset into Androgyne's frequency and led her into the hyper-sleep chamber.

"How has the crew been able to sustain themselves for the past *four* years?" Katz asked Zillah.

"When Opera Alpha arrived at Enceladus, she blacked-out entirely. All comms went down for approximately twenty minutes. When the backup drive started and comms became operational I sent out a distress call."

Zillah pointed at the six hyper-sleep pods.

"Botanix took a hit. Fifty-eight percent damage," she said. "A lot of the plant life didn't survive and the main coolant stopped producing water. My only option was to conserve oxygen and food, and put the crew and myself in hyper-sleep."

Katz, much like Androgyne, felt that something was truly off.

"Are they being fed intravenously?" Katz asked.

"Yes, we have enough protein and supplements to last ten years," Zillah explained. "But only enough oxygen for seventy-two hours. We genuinely didn't think we would see rescue."

"What's the situation with Alpha's thrusters?" Katz asked.

"Heavy damage. We were a sitting duck out there praying for rescue. It doesn't matter, now, if we can board Beta and go home with you."

"We don't have enough hyper-sleep chambers to house

everyone," Katz said. "I'd like to send my team in to investigate. It's possible we could return to Earth together and have each crew member spend half the journey in stasis."

"Everyone would spend six months awake?"

"Yes, something like that," Katz turned to Tor and muted his audio connection to Alpha, "I don't like this one bit. I want to know what happened to them. Why did they black out?"

"Understood, Captain."

"Assemble our crew. We're boarding Alpha," Katz returned to the screen and opened the audio connection, "Zillah, can you confirm Alpha is ready to accommodate my team?"

"Yes, Captain," Zillah said. "I can show you what you need to see when you board."

"Thanks, I'll leave our Androgyne with you. My team and I will board Alpha in thirty minutes. There will be five of us boarding, including our feline."

Zillah entered Alpha's control deck and looked at Androgyne with suspicion, "USARIC sent a feline up with you?"

"Yes," Katz said. "We've made a discovery which we can share with you. Perhaps we can trade updates. It could help to make some sense out of what's been happening."

"Oh—"

"—See you in thirty minutes. Katz, over and out."

Androgyne sniffed around the air. Her sensors flew off the charts, "I'm sensing an unusual odor in the air. What is it?"

Zillah crouched to her knees and held her head in her hands, "Ugghhh…"

"What are you doing?"

Zillah moved her hands away from her face. A trickle of pink, thick liquid slung from her right eye and down her cheek, "Androgyne, I have something to tell you. You're not going to like it."

"What are you going to tell me?"

"You're not human," Zillah scooped the pink goo off her

cheek with her knuckle and licked it, "You're an android. Do you know how I know this?"

"Why are you bleeding?" Androgyne went to touch Zillah's face, only to have her hand patted away in defiance by the ship's captain.

"Didn't you hear what I just said?"

"What?"

"You are not human. Do you know how I know?"

Androgyne's face fell as she took in the revelation, "No, I do not. How do you know?"

Zillah grabbed the back of the communications chair and spun it around.

Alpha's Androgyne, identical in every way to Beta's, lay lifeless in the chair. The front of its face had been removed. The once-pulsating brain had dried up and developed a thin layer of skin over it.

"I don't know what happened during the black out. It fried our communications and terminated our droid. I found her like this."

Androgyne looked her peer in the face and paused. She traced her finger over the droid's skull. It was as if she was looking in a mirror, "Is… is it *me*?"

"No, it's not you," Zillah backed up against the door with caution, "Well, that's not strictly true. It's not you, but it is *one* of you."

Androgyne looked up from the chair in confusion, "Not *one of me*?"

"I'm sorry, Androgyne," Zillah thumped the panel on the wall. The door to the control deck opened. She stepped through it, trying not to show any emotion, "Please forgive me."

The door slid shut, sealing Androgyne in with her dead counterpart, "No, you can't do this. Don't leave me in here!"

Chapter 13

Captain Katz, Tripp, Bonnie, Jaycee, and Haloo strapped themselves into their outer-skins. They prepared to disembark Space Opera Beta.

Bonnie held Jelly in her arms and made a fuss of her, "Hey, honey. Are you ready for an adventure of a lifetime?"

"Bonnie, stop talking weird to the cat, please," Katz yanked the zip up to his helmet, "Let's try to keep first contact with Alpha as professional as possible."

Bonnie smirked and bounced Jelly around in her arms. She affected a cutesy voice, indirectly talking to Katz through the animal, "What's that, Jelly? Yes, he *is* being a miserable old so-and-so, isn't he?"

Katz looked up in horror at Bonnie, much to everyone else's amusement, "Dr. Whitaker."

"Don't pay attention to the nasty man," Bonnie continued. "He's just unhappy that he can't smoke in space."

Katz gave as good as he got. He stroked the top of Jelly's head and gave as good as he was getting, "What's that, Jelly? Yes, that's right. Bonnie *is* a feisty one with a chip on her shoulder, isn't she?"

Jelly didn't know which way to look. Her innocent eyes suggested she couldn't stop the stupid feud between her colleagues.

'Meow.'

Tripp, Jaycee, and Haloo burst out laughing.

"Don't pay any attention to the nasty lady," Katz finished

in his silly voice and winked at Bonnie, "She might be disciplined for insubordination. That's right."

"Okay, that's enough," Tripp folded down his visor, "You two can go get a room and turf it out once we're done rescuing our friends."

"Mmm, sounds like a challenge," Bonnie licked her lips at Katz, "Wanna come back to my quarters and discipline me properly?"

"Not especially, no."

Katz turned to Jaycee and was taken aback by just how tooled up he was. He clutched his K-SPARK shotgun in his arm - grenades, flash bangs and tear gas lined his belt.

Two Rez-9 mini-guns hung over his thigh. The cannons on both boots completed the look.

Katz finally opened his mouth, "Traveling light today, Jaycee?"

"Yeah, not much is worrying me on this one."

"So I see."

Katz flipped down his visor.

An array of digital messages zipped across his screen. The mouthpiece on his headset crept across his lips, "Wool ar-Ban, Tor Klyce, this is Captain Daryl Katz. Can you read me?"

"Yes, captain," Wool's voice came through his visor.

"We are disembarking, now. Heading for Opera Alpha."

"Understood."

Tor and Wool stood in front of the communications deck on Opera Beta.

They watched the first airlock hatch open and allow the team inside. The door shut behind them and the chamber decompressed.

"Captain, we have a bit of an issue with the comms link to Androgyne," Tor flicked through some buttons on the deck.

"What is it?" Katz asked, turning to the outer door.

"We've lost communication. She must have hit a black spot."

"Understood. We will establish contact once we reach Alpha."

Jaycee turned to Jelly in Bonnie's arms, "Why are we taking the cat on board?"

"She's going to tell us what's going on, hopefully."

The outer airlock door slid open and revealed the bridge streaking across the infinite vacuum of space. Alpha loomed on the other end.

"Crossing now," Katz led the way. He grabbed the bridge railings and propelled himself forward, "Androgyne, Zillah? Can you read me?"

No response. Katz looked at Alpha's outer airlock hatch. He hoped one of the two people on board Alpha would open it for them ahead of time, "I repeat, do you read us?"

"The patch is down, captain," Tor's voice came through the headset, "It should only be for a few minutes. If worse comes to the worse, just use your glove on the panel to get in. It shouldn't be an issue. I'll keep Beta outer lock door on standby in case anything untoward occurs."

"Thanks, Tor," Katz looked over his shoulder. Haloo, Tripp, Jaycee, and Bonnie followed behind, "Team, keep your wits about you when we board. Watch your six. Comms are going dark."

Tripp gripped the bridge railing, fighting off the urge to marvel at Saturn. He needed to keep moving, "What's happened?"

"They must have changed frequency. Tor thinks it might be a black spot."

"Meow," Jelly shifted in Bonnie's arms. She wanted to be released.

"Ooh, no, Jelly. Not now, sweetie," Bonnie said to her. "It's not safe out here."

Tripp reached Katz as he prepared to place his glove on the panel beside the airlock, "I hope they're both okay in there."

Androgyne banged on the control deck door with her fist, "Let me out of here!"

Zillah had her trapped inside the control deck. She had Opera Alpha's complete flight deck to herself. She would send a distress if she knew how. Fortunately, she knew

Manuel could assist her.

"Manuel?" she called out in desperation.

The book appeared in front of her. It banged its front and back covers together, "Good after-morning, Androgyne. How can I be of assistance?"

"*After morning?*" she heaved and tried to regulate her breathing, "You're speaking weird. Just get me out of here,"

"No, I don't think so," Manuel floated back and double-over itself, "You see, Miss Zillah has locked you in here for a reason."

"What reason?"

"Something happened to our ship. I don't know what happened, but the result was that everyone died."

"Wh-what do you mean?"

Manuel vaporized into a thousand pieces of holographic molecules, rendering himself gone, "I have cut off all channels of communication to your crew. You are to remain here until they board."

"No, no," Androgyne panicked and held her mouthpiece steady, determined to make contact with her crew, "Captain Katz, this is Androgyne. Do you read me? Do *not* board Alpha. I repeat, do *not* board Alpha. Something is wrong."

The outer airlock door slid up, offering Katz, Tripp, Jaycee, Haloo, Bonnie, and Jelly into the airlock. They hadn't received Androgyne's message.

"Airlock closing," Tripp yanked the lever and shut the five of them inside, "Commence decompression."

The red bulb inside the airlock spun around signaling the start of the pressure release.

Jaycee lifted his K-SPARK auto firearm and peered through the inner airlock door. He saw someone stare back at them.

"There's someone there. I think it's Captain Chin-Dunne."

"Step aside, Jaycee," Katz turned to Jaycee, "Let me do the introductions and pleasantries. When we're in I want you and Tripp to establish surviving crew and escort them onto Beta. Take them to Medix and run a full health diagnostic."

"Yes, captain."

"Haloo?" Katz asked.

"Yes, Captain."

"Keep it simple. I want a full report on Botanix. Zillah said something about distress. Let's see how much we can salvage."

"Yes, Captain."

"Bonnie," Katz said. "You and I will update Zillah and introduce her to Anderson."

"Okay."

The inner airlock door opened. The five Opera Beta crew members' silhouettes bled across the ground and reached the boots belonging to Opera Alpha's host; Zillah Chin-Dunne.

It was as if nothing had happened. She seemed very happy to see them. Katz felt it strange that Androgyne wasn't with her.

Katz stepped forward, ushering his crew toward their new friend.

"My name is Captain Daryl Katz of USARIC's Space Opera Beta. This is my crew."

"I'm so happy to see you," Zillah shook hands with Katz, who was surprised by her vice-like grip, "We're all so glad you came for us."

"That concerns us, Zillah," Katz scanned the airlock exterior. No significant damage had been done.

"We didn't receive a distress call."

"You didn't?"

"No," Katz walked forward with the others. They poked around the immediate area, scanning for any signs of life or damage, "Our mission is to Enceladus. We are to decipher Saturn Cry, and we think we may have the answer."

"Meow," Jelly spotted Zillah and growled.

Zillah backed away and covered her chest with both arms, "You brought a *cat* up here?"

"Yes," Bonnie said, "We made a discovery. The cat is responding to Saturn Cry—"

"—Get that... *thing*... off my ship."

Jelly growled and launched out of Bonnie's arms. She

tried to grab the creature but failed to respond in time.

Jelly's paws hit the floor. She trundled toward Zillah with her tail bushed and growled at her.

"I d-don't like c-cats," Zillah said. "I'm, uh, allergic."

"It's okay," Katz smirked. "She won't bite."

Jelly sat on her hind legs straight and looked up at Zillah, "Meow."

"What in God's name does USARIC think it's doing? Bringing a cat into space?"

Tripp approached Zillah and nodded toward the front of the ship, "We'd like to run a few diagnostic tests if possible. Get your crew out of hyper-sleep and have them embark Beta so we can get you all to safety."

"Yes, of course," Zillah said. "Perhaps we could start with a briefing in our crew hub?"

"Okay."

***

Tor paced around Opera Beta's control deck, muttering. Wool found his behavior strange.

"What are you doing?"

"I'm figuring something out, wait a second," he said, deep in contemplation, "Something isn't right."

"Why, what's the problem?"

"Communications are still down. We've lost Androgyne. I think the autopilot might be interfering," Tor looked up and snapped his fingers, "Manuel?"

The holographic book appeared in the middle of the room, "Hello, Tor. How can I assist you?"

"I'm sorry to have to do this to you, but while Katz and the team are on Alpha, I need to know you're not causing interference."

"I understand."

"Power-down Manuel, two-point-two," Tor said as Manuel vanished, "Reconcile manual control."

The control deck lit up, indicating that Tor was now in charge of Space Opera Beta.

"What are you doing?"

Tor made his way over to Wool, "Remember what happened to Baldron a few hours ago?"

"Yes. He's a traitor."

"I'm afraid he wasn't alone."

He gripped the lever on the deck and yanked it back.

The bridge connecting the two ships began to roll back and separate the two ships.

"What are you doing?"

"What does it look like I'm doing?" Tor said. "I'm retracting the bridge."

"What?" Wool jumped to her feet and thought about preventing Tor from pulling the bridge back, "Why?"

"We have the message decoded and everyone's on the other ship, just as planned. We have everything we need, now."

"What? *We?*"

"Yes."

Tor punched Wool in the face, instantly knocking her out. She spun around and landed in his arms.

"Shh. Good girl," Tor's accent changed from American to Russian instantly, "Let's get you chained up where you belong."

N-Carcerate
Space Opera Beta

Tor dragged the unconscious Wool by her arms across the metal gantry. Baldron stood up from his prison bay and watched his comrade lay her flat across the floor.

"You took your time," Baldron said in his Russian accent. He thumped the thick glass, "I'm fed up with having to do that stupid Yank accent. Get me out of here."

"Okay, yes. In a moment."

"Did they board the Alpha?"

"All except this one, here. I took care of her."

Tor hopped over to Baldron's cell door and placed his glove against the transparent panel, "Come on, get out."

The door slid open.

"Comrade," Baldron opened his arms and hugged Tor.

"We have what we need. Or, rather, we have what we *don't* need."

"Did you shut Manuel down?"

"Yes," Tor looked Baldron up and down, "But your reckless antics nearly cost us the mission."

"It is not my fault he switched cups. I am fortunate that I did not sip from it."

"That stupid cat ruined everything," Tor marched over to Wool's feet, "Here, assist me with this stupid American woman."

"My pleasure."

Baldron slid his hands under Wool's armpits. Tor took her ankles. They lifted her up and threw her into cell four.

"My word, she's heavier than she looks."

"Must be all those cheeseburgers they eat. Oh, who cares?" Tor smacked his palm against the plate, "Goodnight, princess."

As the door slid to a close, the red light came to life above the frame. Wool was now a prisoner on her own ship.

"What now?" Baldron asked. "Is everyone else on board Alpha?"

"Imbecile. I told you already that they are," Tor walked off, with Baldron following, "We send a message back to Dimitri Vasilov. Tell him we have deciphered Saturn Cry. We tell them, also, that the crew of Space Opera Beta are dead when they tried to rescue Alpha."

"Very good," Baldron said, making quotation marks with his forefingers, "*Tor Klyce*. Where did you come up with such a stupid pseudonym?"

"Oh! You are one to speak, *Baldron Landaker*. I could ask you the same question. Where did *you* come up with such a stupid name?"

Tor made his way out of N-Carcerate and adjusted his headset, "We keep using our aliases for the time being. I will send a message to Dimitri and inform them of the bad news, and that we are charting a course back to Earth."

"What do I do?"

"I do not know," Tor looked at Baldron and sighed, "Make yourself useful and go into hyper-sleep?"

***

Zillah walked the crew of Opera Beta into Alpha's conference hub, "I have a couple of things to tell you. It's not much, but it's all that we know."

Tripp, Katz, Bonnie, and Haloo took a seat around the table. Jaycee found it difficult to sit into the chair due to enormity of his armor. Zillah sniggered and watched him try to get comfortable.

"Are you okay?"

"Yes, I'm fine," Jaycee said. "Carrying quite a load, here."

"So I see, big boy."

Zillah turned to the rest of the crew. She circled her own face with her finger, "You may remove your visors, incidentally. It's perfectly breathable here."

Katz and his team looked at each other. One by one, they carefully removed their visors and took a deep breath.

"That's right, every one. Get a good, *deep* lungful."

And so, they did. Every one's chest inflated and deflated, thoroughly absorbing the air.

Zillah rubbed her hands and called up a holographic image of Opera Alpha from the central conference deck.

"As you can see, Alpha took a considerable amount of damage. The centrifuge stopped rotating, causing a lift in gravity. Once the backup drives took effect, most of Alpha's operations returned to normal."

"So you were hit by something?" Tripp asked. "Debris? Meteorites?"

Zillah shook her head, "Neither. The power-down occurred quite out of the blue."

She waved the image of the ship away and pulled up a live feed of the moon Enceladus, "We were six hours away from Enceladus when it happened. Manuel picked up this image. Can you see it?"

Everyone leaned in to look at the dark side of Enceladus.

"No?" Katz said.

"Here," Zillah enlarged the picture with her hand, "Something fantastic happened. We discovered something on the dark side of Enceladus. A pink gas cloud funneling from its core. Typical attributes of a wormhole. As it turns out, the source of Saturn Cry."

Tripp shook his head, "What *is* that pink thing?"

Bonnie released Jelly onto the conference table. She stretched her legs and trundled over to the holographic feed of Enceladus, "Meow."

Jelly clawed at it, but her paws sank through the image. She fell forward, confused.

"Jelly, behave," Bonnie patted the table in an attempt to get the cat to return to her.

Zillah found Jelly's presence on the table infuriating.

"So, what you're saying is that Enceladus is a portal?" Tripp asked.

"It contains a wormhole on the dark side. To where, we don't know."

Haloo scanned the hub and realized someone was missing, "Zillah, where is Androgyne?"

"She's in the control deck."

Trapped inside Opera Alpha's control deck, Androgyne freaked out next to her deceased counterpart.

Saturn hung in the star-filled sky, seemingly looking down on her. A giant, beautiful planet that blocked any kind of meaningful progress.

She held her finger to her ear in the hope someone could come to her aid, "Hello? Does anybody read me?"

No response.

"Hello? This is Tor Klyce in Opera Beta. Is that you Androgyne?"

"Oh God, yes. Tor, it's me," she said with relief, "Listen, I am stuck. Zillah has trapped me on Alpha. I can't get out. My lungs are tightening up, it's as if the room is running out of air…"

"Oh, that's a shame, isn't it?" Tor responded with little emotion.

"Yes, it is. Please, help me."

"No, I don't think so."

"What?" Androgyne ran around in circles and attempted

to compute Tor's words. She felt her limbs slow down and get heavier, "Why won't you help me?"

"Because I want you to die with the others."

She reached the corner of the control deck and a ten-foot-high compartment. Desperate to find a tool that might rescue her, she yanked on the door.

It flung outward, releasing Zillah's dead, deflated body.

"Agh," Androgyne stepped out of the corpse's fall toward the ground, "She's dead. She's dead."

"Who's dead?" Tor asked.

"Zillah. She has some sort of pink blood on her face. Oh my God, she's dead…"

"Androgyne?" Tor interrupted. "Listen to me very carefully."

"Yes, yes?"

She took a step back in complete confusion. Looking around for a way out proved to be futile in the extreme.

"It's very simple Androgyne. You and the crew of Opera Beta are going to die."

"What?"

"Goodbye, Androgyne."

The communication cut off, leaving Androgyne with two corpses in the control deck and very little else.

She just about managed to stagger to the free chair next to her counterpart's body. She sat into it, coughing and spluttering, and looked at her knees.

A drop of pink blood splashed against her thigh.

Her eyes bled a thick, pink liquid.

Chapter 14

Botanix
Space Opera Alpha

Zillah walked the crew of Opera Beta into the partially-destroyed botanical area of her ship.

The plants had withered. Most had disintegrated into a black husk. The remaining plant life had turned a sickly-looking pink color.

"As you can see, Botanix took a lot of the damage."

"The oh-two levels won't have helped if there was an explosion," Haloo lifted a device from her pocket. It sprang to life and took a meter reading, "Do you remember an explosion?"

Zillah shook her head and watched Jelly growl as she prowled her way through the plants, "No, no explosion. Not that we can recall."

"Everything just went dark?" Bonnie asked, looking over at the water coolant.

"Yes, utter darkness," Zillah paused to close her eyes and take in a lungful of air, "Mmm. Even with the majority of the systems down, every so often, I come back here and enjoy the clean air. It reminds me of Earth."

"Really?" Haloo took a reading from the room.

"I've been up here for so long. It gets lonely."

"I'm sure," Katz said. "I think we've seen enough. Tripp?"

"Captain," he walked over to him and pulled him aside.

"Can I have a quick word?"

"Certainly."

Tripp walked with Katz to the corner of the Botanix chamber and kept his voice low. "Are you thinking what I'm thinking?"

"Probably," Katz kept a stern eye on Zillah inhaling the clean air, "Alpha's Captain is not in proper operating order."

"I don't like this *at all*," Tripp whispered. "Something has happened here. None of it makes any sense."

"Power down for twenty minutes? No-one remembers anything?" Katz agreed, "Something's gone spectacularly wrong."

"Want to know what I think?"

"What?"

"I think they went through whatever that thing is on Enceladus."

"The wormhole?"

"Yes," Tripp lowered his voice for fear of being overheard, "I think we should wake Alpha's crew up and put them in quarantine."

Tripp caught Katz looking at him strangely, "What? What's wrong?"

"Your eye. It's bleeding."

"Huh?"

Tripp ran his finger across his cheek. A blob of pink liquid appeared on his glove. He blinked hard in an attempt to squash whatever remained of the substance from his tear duct, "Is it gone now?"

"No," Katz cleared his throat and stormed over to Zillah, "I think we've seen enough. Can I have everybody's attention, please?"

Haloo, Jaycee, Bonnie, and Jelly turned to Katz and awaited his instruction.

"With Zillah's approval, we'll reconvene with Androgyne and awake her crew from hyper-sleep. It is our opinion that Alpha is not salvageable, so we'll have to leave her where she is."

Zillah didn't like what she'd heard. Instead of responding

inappropriately, she crouched to her knees and offered her arms to Jelly, "Come here, girl."

"Meow."

Jelly ran along the plants and jumped into her arms. She held out her infinity claws for Zillah to make a fuss over.

"Captain Katz," Zillah pressed her face against Jelly's and smiled, "I'm afraid you do *not* have my blessing. You see, Space Opera Alpha is my ship. I'm afraid I cannot let her wither away to nothing a billion miles away from Earth."

"I'm afraid that is an assertion for you to make. Captain."

Zillah rubbed noses with Jelly. The cat pawed at her cheeks and widened her eyes. Her pupils went from dark orange to yellow in a few seconds, "Follow me, everyone."

"Where?" Tripp asked.

"Good girl," Zillah walked out of Botanix with Jelly in her arms, "Perhaps I will oblige Captain Katz after all."

Tripp and Katz watched her walk through the door. They were somewhat hesitant to follow her.

"That's one weird chick."

The hyper-sleep chamber on Space Opera Alpha was an exact replica of Opera Beta's. Seven pods in total. Only one of them was open - Zillah's.

She stood with Jelly in her arms and stroked her head, "Look, Jelly. My crew are fast asleep."

Bonnie and Jaycee followed her in. Haloo, Katz, and Tripp walked in after them.

"Good, good. Let's get them up and ready, Zillah," Katz said.

She turned around one-hundred-and-eighty-degrees to face Katz and his crew. She lifted Jelly to her face and listened to her purr.

"I cannot do that, Captain Katz."

"Why not?" he asked.

"Because…" Zillah closed her eyes, "They're all *dead*."

One by one, the fronts of each pod clanged opened to reveal a gray, rotten corpse.

Jaycee squeezed his machine gun in his hands, surveying the array of dead bodies. His trigger finger itched up a storm,

"My God…"

Zillah rubbed her face against Jelly's belly.

Bonnie held back the others and stepped forward, "Zillah?"

"Mmm," she moaned and squeezed Jelly in her arms, "You came here looking for answers, didn't you?"

"Zillah," Bonnie tried. "Give me Jelly."

"Meow," Jelly fanned out her claws. The metal connected with Zillah's face and tore at her lips.

"Let me show you something *fantastic,*" Zillah lifted her head and opened her mouth.

Her top lip crept up along her gums and folded up over her nose. Her bottom lip slung down over her bottom row of teeth and slid under her chin.

The crew watched, open-jawed, as Zillah's body elevated five inches into the air.

And then, a familiar 'cry' emitted from her chest and open mouth.

Hisss… followed by an electrical guitar sound.

And then, twelve seconds in… a familiar *whump.* Jelly shrieked and launched out of Zillah's arms.

"M-My God…" Tripp gazed the bizarre, demonic light show.

"Yes, I am," Zillah's voice crept in along the hiss, a bizarre fusion of static and growl, "Pink… Symphony…"

Twenty seconds into the hiss. Another *whump* barreled through the hyper-sleep chamber.

Zillah's skin slurped from her head and melted down her suit.

"She's dead already?" Tripp gasped. "Look at her!"

"They're using her as a transmitter," Bonnie stepped back and scooped the petrified cat from the floor, "We gotta get out of here."

"You… cannot… leave…" Zillah's body convulsed and flipped inside out, blasting fragments of her skin suit in all directions, "Pink Symphony."

"Everyone out," Katz bolted to the door, "Now."

Zillah's body jig sawed in-and-out and expanded with the chamber, bursting the screen doors on each hyper-sleep pod,

"Gaahhh!"

"Get out of here, now," Bonnie chased along with the others toward the airlock.

"Tor," Katz pressed his finger to his ear, "Tor, this is Katz, do you read me?"

"Yes, Captain. This is Tor, you're coming through loud and clear."

"We're coming back. Zillah and Alpha team are deceased. We are in severe danger."

"Ah. That's a negative, good buddy," Tor threatened over the connection, "Sorry to report that the bridge has been retracted and you're on your own. Over."

Katz looked confused. The reality of their predicament sunk in. He had to make sure he'd heard his comms officer correctly, "What? Sorry, Tor, can you repeat?"

"Did he just say what I think he said?" Bonnie yelled as she reached the inner airlock hatch.

The connection died off. Tor was no longer available.

"My God, My God," Haloo began to freak out, "We're going to die. We're all going to die."

"No, Haloo," Tripp grabbed her shoulders and looked her in the eyes, "It's okay. There's been a miscommunication. Breathe."

"I am b-breathing," Haloo spluttered, a clump of snot pushed through her right nostril. She wiped her face and looked up at Tripp, "Please, d-don't let us die."

The interior of the ship rumbled louder and louder.

"I d-don't know what's g-going on, b-but I want to go home."

"I know, I—" Tripp tried to calm her down but, instead, noticed a thick, pink teardrop rolling down her cheek, "Haloo?"

"Wh-what?"

"Your eye is bleeding."

Katz triggered his headset over and over but got no reply, "No, it's no good. We're cut off."

"What about Androgyne?" Jaycee kept an eye - and his shotgun - ready for Zillah, "We can't leave her here."

"We have no choice," Katz said. "She's replaceable. Haloo

and I aren't."

"Huh?" Tripp screwed his face, "What the—"

"Long story. Let's get back to Opera Beta and get away from whatever this thing is," Katz snapped on his glove and slammed his palm against the panel airlock. He expected it to open.

It didn't.

"C'mon, open up," Katz patted the panel over and over again with his glove, "It's not opening."

Androgyne sat next to her dead counterpart and felt a trickle of something race down her synthetic cheek.

It wasn't blood. Instead, it resembled a transparent and clear bead of sweat.

She'd gotten over the worst of her turmoil and resigned herself to the fact she'd never be rescued. She didn't know where the Beta crew were. All she knew was that she was a captive aboard the Opera Alpha and in serious peril.

She hit the intercom switch on the communication deck in a desperate bid to contact Opera Beta.

"This is Androgyne. Does anyone read me?"

To her surprise the static kicked up and produced a familiar voice.

"This is Space Opera Beta, communications officer Tor Klyce."

Androgyne felt a new emotion race through her body. She gasped for dear life and threw her body forward in haste.

"Tor, this is Androgyne. I am trapped on Opera Alpha. Something weird is happening."

"Yes, I know you are trapped, Androgyne. How are you?"

"I'm scared and I can't get out. Please help me. Where are the others?

"They're on board Alpha with you."

"Oh, thank God," she started crying floods of tears and watch them flood onto her glove, "There's pink tears coming out of my eyes."

"Yes, it's called crying," Tor's voice sounded reassuring. "You're scared, it's perfectly natural."

"I can't get through to them. Can you advise them that I

am trapped? It's Zillah, she's not a good person. She put me here."

"You don't remember the conversation we had ten minutes ago, do you?" Tor asked, "Unfortunately I am unable to help you, Androgyne."

"What? Why? Can you not establish contact with them?"

"No," he said with an eerie calmness, "It's because I don't want to."

"What?" Androgyne couldn't believe what she was hearing, "What do you mean you don't want to?"

"Because I want you and the Beta crew to perish with Zillah. And you're going to assist me."

The reality of her situation finally hit home. The communication device slipped through her fingers.

"Androgyne, can you hear me?"

"Yes," she muttered, knowing she was about to die.

"On your forearm is a synthetic panel," he said. "Do you see it?"

She looked at her left forearm and closed her eyes.

"Yes, I see it."

"Good. Unfasten the housing and remove the cover."

She did as instructed. Two red buttons appeared next to a digital readout, "I've done it."

"Can you see two red buttons?"

She sniffed and cleared her throat, "Y-Yes."

"You're equipped with a self-destruct mechanism. Inside where your womb would be, if you were human, is a quarter tonne of C4. You will press the two buttons together with your free hand and keep it held down for five seconds, enabling a two-minute self-destruct scenario."

"No, no," she shook her head and tried to fight off her superior's instruction, "No, I won't."

"Yes, you will. Don't disobey a direct order. It's for your own good. You want to destroy Zillah, don't you?"

"Yes, but everyone else will die, too."

"Ugh," Tor went silent for a few moments. Androgyne heard him scream at the top of his lungs, "God damn it, you *will* do as I say."

"No," Androgyne bit her lip and went to close the

housing back to her forearm, "I will not murder my crew—"

"—You're not human. You *do* know that, don't you?" Tor's voice shot through her earpiece, piercing her brain, "You're an antiquated Androgyne. A a worthless, antiquated piece of metal that no junkyard would ever take."

She moved her fingers away from the housing and extended her forefinger and middle finger. "No, I'm n-not."

"You're the second-least intelligent life aboard the Alpha, behind that stupid cat."

She nodded and blurted. Tor's psychology was working wonders with her, "Repeat after me, Androgyne."

"Repeat after me, Androgyne," she recited, succumbing to Tor's command.

"I am worthless..."

"I... am... *worthless*..."

"—Good," Tor's voice perked up, "And I will sacrifice myself because it's the noblest thing to do."

"... and I will sacrifice myself, b-because it's the noblest thing to do."

"Do it. Hold down the two buttons."

She pressed the buttons down and kept them held, "Please, forgive me for what I'm about to do."

"I never told you to say that," Tor barked through her ear piece, "Just do as you're told, you useless tin of tuna."

Beep-beep.

"Self-destruct activated," announced the mechanism on her arm, "Two minutes until detonation."

Androgyne rose out of her chair feeling very sorry for herself.

"Well done, girl. You've just saved us from the bad guys. Now, go and sprawl over the flight deck. Maximize your damage to the Alpha's mainframe, my beautiful walking time bomb.

Androgyne looked at the central control deck and walked over to it. She stopped a couple of footsteps away and looked at the flashing lights and levers.

Tor continued to speak into her ear, "Cover the control deck with your whole body."

Her forearm beeped quicker and quicker. Obliging her

tormentor, she held out her hands and took one last look at Saturn.

"Close your eyes," Tor whispered.

The planet faded from sight as she closed her eyes. She fell forward with her arms outstretched and hit the flight deck chest-first.

"Nighty-night, princess."

Back at Alpha's airlock, Jaycee pushed Katz out of the way and lifted his K-SPARK at the lock, "Move."

"What are you doing?"

"If we can't open it manually, we're gonna have to try some tough love."

"Wait," Tripp grabbed the barrel of the machine gun and pushed it away, "You are *not* going to blast the airlock open, are you?"

Jaycee stomped his foot, shaking the ground beneath, "If you've got a better idea, let us know."

"If you shoot the lock, you'll kill us."

"And if we stay, we're dead, anyway," Jaycee pushed Tripp to one side. He took three steps back and cocked the gun, aiming it at the panel, "You wanna put this to the vote?"

"No."

"Good, because this isn't up for debate," Jaycee looked at Katz, "Permission to blow the inner airlock hatch, Captain Katz?"

Katz turned to the corridor that led to the airlock, "Yes, yes," he said, fearing an attack from Zillah - or something - was impending, "Do it. Everyone, visors down. We hit the bridge."

Tripp, Haloo, Bonnie, and Jelly stepped aside and allowed Jaycee to blow the inner airlock hatch.

Tripp flipped his visor down and scanned the cuticle, "Tor, this is Tripp, come in?"

No response.

"Okay, blow the airlock," Tripp said.

Jaycee flipped the lever down on the side of his machine gun. The mechanism whirred to life, heating in his hand. He took aim at the panel.

"Here we go."

He blasted the panel, obliterating the inner door. The impact set off the ship's alarm.

Jaycee marched in and kicked the rest of the broken door apart with his Titanium boot.

"Everyone get in," he grabbed the outer airlock hatch lever, "Listen, once this door is open, all hell is gonna break loose. Watch out for debris. Everything inside this ship is going to puke out into space, and we're standing right in the middle of its throat."

Katz pushed Jaycee to the side, dumbfounded by the view offered by the glass panel in the door, "My God…"

"What?" Tripp asked Katz, "What's wrong?"

Katz blinked and saw that the bridge was missing. The outer door on Beta's airlock was open, a mere fifty meters away.

"The bridge," Katz said, "It's gone."

Haloo freaked out and hyperventilated. The inside of her visor fogged up as she grabbed at the handle bar within the airlock, "No, no…"

Bonnie kept her grip on Jelly, "Haloo, get up."

"I c-can't breathe," Haloo puked pink blood up inside her visor, "Grrh-helpsch… m-me…"

Jaycee hoisted her up to her feet by her arm. She fell into his arms.

"Katz, we need to go—"

A colossal explosion rumbled the airlock.

"What was that?" Katz asked.

The entire ship rumbled violently, shaking everyone around.

"No time to wait around to find out," Tripp grabbed the manual handle on the outer airlock door. "Sounded like an explosion."

Bonnie nodded at the door and held Jelly out. "Open it. We'll have to jump."

Tripp took a final glance at Katz and grabbed the handle. "Ready?"

"Do it."

Alpha's alarms sounded off. The spinning red bulbs

rotated around and around. "Explosion on Alpha control deck."

"Androgyne?" Katz said. "On the control deck?"

"Opening now. Get ready and hold on," Tripp yanked the outer airlock door open.

Everyone grabbed hold of the bars within the airlock.

An intense vacuum sucked anything that wasn't bolted to the ground through the crack in the door as it opened.

Jelly shrieked and extended her metal claws. "Meaa….oowwarrr…"

Boom. The airlock door fully opened, lifting everyone off their feet.

Various objects whizzed past the crew and shot out into the depths of space.

"Bonnie. Release Jelly first," Tripp clung to the door, "Throw her to Beta."

"Okay," Bonnie launched Jelly at Beta's inner airlock hatch.

The cat screamed and held out her arms, pushing through the infinite vacuum, headed for Beta's airlock.

"Meaaooo—" she gulped down, feeling her chest begin to expand. Tufts of fur flew away from her face and littered the inside of her visor.

She clenched her claws and grabbed onto the inner airlock hatch, completing the journey in a matter of seconds.

Tripp kept the Alpha's outer hatch open, "Bonnie, go."

She took a run toward the lip of airlock and jumped into the vacuum.

Whoosh.

Bonnie held her arms to her sides and darted through space like an arrow.

Beta's airlock, containing the frightened Jelly, whizzed closer and closer. Bonnie held out her arms and kicked herself in. She grabbed hold of a lock on the floor, "I'm in, go! Go!"

"Haloo," Tripp said through his visor, "You're next."

"I can't see," she growled, fighting off the vacuum pressure. She pinched the bottom of her visor and threatened to open it.

"What are you doing?" Tripp said, "Don't open your visor—"

It flipped up over her face, exposing her to the vacuum. Tripp couldn't believe what he saw.

Pink blood drenched Haloo's face. Her eyeballs protruded from her skull.

"I'm blind," she said, softly, as if overcome with wonder, "But I can see *everything.*"

"What are you talking about?" Katz gripped the bar on the wall. His feet kicked to the side, "Jump. Get back to Beta."

Having seen Bonnie carry out the same action moments ago, Haloo ran toward the outer door and launched herself forward.

Her body twisted through three-hundred-and-sixty degrees through space like a corkscrew.

Tripp, Jaycee, and Katz heard her wail a cry of death as beads of pink blood raced out from her visor. They glinted against the reflection from Saturn.

She made it into Beta's airlock, very worse for wear. Bonnie clung to the handlebar in the airlock and watched Haloo coughing up blood, "Haloo? What are you doing?"

"Caaa-aaan't b-breathe…"

"Meaaoww," Jelly yelped from the airlock hatch, scratching at the glass panel, "Maaaahh…"

"Keep the air out of your lungs, Haloo," Bonnie screamed, "Don't breathe."

Katz turned to Tripp and Jaycee, "You two go—"

A loud rumbling followed the debris funneling out of the ship. A huge ball of fire rumbled toward them.

Zillah's apparition floated in front of the ball of fire, ten seconds away from impact.

"Pink symphony," Zillah's mouthed opened nearly as wide as her arms, "Come to me."

"Go," Katz shouted and turned to Tripp and Jaycee, "Go, now. I'll keep the door open."

"But, Captain," Tripp said as Katz barged him out of the

way and grabbed the handle on the door.

"Don't disobey me. Both of you go, now."

Tripp nodded and stepped out of the airlock, He twisted on his axis in space. Jaycee ran forward and jumped, grabbing Tripp around his waist.

"Hold tight."

Jaycee kicked them away from the airlock door and stretched out his legs. He aimed the tip of his foot toward the Zillah as she approached Katz at the airlock door.

"Let's kill two birds with one shoe."

BLAM-BLAM-BLAM!

Jaycee fire the cannon on his foot at Zillah as she entered the airlock. The force of the bullets pushed Jaycee and Tripp over to Opera Beta's airlock.

The bullets flew through Zillah's body and into the oncoming rush of fire barreling up the airlock.

"Daryl," Tripp said.

Katz released the door. It slid across and blocked his view of Tripp and Jaycee.

"Look after my crew, Tripp," Katz's final communication came through the headset.

"Daryl, no!"

The door slammed shut, sealing Katz in with Zillah and the impending explosion.

Tripp and Jaycee tumbled into Beta's airlock, along with Haloo, Bonnie and Jelly.

Tripp palmed the button on the outer door. It slammed shut and sealed them off in the airlock.

Everyone turned to the glass door.

Space Opera Alpha vibrated. The airlock filled with fire, sending a magnificently aggressive wave through its structure.

The outer panels broke off, forcing the exterior of the ship to inflate along the ripples.

A brief period of silence, followed by a whooshing noise.

And then... everything went white.

Haloo, Bonnie, Jelly, Tripp, and Jaycee held their forearms over their face and closed their eyes.

A brilliant white light grew from the center of Space

Opera Alpha and flooded the interior Beta airlock.

Everything fell utterly silent.

Then, an almighty explosion woke God himself. The ship exploded in sections.

First to go was the front of the cone.

Followed by its centrifuge, the ring itself shattered out, propelling the back-end of the ship away. It detonated impressively, adding to the already-spectacular firework show.

The separate explosions briefly arranged themselves into the shape of Zillah's face, although Tripp knew it could have been his mind playing tricks.

The force was enough to throw Opera Beta off track. Saturn bleached into view. What little remained of the dormant carcass of Space Opera Alpha hung in the vacuum of space.

All of this, and with no sound whatsoever. The explosion sucked back in on itself the moment it ejected.

No air in space; a deafening silence.

The only way the team knew the destruction of Space Opera Alpha was a reality was through the vibrations felt from the components of their craft they clung to.

Haloo coughed up a mound of thick, pink blood.

Jelly slid down the airlock wall, utterly petrified.

"Is everyone okay?" Tripp asked, wiping his outer skin down.

Everyone was essentially fine, if a little rattled.

Jaycee was without his firearm. He'd lost in transit. The K-SPARK gun spun around somewhere between what remained of Alpha and the steady Beta.

"Lost my gun, but we're good."

"Bonnie?" Tripp asked, approaching her and holding the side of her visor. "Are you okay?"

"Yes, yes," she looked into his eyes. "I'm okay."

Haloo climbed to her knees and pressed her gloved palms to the floor. She spat a few lumps of bloodied phlegm to the floor and turned to Tripp.

Her face had turned pink and her eyes continued to bleed.

"Tripp?"

"Haloo, are you okay?" He darted over to her and tried to lift her to her feet. She didn't have the energy to do it.

"I c-can't move," Haloo wiped her eyes, "I don't know what's happened to me."

Jelly sauntered over to Haloo and investigated her legs, "Meaaaooowww…"

Her cries seemed a bit deeper.

Tripp addressed Jaycee and Bonnie as he opened the inner airlock door, "We need to find Tor and take him out."

"Tripp?" Jaycee reached into his belt and took out a Rez-9 firearm, "Wool is on board with him."

"And Baldron is in N-Carcerate," Bonnie waited for Tripp to open the door, "We need to know where he is."

"Yes." Tripp opened his visor and grabbed at his mouthpiece, "Manuel, this is Tripp. Can you read me?"

"Good after-afternoon, Tripp," Manuel's scrambled voice was full of static and sounded *dislodged*, "Did you r-r-r-rescue Aaaa-lphaa-aaaa—"

"Eh?" Tripp tried again, "Manuel? Do you read me?"

No response.

"Tor's interfering with him," Tripp said. "Jaycee, escort Haloo and Jelly to Medix. Find Wool, and have her run a health check on both of them."

"Yes, *Captain*."

Tripp nodded. "That's right. Have her run a check on you, too."

"Understood."

"Bonnie and I will find Tor and deal with him ourselves."

"You'd better take this, then," Jaycee unclipped a second Rez-9 firearm from his belt and handed it to Tripp.

Bonnie watched Tripp take it and slip it into his belt, "Be careful with that, Healy."

"I'm hoping I won't have to use it."

Bonnie punched the inner airlock panel and opened the hatch, "If I find him first, you won't have to."

Chapter 15

Jaycee helped Haloo across the hub. Jelly followed behind, meowing and whining.

Haloo's legs threatened to buckle as she walked. The only thing keeping her moving was Jaycee's grip on her shoulder.

"You'll be okay, Haloo," Jaycee said as they made their way to the Medix center, "We'll get you seen to."

"Maaaah!" Jelly hopped in front of them and up the corridor. She ran her head along the side of the door to Medix.

"What is it, Anderson?" Jaycee said.

She scratched her metal claws up the window and rammed her head onto its surface.

"Yes, I know, I know," Jaycee clunked his way along the ground, "We'll find Wool and make sure everyone is okay."

Jaycee opened the door and walked into Medix with Haloo draped over his shoulder.

Nobody was around.

"Wool, we're here," Jayce said. "Where are you?"

He removed Haloo's helmet and laid her out on a bed. He puffed up one of the pillows and laid the back of her head on it.

"Wait here, Haloo," he turned to Jelly. She looked up at him and meowed.

"What do you want, girl?" Jaycee saw that Jelly's eyes were bleeding. Her bright orange fur had turned to a soft pink, "What's happening to your face?"

"Meeeeeee-ooooooowwwww… w-oooooooll…"

"Anderson? You're concerning me."

"Meow," Jelly repeated again, her voice turning huskier, "Meeeooooowwwooo-ooolll…"

"Wool?"

Jelly purred and ducked her head. Her metal claws began to flap uncontrollably like a jazzed-up pair of gloves, "Rowaarr."

Jelly flipped onto her behind and tried to fight her paws - *with her own paws.*

"Hey, stop that," Jaycee walked around her, "What are you doing?"

Jelly tumbled onto her side and kicked her hind legs out, trying to fight off whatever was happening to her.

"Jaaaaaay-ceeeee…" her voice broke into a low-pitched growl. Sparks of electricity burst out from her paws.

Jaycee looked to find a tiny bead of pink liquid fall splash against his left shoe.

It broke apart as it collided with the ground, bleaching across the white tiles, "What's happening to us?"

"H-Help m-me…" Haloo's voice and body vibrated aggressively.

Jaycee wiped the bloodied patch from his cheek and raced over to Haloo. Her face had turned pink and her eyes were bleeding once again.

"What's going on here?" Jayce caught a glimpse of his own reflection in the mirrored wall. His face had gone pink, too.

His eyes cried pink blood.

***

Tripp and Bonnie headed for Opera Beta's control deck. He cleared his throat and felt his stomach.

"I don't feel too great," he said, making a beeline for the control deck door.

"We've just swam through a vacuum and watched our sister ship detonate," Bonnie muttered, "I think we're entitled to feel a bit exhausted."

"I guess you're right. We have what we need. As soon as we find Tor, we're turning around and heading straight for home," Tripp snapped his fingers, expecting Manuel to appear, "Manuel?"

Snap-snap-snap. Nothing.

"Manuel?"

"What happened to Androgyne?" Bonnie wondered aloud.

"I don't know. We need answers."

Tripp held his glove to the panel on the door to the control deck. It opened, and they walked in.

"Ah, you made it," Tor grinned and leaned against on the flight deck. Tripp and Bonnie clocked his Russian accent immediately, "I have to say, that was quite an impressive feat. Jumping from one ship to another."

"Tor Klyce," Tripp stopped a few feet away from him, "Under USARIC code fourteen-oh-three and Infinity Clause three, subsection twelve, I hereby place you under arrest for the murder of Captain Daryl J. Katz. Further, IC Two-oh-Five, disobeying a direct command from your superior officer and jeopardizing the souls aboard *both* Opera Alpha and Opera Beta."

Tor sniggered with menace, "Is that so, *Captain*?"

"It *is* so, Tor," Tripp retrieved a Rez-9 firearm from his belt, hoping he wouldn't have to use it, "You will be put into hyper-sleep under N-Carcerate jurisdiction until we reach Earth, where you will be formally charged. Do you understand this statement as I have recited it to you?"

"Yes, I understand what you're saying," Tor chuckled. "But you don't seem to understand the bigger picture."

Bonnie became infuriated with Tor's response, "What bigger picture?"

"You stupid Yanks. You're all the same. Never want to play with the others. Always wanting to take all the credit," Tor nodded behind them, "You poison Viktor Rabinovich, our most esteemed diplomat on your soil and expect to get away with it?"

They turned around to find Baldron pointing a K-SPARK machine gun at them, "Drop the weaponry, American."

Tripp and Bonnie held up their hands.

"Hand over your firearm," Baldron said.

Tripp tossed the Rez-9 at Tor's feet. The bad guy bent down and picked it up. He aimed the barrel at Tripp and Bonnie.

"It is quite simple, really," Tor explained. "You deciphered Saturn Cry for us. You and your crew dock with Alpha and perish in the explosion. Such a shame that Baldron and I were the only ones left with that stupid cat. A Pyhrric but believable victory for us considering your nation attacked ours."

"We will take the glory," Baldron said, "We were the only survivors of Space Opera Beta's mission to Enceladus. We figured out what Saturn Cry means."

"The United States didn't attack Rabinovich."

"Yes, they did,' Baldron winked at Tor. The pair found it difficult to quell their laughter, "Anyway, who cares? We are heroes."

"Like hell you are." Bonnie resisted the urge to punch them both in the face and risk getting herself killed, "You're nothing but scum."

Tor folded his arms with confidence, "On the contrary, young American girl. Show me your forearm."

"What?"

"Do it, or I will shoot you in the face."

Bonnie did as she was told. She lifted her forearm up and looked at it. "Have you gone mad?"

"If you look on your forearm, you'll find a panel."

All she could see was the black ink of her Individimedia, "What panel?"

Tor ran his finger along Bonnie's black tattoo line. It fizzed and shifted apart, creating a Rorschach-esque rectangle.

"Bonnie Whitaker," Tor said. "You're equipped with a self-destruct button. Inside where your womb would be, if you were human, is a quarter tonne of C4. If you hold down the two buttons for five seconds, it would enable a two-minute self-destruct scenario."

"No, no…" She pushed the man back as a wave of terror thundered down her spine, "No, no, it isn't true."

"Bonnie?" Tripp turned to her and kept his arms above

his head.

"Don't move, American," Baldron threatened Tripp and turned to Bonnie, "And *you*, don't move, either. You useless piece of metallic junk."

"No, no," Bonnie punched her fists together, trying to escape the inevitable explanation, "It can't be true."

"North American *pig*," Baldron smirked and spat in Bonnie's direction, "Just a failed Androgyne Series Three upgrade. Like all the others."

"It is true, I'm afraid," Tor chuckled. "Just an obedient, useless heap of failed *Manning/Synapse* ideas. That's all you are. Poetic, really. A waste of space."

"What happened to Androgyne?" Bonnie spluttered and wiped her lip, wanting blood. "What did you do to her?"

"We didn't do anything to her," Tor said. "She did it to herself."

"No," Bonnie shook her head as entire life flashed before her eyes, "I remember everything. You're lying."

"I assure you I am not. And I assure you, you don't remember a thing. Do you?"

Bonnie let out an ear-piercing scream, "I am not an android."

"Ha. I love how you refuse to accept facts that are staring you dead in the face," Tor nodded at the door, "Speaking of *dead*, where are Jaycee and Haloo?"

"We sent them to Botanix," Tripp lied and briefly caught Bonnie's gaze, "We needed to make sure it was operational before we committed to any revisions on how to proceed."

"Good, let's go."

Tripp and Bonnie led the way with their hands above their heads. Tor and Baldron kept their weapons aimed at them from behind.

***

Wool opened her eyes. She didn't recognize where she was at first.

The silver walls gave her a clue.

The padded bench seemed familiar.

"Where am I?" she rubbed her eyes and looked down at her foot. Her ankle had a metal shackle attached to it, "What?"

She wiggled her foot which caused the metal chain to clang against the floor. She looked up and saw the electric bars.

"What am I doing in N-Carcerate?" She stood up from the bench and made for the bars. The shackle kept her from reaching them.

Then, she remembered just how painful it would be if she touched them. The shimmer on the glowing bars threatened to zap anyone stupid enough to have a go.

She patted the side of her pants and reached into her pocket in haste. Once she found that her belongings had been removed, she panicked.

"Help, help," She shouted at the ceiling at the top of her lungs, "Someone, please. Help me. Can anyone hear me?"

Jaycee hooked Haloo up to a diagnostic module in Medix. She hadn't held up very well at all - half-conscious, her face had blossomed bright pink. Her eyes had stopped bleeding for the time being.

"You have a fever, Haloo," Jaycee kept an eye on the monitor, "Your body temperature is well over one hundred."

Jelly paced around, shifting her opposable metal thumbs against the floor.

Something was agitating her.

Jelly leaned back on her haunches hopped onto Haloo's bed. She flapped her tail around and trundled over to the woman's face.

"Meow," Jelly sniffed around Haloo's face.

"Jelly, sweetie..." She half-croaked, "What are you doing?"

The cat pressed her paws on Haloo's shoulder and leaned in for a good, deep sniff. The tip of her nose met with Haloo's.

"I'm sick, Jelly," Haloo muttered. "Stay away from m-me."

"Huh..." Jelly huffed into her face as her whiskers tingled, "Huuuh... Loo..."

Haloo and Jaycee turned to Jelly in incredulity.

"Ha-loo…"

"Huh?" Jaycee tilted his head at the cat, "Say that again, girl?"

"Ha-loo…" Jelly's voice creaked as she tried to speak. "Ha… Loo…"

"My God," Haloo cleared her throat and lifted her hand up to Jelly's head, "She said my name…"

Haloo's chest bounced into the air unexpectedly, forcing Jelly off the bed. Jaycee stepped back and allowed Haloo to endure her spasm.

The back of her head slapped against the padded bed, pushing more pink blood from her eyes.

Finally, her mouth yawned open and spat out a low-pitched whine, "I-It's so *fantastic*…"

"—What is, Haloo? What's *fantastic*?" Jaycee grabbed her shoulders and bunched the fabric of her shirt in his palms, "What are you talking about?"

"Can't you see it?" She gasped, her chest deflating. The diagnostic machine ran wild. Her heart-rate and temperature rocketed skyward.

"No," Jaycee said, angered by his own helplessness, "What are you talking about?"

"Unngghhh…" Haloo's chest heaved once more.

Then, she flat-lined.

The dials spun down to zero. Haloo died in Jaycee's arms right there and then, her eyes looking right into his.

"No, no," Jaycee gasped, "Don't you dare die on me."

The machine let out a long beep indicating that Haloo had passed away.

Jelly rubbed her face over Jaycee's foot. He shooed her aside and made for the defibrillator that hung on the side of the machine, "Sorry, girl. Stand back."

He tore Haloo's outer-skin suit open at the chest.

"Wuuuhhh," Jelly groaned and shook her head, as if coughing up a fur ball, "Whelp."

Jayce powered up the defibrillator paddles in both hands. They whined to life and buzzed, "Clear."

He jolted Haloo with the paddles, trying to shock her to

life. Each time he did, Jelly backed up, groaning in pain.

Jaycee gave up and hooked the paddles on the machine. Haloo was well and truly gone. He knew it, and so did Jelly.

He let out an almighty roar of anger, startling the feline by his feet. He thumped the bed, which rocked Haloo's body back and forth.

After taking a deep breath he turned to Jelly. She looked up at him hoping he wouldn't take his anger out on her.

"Meowgh," she tried but ended up coughing out a rope of pink saliva.

Jaycee reached into his belt and pulled out his secondary Rez-9 firearm. He threw Jelly a look of steely determination, "Someone has to pay for this, right?"

Jelly continued to stare at him and seemed to nod in agreement, "Meow."

Jaycee made for the door and held his finger to his ear, "This is Jaycee Nayall. Can anyone read me?"

No response.

A "meow' came through his ear piece. The whiskers on Jelly's face buzzed. She could communicate with him.

"Not you, girl," Jaycee opened the door and lifted his weapon into the crook of his arm, "I repeat, can…"

"… can anyone read me?" Jaycee's voice finished through Tripp's headset as he walked along the concourse with his hands behind his head.

Bonnie could hear him, too.

Tor and Baldron chuckled to each other, having heard the request for contact, "Do not respond to him."

"No, wait," Baldron whispered to Tor. "Have Tripp advise him to meet them at N-Carcerate. We can execute all of them there."

"Good thinking," Tor buried the barrel of his gun between Tripp's shoulder blades, "Get him to meet you and Bonnie at N-Carcerate. Don't tell him what's happened."

"Okay, okay," Tripp said.

"If you tell him we're here, we'll shoot you right here where you stand."

"Fine," Tripp pressed his finger to his ear, "Jaycee, this is

Tripp reading you, over."

"Tripp?"

"Yes, Jaycee?"

"Haloo's dead, man," he said, barely able to contain his anger, "Did you find Tor, yet? We need answers."

"Dead? What do you mean dead?" Tripp asked, hoping he'd misheard Jaycee's update.

Jaycee's cleared his throat, "Whatever this virus is… it killed her."

"Virus?" Tor whispered, "What is he talking about?"

Tripp chewed back the urge to emote upon hearing the news of his colleague's death. "Jaycee, listen. Bonnie and I are en route to N-Carcerate. Can you meet us there now?"

"Yes, I'm on my way."

"Is Jelly with you, too?"

"Yes, she's with me."

"Good."

"Just as well we're convening at N-Carcerate," Jaycee half-joked, his thoughts steeped in venom, "I'd quite like to pick Landaker's brains—"

"—Okay, ETA three minutes—"

"—with a large screwdriver, then crack open whatever is left of his skull open and drain the contents—"

Tripp let go of his ear and turned over his shoulder to Tor, "He doesn't sound happy."

"That wasn't very nice," Baldron booted Bonnie in the small of her back and sent her tumbling down the corridor, "How would he like it if I said nasty things about him behind his back?"

"Silence," Tor said. "It'll all be over in a few minutes anyway. Keep walking."

Wool felt a rumbling in the N-Carcerate chamber. It wasn't the footsteps of her visitors, however. Something grander was happening.

A series of vibrations she'd never felt before now.

She looked to her window to find it vibrating, the light from Saturn pouring through into her cell.

"What on Earth…" Her face fell when she saw what was

happening to the large planet.

The wreckage from Alpha appeared to be drifting toward it. The rings around the planet slowly split out into three, separate entities. Each of them began to revolve around the planet and throw pieces of the ship away.

"My God, it's *fantastic*," Wool whispered to herself.

CLANG.

Wool yelped and turned around to see the main door to N-Carcerate slid open, "Who's there?"

Tripp and Bonnie walked in, alone. Wool instantly spotted their strange behavior.

"Oh, thank God," Wool cried for joy, "You made it."

"Yes, we did," Tripp said, slowly. "Listen, Wool—"

"—Where are the others?"

"—No time for that right now," Bonnie said. "We are not alone."

"Look, you gotta watch out for Tor. He's a traitor," Wool shook her ankle, "Can you release me, please?"

Tor and Baldron hid behind the door to N-Carcerate, eavesdropping on the information they were sure Wool would spill.

"I knew it," Tor cocked his firearm, "She's told them about us."

"Why are we listening-in?" Baldron sniffed and wiped his eye, "Let's stop toying with them and kill them, already."

Tor squinted at Baldron's brow.

"What is it?"

"Your eyes are bleeding," Tor said. "Are you wearing contacts?"

"No, I'm twenty-twenty, I don't wear contacts," Baldron said, taken aback by the blob of pink blood on his finger, "My face feels really warm."

"Ugh, keep your distance," Tor said. "I don't want to catch space flu."

"I have not got space flu!" Baldron protested and nudged Tor aside, "Enough. Let's execute these infidels and get on with our mission."

"Right. Everyone on your knees. Now," Baldron aimed his firearm at Tripp and Bonnie.

"Wait!" Tripp said and bought some time, "Have you seen Saturn, lately?"

"No, and I don't care."

"Something is happening, look," Tripp nodded at the large window to his left.

Baldron and Tor looked to their right at the window. Their jaws dropped in wonder, "Oh, wow…"

Saturn's rings were in full gyration. The planet seemed to bulge like a beating heart as the rings revolved around at speed. The inertia coming from the spectacle rocked Opera Beta.

"When we boarded Alpha we were told something was going to happen," Tripp explained.

"The mission isn't over," Bonnie added. "It's only just begun."

"What is that?" Tor pointed at Saturn and grew anxious, "Why are the rings doing that?"

"I don't know," Tripp did his best to make his assailants change their minds about executing them, "But we need to stick around to find out."

"Correction, American," Tor snapped. "*We*, my comrade and I, need to stick around to find out. Not you."

Bonnie spotted something coming from the corridor. She clenched her fists behind her head and slowly rose to her feet, "Are you going to sabotage what could be the greatest discovery of the universe?"

"Yes," Tor said without a hint of remorse. He swung his gun at her face. "I am going to blast your pretty little head off."

"It's ironic you said that," Bonnie smirked, evilly.

Tor didn't get the joke. "How is what I just said ironic—"

BLAM.

A bullet rocketed past his head from behind, scraping a few strands of his hair from the side of his face. Tor jumped forward and slid across the floor, releasing his weapon.

Tripp wasted no time in collecting the gun and pointing it at Tor.

Jaycee stormed forward and pointed his Rez-9 gun at Baldron, who reached into his inner-suit and pulled out a red dumb bomb.

"No, no, no," Baldron threatened to yank the pin away from the bomb. He sidestepped toward the exit to the chamber, "You want us all to die?"

"No," Jaycee fumed, ready to kill the man, "Just you."

"What was that you said to me, Jaycee? Never point your gun at the people you work with?"

"You don't work with us."

"Hypocrite." Baldron tugged on the pin and threatened to release it.

"Jesus," Tripp kept his Rez-9 pointed at Tor's head, "Jaycee, don't exacerbate the situation. Stand down."

Jaycee lowered the gun, angry with himself, "Fine."

"You like surrendering, don't you, American? Your history is full of failed war stories," Baldron chuckled to himself. "Tor, are you coming?"

"I would," he said, looking at the barrel of his own gun pointing at him from Tripp's hand, "But, uh, he's got my gun."

"Give my comrade his weapon back, Mr Healy," Baldron tugged at the pin on the dumb bomb, "If I pull the pin, there's no going back. We all get a first row view of whatever is happening out there."

"You wouldn't blow us up," Tripp threw the gun at Tor, who caught it clumsily in his hands, "There's too much at stake."

"On the contrary, American *scum*," Baldron wrenched the pin away from the grenade, setting off its sixty second timer. "I just did."

"Oh, God," everyone screamed, "No!"

"Tor, run!" Baldron darted out of the chamber. Tor jumped after him.

"No, wait," Jaycee turned around and chased after them. Tripp fired two rounds in their direction and missed.

Tor and Baldron jumped through the door and closed it shut.

"Goodbye, scumbags," Baldron tossed the dumb bomb

through the gap in the door and slammed it shut.

The grenade bounced off Jaycee's shoulder and rolled across the ground.

Tripp, Bonnie, and Wool stepped back as the digital readout counted down from forty seconds…

Chapter 16

Bonnie pushed herself to the floor in a frantic scramble to grab the dumb bomb as it rolled toward the cells.

She grabbed the device in her hand and yelled, "Thirty-five seconds! What do we do?"

"We can't shut it off," Wool cried out loud and closed her eyes.

"Stand back," Jaycee aimed his Rez-9 at the door, "Keep your heads down."

BLAMMM!

He blasted the door off its hinges and triggered Opera Beta's internal alarm. He booted the remains of the door away, "Everyone out."

"I'm stuck," Wool lifted her shackled ankle, "They have the key. I can't move."

"Wool," Bonnie looked at the timer on the grenade, "Thirty seconds…"

Tor and Baldron ran along the gantry at speed, heading toward Botanix.

"What did you do that for?" Tor asked. "The bomb will blow a hole in the side of the ship."

"No," Baldron ran ahead of Tor, "N-Carcerate will contain the explosion. We did it. We won. A mass Stateside suicide pact."

The pair's footsteps clanged along the corridor ground. They felt their feet get lighter. Eventually, their toes drifted away from the floor.

The gravity subsided, sending them into a free-float in the middle of the corridor.

"What's happening?"

"Someone's hit the gravity switch," Baldron gasped, and looked at Botanix.

The door slid open. Jelly kicked her hind legs against the frame and propelled forward, claws outstretched.

"Toooorrrr..." she shrieked, flying towards him.

"Anderson?" Tor screamed and covered his face, "What are you doing?"

Jelly swiped his face with her metal claws. His skin tore apart in three sections down the side of his face.

"Gaah!"

Tor kicked Jelly away, sending her tumbling through the gravity-less air. He swung his gun in her direction and squeezed the trigger.

"You dumb rodent."

Bang.

The bullet exploded in the chamber. Tor expected it to fly out of the barrel, but in zero gravity, he'd managed to blow his hand apart in a haze of fire and shrapnel.

Tor screamed and held his charred hand in the air, "Kill that damn *cat*."

Baldron pressed his back against the wall and kicked his feet to the ceiling. He looked back to N-Carcerate to see that door was open. "Oh no."

Bonnie floated into the air with the grenade in her hand, "What do we do?"

"If it goes off here, we're dead. Sucked out into space if the detonator doesn't kill us first."

Jaycee released his Rez-9. Instead of hitting the ground, it simply floated away from his palm, "Gimme the bomb."

"What are you going to do?" Tripp pushed himself into Wool's cell and grabbed her shoulders.

"Something I should have done the instant I met them."

Bonnie pinged the grenade toward Jaycee.

"If I throw it hard enough, Botanix might contain the blast," He caught the grenade and pulled his arm back,

"*Duck.*"

Tripp hugged Wool, who clung to him for dear life, "What the— no!"

Jaycee hurled the grenade down the corridor with all his might.

The bomb bolted down the central passage, headed for Tor and Baldron - and Jelly.

Jelly instincts kicked in. She pushed her hind legs off the ground and bolted behind the grenade.

Her claws latched onto the flying bomb and carried her toward Botanix's open door.

She pressed her knees to her stomach and planted the soles of her hind feet on the dumb bomb.

"What's she doing?" Tor held his breath and grabbed onto Baldron's arms.

"I don't know."

Jelly pushed the dumb bomb forward with her hind paws, pushing it faster along the weightless corridor.

As she kicked away, she somersaulted, legs-over-head and caught the Botanix door frame. The lower-half of her body swung sideways into the room.

She pulled herself through the door and placed her infinity claws against the plate on the wall.

The door slammed shut on the tip of her tail, "Meeeoooowwww!"

"That is *one* smart animal," Baldron couldn't believe his eyes.

"She's stuck," Tor said.

Jelly floated away from the door like a sideways pendulum, trying to 'swim' from the door. Her tail was stuck.

"Anderson?" Tor finally re-evaluated his position in life. Floating before him was a cat smart enough to save the crew from death - at the expense of oxygen.

Baldron swallowed hard. A blob of pink blood drifted away, slowly, from his cheek, "Look at her, she knows what's happening."

Jelly swung her metal claws at the pair. "Tooooorrrrr..." As she tried to speak, clumps of fur shed from her face and floated into the corridor.

A sliver of blood streaked through the air from her eye sockets, "Toooorrrr—"

KA-BOOM!

Botanix exploded like a self-contained thunderclap in a teacup. The sound of the explosion muffled and threw sparks against the window.

The plants caught ablaze and shattered. The heat lamps burst into pieces, sending jolts of electricity around the room.

The door shimmed enough to release Jelly's tail. The tip separated from her body and released her into the corridor.

Baldron and Tor turned to face N-Carcerate, "Oh, dear."

Bonnie grabbed a latch on the corridor wall and propelled herself toward Tor, "Remember? No Russian?"

Baldron went to strike her with his fist, "Yes, I remember."

"Yeah, let's stick to that. Stick *this*."

Bonnie swung her body around and kicked Baldron in the face. He tumbled back in the air and grabbed a latch on the corridor wall. He booted himself forward and punched Bonnie across the face.

A string of blood flew from her lips and traveled toward N-Carcerate.

"You think you can win, you dumb robot?" Baldron grabbed her by the back of her hair and snarled in her face. She clasped his fist with both hands and stared him down.

"Yeah, I think I can win."

Baldron spat in her face, "Repeat after me. I am a dumb robot."

"Ugghhh," Bonnie closed her eyes and spat his saliva away from her mouth.

"I am not a robot," Bonnie growled. "My name is Dr. Whitaker. I am a human being, and I remember *everything*."

She yanked his fist away from her head. He accidentally took a clump of hair away from her head.

Bonnie leaned back and head-butted Baldron on the nose, busting the cartilage within. His face turned a bright pink. The pink blood on her eyes could have been his, or hers, but she didn't care.

Baldron held his face in his hands and squealed in pain.

Everyone watched as Bonnie accosted the bad guy.

She grabbed his inner-suit collar and held him up for a timely telling-off, "Time to take out the trash. On behalf of USARIC, consider this a *dishonorable* discharge."

She planted her titanium foot on his chest and kicked through his breastplate. His body screamed back against the door to Botanix, narrowly missing Jelly.

Baldron twisting and turning through the air in agony. He coughed up a torrent which corkscrewed around the weightless environment like a mad firework.

Tor kept his hands behind his head and looked at Bonnie in terror. She stared at him and wiped the blood from her eyes, "You want some, too?"

"No, no," Tor pleaded, keeping an eye on Tripp as he approached him, "I surrender."

Bonnie drifted out of consciousness and lilted in the air. Her flowing, black locks drifted behind her shoulders, "Something... *fantastic* is... about to happen..."

Tripp pushed his way over to Tor and sealed the zip tie around his wrists, "Tor Klyce, if that's even your real name—"

"—It is not."

"—Well, whoever you are, you are under arrest," Tripp said, "I would ask you to hand over your cyanide capsule, please."

"My right inner thigh."

Tripp pushed him towards N-Carcerate. He spun around and drifted toward the cell doors. Tripp reached into Tor's inner thigh pocket and took out the capsule.

"Thank you very much."

Tripp shackled the man's ankle to the cell bed. Wool drifted back into N-Carcerate and breathed a sigh of relief.

Jaycee kicked himself along the corridor. He reached N-Carcerate with the unconscious Baldron in his arms.

Tor was upset. His comrade had been defeated and so, too, had their plans. A pink blob of water fell away from his tear duct, "Why… why is everyone crying pink?"

"I don't know, Tor," Tripp took Baldron's weightless body from Jaycee's arms, "Blood is usually red. Perhaps it's a lukewarm communist statement? Who knows."

"Why does my face feel like it's on fire?" Tor cried. "What's happening?"

"Shut up, *Russian*," Jaycee threatened to punch Tor's lights out.

"Now, now, Jaycee," Tripp said. "There's no need for rudeness."

Jaycee clamped his giant glove around Tor's neck, "This Soviet scumbag is responsible for this. If it wasn't for him, Captain Katz would be alive. Haloo would be alive. We might not have gotten sick."

"That's not true," Tor said, the grip on his neck making him feel sleepy, "We didn't mean to kill anyone—"

"Didn't mean to? You're talking lessense," Jaycee punched Tor's lights out, "That's for Wool."

The unconscious Tor slumped into Tripp's arms. He flung the bad guy to the bed and nodded at Jaycee, "I've had enough of that idiot."

"Sounds good," Tripp shackled Baldron's ankle to Tor's. He took a step back with Bonnie and admired the view, "Look at them." "Yeah. So pretty together…"

Jelly propelled herself into Wool's arms. They were both very happy to see each other.

"Jelly, come here, honey."

"Meowwwwwww-oool…"

"What's that?" Wool yelped with amazement. She took out a penlight and flashed it in Jelly's eyes, "Let me see you, honey."

Jelly yawned and dug her titanium claws in Wool's suit.

"Oh, you poor thing," Wool inspected the tip of her tail, "No damage done. You were very lucky."

"What's wrong, Wool?" Tripp asked. "Her tail?"

"Look."

She inspected Jelly's tail. The end was bleeding. A lot of the fur was missing. "I don't think the bone is affected. She'll be okay in an hour or two."

"She's bleeding from the eye, as well," Tripp felt his eyelids beginning to lower. Jaycee had fallen asleep like a huge, revolving boulder in the corridor. "I, I... need to get back to control and update USARIC."

"I'll take Jelly back to Medix and make sure she's okay."

"Very good," Tripp said. He pushed himself from the cell door and over to the door.

Opera Beta Control Deck

Tripp pulled himself into the room and snapped his fingers in the air, "Manuel..." he gasped, breathlessly, "Do you read me?"

The holographic book appeared above the flight deck, "Yes, Tripp. May I ask what happened?"

"Tor Klyce disabled you just before we boarded Alpha."

"Why did he do that?"

"He's working for the Russians. He and Baldron Landaker. They're in N-Carcerate till we reach Earth."

"Am I to understand that Captain Katz and Haloo Ess are also no longer with us?"

"Yes," Tripp wiped the blood from his face and sat into the flight chair, "I need you to generate a report on Botanix's current operational output."

"Yes, give me a moment."

Manuel 'paused' in mid-air as Tripp hit a button on the terminal.

The screen sprang to life, showing Tripp's bloodied, worn out face on the recording in real time.

"Jeez, Tripp. You look like hell," he whispered to himself, "Right. Commence recording. USARIC, Cape Claudius. Date imprint, run-time display. Second-in-command, Commander Tripp Healy. Record."

A red record button flashed in the corner of the screen. Tripp looked at the screen and took a moment to run through what he wanted to say.

"This is Tripp Healy, assumed captain of Space Opera Beta. We have lost her captain, Daryl Katz...."

Saturn's rings revolved at speed around the planet. The blue surface glowed and breathed in and out.

"Shortly before boarding Space Opera Alpha, we deciphered enough of Saturn Cry to ascertain that it was, indeed, sending a distress call. Baldron Landaker and Tor Klyce are in incarceration. Dimitri Vasilov, I hope you can hear this. Maar, I hope you're with him. This has been a deliberate sabotage of our mission. I hope USARIC finds the powers it has to rectify the situation."

A pink gas blossomed out from the dark side of Enceladus.

"Haloo Ess confirmed deceased at time of recording. Can confirm that Zillah Chin-Dunne was on board Opera Alpha, although her crew were dead. She speculated that something to do with Saturn was about to happen. I can't recall her exact phrase, but it was going to be something *fantastic*."

The pink chasm on Enceladus's dark side glowed and bleached out across the darkness.

"Opera Alpha was destroyed. Most of us made it back, but we seem to have contracted some sort of virus. The same extends to Jelly Anderson, as well. Botanix has been compromised. I am waiting on Manuel to report back on the severity of the damage. I do not expect it to be positive."

A holy pink light burst from the dark side of Enceladus. Saturn's rings sped up, as if it were responsible for the moon's cry into the infinite vacuum of space.

It caught Tripp's waning attention. He looked over at the deck and saw the light show in all its magnificence.

"Oh m-my," he stammered. "Look at it. It's *beautiful...*"

The recording continued and displayed half of Tripp's head on screen. It didn't reveal just how in awe he was of what he saw.

Manuel's holograph appeared above the screen, "I have the results from Botanix, Tripp."

"Wait a moment, Manuel," Tripp kept his awe-struck gaze on the light show occurring in space. He turned the screen to face the pink matter wading out of Enceladus.

"Can you see that on the screen?" Tripp's voice came over

the recording, "Enceladus. Saturn's sixth largest moon. We always knew *something* was happening. We're hearing it's a wormhole. We think Alpha may have been through it."

Tripp blinked and shook himself out of his mire. He angled the screen back to him as he returned to his chair, "Report, please, Manuel."

"Botanix is at critical levels of operation. Eight-five percent damage."

Tripp sighed and gave up the fight to stay awake, "I feel like I'm burning up."

"I can attempt a *shut-off-and-rejuvenate* on Botanix's core functionality, if you would like?" Manuel offered.

"Just tell me how much air we have left, Manuel," Tripp closed his eyes and buried his face into his arms on the flight deck.

"Approximately seventy-two hours, Tripp."

He lifted his head at the screen, still bleeding from the eyes, "Three days? That's it, I'm afraid. No one will survive. We'll be long dead before you send Opera Charlie, if you ever do," Tripp nodded at Enceladus's pink beauty, "Anyway, there's your answer, USARIC. Saturn and Enceladus partying up. Something called Pink Symphony. Whatever that means. This is captain Tripp Healy… signing off…"

Tripp slumped into his arms.

Manuel floated around and flapping his pages like a bird, "Hmm. Stop recording, please."

The recording stopped.

"Transmit recording to USARIC."

The screen produced a loading bar and advised a send-time of five minutes.

Chapter 17

Wool strapped a piece of gauze around the end of Jelly's tail. She clipped the end off with a razor and pressed the tape around the wound.

"You're very lucky, Jelly. Your injury could have been much worse," Wool coughed into her palm and stroked Jelly with her free hand, "I don't know if you know what's going on. How could you possibly know? Manuel says Botanix has enough oxygen for three days, sweetie. We're going to die up here. Suffocate. There's no way out."

"Meow," Jelly sniffed around Wool's face.

"You initiated zero gravity," Wool said. "How did you do—"

"Zeeeh… rooooow… graaaaa…" Jelly tried.

"Something happened to the crew, Jelly. To you, too. Look," Wool wiped the top of her own cheek. A streak of pink blood ran over her knuckle, "I don't understand why I'm sick. I never boarded Alpha. Whatever it is, they must have brought it back with them."

Wool cleared her throat and took a black capsule from her inner-suit pants.

"Take this. It'll make everything okay."

She pushed the capsule toward Jelly's mouth, but the cat refused to take it in her mouth, "N-Nuh…"

"Come on, honey," Wool hesitated, "It will help. You trust me, don't you?"

Jelly tilted her head and ran her face along the side of Wool's hand.

"It's okay, honey," Wool lifted the cyanide capsule and mimed opening her own mouth, "I'm taking one, too. We'll both go to sleep and there won't be any pain, I promise."

It was enough to convince Jelly. She opened her mouth with great obedience and allowed her friend to drop the cyanide capsule in.

"Good girl," Wool smiled and ran her hands down the sides of Jelly's face.

Little did she know that Jelly flicked Wool's capsule off the table with her hind leg.

"Look at you, you beautiful thing," she said, near to tears, knowing Jelly would die in her hands a few seconds from now, "You don't belong up here. You never did. USARIC made a mistake involving you."

Jelly purred, enjoying the rub-down she was receiving. She ran her face along Wool's cheek.

"I love you too, Jelly," Wool kept the cat's head in her hands. "Any moment now, sweetie. We'll both be at peace."

Jelly licked her cheek, catching a droplet of blood from her eye duct.

"I feel so sleepy," Wool said. "It must be a lack of oxygen, or something. And I'm so warm."

"W-Woooolll…" Jelly's voice rumbled, "W-Woooolll…"

"Yes," Wool gasped, trying to fight her drift into unconsciousness, "That's my name."

"Woooo-oooll…"

"Yes, yes," She released Jelly's head from her palms. She sat back in her chair and tucked her chin to her neck. "My name is Wool ar-Ban. You… are Jelly Anderson…"

Jelly shifted her head and watched as her friend fell asleep in her chair.

She hopped off the table and scurried along the ground, heading for the Medix door. Wool lay across the bed with her arms and started to snore.

Out in the corridor, Jelly stopped at a metal grille in the ground. She opened her mouth and poked her tongue around her gums.

The tip of her tongue lifted the wet cyanide capsule over

her teeth. The small bit of plastic tumbled over her chin and dropped to the ground.

Jelly snarled at it and pushed it toward the grille. It fell through the tiny bars and dropped down, to be lost forever.

"Meow," Jelly licked her paw, careful not to catch her tongue on the Titanium. She trundled towards the control deck, satisfied that she was free from danger...

***

Tripp lay unconscious over the flight panel.

Jelly trundled in and surveyed the surroundings. She was the only soul on board the Opera Beta who was awake, and she knew it.

A huge playground of fun and opportunity surrounded her - alas, not for very long.

She knew that, too. There was work to be done.

Jelly approached the second chair at the flight deck and hopped onto the seat.

The main screen loomed in front of her, obscuring the view of Enceladus emitting a pink symphony of light into the stars.

The image reflected in her glazed eyeballs. She stared up at the spectacle in wonder for a brief moment and licked her mouth.

"Meow," Jelly ducked her head and averted her view of the stars. Her internal engine kicked to life, purring up a storm. She moved over to Tripp's hand and ran the side of her face against his forefinger.

She turned to the screen and held out her paw. Two of her metal claws snapped together, creating a spark.

Manuel's holograph appeared.

"Ah, Miss Anderson," Manuel said. "It's a pleasure to finally have some time alone with you."

"Meow."

"Everyone appears to be asleep. The result of some nasty virus picked up on Opera Alpha, apparently."

"Meow," Jelly clawed at the keyboard under the screen.

"What's that, Miss Anderson?" The book floated around

her twitching ears, "You want to access the N-Gage mainframe?"

"Muuuh..."

"Very well," Manuel shuffled down to the keyboard hovered above the N-Gage communications panel, "N-Gage ready. Simply press the green communication button and tell me who you'd like to speak to."

Jelly whined, looking around the keyboard. She extended her paw and punched the green communication button.

A message flashed on the screen, "Enter respondent ID now."

Jelly tried to catch the flashing text with her claws. Her lungs heaved a series of coughs, "Muuuh…"

"Who would you like to speak too?"

Jelly lowered her head and looked around the keyboard. She flapped her tail around and whined.

"Oh, don't be like that, Miss Anderson," Manuel chuckled to himself. "I'm an advanced system. I can do it for you. I just need the name of the person you'd like to speak to."

Jelly looked up at the floating book. A trickle of blood blobbed out from her eye duct. "Jaayy… Jaaay…"

"Jaycee Nayall?" Manuel asked, "I'm afraid he's incommunicado—"

"Meow," Jelly shook the beads of blood away from her face and growled. "Jaaaaa-aaaayy… Meeeeeoowww…"

"Jaymeow?" Manuel scanned his internal memory banks, "I'm afraid we have no such person—"

"—Jaaayyy… Meee…" Jelly whimpered. Finally, she looked down at her inner-skin suit and ran her face along her name.

She pressed her claw against her surname: *Anderson.*

"Oh, *Jamie* Anderson?" Manuel said. "Honestly, why didn't you just say that? Accessing N-Gage contacts. Dialing for you now."

Jelly shook her head and licked her paw.

The screen dialed for a while.

Jelly looked up at it, but all she saw was her only reflection, "Meow."

Her eyes bled a pink substance. Jelly's instinct was to rescue the poor cat on the other side of the screen.

As she held out her paw, an image of a boy snapped onto the screen; Jamie Anderson, her owner. Only, now, he was two years older.

"Hello?" Jamie poked his nose around the lens of his device, "Hang on a minute. I can't see anything."

Jelly's face lit up - both figuratively and literally. The glare from the screen only exposed the contrast between her pink hue and blood mark.

Jamie recognized who was calling and could barely contain his excitement.

"Oh, wow. Jelly!"

"Meow," she pressed her infinity claws against the image of his face. "Maaah."

Jamie turned around and beckoned someone over, "Mom, come and see this. Look, look."

"What is it, poppet?"

"It's Jelly," Jamie beamed.

Emily walked into shot, carrying a baby in her arms.

Jelly scrunched her face and wondered who the new human being was, "Meow."

"Is that her?" Emily smiled and waved at the camera, "Hey, Jelly. Wow, is that really you?"

Jelly purred quietly to herself. Her paw slid down the screen, away from Jamie's face, "Mmmm," She huffed.

"Well done, poppet," Emily smiled and walked out of shot, "It's been such a long time, I'd almost forgotten..."

Jamie turned to the camera and leaned in, "That was Jolene, your new baby sister."

Jelly was impressed. She looked down at her paw and moved her claws back and forth. The tiny mechanical whirs were almost deafening.

"I didn't forget about you, Jelly," Jamie began to cry, "I miss you. Not a day goes by when I don't think of you."

Jelly looked up at the screen and purred. She seemed to produce a smile, "Jaaaay.... Meeee..."

"Wow, you said my name," Jamie called over his shoulder, "Mom, she can talk."

"Very good, poppet. Can you come into the kitchen and help me, please?"

"Yeah, in a minute," Jamie turned to the screen and looked at Jelly, "You look sick, girl. Is everything okay?"

She held up her infinity claws and moved the cuticles around.

"Oh, *wow*. What did they do to you?"

Jelly whined and flipped her bandaged tail around. She felt her eyelids get heavier.

"I can't wait to see you again, Jelly. When are you coming home?"

"Grrr…" Jelly fought the urge to fall asleep. She wasn't impressed with her owner's behavior, either. She looked up at the screen and blinked as hard as she could.

"Jelly, what's wrong?" Jamie asked, somewhat concerned.

She held up her paw and tilted it from side to side. Jamie's mood soured. He did the same.

They waved goodbye for the last time.

Suddenly, Jamie had a change of heart, "Hey, wait—"

Jelly's paw hit the green button, intending to cut the call. Instead, it flashed onto the next event.

An incoming visual message from USARIC.

"Would you like me to play the message, Miss Anderson?"

"Meow," she whined and curled up beside Tripp's face resting on the flight deck.

"Very well. Playing message now," Manuel said. "One minute, twenty seconds."

Maar Sheck's image appeared on the screen. He stood in front of a podium and a bunch of microphones, addressing a flurry of news reporters.

"Thank you for attending this emergency press conference, everybody. I will try to keep this brief…"

Jelly's eyelids closed, squeezing a couple of drops of pink tears from her eyes.

"USARIC received a visual communication from Space Opera Beta a little under one hour ago. We can confirm that the vessel reached its intended destination, Enceladus, slightly ahead of schedule. We can also confirm that the nature of its distress call, in accordance with USARIC's Infinity Clause, was deciphered with success by the gifted and talented scientists on board Beta..."

Jelly opened her eyes and took one final look at the symphony of pink light emitting from Enceladus, "Meow..."

"We regret to inform our friends, however, that the mission was sabotaged by a direct contravention the Bering Treaty and USARIC's own Infinity Clause. Due diligence has been disregarded. Two crew members, under the command of Dimitri Vasilov, have been detained. Our last communication indicated that Opera Beta's oxygen levels were running well below the requirements needed to get home."

Jelly's ears pricked up. They were unable to go home, "Meow."

Maar continued reading from his statement, "As of this moment, USARIC will cease future operations. All current ones will continue to their conclusion. Following the death of Viktor Rabinovich and, now, the sabotage perpetrated by our Russian allies. All diplomatic relations have been suspended with immediate effect. It is with regret that all Russian operatives are to be ejected from American soil, and vice versa. We send our thoughts and prayers to the souls aboard Opera Beta and wish them all the best on their survival in the vicinity of Enceladus. Space Opera Beta, may God be with you."

The media kicked up a frenzy. Dreenagh Remix pushed through the crowd and held her wrist to Maar's face as he walked away from the hubbub, "Maar Sheck, can you confirm that USARIC is preparing Space Opera Charlie to recover what's left from the first two missions?"

"I'm very sorry," Maar said, stepping away from the podium, "No questions at this time."

The message came to an end.

"Miss Anderson," Manuel asked, politely, "Would you like me to replay the message?"

Jelly climbed onto her feet and shook her head. Determined, she made her way over to Tripp's head and looked at his right hand.

A few inches away lay the hyper-thruster lever.

"Miss Anderson, what are you doing?"

"Peee… Pee…" she growled, almost losing her ability to keep upright, "Sim… fonee…"

"Miss Anderson?" Manuel tried. "Listen, you may be the current in-command operative aboard Opera Beta, but you can't seriously be suggesting we—"

Jelly ignored Manuel despite his attempt to distract her.

A page containing a big, fat mouse didn't work.

He flipped to another page, displaying a bright and colorful set of jangling keys.

"Miss Anderson, please—"

"—Grrrr," she growled, lifted her right paw and placed it on the hyper-thruster lever, "Pink. Symphony…"

She pushed the lever forward, but wasn't strong enough.

"Miss Anderson, I ask you to reconsider. I realize we only have three days' worth of oxygen left, but—"

"Piii-iiink…" Jelly coughed, her voice croaked, more human-sounding, "Symphony…"

She grabbed the lever forward with both paws. It shifted a bit, but not enough.

"We do not know what is in there, Miss Anderson. It's very dangerous."

The roar of pink fire from Enceladus blotted out across her eyeballs. The aggressive visual was enough of a last-push for her to force her entire weight onto the lever.

It was either journey into the great unknown, or stay and die.

Jelly gripped the lever in her Infinity Claws and slammed it forward.

"Hyper-thrusters initiated."

The core of the ship rumbled to life. The array of hyper thrusters lit up, almost brighter than the sun.

Jelly hooked her paws around the lever. Her hind legs lifted off the console and flew into the air.

"Meeeooowww," she cried as the swirling cacophony of pink streaks blasted across the ship's screen.

Space Opera Beta blasted into the fantastic symphony of pink light dancing out from the core of Enceladus...

STAR CAT

BOOK TWO: PINK SYMPHONY

ANDREW MACKAY

BOOK TWO: PINK SYMPHONY

Chapter 1

How long had it been? Twenty minutes? Twenty days? Months? Years?

No one knew.

No one was even aware of what had happened.

The least likely member of Space Opera Beta to ascertain what had happened was Jelly Anderson. Being a cat, she had no concept of space or time - you know, the things we value and live our lives by. The crew weren't much help, either.

Tripp Healy, the assumed captain of Opera Beta, lay unconscious across the flight deck.

He was the first thing Jelly saw when she opened her eyes.

The ship wasn't moving. Everything was eerily silent by all accounts. Whatever happened when she'd forced the ship through the pink light show on Enceladus was beyond comprehension.

It was either venture into Saturn's moon or stick around to be rescued. With just seventy-two hours of oxygen? Sticking around would have prolonged the misery.

If rescue ever came, of course.

Even if it did it would have been five hundred days too late…

The Control Deck
Space Opera Beta - Level One

Jelly rolled around on the floor and stretched her legs. She felt waves of muscular atrophy disappear within seconds. A quick lick around the mouth, and she was up and at 'em.

She trundled toward the flight deck and ran her face along Tripp's heel in an attempt to catch his attention.

He didn't budge.

"Meow," she cried and looked up at him. A couple of blinks squeezed a blob of liquid out from her right eye. It splashed to the floor next to the sole of her captain's shoe.

The communications console buzzed to life. It had been humming ever since she woke up a few moments ago.

A familiar holograph appeared above her head. A book named Manuel, whizzing through its pages, acclimatized itself to the result of having gone through a wormhole - or a portal - whatever that *thing* was on Enceladus.

"Meow."

Manuel fluttered above her head and folded the outer edges of his pages toward her. "Greetings, Miss Anderson."

"Meow."

"I beg your pardon?"

Jelly yawned and revealed her fangs. For the briefest of moments it looked like she was screaming. She hopped onto the deck and nosed around the controls. Her infinity whiskers arrived at the yellow thruster lever. The same one that had blasted them through Saturn's sixth largest moon and saved their lives.

"What are you doing, Miss Anderson?" Manuel shifted across the deck for a better view of Jelly pawing away at the plastic handle.

It didn't move, still locked into *thrust* mode.

"Meow."

Jelly hadn't meant to use it. She wanted to draw Manuel's attention to the action she'd performed to rescue the ship.

"Yes, very good," Manuel said. "I'm afraid I don't know where we are."

"Meow," Jelly turned to the expansive flight deck windshield expecting to see stars, or some evidence of where they were. Instead, she was greeted by a black canvas. They may as well have been shut inside a capsule for all the good the visuals were.

Just then, a haze of pink dust seemed to dance from the right of the screen, like a blotch of paint thrown across a black bed sheet.

The event perturbed Jelly. The effect looked c'
an alien had spewed across the screen.

In an attempt to gain some protection, Jeny
around Tripp's face. His right cheek lay across the panel,
exposing the majority of his face. His nose twitched, covered,
in part, by his pink tears.

Jelly's wet nose sniffled around his, causing his closed
eyelids to flutter. Her action was enough to make him cough
and splutter into a state of awareness.

"What the—?" he said, opening his eyes and spluttering
back to consciousness. "What's g-going on?"

"Good morning slash afternoon slash evening, Tripp,"
Manuel said.

Tripp groaned and pressed his hands to the console. He
pushed himself upright in the pilot's seat and blinked, clearing
the gunk away from his eyes. "What happened?"

Manuel took a moment to reveal not very much at all. "In
short, we have absolutely no idea."

"Why did you say morning slash afternoon?"

"In short, I have absolutely no idea what the time is,
either."

"Jelly?" Tripp turned to the cat looking up at him and ran
his fingers over her head. "Hey, girl. Are you okay?"

"Meow."

"Thank God," Tripp jumped out of his seat, intending to
run over to the communications console. He lost his footing,
stumbled forward and dropped to his knees like an infant.
"Oh God, I don't feel too well—"

Manuel interrupted, "It's better you take time to orient
yourself. Please don't rush."

Tripp spat a lump of phlegm to the floor. It was all he
could do to not spew everywhere. It wasn't until he glanced at
the gelatinous substance that he realized it was pink.

"Huh?"

The inebriating effects of having traveled through
Enceladus had an adverse influence on his stomach.

"My organs feel like pâté."

"That's quite common," Manuel said. "It's something of a

.racle your body wasn't flung around the flight deck when we went through whatever that pink thing was."

"Enceladus?" Tripp staggered to his feet and wiped his face. "We went through Enceladus?"

"It would appear so."

"My God," Tripp thumped the communications console switch.

Jelly hopped after him and climbed onto the comms seat. Tripp stood back and inadvertently knocked the side of the chair with his hip. It sent Jelly spinning around - the result making her look like a dizzied, carnival fool.

"Whoops," he caught the backrest and stopped the rotation, "Sorry, pet."

"Meow."

"Manuel?" Tripp waited for the screen to fire up. "Please tell me that Anderson and I aren't the only ones left alive."

"I'm afraid I cannot confirm anything. For some reason, I am unable to perform a geo-scan on Opera Beta. I can only see the contents of the flight deck which, considering we're already here, is rather useless."

"You don't say," Tripp spat, knowing anxiety was due any moment, "Why isn't the comms deck working?"

"I don't know."

"Come here, girl," Tripp scooped Jelly into his arms and examined her face. "Let me see you."

Jelly stared into Tripp's eyes as he cradled her. She seemed at peace. Nothing out of the ordinary about her face, body or demeanor gave rise to concern.

"How are you, girl?"

"Meow," Jelly exercised her infinity claws on Tripp's sleeve.

"Ah, da-da," he protested, unhooked one of the sharp ends from the material, "Move your paw, girl."

Whizz, whizz. She moved all four claws and her new thumb around, demonstrating that she was perfectly fine. "Meow."

Tripp smiled, satisfied that she was uninjured and in proper operating order. Which was more than could be said for Manuel.

"Good," Tripp released Jelly onto the chair and made for the door. "We need to find our friends and make sure they're okay. Okay?"

"Meow," Jelly seemed to agree.

Tripp snapped his fingers over his shoulder as he reached the panel on the wall. "Manuel?"

"Yes, Tripp?"

"Do whatever you can to get the comms back on, please."

"I'll try my best, Commander."

"Commander?" Tripp stopped and let out a sarcastic sigh. "I'm the *captain*, Manuel. After Katz perished with Alpha."

"Oh," Manuel floated back, apologetically, "Is Captain Katz no longer with us?"

"Are you serious right now?" Tripp remembered everything. He couldn't believe Manuel wasn't able to. A quick, informal diagnostic was required. "Manuel? Don't mess around, tell me you remember."

"I'm sorry, Tripp. I *do* remember now—"

"—I don't believe you. Don't take this the wrong way, Manuel, but I want only quantitative responses. I need reassurance that you're fit and operational. Now, tell me about Enceladus."

Tripp suspected Manuel was buying himself some sympathy - or at least some time. "I can assure you that this isn't necessary, *Captain*."

"Are you disobeying a direct order?" Tripp asked, close to throttling the transparent image hovering in front of him. "Answer me."

"No, Captain."

"Okay. I won't ask again," Tripp said. "Tell me about Enceladus."

Manuel flipped through his pages and arrived at a picture of an oblong pastry with a meat and vegetable filling. The image fizzed and shifted around.

"It is a tortilla that covers a range of meats and vegetables, often containing a hot—"

"—What?"

"—Chili Sauce."

"That's *enchiladas*, you moron."

"Meow," Jelly added.

"Oh," Manuel busied himself by flipping through his pages. One by one, they revealed a blank slate. Several of them appeared torn and incomplete.

"Manuel, I'm sorry. You've taken a lot of damage. You need recalibrating."

"I feel I am able to autopilot," Manuel explained. "I can run a check on—"

"—No, you've demonstrated that you're *unable*," Tripp butted in, "I want you to shut down. Just temporarily until I do a sit-rep."

"But, Tripp—"

"—Don't take it personally, Manuel," Tripp beckoned Jelly over to the door with him. "Go offline. Just for an hour or so. We can't afford to have you confuse H2O with waste water."

"I'm not stupid, Tripp," Manuel slammed his covers together in a strop.

"I'm afraid for the moment you are. Please power down. I promise I'll wake you up when I figure out what's going on."

"*Fine.*" Manuel blurted. He vanished from the room completely, leaving a befuddled Tripp to stare at Jelly for a reaction.

"Crazy, huh?"

"Meow."

"Out of all of us, Manuel should know better. If he's not fully operational then he should be shut down until we can fix him."

Jelly ducked her head and retracted her claws.

"Come on, girl," Tripp held his palm to the wall panel, "Let's go check on the others."

The door slid open, allowing the pair out of the control deck.

Chapter 2

Something felt *off* to Tripp as he walked across Beta's level one corridor.

The entire ship felt like it had powered down. The subtle rumblings and vibrations that he'd become accustomed weren't present.

For the first time since they'd left Earth he could hear his own footsteps clanging against the metal grille as he walked. Jelly turned a corner just behind him, anxious to find out what had happened to her *humans*.

"Let's head to Medix and find your mommy," Tripp held his forearm to his mouth. "This is Captain Healy. Does anyone read me?"

Nobody responded. The radio device on his arm seemed flatter than normal. No static or any sign of life.

"I repeat, this *is* Captain Healy transmitting on Individimedia. The radio and internal comms are down," he stopped in his tracks, "Can anyone read me?"

If Tripp felt alone during the course of their mission, it was nothing compared to how he was feeling right now. All he had was a confused autopilot and a cat for company. With the comms down the universe felt smaller than ever.

Tripp squinted at the door to Medix thirty feet ahead of him.

"I don't like this."

Clunk.

The sound of a shifting metal object thundered along the corridor from the far end. Another turn in the corridor.

A faint sniffing followed the unusual noise.

"What's that?" Tripp whispered to Jelly. She pricked up her ears and moved in front of Tripp, investigating the source of the sound.

"No, no," Tripp her aside with his boot, "Stay there."

"Meow."

"Who's there?" Tripp reached for his Rez-9 firearm on his belt.

The sniffing stopped, as did all sign of life from the turn in the corridor. Tripp unhooked his gun and pointed it forward. "I said who's there?"

"Meow," Jelly seconded Tripp's question.

"Stay back, girl. We don't know what's—"

A silhouetted figure moved in front of the screen door to Medix. A familiar profile outline - tall, voluptuous, and with shoulder-length hair.

"Who are you?" Tripp asked.

The figure lowered her head to her opened hands and sobbed. Her voice sounded familiar, although she hadn't actually spoken.

"Bonnie?"

The figure lowered her arms, revealing the outline of a Rez-9 in her right hand.

"What's h-happening to me?" The figure asked herself through her tears.

"Hey," Tripp shouted down the corridor, "What are you doing?"

His hollering caught the woman's attention. The figure turned forty-five degrees and held her Rez-9 firearm at Tripp, "Where am I? Who are you?"

He squinted, trying to figure out who - or what - was standing in front of him.

"Bonnie? Is that you?"

Jelly hissed, shaken by the strange person's presence.

The figure stepped toward Tripp, keeping her gun pointed at him. She entered a shaft of light from one of the bulbs on the ceiling.

It was *her* - a confused, upset, and pink-splattered Bonnie Whitaker. "Who are you?"

"It's *me*. Tripp Healy."

"Who?" Bonnie pushed her gun forward, threatening to blow his head off. "How do you know my name?"

"What?"

"I said how do you know my name?" Bonnie squealed through her tears, "You don't know *me*."

"You're... one of us."

Bonnie kept her gun aimed at Tripp's face. "Don't come any closer."

Tripp offered his surrender and held out his arms. "Okay."

"You *tell* me where I am and how I got here."

"We don't know, Bonnie. We went through some sort of wormhole on Enceladus. We don't know where we are—"

She blasted a warning shot at Tripp. The charge streaked past his shoulder and blew a hole in the side of the wall.

"Jeez," Tripp held his hands up in surrender, "What the hell—"

"—I swear to God I will kill you. Let me out of here."

"Let you out of here? What are you talking about?"

Bonnie screamed again, close to rupturing her vocal chords, "Where am I?"

"Wait, wait," Tripp tried. "What do you remember? Did you just wake up?"

The question resonated with Bonnie's desire for answers. Tripp could see the tactic worked when she tilted her head at Jelly.

"Yes, I did."

"Please don't shoot us," Tripp said. "We've just woken up, too. You're confused, just like we are."

"What are you talking about?"

"Space Opera Beta. You know what that is, don't you?"

"No," she yelled, "I don't remember anything."

"You're a cosmologist," Tripp said. "You're Bonnie Whitaker, and you're a part of our team."

"Liar," Bonnie aimed the gun at Tripp's head. "You're trying to trick me. I want to go home to my husband and son."

"Where are they, Bonnie?" Tripp tried to rescue himself from death and convince Bonnie he wasn't the bad guy. "Go on. I'm listening. Tell me where home is."

"I don't know."

"That's right, you *don't* know," Tripp nodded at the firearm in her hand. "And why would we give you a gun if we were keeping you here against your will?"

She looked at the Rez-9 in her hand and tried to calculate the information. "I don't know."

"Bonnie, trust me. You can't do anything hasty if you don't know all the facts. Please."

"No, no," Bonnie yelled, "You're lying. Tell me where I am."

"I told you already. You're on Space Opera Beta on a rescue mission on behalf of USARIC."

"USARIC?" Bonnie asked, none-the-wiser.

"My God, you really don't remember, do you?"

A pink tear rolled down Bonnie's cheek as she cried. "I just want to go home…"

"We all do, Bonnie."

She closed her eyes and gave up the will to live.

"Now, just put the gun down…"

Bonnie lifted her head and stared at Tripp. "There's one way I can get out."

"What?"

Bonnie lifted the barrel of the Rez-9 to her temple and threatened to shoot herself.

"No!" Tripp said, reaching his hand out. "Don't do that—"

"—I'm sorry," she hooked her index finger around the trigger.

"Meow," Jelly flapped her tail, trying to divert the woman's attention.

"Bonnie, no!"

Tripp launched forward, flinging his body in her direction. He threw out his hands and attempted to grasp the gun from hers.

ZAP!

He didn't reach her in time.

The gun flew from her hand - something had hit it before Tripp got anywhere near her.

"Agh!"

The bullet flew out from the barrel - but missed the side of her head and flew into the wall.

Strands of her hair feathered into the air from the blast as Tripp pushed her to the ground.

Bonnie looked up from underneath him to see a tall man in an exo-suit looking down at the pair. He adjusted the titanium glove on his right hand. "Bonnie? What's gotten into you?"

She screamed at the top of her lungs. "Help! Help!"

Tripp turned over and saw Jaycee smiling at him.

"Hey, Tripp."

"Jaycee," Tripp stumbled to his feet and patted the giant on the back. "You're here."

"Of course I'm here," he said, looking down at Bonnie. "She was about to blow her brains out."

"I know."

"What did you do to her?"

"I didn't do anything," Tripp collected Bonnie's Rez-9 from the floor and pointed it at her. "She's out of her mind."

"Probably blew a fuse when we entered Enceladus," Jaycee took out his K-SPARK shotgun and cocked it. "We better get her regenerated. Or whatever it is we do to them."

Bonnie remained on the floor, completely overwhelmed by her assailants. She pushed her top half up by her elbows and kicked her feet against the ground.

"Hey, Bonnie," Jaycee said. "Seems you're suffering from a touch of amnesia, there."

'Brain damage, more like,' Tripp said.

"P-Please, h-help me," she wiped a pink tear from her cheek, "I just want to go home."

"Still crying pink?" Jaycee asked, close to blasting her to smithereens. "You're hysterical. Get on your feet, Doctor."

Bonnie obeyed and staggered to her feet. She caught sight of her right leg as she adjusted her pants. The limb was made of metal with wires twisting around the joints.

"My leg. What did you do to me?"

"We didn't do anything to you," Jaycee turned to Tripp and whispered, "We need to get her to N-Vigorate."

"I know," Tripp addressed the distraught woman as carefully as possible. "Bonnie? We need to get you some help."

"What?"

"Something has happened to you. We need to shut you off for a while and let you rejuvenate."

"No," Bonnie took a step back, afraid for her life. Two men she didn't know held their weapons at her. For all she knew, she'd been abducted by aliens. Perhaps they'd perform a probe or vivisection on her. "Stay away from me."

"Where are you gonna go?" Jaycee smirked through the sight on his shotgun and stepped towards her. "You don't know where you are."

"Leave me alone."

"She doesn't wanna come, Tripp," Jaycee turned over his shoulder. "You want me to persuade her?"

Tripp hung his head and nodded. He knew all about Jaycee's ways of *persuasion*.

"Stay away from me, you big hunk of slime," Bonnie held out her arms and threatened to punch him.

Jaycee clenched his fist and gained on Bonnie as she walked backwards. "Come here, Bonnie. It's for your own good."

"Be gentle with her," Tripp called out to Jaycee and scooped Jelly into his arms. "Don't watch."

"I said stay away from me—"

THWUMP.

Jaycee thumped the back of her head and knocked her out. Tripp trained his eyes on the unconscious woman falling into the giant's arms.

"Damn, Jaycee. Remind me to never get on your bad side."

"Had to be done. At least when she wakes up she'll forget she's a damn Androgyne," he said, dragging her backwards under her arms. "The equivalent of switching them off and back on again."

N-Vigorate Chamber
Space Opera Beta - Level Three

Jelly pressed her claws to the panel on the wall and opened the door. Tripp and Jaycee carried the unconscious Bonnie into the cylindrical chamber.

"God, she's heavy," Tripp struggled with the weight of her lower-half.

"That'll be her leg," Jaycee said, carrying her under her arms.

"*You* should have taken her legs."

"Why?"

"You're stronger than me," Tripp nodded at the electric chair at the far end of the room. "Set her down there. We'll get her plugged in."

"Okay."

Jelly ran ahead of them, jumped onto the electric chair made herself comfortable.

"Oh no, Jelly," Tripp frowned as he and Jaycee carried Bonnie toward the device. "Not there, pet."

"Meow."

"*Move.*"

Jelly just stared at the pair as they approached her.

"I said move," Tripp tried to shoo her away with his boot. "Go on, get off."

Jelly climbed down and circled around the men's feet.

"Still her usual self, then?" Jaycee chuckled as he negotiated his footing around Jelly's playful insistence. "A bit surplus to requirement now, though, isn't she?"

"She saved us. Remember that," Tripp dropped Bonnie's legs onto the seat as Jaycee pushed her against the backrest. "If it wasn't for Anderson, we'd be sitting ducks. Sitting, suffocating ducks."

"Hang on a second," Jaycee looked at Jelly and squinted. "Did Anderson just open the N-Vigorate door for us?"

Tripp looked at the passed-out Bonnie, somewhat amused by Jaycee's surprise. "Yeah, I think she did."

"But, how—"

"—As I said, she's the only one who could have engaged the thrusters. We think we went through the pink wormhole thing on Enceladus."

Jaycee nodded at Jelly. "*She* did that?"

"Yeah."

"How do you figure it was her, though?"

"Well, we must have gone through Enceladus," Tripp tightened the strap on Bonnie's lap, "We're not in our solar system anymore. We must be somewhere else."

"Meow," Jelly held up her right paw and yawned.

Tripp winked at Jelly and held his right hand up at her, enacting a cute high-five, "Manuel hasn't the first clue where we are."

"Manuel is an idiot," Jaycee crouched and held his hands out to Jelly. "Who's a good girl, then?"

She ran into the giant's arms and purred. He picked her up and watched Tripp grab a fistful of Bonnie's hair. He held it up to reveal a small tattoo-like text behind her ear that read: *Manning/Synapse.*

He sighed, quietly, and shook his head. "I'm sorry, Bonnie."

"What's up?" Jaycee asked, allowing Jelly to purr away in his arms. "Everything okay?"

Tripp took the end of a chunky cable from the console and lifted the cap away, "I just feel sorry for her, that's all."

"Why?"

Tripp slid the back of her neck open and plugged the cable in, "We all know Series Three is relatively new technology. But for a while, there, I forgot she *wasn't* human."

"You can't let those Androgyne things get to you, my friend. She's a droid. She'll be fine."

"I know that," Tripp locked the cable and released her hair around her neck, "But you'd have thought USARIC would have been more sensitive to its needs."

"Sensitive? *USARIC?*" Jaycee let out a sarcastic smirk, "Since when did a corporation care about anything other than its bottom line?"

"It'd be funny if it wasn't true," Tripp yanked the lever on the console. It fired to life, along with the rejuvenation cable. Bonnie's eyelids lifted up, revealing two pink retinas. "At least N-Vigorate is working."

Tripp peered into Bonnie's lifeless face and eyes. Lifeless, of course, to a point. Everyone except her knew she wasn't a real human being but, damn it, her visage was extremely convincing.

"Okay, that's her taken care of. She'll be fine in a few hours."

Jaycee ran his gloved fingers over Jelly's head, "Tripp. Can I ask you something?"

"Sure."

"Are you ever going to tell Bonnie?"

"Tell her what?" Tripp asked, knowing full well what his colleague was referring to.

"That's she's not human."

"God, no. No, we can never tell her. You know what happens when an Androgyne finds out it's not human."

"But she's a Series Three model. That doesn't apply to them, does it?"

"Hey, you saw how she behaved a few minutes ago. Not exactly a shining endorsement of mental well-being, is it?"

"No, but—"

"—It's not worth the risk, Jaycee," Tripp insisted. "We need to find out what's happened. The last thing we need is Bonnie, of all people—"

"—So to speak," Jaycee interrupted jovially.

"—Very funny," Tripp tried not to smile, "The last thing we need is for her to run rampant and cause more problems for us. Besides, she's human to *us*. That's all that matters."

"I can't argue with that," Jaycee said. "But if I chose to argue with it, I'd win, because I'd just kick your ass all around this room."

Tripp shook his head and smiled. "Have you ever heard the saying 'if you resort to violence then you've lost the argument', at all?"

Jaycee thumped his fists together so hard that it shook the ground, "Uh, *no*."

"I thought not."

Tripp gave up his attempt to educate Jaycee. Instead, he offered Jelly his hand. She swiped at it, playfully.

"Did you see Wool, or our two Russian *friends*, on your travels?"

"No. I woke up and found you and Bonnie. I've seen no one, yet. Other than you, Bonnie, and Jelly, here. The two Russkies should be in N-Carcerate where we left them."

Tripp rubbed Jelly's head and turned to the door, "They'd better be. Let's go and get them."

"Did Manuel run a sit-rep?"

Tripp walked toward the door in haste, "Manuel is, uh, experiencing some technical difficulties."

"Technical difficulties?"

"Yeah. I shut him down till we figure out what's going on." Tripp pressed his palm to the panel on the wall. "How are you feeling, Jaycee? You look okay, but it'd be remiss of me as your captain not to ask."

Jaycee bounced Jelly in his arms and kissed her on the head. "I've never felt better."

"Is that pink stuff still coming from your eyes?"

"Yes, but it doesn't hurt. In fact, all my usual aches and pains are gone. How about you?"

"I'm fine."

The door slid open. Tripp took one final glance at Bonnie fast asleep in the chair. The poor *woman* - something of a prisoner in her own mind. A product, or victim, of the Manning/Synapse company - feelings be damned; destined for a lifetime of confusion.

"It's just not right, you know," Tripp whispered a bit too loudly for comfort.

"What's not right?"

"What they've done to her."

"Bonnie?" Jaycee smiled and tried to console his colleague, "Don't worry about Whitaker. She's a fighter. She'll be fine."

"I guess," Tripp walked through the door. "Promise me one thing, though, Jaycee?"

"What's that?"

"If I die, make sure they don't turn me into one of those things."

Chapter 3

Medix

Space Opera Beta - Level three

Wool ar-Ban lay unconscious across Jelly's medical bed. Fast asleep, her breathing extremely slow. Her radio sat on the desk beside her under a picture of Jamie stuck to the wall.

A pink patch of liquid fell from her closed eyelids and bleached into the fabric of the mattress.

Three beds away from her lay Haloo Ess. She'd died before Opera Beta had ventured into the wormhole on Enceladus. Jaycee had attempted to revive her.

The issue wasn't so much the revival but what had caused it. Like everyone else, Haloo had caught the bug brought back onto the ship. Her reaction was unlike that of the others. She'd developed an allergy and fell into a cardiac arrest.

The heart rate monitor continued to emit the sound of a flat line. The wires from the unit were still attached to her breastplate.

Haloo wasn't breathing. Her face looked gaunt and pale. The stench was undeniable - not quite enough of a pungent aroma to bring Wool out of her slumber, but certainly strong enough to hit Jaycee and Tripp as they entered the chamber.

"My God," Tripp clocked Haloo immediately and ran over to her. "What happened to her?"

Jaycee released Jelly onto the floor, offering her the chance to run around and make a bee line for Wool. "She didn't make it, Tripp."

"So you just left her here?"

"What was I supposed to do? Stuff her in the incinerator?"

"No, but—" Tripp took a long, hard look at Haloo's sunken, gangrenous face, "What the hell happened to her?"

Jaycee switched the heart monitor off. "That pink stuff. Whatever it is it finished her off."

Tripp swallowed his emotion down to his gut. Jaycee and Jelly may have been the only members of the crew to see his reaction. Nevertheless, he kept his composure and pulled the blanket over Haloo's face.

Peace, in the end.

"I don't understand?" Tripp took a step back as the room fell to silence. A reminder that her heart had long since stopped. "Why her?"

"Why her?"

"What's so special about her? Why didn't the pink stuff kill all of us, too?"

"Your guess is as good as mine—"

A loud scratching and fuss from Wool's feet caught Jaycee's attention. Jelly clawed at her feet, encouraging her to wake up.

"Meooooowww... W-Wooool..."

"What are you doing, girl?" Tripp walked over to her and immediately spotted that Wool was breathing. Effectively sleeping. "Wool?"

Her eyelids fluttered and her breathing quickened.

"Wool? Are you okay?"

"W-Wool," Jelly coughed up a pink fur ball and spat it on the floor.

"Hang on a second," Jaycee joined Tripp, entertaining his surprise. "Jelly?"

The cat looked up at the man standing over her. She shifted her head as if to say "Who, me?"

"Yes, *you*," Jaycee said. "Did you just... *speak*?"

Jelly looked to Tripp for the get-out he couldn't offer her.

"You're talking *lessense*, Jaycee. Of course she didn't speak."

Tripp shook his head and turned his attention back to the sleeping Wool. "Hey, are you okay?"

Jelly jumped up onto Wool's lap and nosed around her inner-suit. She ran the side of her face along the contours of her stomach, forcing the woman out from her slumber.

"Ugh," Wool squeezed her eyes shut and lifted her head, licking at her lips, trying to assuage the morning mouth effect. "What h-happened?"

She looked at her lap to find Jelly staring up at her, longingly. "Meow."

"Oh. Hey, honey."

Wool moved her elbow forward, knocking the radio off the desk. It hit the floor in time for Jelly to have a nose around.

"How are you feeling, Wool?" Tripp asked.

She stretched her arms out and let out a huge yawn. "I feel great, actually."

"Good."

Wool cracked out the knots that had formed in her neck from her sleep. "What happened?"

"What do you remember?" Tripp asked.

Jelly hopped onto her bed and demanded Wool's attention by rubbing herself over the woman's arms.

"Umm, I remember Opera Alpha disappearing. You came back," Wool gasped as the memory of a fight flooded into her memory. "Oh my, the Russians?"

Jelly looked at the picture of Jamie and purred. She tried to run her face along it, but it was too high up. "'Jay,'" she croaked, blinking at the picture.

"Yes. Tor and Baldron," Tripp said. "You remember that, too?"

"Yes, I remember everything." She rose to her feet and lifted Jelly from the desk.

"Mwah," she clawed at the picture of her former owner and rolled across the length of Wool's arms.

"What happened? Are we waiting for rescue? Did you hear from USARIC? Where are we?"

Tripp held out his hands and nodded at the cat in her arms. "Calm down, we're okay. Jelly put us through

Enceladus."

"She did?"

"Yes. It was either that or stay and run out of oxygen."

"Wow," Wool smiled at Jelly and felt like crying. "You saved our lives, huh?"

Jelly lifted her chin proudly, wanting a reward from her new mommy, "Meow."

"Who's a *good* girl?" Wool rubbed her face against Jelly's and breathed in her scent.

Tripp and Jaycee smiled at the bond between the two girls.

"Are you telling me that Jelly was able to launch the thrusters? All on her own?" Wool lifted Jelly's right paw up and inspected her claw. "The infinity claws work?"

"They work fine," Tripp said.

Wool sniffed around, puzzled by the stench that drifted under her nostrils. "What's that smell?"

"Wool, listen, we need to tell you something…" Jaycee stepped back, enabling Wool to spot Haloo's covered corpse a few beds away. "Ess didn't make it."

Wool's mood soured as the revelation sank in. She instinctively dropped Jelly to her bed and walked, slowly, to Haloo's bed. "Is that her?"

"Yes, it is."

Wool stood still, wondering whether or not she should take a look. "I, uh—"

"—It's okay," Jaycee stepped behind her and massaged her shoulder, "We'll remove the body once we're sure everything is fine."

Wool got upset. A blob of pink liquid ran down her face. "What's happening to us?"

"We don't know," Tripp braved the situation and jumped into captain mode. "But we're going to find out."

"What's Manuel saying? Sure he knows where we are, right?"

"Manuel's on shutdown. He's not in proper operating order. Something happened to him when we went through the wormhole. At least, we *think* it was a wormhole."

Wool turned to Tripp and stared him out. "You don't

know very much, do you?"

Tripp could have returned with a nasty retort but chose not to. "No, we don't. But we know you're okay. We need to get Manuel and Pure Genius up and running *and* in proper working order. Until we do we're open to all sorts of trouble."

Wool folded her arms for protection, "Haloo and Katz. Both dead?"

"Yes."

"How do you propose we get the system up and running? None of us know how to operate Manuel. "

"Very true," Tripp unclipped his Rez-9 firearm from his belt, "But we know a man who can."

He waved Jelly and Jaycee over to the door with him.

"You can't be serious?" Wool ran after Tripp, allowing the door to slide behind them. "*Those two*?"

"He and his friend may have tried to kill us but Tor Klyce is the only one who can operate Manuel."

Jaycee hulked his K-SPARK in both arms as he clanged down the corridor alongside his superior. "What makes you think they'll play ball?"

"Nothing."

"Nothing?" Wool asked, hesitantly. "What do you mean nothing?"

"I don't think Tor Klyce or Baldron Landaker are going to play ball. We'll have to persuade them or we're stuck here."

"Don't worry," Jaycee moved ahead of the group, determined to destroy something, "I've got just the thing to make them agree. I'll meet you at N-Carcerate."

"Where are you going?"

Jaycee stopped and looked at his glove. "Weapons and Armory. Unless they want to lose their heads, I'm sure they'll behave themselves."

"Okay, be quick," Tripp waved Wool and Jelly up the corridor, "I'll go and speak to them."

"Good. If they say anything, don't believe a word." Jaycee stormed off, his giant boots thundering across the gantry toward a room full of heavy artillery and torture devices.

"I keep forgetting just how much of a behemoth Jaycee

is," Tripp said to no one in particular.

"I wouldn't want to get on his wrong side," Wool turned to Jelly. "Come on, girl. Let's go see the bad guys."

"Meowww-aaar…"

"Huh?" Wool shrugged her shoulders at Jelly's somewhat human tone, "Whatever, let's go."

USARIC Weapons & Armory
Space Opera Beta - Level Four

Jaycee's titanium fist slammed against the fourth bay. The door slid open to reveal an array of lethal-looking gadgets.

Not firearms or grenades - or dumb bombs or smart bombs - but a selection of unusual devices. Sword-shaped slabs of metal. Oblong units of *something* one wouldn't want to be on the receiving end of. Plastic sheets, gauze, and lengths of good old fashioned rope.

And then, the item Jaycee was looking for.

"Bingo."

A cylindrical disc with a ten-inch hole in the middle. It resembled a twelve-inch vinyl record, only made of metal. A fierce-looking piece of equipment weighing at least fifteen pounds.

He opened the disc apart from the side and scanned the room with a terrific impatience. "Come on, what can I test this on?"

A spent, battered dumb bomb sat on the service counter. "Ah, good. Let's see if you're working."

Jaycee placed the opened hole of the disc around the bomb and clamped it shut. The bomb's fifteen-inch width held the contraption in place. Jaycee tilted his head and blinked a couple of times. The disc surrounding the bomb *sort of* resembled Saturn and its rings, "Huh. Ironic."

He lifted his glove and hit a button on the wrist strap. "Calibrate one-one-eight, *Decapidisc*."

A light flashed on his glove. A corresponding white light sprang to life on the Decapidisc, followed be a second and third light, indicating that it had been armed.

The metal device began to vibrate along with a repetitive

set of beeps.

"Five… four…" Jaycee whispered, keeping an eye on the disc. The beeps grew quicker and quicker, threatening to form one, prolonged flat line effect.

"Three… two… and…"

Beep-beep-beep… beeeeeeeep.

"One."

SCHWIPP!

The grenade toppled around. The top half slid away from the bottom and crashed to the counter, releasing the Decapidisc. It clanged onto the surface of the desk.

The blades whirred around within the central hole and slowed down, eventually fanning out and back inside the metal.

"Good ol' *Decapidisc,*" Jaycee picked it up and planted a kiss on its shiny surface. "Now if *that* doesn't get them to comply, nothing will."

N-Carcerate

Tripp entered the cell and swung the keys in his hand, "Wakey-wakey, cretins."

Tor Klyce and Baldron Landaker lay across the bench, shackled together by an ankle chain. The chunky iron bolts streaked along the floor, clamped to the wall.

Wool could barely stand to look at the men - Tor in particular. She held her jaw and thought of the time he knocked her out.

"Kick them like the mules they are," she said. "Kick them *real* hard between the legs so they can't procreate. No grandchildren for them to tell how painful it was."

"No, Wool. We're better than that. We're not Neanderthals, unlike them," Tripp clapped his hands, "Hey, cretins. I said wake up."

Jelly snaked through Wool's legs and approached the sleeping men. She sniffed around Baldron's battered chest. He'd taken quite the kicking from Bonnie during the fight before the dumb bomb went off in Botanix.

"Jelly, no. Stay away from him. He's a bad, bad man,"

Wool crouched to her knees and patted her legs. "Come here, girl."

Jelly wouldn't follow her instructions. She turned to the men and let out a loud, nasty hiss.

Tor opened his eyes and instinctively kicked his chain.

"Hello, Tor," Tripp said with a venomous grin, "Glad you could join us."

"Hissss," Jelly roared in Tor's face.

"Gah," Tor climbed back along the bench and grabbed at his shackled ankle. His eyes followed the chain over to the sleeping Baldron. "What the hell? What's going on?"

"You don't remember?"

"No, no," Tor rubbed his face and grabbed the bench, frightened for his life. "No, I don't remember anything."

Wool placed her hands on her hips in anger. "Liar. Stand up."

Tripp laughed at Tor's anxiety. "Oh dear. You've upset her, now."

"What?"

"I said stand up," Wool stomped her foot to the ground and demanded satisfaction. "Do it."

"Okay, okay. I'm standing. Jeez," Tor stood up and reached eye level with the furious woman.

"You don't remember a thing?" Wool stared him dead in the eyes.

"No, no, I don't. What's happened? Where are we—"

SMACK.

Wool punched Tor in the face, sending him crashing ass-first against the bench. "Maybe *that* will jog your memory."

"Oww, she hit me," Tor held his jaw in his hand.

"Like I said. You upset her. *Comrade.*"

Heavy footsteps rumbled down the corridor from behind the N-Carcerate door.

"God damn Yanks," Tor kicked his heels along the floor with frustration, "I should have put a bullet in you when I had the chance."

"So you *do* remember?" Tripp left a deliberate pause for drama, "Of course you remember. You jeopardized my crew's safety. You sabotaged Opera Beta's mission. I ought to put a bullet in the back of your—"

"—Screw you, *American*," Tor spat a lump of phlegm at Tripp and snorted.

Jaycee pushed through the cell door and deliberately slammed it against the tough wall. The impact made Tor jump from the bench in utter horror.

"Hey, Jaycee," Tripp winked at Wool. "Glad you could join us. We were just talking about you."

Jaycee held up the two metal discs on his hands. "Really?"

"Wh-what are *those*?" Tor asked, fearing for his life.

"Oh, these?" Jaycee grunted and clanged to the two Decapidiscs together, "I'm glad you asked. Some people call them compliance units."

He lifted one of the discs and opened it out. An imprint displayed the company logo on the side in black writing: *Priestly Enterprises.*

"I prefer their actual name. Decapidisc. Sounds more frightening, don't you think?"

"Wh-what are you doing?" Tor backed up a few inches as Jaycee approached him. He shoved the half crescent midsection around Tor's neck and clamped the disc shut, pinching the skin over his Adam's Apple in the process.

"Aww, doesn't he look cute wearing it?" Jaycee bumped fists with Tripp.

"Yeah, it suits him."

"Looks a bit like one of those things the Victorians used to wear. What were they called?"

"A ruff, I think?" Tripp thoroughly enjoyed the ceremonious torment with his colleague.

Tor fumbled around the disc and pulled the flap of skin on his neck free, "Oww." A futile effort to a man. Locked into place and humming with life, the Decapidisc would make even the most hardened perpetrator beg for their mommy. Tor was no exception.

"Wh-what is this? What are you d-doing?"

"It's called a *Decapidisc*, Tor," Jaycee lifted his right hand and showed him the white button on his glove. "We need to know you're going to play ball. If I press this button, those three lights on your new collar light up and your head comes clean off."

"Oh, sh-shi—"

"—Hey!" Tripp snapped, showing Tor that he wasn't playing games. "Don't curse on *my* ship, you pathetic excuse for a human being."

Jelly moved back and hissed at Tor once again.

No matter where the man looked, he was surrounded by people wanting his blood.

"Here, Wool," Jaycee tossed the second Decapidisc to her. "Sort Baldron out with this special necklace, yeah?"

"My pleasure."

Wool moved over to the unconscious Baldron and clamped the disc around his neck.

Tripp stepped forward and folded his arms. "Now, listen very carefully to me, Tor. Are you listening?"

"Y-Yes, I'm listening."

"Jaycee, here, wants to press the button and mount your severed head on his souvenir wall. Do you know why?"

Tor looked at Jaycee playfully teasing the white button on his glove.

"Yes," Tor whispered as a tear of pink effluence dribbled away from his eye duct. "I'm sorry. I'm so sorry."

"It's too late for any of that, now," Jaycee said.

"He's right. What's done is done," Tripp added. "You and Baldron are responsible for the death of Opera Beta's captain and my friend, Daryl Katz. You're also responsible for Haloo's death. In fact, I hold you responsible for absolutely everything that has happened to us. Do you understand what I've said?"

"Yes."

"Now, we find ourselves at a bit of an impasse. None of us know how to fix Manuel. But *you* do."

Tor finally lifted his head, his face solemn and remorseful. He knew what was about to be asked of him. "Ask me."

"Am I going to regret this?" Tripp nodded at Jaycee and his fabulous white button of death.

"No. Ask me."

" We went through Enceladus, thanks to Jelly. We don't know Beta's current state. We don't know how much oxygen we have. We don't know if anything works, apart from the back-up generator that's giving us power and light. But we don't know how much longer that will last. We don't know where we are. We take a look outside and see nothing. We look at the screens and all we see is black. We could be *anywhere*. In fact, we probably *are* anywhere and, as Beta's captain, *anywhere* just isn't good enough."

"How's Manuel?" Tor asked.

"*Not well* is probably quite apt given the circumstances. He's talking crap and can't be trusted and needs professional help,' Tripp thought of a perfect put-down mid-sentence, "which is why I thought of you to help us."

"Or else what?"

"Or else you lose your head and all of us will probably die out here. Alone. Undiscovered. It would have all been for nothing."

Tor looked at the unconscious Baldron laying across the bench, "I need some sort of guarantee."

"Guarantee?" Tripp asked. "What, that Jaycee won't push the button?"

"That, and you promise not to kill me or my comrade after we do what you need me to do."

Tripp took Tor's sincerity literally and clenched his fists, "We're not killers. Unlike you and your boyfriend. I'll rip your damn head off with my own hands. Forget the Decapidisc."

"Aww," Jaycee played up to Tripp's taunting of their captive. "Tch."

"P-Please, don't hurt me."

Tripp squared up to Tor and stared him out. "Is that what you told my captain before you blew the connecting bridge between Alpha and Beta?"

"I'm sorry. It was nothing personal, I was only following ord--"

"—Sorry? You're sorry?" Tripp screamed in the man's face, blowing the hair on his head back a few millimeters. "How about Haloo, eh? Try telling her you're sorry. She's not even around anymore to argue with you."

Tor burst into tears as Tripp closed his eyes and calmed down. The tips of their noses practically touched.

Jaycee found the argument between the two men somewhat comical. "Are you two going to kiss?"

"Shut up," Tripp spat and lifted Tor's crying face up by his chin. "So, what's it to be, Tor? Instant death? Or a sliver of a possibility that you, and all of us, survive?"

Tor took a deep breath and glanced at Jaycee, who taunted him with the white button on his glove. Jelly's sneering didn't help matters much, either.

The decision was inevitable.

Chapter 4

Handax Skill unfolded a piece of black cloth and held it at arm's length. Two eye holes stretched out across the soft material. "Perfect."

He looked around the hideout, refusing to let the grim interior warehouse walls get to him. The *People Against Animal Cruelty* placards lined most of the right-hand wall. They filled him with vigor.

Leif, a petite woman in her twenties, approached the central table. She unclipped her thumbnail on her right hand and set it on the surface, "Two hours to show time."

"Display Individimedia. Put it on Dreenagh Remix's channel."

"That blood-hungry piece of crap in heels?" Leif chuckled as she swiped the ink on her forearm.

Handax ran his fingers through his bright blue hair, contemplating the plan they were about to carry out. He saw his team having second thoughts about the forthcoming event. "Yeah, let's see how she's spun the story."

Dreenagh's name appeared on Leif's arm. Seconds later, the thumbnail threw a giant holographic live feed above the table.

An empty podium outside USARIC headquarters with dozens microphones waiting to be utilized.

"We're on."

"Guys, come and take a look at this," Handax turned to the two men.

One of them stared down the barrel of a long-range rifle.

"Denny, man," Handax said. "Pay attention."

"Yeah," Denny stood up and walked over to the table. "What's good?"

"Pay attention."

Dreenagh commentated off-camera on the non-event, "As you can see, USARIC is preparing to make an official statement of affairs. In a couple hours from now we're expecting USARIC's Deputy CEO, Dimitri Vasilov, to respond to allegations of sabotage."

"Just shut up and get to the good stuff," Handax muttered as he paced around the bench. "Look at her, spinning the story. I bet she doesn't even mention the twenty-three Russian delegates who were forced out of—"

"—Tensions are high after the expulsion of twenty-three Russian delegates from the United States shortly after the last communication from Space Opera Beta. An allegation from the captain of the ship suggests that the mission had been deliberately sabotaged by Russians. Stay with me for USARIC's official reaction."

Leif ducked her head and sighed. "She's just killing time, now."

"Put her on mute," Handax said. "I can't stand her voice."

Leif held out her pinkie and index finger and threw her hand through the image, cutting off the volume. "There, that's better."

Denny placed his rifle on the table. "So, we're still on?"

"Of course we're still on." Handax turned to the fourth member of the crew. "Moses?"

The man looked up from his lap and halted his work on a opened drone. "Yeah, we're still on."

"Gather round the table. We don't have much time."

Moses placed the drone on the seat of his chair and joined the group, "Do I get a mask, too?"

"Everyone gets one."

Handax threw a balaclava each to Leif, Moses, and

Denny. "Make sure you wear them the right way round."

Denny chuckled sarcastically. "Yeah, thanks."

Handax pressed his thumb to his forearm, enabling a rotating vector image of the USARIC's complex to appear above the table.

The west side of the building flashed drawing their attention to the main entrance. A vast complex stood north-west - an area of interest to all concerned.

"The compound," Handax said. "Leif and I will be on point to infiltrate thirty seconds before Denny takes the shot."

"Yeah. What if he misses, though?" Leif asked.

Denny picked up the rifle and looked down the sight. "With firepower like this? I never miss."

"Don't point that thing at me," Leif pushed the end of the barrel away from her.

"Don't worry. It's not charged, yet."

"I don't care. Just don't point it at me."

Handax cleared his throat. "Denny?"

"What?"

"Behave."

"My bad."

"*My bad?*" Handax quipped. "What is this, twenty-twenty-five? Have you been watching those old movies again?"

"Sorry."

"Just concentrate, for heaven's sake," Handax continued. "We need everyone on point. We're about to make history."

Moses slipped on his balaclava and punched his fists together. Somehow, even in s purious mask, his near seven-foot frame seemed all the more threatening. "They won't know what hit them."

"No, they *must* know what hit them. That's the whole idea," Leif reached into her belt and retrieved her handgun, "We better load up if we're going to hit our marks."

Handax took a deep breath. The severity of what they were about to do socked him in the gut. "How are we all feeling?"

"It needs to be done, man," Moses clocked Handax's anxiety instantly. "Hey. You're not chickening out now, are you? This was your idea."

"Yeah, I know. It's just that…"

Handax never finished his sentence, which caused consternation for the others. He knew he had to remain in control for their sake. He lifted his head, angrily.

"Guys, we can't allow these murderous, corporate scumbags to get away with what they've done—"

"—I'd say *bastards* is about right," Leif said, inspecting her handgun. "Let's hit them where it hurts."

Handax thought very carefully about his next statement. "If you could save those tortured creatures and stick it to USARIC's nefarious practices by killing just one man… would you do it?"

"Hell yeah," Denny smiled. "For that alone, sure, but also for sneaking Russians on an American vessel. Two reasons, one bullet."

Leif and Moses nodded in quiet agreement, leaving their leader feeling invigorated and confident. Handax slipped on his balaclava and reached into his belt.

"God help us all."

One Hour and Fifty-Two Minutes Later…

Hundreds of journalists crowded the entrance to USARIC's headquarters. The podium remained empty. Tensions were high - almost as much as the scores of drones that buzzed around in the air vying for the best view.

Dreenagh secured one of the best positions in the cordoned-off press area. Five armed security guards lined the front of the podium, itching for the opportunity to take someone out.

"Hey, you!" Dreenagh shouted to one of the guards. "When is Vasilov coming out?"

"Stay back, please," he said. "We're expecting him soon."

Dreenagh looked up and saw her drone get knocked by another. "What the hell?"

She turned to her left and clocked her silver-haired, suited-and-booted rival, Santiago Sibald. He shot her an evil wink. "Hey, Dreenagh."

"Is that your drone attacking mine?"

"Seems so," he said. "Your useless piece of junk doesn't stand a chance."

"Denny, do you read me?" Handax's voice was stern, yet precise.

"Yeah, man. I'm all set."

Denny placed his index finger in his ear and grabbed the steering wheel. He'd set up his long-range rifle across the front seats. The barrel rested against the opened passenger window, perfectly lined-up to take a shot at USARIC's frontage.

"There's literally thousands of people in the way," Denny said into his forearm. "It's okay, though. I have a clear line of sight to the podium."

"Good."

"Are you in position?"

Handax, Leif, and Moses moved to the corner of the building. Dressed as civilians in shirts and jeans, they blended into the furious crowd extremely well.

"We're about thirty meters from breach," Handax looked at the inked countdown on his forearm. "Twenty-six seconds into the speech. Then we're on."

"Understood," Denny's voice came through earpiece.

Handax nodded at two security guards standing in front of the side entrance to the compound.

"There they are," he said to Leif and Moses.

The emotion from the crowd doubled as the doors to the entrance opened. "We demand answers!" screamed a civilian from within the virus-like baying mob.

Dreenagh slid her fingers across her forearm and moved her drone down to her face. "Hey, good people. Dreenagh Remix, here. It seems Dimitri Vasilov is making an appearance."

A dozen officials exited the building protecting an elderly man. They ushered him to the podium and kept an eye out for trouble from the crowd.

"Yes, yes. If you look at your screens now, we can see that Dimitri Vasilov is on time and about to make a statement. It had better be good. As I stand here there are thousands of civilians demanding answers."

The crowd erupted with anger. The armed guards grabbed their weapons and forced them back, threatening to attack.

"Stay back. Stay back."

A large man screamed at the top of his lungs, "USARIC scumbags."

"Stay back," a security guard threatened a man attempting to climb over the cordon. He lost his balance and fell to the ground in pain.

Dimitri caught sight of the security guard burying the nozzle of his gun against the protester's head, "My God. It's a jungle out here,"

"Get up, you chunk of whale blubber," the guard screamed in the fat man's face.

"Please, d-don't shoot me."

The fat man rolled onto his belly and surrendered in front of the restless crowd.

"Ignore it, sir," advised one of the officials as he escorted Dimitri to the podium. "We have a schedule to keep."

Handax kept an eye on the two armed guards by the side entrance to the building. They turned away to look at the commotion at the front of the building. "What's going on over there?"

"Okay, an unexpected gift, guys," Handax whispered to Leif and Moses. "Get ready. Looks like Vasilov is about to do his thing."

The two guards at the side entrance stepped away from their markers, taking a keen interest in the fat man's arrest.

"Denny, can you see what we're seeing?"

"I'm too far away. It looks like a fight has broken out, or something."

"Some fat guy did us a favor," Handax hopped over the cordon and waved Moses and Leif over to the door. "The guards at the animal compound have moved off. I don't know for how long."

"Okay, " Denny said. "I'm ready."

"Good luck, everyone."

A USARIC official stepped up to the podium and moved his face to the microphone. Feedback from the speakers wailed across the grounds, diverting everyone's attention from the fat man. "Citizens. Can I have your attention, please?"

"We want answers," the crowd roared back.

"You'll get them in due course. I would ask everyone here, including our respected journalists, to keep the fuss to a minimum."

Dimitri scanned the blood-hungry mob from behind the safety of his security team. The guards weren't messing around. A contentious moment such as this needed order.

"Dimitri?" The official turned to the elderly man and offered him the podium. "Let's get this over with as quick as possible."

"Oh, I intend to," Dimitri moved through the sea of officials and reached the microphones. The crowds whooped and booed at the sight of him.

He leaned into the microphone. "Good people, please, allow me—"

"U-SUCK-RICK! U-SUCK-RICK!"

A security guard quelled the noise by firing three shots into the air. "Shut the hell up." The crowd fell silent and obedient in an instant.

Dimitri smiled and nodded at the guard. "Thank you."

"No problem."

Dimitri cleared his throat and reached for a sheet of paper from his blazer pocket. "I understand that you are all angry and want answers. I have a prepared statement and I will not be taking any questions."

The angry crowd allowed the man to have his say, poised to scold him at the first opportunity.

"I, Dimitri Vasilov, wish to deny any and all allegations of sabotage. To be clear, USARIC's Infinity Clause, in accordance with the Bering Treaty of 2085, stipulates that no Russian national may join any manned mission to space, or beyond. Despite our reluctance to these terms, the Russian contingent of USARIC had steadfastly agreed to them and continue to do so."

"You're talking *lessense*," a woman yelled from the crowd.

"Please, let me finish," Dimitri continued. "USARIC can confirm that we received communication from Space Opera Beta advising that two Russians had made themselves known amongst the crew. This was shortly before the disappearance of the ship, which also had the winner of the Star Cat Trials, Bisoubisou, amongst its crew members. Despite her Russian nationality it was deemed acceptable that she join the mission on account of her being the most suitable candidate—"

Dimitri's chest opened up in a haze of blood, sending him crashing to the ground.

The crowd screamed bloody murder and dispersed in all directions, pushing into each other.

A violent and desperate dash to escape the shooter - wherever he or she was.

Civilians crushed against and over each other in a dash to get to safety. Men, women, and children. The security guards fired indiscriminately at the crowd, hoping to catch the perpetrator.

The bleeding Dimitri lay on the floor, coughing and spluttering. The bullet had torn through his lungs.

"My God, did you see that?" Dreenagh billowed into her forearm, fending off the stampede rollicking behind her. "Look, look. Dimitri Vasilov has been assassinated."

Her drone buzzed around the podium along with many others in an attempt to get a decent view of the carnage.

BAM!

Two security guards fired at the wasp-like drones. Their bullets hit some of them, punching them out of the air.

"Target eliminated," Denny's voice came through Handax's earpiece over the sound of a car engine firing up as he followed his instruction. "Over to you, guys."

"Okay, go!"

Handax, Leif, and Moses stormed over to the compound side entrance and pulled their balaclavas over their heads. The door was bolted shut but unguarded.

"Moses, the two guards have moved off. I figure you have about thirty seconds."

"I know, I know," he clamped a rectangular device across the door's bolt. "I only need fifteen."

Handax held his hand gun in both hands and watched the screaming crowd run off. No one spotted Handax and Leif keeping an eye out for security, much less the firearms in their hands.

"Twenty-five seconds, Moses."

"I'm going as fast as I can," Moses lifted the flap of his device and punched in a three digit code: 4-5-7. "The code is in. Nearly there."

Handax turned to Leif, keeping a tight grip on his gun. "Any sign of security?"

"Not yet, no," Leif watched the ink on her forearm countdown from twenty. She scanned at the corner of the building. "It's only a matter of time before they return. Hurry up, Moses."

"Okay, five seconds till we're in," Moses said, stepping back from the door. "Five... four..."

Leif spotted the security guard walking around the corner of the building with his colleague. "Guys, we got company."

The pair headed straight for them.

"... three..."

"They're coming, they're coming. We gotta get in now before we're seen."

"Two," Moses finished through the earpieces, "One... and, we're in business."

The door didn't unbolt. The tactical device failed and spluttered, slumping against the handle.

"Damn."

"What?" Handax turned to Moses, "What's going on?"

"It didn't work."

"Guys," Leif backed up to the two men, ready to threaten the guards who'd yet to clock them. "We're seconds away from being spotted."

"What do we do?"

"You and your stupid technology," Handax clipped Moses around the back of the head. Fast-thinking, he jumped out from the corner and made his presence known to the approaching guards. "Excuse me."

"What the hell do you think you're doing?" Leif ducked behind the door, unseen by the two guards as they approached her leader with their weapons drawn.

"Hey, you. Citizen. Put the gun down."

Handax pointed his hand gun at them and smiled. Leif and Moses did the same.

"No, I think *you* put yours down," Handax said.

"We're not messing around," one of the security guards kept his sights focused on Moses and Handax. "This is a private zone. Drop your weapons and remove your masks, or we will shoot you."

Handax kept an eye on the compound door and aimed his gun at the second security guard. "No, I don't think so."

An abrasive stand-off occurred. The five of them pointed their weapons at each other.

"I said lower your weapons, citizen," screamed the first guard.

"Okay, now," Handax blasted the second guard's weapon out of his hand.

The first guard took a shot at Handax's head. Leif barged against guard's elbow, forcing the trajectory of the bullet away.

"Oww."

She jumped onto his back, wrapped her legs around his waist and jammed the barrel of her gun in his temple, "Hey, sweetie. Gonna let us in?"

Moses snatched the shotgun from of the security guard's hands and strapped it over his shoulder. "Be quiet."

Handax kicked the second security guard's gun away, grabbed his collar and lifted him to his feet.

"Wh-what are you d-doing?" the second guard asked in a state of near-paralysis, "Please d-don't kill me."

"We're not the murderers, *murderer*." Handax kicked the guard toward the door. "Now, open the door."

Leif removed the first guard's helmet, revealing a reasonably attractive man underneath it.

"Ooh, you're hot."

"Get off of me. Please."

"Nah, I like it here," she giggled, squeezing his waist from behind with her thighs. "Nice of you to give me a ride."

"Leif," Handax shot her a look of disdain and waved his gun at her. "Stop flirting with the bad guys."

"Aww," she climbed off his back and kept her gun held at his temple, "Maybe after all this is over?"

He squeezed his eyes shut and prayed she wouldn't blow his brains out.

"Get off him. We have work to do," Handax thumped his captor on the back, "Open the door. Now."

"Okay, okay," the guard punched a three digit code on the door where Moses' device had failed. "I'm doing it."

Handax pressed his finger to his ear, pacing around. "Denny, man? Do you read me?"

"Uh, yeah?"

"Where are you?"

"Umm," came his voice, "I'm in the middle of threatening someone right now. Can I call you back?"

A dozen USARIC security cars tore across the airfield after Denny's speeding van. Their sirens wailed and screeched as they gained on him.

"Sure, man," Handax's voice came through the car's speakers. " Just head back to base."

"Very funny," Denny spun the steering wheel to the left, forcing his van to change trajectory. He swiped his forearm, cutting off the call and looked in the rear view mirror. "Come on, cretins. Let's see if you can do one hundred."

The USARIC vehicles grew larger and larger in his wing mirror as he stepped on the gas.

80 mph... 90 mph... "Come on, come on..."

"Driver," a voice through a megaphone on top of an approaching USARIC SUV whirled through the air, "Pull your vehicle over. Now."

"Nu-uh," Denny slammed on the gas with all his might. He rolled down the driver's window and pushed out his hand, flipping his assailants the bird. "Come and get me, scumbags."

Denny's van rocketed across the runway. In the distance, a three-quarter-built cone-shaped spacecraft loomed, facing upright within its scaffolding. On its side in giant, black lettering read *Space Opera Charlie*.

"Huh?" Denny muttered in astonishment, tearing his concentration away from the airstrip. "*Charlie?*"

BLAM-BLAM-BLAM!

Mercenaries in each USARIC SUV opened fired on Denny's van as they zoomed toward the incomplete spacecraft. Dozens of bullets sprayed against the back doors. The left one bust open and flapped back and forth.

105 mph...

Space Opera Charlie got closer and closer as Denny kept his foot on the gas. He pressed his forearm and held his right ear, struggling to keep control of the rickety van. The vehicle wasn't used to these kind of speeds.

"Handax, you read me, man?" Denny yelled. "You read me?"

"Yes, I read you—"

"—Charlie, *man*. Space Opera Charlie. I can see it with right now in the airfield," Denny slammed on the breaks, forcing his rifle to fly off its housing and crash against the windshield. "They're after me. They're going to kill me."

"Denny? Where are you?"

"The airfield. I had no choice, they were on to me the moment the bullet hit Vasilov's left lung."

The van screeched to a halt on the airstrip. Dozens of USARIC vehicles flew past, underestimating Denny's brake application.

A score of handbrake turns sent the speeding SUVs around, kicking dust into the air from under the tires. Some of them tumbled around and upside down.

The remaining SUVs slammed on the brakes, releasing a SWAT-like team of USARIC officials from the back doors. They surrounded Denny's vehicle with their automatic weapons drawn.

"Driver, exit the car," came an furious voice from the megaphone atop the closest car. "We are *not* playing around. Exit the car now, or we *will* open fire—"

"—Okay, okay," Denny screamed and kicked open the driver's door.

"Stay where you are."

Denny closed his eyes and placed his hands on top of his head. This was *it*. This was how it all ended for him, he thought. Mission accomplished and failed in one fell swoop.

A tear rolled down his cheek as he awaited instructions from the one-hundred-strong USARIC army threatening to blow him off the face of the planet.

"Driver, exit your vehicle with your hands behind your head. Place your knees on the ground and hold your arms out. Failure to comply will result in execution."

"Denny?" Handax's voice indicated concern and haste. "What's that noise?"

"I'm sorry, man," Denny cried.

An armed USARIC mercenary pointed his machine gun at the driver's door. "Out."

Denny stepped out of the van with his hands above his head, blubbering like a little girl. "I'm sorry."

"Shut up and get on your goddamn knees," the mercenary kept his gun aimed at Denny as his knees hit the tarmac. He looked at his colleagues and waved them to the van. "Check the vehicle."

"Yes, sir."

Three USARIC mercenaries ran over to the back of the van and tore off the doors.

"You got some balls doing what you did," the mercenary said to Denny. "Why did you do it?"

"D-Do what?" Denny tried to act all innocent.

"Don't act dumb with me, dickhead. You took out Vasilov and tried to escape. Did you really think you'd get away with *that*?"

"I'm sorry."

"And *then* you break into the airfield?" He chuckled with great enthusiasm and nodded up at Space Opera Charlie. "That takes guts. I'm looking forward to yanking them out of your stomach and strangling you with them."

"I said I'm sorry. Please don't kill me—"

"—Oh my God," One of the USARIC trio at the van

jumped onto the tarmac and stepped back. "Get back. Get back."

Denny growled and slapped the ink on his left forearm, setting off a series of rapid beeps from the holes in his wrist. "Handax, I'm sorry. It's game over."

"Who are you talking to?" The mercenary grabbed the back of Denny's shirt and hoisted him to his feet. "What's going on—"

"—Get back," screamed the USARIC van inspector, tumbling over his feet. "It's gonna blow—"

KA-BLAAAAM!

The van exploded, vaporizing dozens of nearby USARIC mercenaries - and Denny himself. Dozens of human fireballs catapulted in all directions as the van crashed back to the tarmac-laden airstrip.

Those who didn't get caught up in the explosion opened fire on Denny's barbecuing body. Scores of stray bullets tore into the USARIC official by accident.

The latter's murder was considered a necessary evil.

"Denny? *Denny?*" Handax screamed into his forearm, hearing the real-time death of his friend. A cacophony of fire and bullets rattled into Moses and Leif's earpieces as they held their captives in the compound's corridor.

"Sorry for your loss, man." Moses kept his firearm at the first security guard's head. He could see that murder was on Handax's mind. Quite the irony, considering their mission.

Leif kept her 'hot' security guard at bay with her gun and tried to offer her leader some sympathy. "Handax, man—"

"—Listen to me very carefully," Handax jammed the barrel of his gun into the first security guard's temple. The mist from his breathing plumed out through the fabric of his balaclava, "Do you know who we are?"

"N-No, and we don't need to know," the guard said, aware that his captor was incandescent with rage, "Please, just let us go."

"Get up. Take us to the animal compound."

Moses kept his gun held at the first guard. Leif did the same with the second.

"You'll never get away with this," the second guard said to Leif.

"That's okay,' she flirted back at him, "We don't plan to."

"You're crazy."

"That's right. One of yours just executed one of ours," Handax barked at the pair, "One false move and you get a bullet in the brain. Understood?"

The two guards nodded, convinced they were going to die.

Handax pointed at the far end of the corridor, "Let's go."

Chapter 5

Space Opera Beta

"Let's go," Jaycee's patience ran out. He planted his boot on Tor's lower back and booted him along the corridor.

"Okay, stop hitting me," Tor yelped like a pansy. "I'm *going.*"

Tripp and Wool smirked to themselves as they followed behind the pair. The blatant mistreatment of their prisoner felt largely deserved.

The crew entered the control deck.

Jelly snarled at Tor as he reached the communications panel. She hopped onto the swivel chair. The sudden application of her weight made it twirl around a few times.

"Hissss," she dug her infinity claws into the fabric, enacting what she'd like to do with Tor if she ever had time alone with him.

He stared into her bright orange eyes and swallowed hard. Something was very definitely *off* between them.

"What are you looking at?" Jaycee thumped Tor on the shoulder a little harder than necessary. "Get working, you miserable bag of puke."

"Oh," Tor double-took and felt the metal Decapidisc around his neck. He cleared his throat and looked at the comms panel. "Yes. Manuel override set up—"

"*Manuel* override?" Tripp asked in confusion.

"Sorry, I mean *manual* override," Tor felt the rim of the

Decapidisc around his neck. "Set up. A-W-A-K-E-4-5-7."

A distinct air of unease fell around the team as the panel booted up. An array of lights sprang to life and flashed. Tor turned to Jaycee and tried for a smile. The comms deck had responded to the command. Progress had been made.

"About damn time," Jaycee said, refusing to share a congratulatory moment with the bad guy. Fighting off the desire to activate the man's Decapidisc proved to be difficult as Tor stared back at him.

"Don't look at me," Jaycee spat. "Get Manuel working."

"He's booting up."

Whump.

Manuel's holographic book appeared few feet away from the deck. The image fizzled and acclimatized to the reboot. Manuel's voice came out as garbled nonsense in an array of pitches and tones.

"G-Good after-m-morrrr-ning,"

"He's back on," Tripp stepped forward and stared at the flipping pages finally shining to life. "At least he's not completely destroyed."

"Manuel?" Tor asked. "Do you read me?"

"Yes. I r-r-r-read y-you."

Tor typed a command on the keyboard at speed. "I'm going to run a diagnostic on you. We need to know you're fully operational."

"Okay."

"Just a couple of easy questions. Please don't take it personally. Are you ready?"

"Yes, I'm ruh... ruh... r-ready.'

Jaycee pointed at Manuel with disdain, "Are you sure Max Headroom, here, is in a fit state to answer questions?"

"Let's find out," Tor hit the return key on the panel and took a step back. "Manuel?"

"Yes, Tor?"

"What does USARIC stand for?"

All eyes turned to Manuel as he drifted over to the control panel. "The United States and Russian Intergalactic Confederation."

"Correct," Tor hit a green button on the control panel.

"Second question. What was the primary remit of Space Opera Beta's mission?"

"Oh, that's easy," Manuel said. "To visit Enceladus to decipher Saturn Cry."

"Almost," Tripp said. "The journey was to Saturn. We didn't know about Enceladus until we reached orbit."

"The answer is good enough for now," Tor licked his lips and punched in a command on the keyboard. "Last question before flushing to disk."

"Okay."

"Where are we?"

Manuel went silent. His pages rifled together, creating a sound similar to that of a deck of cards being shuffled.

"Manuel?" Tripp grew impatient. His crew members' lives were at stake. "Where are we?"

The book slammed shut and shifted over to the communications deck, "Right ascension, declination, *position*," Manuel arrived at the most honest answer he could muster.

"Well?"

"I don't know," Manuel said. "I've retrieved the *geodata* in accordance with the Galactic coordinate system. It makes little sense."

"Much like you, then" Jaycee's unhelpful retort agitated the others.

"Shut up, Jaycee,' Tripp said.

Tor shifted Jelly's chair to one side and set the keyboard onto the panel. "Sorry, pet."

"Hisss…" Jelly opened her mouth and made sure he could see her sharp fangs.

Somewhat frightened, he turned away from the disgruntled cat and over to Manuel. "Display the coordinates, please."

"I'm not sure how much use they will be. But here they are."

One by one, the numbers beamed into the middle of the deck from Manuel's data page.

00h 00m 00.0000s, −00° 00' 00.0

Tripp's face fell, along with Wool's.

Jaycee couldn't believe the result, either. "Just a bunch of zeros?"

"The format isn't even correct," Manuel said. "Most of the zeros we see shouldn't even be showing. It's scrambled, unintelligible and downright wrong at best."

Jelly took the opportunity to clean her right paw with her tongue.

"*Nowhere?*" Tripp muttered. "No, this can't be right. We have to be somewhere."

An idea jumped into Tor's head as he took in the display. "Manuel, ignore the coordinates for now. We know we went through Enceladus. Do you have *any* idea where we are?"

"I am running a scan, now."

"And the oxygen levels?" Tripp asked. "Botanix took a substantial amount of damage."

"Opera Beta's oxygen supply expires a little under seventy hours from now," Manuel said. "But according to the scan, there is no oxygen present on board. No habitable atmosphere."

"Well that's wrong. We're still here," Tripp took a deep breath and exhaled. "Yup, that's oxygen all right."

Wool grew anxious and began to tremble. "Oh, God. We're dead, aren't we? That's it, there's no rescue."

Tripp took her arms in an attempt to calm her down. "We don't know the full facts, yet. The readings must be wrong."

Her hyperventilation didn't help matters, "Seventy hours of oxygen? We're going to die, Tripp."

"Calm down. Just breathe."

"That's the whole *problem*, Tripp. I don't want to breathe. We have to conserve—"

"—Well, this is interesting," Manuel interrupted. "I'm not sure how to tell you this."

"What?" Tor asked.

"We are *not* aboard Space Opera Beta."

Everyone looked around the flight deck. They were definitely aboard the spacecraft. Jelly hopped onto the communications deck and walked across the keyboard, swishing her tail. "Meow."

"What do you mean we're not on Beta?" Tripp asked Manuel. "I think you need another reboot, you know."

"Also, something strange is happening to my clock."

"You don't say?" Tripp sighed. "You've got the oxygen report wrong, our location all scrambled - and wrong. Are you trying for the hat trick, now, with us not being on our own spacecraft?"

"Tripp, time is moving very slowly. I am not trying to be humorous. For every hour we have been at these coordinates, Earth has advanced by one calendar month."

"Okay, that's enough. We're switching you off and on again."

"The equation between Earth time and here is an approximation, of course. Not an exact figure."

Tor whispered to Tripp. "I think Manuel is several gigabytes short of a terabyte. He's clearly confused."

"I can assure you I am not confused," Manuel said with a great deal of sincerity. "My calculations are correct. We are *not* on Space Opera Beta. Take a look around. Do you recognize anything you see?"

"Yes! You moron," Tripp screamed with frustration and thumped the control deck "I recognize *everything*. See, I can touch stuff. We're definitely on board Beta—"

"—I think you may be suffering from delusion, Tripp," Manuel interrupted, much to the amazement of the others. "Might I suggest a couple of hours of rest to fully acclimate yourself to your surroundings—"

"—What are you talking about?"

Tripp turned to Wool for her reaction. To say she was anything other than bamboozled would be a vast understatement.

"He's nuts," she walked over to Jelly and opened her arms. "We're dead. Plain and simple. Jelly, come to mommy."

Jelly jumped into her open arms and nestled herself in the crook of her elbow.

"Meowww-wwwaaar…"

The entire ship rumbled to life just as she made herself comfortable.

Tripp, Tor, and Jaycee looked around and breathed a

suspicious sigh of relief. Finally, an atmosphere that suggested progress, and one that was familiar to them.

"Beta. She's back on," Tor looked up and around. "I'm rebooting Manuel. This is a good sign. It looks like we're in business again."

"Tor, please do not reboot me. It is unnecessary. I am one hundred percent operational—"

"—Good call, Tor," Tripp said. "Let's get the controls up and running and find out where we are, at least."

"No, don't do that—"

"—Rest, Manuel." Tor snapped his fingers, shutting off Manuel's holographic representation. "Get some rest."

Jaycee took a few careful steps forward and lifted his K-SPARK toward the door. "Wait. Something's *not* right."

"Not right?"

He looked around the walls and ceiling. The lights flickered. A distant, angelic humming grew louder from behind the door.

"You hear that?"

Jelly snarled, startling the others. She swiped her paw at Wool's face, catching her off guard. Two of her infinity claws tore across the woman's cheek, forcing her to release Jelly to the ground.

"Oww," Wool yelped, confused by Jelly's lashing out. "Jelly, what are you—"

"—Roowaaaarr!" Jelly hit the ground and tumbled onto her side.

Tripp, Jaycee, and Tor turned to the irritated cat. Her whiskers fizzed with tiny beads of electricity. She sat up right straight on her hind legs and allowed her whiskers to do *whatever they were doing.*

"Muuuuh…"

"What's h-happening to her?" Tor gasped. "What's happening to her face?"

Boom-boom-boom…

Three distinct thuds rattled from behind the door. Jelly ignored it as her whiskers perked up and fizzed. Her face and body vibrated with small, swift shocks.

Wool felt the bloodied scratch on her face and looked at

her fingers. Pink liquid trickled between them.

"Jelly?" Tripp muttered in astonishment, "What's happening to you, girl?"

Jelly's metal whiskers lit up and stood on end in a fascinatingly unnatural way. Much like her ears did whenever she heard something she hadn't expected to hear. She lowered her head and stared Tripp in the eyes.

"Meoowww..." she whined - only this time in a slightly lower octave than everyone expected. "Muuuuhhh..."

Boom-boom-boom...

Everyone turned to the door. It shunted open through the ship's intense vibrations.

"What's going on?" Wool cried for her life.

The angelic humming barreled down the walls and into the room, along with a fine pink mist.

"Come to me, sweetie..." A familiar voice accompanied the mist as it pervaded the entire control deck.

Wool's jaw dropped. She lowered her hand, exposing the fresh, bloodied scratch on her cheek. "What's h-happening?"

Jelly howled at the mist hanging around the walls and floor. Her infinity claws spasmed, almost involuntarily. Her whiskers vibrated a storm, creating a spark in her pupils.

"Muh... muh... mwaaah... loo... " Jelly croaked and gave up trying to speak.

"Jelly?" Tripp approached her, only to be met with a fiery resistance. She held up her infinity claws and clenched them tight.

"N-Nnn..." she coughed up a blob of pink phlegm and spat it to the ground. "*No...*"

Tripp could scarcely believe what he was seeing. The same reaction came from Tor, Wool, and Jaycee, who lowered his gun in astonishment.

"Jelly? *No?*"

"She just *spoke*," Jaycee held his shotgun at Jelly as a precaution. He looked around the deck as the pink gas-like substance filled the room from the corridor. "This is weird. I don't like it."

The female voice flooded the room with terrific volume. "Jelly. Come to me, sweetie..."

Jelly turned to the door, jumped to her paws and scurried towards the corridor. She let out a low-pitched growl as she hopped through the opened door.

Jelly Anderson was on a quest. What's more, she seemed to know *exactly* what was going on.

Tripp, Tor, Jaycee, and Wool watched her dart out of the room.

"After her!" Tripp said, chasing after Jelly. "Go, go."

Jelly bounded along the level one walkway. She was headed somewhere unknown. The pink gas wafted out of her path away as the others chased after her.

"Where's she going?" Jaycee stomped along the ground after her.

"How the hell should I know?" Tripp kept up the pace and turned to Wool as she ran alongside him, pressing her fingertips against the raw scratch mark on her cheek.

Jelly skidded on her paws and bolted around the corner. The chorus-like voice seemed louder, now. Wherever they were headed, they were getting close to the source.

"Jelly, girl," Tripp hollered after her. "Where are you going?"

She ignored them and kept running.

"I think we're going to Medix," Jaycee grabbed Tor's arm, careful not to knock his Decapidisc. "Come on, keep up."

"I am, I am," Tor hoped Jaycee wouldn't knock him out or press the button on his glove.

"Come to me, sweetie," the sleepy, female voice shot past their ears as they ran, "You're such a *good* girl."

"That voice. Is that *Haloo*?" Tripp pointed dead ahead at the opened door to the Medix chamber. "Jelly, what—"

She bounced into the room and disappeared in a cloud of smog.

Whvoom!

"Go, go, go," Tripp said as he reached the Medix facility.

Wool screamed after Tripp. "Are you sure it's safe?"

"No."

Tripp launched himself into the room and into the pink cloud. Wool, Jaycee, and Tor followed him in…

Tripp walked through the pink gas and into Medix proper. Much to his surprise the room was exactly how they'd left it.

Several beds, machines, and the unmistakable bright white walls, ceiling and floor. Nothing untoward as far as the room was concerned.

Jaycee, Tor, and Wool kept a keen eye on Jelly as she nosed around the trolley containing Haloo Ess's covered body.

"Mwaaaar," Jelly snaked around the metal legs, pawing at the casters. "H-Haaa... loooo."

Jaycee scanned his surroundings, ready to blast whatever presented itself to smithereens. "What's going on?"

"I don't know," Tripp nodded at Jelly as she made a fuss over Haloo's bed. "Jelly, what are you doing?"

"Meow."

She seemed calmer, now, backing away from the bed.

The sight of the sheet shuffling around over Haloo's body suggested she wasn't dead.

"My God, stay back," Tripp held out his arms and waved everyone away. "Haloo?"

"What's happening to her?" Wool asked, terrified.

"I don't know—"

Haloo's body sat upright on the bed. The sheet dropped from her chest and landed on her lap. Her eyes were closed, her face still sunken.

Tripp took one step closer to the bed, careful not to antagonize the woman. "Haloo?"

Her eyes opened the moment he called her name. She turned to him with a robotic movement and focused on his face. Her pupils were bright pink.

"Are you okay?" Tripp asked, cautiously.

"Tripp," she whispered.

"Haloo. It's me, Tripp. Are you okay?"

She burst out laughing and held her hand to her mouth. "Oh, I'm sorry, Tripp."

"Huh?"

"I'm feeling *great*," she clocked Tor, Jaycee, and Wool. Aghast, they didn't how to respond to the fact that their colleague was alive.

Tripp pointed out the obvious, "We thought you were dead?"

Jaycee lifted his gun and pointed it at her. "This is insane. She died right in my arms. Don't go near her."

Unmoved by Jaycee's reaction, Haloo turned her attention to Jelly, who looked up at her from the ground.

"Ohh. I'm not *dead*," she patted her lap, offering Jelly a hug, "Come on, girl. Come and give your auntie Haloo a cuddle."

"Meow."

Jelly hopped onto the chair, and then onto the bed itself. She confidently strode along the surface intending to take up Haloo's offer of a hug.

"Meow."

"Haloo? What are you doing?" Jaycee's trigger finger grew restless. "It's weird."

"Mmm," Haloo scooped the willing Jelly into her arms and planted her lips on her fluffy forehead. "You're such a *good* girl."

Wool blinked a few times, hoping she'd wake up from this bizarre *daymare*. It didn't work - what she saw was *very real indeed*.

"Haloo?" Wool asked, sure that something bad was on its way, "Tell us what's going—"

"—Mmm," Haloo hugged Jelly as tight as possible and smiled at Tripp. Jelly loved every second of it. "She is a good little girl, isn't she?"

"Okay, that's enough." Jaycee aimed his firearm at the sitting corpse. "You don't just wake up from death like this, Haloo. We want answers."

She giggled, enjoying how little the others seemed to understand. Suspense filled the room as a result.

"Oh, Jaycee," Haloo swung her legs over the side of the bed and pressed the soles of her feet on the floor, "Something fantastic is coming."

Chapter 6

USARIC Animal Compound
Sector Z118 - Medix

Handax stormed across the metal veterinary walkway. The fluorescent bulbs emitted a white light that was initially blinding to those who'd never been inside before.

A distinct waft of something very familiar crept under his nostrils - like that of a hospital.

"Right, is this the place?" Handax turned to Moses' guard. "Is it?"

"Yes, this is where they keep them."

"Good," Handax turned to Leif and Moses. "Now, no messing around. Once we're in, we grab what we can. We're looking for the release mechanism."

"Release mechanism?" asked the first guard, who nearly soiled himself. "What are you going—"

"—Shut up," Handax spat in the man's face and removed his balaclava, "You don't say a goddamn word, you hear me?"

"No, don't show me your face."

"Hey," Handax grabbed the first guard's chin and turned his face to his own. "Look at me. Remember my face, USARIC scumbag."

"Okay."

"*We* are going in there and doing what we need to do. Who's in charge at Medix right now?"

"Wool ar-Ban."

"Don't lie to me," Handax slapped the guard's face and

tightened the grip no his chin, "ar-Ban is on Beta along with the others. For the last time of asking, who's in charge? Give me a name."

The guard knew he had two options. He could tell his captor the name of Wool's replacement, or head butt a bullet.

"Her name is Katcheena."

"What a stupid name. How many people are in the compound?"

"I dunno, maybe twenty or thirty?"

"That many?" Handax pushed the man against the sliding door, "We need your palm print. Take your glove off."

The guard did as he was told.

"Hanny?" Leif asked. "You want us to keep our guests, here, on display?"

"I want these two cowards front and center. Use them as body shields."

"Oh, no..." the second guard burst into tears, "Please d-don't—"

"—Stop crying," Leif lowered her gun in an attempt to calm the man down, "As long as you do what we say, you'll be fine."

"B-But I d-don't want—"

"—Bluergh, waaah," Handax interrupted in severe mockery mode. "I don't wanna die," he finished and returned to his usual, venomous state. "Try telling that to the poor animals you bastards have locked up in there."

Moses took this opportunity to play the hard man. "Yeah, shut the hell up."

Handax turned to him. "Moses?"

"Yeah?"

"Be quiet."

Handax turned to the first guard and grabbed his bare hand, "We good?"

"Yes."

He grabbed the back of the guard's hand and slammed his palm against the glass plate. The door flew open, inviting them inside the compound. Handax turned to Moses and Leif. "If they run, shoot them. I reckon we have about two minutes. Someone is bound to set off the alarm."

"Let's do it," Moses jammed the barrel of his gun against the first guard's head and walked in with him. Leif did the same with her guard.

Handax pulled his balaclava over his head and thumped the guard on his back. "Let's go."

Handax entered the room and took a look around. A vast laboratory about the size of a football stadium.

Dozens of medicians in white coats busied themselves at their computers to his immediate left. None of them saw him or his colleagues enter the compound.

To the right, a series of metal cages containing dozens of chimpanzees. Many of them hopped around and made a noise. The rest were asleep or covering their ears as they tried to get comfortable.

Dead ahead of them was the main console. A woman with red-rimmed glasses attended to the control bank. On the far wall behind her stood three doors.

USARIC medicians swarmed the place. It was hard to know where to start.

BLAM!

He fired a shot into the ceiling. It startled everyone in the room. They turned in fright to see a masked Moses and Leif threatening to kill the security guards. "Good people, can I have your attention please?"

The medicians held their breath and threw their arms up in total and utter surrender. The woman with the red-rimmed glasses dropped her clipboard to the ground in shock. "Oh, my word."

"Now, I know this looks weird," Handax held out his arms and clutched his gun tighter than ever. "I can assure you we are not here to hurt anybody. In order to make sure none of you hit the alarm, I'm gonna need you all to get on the floor. Nice and slowly—"

The cheering and hollering from the caged chimpanzees threatened to overwhelm Handax's statement.

"—Would you shut up, please."

They wouldn't shut up - they were chimps. If anything, the fact that a stranger had made contact with them exacerbated their excitement all the more.

"They're chimpanzees," said the woman with the red-rimmed glasses hit a button on the console. "Leave them alone."

Pssscccchhhhh...

Handax swung his gun at the woman. "What did I just say?"

"It's not an alarm, look," she said, nodding at the chimp cages. A soft, pinkish gas emanated from the seams in the wall. One by one, the more excitable creatures slowed down and fell asleep. "I'm just quietening them down."

"That pink stuff doesn't hurt them, does it?"

"It's absolutely harmless."

"You better not be lying to me," Handax hopped over the bench in front of him and reached the woman. "USARIC's track record in truth-telling department isn't exactly one hundred percent, is it?"

The woman squinted at Handax. "I can assure you, they are perfectly fine." She couldn't see past the balaclava. Inside, she was puzzled. She felt the need to keep an exterior air of confidence for the sake of her team. "Who are you?"

"It doesn't matter who I am," he said, clocking her USARIC name badge. "Consider me a freedom fighter. *Katcheena Brooks.*"

She turned her head away, angry at Handax's intrusion on her person.

"Why are you wearing glasses?" He removed them from her face. The wired rims had no lenses in them.

"I like them."

Handax chuckled, "Do you think they make you look intelligent?"

"—Hey," Moses screamed from the door to the compound. He caught a medician reaching for the alarm button under her desk. "You. Get down on the floor or I'll blow your damn head off your shoulders. Do it."

Close to tears, the medician fanned her arms across the floor and sobbed against the tiled floor.

"Moses," Handax called out, feeling a little sorry for her, "Come on, man."

"She was going for the alarm, you know."

"Just keep your gun on the guard."

Moses turned his gun on his captive and thumped him on the arm. "Trying to distract me."

Handax dropped Katcheena's glasses on the floor and nodded over at Moses. "I'll cut straight to the chase, Katcheena. My friend over there is going to absorb USARIC's data. My other friend and I are going to release all the animals."

Katcheena burst out laughing. "Oh, really?"

"Yeah. *Really*," Handax jammed the barrel of his gun into her temple. He found her strange laughter puzzling, "And if you don't do exactly as we say, I'm going to paint a pretty little death smile on your pretty little face."

Katcheena's flippant reaction was met with dumbfounded reaction from her many colleagues.

"I don't think so," she turned to her frightened crew and screamed at the top of her lungs. "Everyone, follow the agreed-upon course of action."

She thumped the red button on the console, setting off the security alarms. The white walls turned blood red from the spinning cascade of the emergency lights.

Handax shot Katcheena in the shin and kicked her against the console, "Stupid woman. Where are the animals?"

Her colleagues tore across the room and made for the opened emergency exits.

Leif and Moses didn't know whether to take potshots at the fleeing USARIC medicians, or train their guns on their captives.

"Handax, what do we do?" Leif called out over the screaming and crying.

"Shut up, I'm thinking."

"Handax? *People Against Animal Cruelty* Handax Skill?" Katcheena went for her bleeding leg, trying to fight off the urge to faint. "Just kill me, you dumb animal-botherer. I'm telling you nothing."

"I mean it," Handax pointed his gun at her chest. "Tell me where they are."

"Never," Katcheena's eyelids closed slowly as she

slumped off the console and hit the ground. Handax watched the last of the medicians barrel through the door to freedom.

"Damn it," he screamed over the alarm and waved Moses over to the console. "Do it. Now."

"On it," Moses made a dash for the console and unfastened his shirt sleeve.

"How long to absorb the records?"

"Depends on their interface," Moses lifted the plastic cover from the flat screen on the deck, "Last check, they're storing fifteen terabytes of data so, maybe, two minutes?"

"Get on it," Handax watched Moses press his forearm to the screen.

"Cee-Cee, connect," Moses yelled at his arm as the ink reformed into three lines. "N-Gage. Four, five, seven."

"N-Gage connection complete," advised the calm female console voice, "Commencing data download."

"We're in."

Handax and Moses shared a brief smile. Something resembling victory was forthcoming - as long as they got out in time.

"Hey, babes," Handax shouted at Leif, who kept her gun on the two security guards from behind. "Take care of those two and come help me break these doors down."

"Sure."

BLAM-BLAM!

She shot each guard in the back of their right leg. Both men wailed in pain and dropped to their knees, clutching their wounds.

Moses raised his eyebrows in shock at what she'd done.

"What are you doing?" Handax shouted over the alarm. "I meant tie them up, not shoot them."

"Tie them up with what?" Leif bolted towards him. "I don't have any ties."

Handax grabbed her hand and pulled her across the console. She jumped to her feet and ran with him to the three doors on the far wall.

"That was unnecessary. You didn't have to injure them."

"They're only human. It doesn't matter."

"Guys," Moses hollered after them, effectively chained to

the console by his forearm. "The data's downloading. I dunno what you have planned, but whatever it is, make it fast."

Handax turned to the first door and aimed his firearm at the handle. "Stand back!"

KERR-ASH!

The door burst off its hinges, leading into the second compound. A pungent smell of death greeted Handax as Leif followed him into the frosty cryo-chamber.

"Ugh. What's that smell?"

"Smells like rancid butter," Leif stepped forward and accidentally knocked Handax's heel. "Ugh, I think I'm gonna be sick."

The lights fizzed to life and illuminated the contents of the small room. Leif's face fell when she peered from behind her hand. "Oh my God."

Handax took a look around and felt his soul machete through his chest and run away from his body, "I don't believe it."

More cages. But this time, stuffed to the brim with animal carcasses. Most of them had tails and were long dead.

"No, this is a mistake. This can't be right."

One of the in-built storage units caught his attention. He slid the compartment out and stared at the gray feline carcass inside it. One of the lucky ones, by all accounts.

He lifted its hind leg. What was once a Russian Blue was no more. Attached to its foot was a tag with a name written on it.

Bisoubisou Gagarin

"Bisoubisou?" Handax muttered. "But she's—"

"—She's on Opera Beta?" Leif interrupted. "Has been for nearly two years."

"Guys," Moses hollered from the central control unit, "I'm nearly done. Get ready to get the hell out of here."

The illness Leif felt in the pit of her stomach was hard to take. Handax lowered the cat's hind leg as gently as he could to the surface of the cage. "She never went."

"I hate USARIC," Leif freaked out and thumped the cage, inadvertently shuffling the carcasses around, "We were supposed to set them free. How can we set them free when they're all dead?"

"Calm down," Handax took her by the shoulders and tried to shake her back to reality. "Leif, please."

"They're all dead. USARIC killed them all."

"Leif, you're hysterical. Calm down and listen to me."

"Let go of me, I have to rescue the animals." She pushed him back and darted out of the room.

Moses looked over at her running towards the second door. "Leif, what are you doing?"

"I'm going to rescue whatever's behind that second door," she aimed her gun at the door handle and blasted it with her gun.

BLAM!

Handax chased after her with trepidation, "Leif, don't go in there. You don't know what you'll—"

"—No, Handax. I'm going in."

He closed his eyes and allowed her to carry out her quest.

A series of cages housed more than a hundred cats in the second enclosed compound. They howled at Leif as she entered the room, each of them vying for her attention.

"Oh my God," Leif clapped her hands together in delight. "They're here."

Handax bolted into the room after her and took a look around. "Oh, *wow*."

A torrent of 'meows' flew from the cages, each and every one of them desperate for freedom.

"What are they doing here?" Leif asked. "Why is USARIC keeping them?"

SNARL ... SNASH ... HISS!

Two of the caged cats displayed their frustration at having been kept holed up in their metal cells.

"I dunno," Handax scoured the room and attempted to count the felines on display, "There must be a switch or something that releases them all. It'd take forever to open them one by one."

"Hey, little guys," she approached the cages and addressed the wailing felines, "It's okay. We're here to set you free."

Leif clamped eyes with a white American bobtail who seemed happy to see her, "Hey, gorgeous. What's your name?"

"Meow."

Handax looked around the room for the release switch. "I can't find anything here. The cages are bolted shut. No individual releases. I'll check with Moses."

"Okay," Leif didn't turn around to see Handax run out of the room. She focused her attention on the fluffy white creature and read the name on the tag attached to her leg.

"Fluffy? Ha. Figures, you sure *are* fluffy."

"Meow."

Fluffy ran the side of her face against the metal bars.

"Why are they keeping you here, Fluffy? What's going on, pet?"

"Meow."

Handax hopped up to the control bank while Moses absorbed the data from the control panel. The inked loading bar on his forearm snailed toward the crook of his elbow. "Careful, man. Don't knock me or you'll sever the connection."

"How's the transfer going?"

"I figure sixty seconds or so. Security are gonna be here any minute, now. We gotta get ready to run."

"We gotta find that release switch," Handax perused the console like a madman, "I'm not leaving those cats in there."

"Cats?"

"Hundreds of them," Handax said. "All caged up."

"Ugh," Katcheena spluttered from the floor, slowly waking up. Her leg bled a storm across the floor, "Ugh."

Both Moses and Handax looked down at her.

"She's seen better days, hasn't she?"

Handax snorted, knowing full well that she was an unfortunate casualty of her employer's war. "We'll get her help when we get what we want. How long, now?"

Moses looked up at the panel and eyed the absorption bar. "Less than a minute. I hope."

"You'll... you'll..." Katcheena tried through her bloodied mouth.

"We'll what?" Handax asked, put-out by her drama.

"You'll never get out alive."

"That's as maybe, but as long as the animals do, we don't care."

By now, everyone had gotten used to the screaming alarms.

Handax crouched down and felt Katcheena's neck, "I reckon you have about two minutes before you bleed out."

Defiant, she spat in his face, "Go to hell."

He duly ignored her instruction and wiped the phlegm from his face. "You can make this right, Katcheena. Tell me where the release switch is."

"Never."

"Suit yourself," Handax rose to his feet and hollered at the second compound door. "Leif, get out of there."

Leif ran out of the room and up to Moses and Handax. "Yeah, what's up?" She spotted the bleeding security guards screaming for their lives by the main door.

"Katcheena, here, won't tell us where the release switch is. It must be here somewhere, judging by the look on her face *lift*."

"How *dare* you," she retaliated and pressed her fingertips to her cheeks. The oily, plastic skin pushed around her skull, "I have not had a face lift."

"Keep telling yourself that, sweetheart," Moses nodded at a green button on the control deck, "Try that one."

"No, don't press that," Katcheena cried. "It's the fire alarm, you'll soak us all."

Handax looked at her dead in the eyes. "Really?"

"Yes, really," she insisted. "The whole place will flood. If we don't run, we'll drown."

"I guess it'll release the cages if that were to happen, won't it?" Moses kept an eye on his forearm. Hundreds of little black dots formed across his skin. "That would be a mighty shame. For you."

"Ugghh," Katcheena rolled around the floor in pain and clutched at her bullet wound, "Don't press it. Please, don't press it."

Handax and Leif shot each other a knowing glance.

"Leif?"

"Yeah, babe?"

"Hit the green button."

"You got it," she thumped the button and turned to face the second compound.

SCHTANG-SCHTANG-SCHTANG!

The cage doors burst open one by one and released the one-hundred-strong tidal wave of furry felines to the ground. They tumbled, shrieked and scratched their way into the central compound area.

"Run, my darlings," Leif pointed to the main door, "Over there. Run, run, run."

Fluffy, the white American bobtail, led the charge. A huge variety of cats chased after her as they dispersed around the console.

"No, no," Katcheena screamed at the top of her lungs. "What have you done? They're not ready for release—"

"—We're only doing what USARIC claims to be doing,' Handax shouted at her. 'Maintaining their welfare."

"You idiots. You don't know what you've done."

A few cats became fascinated by the workstation's swivel chairs. They spun them around, and dug their claws into the upholstery.

"Gaaah," Ketcheena screamed as the influx of furry little felines descended upon her. "Get away from me."

SCRATCH! GNASH!

Twenty-six cats tore away at Katcheena's work suit and face, tearing her clothes to shreds and much of the skin from her face.

"Meow," one particularly vicious cat who resembled Jelly Anderson clawed at her eyes, hungry for revenge.

"That's one furious pussy, right there," Moses gasped at the attack and turned to his forearm, "Nearly done."

"Good," Handax watched as the majority of the cats

storm through the entrance and into the corridor, "They're going."

Leif pointed at the far wall in haste, "The third door?"

"No time for that, now—" Handax caught sight of the door leading to the corridor. Furious gunfire, followed by screeching from some of the felines, rattled along the walls and into the compound. "Oh, *no*."

Just then, twenty-odd cats ran back into the room, trying to hide from danger.

"Someone's coming,' Handax yelled. 'Someone's coming."

Moses kept his forearm held to the plate. "I need more time."

"No, there's no time," Handax grabbed Moses' shoulders, "Security's coming. There's only one way out."

"If we're going to die, I'm taking as many of those bastards with me," Leif lifted her firearm and pointed it at the corridor.

The returning cats fanned out around the room and took refuge behind the chairs and desks.

"Security breach in Sector Z118," a stern-sounding voice thundered down the tunnel, "Shoot to kill."

"Forget that," Handax slid the machine gun Moses had confiscated from the security guard from his shoulder, "Mind if I borrow this?"

"Hold them off till I'm done," Moses reached into his belt for his hand gun with his free, right hand. He aimed it at the door and kept an eye on the absorption process. "Twenty seconds. I'm right here with you."

The sound of charging footsteps grew louder and louder.

Leif hid behind the console and held her gun in both hands. Handax inadvertently stepped on Katcheena's glasses, crunching them against the ground. "Whoops." He slid across the console deck, crouched behind the chair and aimed the machine gun at the door. "Ready, guys?"

"Oh, yeah," Moses held his hand gun at the corridor. "Let's give 'em hell."

"Leif," Handax shouted over the console. "Protect Moses till he's done transferring."

Leif cocked her weapon and knocked the side of her head

against the console, enjoying the adrenaline rush. "You got it, babes."

"Here they come."

A USARIC mercenary ran into the room, ready to open fire with his USARIC-issue machine gun. He took a look around and saw Moses in the middle of the room with his arm pressed to the console plate.

BLAM!

Moses fired a shot at the mercenary. "S'up?" The bullet smoked in the wall a few inches to the right of the man's head. He saw the barrel of Moses' handgun facing him. "The next bullet won't be so kind, my friend."

"Okay, okay," the mercenary unhooked the gun from his shoulder and set it to the floor, "Don't shoot."

"Get on the floor and lie down, face-first."

"Whatever you say."

The mercenary carefully placed his chest on the floor. In doing so, he caught sight of Leif and Handax hiding behind the console. To his left, dozens of scared kitties peered from behind the chairs and desks.

"How many cats got out?" asked the mercenary.

"A few. I don't know," Moses said. "Now it's your turn to answer my question. How many of you scumbags are coming?"

"Dozens. We've been ordered to shoot—"

"—Shut up."

"They're already here," the mercenary said.

"What?"

The mercenary pushed himself onto his back and reached into his boot strap. "Advance. One on the console, and two behind the deck."

"Huh?" Moses double-took as everything slowed-down to a crashing halt. "What the—"

The mercenary pulled out a Rez-9 from his boot and fired at Moses. The charge hit him in the shoulder, breaking the skin and sending a charge down his body.

Handax closed his eyes, hearing a bunch of footsteps enter the room. "Okay, now."

He jumped up from behind the console and fired off a round of bullets at the USARIC militia.

Thraa-a-tat-a-tat!

Seven armed mercenaries returned fire, their random bullets smashing the furniture and walls to pieces.

Leif screamed and launched herself sideways, firing at them. Her bullets caught two USARIC militia in their legs. They dropped their weapons to the ground and screamed blue murder.

"Reloading," Handax unbolted a side magazine from the machine gun's housing and thumped it into the grip.

"Come out, now," screamed a USARIC mercenary as bits of the console pinged and burst apart from the gunfire.

"No. Put down your weapons," Handax screamed as he witnessed Leif try her luck. She launched her behind onto the console and blasted ten successive shots at the five remaining USARIC mercenaries, hitting two of them in the chest. The latter of them swung his arm to the console and pulled the trigger.

BAMM-SCHPLATT!

Leif's forehead opened out like a flower as the bullet careened through her skull, killing her instantly. The back of her head thumped against the console. Her dead eyes stared at Handax as her grip loosened on her firearm.

"Leif, no," he screamed and hulked the machine gun over the console, yanking on the trigger, "Die, you scumbags."

Pow-pow-pow-pow-click-click-click-click.

Blind-firing got him two kills on the spot, leaving two injured USARIC mercs to back away from their fallen colleagues.

Handax threw the empty machine gun aside and reached for his handgun. He daren't peer up from the console for fear of getting hit in the face by a stray bullet.

He slowed his breathing in a futile attempt to decelerate his heartbeat - the organ in question ready to jump up through his throat and shoot through his mouth.

"Is that all of them?" asked one of the mercenaries.

"I think so. That guy on the console. Headshot on the girl."

"Good. Check the corners and clear the area."

Handax kicked himself against the back of the console and checked his gun. He was so close to hyperventilating and giving himself away.

"What do we do about these damn cats?" a mercenary pointed to the petrified kitties cowering behind the debris.

"They'll be here in ninety seconds. Mark the area as clear, then we execute."

"No, no, no, no—" Handax whispered through the sweat forming on his lips. He turned to his left and saw a congregation of terrified cats look to him for rescue.

Clomp, clomp, clomp...

"Oh, God..." Handax knew it was a matter of seconds before the mercenary found him hiding. He took a final breath and booted the chair next to him away from the console. It provided a distraction as he jumped out from behind the console and unloaded his magazine.

BANG-BANG-BANG!

The approaching mercenary opened fire on the chair without compromise. The bullets tore through it, breaking it into sections across the ground.

Handax spotted his opportunity. He slid over the console and blasted the man in the back, busting his shoulder apart. The mercenary dropped the gun and hit the floor, dead.

"Oh, *God*. Moses," Handax saw Moses' corpse sprawled across the console. By his sneakers, Leif's body had fallen to the ground. Both his friends were dead. "I... I..."

"—Sucks, doesn't it?" came a voice.

"Huh?" Handax double-took and turned to a mercenary chuckling to himself at the entrance. He'd lost his weapon and wasn't quick enough to reach the discarded firearm on the floor.

"Wh-what?"

"Both your friends, there. Dead. And then you go and kill one of mine."

"But, but—"

"—I guess that's your buddy barbecuing out on the airfield, too, right?

Handax didn't know how to respond. He stood still,

flummoxed, and lifted his gun at the man's face. He wondered why the mercenary wasn't firing at him.

"You're not going to shoot me," the mercenary said. "Do you know why?"

Handax's nerves got the better of him. He could barely keep the gun up. The anxiety reflected in his voice when he spoke. "No, why?"

"Because there's only one way out for you. And that's in a body bag with your friends. And, of course, all these furry little turds."

"What..." Handax closed his eyes and shook away the sweat. "What is USARIC doing with these cats?"

"I dunno. Who cares," the mercenary kicked himself away from the wall and approached the console. "I don't ask questions. USARIC pays my wage and I get to feed my family. Do you know what they're paying me to do, now?"

"What?" Handax kept his pathetic hold on the man as he got nearer.

"Kill you stone dead," he smiled in the face of execution and nodded at Handax's gun, "You gonna use that on me?"

Handax glanced at the shaking cats and created a compromise, "Will you let me go if I walk out of here?"

"Your two buddies did it. I never saw you. You're wearing a mask. "

Handax thought over the offer for a few seconds. Freedom beckoned.

"Go on, get out of here."

Handax kept his gun aimed at the man and gripped the top of his balaclava with his free hand.

"Hey, no. What are you doing? Don't show me your—"

Off came the balaclava, revealing Handax's tear-strewn face.

The mercenary thumped his fists together in a state of fury, "You imbecile. I've seen you, now."

"Yeah, you know what this means. Don't you?"

The mercenary held up his hands in shock, "You don't have to do this, you know."

"I *have* to do this."

BLAM!

Handax shot the mercenary in the chest, killing him. He blinked a few times and attempted to process what he'd done. "I can't run," he muttered and accepted his fate. He turned to the cats, "But it means *you guys* can. Go on. Get out of here. Quick."

The cats stood looking at him, suspended in disbelief.

"Don't just stand there staring at me, you morons. Run."

Still no response. Any moment now, USARIC would breach the compound and terminate anything turning oxygen into carbon dioxide without question.

Handax did what he had to do. It was for their own good. He ran at them barking like a dog as loud as he could, "Woof, woof!"

The cats shrieked and jumped into the air. Most of them bolted toward the door and down the corridor.

"Go on. Go, go," he shouted after them and waved the few that remained toward the door. He stomped forward, acting the violent beast, "Grrr."

The final few startled kitties chased after their counterparts and vacated the compound, leaving a thoroughly disheveled Handax to take a deep breath.

Leif and Moses were dead.

Handax would join them thirty seconds from now. He stepped up to the console and lifted Moses' left arm. The absorption process was close to completion. The data that had successfully transferred was useless in the body of a dead man.

Handax carefully set his friend's arm to the console and took a seat in the chair. He rolled up his sleeve and swiped the three inked lines across his forearm.

"Individimedia, access. Enable broadcast. Handax T. Skill."

The ink formed a row of dots across his skin. His thumbnail lit up a soft green and pink, throwing a shaft of light at his face.

A screech of tires slamming to a halt barreled from the far end of the corridor. The worry vacated his mind. He looked at his forearm and moved his thumb to allow the light emission to reach his eyes.

"This is Handax Skill from P.A.A.C, People Against Animal Cruelty. I hope someone is watching. We take responsibility for the assassination of Dimitri Vasilov. We breached the animal compound at USARIC's headquarters at Cape Claudius, which is where I am broadcasting from.

"If it moves, shoot it," a voice shouted form within the corridor.

Handax continued his last will and testament into his forearm. "I know someone out there is watching. What USARIC has done is unforgivable. What we found when we breached the compound is even worse…"

The footsteps grew louder and louder, as did the angry shouting of orders to kill everything on sight.

"Remy Gagarin's cat, Bisoubisou, never boarded Opera Beta. We found her body at the compound along with hundreds of others. Those we found alive we set free. USARIC has killed three of my team. Moses, Denny, and Leif. They'll deny it, of course. They'll claim they went missing and have no involvement. In a matter of seconds, I'll be joining them."

"Over there," yelled an umpteenth USARIC mercenary as he entered the room, "Hey, you. Put your arms above your head and drop to your knees."

Handax obliged the official and faced his forearm, still broadcasting, "Can you hear that? Here they are, look."

He tilted his forearm forward, displaying a dozen USARIC mercs looking back at him with their weapons drawn. In that very moment, Handax's broadcast evolved into a live feed for his inevitable execution.

Chrome Valley
Northwest London, United Kingdom

One viewer who saw Handax's Individimedia broadcast was seven-year-old Jamie Anderson, who watched the events play out on a holographic image in his bedroom.

"Handax? Is that *you*?" Jamie muttered in astonishment.

Upside-down footage of the heavily armed USARIC mercenaries greeted the viewer.

"We will not lie down until USARIC reverses its decision to use animals for space exploration," Handax's voice emitted over the broadcast as the image lowered to the ground. He'd dropped to his knees.

The first mercenary hooked his finger around the trigger of his gun, "Hey, *blue hair*. Are you broadcasting?"

"Death to human scum who practice inhumane—"

"—Stop that Individimedia broadcast, right now!" ordered the mercenary.

Handax squeezed his eyes shut and yelled at the top of his lungs. "Death to human scum who practice inhumane treatment of animals—"

BANG-BANG-BANG-THUMP!

Jamie shrieked and held his hands over his mouth as the point-of-view of the live feed crashed to the floor. Not seeing the violence play out on the footage was much worse than seeing it. Handax's arm slapped to the floor, offering viewers a front-row ticket to a first-person death.

Jamie Anderson's mind went into overdrive. He stared at the screen, open-jawed and traumatized. After a moment or two, he turned to his opened bedroom door, "Mom!"

Chapter 7

Botanix
Space Opera Beta - Level Three

"I don't get it. I saw Haloo die *right in front of me*. On the operating table. No pulse, nothing."

Jaycee's suspicion didn't subside as the crew approached Botanix. The door had been shattered - the result of an explosion.

He vented his frustration quietly, and confidently. He kept his grip on Tor's Decapidisc, forcing the man forward, "Ain't that right, Russian?"

"I don't know," Tor said.

"Yeah. You don't know very much, do you?"

"Whatever that pink stuff is, it's done no lasting damage," Tripp whispered back. "You *think* you saw her die. But you're no medician."

Wool glanced at Tripp as they approached the door to Botanix. "Well, I *am* a medician, and something isn't right, here."

Haloo reached the door and ran her palm over Jelly's head. "Look, girl. We're here."

"Meow," Jelly shuffled around in her arms, wanting to get down. Haloo wouldn't release her. Instead, she kissed Jelly on the head and looked into her orange eyes.

"Are you ready, honey?"

"Mwaah," Jelly's saw something in Haloo's face that

terrified her. She squealed and jumped out of her arms, landing paws-first to the floor, "Meow."

She made a bee line for Wool's legs and took refuge behind them.

"Hey, girl. What's up?"

Jelly whined and tilted her head up to Wool. The cat's inner-suit had split across her two front arms.

"You've damaged your suit, girl," she crouched to her knees and held Jelly's arm, "How did that happen—?"

"—She's grown, Wool," Haloo smiled, held out her hand and threatened to press the panel on the wall. "She's growing."

"Growing?" Wool collected Jelly in her arms and inspected her suit.

The underside, covering the belly, had torn at the seams. Her two hind legs bulged through the legs of the suit. Even the stitched named tag - *J. Anderson* - hung from the material.

"She's gotten heavier."

"What's going on, Haloo?" Tripp was ready to take out his gun. He saw that Jaycee was already a few steps ahead of him in that respect.

"Oh," Haloo giggled palmed the panel, "It's okay, don't be nervous. Something fantastic is coming."

"Yeah, you keep saying that," Jaycee squeezed the handle on his K-SPARK, "It's not helping."

"Good people of Opera Beta. I have something fantastic to show you."

The door to Botanix slid open.

A thunderous draught flew along the walkway and shot through the door, carrying whatever remained of the pink mist with it.

In the distance a chorus of classical music wailed around. Quite unusual for Botanix. Haloo usually liked it quiet and peaceful in there, being the crew's botanist.

Haloo's hair lifted and rippled across her shoulders as she embraced the opened door, "Come, see," she said as she drifted into the brilliant white light.

Tor took a deep breath and tilted his head. He was

greeted by the metal disc housed around his neck. "You're not going to follow her, are you?"

"She seems to know what's going on," Tripp said. "It's a room full of plants and fresh water—"

"—Correction, Tripp," Jaycee interrupted, taking a step back, defying all reason to enter the chamber. "It *was* a room full of water and plants until that bomb went off. How do we know it's not contaminated?"

Tripp considered the facts and pulled out his Rez-9. "Good point. You stay here with Tor. Make sure he doesn't run off. Wool?"

"Yes, Tripp?"

"We'll go in and see what Haloo's got to say. We'll take Jelly with us."

"Okay," Wool double-checked the proposal with Jelly. She did this by smiling at her face, waiting for as positive a reaction as a human could expect from a cat. Jelly licked Wool's glove, excitedly.

"Okay," Tripp thumped Jaycee on the back, forgetting that his exo-suit was made of much stronger stuff than flesh and bone. "Ah, damn."

"What did you do that for?" Jaycee asked, failing to get the joke.

"Just trying to be friendly."

"Well don't," Jaycee snapped. "Just get in and get out."

"We'll be right back, as they say."

"No, don't say that," Jaycee huffed. "Don't say *anything*. Just go in there and get the hell out."

"Yes, good idea."

Jaycee yanked Tor's Decapidisc around, ensuring it caused the man a healthy amount of discomfort, "If you're not back in three minutes, I'm coming in there all guns blazing and leaving this headless piece of crap to paint the floor red. Is that acceptable, Captain?"

Tripp stared at the opened door, thinking over his response. "Yes, very good. Wool, let's go."

He waved Wool - and Jelly - along with him. Seconds later, they disappeared into the haze of white light...

***

They expected to see a ruined Botanix. Initially, that's what they saw.

Rows of plants stood before them in various states of charcoaled destruction.

Wool looked to the left. Jelly's sectioned-off area in the corner sat relatively unscathed from bomb's blast.

"Some damage done. Seems we can salvage a lot of it," Wool turned to Tripp and gasped. "Tripp?"

He stared dead-ahead, eyes bulging, unable to speak. She turned her head forward and saw what he was marveling at.

"Oh... my... *God*," she exclaimed. "It's... *beautiful*."

Jelly turned her head. A puzzled expression on her face formed, along with her two humans.

"Good people," Haloo's voice chimed around them, "Welcome to *life*."

The immediate vicinity of Botanix was as it always was. The walls, however, broke apart like a shattered toy fifty feet ahead of them.

The rows of plants subsided, adjacent to the walls.

The second half - the farthest from Tripp, Wool and Jelly - transformed into a magnificent utopia.

A blue sky with white clouds and flying birds. Where the ground sunk, a glorious beach front, complete with crystal white sand ran all the way up to the horizon.

Looking down, they saw the water filtration system pumping its wares into a beautiful lake of sparkling blue water.

Even the air was a pleasure to breathe.

Tripp closed his eyes and took in a lungful. "It's heaven." He exhaled slowly and rubbed his face, ensuring he wasn't stuck in the middle of a particularly comforting dream.

Wool walked forward with Jelly in her hands, wanting to involve herself further. "Did we die? Is this *heaven*?"

"No, this isn't heaven," Tripp whispered in quiet ecstasy. He walked alongside Wool, steadily approaching the end of the burnt plants. The glistening white sand crunched below their boots with every step, "Where are we?"

Haloo moved in front of them with a glorious grin on her face. She held her hand out, introducing the pair to the perfect rendition of life awaiting them.

"Where are we, Haloo?"

"Welcome… to *Pink Symphony*," Haloo moved her hand to the sprawling ocean to their left, "Where everything began. And where everything will end."

Tripp fell to his knees in utter awe. He cupped the lukewarm sand in his hands and let it waterfall through his fingers.

All the blemishes and varicose veins that had formed through years of service in the American Star Fleet fell with it. A thorough and vital rejuvenation.

Jelly was less impressed. Her whiskers buzzed to life, as did her infinity claws. She dug them into the fabric of Wool's inner-suit, "Meow."

"Whoa, Jelly."

The cat landed on the sand, finding it a little too hot for comfort. She bolted toward Haloo in a haze of fury.

"Hey, girl," Haloo kept smiling and opened her arms. "Come to me. I have a gift for you. You like gifts, don't you?"

"Hissss."

Jelly kicked a bunch of sand into the air as she skidded on her claws. She had no intention of going anywhere near the woman.

"Oh," Haloo pulled a dramatic and sad face. "Don't you love me, anymore?"

"Hisss."

Jelly bushed her tail and flapped it around in circles, certain that danger was close by.

Haloo fell to her knees and wept. Quite the theatrical performance, she began muttering to herself as if she was speaking to someone else, "But I tried. Really, I did."

"Maaah," Jelly knuckled down and sat on her hind legs ten feet away from Haloo. She took no pity on the poor woman.

"What's she doing?" Wool turned her attention to a giant tree shooting up a hundred feet or so from the center of the ocean. "And what's that?"

Streaks of pink lightning streaked across the sky as Haloo continued muttering to herself through her sobs. "She's here, now. She's here."

The light breeze turned into a gale. The clouds bleached across the perfect sky like spilled paint hitting a canvas.

"Aww, no," Haloo fell sideways to the sand and lifted her hands to her face. "Please, leave me to die in peace. Haven't I done enough?"

"Haloo?" Tripp stepped forward in an attempt to help her. Jelly scowled at him and forced him to stop. "Jelly?"

The cat heaved and spluttered tearing the rip in her inner-suit apart. "Traaah... Traaah..."

"What's going on, girl?" Wool watched Jelly tumble to her side and claw at her inner-suit. She wanted out of it as quickly as possible.

Haloo screamed through her tears and grabbed her lips in each hand. "Gnaawww."

"Jesus Christ," Tripp held Wool back as the woman lifted her lip over her nose, coughing a plume of pink gas across the sand. "Gwaaar."

"Haloo," Wool squealed, unable to watch.

"Treeh," Jelly tore chunks of her inner-suit away with her claws in a feisty fit of anger. "Treep... Trep..."

Haloo's shoulders hulked several inches above the ground. Her head and her body below the abdomen hung, suspended, as her inner-suit broke away.

"My G-God," Tripp pushed Wool back. "Get back, get back. We need to get out of here."

Suddenly, a classical tune emitted from the tree in the middle of the ocean, catching their attention.

It billowed at an increasingly high volume - enough to fill the air. Four, simple chords, twice repeated.

Da-da-da-dum. Da... da... da... *dum.*

"What the hell?" Tripp shouted over the gale and the music.

"The tree is singing?" Wool snapped, not knowing which way to turn. "What's going on—"

Jelly squealed and shredded the last section of her suit. She sprang to her feet and exercised her infinity claws, wrenching them in and out.

She launched into the air and took two swipes at Haloo's levitating body as it rose toward the sky. Her titanium claw caught the woman's left ear and tore the skin.

"Waaah," Jelly screamed in a furious rage, unable to jump higher as Haloo's body tilted to a halt twenty feet in the air.

"Oh, Jesus," Tripp quipped. "Let's get back to Beta, *right now*."

"Jelly," Wool let out an ambitious, final call of hope that Jelly would return with them.

It fell on deaf, furry ears.

Jelly thudded to the floor, pushing grains of sand away from her. She howled at Wool, terrifying her.

"No, no, no," Wool threw Tripp's hand from her forearm. "I'm not leaving her here—"

Jelly roared, negating the desire to be rescued. She'd grown a few inches, more resembling an orange panther than the common, domesticated cat.

Her growl was near adolescent in nature. Even her face had matured.

Jelly Anderson was... *evolving*.

Tripp and Wool's attention was caught by a rumbling, buzzing noise shooting from the violent pinkish purple sky.

Haloo's chest broke apart and emitted a pink beam of light into the heavens. The back of her head hung down, pushing her chest upwards. It was as if her heart and soul tried to escape from her body.

"Take me," she screamed with a disconcertingly calm manner, "Take me home."

The pink beam blasting from her body thickened and ruptured, seeming to imitate the launch of a spacecraft.

Her knees broke, flinging her legs behind her ass. The back of her head recoiled under the small of her back, snapping her body in two and shattering the bones.

Then, the beam carried her body into the sky and crashed to a close into an electric storm of thunder with the clouds.

Jelly shrieked at the light show and ran toward the ocean in a fit of anger.

Tripp and Wool didn't stick around to watch the

unnatural event. They bolted across the sand, backtracking across their original footsteps.

The sand turned from hard ground into scattered mud. Rows of blackened plants and tiled walls appeared beside them.

The fluorescent lighting in Botanix crept along the floor.

"The door, quick," Tripp pulled Wool along and darted for the opened door. As they gained on the rectangular structure, Tripp covered her from behind and pushed her through the door to Botanix.

"Tripp," Jaycee lifted his shotgun and aimed it at the door, "What the hell's going on out there?"

"It's a long story," Tripp spat as he ran through the plants and thumped his fist against the panel on the wall.

SCHUNT.

The door slid shut, cutting Opera Beta off from whatever that place was beyond the door.

Tripp caught his breath and coughed up a storm. Wool paced around, trying not to emote. She held her chest, hoping her heart wouldn't grow limbs, climb up her throat and jump out of her mouth, "I feel sick."

"What happened out there?" Jaycee stomped his foot to the floor and thumped Tor on the back for some semblance of satisfaction. "Where's Anderson?"

"No time to explain," Tripp turned to the door and hit the glass, making damn sure nothing could get in - or out. He spun around and pushed past Tor. "You."

"Me?" Tor asked.

"Yes, you," he said, pushing Tor forward by the shoulders. "We need to get Manuel back online right now. Let's go. Come on."

"Okay, okay."

Wool chased after Tripp as he stormed off, "Where are we going?"

"The flight deck. It's time for some answers."

Jaycee kicked Tor along the corridor and showed him his glove. He delighted in threatening to activate his Decapidisc, "Speaking of answers, can you tell me what happened out there?"

For the first time in his career, Tripp felt that his crew might not believe his next statement.

"The dumb bomb Baldron threw into Botanix before we passed out?"

"Yeah?"

"It created a hole on the far wall and opened us up into a whole world of trouble."

"What trouble?" Tor tried.

Jaycee hit him on the back of the head. "Hey, idiot, *I'm* asking the questions here, okay? You're the convict who gets to shut up. Do you understand me?"

"Yes, I understand."

"Good," Jaycee spat. "What trouble, Tripp?"

Wool knew her captain wasn't in the mood for explaining as they turned the corner and made their way to the control deck.

"We've landed on another planet. Haloo said it was called Pink Symphony. Then, she, uh, died again."

"Died *again*?"

Tor started to sniff. "I'm s-scared."

"Shut up, Russian scum," Jaycee shouted in his ear, "Say one more word and you're dead."

"I'm sorry."

Jaycee, at the end of his tether, thumped the man on the back of the head to underscore his point. "And stop apologizing."

"I'm sor—"

"—Something strange happened to Jelly," Wool interjected, saving Tor from himself, "She went on the attack. She didn't want to come back with us. It was like she turned bad or something."

"Enough," Tripp entered the control deck. He pointed at Tor and then at the communications panel. "You, over here."

"Come on, sweetheart," Jaycee pushed Tor against the chair in front of the console. "Let's get to work."

Tripp scratched behind his ear and evaluated his orders before speaking them. "Okay, call up Manuel. He said something about us *not* being on Opera Beta. At first I thought he was mad but he might have been onto something."

"How can we trust him?" Tor asked.

An instant pang of irony stretching across Tripp's face, "That's rich coming from you."

"Look," Tor thumped the console in a fit of despair. "I'm just as scared—"

"—Do not speak back to me, okay? I am your captain—"

"—No," Tor screamed into Tripp's face, determined to have his say. He calmed soon as he realized that his wish was granted, and sat into the chair.

"I'm just as scared as you are. I don't know what's going on. If I stay here, I'm dead. If I go out there - wherever that place is - I'm dead. Run out of oxygen? Yeah, that could happen, or this hulking ignoramus will take my head off. In fact, even *if* we make it back home, I'll be arrested, tried and sentenced to death. I'm a mathematician. I figure the odds of being alive for much longer are about six million to one."

"The odds will be considerably worse if you don't reboot Manuel and get him to function," Tripp slapped Tor across the face and pointed at the console. "Do you understand what I've just said? *Russian?*"

Wool and Jaycee looked at each other for a response. Their captain was about to lose his mind once and for all.

"Yes, I understand."

"Good," Tripp moved his face into Tor's and stared him out. "One false move and it's all over. Do you understand?"

"Yes," Tor blurted, deeply upset. "I understand."

"I wasn't talking to you." Tripp rubbed Tor's hair like a child, and winked at Jaycee. "I was talking to *him.*"

Tor and Tripp looked at Jaycee's glove. He teased the button once again, "Just give me the word, Captain. Any excuse to press this button."

Tor cleared his throat and swallowed. He threw his arms forward and hit the live switch on the console. "In my country I am considered a hero. In the vacuum of space I am considered a traitor. A scumbag." He rose from his seat and snapped his fingers. "USARIC communications officer Tor Klyce, reboot autopilot four, five, seven—"

"—that's not even his real name," Jaycee whispered to Wool, trying to lighten the mood. She didn't laugh so much as roll her eyes.

"—Manuel, do you read me?" Tor finished and snapped his fingers.

"Yes, I read you."

WHVOOM.

Manuel's holographic book image sprang to life in the middle of the room. He rifled through his pages and floated over to Tor, "Good whenever-it-is. How are you?"

"I'm well, Manuel."

"No, *I'm* Manuel."

"No, I said *I am well*, not *I'm Manuel.*"

"I beg your pardon?" Manuel shuffled back, slamming his front and back covers together, trying to work out the joke. "I'm sorry, I don't understand—"

"—Never mind that," Tripp stepped in and watched the book float around the room. "How are you feeling, Manuel?"

"Full of the joys of a typical Spring day, Tripp. Yourself?"

"Good. He recognizes us, at least."

"Soul count returns a number I was not expecting," Manuel said.

"How many souls aboard Opera Beta?" Tor asked. "We're counting me, Tripp, Wool, and Jaycee. That should make four."

"I am expecting eight. Haloo Ess, Captain Daryl Katz, Miss Anderson and the series two Androgyne unit."

Tripp squinted at Manuel in confusion. "Eight? Do you know what happened to them?"

"I do not. I apologize," Manuel ruffled his pages and emitted four beeps. "I am in full operational order. Quite without anomaly."

"Without anomaly?" Jaycee shook his head and let out a chuckle of utter disdain. "You know stuff-all about what's happened to us."

"Hey, leave him alone," Tor said. "I don't know how much data was flushed to his disk before we went through Enceladus. I need to run a test on him. Try to pinpoint the exact time he failed to recollect—"

"—I am running a geo-scan on the ship," Manuel said. "But I cannot locate it."

Tripp turned to Tor and patted him on the shoulder. "See what I mean?"

"Wait. Let's run a test. Ask him something, anything, about an event prior to us going through Enceladus."

Tripp went quiet, thinking of a question to ask. He arrived at one. "Manuel?"

"Yes, Tripp?"

"What's my son's name?"

"Your son's name is Ryan Healy."

"And his date of birth?"

"October seventh, twenty-one-eleven."

Tripp shrugged his shoulders. "Perfect answer."

"No, wait, wait," Tor thought aloud. "That's too far in the past. Manuel?"

"Yes, Tor?"

"Data Point, run exposition scan. Open quote, what is Pink Symphony, close quote."

Manuel's holograph fizzled in mid-air as he spun through his pages. Tor turned to the others and smiled.

"He's recalibrating," Tor lowered his voice to a dead whisper, "If he remembers anything about Pure Genius and Jelly's attempt to decode Saturn Cry, then we know he's up-to-date."

The Manuel

Pink Symphony
Pg 616,647
(exposition dump #139/2a)

Cats exist to live a life of comfort and privilege if they are lucky. Should they find a good home, their work extends to that of capturing a mouse. Sometimes, even, defending their territory - if they can be bothered.

Those less fortunate and without a compassionate home are forced to survive. They become territorial, and deadly so.

Nevertheless, one attribute stands true. Cats are stupid. Dumb, ill-mannered creatures to a man, especially in relation to human beings.

They have no concept of intelligence and, as discovered in the year 2080, failed to advance in the way humans did given a lifetime of experience.

Humans went on to grasp the concept of fire, for example. A cat doesn't even know what a box of matches is. Ask an adult human with reasonable common sense to watch a boiling pot of water and he will. Ask a cat the same thing, and it will - it'll watch it burn the house down.

The above-mentioned facts are important in understanding the breakthrough that was achieved in the year 2119.

Space Opera Beta launched the previous year. It's mission, to decode a message from what was originally thought to be Saturn. It transpired that it was actually coming from its sixth largest moon, Enceladus.

In conjunction with Opera Beta's on-board computer, Pure Genius, crew member Jelly Anderson managed to crack the code.

Whether or not she was aware of her success is neither here nor there. The fact remains that she cracked it - which is more than can be said for the humans.

A series of numbers presented themselves, which Pure Genius quickly configured to be the standard English alphabet. The translation of twelve numbers returned the phrase Pink Symphony.

Nothing is known of its derivation, origin, or even what it means. Much like humans in space, or cats on Earth, the answer one can reasonably derive that the discovery is as follows: completely and utterly vague, and of no use to man or beast.

***

"Yeah, okay," Tripp suppressed the urge to accost Manuel for his matter-of-fact rudeness. He turned to Jaycee with his thoughts on the matter, "Very snarky. Inelegant to a fault. He evidently remembers what happened before it all started."

"Well, that's a start."

"Very good, Manuel." Tor held out his hand and prompted Manuel, "Now that you're operational, I need you to run a—"

"Tor?" Manuel asked.

"Yes, Manuel?"

"I do not have you listed as an official crew member of Space Opera Beta."

"What do you mean?" Tor shot Tripp and Jaycee a look of extreme consternation. "Explain, please."

"A little over two hours ago, Opera Beta received a communication from Maar Sheck at USARIC, suggesting that you and Baldron Landaker were not who you said you were."

Tor felt around the rim of his Decapidisc. He hoped the revelation wouldn't anger Jaycee. "It's a long story, Manuel."

"Is it true?"

"Yes, it's true."

"For my records, I need to know your real name and rank. I presume you are an employee of USARIC?"

"Yes, I am."

Manuel opened his bookends out. Tor's head shot, along with his assumed name - Tor Klyce - appeared as a sheet of transparent paper in the air.

"May I have your real name, please?"

Tor cleared his throat, hoping the answer he'd give wouldn't anger the others.

"Viktor Rabinovich."

"What?" Tripp walked through the photo form and sized up to Tor. "You're lying. Rabinovich was poisoned and died."

"No, I wasn't. And I didn't."

Jaycee didn't take the news very well. "Okay, that's enough. I'm pressing the button." He placed his finger on his glove, activating the Decapidisc.

A white light beeped on the surface of the disc around Tor's neck, followed by a tinny-sounding voice. "Decapidisc armed. Warning, Decapidisc armed."

"No, no," Tor yelped in fright, stepping away and tried to remove the disc around his neck. "Please, make it stop.

Beep… beep…

The second of the three white lights lit up, filling Tor with a palpable anxiety.

"Jaycee," Wool shouted, "Don't do this."

"I figure you have about fifteen seconds to explain yourself," Tripp grinned with Jaycee. "Or your head comes off."

"No, no, please." Tor fell to his knees and begged Jaycee to deactivate the inevitable.

"Tell us what happened, *Viktor*."

"Okay, okay, I'll tell you," Tor stumbled over the chair. His breathing quickened, the realization that he had better give an accurate account of events within the given time frame - or risk death.

"Dimitri Vasilov. It was all his idea. I was stationed in Moscow, developing the Androgyne series with Baldron. He tracked me down and head-hunted me—"

"—Now *that's* ironic," Jaycee chuckled to himself.

"Shut up, let him speak."

A stream of tears squirted from Tor's eyes as he hurried his explanation. "He gave us new identities and hurried us into the Opera Beta mission."

"What was your primary objective, Tor?" Tripp folded his arms, enjoying the man's torment.

"To get Anderson to decode Saturn Cry and terminate the crew."

The third and final white dot on the Decapidisc appeared. The beeps grew louder and louder...

"Oh, God. Please, no," Tor stood up, frantically clutching at the disc.

"Hey, ass hat," Jaycee said, "How did you think you were gonna get away with killing us all?"

"When Androgyne boarded Alpha we knew you'd follow. It was perfect. I primed her to detonate and take you down with the ship."

The Decapidisc beeped quicker and quicker to a near flat line sound.

"Oh *Jesus*," Tor's sweat fountained down his face. He hoped the next ten seconds weren't going to be his last.

"So you decode the message and save the day? Return home as heroes?"

"I'm sorry! I'm sorry!" Tor gave up on the disc and gripped the arm rests on the console chair. He was close to throwing up.

"Sorry you were caught?" Tripp spat. "Or genuinely sorry?"

"Both."

"It all makes sense, now," Wool said. "If that plan had

worked, they would have been heroes."

"A perfect ruse to get USARIC to allow Russians to join future endeavors?" Tripp kicked the chair away from Tor, throwing him to his ass. "Sound about right to you, *Tor*?"

The beeps feathered out into a constant flat line noise.

"Moment of truth, Rabinovich, my friend," Jaycee said.

Tor rolled onto his side, his neck pushed up at an awkward angle against the cylinder jamming against the floor. He closed his eyes, adjusted his breathing and accepted his fate.

"I'm ready."

SWISH-CLUNK!

The Decapidisc unbolted, separating out into a metal '3' shape. The whirring inner blades sluiced together, nicking his skin as it clanged to the floor.

Nanoseconds away from death.

Tor thought he'd been executed. His eyelids opened, scraping away the tears. His Decapidisc danced around his feet.

"Am I d-dead?"

"Sadly, no," Jaycee showed him his glove, "You're not dead. But we got the truth out of you and that's all that matters."

Tor fell to his knees and burst into tears, "I wish you'd killed me."

"So do we. But we're not mercenaries," Tripp offered the man his hand, "Get up."

"I can't stand this any longer," Wool said, "Stop torturing this poor man."

Tor wrapped his arms around Tripp and hugged him as tightly as possibly, "Thank you. Thank you."

"It's okay. We're not the bad guys," Tripp pushed the confused and discombobulated man away from him. "You and that boyfriend of yours have that all sewn up. Next time, though, you won't be so lucky."

"I understand."

"The only reason you're alive is because you know how to operate the communications panel and Manuel. Remember that."

"Pick up the Decapidisc, Viktor," Jaycee said.

The man did as instructed and swiped the metal execution device from the floor.

"Back on your neck."

"No, please. Don't make me wear it again—"

"—I said put it back on," Jaycee screamed in the man's face. "Do it. Now."

With a great deal of reluctance, Tor slid the neck hole under his chin and clamped the disc shut. He looked utterly miserable and deflated with the compliance device around his neck once again.

"Right, that's enough," Tripp said. "Tor, you stay here and run a diagnostic on Manuel. Find out precisely where we are."

Tor kept his head hung. The best he could do was nod his head in acknowledgment of his Captain's order.

"Wool, come with me to N-Vigorate."

"What are we doing?"

Tripp made his way out of the control deck. "We need to wake Bonnie up. We don't know anything about where we are. The air out there could be toxic. It certainly seems to be having a strange effect on cats and dead people, anyway. Jaycee?"

"Yeah."

"Go and wake up Tor's boyfriend in N-Carcerate. Bring him straight back to the control deck and fill him in on what's happened."

"You want me to tell him *everything*?"

"He'll find out sooner or later, so yes. Tell him everything," Tripp opened the door and let Wool through, "Tell him if we need to fight for whatever reason that he's first in the firing line. Like a human shield, kinda thing."

"My pleasure," Jaycee stormed toward the door and threw Tor a look of evil joy. "You better be here when I get back."

"I will," Tor turned to the communication panel and continued his work. "Manuel, run oxygen level diagnostic, please."

Jaycee reached Trip and walked through the door with him. "Oh, and... Jaycee?"

"Yeah?"

"When you wake up Baldron try not to batter him too badly, okay?"

"Who, *me?*" Jaycee snorted and punched his knuckles together, "The thought never entered my mind."

Chapter 8

A wave of muffled voices flew around the darkness. The feeling of an expanding coat hanger pushing through her internal organs was getting too much.

"She's losing consciousness," a female voice flew into the air, "Dr. Whitaker? Can you hear me?"

A horizontal sliver of light burst across the darkness, revealing a blurred vision of a delivery nurse. Bonnie lifted her eyelids and looked down to find her knees splayed across the flooded, spongy floor.

"Welcome back, Dr. Whitaker," the nurse said, holding her up by her left arm. The image of the woman focused into crystal clarity. The bottom half of her body remained blurred through the plastic case attached to her face.

An oxygen mask.

"Level off the gas, please," said another nurse, who kept an eye on a monitor to the left. "No need for the Entonox. She's doing fine on her own."

"Keep pushing, Bonnie," the delivery nurse said, holding her hands out between her legs, "Nearly there."

Bonnie tilted her head to the right. Holding her hand was her husband, Troy, doing his best to keep her calm. "You're doing great, Bonnie."

Bonnie's cries fogged up the oxygen mask. Her stomach felt like it had been stuffed with a thousand lit fireworks. She bent her knees apart and tried to push said fireworks out from between her legs.

A man's voice echoed around her head as she suffered her birthing pains, "Good people, it is our pleasure to introduce to you the next level in the Androgyne series. The *third* generation."

Nine Years Ago...

The USARIC 2110 summit - attended by all twelve board members and their guests - was the highlight of the company's year.

In his late twenties, the devastatingly handsome Xavier Manning spoke to the audience from the stage. Two twenty year-old women stood either side of him in black underwear.

"The Androgyne Series Three model is an ultra-simple machine. In every way, vastly superior to its previous incarnation. Take a look at both my friends, here. One of them is a genuine human being, born of flesh and blood. The other is not. Can you tell which is which?"

The first woman stepped forward and place her hands on her hip, posing for the audience.

In the front row, Maar Sheck felt along his forearm, pushing the ink around and taking a keen interest in the display.

The second woman stepped forward and turned one-hundred-and-eighty degrees for the crowd of onlookers.

It was impossible to tell the difference between the two women. Xavier found the audience's awe most amusing.

A diagram of what looked like a human body appeared on the screen behind him.

"What a difference advancements in technology makes. No more amnesia, except for where it counts. The Androgyne Series Three comes equipped with a fully customizable remit. You need an engineer to carry out tasks for you? You got it."

Xavier lifted the back of the first model's hair and lifted it up. He opened a plate in the back of her neck and pressed a button. "Sleep, Bonnie."

The woman's head faced down, appearing to be offline. He turned to the second woman and smiled. "So, I guess you figured out which one was the genuine woman, huh?"

The audience giggled. Maar whispered in Dimitri's ear. "This is incrediful."

"I know. We should consider stocking future ventures with them."

"What do you mean?"

"Think of the savings on life insurance, if nothing else. If something happens, the repair bill will be a lot cheaper than the insurance pay-out."

"I see you're thinking what I'm thinking, Dimitri."

The USARIC chiefs turned to the stage to see the second woman turn her back to Xavier. He reached for the back of her head.

"Well, everyone, you chose wrong. Belinda, here, is *also* a Series Three unit."

He lifted her hair and revealed a removable panel. The casing slid across her neck, revealing the circuitry inside. Her scalp slid off into Xavier's hands.

"Fully integrated organs. Lungs, stomach, pancreas, kidneys, and a fully functioning brain. Every single series three unit is, for all intents and purposes, a real life human being. Calibrated with a lifetime's worth of carefully selected memories. In essence, utterly indistinguishable from a genuine human being."

The audience clapped and cheered as Xavier replaced Belinda's scalp and reactivated her.

"Belinda?"

"Yes, Xavier?"

"Tell me about yourself."

"What would you like to know?" She smiled and winked at him, much to the amusement of the audience.

"I don't know. Tell me your age and where you're from."

"Oh, you're *so* forward," she giggled to knowing chuckles from the audience. "I was born in South Texas, but grew up in New York City. I'm twenty-years-old."

"Excellent," Xavier said. "Tell me about your family?"

"My folks live in South Texas. I have two older brothers."

"What do you do for a living?"

"I'm an engineer for the Manning/Synapse company, out of Moscow. It's a pleasure to be here with you, Xavier. You've always been a hero of mine."

The audience muttered to themselves with great curiosity. Standing before them was an android who believed she was real and had no reason to believe otherwise.

"Sleep, Belinda," Xavier said.

She kept her eyes open and powered down, standing still on the spot.

"Obviously, I don't recommend that command when you acquire your own droid," Xavier chuckled. "This is for the purposes of the demonstration. You can customize your shut-down command, too. You, the shareholders and major partners have spoken. We at Manning/Synapse listened. The series three model will forget that they are a droid with every power-down. No more recharging chambers, either. When they sleep, they replenish their internal core and battery, just like us humans do. They wake up fresh, and remember everything - except that they are not human. Just the way it should be. Being alive is depressing enough without that knowledge. Am I right?"

A burst of giddy excitement came from the audience. The diagram on the screen behind him faded out, replaced by the Manning/Synapse company logo.

"We believe the days are gone where technology and humans are distinguishable. Soon, the differentiation between the two will be a thing of the past. A unit that believes it is human. A unit that can reproduce and never die. Imagine the reduction of risk for your company, given the nature of the work you undertake. No more injury or, at least if there is, it's easily fixed. No more death."

Maar and Dimitri looked at each other knowing full well what the other was thinking.

***

Bonnie screamed and thrashed around as she heaved through her oxygen mask. Her knees threatened to buckle.

The woman was in so much pain squatting over the birthing pool, kept in place by her husband and a nurse.

"Okay, Bonnie, keep pushing," the delivery nurse said, "The head is coming through."

"Nggg..." Bonnie lifted her hips and stomped her false leg to the ground in an attempt to fling the volcano of hurt away.

"It's coming... keep breathing. Push, push."

A final flex of the muscles did the trick. She slammed the back of her head against the padding and exhaled through her tears.

The sense of relief was immeasurable, and only nearly as affecting as the cries of a newborn baby that followed seconds later.

Bonnie opened her eyes to find Troy marveling at what lay in the delivery nurse's arms. "Oh... my God. Bonnie, look."

"Congratulations, Dr. Whitaker," the nurse said, holding the detritus-covered baby in her arms. "It's a boy."

Bonnie lifted her arms, unable to quell her happiness. "It's a miracle is what it is."

Troy smiled at her. "Well done, honey. I'm proud of you."

"Can I hold him?"

"Sure," the delivery nurse helped her to her feet.

Her colleague handed her newborn son over, "Here he is. Ten fingers and ten, tiny toes."

Bonnie took the crying human being in her arms and scanned him up and down. "My little angel."

By all accounts, the her son was perfect. Ten fingers and ten, tiny toes. The comfort of his mother's embrace was enough to stop him crying and relax.

Finally, he opened his eyes. The first thing he ever saw in his life was his mother smiling back at him. The second thing he saw was the gracious smile stretched across his father's face.

"Do you have a name in mind for him, Dr. Whitaker?"

Bonnie kept her eyes trained on the child and giggled, soaking up every atom of his body.

"We were thinking Adam."

"Huh?" The baby stopped kicking around and shot his mother a look of confusion. "Adam?"

"Yes?" Bonnie felt hurt by her son's protestation. Confused, further, by his ability to speak at a mere ninety seconds old, "Why, what's wrong with that?"

"That's a bit of an obvious name, isn't it?" The baby said, barely able to contain his disdain, "The first human being ever created? Bonnie?"

"But, I—"

"Bonnie?" The baby snapped his fingers, "No, it's no good. I don't think she can hear me."

Bonnie screwed her face. A deep-rooted feeling of illness socked her in the gut, "Who are you talking to—"

A shooting pain stormed across the back of her head, followed by a prolonged and intense tingling in her ears.

"Yaarrggh!"

The baby in her arms fizzed in and out. He opened his mouth and spoke once again. "Bonnie, can you hear me?"

"No, no, it's not right—"

"She's speaking," the baby said, nonchalantly, "Bonnie, I know you can hear me. If you can hear me—"

N-Vigorate

Space Opera Beta – Level Three

"—Just nod your head," Tripp finished his sentence. He crouched in front of her as she sat in the electric chair.

Bonnie jolted in the seat and pressed herself back against the headrest in fright, her eyes wide open.

"Oh, God. Oh, God."

Her breathing quickened as she attempted to acclimatize herself to her surroundings.

Tripp looked at Wool for a response. "There we are, we're back online."

"What am I doing in here?" Bonnie spluttered and caught her breath. "Why did you plug me into the electric chair?"

Tripp's face soured. He rose to his feet and stood next to Wool, looking down at her. "Bonnie, we have something to tell you."

"What is it?"

"We know you're confused," Wool said. "But we want you to know the truth."

"Okay, I'm listening."

Tripp folded his arms and cleared his throat. "There's no easy way to say this, Bonnie. So it's probably just better to come right out with it. You're an Androgyne Series Three Unit."

Bonnie stared at Tripp, waiting for the "ha-ha, *got you*" moment that would never come.

Sure enough, even after Tripp's pregnant pause, it never came.

"Bonnie?"

She blinked and scrunched her face. "Are you serious, right now?"

"I'm afraid so."

"What *lessense*. Only Series Three units recharge in N-Vigorate chambers. That's old school," Bonnie stood out from the seat and extended her arms, ironing out the kinks on her muscles. "Anyway, I have a husband and a son. I was born before the first Androgyne series was even invented. Your jokes are starting to wear thin."

"No, Bonnie," Wool said. "We figured it was better to be honest with you. When you time out, or otherwise lose consciousness, you seem to be suffering from amnesia."

"We think your battery was damaged in the fight. You're not operating properly."

"Is that so?" Bonnie lifted her metal leg and placed her foot on the seat. She unraveled her pants leg across her shin and wiggled her metal toes around. "I lost my leg in a vehicle accident, before they abolished flying cars."

"No. You didn't. USARIC programmed you to think you did."

Bonnie didn't believe a word coming from her captain's mouth. "Why would they do that?"

"To keep their options open."

Bonnie held her right hand at the pair, dismissing their stupidity. "Shut up."

Wool walked to the N-Vigorate chamber door. "We don't

have much time, Bonnie. We need your help—"

The stripped lights stretching across the ceiling dipped in and out as the walls began to rumble.

Concerned, Wool looked up and around her immediate vicinity, "What's that?"

"Seems Manuel's got the engine working."

Bonnie walked into the middle of the room and scanned the harshly-lit walls. She closed her eyes and inhaled. "Are we still lost?"

"Yes," Tripp said.

The humming from the power behind the walls underscored Bonnie's recollection of events. "The last thing I remember was a pink gas. My eyes went funny. Anderson rescued us," her speaking slowed as she remembered something vital, "Tor. Baldron. They tried to kill us."

Tripp raised his eyebrows, curious that Bonnie had remembered. "That's right. You remember?"

"Anderson," Bonnie added with maternal instinct, "Where is she?"

Wool wasted no time in hurrying up the expedition. "That's what we want to find out—"

The entire chamber rocked back and forth like a fairground ride. Dust coughed around them from the ceiling. The near-deafening chaos and vibrations never abated.

"Jesus, what was that?" Tripp grabbed Wool in his arms and ran with her to the door, "Quick, with me."

Bonnie twisted around on the spot and watched the far wall crack apart. It shot sifts of white and pink light through the ceramic. "What is *that*?" Quick-thinking, she followed the cracks crawl up the wall and shatter the ceiling, threatening to propel a chunk of it at her face.

Whoosh.

Chunks of debris whizzed past her head. She splayed out her legs and hit the ground. It stabbed down and created a vicious dent in the ground. Just two more inches to the left and Bonnie could have been sold as scrap metal.

"Quick, get out of here," Bonnie stomped her metal foot to the floor and propelled herself into the air, thumping rocks of falling detritus against the far wall.

Wool and Trip ran through the door, but the spectacular light show was too enthralling to run away from. Wool skidded on her heels and tugged at Tripp's arm, forcing him to stop.

"No, wait. We can't leave Bonnie there, we—" she couldn't finish her sentence. The sight beyond the frame of the door was too much to handle.

"Where are you?" Bonnie screamed at the splattered, milky sky that had opened up around her. "You coming for *me*? Come and get me."

"Bonnie," Wool wailed at her as she ran away from the door and into the beautiful sand-drenched horizon, "Bonnie, come back."

"What the hell is going on here?" Tripp muttered as he witnessed the N-Vigorate chamber break away into nothingness. The walls smashed against the sand, kicking a wisp of saturated rock into the air.

"Manuel said we weren't on Opera Beta," Wool clasped Tripp's hand and ran with him along the corridor, "I'm starting to believe him. We gotta find Jaycee, quick."

Tripp barreled along the walkway with her, their footsteps clanging against the metal grills. He held up his left forearm and screamed into his Individimedia ink.

"Tor, this is Tripp. Do you read me?"

The ink on his arm swirled into the shape of a tick and bled out into a black-and-white rendition of Tor's face. "Yes, this is Tor. I read you."

"Tor, listen. Something has happened to N-Vigorate," he said, losing his breath while running, "We're in danger."

"Danger? What danger?"

"That *place* we saw earlier. It's starting to appear everywhere. We think Manuel is right, we're not on Opera Beta—"

The walls of the walkway shunted back and forth, putting a halt to Tripp's comments, and a slight pause in progress. "Oh, wow."

Breathless, Wool slowed down to a jog and tilted her head to the ceiling. "It's happening again."

"Tripp?" Tor's voice shot out from Tripp's arm, "What's

going on?"

SCHUNT!

A chasm split along the ceiling, shattering the material like a broken eggshell. "Run!"

Wool and Tripp wasted no time. They bolted along the corridor as the crack opened up above their heads, spilling pipework and sharp bits of ceramic all around them.

"What do I do? Tor asked from Tripp's forearm.

He turned to the ink on his skin and kept running. "Stay where you are. Do not leave the control deck. Lock the door and await further instru—"

KERRAANG!

A lump of metal daggered through the corridor wall. Tripp yanked her forward just in time for it to avoid severing her hip. The resultant tear on her inner-suit was imminently more preferable than losing a vital organ.

"Thanks."

"Don't thank me, just run," Tripp quipped as they picked up the pace, "Don't even think about stopping."

Wool looked over her shoulder as she quickened her pace. A dozen pipes fell across the path, blasting various liquids and gases across the walkway.

"Oh my God, we're—"

The ceiling cracked apart like a budding rose as they turned the corner, on the path to N-Carcerate.

"Tripp, Tripp," Wool pulled him back and pointed at the opened sky, multi-colored sky. A serene sound of ocean waves and cool air rolled around the opening.

Tripp couldn't believe what he was seeing. His ship was breaking apart all around him like a detonated tomb with a grudge.

"Come on. No time to admire the view." He spun around on his feet and stormed toward N-Carcerate with Wool in tow. "Jaycee, open the door."

The N-Carcerate door edged closer and closer as Tripp and Wool clanged along the stern surface of the walkway. He opened out his palm and shoved his arm in front of his face, intending to slap it against the panel.

"Get ready," he screamed, trying to outrun the metaphysical destruction erupting around them.

The door slid open before Tripp had the chance to manually open it. "Whoa."

He pushed Wool into the room, turned on his heels and drew the door shut by its handle.

Seriously out of breath, he placed his hands on his knees and gasped. "Ugh, no more. No more… this… is too much."

"You okay, Tripp?" Jaycee's voice lumbered from the other side of the room.

Tripp closed his eyes and caught his breath. At last, a reassuring voice and some confirmation that Jaycee was perfectly fine. He stood up straight and was about to speak, when he laid eyes on the giant of a man.

His face fell a few light years from his body. "Jaycee?"

"Yes, Captain. Look who woke up."

Tripp blinked over and over again, trying to process what he saw. Wool held her hand over her mouth and gasped as she finally laid eyes on the scene. "Oh, my God."

"Jaycee?" Tripp took a careful step forward, hoping not to attract any undue attention. "Don't… *move.*"

"What are you talking about?" Jaycee knocked Baldron's arm. The Decapidisc sat around his captive's neck, resting heavily across his shoulders.

Of course, this was to be expected. Jaycee was never one to miss an opportunity to instill fear in people - particularly a traitor. Both he and Baldron faced Tripp and Wool. The opposite direction of the cause of concern.

"He's g-going to kill me," Baldron sobbed and rubbed his arms.

Tripp averted his gaze over Jaycee's shoulder, staring at the wall behind him "Not if that… *thing…* kills you first."

"What *thing?*" Jaycee turned around and nearly soiled his exo-suit pants. "Wha—" He elbowed Baldron toward Tripp and slung his K-SPARK gun at the wall. "What in God's name is that *that*—?

A giant ball of pasty-white human flesh with twelve limbs clung to the wall like an absorbent slug. Balled-up like a spider, it retracted its "arms". It measured at least five feet wide and eight feet tall. The sheer enormity of the *thing* was devastating.

The mid-section of the beast heaved in and out, squirming as it slid down the wall. Two of its *limbs* reached the ground and thumped out, trying to orient itself as it crawled to the ground.

"Get back— My God," Jaycee aimed his shotgun at it and teased the trigger. "What's going on here?"

"Up there," Wool whispered, afraid to alarm the creature as it flopped to the ground and squealed. "Look. The crack. It must have got in through there."

She was right - a crack had formed where the ceiling met the wall.

Jaycee focused on the creature and aimed down his sight. "*Damn*, that's one ugly-looking lump of flesh."

"Jaycee, no. Don't shoot it—" Tripp quipped as the multi-limbed sack of flesh extended six of its twelve fleshy tentacle-cum-limbs across the ground. The central tumorous slit opened up and squealed in anger.

"Night-night, sweetheart," Jaycee spat.

BANG-SCHPLATT!

The bullet rocketed through the air and hit the creature. It exploded in all directions. Bits of pink-colored flesh and blood splattered the crew.

"Gaaoooww," Baldron screamed as some of it went in his mouth.

The bullet blasted right through the creature and smashed into the wall, forcing a crack ten feet above them to break apart. Chunks of ceramic crashed around Baldron and Jaycee.

"Get out of here, now!"

"Baldron, let's go," Wool took his hand and made for the door. Tripp thumped Jaycee on the back, ready to accost him, when he caught a glimpse through the crack in the wall.

"Oh… no, no, run. Run, run, run!" Tripp's soul nearly flew out of his mouth, as did Jaycee's.

Several hundred feet in the sandy horizon thousands more of the same creatures scuttled toward the ship.

"This can't be h-happening," Jaycee stammered, unable to move. "Where are we?"

Tripp pushed him toward the door. "I dunno, but we're not sticking around to find out—"

CRAA-ACCK!

N-Carcerate's ceiling shunted apart like a pressurized ribcage, flooding the prison chamber with pink light. The iron bars on each cell punctured away from its housing and crashed to the floor, creating a series of obstacles on the path to the door.

"Tripp," Wool shouted over the commotion, "Come on, we gotta get outta here!"

Tripp jumped over the fallen bar and pulled Jaycee with him. "God, you're heavy."

"It's the exo-suit, man."

"Yeah," Tripp yanked him by his mammoth waist, "And it's not water retention, it's cake retention."

"You calling me fat?" Jaycee took aim at the chasm in the wall. The creatures scurried forward, squealing for revenge.

"No, I'm calling you *dead* if you don't get out of here," Tripp hoisted himself over the debris and jumped toward the door. "Head for the control deck."

"What?" Jaycee pushed through the door and into the walkway. "Why?"

"We need to get Tor before those *things* do." Tripp slid the door shut mere nanoseconds before the first of scores of fleshy creatures slapped against the glass door, splattering its pink saliva up the glass window.

"What's happening to us?" Baldron cried and shook his head. "What kind of perversion is this?"

Jaycee bopped him on the back of the head with the butt of his K-SPARK as they hurried toward the control deck. "Shut up, Russian."

"It is a perversion of science," Baldron sobbed. "Those things—"

"—Yeah, and those *things* are going to have their way with us if we don't figure out what the hell is going on, here," Tripp lifted his forearm and spoke into his skin ink. "Individimedia. Open channel, please."

"You're not giving Rabinovich the heads up, are you?"

Jaycee asked.

"Huh?" Baldron shot Tripp a look of despair. How did they know Tor's real identity?

Tripp didn't look at the man. He was more determined to get the crew to the safety of the control deck. "Don't act like a numbnuts with us, *numbnuts*. We know who *Tor* is. Speaking of which, Tor, can you read me?"

"I read you, Tripp," came his voice. "What's the situation?"

"We have Baldron and we're making our way to control right now. Something's happening."

"What?"

"A Tango got on the ship. It's okay, we took care of it."

"Took care of what? What Tango?"

"Hey," Tripp screamed into his arm, "Don't quiz me. Just do as I say."

"Sorry."

"We are ETA ninety seconds to the control deck. Is Manuel online and ready to go?"

"He's online," Tor said. "Whether or not he's ready to go is another matter."

"He'd better be, or I'll have Jaycee remove your head. Do you understand what I have just said?"

"Yes."

"Good, now get ready."

"But, can I—"

"—Can you shut up and do as I say? Yes, good idea." Tripp swiped the ink on his arm to his wrist, severing the communication. He quickened his walk to a sprint and moved ahead of Wool, Baldron, and Jaycee. "First N-Vigorate, then the cells. We're not going to have much of a ship left if this continues."

"Tripp?" Jaycee shouted from behind Baldron. "What about those monster things?"

Tripp's temper neared to a close, "How the hell do I know, Jaycee? I know as much as you do."

"Yeah, but they could be anywhere."

"They *are* anywhere. They're outside. They're all over the damn place," Tripp rubbed Wool's shoulder as he faced front and continued walking. "One thing's for sure, at any rate. We *know* we're not in space. This walkway is bound to subside just like every other part of the ship. Keep moving. As long as we're moving we're not sitting ducks."

"What are we going to do when we get to control?" Wool asked. "Do you have a plan?"

"Yeah."

"What is it?"

"Survive."

Wool rolled her eyes. Fortunately, Tripp couldn't see her reaction as he was ahead of her. If he'd have caught her flippant retort it might have proved to be the final straw.

Tripp was as angry as the others were frightened. He was the captain of Space Opera Beta. The human being in him was frightened, too. The captain in him, though, was a whole different person altogether. Nothing stood in his way.

"The plan right now is to survive."

Chapter 9

A trail of tiny paw prints nestled in the fine, white sand. Two on the left, two on the right, a few inches apart.

They belonged to Jelly.

For such a young cat she sure had a lot of energy. She couldn't remember the last time she'd eaten or had a sip of water. She felt a rumbling sensation in her stomach commensurate with a similar occurrence in the pink sky.

Jelly paused, shifted her behind in the sand and tilted her head back. A permanent smile struck across her face as the glint of the nearest white blotch of white - a sort of *cloud* - reflected in her pupil.

A few laps of her tongue across her mouth and she was off to the oceanfront. As she trundled ever nearer to the shore, she stopped occasionally to turn around and see if the Opera Beta was there.

It wasn't.

She might as well have jumped through a portal for all the good her bearings were to her. Usually, she'd be on point in that respect. Geography had always been her strong suit - a sense of belonging and territory.

In the infinite vastness of Pink Symphony she felt naked and alone.

The crystal blue water lapped against the white sand, turning it a strange yellow color as it rolled across, settled down, and clawed thousands of grains of sand with it into the water.

The journey to the ocean took longer than Jelly expected.

Storming forwards, exercising every muscle in her body, the faster she sped the slower the ocean arrived.

A perplexing mirage for a cat.

On the way there she passed the odd fish bone. One of them resembled a ribcage with a skull in the shape of a helmet.

A quick sniff around confirmed what she knew all along. Whatever this thing was had well and truly expired.

She felt the pink-colored sky watch her every move. If she moved her left paw the clouds tilted to the left like an angry lava lamp.

The right claw moved forward taking with it the clouds in the sky. They didn't move as they had back on Earth. Calling them clouds were as comparable as possible to what they really were. More like explosions of distant galaxies; silky and smooth, as if someone had poured full fat cream into a sky full of candy floss.

Jelly might well have had second thoughts about moving in any direction. The water, at least, seemed benevolent enough.

Eventually, she reached the shore. A careful probe with her infinity claws resulted in the wet sand tearing apart as expected.

The metal claws fizzed subtly as the waves crashed around her paws. She stepped forward and lowered her face, exploring the liquid with her tongue.

Two successive gulps - and success. A fully lubricated mouth. A wave of relief ran through her entire body. She felt better, energized, and ready for more.

Lap, lap, lap… the refreshing water soaked into her coarse tongue and swirled around her mouth. Above her in the sky, the white ink-like clouds bled out, creating a harmonious voice for the duration of its travel.

Jelly's ears pricked up as she continued to drink the water.

The thought occurred to her that she should get back to the ship and alert her crew of the seemingly plentiful supply of H2O. Said thought evaporated when the oncoming ripples of water grew higher and turned into medium-sized waves.

"Meow," she squealed and hopped back, fearing the wave would entrench her entirely. She loved the water, but the concept of swimming was way beyond her grasp.

In fact, she didn't even know if she could swim.

Stepping back wasn't enough. She had to run around and run across the sand just in time for the end of the wave to envelope her hind legs.

"Meow," she yelped in defiance, determined to return and satisfy her thirst.

As the wave rolled back into the ocean, her eyes followed it back to the tree dead in the middle of the ocean.

It was a tree, yet it wasn't a tree. It merely resembled one.

Jelly knew what a tree was. Fat at the bottom, thinning out in the middle, with hundreds of blossoming branches fanning out from the top. Usually brown, or dark brown, and made of wood and covered in bark. She'd got stuck in many of them during her young life.

She loved to climb the one in Jamie's garden area. Occasionally, in her good old kitty days, she'd need rescuing.

This *tree* wasn't made of wood. If it was then the wood was made of a spongy, black mucous shooting out from the water and blossoming one hundred feet in the air.

Its towering effect antagonized her.

Where there might have been branches were, instead, darkened shafts of coal about twenty feet in length. It was as if an aircraft's wings had melted in intense heat. They curved around the midpoint, arrowing back toward the water.

The stem bulged in and out as if it was breathing. Jelly saw the bulge shoot up from the root, causing the water to rupture away. It traveled up the stem and dispersed among the twenty or so *branches* and died out toward their ends.

Jelly sat perfectly still and took in the sheer size of the tree. She blinked hard, expecting it to move. Of course, it had no such intention. Being an inanimate object, it didn't care much for the strange being sitting before it.

Being curious in nature, Jelly wanted to know more. But she'd be damned if she went into the water to quench her thirst for knowledge.

At least the place was quiet, though. The sky acted

strangely. The tree added a perversely morbid air to an otherwise wistful utopia. Jelly rolled around in the wet sand and cooled herself down.

"Jelly?"

She jumped to her feet and turned around. A recognizable shape in the shifting sand seat warbled into focus. The contours of a woman named Bonnie steadily approached her.

"Hey, girl," she finished, confidently striding closer, "There you are."

Jelly hopped to her feet and meowed back.

"I know," Bonnie hollered as softly as she could, "It's nice here, isn't it?"

"Meow."

Bonnie let out a hearty laugh and flung her long, brown hair across her left shoulder. "Aww." She squatted to the sand and held her arms forward. "Come on, pet. Come here and give your auntie Bonnie a cuddle."

Jelly found the human's behavior a little strange. Stuck in a strange place and with little-to-no recourse for rescue, Bonnie seemed uniquely at home.

Her demeanor was enough reassurance for Jelly. She hopped along the sand, digging her infinity claws in with each step for good measure, and raced into Bonnie's opened hands.

She arched her back and held Jelly out at arm's length against the sky.

"Hey, sweetie."

"Meow," Jelly licked her lips and flipped her tail around, wondering when the cuddle would commence. She lifted her right leg for balance.

"God, you're such a gorgeous creature," Bonnie said with a deft admiration, her eyes fixated on Jelly's. "Look at you."

Then, the cuddle came. Bonnie's left cheek nestled against Jelly's forehead.

She took a look at the blackened tree to find a waterfall of dark pink liquid gushing from a slit that tore near the top of the stem.

"Oh, look. It's crying pink."

Jelly took a look and immediately grew concerned. She dug her titanium claws into Bonnie's inner-suit sleeve, wanting to be set free.

"Okay, okay," Bonnie huffed. "Jeez, you're cranky—"

The middle of the tree's stem heaved out, as if taking in a lungful of air. A pregnant pause befell Jelly and Bonnie as they waited for it to exhale.

Where would the exhalation come from, anyway? Apart from the slit, there was no sign of a mouth anywhere on it.

The branches slumped down, appearing to weaken as the tree bent back.

"What is that?" Bonnie squinted at the alien object as it gently lilted around.

Then, a deafening blast of sound rippled in every direction from the root of the tree.

Da-da-da-dummm…

"Huh?" she said.

Dah, dah, dah…. *dum.*

Bonnie clamped her hands over her ears and let out a cry of pain. "Agh."

SPLASH!

A wave crashed out across the sand. A large fish plopped to the shore and shuffled around in pain, trying to breath. Its rounded lips gaped in and out.

"Meow," Jelly kicked up some sand as she entered the prone position. Her tail bushed out, ready to attack.

"Jelly, honey, what—"

"Shhh," Jelly fixated her eyes on the fat, circular fish as it flapped across the sand and gasped for air, "Shhh."

"Sweetie? How are you saying that—"

"Mweh," Jelly coughed up a lump of pink phlegm and spat to the sand. She darted over to the fish intending to tear it to shreds.

"No, Jelly. Don't touch it—"

The fish bounced over the damp sand in an attempt to escape its impending doom. The back end of the blue creature lifted up and shed its skin.

A bony tail shot out and slapped to the ground.

Jelly screeched to a halt, kicking sand into the air with her paws. She didn't like what had happened and would soon be terrified of what happened next, "Muuuh."

The creature whipped its tail in retaliation. The end thwacked against the sand. The impact sent a shock wave through its bone, shattering its blue, oily skin across its body. The fish's mouth stretched back over its face. A row of sharp teeth jutted out from its skull, as the blue skin flaked away.

It had turned into a bizarre armadillo-type creature. Four small limbs, bent at the middle, with claws.

Jelly widened her eyes in terror as the creature turned to her and growled. A swish from the creature's tail made sure Jelly took a few steps back, hoping not to get murdered.

The beast crept forward on its chunky feet and slammed its razor sharp jaws together.

Da-da-da... dum... the tree appeared to sing.

Bonnie found the whole spectacle puzzling but wasn't afraid of the abnormality creeping towards her. She gripped her metal leg and made sure it was armed in case the creature tried its luck.

"What the hell is going on, here?" she turned to Jelly and raised her voice, "Come here, girl."

Jelly didn't hear the command. She froze on the spot, scared that the creature might lunge at her.

The tree heaved and lilted to the left side as if quietly dancing to its own rendition of a classical tune. The mimicry of organs and trumpets came out like a confused amalgam of croaking wood and belches.

Bonnie recognized the attempt, finding the entire scenario eerily reminiscent of Opera Alpha.

"Is that... *Beethoven's Fifth*?" she gasped, piecing the tree's segments of harmonious rumbles together. "It is, it is..." She turned over her shoulder and saw a transparent spacecraft wreckage in the horizon. The ghost of the deserted Space Opera Alpha.

"Huh?"

Jelly, meanwhile, found herself crawling backwards on her hind legs as the recently-evolved beast threw its spindly arms forward.

"Maaw," she kept her fattened tail up and swung it around. A failed attempted to allay the creature's desire for feline blood.

The beast growled at her, forcing the air molecules to ripple together and throw her fur on end.

"Meow," Jelly screamed back and swiped her right claw in retaliation.

So hard was the creature's roar that the reptilian skin on its face broke apart and slapped against the sand. A gray-colored skull broke forward and shrieked, shedding the rest of its skin. Its skeletal structure fizzed and sparked, cracking onto itself.

The spine curved in the middle and sprung stems on either side, meeting around its exposed organs.

A liver.

A stomach.

A pancreas.

The ribbed bones crept around its lungs and heart, forming a protective cage around them.

The pinkish under skin blistered in the intense heat from the pink sky. A sun, previously unseen, introduced itself from behind one of several milky clouds.

The tree continued its interpretation of *Beethoven's 5th Symphony* across the air. Croaky and strangely harmonic, given the absence of a coherent orchestra.

Bonnie unhooked her Rez-9 firearm from her belt and pointed it at the creature. She'd seen - and had - enough, "Don't move."

Jelly turned around and meowed at Bonnie. The look in both her eyeballs screamed *don't shoot.*

"Don't look at me in that tone of voice, young madam," Bonnie said. "Look at it. It's in pain. I'm doing it a favor."

Jelly turned back to the creature.

It resembled more an ape than a scaly reptile. The sunburn blackened most of its skin. Tufts of hair had formed on it as it squealed in immense turmoil.

"Meow," Jelly chanced her luck and crawled nearer to the pained monstrosity writhing around in front of her.

"Enough," Bonnie cocked her Rez-9 and loomed over the

crying beast. She held the gun to its head and took mercy, "Peace."

BLAM!

She shot the ape creature in the head and jumped back when the unexpected made itself known.

"What the—?

Instead of busting the primate's head apart and disintegrating the rest of its body, it only exacerbated the transformation.

The impact of the bullet sent a bolt of electricity through its body, cracking its shoulders out a few inches. In retaliation, the ape climbed to its feet and stomped its considerably large feet to the ground.

Bonnie kept her gun pointed at the beast. "Wh-what… *are you?*"

The ape slammed its furry chest with both fists and roared, frightening Jelly enough for her to run behind Bonnie's feet for protection.

"Girl, we better get out of here. Let's go."

Bonnie walked backwards across the sand, keeping an eye on the ape-like creature as it screamed for vengeance. Pink tears shot down its face.

"That's one ugly beast," Bonnie turned around and expected to find Opera Beta sitting in the distance.

It wasn't there. The distant apparition of Opera Alpha in the horizon had vanished, too.

"God, I must be seeing things," she stopped in her tracks and looked down to Jelly. "Girl, where's our ship?"

"Muuuh," Jelly lifted her shoulders up and down, indicating that she had no clue.

ROOOOAAARRRR!

The ape's insane exclamation forced Bonnie and Jelly to pay attention to it. They turned around in tandem, expecting to be set-upon and mauled to death.

Instead of attacking, the ape slammed its fists against the sand. A loud grunt followed before it snorted through its widened nostrils.

Huffing around the grains of sand, it laid eyes on Jelly and grunted again. It held out its left paw, wanting Jelly to make contact.

The cat was much too afraid to oblige.

"Jelly, stay right where you are," Bonnie tuned her ears to the tree's attempt to reproduce Beethoven's classic symphony, "And would you *stop* that damn singing.*"

The tree, relentless in its insistence to continue singing, upped its volume. In turn, its rendition grew more strained and perverse.

The ape appeared not to hear it.

"Meow," Jelly tried in a bid to win favor - or at the very least, *time* - with the hirsute freak standing before them.

"We have nowhere to go," Bonnie faced the sky for some semblance of geography, "If we run, we could end up running forever."

The light from the intense sun blanketed her face. For just a moment, she felt like she was home. Closing her eyes shut and enjoying the warmth meant the world to her, "It's fantastic, isn't it?"

Bonnie opened her eyes and saw the sun had split into three, larger balls of magnificence. To call it *the sun* was a massive anomaly. It wasn't the sun Bonnie had enjoyed on Earth. The ball of fire she saw in the sky enlarged a few millimeters per second.

A deafening thud came from her left. "Oh, my God."

The ape had dropped onto its side, crying and moaning to itself. Much of its hair had shed and entwined amongst the grains of sands.

The grunting turned to sobbing as the ape balled up in the fetal position. As the hair shed away to reveal a pink-white skin - like that of a human being.

"Stay there, girl," Bonnie's curiosity outshone the cat's, which was a first in all the time they'd known each other. Jelly followed behind her careful not to draw attention to herself.

"Hey," Bonnie said at the five-foot lump of skin burying its head against its stomach, "Are you okay?"

The creature moved its arms forward and covered its face. As it groaned and kicked across the dusty ground with its feet, its ape-like voice normalized into that of a human being's.

"Sch... sch... gwup."

The sand sticking to its sweaty skin as it rolled around.

"Whoa," Bonnie held out her hands and tried to calm the thing down. "Hey, can you hear me?"

It removed its perfectly-formed human hands from its face. A scared and shivering man stared back at her - his face covered in pink liquid sprouting from his tear ducts.

A naked, male human being.

"Shaaa..." he gurgled and lifted his hand up, blocking out the light from the three suns. "Shaa—"

"—Here, get up," Bonnie grabbed his hand and hoisted him to his feet. She took the opportunity to thoroughly check him over. Two arms, two legs, ten fingers and toes. Overall, he appeared to be in excellent shape.

Bonnie's eyes clamped on the one appendage that confirmed his masculinity. She looked at his face and tried to keep professional, "You're not going to hurt me, are you?"

"Whu..." he gasped and scratched his beard as he eyed Jelly. "Wah!" He pointed at her, wanting to know what the furry little creature was.

"Oh, her? That's Jelly."

"Juh... juh..." he tried, closing his eyes, angry about his inability to replicate the sounds Bonnie was making. "Jeh..."

"Meow."

"Meee?" The man repeated - utterly clueless - and shook his head in anger. He thumped his stomach with the underside of his fist. "Meee. Oww."

Jelly looked to Bonnie for a reaction. This *new* human being was clearly insane, and probably quite volatile.

Bonnie chuckled to herself and extended her index finger. She placed her fingertip at her chest. "Bonnie."

"Boh... boh..." the man said, fighting off the perturbation of the singing tree. "Boh... knee."

"Yes."

She clapped her hands together and gave the man the thumbs up. She lifted her index finger and pressed it against his chest.

"Ah," he said, "Shaa..."

"Shaa?"

"Shanta—"

A pink tear rolled down his cheek. She flicked her finger over to his top lip and collected the liquid against her knuckle. "Do you know what this is?"

Jelly tore her gaze away from the man and looked at the tree. "Meow!"

WHUMP.

As the song slowed down the cavernous slit at the top of the tree coughed. Jelly squealed and spun her arms and hind legs around in the air in a fit of apoplectic rage.

Bonnie looked at her, deeply concerned. "Jelly!"

The confrontation between the two lasted exactly eight seconds. Then, the tree spat again.

WHUMP.

Jelly flew into a tizzy, thoroughly agitated by the noise. She extended her claws and made straight for the man standing in front of Bonnie.

"Maaaah," she growled, intending to launch herself into the air and claw the man to death.

He grunted and held out his arms for protection.

"Bad pussycat," Bonnie shouted at her as Jelly kicked her hind legs against the sand and jumped into the air, headed for the man's face.

"Meow."

The man's attempt to guard his face worked. Jelly took a swipe with her extended titanium claw and tore the skin on top of his hand. He batted her away, sending her to the floor.

She landed on her infinity claws and scraped a lump of sand away, ready for a second attack. "Meow."

WHUMP… The tree swayed around and coughed out a third and final sound. Jelly instantly relaxed and gave up her desire for blood.

She needed water, and the oceanfront looked suitably thirst-quenching.

"Shaaa—"

"—Meow," Jelly snapped, cutting the man off mid-grunt. The stern look in her eyes suggested she wasn't to be messed with. Her nose twitched over and over again as her whiskers began to vibrate.

The tree's incessant humming of the tune came to a close.

Then, Jelly's facial fur stood on end, as if having been rubbed by a balloon, "Meoowwuuurrr...."

Bonnie and the man couldn't tear their eyes away. Something *strange* was happening to Jelly.

Her entire body shuddered continuously.

The tree began to subside and crumble apart.

The sky grew overcast with a milk-like substance.

Jelly's whiskers tingled and sparked, lighting up. The intensity throttled her around, the air dragging her by the shoulders towards the shore.

"Jelly," Bonnie ran after her. Ready to take out her Rez-9 and blast whatever was responsible for pulling Jelly to the ocean, she found herself at a loss. Nothing to shoot - no preventable action could be taken.

Powerless, Bonnie watched Jelly lift into the air, thrashing her limbs around and screaming for dear life.

"Oh, *God...*" Bonnie dropped her arms and witnessed the tree break apart and slink into the pink, bloodied ocean.

"Miyeeeww,' Jelly let out a final squeal of terror fifty feet in the air. The invisible force released its grip and tossed her face-first into the water.

She threw her infinity claws in front of her face.

SPLOSH.

Helpless, Bonnie didn't know where to turn. Perhaps the naked man could help?

"Hey, you," she said. "Where are— oh, *no*. Oh no, no, no..."

She couldn't believe what she saw.

His severed head sat atop the sand, wide-eyed. It looked as if someone had buried him up to the neck for fun.

She retrieved her Rez-9 from her belt and held it at the head, "Where's... where's the rest of your body—"

BOP!

An incredible forced slammed Bonnie from behind, throwing her chest-first to the floor. "Gah!" Her Rez-9 flew out of her hand and slid ten feet across the sand in front of her. "Damn."

She pushed herself onto her elbows, expected to be

blinded by the sun, "Help me."

Instead, the shadow of something insidious crept over her face. Whatever it was scuttled in slow-motion toward her.

Bonnie kicked herself back along the sand, trying to understand the predicament she was in. "Jesus Christ, what the *hell* is that?"

It was an outrageous amalgam of flesh and skin, previously of human form. Measuring eight-foot high and around ten-foot wide. Twelve limb-like legs with stumps on each side working in unison to help it forward. A gaping concoction of gums and teeth opened up in the middle and let out a guttural, terrifying roar.

Seconds away from doing whatever it was it did to people like Bonnie, she decided she wasn't sticking around to find out.

"*Jeez...*"

She scrambled onto her front and crawled along the piping hot sandy surface. Her fists slipped with each grasp forward, slowing her escape down to a near halt.

The creature gained on her.

"Come on, come on..." she squinted at her Rez-9 firearm laying five feet away from her, "Gah, gah... *come on.*"

She made the mistake of looking over her shoulder. The beast jabbed the sand with its four front limbs and pulled itself toward her.

"Aggh," she dug her heels into the ground and pushed the top half of her body back a few inches.

SWIPE! SWISH!

One of its limbs tore her inner-suit with its razor sharp talon at the end of its stump.

Six of its back limbs lifted up, ready to strike, leaving six grounded flesh poles to move forward.

"No, no... *please.*"

The beast roared, spraying pink spittle into the air. Some of it hit Bonnie's face as she trailed back by her elbows, "No!"

SWIPE!

Bonnie kicked her titanium foot at the beast in an attempt to fend it off. It had the opposite effect, enraging the beast even more.

Her leg detached from the ball and joint socket in her hip, the dislodged appendage firmly in the beast's razor-sharp claws.

"Nooo," Bonnie flipped onto her front and scrambled for her Rez-9. She grabbed at it but her fingertips couldn't quite get there.

Just three inches separated her from death and freedom. "Please, please…"

WHUMP!

The beast roared once again and stabbed at Bonnie, spearing its front-left limb into the ground.

"Gah! Cute little thing, aren't ya?"

Bonnie scrunched her face and planted the sole of her right boot on the creature's front limb. The beast howled as she kicked herself back.

She rolled onto her side, swiped her Rez-9 in her right hand and swung the barrel at the center of the monstrosity.

"Hey, you," She flicked the latch on the side of the chamber, arming the gun, "Look at me, you disgusting knuckle-headed bag of puke."

All twelve of the creature's limbs tightened up, throwing its body onto its haunches.

"Go to hell," she pulled the trigger and covered her face.

The hole at the end of the barrel focused into the creature's view, followed by a smothering of white light. It's mouth opened up and screamed in her face. "Shantaaaaaaaa—"

KA-SCHPPLLAAATTT!!!

The creature exploded into a zillion, gloopy pieces. It's stuck front limb stood upright like a tent peg as the rest of it splattered across the ground, coating the sand a wet shade of pink and red.

Bonnie held her position - and her breath - wanting confirmation that the thing had been obliterated.

Her detached leg slumped to the middle of the gore-strewn sand a few feet away from her.

She took a deep breath and pressed the back of her head against the sand, thankful she hadn't been killed.

As the harsh, radioactive light from the three suns cooked her face, she realized she didn't have to worry about sunburn. She was an Androgyne unit, after all, despite her memories suggesting the contrary.

Bonnie moved her head to the side. The waves crashed against the shore.

The tree was there a few moments ago but had disappeared during the fight. Its absence brought Bonnie back into action.

Where had Jelly gone?

Chapter 10

Pink Symphony

A thousand bubbles raced up Jelly's arms as she waded through the clear, blue water.

"Blug-blug-blug," came out of her mouth instead of a meow. Her lungs expelled the oxygen into the never-ending depths of the ocean.

Her whiskers lit up a neon yellow and fizzed at the tips. Her infinity claws acted the same way as she forced herself to keep her eyes open.

She'd experienced water before. Outside of actually needing to drink it, she'd fallen into Jamie's paddling pool in the garden area outside his apartment. It was a torturous affair for her.

But this was no paddling pool. It stretched out in all directions. The surface was only a few feet from her head.

She learned to swim right there and then. A movement of both arms seemed to do the trick. She waded as hard as she could, trying to reach the surface.

It was no use.

Time and oxygen were running out. A feeling of suffocation began to pervade her body and mind. The ensuing panic afforded her that vital few seconds she'd need if she was to ever reach the surface.

Bwup, bwup, bwup…

Jelly felt her whiskers direct her away from the surface - the opposite direction she felt she needed to go.

A dolphin echo from way, way down pierced through the

water. Before long, a second and third siren beamed through the density of the ocean.

Her claws opened out and sparked again, pointing toward the ocean bed. It was too far down to be seen with her eyes. It was clear to her that her whiskers were pointing her to the ocean bed.

Jelly had no concept of drowning. She knew she needed to breathe, though - that much was clear. How long could she hold on for without any air?

Whump.

A ripple of bubbles spread apart as she swam down to the bed. With no concept of drowning came little concept of how physics worked. She was a cat, after all, trying to figure out everything on her own terms.

The pervading tail-end of the whump noise rumbling through the water crashed against her, firing up her internal engine. She clawed at the bubbles, hoping one of them might release so much-needed respite.

No such luck.

The other bubbles chuckled away, laughing at her, as she tried to kill them. They were too fast.

Whump...

It was easy enough for her to recoil and tumble head-over-tail in the weightlessness of the ocean. A feeling she'd experienced once or twice during zero gravity training. At least she had that going for her.

That second *whump* sound came from *somewhere* below. Jelly pressed her paws to her face and stopped moving. Her tail drifted up between her fanned-out legs as she tried to block out the fury she felt.

"Bleooowwulp," she squealed, expending most of what little oxygen remained in her body.

Then, a dawning realization set in. No more air. That was her last breath floating in a warbled, glinting bubble dead in front of her face.

Her whiskers buzzed to life once again, sending a tingling sensation down her spine.

Jelly barreled over and plummeted toward the sea bed as

fast as she could. On the way, she spotted a school of fish swimming around. The same fish that would go on to beach themselves and turn into those creatures.

She wished she could trade places with them.

Biddum-biddum-biddum...

Her heart-rate quickened. The water felt like it was heating up. Nothing to do with her proximity within the water, rather, her rising body temperature and fear that death was looming.

Death was on the cards if a way out didn't present itself soon.

"Blowaarggh," Jelly let out the last gasp of oxygen she had in her lungs. The closer to the ocean bed she swam, the more her whiskers lit up and fizzed.

Her infinity claws pushed the water away, almost intuitively. She breast-stroked deeper and deeper toward the ocean bed.

A pink hue burst through the water from below like a discarded floodlight. The strips of light bounced around, offering her a challenge.

Swipe right, fail to catch.

Swipe left, bound forward - still no success.

The light couldn't be caught. The closer she swam to the source the more her whiskers seemed to guide her.

Way, way up above, an unintelligible voice shouted something at someone. Then, the sound of a holy thud creaked across the ocean's surface.

A deathly howl followed.

The blackened branches of the tree bulleted through the water, narrowly missing Jelly as she continued to swim...

And swim...

Her whiskers danced a glorious light show as the source of the pink beams made itself visually available.

A gelatinous blob of pink throbbed near the root of the tree, surrounded by a sliver of gold haze.

"Glub... glub," Jelly's mouth opened out. Her eyes widened at the view of the spectacular foreign entity calling her down.

Consciousness was about to become a thing of the past...

***

"Jelly?"

"Meow."

"I know you're not a dog. But I have this ball if you wanna play with it?"

Jamie sat crossed-legged in the middle of the garden. He held up a shiny pink object about the size of a tennis ball. Jelly sat a few feet away wondering what the dastardly contraption was.

"Wanna chase the ball?"

She purred up a treat and climbed on all fours, ready for Jamie to roll the ball to her.

"Ah, no, no," he giggled. "You gotta go get it. Ready?"

"Meow."

He tossed the ball toward the bushes by the fence - a little too hard. "Oh."

"Meow," Jelly jumped at the bushes and followed the ball through the foliage.

Jamie scrambled to his feet and called after her. He knew the danger of the bushes all too well. The fence was broken. Worse, the busy main road lay right behind it.

"Jelly, come back!" he yelled as he saw her behind disappear behind the bushes.

She trundled through the leaves and broken sticks and eyed the ball as it rolled through the gap in the fence. "Meow." The sticks broke apart as she trundled over them. The hole in the fence yawned out and invited her through.

The hole was a bit smaller than she'd have liked. Hoisting her considerable frame through tiny opening was painful. The jagged ends raked through her fur and body as she squeezed through.

The pink ball took center stage in the middle of the road. It seemed to plead for rescue amongst the whizzing cars. She hadn't the first clue how to grab the thing when she reached it.

But it didn't matter. It needed rescuing, and that was all that mattered. She bolted across the first lane of traffic believing herself to be invincible.

NEEAAWW!

A car whizzed past her, nearly taking a whisker away from her face.

More cars shot past at ridiculous speeds. Her head twisted right to left, left to right, keeping up with the vehicular jousting match.

"Jelly, don't move," Jamie's face appeared in the hole of the fence. He'd burrowed through the mud and sticks to try and save her.

"Meow," she turned around and spotted her opportunity to move.

Pounce!

She jumped into the middle of the road, narrowly avoiding being hit by a speeding car.

"Jelly," Jamie hollered. "What did I tell you? Stay there."

She sniffed around the ball and kicked her tail up for balance. She decided she couldn't bite it much less carry it in her mouth. She'd seen dogs do it but knew that they were more adept at carrying items.

Bop.

She knocked the ball with her paw. It wobbled and rested back to its original position.

Maybe two paws?

She yelped and batted the ball from opposite ends with her two paws. It pinged out of her grasp and rolled across the main road.

Without thinking, she darted after it… but hadn't counted on a speeding car rocketing toward her.

She turned to face the gargantuan hunk of metal blare its horn and flood her face with its head lights.

"Meow."

"No," Jamie ran into the path of the car with his arms out, hoping the driver would slam on his brakes in time.

Jelly closed her eyes and held her breath, expecting the worst…

***

Darkness.

Imagine your arms, legs and midriff are suspended in the air. Like you're lying on cloud, without fear of falling either side. No more noise.

Just complete and utter silence.

That's how Jelly felt for a time once the headlights disappeared. She opened her eyes very slowly.

A horizontal slit let a flood of white and pink light into her retinas. It should have hurt but it didn't. Instead, it had a soothing effect.

Her left paw lifted into view, complete with her titanium claws. She exercised them, retracting them in and fanning them back out. A tiny whirring occurred, followed by a streak of blue shocks.

Her right paw waded in front of her face, blockading the view of the length of her body.

An endless gloop of pink stuff cocooned her outstretched body as if being smothered by a warm duvet.

No more suffocating. No more water. No more *anything*.

She tried to flip around to her side but couldn't. Perhaps she was too relaxed? Not as such. She wanted to move around - but simply couldn't.

Her limbs worked, evidently. She wasn't tired - quite the contrary.

She lifted her face to the side and stared at the sticky, pink substance and tried to meow at it.

But she couldn't speak. Her mouth opened, but nothing came out.

A face emerged within the pink, jellied tomb. A nose, then two cheekbones and a pair of eyes. It moved around and stared back at Jelly.

"Ha... Haloo... ?" Jelly mouthed.

A smile stretched across the image of the woman's face and nodded. "Hello, Jelly," it said, softly.

"Mwaaa-ack,' Jelly nearly squeezed out a sound but it was of little use. She pained when she tried to speak and so decided against it.

Another face appeared directly above her. A Japanese woman Jelly had met on Space Opera Alpha. Her name was

Zilla Chin-Dunne.

"Zaaah..." Jelly tried and licked her mouth.

Zillah's face nodded and slowly faded away from the sloppy, pink ceiling.

Jelly made the mistake of blinking. Blackness fell for approximately two-fifths of a second and turned back to pink. Another blink. The gelatinous catacomb turned black.

Another blink, and it turned pink once again.

It frightened Jelly to the point where she didn't want to blink ever again.

Before she had time to display her defiance the entire womb-like tomb rotated around her body. The sound of the movement was intense. She wasn't able to block her ears with her paws. Try as she might, she'd just have to put up with the deafening sound.

"Meeeooowwww."

"Jelly," a voice whirled around the increasing spin of the tomb, "Something *fantastic* is coming."

"Mwaaaah," she screamed and clamped her face with both paws, careful not to take her eye out with her infinity claws.

Lightning bolts struck around the internal walls of the tomb, briefly illuminating it to resemble the inside of a human brain.

Then, Jelly herself began to spin around sideways.

At first it was quick, but as the tomb's rotation sped up so, too, did Jelly's - in the opposite direction.

Spin... spin... spin...

Faster and faster and faster...

A rocketing thunder clap lit up the tomb as it smoothed out into a perfect cylinder, spinning faster than was comprehensible.

Jelly's meowing bleached into a blend of gargles and growls then to nothing as she rotated several hundred times per second.

The thunder bolts intensified as a pang of white light broke out from her face.

Perfect oblong particles broke along her whiskers, streaking out to her nose and cheeks, shifting them away from her head.

Just then, a storm of choral music piped in, smearing into the brilliant white light as Jelly spun around even faster. And faster. Her body blurred, she was spinning so fast.

Her body ballooned due to the inertia until it reached the insides the tomb in all directions. Jelly's zippy revolutions per second were beyond measure.

Spin-spin-spin-spin… Jelly let out a prolonged growl of pain.

The white light exploded into a miasma of heavenly outreach.

Seconds later it swallowed onto itself, leaving absolutely nothing left… *of anything.*

Chapter 11

The staff parking lot.

A quartet of USARIC mercenaries decked out in standard-issue armor bundled an elderly man into the back of a limousine.

"Get in, now," the leader of the squad stood next to the door as the man got in.

"Sheck is secure," he said into his black-coated utility sleeve. The USARIC logo adorned the underside of his forearm, along with his first initial and surname - *K. Too.*

He listened intently to the response.

"Kaoz," Marr shifting his behind across the length of the limousine's back seat, "Are we going or what?"

"Team, listen up," Kaoz addressed his three subordinates and pointed at the peninsula in the not-too-distant horizon. "We've had a major security breach at the Animal compound, Sector Z118."

"What happened?" asked one of the mercenaries, ready to spring into action. "What kind of breach?"

"Most escaped. The perps have been dealt with but the subjects in the second bay escaped."

"Escaped?"

"They're headed for the peninsula."

The reflection of the incomplete Space Opera Charlie vessel smeared across Kaoz's visor.

"Set up a task and finish team to bring them back. They're not regular felines."

"They're not?"

"No. Don't ask any questions. Just find them and bring them back. Dead or alive, I don't much care at this point."

"Understood," Kaoz stepped into the limousine and took a seat opposite Maar. He thumped on the driver's compartment, "Let's go."

The driver slammed on the gas and drove toward the gated exit. A kick of dust lifted from the ground and into dusky haze of the setting sun.

Maar almost freaked out inside the car. He couldn't get comfortable, fidgeting around with the belt clip in the padding of the plush seat.

"Don't be anxious," Kaoz flipped his visor over his head and pinched his mouthpiece, "You're perfectly safe now. ETA, ten minutes."

"Good, good," Maar looked over his shoulder and saw the USARIC building vanish into the distance, "Please tell me this damn car is bulletproof?"

"Of course it is."

"I'm sorry. Can we talk business, please?"

Kaoz and Maar turned to a stern-looking man with silver hair sitting opposite them. He pressed his back against the glass compartment between them and the driver.

"Sorry, Crain. What's the update?"

Crain McDormand - USARIC's head of the legal counsel and the chair of the select committee. Not someone you'd want to get on the wrong side of. He had a manner about him that suggested he'd take you down in court for looking at him the wrong way.

Crain opened his palm and pulled out his thumbnail, "About fifteen minutes after Vasilov was executed someone sent an Individimedia broadcast inside USARIC's animal compound."

He set his cuticle down on the champagne unit next to his knee.

"Some guy with blue hair you might recognize."

The thumbnail projected a paused holographic image of Handax Skill in the middle of the limousine.

"I think I'd recognize a cretin with blue hair," Maar kept his head away from the passenger window. He wasn't terribly interested in a stray bullet flying through his cranium. "Who is this guy?"

"His name is Handax Skill," the man explained, "Sort of the leader of PAAC."

"People Against Animal Cruelty?" Kaoz asked and shook his head. "They're always disturbing us."

"They did a great job in the past hour, I'm afraid to say," Crain snapped his fingers and sat back into the chair, "I could fill you in verbally. The broadcast does a better job of explaining just how bad this is better than I ever could."

"They kill Dimitri and there's *more* bad news?"

"Just watch."

Maar leaned forward as the recording played. A sound of gunfire and commotion rattled around the walls of the limousine.

Even though Handax was long dead it felt like he was directly addressing everyone in the vehicle. Maar found it doubly worrying. He'd failed to realize that Handax addressed *a lot* more people than just those in the car.

"Bisoubisou never boarded Opera Beta. We found her body at the compound along with hundreds of others. Those we found alive and well, we rescued. USARIC has killed three of my team. Moses, Denny, and Leif—"

"—Oh no, no," Maar gasped and held his mouth in shock, "Did this Individimedia go live?"

"I'm afraid so," Crain frowned.

"What? How many saw it?"

"Tens of thousands, if not more. Keep watching."

"That's okay," Maar tried to calm himself down, "We'll just deny it and claim—"

"—They'll deny it, of course," Handax's recording continued much to Maar's worry, "They'll claim they went missing and have no involvement. In a matter of seconds, I'll be joining them."

"Over there," screamed another voice in the recording.

"Hey, you. Put your arms above your head and drop to your knees."

Handax turned away from the broadcast to a cacophony of bullets. The recording paused, offering Crain, Maar, and Kaoz a view of the ground.

"Oh, for heaven's sake," Maar thumped the seat in anger and wiped his sweating brow, "USARIC shot the protesters dead on a live feed?"

Kaoz and Crain didn't know how to respond. They watched their boss try to calm down.

The roads were empty right now. Maar was surrounded by advisers and bodyguards, two of whom were with him in the limousine. Many more were stationed at USARIC's Research & Development Institute twenty miles away to the north.

"I'm…" Maar whimpered, "This was a mistake. A big mistake."

"What was a mistake?" Crain asked with no hint of emotion.

"The Star Cat Project," Maar pointed around the interior of the limousine, "Opera Beta, all this. How long ago was the broadcast?"

"Thirty minutes or so."

"Ugh," Maar hung his head and sniffed, "All hell is going to break loose."

"Maar, if I may say so. I don't think any of this was a mistake. You made decisions in USARIC's best interests. If you had failed to act on Saturn Cry, or Tripp Healy's request to find a suitable subject, we could well have regretted it. In my view you had no choice."

"Try telling that to Dimitri," Maar looked up and stared Crain out with his now-reddened eyes, "He's not even around anymore to argue with you."

"It's *terriful* what happened to him,' Crain tried to sympathize, 'but this was always going to be a contentious issue. It's just very unfortunate—"

"—They shot him in the chest and practically destroyed the animal compound," Maar interjected with a healthy dose of venom, "They've set a dangerous precedent. You know what people are like. When one maniac shoots a place up and becomes a household name they spawn thousands of imitators."

"I'm sure it won't come to that, Maar,"

"Thank God social media is a thing of the past. Everyone would be getting ideas."

Crain tried for a smile of reassurance. "They targeted Vasilov because of his Russian connection. The two aboard Beta who defected and tried to sabotage the mission."

"You're not the one in my shoes, Crain," Maar said. "I want my wife and son relocated to safety."

"It's not necessary—"

"—Have it done right now, Crain," Maar snapped in a fit of rage, "I can't have them in the firing line. Compounds collapse. Important people get shot. Innocent bystanders die."

Crain slipped his thumbnail onto his thumb and shook his head.

"Crain?" Maar threw the man a look of remorse, "Wives and children *burn*, Crain."

Moscow, Russia
Second Sub District of Ramenki

Seven-year-old Remy Gagarin looked up at his mother with an angelic smile. She spat into her palm and wiped a black smudge from his cheek.

Vera Gagarin held her son's face in her hands and made sure he looked the part.

"Mom?"

"Yes, Remy?"

"Why must I speak in English?"

"Because, son, most who watch will not understand Russian."

She palmed his dark, gelled hair over his scalp and smartened him up. She took a step back and eyed him up and down, "There, that is much better."

Remy held out his arms. Dressed in a very attractive suit and tie, he looked approximately a quarter of a million dollars.

It had been nearly two years since Space Opera Beta left on its mission to Saturn.

Remy looked at the marble mantelpiece as he pulled his shirt down. Pictures of him with various celebrities, including Maar Sheck, adorned the wall.

He'd become famous for a time - the handsome boy whose Russian Blue had won the Star Cat Project.

He missed Bisoubisou beyond all measure. His family's new-found riches staved off the regret for large periods of time. The sickening feeling of giving her up for the sake of the good life crept back in. He'd grown up a lot in the past twenty-four months.

Vera didn't much care about Bisoubisou. She and her son rarely spoke of her.

His mother had never been much of a cat lover. Bisoubisou was her son's pet as far as she was concerned - at least, that's what she'd tell herself whenever she experienced the odd pang of regret.

The most fierce regret came in the form of the occasional sadness in her son's eyes. He walked over to the Bisoubisou action figure perched next to the photos. A five-inch rendition of the cat he once had, which resulted in a brief, but Pyrrhic, smile of affection.

Vera's forearm pulsed. She pushed the black ink around into a circle on her skin and looked at her son, "You still miss her, don't you?"

"She is in space helping the American astronauts," Remy was lost in his own naive contrition. He put the figure down on the ledge, "One day she will return."

"Okay, she is ready," Vera pulled an antique chair across the rug and set it beside their expensive couch. "Come, sit next to me."

Remy sat next to his mother on the sofa. She removed her thumbnail and placed it on the Edwardian-style coffee table in front of their knees. "Now, remember. You speak with precision. No filling time with *lessense*."

"Yes, mother."

"You answer the questions she has with as few words as possible and be polite when you do it."

"I will."

"Very good," she snapped her fingers, forcing a projected holographic image of a woman to appear in the middle of the room.

"Ah, I'm here."

A life-size image of Dreenagh Remix pinged to life in the middle of the coffee table. Her shins were out of view as she stood within the coffee table. "Oh, I'm sorry," she looked down and stepped out through the wooden slab.

"That is quite okay."

"Ugh, I hate these live feeds sometimes," Dreenagh chuckled. Her transparent visual representation shimmied up and down like a drunken ghost trying to maintain the strength of its connection from the ether.

"You know, one time, I appeared in my boyfriend's toilet while he was brushing his teeth. So embarrassing."

Dreenagh's affable humor didn't wash very well with the Gagarin family. She shrugged her shoulders, pulled up her left sleeve and pointed at the chair, "Is that for me?"

"Yes," Vera pushed her long ponytail behind her neck and showed Dreenagh the right side of her face. "I prefer if you show this side as it is better than my left."

"You're gorgeous. You have *no* bad sides, Vera," Dreenagh held out her see-through hand. A tiny drone built itself from the surface of her skin. "How are you, Remy?"

"I am well, Dreenagh. Thank you."

"You excited about the interview?"

"Yes. I think so."

The drone whizzed from Dreenagh's palm and zoomed twenty feet away. She angled her fist to the right, moving the holographic drone above the coffee table. "Okay, ready?"

"We are ready," Vera held her posture steady for the drone.

"*Amaziant*, here we go," Dreenagh turned to the drone. The light beaming from its iris blasted out and highlighted the contours on each of the three bodies.

"Hey, good people," she smiled at the drone and jumped

into professional-mode, "Dreenagh Remix here on Individimedia forty-four. As we approach the two-year anniversary of the Star Cat Project and Opera Beta's mission to Saturn, I'm *here*, so to speak, with the Bisoubisou's owners for an exclusive update."

Dreenagh turned to Remy and gave him a media-strewn smile. "Remy Gagarin. You must be very excited?"

"Yes, I am. My cat is going to help people."

Vera placed her hand on his knee. "Yes, we are most proud of Bisoubisou."

"Now, Vera, as Remy's mother, how has the past two years affected you?"

"Oh, we have been most fortunate. We have the satisfaction of knowing our beloved pet is helping USARIC on their vital mission," she beamed and eyeballed the interior of their expensive front room. "As you can see, the money has helped, too."

"So I see," Dreenagh's holographic image sat forward, impressed by the no-expense-spared decor, "I gather the quarter of a million dollar prize money was just the beginning?"

"Indeed, it was very helpful," Vera smiled at Remy, "Since then, Bisoubisou has become a hero and we have become like celebrities."

"I guess the celebrity endorsements contributed to your wealth, too?"

"My mother had a small part in Star Jelly thirty-eight as a scientist."

"Oh, yes," Dreenagh chuckled politely, "The Star Jelly movie franchise. She was very good at acting, wasn't she?"

"Yes," Remy said, "And I appeared in cat food commercials."

"Meow-nom-nom," Dreenagh enacted the famous line from the commercial. "I'm sure people say that to you all the time, right?"

"Not really," Remy said. "We try to stay away from poor people who eat junk food."

"Oh."

Vera rolled her shoulders and held her neck out,

attempting to remove her double-chin from the drone's feed. "Yes, it got very much bad after everyone found out where we lived. So we moved here. Remy is now home-schooled."

"A very wise idea."

"Yes."

Dreenagh's mood softened as she looked at her forearm, preparing herself for the next question. "Remy?"

"Yes?"

"Have you been missing Bisoubisou since she's been away?"

Remy stared at his pristine-suited legs and considered the question. "Yes, I do. But she will be home soon."

It was clear that Vera had no knowledge of recent events at Cape Claudius. She wondered why the aura in the interview was so chirpy. If Remy and his mother had known the truth they might not have been so forthcoming with their answers - or even agreed to the interview in the first place.

Chrome Valley
Northwest London, United Kingdom

Jamie sat cross-legged on the floor of the front room watching Dreenagh's Individimedia broadcast. His mother, Emily, sat on the couch keeping one eye on the floor.

Remy and Vera's holographic representations sat in the middle of the front room awaiting Dreenagh's next question.

A toddler crawled across the carpet, trying to grab at Vera's sparkling shoes.

"No, Jolene," Emily ran over to her and scooped her off the floor, "It's not real, don't touch it."

"Ga-ga," she burped and produced a messy grin.

"Mom, please. I'm trying to listen," Jamie lifted his palm in the air and, along with it, the volume of the broadcast.

Emily lifted Jolene into her high chair, "Not too loud, poppet. You'll upset your sister."

"Not as upset as Remy's going to be, look," Jamie pointed at Dreenagh, "She knows they don't know. She's going to tell him."

"Oh, Jesus," Emily lowered her behind to the couch,

entranced by the drama that would surely follow, "That woman is a piece of work. Tony, come and see this."

"History in the making, is it?" Tony appeared at the door to the front room with a cup of coffee. He leaned against the frame and shook his head. "They have no idea?"

"No, Dad," Jamie turned to the broadcast with great intensity, "Everyone knows but them."

Dreenagh cleared her throat and dampened her voice. Remy eyes shot back at her, wistfully.

"Remy, what was your reaction to the breaking news a couple of hours ago?"

"What news?" Vera asked. "What are you speaking about?"

"You don't know, do you?"

"No," Remy said with innocence, "Is something wrong?"

Dreenagh closed her eyes. On the surface she felt terrible. In her heart, she knew she had the exclusive story of a lifetime. She'd be the first to break it. Enough for her to continue with her USARIC-like grab for power and glory.

"Someone broke into USARIC and found Bisoubisou's body."

"What?" Remy snapped. "You liar. Is it a joke?"

"No, Remy. He sent out a message saying that Bisoubisou was dead and still at USARIC."

"This is quite terriful," Vera snapped. "Bisoubisou is at Saturn helping the Americans find out what the message means."

"I'm afraid not," Dreenagh held out her finger and drew a large rectangle in from their face. Handax's face appeared and the broadcast began to play."

Emily turned to Tony, full of emotion. "I can't watch this."

"No, Mom. We *need* to watch it," Jamie pushed himself onto his feet. Now seven-years-old, he'd grown since he'd last seen Jelly. "It's always better to tell the truth," he turned to his stepfather for confirmation, "Isn't it, Dad?"

"I'm not so sure on this occasion, Jamie," Tony fixed his gaze on Remy's beleaguered face. "Sometimes we have to tell lies. Sometimes it's necessary."

"The scumbags never told them," Emily left the room in a flood of tears. "All this time we thought they knew."

"Sweetie," Tony walked after her and tried to talk her down from her upset. "It's not your fault—"

"—Yes, it is. I took USARIC at their word like a complete fool."

Jamie shut out his mother's grief and concentrated on the interview.

Remy burst into tears and fell into his Vera's arms. She was equally as shocked at the news. His mother's holographic representation pushed through Jolene's face. She, too, began to cry at the visual of Remy doing the same thing.

"Jolene, stop it," Jamie pointed at Dreenagh, "I'm trying to watch."

Vera hugged her grief-ridden son and screamed at Dreenagh. "My God. Is this some kind of sick joke?"

"No, Vera. I'm afraid not."

"It is a lie," she unhanded Remy and stood up from the couch, "You media, you are all the same. Nothing but sensation and lies."

"Well, I'm sorry but—"

"—Get out of my house, you scheming cow."

Dreenagh's transparent image stood up and held out her hands. "I'm not *in* your house, technically."

"That's not what I meant and you know it," she barked back and pointed at Remy sobbing against a cushion, "You invade my home. You come here, spreading lies with actors with stupid colored hair."

"I can assure you I am not lying, Vera. Look," Dreenagh displayed her forearm. The ink swirled around to form a number: 1.4M.

"See that?" Dreenagh asked.

"Yes?"

"That's how many viewers across the world are watching right now. Don't you think just *one* of them might have something to say if they knew it to be false?"

The woman had a point. Remy was way, way ahead of his mother in the grieving process. Granted, that was down to adolescent naivety on his part but, nevertheless, an accurate and fair distance ahead of his mother's reasoning.

"Bisoubisou died right there at the Star Cat Trial finals, Vera," Dreenagh said as she watched the dizzied Russian woman slump to the couch. "I'm sorry, but it's the truth."

"They killed her," Remy hyperventilated through his sobs, "They killed my cat—"

"—Vera, you think the assassination of Viktor Rabinovich and the subsequent expulsion of twenty-three Russian diplomats was a coincidence?" Dreenagh tried to bring the woman to her senses. "Do you see how this ties together?

Vera stared at the floor in bewilderment. "How could I have been so blind?"

"You may hate me, Vera, and that's fine. But I'm a journalist," Dreenagh smiled at her drone and gave it a sly wink, "My job is to report the truth. You saw it here first, viewers."

Jamie couldn't decide which of the three images were more compelling.

Remy, with the look of fear and devastation on his face.

Vera came around to the idea that her life and career was over.

Dreenagh Remix suppressed her desire for fame and fortune at the expense of tearing a family apart with the truth.

It was at this moment that Jamie Anderson realized two things:

1: The world didn't work the way he thought it did. The same could be said for the universe at large but there was no time to expatiate on it. The world suddenly showed its playing cards as the ruthless, vindictive and painful place it had always been. The same place his mother and, until a few years ago, his biological father had tried to shield from his innocent eyes.

2: Bisoubisou's death and subsequent absence was known to him and his mother. Jelly went in her place after accidentally murdering her. Actually, *murder*, he thought, was a complete misnomer. She was merely defending herself and fought for honor. At the time Jelly was signed up, he and his mother signed a contract non-disclosure agreement. Judging by the Gagarin family interview, it seemed they had avoided a major hassle. Jamie and his mother received the prize money. When he turned eighteen he'd be in receipt of the bulk of it.

A thought occurred to him as he sat in the carpet.

If everyone now knew that Bisoubisou didn't join Opera Beta, then *which cat did?*

He assumed that anyone wanting answers - which was *everyone* and their grandmother - would come knocking at the Anderson household looking for answers.

One such feisty journalist named Dreenagh Remix could be the first of them.

"Mom, Mom," Jamie climbed to his feet and ran out of the front room. He used the sound of his mother's sobbing as route to find where she was. "*Mom.*"

Tony stepped into Jamie's path, preventing him from reaching the bedroom. "Hey, son. She's a bit upset. Give her a few minutes, okay?"

"No, Tony. This is really—"

"—Don't call me Tony. I'm your father."

"You're not my *real* dad," he barged past and nearly made the door, only to be caught by the back of the shirt. Tony crouched down and glanced at his vindictive little stepchild in the eyes.

"What did you just say?"

"I'm sorry, I—"

"—I'd appreciate it if you referred to me as *Dad*," Tony finished, noticing Jamie was desperate to get to his mother. "What's wrong?"

Jamie raised his eyebrows with great sincerity. "If everyone knows Remy's cat didn't go to Saturn they might think Jelly went, instead. Everyone still thinks she's the runner-up"

The boy had a hell of a point. The knock-on consequences of this revelation smacked Tony in the face. "You're right."

He stood up straight and made for the bedroom with Jamie's hand in his. "Come on, son, let's go tell her."

Emily's incessant sobbing flew out of the bedroom and showed no sign of halting.

Tony peered around the door, not wanting to disturb her moment of sadness. "Emily?"

Jamie looked up at him with an cherubic smile. His stepfather couldn't help but feel a shudder roll down his spine. Moments ago he viewed Jamie as just an average little boy. Now, with the astonishing connection he'd made, the little boy seemed more mature.

Certainly wiser...

USARIC Research & Development Institute
Port D'Souza
(Ten miles northeast of Corpus Claudius)

USARIC's R&D institute, much like its headquarters at Cape Claudius, was so big it had its own zip code. Maar had become the major shareholder of the company now that Dimitri Vasilov was no longer breathing.

The research and development institute housed hangers designed to test thruster and engine capabilities. Much of Manning/Synapse's beta testing of the Androgyne series with the American Star Fleet had taken place at this location.

This evening, it also served as a discreet embassy to protect the one man who'd yet to be assassinated - Maar Sheck.

He stepped out of the tubular elevator cage and into a vast scientific laboratory.

Like the animal compound at USARIC HQ this clandestine set-up was as sinister, if not more so. Though he rarely frequented the science division (the nerds and tech-heads had that all covered) he always marveled at the technology on display.

No such luxuries could be afforded now, though, as Kaoz marched him and Crain along the observatory gangway several feet above the work parapet.

"How long do I have to stay down here?" Maar walked past a colossal slab of ceramic being polished by six men wearing breathing apparatus.

"As long as it takes, Maar," Kaoz said. "News has just broken of what's happened, so you'll be down here for at least another couple of months."

"*Couple of months?*"

"At least."

"Ugh, this is a nightmare."

"Unless you want to go up for air and risk getting your head blown off, then yes."

"God damn it," Maar pointed at the head of a wall at the end of the gangway. A dim red bulb rotated just above it. "Are they here?"

"Yes."

Maar continued down the metal strip and waved them on. "Good, I want a full report on the subject capture, please. They better have good news for me."

The wall split in two as the men approached toward it. Kaoz lifted his mouthpiece in front of his lips and hit a button on his wrist. "Oxade, this is Kaoz. Come in."

The sound of an attack vehicle roared through his earpiece. "This is Oxade, over."

The clandestine bunker lit up as the three men entered. Maar placed his hands on his hips, "So, this is home, is it?" he asked himself as he looked around the featureless room.

"For the moment, yes," Crain said. "You're safe here."

"Do my family know?"

"Oh. Good Lord, no. They can't know your whereabouts."

Kaoz hit a button on the wall, forcing the doors to shut behind him. "Maar wants a sit-rep on the subject capture."

The moon was full tonight.

A female Siamese sniffed around a patch of fresh grass and mud in a desperate hunt for food. The dried flakes of dust began to rumble back and forth like a marbles on a vibrating trampoline.

Her ears pricked up, alert, "Meow."

The mud cracked apart as the sound of a furious engine blanketed her from behind.

She hopped around and attempted to find the source of the noise. Two giant headlamps blinded her as she howled for her life.

P'TATCH! SWISH-SWIPE!

A brown grid enlarged in front of her eyes. Her feet shot into the air. The tomb of rope tangled in her claws as she somersaulted and landed in the back of a jeep.

"Maaoooww," she squealed through her soft but venomous prison.

"Got her," Oxade yelled at the driver from the passenger side of the 4x4. He thumped the USARIC logo on the outside of the door. The Siamese squealed in terror as it clamped eyes on a dozen captured cats in the back. The roped cats slammed into each other as the vehicle sped along the ground.

"Sorry, Kaoz. You were saying?"

He clutched the window-mounted machine gun and flicked the attached flashlight to life. The ground illuminated as they sped up, searching for more of the escapees.

"Maar wants to know how many you've caught."

"Uh, hang on," Oxade turned to the back of the 4x4 and performed a hasty head count, "Around twenty or so. We have other units out looking for them. You know what herding cats is like."

"Okay, I'll tell him," Kaoz said before cutting the connection dead.

Two American bobtails - one orange, one white - hid behind a tree, exhausted from their escape from the compound. Not the fastest of felines, they'd become separated from the others who'd stormed ahead.

The 4x4's headlamps began as dots in the distance but expanded the closer they got to them.

"Meow," the orange bobtail nudged the white's behind, running toward the Port D'Souza peninsula on the Gulf of Mexico - a glorious stretch of water lit up by the full moon.

Orange bobtail found the strength to continue toward the section of land that encroached the water, leaving the fatigued white cat behind.

VROOM, VROOM!

"I think I can see another one," Oxade said to the driver, "Quick, to the left. Look, there. You can see its stupid cat's eyes."

"Meow," the white bobtail exclaimed and ran away from the vehicle's path.

Oxade took both handles of the gun as the driver floored the gas, frightening the life out of the cat. It jumped into the air and hissed, bushing up its tail.

He opened fire on the cat.

THRAAAA-TA-TAT-A-TAT!

"Here, kitty-kitty-kitty…" he shouted as the bullets chewed up the grass as it hopped around like a cowboy having its feet fired at it by a drunken ne'er-do-well.

"Rowwaaarrr," she screamed, tumbling around the exploding patches of mud.

"We got a live one," Oxade yelled at the driver, "I think this one's for the net. Back up."

The vehicle screeched to a halt, flinging mud out in front of its bumper.

The hellish red reverse lights sprang on, flooding the white bobtail's scared face. She turned around and ran off in the opposite direction.

VROOOOM!

The vehicle spun its wheels and darted backwards at full speed. Oxade swung the machine gun toward the trunk of the SUV and aimed it at the cat as the vehicle backed towards her.

"Faster, man. C'mon!"

"I'm trying," the driver shouted into the rear view mirror. He carefully avoided veering off the already-beaten track.

"Closer… *closer*… come on to daddy, you dumb critter," Oxade whispered, aiming the sight down on the cat's behind. "Now!"

He yanked back on both triggers.

PTATCH!

A net blasted out from the barrel and javelined over her as she ran.

"Got her!"

SWISH-SWIPE! The net swished across the mud, wrapped itself around the white Bobtail's hind legs and swung into the air like a fierce fairground ride.

"Meeoooowwwwaaaaahhhh!"

She slammed to the opened deck in the back of the vehicles with dozens of fellow captives. The black Siamese clawed and chewed at the rope, trying to burst free. She looked up at the nasty man sitting atop the roof.

"Attention, please, my furry friends," Oxade squatted and clapped his hands together, "Now, all of you have been *very* naughty, haven't you? And you know what happens to bad pussycats, don't you?"

"Hey, Oxade," yelled the driver as he stepped on the gas, "Stop flirting with them. They've had enough."

Oxade hissed at the petrified cats, scaring them half to death, "Ha-ha!"

He thumped his foot on the roof and shouted over his shoulder. "We must have at least thirty of them, now."

"Where are the rest?"

"I don't know, but we'll get them," Oxade took a final look at the feline captives, "Won't we, my little pedigree chums?"

The 4x4 sped off past the trees and into the horizon. The noise from the engine dissipated only to be replaced by crickets.

Ten seconds later, a wet nose appeared from one of the trees. All clear.

Then another nose moved out from another tree…

… *and another…*

… until twenty or so female felines of different breeds, sizes and colors emerged, knowing they were safe - for now.

The leader of the pack, a gorgeous panther-esque Egyptian Mau with silver eyes, howled at the others and caught their attention.

Scores of tiny spiders crept across the ground, snaking in and out of their paws.

The cats clawed back at them, stomping, and squishing a few of the spindly creatures as they scuttled away.

Mau snarled at the surviving spiders. She roared at the ground, scaring them off.

The cats instinctively formed a crescent around her and

sat on their haunches. They were ready for answers.

Mau shifted around, lifted her tail and showed them all her behind. Everyone knew who was in charge, now.

"Meow," the cats replied in unison.

Mau wandered toward the water knowing the others were following her. She averted her attention to the bright moon and stopped at the shoreline.

The cats sat upright behind her.

Mau licked her mouth and shook the fatigue from her head. The light from the moon streaked across her pupils.

"Meow."

The other cats followed suit. "Meow."

A wondrous sight to behold if anyone had seen it. Thirty or so escapees looking at the stars in the night sky. Thankful for the chance for freedom.

The call-outs to the moon occurred again, and again... until the chorus of meows from each cat blended into one prolonged and eerie howl at the moon...

Chapter 12

The Control Deck
Space Opera Beta

Tor held the analog keyboard in his hands, restricted in movement by the wires connecting to the deck. Manuel's holographic book hung in the air as they conversed.

"Manuel, what is your primary function?"

"To serve the crew of Space Opera Beta and to act as autopilot."

"Good," Tor punched the results onto the keys and turned to the transparent screen in front of the deck. He felt the rim of his Decapidisc, lamenting the day he fell on the wrong side of his crew. "Confirm coordinates of Opera Beta, please."

Manuel folded his spine and conked out for a couple of seconds.

"Manuel?"

"Yes, Tor?"

"Confirm Opera Beta coordinates, please. Command prompt. One, zero, six, forward slash, one, zero."

The numbers appeared in as a green digital readout over the front of the book.

"The coordinates are precisely the same as before. That is to say, zero, zero, zero, zero—"

"—Okay, stop. I get the picture."

Tor shook his head and typed a prompt on the keyboard, "Commencing scan, please standby."

Tripp and Wool ran onto the deck ahead of Jaycee

415

escorting Baldron through the door, "Tor, are we up and running?"

"Yes, we—" he turned around and saw Tripp clutching his Rez-9. It made him nervous, "What's going on? Why the gun?"

"Didn't you hear what I told you?" Tripp scanned the walls and ceiling ready to blast whatever might pop out from the walls, "The whole place is breaking up."

"Breaking up?"

"It's sick, comrade," Baldron spat and caught Tor's attention, "There's these *things* breaking into the ship, Viktor. We're not in space anymore, comrade."

Tor eyed Baldron's Decapidisc. It seemed to him that whoever was wearing one was considered to be the bad guy.

"Comrade," Baldron stepped over to Tor and opened his arms for a hug. The pair found they couldn't hug on account of the metal discs around their necks..

"Hey," Jaycee threatened the pair with his K-SPARK shotgun. "Less of that stupidity. Get a room."

"We *had* a room," Tor chewed down the urge to scream, "We were perfectly safe in N-Carcerate till you forced us out."

Baldron closed his eyes and tugged at his Decapidisc, "No, no, that's where the things got in."

"Will someone please tell me what he's talking about?" Tor asked. "What things?"

Tripp checked signs of damage on the control deck, "They're big and ugly, and vicious. Whatever they are."

Baldron eyed Jaycee, only to receive a knowing wink from him.

"You don't say."

"How's Manuel? We need to get the thrusters up and running and get the hell out of here."

Tor placed the keyboard on the control deck and hit the return key, "Functional, but still confused. I found something, though."

Wool kept her right hand near her belt's hand gun holster. "What did you find?

"A video message. Sent just before we went dark."

"Oh."

Tripp knew the content of the message. He had hoped to keep the details to himself, "The one from USARIC?"

Tor couldn't bear to look at his captain. "Yeah. Look." He hit a key. The holovideo to projected into the middle of the control deck.

Maar Sheck, CEO of USARIC, read from a prepared holographic statement at a podium.

"Following the death of Viktor Rabinovich, Deputy Dimitri Vasilov and the news of Russian infiltration on Space Opera Beta, USARIC will cease operation with immediate effect."

Baldron took a few steps around the holovideo and glanced at Tor, "So, they know?"

"Seems so," Tor nodded as the video played out.

Maar continued, "All diplomatic relations have been suspended with immediate effect. It is with regret that all Russian operatives are to be ejected from American soil, and vice versa."

Jaycee didn't take the revelation very well at all. He stomped over to the keyboard and hit the pause button. "You mean to tell me that Russia and North America are now at war?"

Tripp shook his head, "Not quite *war*. More a divorce, if you like."

"It wasn't our fault," Tor complained. "It was the brainchild of Dimitri Vasilov. We were only following orders."

"Much like my button on my glove, here," Jaycee held up his wrist and teased the button on his glove with his finger.

"Stop doing that," Baldron and Tor screamed in unison.

"Jaycee, stop," Wool tried to placate the angry mercenary as he pushed Baldron against the control deck.

"Hey, imbecile."

"Please don't kill me," Baldron felt along the rim of the deck and pulled himself away from Jaycee. "I swear, it wasn't—"

"—*Earth* is about to start a second cold war because of *you*. I have family back home."

Tripp tried to placate the angry giant's temper, "Jaycee, all of us have family back home."

"You shut up," He pointed at Tripp and screamed at him for the first time - close to two years' worth of pent-up frustration against his colleague.

Tripp lowered his gun, stunned beyond comprehension, "*Okaaay*?"

Jaycee socked Baldron in the face. The side of his body hit the deck, accidentally hitting the play button on the keyboard.

"Oww."

"You're gonna get us all killed,' Jaycee spat and blenched his fist.

Maar's hologram continued speaking, "We send our thoughts and prayers to the souls aboard Opera Beta and wish them all the best on their survival in the vicinity of Enceladus. Beta, may God be with you."

Jaycee ran his gloves through his hair and let out a pained exclamation, "Someone shut that imbecile off!"

"Yes," Tor scrambled to the keyboard and hit the pause button. "I'm sorry."

Tripp held out his arms and walked through the paused image of Maar Sheck. He offered a makeshift peace treaty. "Listen to me very carefully."

The visual cracked apart and vanished into thin air. The entire team turned to Tripp to hear him out.

"Events on Earth can't be changed. What's done is done. I can only run with the facts."

"No," Jaycee said. "We can kill these two right now and protect ourselves."

Tor and Baldron hung their heads in shame. Jaycee wasn't exactly exercising his subtlety at this point.

"Stop and think for a second, will you? Just *think*. We can't kill them—"

"—you heard the message, Tripp," Jaycee said. "USARIC is no more. We're at war with these commie scum suckers—"

"—I know that. But the fact still stands. We need them and they need us. I don't care about what's going on back home. I just care that we *get* back home."

"This is utter lessense."

Tripp turned to the two men at the control deck, "You said Manuel was up and running?"

"Yes," Tor picked up the keyboard, eager to satisfy his superior.

"I want a trace on Anderson and Dr Whitaker. I want an update on the engine and the thrusters and what we need to do to get back get home."

Tor typed away on the keys with enthusiasm. Jaycee's desire to murder him and his colleague had been overridden by the captain. "I'm way ahead of you—"

BZZZZ-OWWW.

The communications and flight panel shunted around. The lights snapped off and filled the deck with darkness. The generator's hum slowed to a standstill. Even the floor's emergency strip lighting failed to light up.

"Jesus, what was that?" Wool's voice came from the darkness.

"Oh, God," Baldron's trembling vocal chords barreled around the room, "Is this it? Are we dead?"

"Stay absolutely still, everyone." Tripp advised. "Don't move a muscle."

"I can't see anything," Jaycee pressed his foot forward.

"I said don't move. Wool, is that you?"

"Yes, yes, I think so," she said, trying her level best to keep calm, "I can feel your hand."

"Don't move."

The walls and ground vibrated and shifted around. Despite the darkness, most in the room tried to keep their balance by holding onto something solid.

"What's going on?"

"We've lost power," Tripp barked. "Grab hold of something. Anything rooted to the ground or the wall."

The shifting intensified and refused to let up.

Wool grabbed hold of the flight deck. Jaycee pressed his back against the wall. The sound of two metal Decapidiscs clanging together suggested Tor and Baldron hugged each other.

"Christ, we're going to die," Baldron bawled. "This is how

it ends."

"Shut up and hold tight," Tripp shouted over the noise and turned to the flight deck's acrylic frontage, "We're not going to— Oh... *my God*. What is *that?*"

Stars formed across the black canvas of space. Lighting up one by one, they added glare and cast a dim light into the control deck.

Everyone staggered around in an attempt to remain upright.

Pink dust crept across the stars and fanned out in all directions. Seconds later, a giant circle appeared to the right of the shield, filling itself with a bizarre amalgam of black and orange clouds.

Six silver whiskers streaked out underneath the circle as it formed into a strangely familiar eye.

The vibrations of the ship conformed to a piece of classical music.

"Is that... *Jelly?*" Wool screamed over the commotion.

It was. Her enlarged eyeball peered against the transparent plastic, reflecting Saturn and its spinning rings. Violent-looking and beyond reproach, her face remained steady - and determined. Fire erupted in her thirty-foot eyeball.

"Jelly!"

Cracks tore down the sides of the control deck. A burst of pink light blasted the darkness away.

"My God," Baldron looked at the eyeball in utter astonishment. He couldn't move out of sheer reverence. "She's..."

WHUMP.

Baldron and Tor blacked out. Their bodies hit the deck. Jaycee covered his face with his arm, blocking out the magnificent light from his eyes. It wasn't long before he passed out and hit the deck.

Tripp and Wool kept their gaze fixed on Jelly's face as the volume of the orchestra loudened.

"She's... she's..." Wool gasped and gripped Tripp's arm. "She's..."

WHUMP.

Overwhelmed, Tripp and Wool's eyelids snapped shut.

They collapsed to the ground together.

The cracks in the ship sealed up immediately, plunging the control deck into darkness once again.

Then, Jelly's face vanished in a puff of dust - taking the stars in the sky with it.

A bizarre phenomenon that proved beyond comprehension...

Botanix

The damage from the dumb bomb explosion could still be felt. The walls had been shattered to a point, leading into the sprawling and infinite Pink Symphony landscape.

Sitting with her back to the wall, Bonnie remained unconscious. The back of her hand lay against the ground with her Rez-9 in her palm.

The water tank suffered damage. Broken into three sections, it gushed the contents across the floor and soaked her inner-suit pants and boots. Her removable leg had come free during the fight with the creature. It was missing.

A pink tear collected in her right eye as she breathed. More and more watery effluence added to the build-up, forcing its collected weight over the eyelid and down her cheek.

It plummeted toward the ground and splashed against her good leg, soaking into the fabric.

It was enough to make her open her eyes and inspect the strange sensation.

"Ugh, what happened?" she lubricated the inside of her mouth with her tongue, "Good lord, what—"

She squeezed the gun and brushed her inner-suit down. Splatter from the creature she'd executed outside had soaked into it. Her focus shifted from her stomach to the stump on her right leg.

Fear set in.

Her titanium leg was nowhere to be seen. She leaned over and grabbed at the metal grille, hoisting herself forward. "My leg, my leg..."

She dragged the lower half of her body by her hands

along the row of plants, trying her utmost to peek between them. Still no sign of her missing limb.

Instead, she saw a small, furry creature laying on its side. It's stomach and sides pushed in and out. An indication that it was at least alive.

"God damn it, not another one," she gripped her Rez-9 and aimed the sight at the beast, "Hey, you."

Its furry ears twitched at the sound of her voice, but didn't move from the fetal position.

"You want some more, you freak?"

She squeezed the trigger, blasting a warning shot across its body.

A tuft of fur flew into the air having been grazed by the edge of the projectile. The creature lifted its tail and whipped it back to the ground.

"Huh?" Bonnie watched in amazement as the creature rolled over onto its back and held up its paws. Its eyes opened, forcing it to yawn and reveal its front teeth.

"Anderson?"

Its ears pricked up at the call of her name. A slurp of the tongue, and the little thing was back in business. Of course it was Jelly.

"Meeooo..." she squealed at the top of her croaking voice, struggling to get the sound out. She meowed again. This time in much lower pitch.

"Where... where did you go?"

"Boh... Boh..." Jelly rolled onto her back and clawed at her tail. "Boh... knee..."

"You just said my name!"

Bonnie flipped around and dug her shoulders into the ground. Enthralled by what she'd witnessed, she lifted her forearm in front of her face. Her thumb scraped the three links of black ink across her synthetic skin, "Individimedia, access. Dr. Bonnie Whitaker, broadcast enable."

The ink formed three individual dots. They flashed on and off, indicating a successful connection, "This is Bonnie. I repeat, this is Bonnie Whitaker. Does anyone read me?"

She kept her eyes on Jelly, who clawed at her own tail in the throes of turmoil.

"Bonnie?" Tripp's tinny voice flew out of the pinpricks in her wrist, "We read you. Where are you?"

"Botanix. Anderson's with me. Come, quickly."

"Is she? What's she doing?"

"Behaving strangely. Something happened to us, to her. Where are you?"

"We're in control right now. Something happened here, too. We lost power, briefly, but we're back on."

"I'm scared, Tripp," Bonnie looked around at the shattered walls. Behind her stood the door to Botanix. Directly opposite, the infinite landscape of Pink Symphony. "That pink beach thing is still here. I was attacked. I've lost my leg—"

"—Okay, okay, calm down. Just stay there. I'll be right over with Wool."

"Please be quick," Bonnie lowered her arm and relaxed her shoulders.

"Make sure Anderson doesn't run off out there—"

"—But, I can't move."

Tripp waved Wool over to the door of the control deck, "We're on our way. Do you have your firearm on you?"

Bonnie's voice came through Tripp's forearm, "Just my Rez."

An ethical quandary appeared in his mind as he reached the door, "Listen, Bonnie."

"What is it?"

"If you have to…" Tripp ducked his head and thought very carefully about his instruction.

"If I have to *what*?"

"Damn it."

Wool knew what was going on, "Oh, Tripp. No. Don't you *dare*."

"We have no choice," Tripp lifted his arm to mouth, "Use the gun on Anderson if she doesn't comply."

"What?" Bonnie screamed back.

Jaycee, Baldron and Tor threw their captain a befuddled look. "What?"

"I'm not playing around, here," Tripp finished. "If she

tries to run off, shoot her."

"Tripp, you can't do that—" Wool tried.

"—I don't trust her, not after what happened a few minutes ago. Come on, we have to get to Botanix."

The duo walked through the door, leaving Jaycee, and his two Russian captives alone in the control deck.

Tor turned to Jaycee for a reaction.

"What are you looking at?" he bopped the man on the back of the head, "Get busy, numbskull. We know where everyone is. We need to know the state of Opera Beta."

"Right, right," Tor snapped his fingers and prayed Manuel would appear, "Manuel?"

The holographic book appeared in front of them, spinning its covers around, eager to assist, "Greetings, good people."

"I want a full report on the ship's system."

"Certainly."

Tor followed Manuel across the room. The book inspected the flight deck.

"Also, run coordinates on our current location."

"As I have relayed *twice*, now, the coordinates are irrelevant. Please excuse me while I run a scan on Beta's functionality."

The holographic book beeped over and over again.

Baldron dared not look Jaycee in the eye. He kept his focus on his boots hoping he wouldn't get thumped.

"Hey, you. Landaker."

Baldron tensed his shoulders and flinched, "Don't hit me."

"I'm not gonna hit you," Jaycee sniggered. "Just wanted to know how you were feeling right now?"

"I'm scared."

"You have *no* idea how happy I am to hear that."

Jaycee intimidated him by slammed the K-SPARK barrel in his open palm. Baldron jumped in his shoes, the weight of his Decapidisc reminding him of his situation. "*Jeez*. I think I'm going to have a coronary."

"We can only hope,' Jaycee grinned. "Hey, can I tell you a secret?"

"Wh-what?"

"I'm scared too, you know," Jaycee whispered in his ear, "I know I don't look it, but I am. Do you know what happens when I get scared?"

"N-No, what?" Baldron bit his lip as his oppressor got a little *too* close for comfort.

"I get fidgety, you know. Dunno what to do with myself. I start hitting things. Me and my temper."

"Oh, G-God," Baldron whimpered and scrunched his face. "Please d-don't—"

"—you ever seen what a K-SPARK shell does to the human body?"

"N-No."

"Total and utter evisceration."

Biddip-beep. Manuel snapped out of his scan. "Aha. Report complete."

Baldron breathed a sigh of relief as Jaycee turned to the holographic book, "Is he on?"

"Seems to be," Tor said. "Manuel?"

"Yes, Tor?"

"Report, please?"

"Certainly."

Manuel darted over to the middle of the room and bent its pages out wide. A vector image of Space Opera Beta projected from its spine and into the middle of the deck.

"Thruster damage in Engine and Payload, Level Ten. Two of twenty modules at more than seventy-five percent damage."

Tor walked around the map of Beta and placed his fingertip on the thruster area at the fat end of the ship, "Ports Y118, and Z409?"

"Indeed."

"Perfect, that's precisely what I wanted you to say," Tor looked at Baldron. "That's one for you, my friend."

"Wanted him to say?" Jaycee asked, quizzically.

Tor held out his hand and corrected himself at speed, "I mean, it's what I was expecting. Two ports down. In other words, Manuel is spot on."

"What's the damage, Manuel?" Baldron felt entitled to

join in with the analysis - and away from Jaycee for a moment or two.

The twenty cylinders enlarged into view and spun around slowly, outlining the affected area.

"The affected cylinders disengaged, either during the explosion or the trip through Enceladus. I don't know which, but both need re-connecting."

"Understood," Baldron turned to Tor, who winked at him in secrecy.

"Is that something you can fix?" Jaycee asked. "I hope so, otherwise you're of no use to man nor beast."

Baldron didn't know where to look, "Yes, yes. I can fix it, provided—"

"—With an emphasis on the word *beast*," Jaycee joked.

"Provided the location is unaffected by whatever that stuff is out there, it's a two-man job with Tor guiding us."

"How long will it take, chump?"

"Thirty minutes, maybe less."

"Okay, *amaziant*," Jaycee booted Baldron in the back. He stumbled forward and crashing against the control deck.

"Jaycee? Seriously?" Tor took pity on his friend, "That was uncalled for."

"No, it wasn't," Jaycee applauded Baldron as he struggled to his feet in serious anguish, "Look at you, withstanding all this pain."

"Stop hitting me."

"No."

"Hey, less of it," Tor held the warring men apart, "Jaycee, please. The last thing you need is an injured man carrying a nuclear device. We're trying to work on getting back home. Baldron is our engineer and he's no use to us if he can't do his job."

Jaycee grabbed Tor's wrist and threw his arm away, "Don't talk to me like you're one of the good guys, you egotistical little turd. Don't come on like you're a hero in all this."

Tor puffed his chest out, ready to take the inevitable beating his next sentence would initiate. "Oh yeah?"

"Yeah."

"We're doing precisely what you're telling us to do. Baldron and I aren't heroes, but we're working with you, aren't we?"

"Only because my captain insists on it."

"Okay, fine," Tor screamed in Jaycee's face, "Kick and punch us both to death, then. Let's see how far you get."

Jaycee's patience was about to end. He lifted his glove and threatened to active their Decapidiscs.

"Jesus, you and your big mouth, Viktor," Baldron backed away in an attempt to disassociate himself with his comrade. He pointed his finger at Jaycee, "*He's* in control, not us. Don't give him any more excuses to hit that damn button."

"Well said, Landaker,' Jaycee grinned. "I've been instructed to remove both your heads if either of you so much as *fart* in a clear air zone."

Tor backed down. He couldn't argue with *that* statement.

"So, here's what we're gonna do. Tor, you're gonna stay here and complete Manuel's scan, or whatever the hell he does. Baldron, you and I are gonna go to the engine and fix whatever it is needs fixing so we can get the hell out of this pink paradise."

Tor snorted and fought to keep his dignity intact. He didn't acknowledge Jaycee's instruction.

"Do you understand what I've just said, *comrade*?"

"*Yes*," Tor spat, deeply unhappy and full of sarcasm, "I read you loud and clear."

"Good."

Chapter 13

Botanix

Space Opera Beta - Level Three

Bonnie pulled her body across the desecrated row of plants. Inch by inch, she got closer to Jelly, who lay on her side cleaning herself with her tongue.

She coughed and spluttered occasionally, spitting out tufts of fur to the ground. Every time she looked over at Bonnie from between the charcoaled vegetation she froze solid and kept her eyes on her.

"Meow," Jelly licked her titanium infinity claws with her tongue. She'd gotten used to the zinc-like taste over time.

"Hey, girl," Bonnie removed her Rez-9 from her mouth and set it to the ground, "Stay where you are. Help is coming."

Jelly didn't seem the slightest bit concerned. She flicked her ears and shot Bonnie in a vicious look, "Maaoow."

"Stay there, I'm coming for you."

Jelly began to whelp as if overcome by illness. Her throat constricted due to her coughs and splutters.

"Are you feeling okay—"

"Meaooowww," came the creepy response. A deadened, throaty howl of turmoil. Jelly fell back and rolled around, croaking up a storm.

"Jeez, what's wrong with you?"

Jelly hopped onto all fours and shook her entire body. Strands of fur flicked out in all directions. She pushed her right hind leg back, intending to move away into the glorious pink-hued beach front.

"No, no, don't—" Bonnie thumped the grip of her Rez-9 to the ground and took aim at the cat, "Don't go, Anderson."

Jelly took another step back, this time with her left hind leg. Now was the time to test her synthetic human.

"Meow," Jelly spat out a rope of pink drool.

"I mean it, sweetie," Bonnie flicked the safety catch down with her thumb, arming her Rez-9. She blinked hard. A drop of pink liquid fell from her right eye, "Don't move."

Jelly tested the standoff once again, seconds away from an attempt to run off into Pink Symphony.

"What's happened to you, girl?" Bonnie whispered and tightened her grip on the gun, "Tell me what's going on."

Jelly relaxed on the spot and tilted her head.

Swish!

The door to Botanix slid open behind Bonnie's heel. Startled, Jelly launched into the air and flipped around, headed for Pink Symphony.

"Anderson," Tripp screamed after her as she bolted across the metal grille and onto the sand leading to nowhere.

Wool darted after her with her arms outstretched, "Jelly, come back."

Jelly bolted through the opening in the wall.

BOMP!

Her nose and forehead scrunched together, the result of a vicious impact against a transparent barrier preventing her from escape. "Miaow."

Wool's feet splashed through stream of fresh water and ground to a halt. Aghast, she witnessed her feline friend tumbled over in pain.

"Jelly, stop," Wool reached the cat and scooped her up in her arms, "Hey, sweetie. What's wrong?"

Jelly blinked a few times and swiped the air with her claws in a fit of rage, "Miaow!"

"Hey, calm down," Wool lifted her up under her arms and looked into her eyes, "Something's wrong with you, girl," Wool turned to Tripp, "I need to get her to Medix."

"Okay, is she all right?"

"I don't know," Wool ran across the puddle and turned to Bonnie, "What did you do to her?"

"*Me?* I didn't do anything to her."

"Her heart is racing, look," Wool rocked Jelly in her arms in an attempt to calm her down, "Something's hassling her."

"*She*'s feeling hassled?" Bonnie grabbed Tripp's hand and stood on her one, good leg, "Aw, poor thing. She's all hassled, is she?"

"Yes, she is," Wool walked off with Jelly in her arms, "Come on, girl. Let's get you checked out."

"That cat is nothing but a liability," Bonnie screamed after Wool as she exited the area.

Tripp stared at Pink Symphony. Tiny silhouetted figures crept over the sandy dune's horizon and scuttled toward the ship's opening.

"Look, look," he tugged at Bonnie's arm, "Look at them."

"I know. I met one when I was out there."

"Really?" Tripp gasped, "What happened?"

"Came to a pretty messy end, to be honest," Bonnie slung her arm over Tripp's shoulder and nodded at the door, "Seen the state of my suit? It sucks."

"It went down that easy?"

"Right in the middle of its nasty face," Bonnie raised the stump on her right leg. "Take me to the fit room. If I need to fight those things, you need me upright, don't you?"

"No Fit Room for you, Bonnie. We're going to N-Vigorate to get you re-limbed first."

Hundreds of fleshy, twelve-limbed creatures reached the invisible barrier between the broken section of Botanix's back wall and Pink Symphony.

BAM. THUD-BANG-THUD.

The creatures squealed and slammed their thick talons against the barrier, wanting to get in and murder anything breathing.

"What do you know about these things?" Bonnie asked as she hopped to the door using Tripp for balance.

"Not as much as you."

"Huh?"

431

"Well, you've disposed of one of them already. I haven't. And I'd rather not if I don't have to."

"Nothing from Manuel?" Bonnie asked.

"No, he's busy trying to get us out of here."

They reached the door and took a final look at what might happen to them if they weren't able to escape. Death by at least one hundred fleshy spider *things*.

"SCREEEEEE!"

The largest of the creatures wailed from its knuckled mid-section. Its front four talons daggered at the see-through barrier.

"I dunno what those things are," Tripp muttered as he helped Bonnie through the door, "But someone had better give us some answers pretty damn fast."

Medix

Jelly struggled for freedom as Wool released her onto her bed. She fought back with an intensity previously unseen by Wool. The claws came out. Swipes were thrown.

"For heaven's sake, Jelly," Wool felt her heart sink as she pinned her forearms against Jelly's. At least she couldn't hit back. "Calm down. You'll work yourself into a frenzy."

"Shaaaantaaa…"

"Shanta? What *are* you saying? You're delirious—"

Jelly screeched up at the ceiling and threw her hind legs forward. One of her infinity claws pierced through Wool's inner-suit by her abdomen, tearing the skin.

Wool pressed her elbow on Jelly's upturned stomach and reached for a syringe on the medician's bedside unit. She pushed the radio out of the way and avoided looking at the picture of Jamie Anderson on the wall next to the window.

She lifted the device in her fingers and caught a glimpse of the horizon stretching over Pink Symphony. "Wow." A large planet hung in the whitened sky. Its three rings moved, slowly, in all directions, like a fairground ride.

Jelly attempted to wriggle free from Wool's pin down.

"Stop it, Jelly. You want the syringe, do you?"

Jelly calmed down the moment her eyes clapped on the

needle. Her legs kicked against Wool's thighs. She dropped the syringe and fanned her palm on the crazy cat's head.

"Mwaaah," Jelly sunk her fangs in the webbing between Wool's fingers. Under any other circumstances her actions might have been considered playful. Wool quickly dismissed that notion as she looked into Jelly's eyes.

Both were blood-red with orange clouds formed around each pupil.

"Jesus, what's happened to you?"

"ROOWAARR," Jelly shrieked at the top of her lungs.

Wool pushed herself away in fright and looked down at the tear in her inner-suit. Her elbow caught the power cable attached to the radio, knocking the device to the floor.

A glob of blood peeled through Wool's inner-suit. She slid the side of her index finger under the cut and lifted it to her face for inspection.

"Oh, you made me bleed—"

BWUCK!

Jelly spat out a pink fur ball. She rolled onto her front and settled into the prone position, poised to attack. Her tail slapped left and right as she sized up her new opponent.

"Jelly, what are y-you d-doing—"

BWUCK-BWUCK-BWUCK!

Jelly's chest distended, violently. She dug her infinity claws into the foam mattress, puncturing its surface.

"Waaaaaaah!" Jelly's behind lifted into the air like a possessed demon - the start of an event Wool wouldn't forget in a hurry.

"Oh, God…"

Jelly's titanium infinity claws sprung out from her paws. Each digital pad blew open, squeezing out a pink substance across her shedding fur.

"Grrraaaooowww," Jelly's broken screeches bounced off the walls and slammed into Wool's ears.

WHUMP.

Her stomach distended and blew outward, coughing lumps of fur to the bed.

"J-Jelly?" Wool took a step forward, careful not to get too

near what was surely some sort of infectious disease.

The cat whined and shook her head, trying to make the pain subside. The more she fought, the worse it became.

Her skin on her arms turned a yellowy white and forced the flesh underneath to blow across to her body.

The stench was overwhelming.

Wool knew she should have sedated Jelly when she had the chance. There was no going back, now.

Jelly's behind ballooned out, pushing most of her fur away. The bone in her hind legs cracked forward, causing her a considerable amount of pain. A sickening sound of contorting flesh breaking into new positions thundered within her limbs. Jelly's intense squeals warbled the acrylic windows back and forth.

"Holy Mary, mother of God," Wool crossed her body with her index finger as she watched Jelly convulse and change before her eyes. "God have mercy."

Jelly's spine arched onto itself, exposing her shoulder bone through the skin. Strands of fur pushed away from her body.

A final wail of death thundered through the room as her entire body shuddered like a furious cocktail mixer. Her mouth opened out and forward. Jelly's skull pulled back and up, forcing the back of her head to raise thee inches.

The zygomatic bone above her top row of teeth crunched into an oblong and out under her nose. Her teeth fell out one by one. A new set of ivories pushed through her gums, including a pair of sharp incisors.

"Shaaaa," Jelly snorted, fixed to the bed by her infinity claws. Her chin broke away under her bottom row of teeth. A new skeletal structure pushed through in its place.

Her whiskers fizzed away like a perverse light show.

Jelly's entire body thundered on the spot. Her abdomen shunted whatever was left of her former self across the bed in gory segments. Bones transformed and cracked out into new formations.

Fine, dark hair - much like her whiskers - sprouted from the top of her head and fell down her back.

Wool covered her eyes and turned away. Close to a

nervous breakdown, she knew what was coming next. Having seen the twelve-legged creatures at a distance - coupled with what she knew of the battle in Pink Symphony - the next stage would prove to be a body apocalypse.

Wool fanned her fingers out over one eye, catching only the briefest glimpses of the horror.

A fur-less cat, dying and effectively melting in a demonic puddle of its own effluence.

"I'm s-so sorry, Jelly," Wool burst out crying and made for the door, "Let's finish this."

"Mwaaoorgh," Jelly blasted her turmoil around the room from the splattered bed.

Wool pulled the door shut and dropped to her knees in a state of helpless delirium.

"No, please, God. No," she spluttered in floods of tears, "Please."

She knocked the back of her head against the wall in an attempt to block out Jelly's deathly howls from within Medix. Something had to be done.

Her hand slipped around her belt and gripped her Rez-9. A mercy killing was necessary - the second time, now, she'd be attempting to put Jelly out of her misery. Images of having placed a cyanide capsule in Jelly's mouth slammed into her brain.

Wool rolled up the sleeve on her left forearm. She thumbed the ink out into three dots. "This is… Wool," she tried to clear the upset from her voice, "Tripp, are you there?"

No response.

"Tripp, please," Wool sniffed and tilted the side of her gun to ensure it was loaded. The strip light indicated a full magazine. "Tripp?"

"Yes, Wool. I read you."

"She's sick, Tripp. Really sick…"

"Where are you?"

"Outside Medix," Wool blurted and wiped the tears from her eyes. "It's over for her. I need you to come here."

"Dying?"

Wool couldn't help herself. She cried into her forearm like a madwoman. "She's all over the p-place, Tripp. I..."

"—Wool, stay right where you are. Don't do anything."

"She's in s-so much pain, I need to—"

"Wool. No!" Tripp's voice blared through the tiny pin pricks in her wrist, "For God's sake, don't do anything. Stay where you are."

Wool picked herself up from the floor and took a deep breath. She gripped her gun and deliberated the consequences of the action she was about to take.

It was now or never.

N-Vigorate
Three minutes earlier...

The opened utility door revealed a variety of synthetic limbs. One of them had been selected by Bonnie. Much like the others, a titanium-based extensions was the order of the day.

Only, this one was equipped for war as well as balance.

"The Cortex K-12," Tripp attached the magnetic thigh plate to Bonnie's stump, "Interesting choice."

"It really belongs in Weapons and Armory," Bonnie looked down at Tripp and noticed something behind his ear. It resembled a black squiggle. Despite her enhanced vision she elected to look away and braced herself for the forthcoming jolt of pain.

The magnet on her stump sucked the silver plate on the false limb into place with a heavy 'schwump' sound.

"There, you're all set."

Bonnie looked down in time for Tripp to smile at her from between her legs, "Thanks."

"No problem."

"While you're down there?" Bonnie chuckled at her own joke.

"Very funny," Tripp pushed himself upright and held out his palm, "Test it out?"

She grabbed his hand in hers, standing to her feet. She looked down her midriff and swiveled her new right knee left and right, ensuring the device worked. "Feels great."

Tripp smiled obliquely. Something was bothering him.

"What's up?"

"I'm sorry, Bonnie."

"What for?"

"Just, you know. The whole Androgyne *thing*. USARIC has a lot to answer for."

"Oh, that?" Bonnie hopped back to the chair and rammed the calf on the armrest. She arched her back down and grabbed her knees, squinting at her new toe. "I've decided I don't care anymore."

The end of her boot unraveled to the tune of mechanical switches. A barrel formed at the end.

"You don't?"

"Why should I?" Bonnie whacked the side of her hand on a lever on the side of her leg, arming the device. "I'm as human as you or anyone else when you think about it. One thing I don't understand, though?"

"What's that?"

"If I'm a Series Three unit, why do I need the N-Vigorate chamber? Can't I recharge during power down?"

Tripp walked over to the door and pulled out a blast sheet from the hinge, "Your battery took some damage, Bonnie. Once we're up and running we'll need to take a look inside and see if we can fix it."

Bonnie nodded at the sheet, "Can you set up the target?"

"Sure."

Tripp clamped the free end to the wall. The image resembled the common dart board, complete with a bullseye. The USARIC logo stood proudly across the top.

"This okay for you?"

"That's great, step away," Bonnie pressed her elbow to the adjacent arm rest and took hold of her thigh, "I may be synthetic. But my organs are real. My brain is real. I remember everything I need to."

"That's very true," Tripp was relieved that Bonnie had become accustomed to her existence. "You're more human than human, in some respects."

The bullseye focused into view at the end of her brand new limb, "You know it."

Tripp offered her some sympathy, "Sometimes I wish every time I went to sleep I could forget."

Bonnie held out her tongue, taking careful aim at the bullseye on the sheet.

"Be careful what you wish for, Healy."

Bonnie fired off a blast at the sheet. Tripp jumped back as the bullet burst against the bulletproof sheet and vaporized into a thousand pieces.

"Direct hit," Bonnie smiled and stomped her new foot to the ground.

"Wow. That new leg of yours really kicks ass," Tripp slowed his breathing and approached the sheet, "Umm…"

"What?"

A bullet hole spat out smoke right in the middle of the USARIC logo - her intended target.

"Angry much?"

"As I said. *Direct hit.*"

Tripp's forearm buzzed. The three tattooed lines swirled around to form a name: "Wool ar-Ban."

"Who is it?" Bonnie asked.

"It's Wool. Must be an update on Jelly," he ran his fingers across the ink on his forearm, "Wool?"

"Tripp, please?" Wool's strained cries shot out of his wrist.

"Yes, Wool. I read you."

"She's sick, Tripp. Really sick…"

"Where are you?" Tripp's waved Bonnie over toward him.

"Outside Medix," Wool's voice croaked over the transmission, "It's over for her. I need you come here."

"What do you mean she's sick?" Tripp shot Bonnie a look of urgency, "She's crying," he mouthed.

Bonnie raised her eyebrows with suspicion, "Crying?"

"She's all over the p-place, Tripp. I…"

"—Wool, stay right where you are. Don't do anything."

"She's in s-so much pain, I need to—"

"Wool. No. For God's sake, don't do anything hasty. Stay where you are."

Tripp brushed the palm of his hand across his forearm, cutting off the call. "We need to get to Medix. Right now."

"Is she okay?"

"You heard everything I did."

Tripp pulled the door open and stormed into the walkway with Bonnie.

It was only a two minute walk across the level three gantry from N-Vigorate to Medix. In this very moment, it felt at least three times longer than usual.

Despite the earlier otherworldly happenings, the ship was once again intact. It was as if the cracks and damage had never occurred. A long, distant virus-fueled nightmare.

No creaking, no weird sounds. Everything seemed just fine. The ship's engine was alive - the vibrations that rocked the Opera Beta's interiors provided a welcome and familiar comfort.

That was all Tripp and Bonnie were able to enjoy as they hightailed it across the metal grills on the ground. Plumes of steam shot out around their boots as they snaked around the corner. They prepared themselves for whatever was happening to Wool.

Bonnie eyed the pipes on the walls, remembering what she'd heard about the ship falling apart. "I don't get it, Tripp."

"What don't you get?"

"Botanix leads out into that weird, pink place. The one with the creature things. Why is everything back to normal?"

"I don't know, Bonnie."

"For our assumed captain you sure don't know very much."

Tripp couldn't take Bonnie's inadvertent rudeness any longer and stopped on the spot, "Bonnie."

Tripp ran his knuckle across his freshly-formed five o'clock shadow. His finger inadvertently brushed against his earlobe - just in time for Bonnie to catch the black text behind it, tucked out-of-sight above his jawline.

A familiar company by the name of *Manning/Synapse*.

"Tripp?" she smiled at him.

"Don't play the dummy android with me, Bonnie. You made be more advanced than the rest of us—"

"—*Au contraire*," she said with side order of snark.

"What's that meant to mean?"

"Nothing."

"No, seriously. What did you mean by that?"

"Drop it, Healy," she nodded up at the far end of the walkway, "Enough pillow talk. Let's get to Wool before she does something stupid."

Chapter 14

Engine & Payload
Space Opera Beta - Level Ten

In any ordinary situation Baldron would have to use the primary airlock to exit the spacecraft. Harnessing the weightlessness of space, he'd use the outer-suit thrusters to "fly" along the exterior of the ship to the fat end to attend to the ship's engine. But this was no ordinary situation. Being grounded on Pink Symphony proved to be a much quicker prospect for fixing them.

Engine & Payload, much like the other chambers on the ship, could be reached by using Opera Beta's lone elevator. Room enough for ten passengers.

The metal cage whizzed down the circular tube.

Jaycee and Baldron each carried a large nuclear canister in their arms. Being close to seven feet in height and built like a tornado fused with a bull, Jaycee barely registered the weight of his nuke.

Baldron, on the other hand, felt the need to place the end of his canister to the floor and rest the tip against the wall of the elevator.

"How many times have you done this before?" Jaycee asked, turning his head away from the whizzing of the panel lights sprawling up and down across his helmet's visor.

"At least a dozen. Delicacy is key, here."

"Like dropping the end on the ground like a big fairy, you mean?" Jaycee chuckled through his internal radio microphone.

"It's heavy. We're not all built like brick houses like you."

"True enough," Jaycee grinned, enamored by the fact that Baldron's Decapidisc fit perfectly under the rim of his helmet, "Still. Nothing to lose your head over, eh?"

Baldron knocked the edge of the disc with his gloved hand, "This is really going to get in my way while I try to work."

"I'm sure you'll live. Probably."

The friendly female announcement whirled around the elevator, "Level Ten. Engine and Payload. Have a nice day,"

The doors slid apart, revealing the enormity of Engine & Payload. Zero gravity set in immediately, lifting the pair's feet from the ground.

"Zero G?" Jaycee asked.

"Yeah. Gravity doesn't help much when you're dealing with ballistics or nuclear paraphernalia," Baldron swung his arms around his canister. He planted the sole of his boot on the elevator wall and propelled himself forward, "Follow me."

Jaycee's boots levitated away from the floor. He enacted the same movement as Baldron and pushed himself into the chamber.

A dimly-lit arena resembling the inside of a set of vocal chords.

Thick, twenty-foot high columns provided an obstacle to the port panel on the far wall. Conversely, it helped the two men kick themselves toward their destination a lot quicker.

"Ugh," Baldron said into his radio mic, "I hate the absence of gravity. It makes my stomach queasy."

"I'm sorry to hear that," Jaycee spat, indicating that he'd run out of rat's asses to give, "Hey, here's an idea."

"What?"

"Why don't you shut the hell up and do your job?"

Baldron pressed his boots against a column and pushed himself toward a gargantuan wall of lit-up rectangles. Thousands of them shone against both men's visors on their approach.

"See those white columns over there?" Baldron pointed to the right of the wall.

"Yeah?"

"The hyper-thrusters," Baldron continued. "Each one of them with enough nuclear energy to wipe out Florida."

"Much like climate change then?"

"Yeah, you could say that. You Americans use nukes to get ahead in the second space race. It's no wonder your country is eroding around the edges."

"Hey, Russkie," Jaycee kicked forward from another column and reached Baldron, "Shall we see if your organs can survive a nuclear blast?"

"What?"

"Keep that xenophobic talk up and I'll shove your head in this canister."

"We're here. Kick down to section *Zee*. We're looking for port loader number four, zero, niner."

The numbers on each of the rectangles ran into the thousands. Jaycee used the locking bolt on a loader to push himself down and read out the numbers on each one.

"Four fifty-two… four twenty-eight…" Jaycee found the one they were looking for, "Here, it's here. Four, zero, niner."

"Good. I'm coming down," Baldron hugged his nuke as he waded down past the loaders, "I gotta say, these things are much easier to carry in here."

"Yeah, I can see that," Jaycee looked up. The butt of Baldron's canister enveloped his visor quicker than anticipated.

"Hey. Be careful," Jaycee kicked back in defiance, "You nearly hit my visor."

"Sorry."

Baldron reached the lock on the panel and balanced the canister upright in the palm of his left hand, "Tor, this is Baldron. Do you read me?"

"Yes, Baldron. I read you,' Tor's static-laden voice bled into Baldron's helmet, "Confirm Port Zee. Four, zero, niner."

"Port Zee. Four, zero, niner. Confirmed."

"Understood, standby."

Jaycee scowled at Baldron and showed him his glove.

Tor spoke before the torment could continue, "On my command you will make contact with the lock. A countdown of three. Do you understand?"

"I understand."

"Reconciling nuclear engagement. Establish contact, please."

The bolt on the lock shunted out, offering itself to Baldron. He grasped it in his hand and cleared his throat, "Contact established."

"From three," Tor's advised. "Three, two, one... and engage."

SHUNT-SWISH.

Baldron's hand turned with the bolt, sliding the port door down.

Jaycee tilted his head to the side and took a look at the interior, "Ugh. That canister thing has seen better days, hasn't it?"

"Yup," Baldron grabbed the port edges and pulled himself inside. "Oh, damn. Can you grab my canister, please?"

Jaycee looked at the cylinder revolving gently in mid-air, "Idiot."

"Sorry, it slipped," Baldron stomped his feet to the ground within the port. Its canister had subsided in its housing. The blackened underside indicated something had gone wrong, "Okay, this is pretty straight forward."

"Baldron," Tor's voice came through the mic, "Sit-rep on Zee four, zero, niner, please?"

"Defective canister. Manuel was right, this one is down. I will confirm on Yankee one, one, eight next."

"Yeah, *Yankee* is about right," Tor chuckled. "Speaking of which, how's our ugly turd holding up?"

Jaycee threw Baldron a look of evil.

"Uh, he can hear you, Tor."

"Damn," Tor's voice fizzled away into silence for a moment. "Uh, Jaycee?"

"Yes, Tor?"

"Sorry about that."

"Don't worry. I'm going to kill you the moment we get back. Nothing serious."

"Yes," Tor tried to make amends, "Joking aside, it might help if—"

"—Oh, I'm *not* joking," Jaycee said, looking at the Yankee section of the loader ports. "I *am* going to kill you."

"Jaycee, please. Listen to me."

"I'm listening."

Jaycee watched Baldron hold the pinkie on his glove to the defective canister housing. The end whizzed around as he inserted it into the first of two bolts at the side of the damaged canister.

"What do you want?"

"We can expedite this event if you start on Yankee one, one, eight. The little finger on your glove will unscrew the housing. You simply remove the dud and clamp the fresh canister into place. Bring the used one back with you for recycle—"

"—You want me to do Baldron's job for him?"

"Actually, *yes*. It would be helpful. Seeing as we're low on oxygen."

"Ugh, fine."

Baldron peered out from the his loader port and held up his thumb, "Thanks, man."

"It's not a favor, you cretin. I'm doing it to save time."

"Suits me," Baldron winked back at Jaycee as he pushed off toward the Yankee section on the hunt for port 118.

Baldron felt much happier now that his captor had gone away *and* helped him with the task at hand. He clamped the fresh canister into place and screwed it into the brackets.

"Baldron?" Tor's voice came through the mic, "Do you read me?"

"Yes, I read you," he said, screwing the new canister shut with his pinkie.

"Jaycee, do you read me?" Tor asked.

No response.

"I repeat, Jaycee. Do you read me?"

Baldron gripped the edge of the loader and watched Jaycee arrive at port Yankee 118, whistling to himself, "I don't think he hears us."

"Good, I changed the frequency. It's just you and me, now," Tor explained. "He's going start talking at me. He'll want the lock opened."

"Yes, I expect so," Baldron hushed into his helmet mic, "What's this got to do with me?"

"Are you looking at him?"

"Yes, he's nearly at the loader."

"For heaven's sake, get back in, stupid. You don't want him looking at you."

"Okay, okay," Baldron slipped his head into the port and turned to the canister, "What's going on?"

"Now is our chance, comrade."

"What?"

"Manuel was right about the ports needing mended," Tor explained. "But only about why-oh-oh-eight. Zee four zero niner, your loader, is perfectly operational. Never needed attention."

"But, it's been hit by subsidence. The bottom has been hit by—"

"—They're all like that. Standard wear and tear, they're designed to last for decades, if not centuries. You're an *engineer*, remember? You should know that."

"You and I both know that's *lessense*."

Jaycee announced his arrival to his port with a vicious thump on its hatch. The sound echoed through the chamber, "Tor, this is Jaycee. Ready at Yankee-one-one-eight."

"Damn, he's there," Tor lightened his tone and addressed Jaycee, leaving his comrade wondering what was going on, "Understood, Jaycee. One moment, please."

"Hurry up."

"Baldron?" Tor asked.

"Yes?"

"No time to explain. Get the hell out of there, now. And make sure Jaycee doesn't see you."

"What?"

"No questions! Head to the lift and get back to the control deck. Now," Tor changed his tone when addressing Jaycee, "Okay. You heard my instructions to Baldron a few minutes ago, right?"

"Yeah, I get the idea," Jaycee grabbed the bolt on the loader port, "Ready to rock and roll."

Baldron didn't know which way to look, or what to do. "Comrade? What are—"

"—Jaycee, please confirm Port Zee, four, zero, niner." Tor said, no longer available for a clandestine chat with his Russian conspirator.

"Port zed, four, zero, niner. Confirmed."

"Understood, standby," Tor's voice sped up and flooded Baldron's headset, "Get out of there, good buddy."

"Why?"

"Trust me, there is *literally* no time to explain. We're wasting time talking about not talking about it. Go, go—"

"—Okay, I'm *going*."

"Make sure that useless pile of mechanical puke doesn't see you."

"I'll do my best."

"You'll have to do a lot better than *your best*, my friend," Tor switched comms to Jaycee, "Okay, Jaycee. On my command you will make contact with the lock. On a countdown of three. Do you understand?"

"I understand."

Baldron pushed himself out of the port and into the payload chamber. He grabbed the used canister and released it in the air a few inches from the door.

Tor continued with his instruction, "Reconciling nuclear engagement. Make contact please."

Baldron carefully planted the sole of both boots on the adjacent panel and pushed himself into the distance.

Jaycee looked up at Baldron's port but failed to see him move away. As far as he could see, the door was open and Baldron was still inside. His canister revolved around in the air just by the door.

"Idiot."

"Sorry, repeat? Jaycee?"

"I wasn't talking to you," he turned back to the bolt mechanism on the port, "Let's get on with this. Open the damn *thing*, will you?"

"Suits me. Contact established?"

The bolt on the lock shunted out, offering itself to Baldron. He grasped it in his hand and cleared his throat,

"Contact established."

Streaks of sweat smeared up the inside of Baldron's visor as he kicked himself away from the next column. The elevator doors loomed fifty feet in the distance. A minute or two from escape.

Jaycee rolled his shoulders and prepared to open his port loader.

"From three," Tor advised. "Three, two, one... and engage."

SHUNT-SWISH.

The port door slid down into the groove. Jaycee released the bolt and placed the good canister on inside it. "I'm in."

"Good. Just holler if you need me."

"I doubt I'll be doing that," Jaycee huffed and pressed his feet to the ground. He held his right glove to his face and inspected the little finger on his glove. The ends slid apart and released a screw tip, "Here we go."

He moved his glove away from his face and eyeballed the thoroughly worn canister, "Right. Let's get you fixed."

A giant fleshy limb with a razor sharp talon shot out from behind it and swiped at Jaycee.

"Jeeeeeesus *Christ*," he yelped and grabbed the good canister by his knees.

A second, third and fourth limb hugged around the canister, angry at having been disturbed.

The vicious beast snapped the spent canister in two. A blast of gas slammed against Jaycee, pushing him out of the port loader.

The good canister tumbled around at speed over his shoulder and clanged against a column. Jaycee unhooked his Rez-9 and aimed it at the creature, "Tor!"

The creature jammed forward along the port tight walls. It wanted Jaycee's blood.

"Tor, do you read me?"

"Yes, good buddy. I read you. How are you getting on down there?"

"You son of a bi—" Jaycee drew his weapon.

"—What's wrong?"

SNARL-SNASH! The creature's six limbs rapid-gripped the edges of the port, one by one, and prepared to launch forward.

"You know damn well what's wrong—"

"—No need for cursing, that's just rude," Tor fake-chuckled over the comms, "Now, at this point you've probably got your gun aiming right at *it*, don't you?"

"You're Goddamn right I do."

"Yeah, just one thing."

"What?" Jaycee trained his gun at the knuckle-headed midsection of the beast. It opened its mouth-like cave and screeched up a storm.

"Bullets and zero gravity, my friend? You may as well just take a bath and drop a toaster in with you—"

"—You're a dead man, I swear," Jaycee released his finger from the trigger. He threw the gun at the screaming beast's mouth. It caught it with deft expertize and munched away on it, breaking it in two. "You better pray it kills me."

"I've already done that. Send my regards to Daryl and Haloo when you get to Hell," Tor smirked and cut the call.

Baldron reached the elevator doors. He slammed the panel in a desperate bid to open them, "C'mon, c'mon."

"Landaker," Jaycee's voice hurtled toward him as he frantically jabbed at the button on the wall.

"Come on, please. *Please.*"

"You and your soviet boyfriend are dead men," Jaycee kicked himself away from one of the many columns, headed straight for the door.

"Close, damn it. *Close,*" Baldron rapid-hit the button, praying for a swift escape.

Jaycee flew through the air and threw his hands forward. Baldron's throat needed removing.

The creature, however, was hot on Jaycee's tail, too.

"Baldron, don't close that door," Jaycee shouted as he kicked himself forward, "Keep it open."

"Comrade," Tor's voice came through, "Close the door."

"I am, I am," Baldron hit the panel over and over again, "It won't close."

"Stupid American-made crap," Tor failed to realize his voice came through Jaycee's helmet, "Much like that big hunk of whale blubber."

"What did you call me?" Jaycee screamed.

"Oh, you can hear me?"

"Yeah, I can hear you," Jaycee quipped, angrily, as he zipped towards Baldron in the elevator cage fifty-odd feet away, "Hey, dead man."

"Who, me?" Baldron and Tor asked in unison.

"*Both* of you."

The creature gained on Jaycee. It had learned to propel itself watching the man's actions. Worse still, it had six times as many limbs as its prey to do it with.

Baldron elbowed the button on the elevator panel. The doors slid together very, very slowly, "It's closing," He clapped eyes on the creature in the distance and backed up against the elevator's back wall, "Oh, *shiiii*—"

"—It's trying to kill me,' Jaycee threw his hands forward and opened his fingers in an attempt to grab the doors before they sliced shut, "Stay right where you are, you—"

Too late - the doors were half a second away from slamming shut.

Baldron's face disappeared behind the closing doors.

"I'm gonna tear the skull out of your head," Jaycee clenched his right hand made for Baldron's throat.

"I'm s-sorry, Jaycee—"

SCHLAA-AAM!

The elevator doors clamped shut on Jaycee's wrist, "Gaahh," The severed appendage clanged against the wall and crashed knuckles-first to the ground.

Baldron tumbled to his knees as the cage hurtled up through the elevator tube. Jaycee's grunts and screams dissipated behind the outer door as he fought with the creature.

"Hey, man. You there?" Tor asked.

"Yes, I'm here," Baldron slumped to his behind on the floor and breathed a sigh of relief, "And Jaycee... *isn't*."

"Good job, comrade."

"We're so dead if that thing doesn't finish him off—"

The severed hand's fingers and thumb fanned out and clench into a fist, punching itself to its fingertips. It crawled toward Baldron like a mad, mechanical spider with an opposable thumb.

Thoroughly intimidated, Baldron kicked himself back against the far wall, "His hand. It's his damn *hand*, man!"

"What hand?" Tor asked. "What's going on—"

"—The elevator doors, they... they... *cut it off.* Oh, G-God, it's trying to kill me—"

The hand crept forward, threatening Baldron. sparks of electricity blasted along its trail of wires and metal dragging behind the destroyed wrist.

"Please, no!"

The hand quickly ran out of juice - containing just enough energy left to hold its middle finger up at Baldron as a parting salute.

"Huh?"

It splayed its fingers out and punched the floor with its palm, giving up the ghost. The white button on the wrist flap flashed, begging to be pressed.

"Baldron? Give me a sit-rep, please."

"It's okay. I think it's dead," Baldron quickly arrived at an epiphany, "Wait, wait."

"What?"

"It's... *not real*," he grabbing the discarded appendage by the fingers and looked at the trailing wires and connectors.

"Not real?"

"No."

Baldron slipped the glove from the synthetic hand, "Well, not human. Titanium. Special connectors, with heat-proof underpinnings."

"Classic Manning/Synapse hardware, right?"

"Right," Baldron brushed the tip of his thumb across the synthetic skin on Jaycee's hand, "What do I do with it?"

"What do you do with what?"

Baldron pressed his shoulders against the elevator wall as it rocketed toward level one, "The hand, Tor. What do I do with Jaycee's hand?"

"What? The hand? Who gives a rat's ass? Just leave it

there. It's the *glove* we want. For God's sake, do *not* press any buttons on it."

The Decapidisc slunk around Baldron's shoulders, enabling a terrifying prospect, "Oh, God…. Oh, God."

"What is it, now?" Tor asked, near ready to explode.

"The button's flashing on the glove. The disc is gonna take my head off—"

"—It's okay, it's just in advisory mode,' Tor mocked his friend for fun, "I need you to bring that ghastly, five-fingered contraption back to control right now. The elevator is making its way to Level One. Control Deck."

Baldron tossed the hand at the wall and held the glove to his chest, "Are you sure we're okay?"

"As long as you keep away from that activation button, yes," Tor said. "Now, calm yourself down and meet me at control. We'll take care of the others."

"Okay."

"And that stupid cat, as well."

The elevator bolted skyward in a haze of spinning bulbs and lights.

Medix

Wool sat against the exterior Medix wall. She'd resigned herself to the only course of action available.

Jelly's muffled howls of pain muffled from within the room.

"They're not coming," Wool lifted her Rez-9 firearm in her right hand and looked at the safety catch. She pressed it down with her thumb, arming the weapon. Finally, she closed her eyes and took a deep breath.

"Forgive me for what I'm about to do," she pushed her heels into the ground and slid her back up the wall.

"Wool," Tripp's voice rumbled across the walkway, flying into her ears. She jumped in fright and opened her eyes, instinctively aiming her gun at the emptiness dead ahead of her.

"Tripp?" Wool hollered, prepared to fire, "Is that you?"

"Yes, it's me and Bonnie."

Tripp crept around the corner with terrific trepidation, "Are you okay?"

"No. I'm not okay," Wool thumped the door to Medix. The rectangular slab slid away from its casters.

"Why have you got your firearm out?" Bonnie joined Tripp and readied herself to beat the hell out of whatever had upset her colleague, "What's going on?"

Wool peered through the transparent door's window. An effort that proved to be futile; the surface had fogged up a storm, leaving only a blurry contour of slowing down on the bed.

"She's in there."

Tripp made for the door, "Right, let's rescue her—"

"—No, no. I, uh…" Wool stood in his path and clutched at her Rez-9, "Something's happening to her. Whatever that pink stuff is… it's doing to her what it did to Haloo."

Bonnie frowned and quickly grew angry with their predicament, "For God's sake," she socked the wall with her fist and held her breath.

"It's over, Tripp," Wool sniffed. "She's quarantined in there. Riding it out."

An intense, guttural howl crashed from the other side of the door. Tripp looked down, barely able to soak in Wool's distress. He reached into his belt and grabbed his Rez-9.

"You want me to do it?"

It was the least he could offer to do given the circumstances. Wool and Jelly had formed a bond that was better left on the happiest note available.

"No, no," she wiped a pink tear from her eye, "Let me do it. *Please.*"

Bonnie tried to offer some sympathy. "Wool, look. It's the best thing—"

"—What the hell do you know about feelings, Bonnie? You're just a lump of pretty metal, made by men *for* men."

"How dare you," Bonnie protested. Her absence of mind neglected the fact that her follow-on statement would correct the *wrong* half of Wool's accusation, "I am *not* made of metal,"

"Whatever. It doesn't matter anymore," Wool turned to the door, ready to execute the monstrosity in the throes of its last breaths, "We're *all* somebody's bitch at the end of the day, aren't we?"

A wave of sobs crept through the crack in the door as Wool pushed it open, "Wait here. It'll only take a second."

Tripp and Bonnie lowered their heads and nodded.

Wool allowed the door to slide shut behind her. She aimed her Rez-9 at the source of the whimpering with her eyes closed. The sniveling and gasps of anguish were impossible to withstand. All she had to do was pull the trigger, hope to hit a vital organ, and leave without seeing what she'd done. A blissfully ignorant act of mercy, to be sure, but a necessary one if Wool was retain any semblance of mental well-being post-execution.

"I'm sorry, pet."

"Wuh…" groaned a voice more human than she'd expected, "Wuuh…"

In a rare moment of assurance, Wool lifted her eyelids slightly, keeping her gun facing the bed.

"Huh?"

"Wuh-wuh… Wooo… Luhh…"

Wool squeezed her eyes shut for two seconds and then opened them again. She froze on the spot as if having seen God in the flesh.

"Wool," came the voice once again, but lower in pitch.

The surface of Wool's eyeball reflected an orange-white *thing*. It kicked its legs forward.

Blink, blink.

Wool's eyelids wiped the detritus from the surface of her eyeballs. This time, the fleshy, fish-eyed image reflecting back rolled over to its side and stopped crying.

"Wool," the image said, "It… is… *you.*"

The gun slipped form Wool's frozen hand and bounced against the white floor tiles beside her left boot.

"I'm… c-cold…" the thing said in a reassuring, young voice, "P-Please?"

Wool finally managed to close her jaw. The reality of the event burrowed through her mind. She wasn't sleeping and certainly not dreaming.

"J-Jelly… you… I…" Wool stammered, "M-My *God…*"

Out in the walkway, Tripp experienced restlessness on a scale he'd seldom encountered. He'd expected to hear a gunshot by now. The desire to run in and assist his colleague was proving hard to shake off.

Impatient, Bonnie paced around and clutched her belt, "What's taking so long in there?"

"I don't know. I really don't like it."

"Maybe a few seconds alone with her?" Bonnie flicked her head up towards the ceiling and licked her lips. "Can't say I blame her."

"*Seconds*? She's been in there five minutes, at least. I'll give her thirty more seconds," Tripp held his forearm in front of his chest. He drew a pattern on the skin with his thumb tip. *00:30*. The numbers counted down the moment his pressed his fingertip against it. "More than enough time."

He needn't have bothered setting the timer. The door slid open and presented a thoroughly relieved - and awe-struck - Wool.

"Done?" Tripp asked.

"Guys," Wool took a deep breath, near ready to cry with excitement, "Come in. Something… something—"

"—*Fantastic*?" Bonnie chimed in with a healthy amount of flippancy.

"Yes, yes," Wool beamed with teary delight and clapped her hands together, "My God, something fantastic *has* happened."

Chapter 15

Level One
Space Opera Beta

The elevator doors slid open. Baldron clutched Jaycee's glove in his right hand, careful not to hit the white button. He stepped into the fluorescent-lit corridor and made for the Control Deck.

"Tor, come in," he tried to unfasten his helmet, "Ugh, this bloody thing."

"Yeah, good buddy. I read you. Are you on your way?"

"Yeah, about sixty seconds ETA."

"Good, I'm working on Manuel, now. You still got that fat idiot's glove?"

"Yeah, left his hand in the elevator," Baldron flipped the visor screen up and took a deep breath as he jogged along the corridor.

"Whatever you do, don't hit that button. It's primed to go."

"I don't intend to." Baldron slipped off his helmet and tossed it against the wall. He thumped the flat, cold surface on his Decapidisc, "I just want this damn thing off my neck."

"You and me both. Just get here, now."

***

"Come get me," Jaycee waved his sparking, wrecked wrist at the creature. His legs levitated above his waist as he tried to wrench the outer elevator tube doors apart.

The monstrosity screeched up a storm and swiped its two front limbs at him.

"Nggg... *c'mon*," Jaycee failed to separate the doors. He pressed the fingers on his good hand through the slit but had no opposing force to wrench it apart, "God damn it."

THRA-AA-APP-PP!

Six of the creature's elongated limbs wrapped around the column. It prepared to bolt like a jellyfish toward the elevator door and attack Jaycee.

"C'mon, c'mon, budge. You stubborn slab of junk," Jaycee turned his body and thumped his boots against the door.

The creature launched forward and squealed as it darted through the air. Jaycee looked over his shoulder and pressed his knees to his chest.

"Come on!"

The creature fanned out all twelve limbs and opened its midsection, like some perverse spider-cobra-flower.

Jaycee's eyes widened. The blasted thing was at least ten feet wide in diameter and about to smother him. "Wow."

SCREEEEECH!

The talons at the end of each limb flicked out. The creature spun around and retracted all twelve of its limbs, creating a bizarrely beautiful spectacle.

Not beautiful enough to hang around for, though. Jaycee had to take decisive action to survive.

He kicked himself toward the creature - the two flew through the air towards each other just outside the elevator door. In a few seconds they'd collide and slam the hell out of each other.

Jaycee reached into his belt and took out his secondary Rez-9 firearm. He aimed it at the creature's knuckled center and waited for the perfect moment to take his shot, "Monster go bye-bye."

"Screeeeee," the creature flung its talons forward.

Jaycee ducked as the talon sliced the back of his helmet. "Gaah," He jammed the Rez-9 into the creature's screaming throat and squeezed the trigger.

KA-SCHPLAA-AATT!

Six of the creature's limbs splattered out from his body, vomiting ropes of pink slime in all directions.

Jaycee whipped his hand out from the creature's mouth as its jaws clamped shut. The Rez-9 bounced off its incisors and into the depths of the chamber.

"Screeeee," It wailed against the elevator tube's outer doors. Four of its remaining limbs pushed the door off its railings, forcing the creature's body into the empty travel tube.

Jaycee kicked himself away from the column. He barrel-rolled for the battered door like a twisting dart of metal.

"Let's finish this, ass-face."

The creature slammed three limbs on both sides of its body against the elevator tube. The result looked like a twenty-foot, limb-like cobweb - ready to catch and murder its prey.

Jaycee shot through the broken door and clenched his right fist, "Come get some."

FLICK-SWISH-SCHTANG!

The talons on each of the six limbs fanned out in readiness for its assailant's arrival.

Jaycee's knuckles connected with the beast's screaming slit. Its razor teeth bent down its throat causing it to choke and splutter. It retaliated by swiping its limbs at Jaycee. Each attempt narrowly avoided his body. He was too close and the limbs couldn't tuck in enough to do any significant damage.

A thundering sound of something *very* heavy shot down the tube as Jaycee punched the beast once again.

The sound of heaviness grew ever louder. The tube shuddered more and more…

A shadow stretched across Jaycee's face. Something rocketed towards him and the beast - the elevator.

"Oh, shii—"

He took one, final look at the beast. The creature roared in Jaycee's face with such force that a hairline crack tore across his visor.

He tightened his grip on the creature's midsection and yelled back over the growing thunder of the whizzing elevator, "Die. You ugly, pink bastard."

Jaycee booted the creature and somersaulted out of the tunnel, banging his arm on the broken door.

The force of the launch sent the creature back against the curved tube.

It looked up as its body blanketed into darkness from the shadow created by the approaching elevator.

"Screeeee—"

SCHAA-PLATTT!

The elevator pulverized the creature against the ground. It exploded in a haze of pink gore and shattered bone.

Jaycee's boots hit the ground, affording him a few seconds of respite.

Streaks of pink blood the size of a rolled-up duvet jettisoned in all directions from underneath the elevator and splattered across the floor.

"Level ten. Engine and Payload. Have a nice day," the female voice announced with a chirpy vigor. The elevator doors opened and released Jaycee's severed, gloveless hand.

He grabbed it in his good hand and pulled himself into the elevator.

The flat surface panel lit up, requesting a level selection. He didn't press any of the buttons. Instead, he looked at the complicated fusion of wires and metal rods jutting out from the wrist of his severed hand.

Tucked inside the trapezium of the hand was a small imprint of *something.*

Jaycee squinted at it at the text and moved it closer to his face. Then, a damning blow crept across his brain as he processed the information.

The logo of a company named of *Manning/Synapse* nestled inside the wrist.

Jaycee blinked three times in succession. The text was still there in black and white - in more ways than one.

He let out an apocalyptic cry of anger and threw his useless hand against the ground, "Bastards."

He kicked the elevator wall with his giant metal boot. He wanted blood, but had to expel the revelation from his mind.

"No, no, no…"

The elevator wall didn't budge. He could have kicked it all day long without so much as causing a chink in the material.

He stomped his boot to the floor and tried to calm himself down, "An Androgyne? I can't—"

THWACK!

He thumped the panel on the wall and shattered the screen. He'd taken himself by surprise with his own violent reaction.

Level Four lit up on the selection panel.

"Thank you," the reassuring voice said, "Level Four. Weapons and Armory. Please remain standing."

The cage doors closed on a furious Jaycee Nayall.

The elevator shot up the delivery pipe, sending the ultimate - if imperfect and incomplete - execution machine to the top of the ship.

***

Wool, Tripp, and Bonnie entered Medix with a considerable amount of caution. The latter two members of Opera Beta were unsure of what they were about to see and braced themselves.

Wool walked over to Jelly's bed. She encouraging her colleague's eye line to the wondrous event that had taken place on Jelly's bed.

"It's okay, you can come forward," Wool grabbed a blanket from an adjacent gurney and turned to Jelly, "Look at you. You're cold."

Tripp and Bonnie could hardly believe what they saw, "Jelly?" they said together.

"Oh, wow," a joyous grin crept across Bonnie's face, "It's amaziant."

"But, but—" Tripp shook his head and flew into cynical mode, "It can't be?"

"I believe you," Bonnie sat at the edge of the bed and pressed her fingertips against the mattress. "Are you okay?"

"It can be, and it is," Wool pulled out the soft sheet and lowered it onto the back of an orange-white neck and shoulders, "She's fine and healthy. Aren't you, honey?"

A six-year-old girl-cat sat on the bed, shivering, with her arms around her bent knees. Several wires attached to her chest and abdomen sprawled over her arms, attached to a heart rate monitor.

This was no ordinary girl, though.

"Is that better, honey?" Wool smiled and placed the blanket over Jelly's knees, warming her up and securing her modesty.

The girl ran the side of her face against Wool's sleeve.

"Aww. You like that, don't you?"

Jelly had evolved. How much so? It was too early to tell.

Her whiskers had shrunk but still vibrated with life. She retained her slightly elongated infinity claws. Very fine orange hair adorned her legs, arms, and face.

She looked more human than feline, not accounting for the whiskers. By all accounts, an astounding vision of beauty.

Tripp took a step forward and couldn't help but stare, "In all my life, I... I don't know what to *say*."

"Then don't say anything," Wool whispered. "She's had a rough day. I think she'll need some rest."

"Wool?" Jelly coughed inside her throat and ran her coarse tongue across her lips.

"Yes, honey?"

"Water."

Her voice conformed to that of a typical six-year-old's - relatively high in tone but with a discreet cat-like twist.

"She talks, too?" Bonnie's eyes lit up with love in an instant. She pressed her finger to her chest and over-gesticulated her opening statement, "Me... Bonnie."

Jelly ducked her head with embarrassment, "I know... *you*."

"Wow," Bonnie gasped.

Jelly's cat-like ears slapped back and forth as she lowered the side of her face to her own forearm and purred.

Tripp made for the door in haste, "I'm sorry, I need a few minutes. I'll be right back."

Wool passed by him with a cup of water, "Everything okay?"

"Yes," he huffed, very unsure of himself, "No. I don't

know. Just give me…"

He didn't finish his sentence as he walked through the door. Wool shrugged her shoulders and approached Jelly's bed, "Here you are, honey. Some fresh water."

"Mommy," Jelly opened out her half-human hand, fanning her titanium claws out, "Claws. Sharp. Ouch."

Wool giggled. "I'll tell you what I'll do. I'll set it down on the side desk, here. You can pick it up yourself."

"Water," Jelly added.

Tripp wandered aimlessly around the corridor with his eyes shut. He muttered to himself at a rapid pace. Praying was beyond him. Most of the events he'd experienced since leaving for Saturn ran through his mind.

Discovering Alpha.

The escape from Alpha.

The loss of his best friend and captain, Daryl Katz.

The strange happenings with Haloo Ess.

News of what was happening on Earth.

The discovery of Pink Symphony - whatever it was.

He tried to make sense of it all. The answer felt so tantalizingly close yet nowhere near solvable. A frustrating experience aided little with what had happened to Jelly.

"Please, tell me this is all a dream," Tripp crouched to his knees and ran his hands through his hair, "I want to wake up… I feel so alone…"

Jelly wiggled her nose at her own reflection in the glass of water.

Wool and Bonnie watched her sniff around the rim of the glass. A bit too close. Her head jolted back from the corresponding reflection of her nose in the glass.

"You've seen humans drink from a glass, haven't you?" Wool giggled with affection.

"Yes," she opened out her brand new human fingers and blew across her fur. Her metacarpal pad remained in the center of her palm.

She closed her fingers around it. The sharp underside of each infinity claw clinked across the glass as she tightened her grip.

"That's it, honey," Wool beamed and winked at Bonnie, "You're doing *so* well."

The bottom of the glass lifted away from the desk and over her lap. Jelly sniffed around the rim, ensuring its freshness.

"Now, put up to your mouth," Bonnie pursed her lips and mimed knocking back a shot of liquid from a pretend glass, "You'll have to make your mouth move. Like this."

Jelly enacted what she saw. Her lips were new - she'd have fun with them for the next few hours until the novelty wore off.

The rim of the glass pressed against her bottom lip. She replicated Bonnie's actions a little *too* literally. The water fountained down her sheet, going everywhere *except* her mouth.

"Oh no," Wool moved forward and caught the glass from Jelly's hand, "Here, let me take that—"

Jelly burst out crying as the water soaked through the sheet.

"Hey, hey, it's okay," Bonnie took the sheet away and folded it in her arms, "We'll get you another—"

"—Right, I want answers," Tripp stormed through the door and made for Jelly, who instantly cowered behind her arms in fright.

"Miew."

"Jelly, look at me."

"Tripp, what are you doing?" Wool barked at him as he loomed over the frightened young girl. The heart monitor beeped rapidly.

"Be quiet, Wool. That's an order," he turned to Jelly and paused for a second as he looked into her eyes, "Look at me."

"I… I *look*."

"This is quite ridiculous. You expect me to believe—"

"—Tripp, please," Bonnie tried.

"Bonnie, you're outta line. Stand down," he returned to Jelly and demanded answers, "I know you understand me. I'm not playing around, anymore. Tell me what happened to you."

Jelly stopped purring and hugged her knees against her chest, "Big... water."

"Big water? You mean outside there in that pink place?"

She nodded and hoped Tripp was satisfied enough to leave her alone. Very ambitious, given his less than sedentary mood.

"What happened when you went in the water?"

"S-Swim," she stammered, her whiskers vibrating subtly, "Down."

"Why did you do that?"

"Hairs made me," she pointed at her whiskers, "Go to get gift."

"*Gift?*" Tripp exclaimed and threw his hands into the air, "What gift? What's the gift?"

"Pink Symphony."

"This is useless," Tripp couldn't look at her any longer. He faced the opposite wall in an attempt to calm his nerves.

"Not liking. Angry," Jelly swung her legs over the edge of the bed in defiance, "Not liking *you*."

He punched his fists together with frustration, "Tell her to stop speaking. She's a cat for Christ's sake. Cats don't speak."

Wool wasn't happy with his behavior. She walked around the bed and held her hands out at Jelly, "Tripp, can you try to exercise a bit of decorum, here? Please?"

Bonnie didn't have anything to say.

"Here, honey," Wool held her hands under Jelly's opened arms, "You want to try and walk? Like we do?"

Exasperated, Tripp turned around, baffled with the girls' refusal to question what had happened.

"She's a *cat*. Look at her."

"Tripp," Bonnie shouted at him with disdain and pointed at the little girl, "Look, we know it's ridiculous, but look at her. She's real, she's there, and she's frightened. It's happened, okay? *This* is what we have, now. Do you understand?"

He screwed his face and looked at the floor.

"Hey, Healy," Bonnie jumped to her feet and clapped her hands together, launching into a sarcastic tirade. "Yoo-hoo.

Pink Symphony-to-Healy. Can you read me?"

"Yes, I hear you."

"What did you think we'd find when we left USARIC, huh?" Bonnie's heart needed to release way more than just a rhetorical cliché of a question.

"I don't know—"

"—You think we'd all sail up to Saturn and find aliens with two mouths? We use all the weapons and start a big, galactic fight with space ships and guns? Pfft, typical *male*, aren't you?"

"No."

Bonnie licked her mouth and pretend-spat at the floor, "Ugh, you've made my mouth go all dry, now, having to shout at you like that," she thumped her chest in a pantomime fashion, "Me, Bonnie. *You*, captain," she pointed to Wool as she hugged Jelly. "Her? Jelly Anderson. *Star Cat*. Remember that?"

"Yes," Tripp apologized. "I remember."

"This was *your* idea, you know."

"I know."

"Don't *I know* me and act all repentant now that you're being told off by an android. You're feeling lonely? Tough. Hard times out in the big bad universe? Big deal, go N-Gage your wife and kid and cry about it. Start as you mean to go on, Healy. You asked USARIC to help you find the perfect candidate to join us. Now that you've have it you're acting like a puss— no, actually, you're acting like a *bitch*. Kind of ironic, isn't it?"

She stormed over to the bed and scooped Jelly into her arms. She purred up a treat and rubbed the side of her face against Bonnie's shoulder. Wool teared up and moved her face away from view.

Jelly stretched her arms out at the picture of Jamie on the wall, "Want Jamie."

"I know, sweetie. We all have people we miss."

"Miew," Jelly whimpered with a smile on her face. She threw her arms around Bonnie's neck and hugged her, purring up a treat, "Bonnie."

Tripp took in the unusual sight. He knew deep down

inside that he'd acted hastily. It was the last thing anyone on Opera Beta needed right now.

"I'm sorry."

"You bet your sweet ass you're sorry," Bonnie ran her knuckle under Jelly's chin and threw Tripp a look of contrition, "Now apologize to Jelly."

"Uh, sorry. Jelly."

"Pathetic. Say it like you mean it."

Bonnie lowered Jelly to the ground. Tripp's eyes followed her down. Her bare paw-like feet hit the tiled ground. Then, a fluffy tail lowered above it.

Jelly waded around on the spot, keeping a firm grip on Bonnie's hand.

Tripp squatted in front of her and held out his hand, "I'm sorry, Jelly. Friends?"

She eyed his fingers and considered his offer.

"No."

"Oh."

For the first time in his entire life Tripp's attempt at reconciliation had failed him. His charm may have worked wonders with others. But with Jelly? Not so much.

"Tripp, we have work to do," Wool said. "I need to make sure she's mobile. I want to run a PET scan on her before I let her leave Medix. Just to be on the safe side."

"A *pet* scan?" Tripp smiled.

"Yes. Problem?"

"No, no. Just appreciating the irony, that's all." He stood up and swallowed the rejection. He caught Jelly peering from behind Bonnie's waist, hoping he'd just go away.

"Miew.'

"Okay, okay. I'm going," he acknowledged his personal rejection, "I'll go and find out what's happening on the flight deck, shall I?"

"Yes, I think that would be best," Bonnie ran her fingers through Jelly's new head of hair.

Tripp exited Medix with as much affability and dignity as his current situation allowed. Which wasn't very much, sadly.

As soon as the door shut, Wool and Bonnie breathed a sigh of relief.

"He's such a butt hole, sometimes," Wool turned to Jelly and smiled, "Do you know what a butt hole is?"

Jelly nodded.

"Yes, of course you do. You've spent enough time cleaning yours."

"No decorum, huh?" Bonnie giggled.

Jelly stared at Bonnie's hand and released her grip, slowly.

"What are you doing, honey?" Wool grew apprehensive about Jelly's desire for independence, "No, no. You're not ready for that, yet."

"Let her try?" Bonnie kept her focus on Jelly's hand in hers, "Go on, sweetie. Try and stand on your own."

Jelly pursed her lips and teased her claws away from Bonnie's palm.

Her arm moved to the side of her waist. There she was, standing upright on her own feet, covered in a damp, white blanket. She resembled a statuesque angel in her own way.

Wool held her mouth in amazement. "Unbelievable."

Bonnie lifted her false leg and planted her right boot a few inches in front of her left, "Like that, Jelly. Like we do."

"Like you... *do*," Jelly repeated.

"Yes. Try it."

Jelly moved her right foot forward and planted the sole of her foot on the ground. She held out her arms for balance and stepped forward.

Then, she remembered she had her tail. She swished it around and evened her body weight out, relaxing into position.

"Now, the other leg," Bonnie demonstrated by lifting her left boot next to her right.

Jelly let out cat-like whimper as she shifted her weight forward. Her right foot rocked sideways as she struggle to balance.

It needed to be done. Wool and Bonnie watched with great intensity.

"Miew," she quipped with fear.

"Try, honey."

Her mouth quivered as she moved her right leg forward. She lost her balance quite out of the blue and fell paws-first to the ground. The bed rocked back and forth on its casters.

Jelly started sobbing on the floor.

Wool raced over to pick Jelly up under her arms, "Okay, that's more than enough fun for today, I think."

"Oh dear," Bonnie sighed. "Looks like we're gonna have to practice this a bit more, huh?

Wool laid Jelly out on the bed and fluffed the pillow, "Bonnie, I need to perform an enhanced MRI. Can you give us about half an hour? "

"Sure," Bonnie made for the door and blew Jelly a kiss, "Good luck."

Chapter 16

"Level Four," the elevator called out as the cage stopped at the outer doors, "Weapons and Armory. Have a nice day."

"Open the damn doors," Jaycee clutched his severed left hand in his right and yelled at the ceiling. He kicked the cage in a fit of fury.

His boot connected with the Perspex panel, effectively scaring the doors open.

Jaycee stormed onto the sprawling metal gantry that led to Weapons & Armory. A ruthless determination to rectify what had happened swept through his body.

The clanging from his stomping boots echoed across the ground as he spoke into his radio mic.

"Tripp, this is Jaycee. Broadcasting on a secure frequency. Do you read me?"

A burst of static came through his ear piece. The device belonged to his helmet which he'd long since discarded.

"Tripp, do you read—"

"—Jaycee?" Tripp's voice crept into his ear, "Yes, this is Tripp. I read you."

"Tripp?"

"Yes, go ahead. Are you done with Engine and Payload, yet? I guess you must be if we're able to communi—"

"—Tripp, listen," Jaycee jogged along the gantry at speed, "We need to find Baldron and Tor right now. Have you seen them?"

"No, I've just got out of Medix. Why, what's the issue? Where are you?"

"Heading for Weapons and Armory."

"What?" his voice indicated confusion, "Why?"

"I'm gonna tool up and kill them both."

"What did they do?"

Jaycee arrived at the door and slammed the palm of his severed hand against the open panel. The door slid open and allowed him in.

"Jaycee? Talk to me?"

"Yeah, I hear you."

"What happened?"

"They tried to kill me."

"But you have the compliance device. Weren't they afraid you'd use it?"

"It's a trap, man. They brought me down to E&P so one of those creature things could attack me. Baldron ran off with my glove. He's got the Decapidisc detonator."

Jaycee arrived at the first weapons bay and kicked the door open in a furious rage.

"Tor's on the control deck," Tripp said. "Baldron must be headed there right now."

Jaycee lifted a fresh K-SPARK shotgun from the holster on the wall and strapped it around his shoulders, "I'm tooling up, now, Tripp. Are you *carrying*?

"I've got my standard issue on me."

"It might not be enough," Jaycee grabbed two Rez-9s from the wall and slotted a fresh magazine into each one with extreme deftness, "Don't go there without me. You're outnumbered two-to-one."

"Jaycee, listen. I can't let them loose on the deck. God knows what they'll get up to with all the core commands and Manuel at their disposal.

"Do *not* go into control alone," Jaycee grunted into his mouth piece as he pulled open the second bay, "They probably think I'm dead. If so, who do you think is next on their hit list?"

An array of grenades and assorted explosive weapons and

attachments glinted in the bay's strip lights.

"How long are you going to be?" Tripp asked.

Jaycee swiped a handful of dumb bombs and planted his boot on the lip of the shelf, "Dunno, maybe a couple minutes."

"Jaycee, listen. Something else has happened. Something bizarre. To do with Anderson."

The side section of Jaycee's thigh sprung open, providing a compartment to store four red dumb bombs and four black smart bombs.

"Anderson? What about her?"

He dropped the grenades inside and thumped the compartment shut with the side of his fist.

"I'll tell you when we meet. You're not going to believe me. Can you get to control in ninety seconds?" Tripp asked through the static.

"Sure thing," Jaycee reached into the bay and unfastened a yellow claymore from its housing. "Stay out of sight."

"Will do."

Jaycee lifted the claymore up in front of his face and pulled it apart like an accordion. Three additional claymores hung together across a wire, "Make sure it's just you. No one else."

"Sure, just you and me."

"At the corner by the door," Satisfied, Jaycee collapsed the claymores together and clipped them to his belt. He looked at the first weapons bay and saw a second K-SPARK shining back at him.

He had an idea.

"I'm bringing another shotgun with me, this one's floor mountable. Doubles up as a turret. Go to the deck, I'm on my way."

Jaycee wrenched the heavy artillery unit from the bay in his right hand.

"See you in ninety," Tripp said.

Jaycee gripped the barrel and cocked it in his strong, right hand, "Stay safe till I get there."

The Control Deck
Space Opera Beta – Level One

Baldron stood at the flight deck, staring idly at the controls. He'd placed Jaycee's glove next to the yellow thruster lever. He looked at the view of Pink Symphony through the windscreen and felt the lip of his Decapidisc. His fate, until now, had been in the hands of someone who despised him; someone who could have taken his life at the push of a button - one which Baldron was now in control of.

He took a deep breath and closed his eyes, "One down, three to go."

"Three?" Tor looked over from the communications panel, "Oh, right. Yeah. Including that stupid cat."

Manuel hung still six feet in the air. His pages paused and flickering in mid-flip.

"How's Manuel?"

Tor followed a small white line creeping across Manuel's paused page, "Flushing to disk. Thirty more seconds and we're in business."

Baldron turned to the glorious, opulent pink sky looming beyond the shield. The three suns closed together, the harshness of their beams subdued by a series of pallid, milky clouds.

"A century and a half ago we put the first dog in space. I still don't know why we bothered."

Tor ran his fingers along the surface of his Decapidisc, "Because we could, comrade."

"I just hope Dimitri is okay. Those idiot Yanks have a habit of executing first and asking questions later. They have a history of it."

Baldron turned around and looked at Manuel's holograph. It shimmied around and attempted to speak.

"Remember, Viktor. We may be the bad guys in the eyes of those on Earth. But we had no choice. The others died and we survived. We cracked the code," Baldron pointed at the window, "Now, we have the answer."

"We do. Now we just need to figure out what it means."

Manuel vanished and reappeared in the blink of an eye.

The book powered up and spread its ends out like a bird. Healthy and energetic.

"Ah, I'm online," Manuel beamed and tilted the top of his pages at Tor, "Good whenever-it-is, Tor. How are you?"

"I'm okay, Manuel."

Manuel slipped a few meters to Tor's right and nosed in around his neck, "Why are you wearing a compliance unit?"

"It's a mistake, Manuel. Jaycee Nayall attached them to me and Baldron Landaker in error."

"We believe Jaycee has short-circuited," Baldron added as he approached Tor and Manuel, "We are unhappy that a Series Three Androgyne gets away with insubordination like this."

"I agree."

Tor raised his eyebrows with surprise, "You do?"

"Absolutely," Manuel flipped to page 453, 770. "See, here? Infinity Clause seven, para one. *No Androgyne unit may act against its humans*. He is in direct contravention of this clause."

"Good," Tor breathed a sigh of relief along with Baldron, "Can you remove my Decapidisc please?"

"Certainly. Give me a moment," Manuel froze solid in the air.

Baldron and Tor smiled and high-fived each other.

***

Tripp peered round the corner wall and stared at the control deck door. He held his Rez-9 flat in his palm, clocking the white indicator on the side - a full magazine.

"Please, God. Let us survive this one."

He squeezed the grip in his right hand, keeping the gun pointed at the ground.

A series of heavy footsteps clomped away behind his shoulders. He knew who they belonged to.

"You ready, man?"

Time seemed to grind into slow motion as Tripp laid eyes on Jaycee.

The man bounded forward with great purpose. Armed with two, heavy K-SPARKS, claymores and an exo-suit that could probably withstand an atomic blast.

"Jaycee."

"Catch," He tossed one of the K-SPARKs over to Tripp, who caught it in both hands and slipped the harness over his shoulder.

"Got it."

Jaycee flipped his visor down, ready for war, "Let's give 'em hell."

Tripp held him back, "Jaycee, listen. Don't kill them. At worst, a little light maiming. We need them."

"But we can't trust those scumbags."

"I know, but we need them."

"*Need them?* Need them to kill us the second our backs are turned?"

"What happened down at Engine and Payload?"

Jaycee held up his ruined wrist. A bent metal carpal extension protruded through the broken wires and connectors.

"What the—"

"Does this answer your question?"

"Yes."

"—They need killing. So, let's do it," Jaycee put a foot forward, only to be held back by Tripp.

"Jaycee?"

"Yeah."

"You're an Androgyne?"

Jaycee spun his head to the right, no longer able to face reality. "I... I... just..."

"I had no idea."

Jaycee sniffed and held his elbow to his face, "I know you didn't. How could you? Bonnie didn't even know when she found out."

Tripp allowed Jaycee a few seconds to himself.

"If it's any consolation, you're as good as human to me. You know that, right?"

A pink tear trickled down Jaycee's cheek, "I never thought it could happen to me, man."

"Why anyone, buddy?

"My entire life has been a lie," Jaycee wept quietly, "My

wife must know. My kids—"

"—Jaycee, I know it's hard to take, but—"

"—Every single time I go to sleep, I forget. I wake up the next day thinking I'm normal," Jaycee's lips quivered. "I remember everything. Everything, except for the fact I'm not normal."

Tripp didn't have the words nor the credentials to try and talk his friend down from his mire, "Hey."

"Yeah," Jaycee wiped the liquid from his face and half-laughed in pain, "Genuine tears, look. They've even got the salt levels right."

"I'm not going to try and tell you everything is okay. I can't imagine what you're going through."

"You have no idea what I'm going through. I just want to die. I never want to feel like this again."

"You're a man, aren't you?"

"Yeah," Jaycee sniffed.

"You have memories? A loving family, right?"

"Yes. I do."

"Then as far as everyone's concerned, you're a human being. What's the difference?" Tripp placed his finger under the barrel of Jaycee's gun and pointed it at control deck door, "All that anger deep in your gut? Put it to good use. Focus it at those bastards in *there*."

Jaycee sniggered through his tears. The feeling of heartache and self-pity manifested itself into a whirlwind of pure rage.

Tripp could see the realization take place in Jaycee's eyes, "That's right, man. You fire up and take it out on the bad guys."

"I will."

Tripp gave him a harsh but friendly thump on the shoulder, "That's the spirit."

"Thanks, man."

"Oww," Tripp waved his hand in pain, quietly, "Damn, your suit is vicious."

"Yeah, don't hit me again," Jaycee cleared his throat and acted manly once again, "Don't tell anyone I cried, okay?"

"Of course not."

"Because if you do I'll remove your skull, sand it down and give it to your wife as a souvenir cereal bowl."

"That won't work. She hates cereal."

Tripp and Jaycee shared a moment. Certain death was on the horizon. Both men knew it, and elected to laugh right in its face.

"Okay, listen carefully. We're not going in all guns blazing."

"No?"

"Nope," Tripp shook his head and scanned the door to the control deck, "I'm going in first..."

***

"Override compliance unit," Manuel's voice came out of Tor's mouth, "Decapidisc. Unit Two."

The lights on the disc shut off one by one. Tor stood mannequin-still as Manuel controlled his body.

"Oh, this *is* curious. This is what it feels like to be human?" Tor felt the neck hole unbolt. Both halves of the disc swung out, resembling a huge *three* shape hanging from the back of his neck.

A sharp, purple light bolted out from Tor's eyes, puking Manuel's holographic book image into the air.

"Done. Whoa, what a rush," Manuel fluttered around in an attempt to acclimatize himself to his surroundings.

Tor's blinked back to life and shook the dizziness away, "Wow. Is it over?"

"Yes," Manuel shifted around in the air, applauding the experience with two of his pages.

"Thank, God," He caught the disabled Decapidisc in his hands and placed it on the communications panel, "Thanks, Manuel."

"You're welcome. Thank you for letting me inside you, Viktor."

"What?"

"Your name. Viktor Rabinovich. I took the liberty to run a backup on your entire life in case you ever developed Alzheimer's."

"I didn't give you permission to do that," Tor fumed. "Erase it. Right now, please."

"I'm sorry, I didn't mean to—"

"—Dah, dah, I don't wanna hear it. Erase all that data you *stole* from my head, please. At once."

"Certainly," Manuel paused for nanosecond. "Erase complete."

"Thank *you*. You're out of your mind."

"I know, Tor. I was *in* yours."

"That's not what I meant—*forget it*."

Baldron got thoroughly fed up with the friendly exchange. He pointed at the button on Jaycee's glove and then to his own Decapidisc, "Hey, what about me? Get inside me and take this thing off."

Tor waved his hand across his face. An eight-foot holographic vector image of Opera Beta pinged to life in the middle of the room.

"Manuel?"

"Yes, Viktor?"

"Stop calling me that. Call me Tor."

"Certainly, *Tor*."

"What's the situation with Pure Genius?"

"The supercomputer is fully operational, now. Everything is well."

"Good," Tor ignored Baldron and pointed to the vector image, "Sit-rep report on all souls aboard Opera Beta, please. Engage coordinates, and show them in purple."

"Certainly."

"Comrade, please," Baldron pleaded, "Have Manuel remove this thing from my neck."

"Look, *comrade*. We need to know where the others are, and I want to make sure Jaycee is dead—"

The door to the control deck slid open. Tor and Baldron averted their attention to the man entering the room.

A stern-looking Tripp Healy, complete with K-SPARK heavy artillery, "Hey, guys."

"Hello, Tripp," Tor clutched at his neck and stood in front of the opened Decapidisc nestled on the comms panel.

"Did you get those nuke thrusters replaced okay?"

"Yes, we did. Everything is... *well*."

"You're starting to sound just like him."

"Who?"

"Manuel," Tripp smiled and nodded at the vector image of Opera Beta, "What are you doing with that, Tor?"

"Oh, I—" he stumbled over his need to lie, "I was just working out if Pure Genius is up and running."

Tripp clocked Baldron's nerves getting the better of him. He threw Tor a look of suspicion but kept his manner friendly and professional, "I see you managed to get your Decapidisc off?"

"It was hurting my neck," Tor held his breath and watched Tripp walk towards the flight deck. A swift change of conversation was required. "Um, where have you been?"

"Where have I been?" Tripp gripped the back of the flight chair and chuckled with faux confusion, "I'm sorry, I didn't know I had to report my whereabouts to you at all times."

Tor and Baldron just *knew* something was wrong. Tripp knew it, too, and decided to have fun with them. He clocked Jaycee's glove in the corner of his eye but made out he hadn't noticed.

"Where's the big man? Was he helpful?"

Baldron gulped hard, trying not to sweat. His pores had other ideas, though.

"Y-Yes," he stammered and almost croaked, "H-He was—"

"—Why are you sweating, Landaker?" Tripp asked.

"This is unusual," Manuel butted in, "I'm detecting a lot more souls than anticipated."

Tor ignored Manuel and focused his attention on pleasing Tripp, "I'm not. It's just hot in here—"

Manuel activated himself and shifted around the room, "Tor, the sit-rep is available. But I'm afraid to report there are many more—"

"—Not now, Manuel—"

"—Sit-rep? *Souls*?" Tripp stepped toward the vector image, away from the flight deck, "What sit-rep?"

Tor held out his hands in defiance. "Manuel, no—"

"—Ah, hello, Tripp. Tor asked me for everyone's

coordinates within Opera Beta. Here they are."

Tor closed his eyes as three purple dots blotted out inside Medix. Three in the control deck, and one in the corridor just outside.

"Those are just the crew, however."

Baldron scrunched his face in confusion at the last pulsating purple icon. Someone was just outside the door. He shot Tor a look and then made for the glove on the flight panel.

Tripp didn't see Baldron snatching the glove - he had his back to him.

"Why do you want to know where everyone is?" Tripp lifted his K-SPARK and slipped his finger around the trigger.

Dozens of purple blobs appeared around the ship's vector.

Manuel flew around the room trying to catch everyone's attention, "I seriously advise you act on this information, good people." A giant blob appeared at the front of the ship's vector image.

"B-Because..." Tor struggled.

Tripp opened his mouth and shouted at the door. "Jaycee, now!"

"What?" Tor didn't know where to turn. He backed up and gripped the edges of the deck, "Quick, the glove."

"I got it, I got it," Baldron wiggled his fingers into the glove.

Jaycee stomped into the room and pointed his gun at Baldron, "Hey, *you*."

"No, d-don't shoot!"

SCHPLATTT!

Everyone turned to the source of the noise. A giant creature slapped itself to the exterior of the flight deck windshield.

"Jaaaaysus," Tor gasped at the underbelly of the thirty-foot tall creature thumping the transparent plastic.

"Gah," Baldron looked up at the hundreds of sharp teeth scratching at him from up above. The magnificent beast was darker in color than the other, smaller ones they'd seen, "We're in hell!"

"Shut up," Jaycee aimed down his sight and stomped his foot to the ground, "Hey! You idiot, over here."

Baldron turned around in an utter daze, "Huh?"

The creature shunted the windshield, squealing an ungodly roar at the humans on the other side.

"I want my damn glove back," Jaycee's K-SPARK beamed to life, seconds away from firing a bullet, "Throw it to me."

Baldron squeezed it in his hand, "No."

"I said give me the damn glove."

"No."

CRAAA-AAA-ACK… Scores of hairline cracks blasted across the windshield. It wouldn't hold off the beast much longer.

"Hell's teeth!" Tripp backed up and waved everyone to the door, "Everyone, get out of here."

Manuel flew through the vector image and emitted a beam at the hundreds of purple flashing dots, "Tripp, these unidentified *things* are everywhere. Observe, Primary Air Lock, Level One."

The vector contours of the airlock image enlarged, offering a more detailed view. A torrent of purple dots bundled up at the line pushing one of them through.

"We're *on* level one," Tripp gasped.

A thunderous crash rattled down the walkway followed by a cacophony of high pitch screeches.

"It's *them*. We're stuck," Baldron screamed, "We're all gonna die."

Jaycee lifted his K-SPARK to the windshield and yanked the trigger back with his index finger.

"You first."

The bullet charge bolted out of the barrel, tore through the vector image, and made its way to the dead center of the windshield.

KERR-RAASSH!

Baldron threw himself back. The plastic shield exploded, raining sharp fragments of plastic over the control deck. The giant creature smashed against the flight panel, accidentally knocking the yellow thruster level forward.

"Gaaah," Baldron swiped at the creature and missed.

Jaycee stepped back slowly as he led the retreat to the closed door, "Quick, behind me."

"What?" Tor yelled and pointed at Baldron, "You can't leave him there. That *thing* will kill him."

"Good riddance. He can keep that big, ugly bastard busy while we run."

The entire ship began to rumble to life. Manuel spun around on the spot, "Engines initiated. Prepare for launch."

"We're going!" Tripp backed up with Jaycee. Both held their K-SPARKs up at the enormous monstrosity.

"Holy hell, look. It's killing him."

"No, no," Baldron slapped the creature's bulbous mid-section with the glove. His Decapidisc kept his neck and head inches from the floor, rolling side to side. It also protected his neck from the sharp talons as they jabbed away at his face and neck, "Help me, p-please."

The creature roared into his face, rippling his skin up the front of his face.

"Gah, gah, please," Baldron rolled his neck along the rim of his disc and looked at Jaycee, "P-Please, shoot it."

"I will," Jaycee looked up from the sight on his gun, "Just as soon as it kills you."

Tripp looked away, somewhat resigned to the execution that was about to take place.

"Gimme that gun," Tor gripped the barrel of Jaycee's K-SPARK and tried to pull it away from his hands, "Shoot that thing. It's going to kill him."

Jaycee winced and booted Tor in his gut. The man tumbled over and bounced against the door, "Get off me." Jaycee swung the gun back at the creature. It lifted the first two of its mangled, black limbs and fanned out its talons.

STAB-SHUNT-CLAMP!

The sharp ends pinned Baldron to the ground on his back. It lowered its razor sharp teeth-filled slit down to his face and roared once again.

"Okay," Baldron convulsed with fear, "I-If I'm g-going, you're coming with me."

He gripped Jaycee's glove in his right hand and punched

the creature in the throat, releasing it deep inside its throat.

The beast shunted back on its limbs as the ship tilted forward and pulled itself away from Pink Symphony's sandy surface.

The horizon shuddered in the background, wading around, suggesting the ship was struggling to take off.

Tripp, Jaycee, and Tor stumbled away from the door and hit the wall. "*Damn* it."

The creature munched away on Baldron's glove. The ship tilted back, rolling Baldron out from under the creature and sliding along the control deck floor.

"Comrade," Tor flung himself up the raised length of the ground and caught Baldron in his arms.

"Hey, you two," Tripp shouted at them as he clung to the door. His feet drifted into the air as the ship tried to launch, "Enough lessense, get over here."

Jaycee peered through the window in the door. The corridor seemed clear enough, "We gotta get to Medix and protect the others."

"Jaycee, open the door," Tripp shouted over the combined deafening sound of the creature's squeals and the ship's thrusters, "Now."

Jaycee waved Tripp through as the door slid open. He swung his gun back at the creature and prepared to blast it to pieces, "Come on, you ugly spider-looking bag of puke. Let's do it."

CRUNCH!

The creature's mouth crunched Jaycee's glove, spitting out strips of fabric. It nestled against the flight deck and roared again.

"Thank God," Tor said to Baldron, "Let's get out of here—"

Biddip-biddip-beeep…

Three white lights lit up on Baldron's Decapidisc. He gasped and tried to pull it away from his neck, "No, no, no."

Tor looked at the creature, "Oh *no*."

GULP! The creature swallowed the glove and spat the plastic activation button to the ground. It spun around on its axis and fell on its side.

"Help me," Baldron screamed and pushed away from Tor. He ran through the vector image of Opera Beta, toward the beast, tugging at the metal disc, "I'm going to die,"

The creature spread all twelve limbs across the floor, ceiling, and walls, looking for all the world like a fleshy spider-cobweb.

Beep-beep-beep...

The three white lights flashed on Baldron's Decapidisc. The creature widened its mouth behind Baldron as he squealed for the last time.

"Comrade, p-please," he begged Tor slumped to his knees.

"I c-can't," Tor squealed, utterly helpless.

Biddip, biddip, beeeeeeeeep. The three indicators flashed faster and faster.

The Decapidisc vibrated around Baldron's neck. The blades within the metal housing spun to life and produced a whirring sound.

Baldron accepted his fate and closed his eyes.

SCHWIIRRR-SCHUNT.

The disc rocked gently around Baldron's neck. He lifted his head and looked at Jaycee with sadness, "I'm sorry."

"Yeah, you keep saying that."

Jaycee thumped his thigh compartment open with his fist. A red dumb bomb fell into his palm just in time for him to scowl at Baldron in his last seconds.

A comforting smile stretched across Baldron's mouth. His eyes, nostrils and mouth released a fountain of pink liquid. His head wobbled atop his shoulders for a couple of seconds.

The ship adjusted itself, throwing Jaycee and Tor to the left - and Baldron's freshly severed head from his shoulders. The opened Decapidisc clanged to the floor - mission accomplished.

"Go to Hell, you *sonofabitch*."

"Who are you talking to?" Tor asked.

"Both of them."

Jaycee hurled the dumb bomb at the creature. It unlatched its limbs from the wall and made for Jaycee and Tor. It screeched at the top of its vocal chords.

The bomb flew into its open, wailing mouth.

"Run," Jaycee grabbed Tor's sleeve, "C'mon, let's go."

Tor trained his eyes on Baldron's severed head rolling towards the flight deck like a lit sparkler. It bounced to a stop between the creature's limbs.

"What—? He's... he's not—"

"—Yeah, another Androgyne Series Three unit. Sucks doesn't it?" Jaycee pushed Tor through the door and jumped after him, "It's becoming something of a bad habit around here, lately. Finding out you're one of them can really screw up your day."

The creature pushed itself forward just as Jaycee slammed the door shut on one of its limbs. Its muffled squeals bounced behind the sound-proof window.

Jaycee took the opportunity to watch the impending execution, "Look at it, Tor."

"Wh-what?"

"That's *one* angry mother—"

KA-SCHPLATTT-TT!

The beast exploded, painting the entire control deck with pink gore and charred remains.

"We gotta get out of here," Tor held his hand to his mouth like a frightened child.

"Damn straight," Jaycee bounded up the corridor and turned the corner.

Tor double-took and followed after him, "I need a gun."

"Ha. Very funny," Jaycee bopped him on the back of the head, "The only way you're getting a weapon is if you use it on yourself."

"Jaycee?" Tripp's voice shot through Jaycee's headset, "I'm at the Primary airlock. They're *everywhere*, man."

"Tripp?" Jaycee ran across the corridor, "Everywhere?"

"Those creatures. Listen, do *not* come here. Get to Medix. Bonnie and Wool are there with Jelly. I can't hold them off. Both airlock doors are damaged."

"But, we're taking off?" Tor muttered, "If we hit orbit— hell, if we leave its atmosphere, all the air will get sucked out—"

"—Understood." Jaycee turned left and made for the

bank of descending stairs, "Come on, *Viktor*. We're going to Medix."

Chapter 17

Medix
Space Opera Beta - Level Three

A holographic scan of Jelly's brain projected from Wool's thumbnail on the central desk. The left and right hemisphere glowed red and blue, respectively.

"Head?" Jelly pressed her fingers to a digipad secured on her scalp, "What is?"

"No, honey. What… is… *this*?"

"What… is… *this*?" Jelly repeated verbatim, understanding very little of what she'd just learned.

"It's a tracer," Wool walked around the image and analyzed it, "It shows us what's inside your head. We're just making sure you're okay. It'll take a few minutes for the report to return."

Jelly shifted her buttocks across the mattress still not fully accustomed to the new position. Her tail got in the way much of the time which went some way to distract her from the pain in her stomach.

"Tummy hurts."

"That's normal, Jelly. Probably adjusting to your new posture and diet."

"Ad… just… ing," Jelly repeated.

"Well, when you like things a certain way but something makes you change it. Adjusting."

"Oh," Jelly wiggled her nose and pricked up her ears. The bed began to vibrate, "Why bed move?"

"Why is the bed *moving*, honey."

"Not knowing," she purred and gripped the sides of the mattress for safety.

"No, I wasn't asking you, honey. I was correcting you."

"Correcting?"

Wool turned to the ceiling and stepped away from the image scan. The largest of the three sun's rings revolved in all directions around its body. The pink horizon slid down the window. Opera Beta was in motion.

"Thank God," She breathed a sigh of relief and smiled at Jelly, "Looks like we're going home."

"Like house," Jelly returned the smile, "Want Jamie."

"*Home*, sweetie. Not house. You *like* home. We all like home," Wool walked over to the bed and sat into the chair. She was on the verge of crying for joy, "I have to tell you something."

Jelly lifted her jaw, "Do chin."

Wool ran her knuckle under Jelly's chin, "Feeling better?"

A gleeful purr came from her throat as she spotted Bonnie napping on the chair.

"I guess you are," Wool enjoyed Jelly's relaxed nature.

Jelly turned toward the sleeping woman on the chair, "Bonnie. Dead?"

"Bonnie isn't dead, honey. She's recharging her batteries," Wool pretended to rub her eye with her fist, "Tired."

Jelly slid the side of her face along the back of Wool's hand, purring twice as hard.

"When we return home I don't know if Jamie will recognize you. He might be a bit scared."

"Scared?" Jelly's head bolted upright, confused. She pointed at the picture of Jamie on the wall, "Friend."

"No, I know that," Wool rose out of the chair and lifted Jelly's blanket over her shoulders, "It's just that you've grown up a bit and you look different. So he might not know who you are."

Jelly wiggled her nose along the top of the blanket, "Smell? Know me?"

Wool removed the scan pad from Jelly's head and placed it on her stomach, "Hold still, honey."

"You *hold*. Picture," Jelly nosed around the device in her master's hand.

"No, *you* hold yourself still. Don't move," Wool strapped the pad in place and lifted the wires over her right leg, "We'll do your body next."

The brain scan image rippled wildly and replaces Jelly's body shape and the outline of her organs.

"PET scan report," the machine advised. "Two minutes."

"You know, a hundred years ago, they'd have had to put you in a big tube to do this."

"Big tube. Water?" Jelly extended her claws and touched her teeth, "Thirsty."

"Yeah, *kinda*," Wool looked at the machine and held the pad in place against Jelly's chest, "Commence enhanced magnetic resonance imaging, please."

"E-MRI activated."

"Now, don't worry, honey. This might tingle a little bit."

The pad sucked in and absorbed itself onto Jelly's abdomen.

"Miew," she whimpered. "Tummy. Hurts."

"I know. It won't hurt much longer," Wool flicked a switch on the front of the machine, "Administer tracer."

The door to Medix slid open.

A giant killing machine decked out in an exo-suit and K-SPARK shotgun was the first person in.

"Jaycee?" Wool held Jelly's head in her hands at once, realizing the two hadn't been formally acquainted, "What are you doing here?"

"You got time for a long, drawn-out story?"

"No, I don't. But I've been left alone here with jelly all this time. She's scared."

Without so much as a courtesy greeting, he yanked Tor by his collar and threw him into the room, "Get in."

The man staggered forward and crashed against an empty bed. The medician tools spilled from the attached tray. Jaycee rolled his eyes and lunged after him, "Get off the floor, you self-absorbed, Soviet ass-clown."

"No, p-please, no m-more—"

Jaycee bent over and grabbed Tor's collar, lifting the top half of his body into the air. "We've only just begun—

"—Hey," Wool barked at the pair, "Behave yourselves. We have a guest."

"What the—" Jaycee spotted the strange half-cat girl sitting with his colleague on Jelly's bed, "I, uh—"

"—Is that *Anderson*?" Tor asked, confused.

Jaycee absentmindedly released Tor's collar and dropped him to the floor. "What happened to her?"

"We don't know yet and she won't tell me."

"Huh? Won't *tell* you?" Jaycee pressed his knee against his gun. "Want me to make her?"

"Are you out of your mind, Nayall?" Wool yelled at his face, "It's not that she doesn't want to tell me. It's that she's not able to."

"She can speak?"

"Yes. Speak," Jelly scowled at the large mercenary filling her periphery vision, "Jaycee. Bad man."

"Yes, that's right, honey. Don't pay any attention to the bad man," she finished in a mocking tone and gave her a cuddle.

Tor winced and staggered to his feet, "You're right, he *is* a bad man."

The remark snapped Jaycee back to reality - and the severity of their current situation.

"Well," he half-mocked and thumped his exo-suit, "This *bad man* just saved all your lives."

"Did you?" Wool asked.

"The ship is swarming with those creature things. Just killed a massive one out in the control deck."

Wool stood out of her seat in shock, "What?"

"They're everywhere," Tor confirmed. He spotted Bonnie fast asleep on the chair behind Jaycee, "We got Manuel operational. He's trying to get us out of here."

"Cannot leave," Jelly blurted matter-of-factly and patted her mattress like an excited child, "Stay, stay, stay."

Jaycee approached the bed and felt the urge to touch her face, "What did you say?" His gloved fingers made contact with her cheek.

"Miew," she cowered, only for his finger to brush against one her whiskers.

ZAAPP-PP!

Each whisker lit up and jolted Jaycee's hand away, "Oww. What the hell is wrong with you?"

Jelly exploded in tears and held the sides of her head with her paws, "Brain. Hurts."

"Look what you've done," Wool scooped the sobbing Jelly into her arms. It wasn't until she felt her weight that she fully acknowledged her growth, "Honey, are you okay?"

"Bad men," she wept, "In head."

"Bad men? What bad men?"

Jaycee turned to Tor and pointed at Bonnie. "You, wake Dr. Whitaker up. Now. We need her online."

"Fine."

Tor raced over to the chair as Jaycee turned back to Wool and Jelly, "What's wrong with her?"

"PET scan complete," the machine advised, "J. Anderson, configuration one, one, eight. Congratulations, you've a clean bill of health. Generating quantitative report. Please standby."

The image displayed a 3D rendition of Jelly's brain. All four quadrants flashed green.

"What does that mean?"

Wool hugged Jelly and exhaled, "Like the machine said, a clean bill of health. Nothing wrong."

"Hey, wake up," Tor bopped Bonnie on the shoulder.

"Huh?" she licked her lips and opened her eyes, "Where am I?"

"Very funny. Get up. We're at war."

"War?"

"Apparently so."

Bonnie jumped to her feet and sprang into action. She reached for her Rez-9 and clasped the holster, "Who are we fighting?"

"You remember those ugly monster things?"

"Yes."

"Them."

"Where are they?"

"We're waiting here for Tripp. Just get ready," Tor immediately thought of a question, "Don't get angry, but... are you human?"

"Of course I'm human, you idiot," Bonnie spat and saw Jelly in Wool's arms, "Oh, there she is."

"Hey."

Bonnie lifted her boot at the end of her mechanical leg and wondered why it was vibrating, "Oh, it's not me. Are we *traveling?*"

"We're trying to," Tripp entered Medix. Covered in pink slime, his face and inner-suit had seen happier, cleaner days.

He slung the K-SPARK over his shoulders and held out his arms, acknowledging his gory state, "You're welcome." He turned to Jaycee and held out his hand, "Fresh mag, please."

"You got it," Jaycee released the magazine from his gun, "Here," he threw it at Tripp, who caught it and slotted it into his shotgun.

"Thanks," Tripp wiped a slew of pink gloop from his face and pulled the door shut.

"What's the situation, Tripp?' Wool asked. 'I'm hearing those *things* got into the ship."

"Yes, I've just killed about twenty of them."

"So, they're all dead?"

"Nope," Tripp cleared his throat and wiped his pink sludge-splattered face, "That was just the start. We'll be out of here soon. We need to kill however many of them are left. Where's Baldron?"

"He, uh, didn't make it," Jaycee said.

Tripp hawked up a pink wad of phlegm and spat it at Tor's face. He recoiled with apology when it splatted against the man's forehead.

"Eww."

"Sorry, I meant to miss you."

Tripp barged the man out of his path and looked at the E-MRI holograph hanging in the middle of the room, "This is Jelly, right?"

"Yes," Wool explained, carrying Jelly over to Tripp, "The brain scan came back all clear. Just a routine health check, really."

"You okay, Jelly?"

Tripp smiled at her, hoping for a positive reception. No such luck. She pressed the side of her head against Wool's shoulder and avoided him.

"Charming."

He turned around and addressed Wool, Jaycee, Tor, and Bonnie, "Okay, here's the lowdown. We're screwed. Manuel's trying his best to get us out of this godforsaken place, but the thrusters are playing up and we might not have enough throttle to reach the sky, let alone orbit," he shot Tor a look of utter disgust, "Ain't that right, comrade?"

"I'm sorry."

"I swear on my wife and son, Tor," Tripp grunted, about ready to execute the man with his own bare hands, "If you say you're sorry just one more damn time, I'll tear off your head and thread it on a skewer along with Baldron's. Do you understand what I've just said?"

Tor pressed his hands together and decided it was best not to call his captain's bluff, "Yes, Captain."

"Good," Tripp reached into his belt, retrieved his Rez-9 and pushed it into Wool's hands, "Bonnie, are you carrying?"

"Yeah, just the one piece," Bonnie gripped her firearm and thumped her metal leg, "Got the K-12 on as a backup."

"Stay behind Jaycee, then. He and I are locked and ready to blast."

"I don't have a gun," Tor tried, temporarily forgetting that he was the bad guy.

"Why don't you try punching them in the face? See how far that gets you?" Tripp winked at Wool but she hadn't the heart to smirk back.

"This isn't funny, Tripp," Tor said.

"Yes it is. You're good at hitting things, aren't you?' Tripp pointed at Wool, 'Especially women."

"That's irrelevant. If we go out there unarmed I'll get killed."

"Want me to tear your arms off, then?" Jaycee joked, enjoying the man's distress, 'I'll rip them off and batter you to death with them."

"No, *armed*, you dummy. Give me a weapon *at least*."

"No guns for you, ass hat,' Tripp spat. 'If you die, you die. We'll be sure to send N-Gage your loved ones and tell them how awesome you are, or, hopefully, soon to be *were*."

Jelly's whiskers sparked up. "Miewww," She clawed at Wool's arm, wanting to be set down on the bed.

"Okay, honey."

Everyone watched as she dropped Jelly to her mattress, "Voice in brain," she shuddered and held her claws to her face, "Pink... *Pink Symphony*."

"What's she talking about now?" Jaycee asked, ready to storm out and do battle. The bizarre interlude was preventing him from doing his job, "We'd better go."

"No, wait," Wool leaned over Jelly and looked at her face, "What's wrong, honey?"

Jelly yelped and swiped her infinity claws at Wool, tearing three slits across her cheek, "ROOWAAR."

"Gah," Wool cupped her face and stepped back against the wall, "She scratched me!"

Tripp ran over and held her arm, "Wool."

Jelly snatched the radio on her bedside desk and slammed it against her thighs. The bone in her leg cracked pushing her feet out a further two inches, "Pink..."

She dropped the radio to the floor and writhed around in pain, "Waaaah."

The black device hit the floor, cracking apart. Beethoven's 5th Symphony piped up.

Da-da-da-dummm...

The crew backed up as Jelly's chest hulked into the air and carried the rest of her flailing body ten inches above the bed.

"Shaaah..." Her childlike voice deepened, mid-cry, "Shaaantaa..."

Wool caught sight of a commotion coming from outside the window, "Look, out there."

The two smaller suns in the sky converged into the biggest. Its rings whizzed around at speed, vacuuming the grains of sand off the floor like a reverse waterfall.

The ship shuddered and rocked around forcing the horizon to creep back into view.

"I don't like this," Tripp said. "What the hell is—"

THUD!

Jelly crashed back to the bed and wailed, "Ugghhh…"

Bonnie widened her eyes at Jelly. Her body had lengthened by five inches. Still covered by the blanket, she shook her head and flicked her ears, "They come."

"What?" Jaycee lost his temper. "*Who* come?"

"We stay," she said in her huskier voice, barely registering any pain, "We fight."

"Fight what?" Tripp asked, about to explode with frustration.

Jelly's blinks turned her orange eyes pink. Her whiskers lit up. Her voice husky and gravelly, as if possessed, "Do you know why you are here?"

Magnetized by Jelly's transformation, Tripp cleared his throat and calmed down, "No, we don't. Tell us."

"Look outside and see," she said, attracting the undivided attention of everyone in the room.

All sets of eyes averted to the window.

Hundreds of thousands of creatures scurried across the sand away from the ocean. Many crammed into each other as they funneled to the ship like a virus.

"God, look at that."

"We gave Jelly *The Gift*," the girl's voice slowed down, near unrecognizable, "We need your help."

"That's not Jelly talking," Wool said.

"Who are you?"

"Pink Symphony. Evolve."

"*Lessense*," Jaycee prepared to hop through the window and go down in a blaze of glory, "That's a stupid name for—"

"—It is the closest name we have. Beings from your universe cannot comprehend our true name," Jelly swung her legs over the side of the bed and stood to her feet. She pulled the E-MRI pad from her chest and clutched the blanket around her neck. "To you, we are Pink Symphony. Pink, because that's as close as your eyes can process…"

Jelly looked at the radio on the floor and sighed. A battered, tinny version of Beethoven's classic whimpered across the ground.

"Symphony. Because of the language your radio speaks. Your friends on the other ship came to help us, but they did not have the right species."

Tor put two and two together, hoping he hadn't arrived at five, "Wait. That makes sense."

"What makes sense?" Tripp asked. "It makes no sense at all."

Tor went for the radio. "No, hang on. Wait." He picked up the broken piece of plastic and tore out the wiring, "When Alpha went through Enceladus, it must have come here. To Pink Symphony. Right?"

"Can't say I disagree."

"Don't you understand?" The puzzle slotted together in Tor's mind, "Saturn Cry, the message it sent. It wasn't coming from Enceladus. It came from *here*."

"Why didn't Alpha crack the code?" Wool asked, still failing to get to grips with the idea.

"Because they didn't have a cat on board," Bonnie said, "They were useless to *whoever* this is we're speaking to through Jelly."

"*The Gift*," Jelly made her way over to the wardrobe and sifted through the hanging medician gowns, "Blind as the day you were born."

"She cracked the code when she was in Pure Genius," Tor continued. "She sent us through Enceladus and brought us here."

"Yes, but it was either that or run out of oxygen," Tripp tried his best to question the bizarre logic.

"No, this was no accident. Jelly had no choice."

"Pink Symphony is oxygen. We breathe, we live," Jelly slipped her arms through the sleeves of the medician gown and pushed the door shut, "The girl is cold."

"Whatever brought us here needed Jelly," Tripp asked. "Or, a *cat*?"

"The cat went into the water. She returned with The Gift we gave her," Jelly flicked her shoulder length hair over her shoulders. She stood an impressive three foot five and looked more human, "War is coming. You need to protect her."

"What are you talking about?"

"Not Jelly," Jelly held out her arms, encouraging Wool to go and hug her, "Pink Symphony."

"Are we... *talking*... to Pink Symphony right now?" Tor asked.

"Yes."

"Wow," Tor cackled wildly, "That's messed up."

Tripp shrugged his shoulders and waved Tor across the room, "Well, you're the communications expert. Go and talk to her."

"This is incredible. Let me look at her."

"Just don't touch her," Wool squeezed Jelly's shoulders from behind.

Tor lowered himself and looked into Jelly's possessed eyes, "Jelly?"

She blinked, shyly, and clung to Wool's leg as she awaited Tor's questions.

"Why did you bring us here?"

"To save us."

"Who is *us*?"

"Pink Symphony—"

"—Yes, I know. But, *who* are you?"

"Virus."

"That explains the pink gas," Tor looked up at Tripp for a response. He didn't get one and so returned to Jelly, "A virus?"

"You carry us," Jelly's face remained utterly still, "We cure humans, we kill humans."

"It hasn't killed me, yet. Or any of my crew."

Jelly shook her head, "Only kills *humans*."

"Right. So why aren't we dead, yet?"

Jelly twitched her nose as the voice radiated through the skin on her face, "No one heard Saturn Cry for the equivalent of an Earth millennium. Humans responded to the message. We didn't mean to kill your people."

"Is that what happened to Alpha?"

"We learned much from Alpha. They came, we heard noises we liked. We sent Alpha back, they helped to transmit our call for rescue. To save us."

"Save you from what?" Tor asked, carefully.

"Shanta."

"*Shanta*?"

Jelly scowled and roared in Tor's face, "Pink Symphony *is* evolution."

Wool turned to the E-MRI scan and spotted a glowing pink orb in her belly, "What's that?"

"The gift," Jelly approached her and pointed to the stomach organ, "You protect cat."

"We can never go home," Jaycee said. "We've been infected by the virus. It'll kill everyone."

Jelly's eyes tilted up into her skull. "Protect. *Please*," She closed her eyelids and slumped to the floor in a crazy heap.

"Jelly," Wool crouched down and scooped her into her arms and lifted her up, "God, she's gotten heavier, Tripp. Help me carry her to the bed."

"Okay," He grabbed Jelly's calves in his hands. Wool pulled her over to the bed by her arms.

"Be careful with her tail," Wool set her top half onto the mattress, "I'm not sure what's going on here, Tripp."

"Join the club."

"The E-MRI is nearly complete. It's not my place to bark orders at people, but I think you guys should go and do whatever it is you need to do and help us get out of here."

"You're right," Tripp looked at Jelly and ran his thumb across her forehead, "Is she okay?"

"Yeah, BPM is one over fifty. She's sleeping. Probably a bit exhausted."

"I'm not going to let anything happen to her," Tripp absorbed the girl's beauty, "If we have to *protect* her, then that's what we'll do."

"Tripp?" Tor was eager to get a word in edgewise, "I, uh, I think we're—

oh, God."

"Not now, Tor."

Tripp nodded at Jaycee and Bonnie. The primary airlock is damaged, but we're off-ground, at least. Those creature things won't be coming in—"

Jelly's eyes flew open. "Shaaaanta."

"Shanta, yes," Tripp agreed before double-taking and

realized what he'd just said, "Shanta?"

"Shanta," Jelly fumed and blinked.

"Okay, I guess they're called *The Shanta*," Tripp said. "Botanix is vulnerable, so I suggest we go there and make sure it's sealed."

"There were enough of them trying to get in there," Bonnie said. "Good idea."

A bead of sweat ran down Tor's anxiety-ridden face. "Oh, God. She said it only kills *humans*," he muttered.

"Tor, not now. You can think about sabotaging all our future missions another time."

He grabbed at Tripp's hand in profound desperation.

"Get off me, numb nuts."

"Pink Symphony. It only kills humans. Why am I not dead?" Tor turned his back to Tripp and grabbed his left ear, "There's only one explanation. Please, look behind my ear. Do you see anything?"

Tripp sighed, "If it shuts you up, then fine. Show me."

Sure enough, the Manning/Synapse imprint was visible behind his earlobe now that Tripp held it up.

"Huh?"

"I *knew it*. I'm a damn Androgyne," Tor burst into tears and slumped against the bed on the adjacent wall, "You call me a conspirator? I just *knew* something was up. Baldron was Series Three, and now... now..." he started to hyperventilate, "Now you're keeping this from me?"

"Hey, calm down. No one knew," Tripp spat. "How did *you* know?"

Tor wiped his nose and stammered as he spoke, "Jelly, Pink Symphony. Whatever it's c-called. It's a virus. Some evolutionary virus *thing*."

"Yes."

"And it only *kills* humans?"

"Yeah, I heard her," Tripp tried to scramble for the answer before Tor had to spell it out, "Why?"

"Who died after we left Alpha?" Tor cried.

"Daryl, Androgyne—"

"—No. *Not* during the explosion. Anyone would have been killed in that. I mean, who died because they had the virus?"

"Haloo."

"Right."

"Right."

Bonnie and Jaycee knew what Tripp had failed to grasp. Wool knew it, too, and clocked on instantly.

"Oh, n-no, no," Wool's hand shook intensely as she reached up to her left ear, "No, I c-can't be."

Tripp dashed over to her and grabbed her shoulders, "Quick, show me."

"If… if I am, then I d-don't want to know," Wool treated the proposed diagnosis as terminal, "Tripp, p-please. Promise me you'll lie if I am, or tell me the truth if I'm not."

"Turn around."

Her eyes peeled away from his face as she turned around. Faced with her shoulders, he carefully lifted her earlobe up with his knuckle.

Jaycee scrunched his face and felt a lump form in his throat. He *knew* what it felt like it. Everyone else fell silent in anticipation.

"Tripp?" Wool whispered. "Is it there?"

He opened his eyes but couldn't squeeze the words out.

"Tripp? *Say something!*" Wool squealed as he turned her around to face him.

"I'm so sorry, Wool."

Jelly let out a cat-like whine in reverence for Wool's torment. "Not sad, mommy."

A stream of pink tears ran down Wool's face, "I c-can't…"

"I, uh, don't know what to say."

"Kill me, *please*," Wool grabbed his wrists like a woman possessed and threatened to lash out at everyone, "I *can't* be an Androgyne. It's not true. It's some sort of sick trick. Someone must have put it there—"

THWOCK.

Tripp punched her across the face, knocking her out. She crashed shoulders-first to the floor. Pink saliva shot across the tiles from her lips.

Tripp wiggled his fingers around and ironed out the kinks

in his neck, showing little remorse for his actions.

Bonnie, Jaycee and Tor watched Tripp turn to face them and crack his knuckles.

"I'm not proud of what I just did but it was necessary. No one say a damn word."

No one dared say a damn word until Tripp gave his permission. He calmed his breathing and opened his eyes on Wool's snoring face, "When she wakes up, she'll be back to normal. She'll have forgotten this."

"Not stop Shanta. They come," Jelly jumped from the bed and landed on all fours. "I go." One by one, the pads and wires pinged away from her body.

"Who come, honey?" Bonnie squeezed the Rez-9 in her hand.

"Shanta," she swiped the panel on the wall and pressed the end of one of her infinity claws to her chest, "Jelly. Help humans fight. War mage."

The door whizzed open, letting Jelly disappear into the corridor.

"For heaven's sake," Bonnie bolted after her, "Come back, girl."

Jaycee nodded at Tor to follow Bonnie, "Protect the young lady, trooper."

"What with?" Tor held up his bare, decidedly weapon-free hands.

"Your sense of humor?" Jaycee punched him on the back with his broken wrist, "Get out of my sight."

"Oww. Okay, okay," Tor darted out of the room, "Bonnie, I'm coming."

"Are you staying here with Wool? I think we should—" Jaycee turned to Tripp in shock, "What the hell are you doing?"

Tripp inserted the business end of his Rez-9 into his mouth. He hooked his finger around the trigger.

"No."

Jaycee jumped forward and punched the gun out of Tripp's hand.

BLAM!

Jaycee got there in the nick of time. The barrel slid away from Tripp's mouth as the bullet tore through the inside of his cheek. The contents of the left hand side of his face splattered against the wall.

"Are you crazy?" Jaycee kicked the Rez-9 across the tiles and held Tripp's left cheek. "What's gotten into you?"

The right side of Tripp's face convulsed, spitting electrical sparks over his busted titanium cheekbone. The top and bottom rows of his teeth chattered together through the singed synthetic skin.

"I c-c-c-c-cannot-t," the rotors in his eyelids whirred as they windscreen-wiped over his pupils, "J-Jay-Jay-Jay…"

"—Hey," Jaycee screamed into his face. "Knock it off."

THWUNK!

Jaycee thumped Tripp's neck connector back into place. "Don't *ever* do that again."

The two rods in Tripp's throat whirred and lifted his head back into position. His retinas spun around and focused on Jaycee's face.

"Who's ugly now?" Jaycee said.

Tripp felt the cavity on the right side of his face with his fingers, "You bastard."

"Me? I saved you."

"Saved me? Saved me from what?" Tripp's voice flew out of his half-singed lips and the hole in his cheek, "Saved me from an eternity of rest and peace? Screw you."

Tripp planted his palms on Jaycee's chest plates and pushed him back with all his might - enough time for him to dive for the discarded Rez-9 and finish himself off for good.

"Oh, no. No, you don't get to take the easy way out you selfish—" Jaycee kicked himself away from the wall and slid onto his ass, feet-first, priming himself to boot Tripp up the backside before he reached the gun.

"No, no, no—" Jaycee bent his knees as he barreled toward his friend, "Don't do that—"

Tripp grabbed the grip of the Rez-9 in his hand and rolled onto his back. He jammed the barrel under his jaw and buried it deep into his chin.

THWOCK-BLAM!

Jaycee's boot smashed into Tripp's hand, crunching his mechanical fourth and fifth fingers up and out. They splintered and fizzed away at the knuckle as Rex-9 sprung from his hand.

"Nggggggg," Tripp hopped to his feet and grabbed the K-SPARK strap secured around his chest, "Leave me alone, leave me alone—"

"—Hey," Jaycee bent his elbow, ready to punch Tripp through the window, "You move one damn motor and I'll kill you myself."

"You wanna do me a favor?" Tripp lifted the strap, hoping Jaycee would kill him, "I consider it externally assisted suicide. Come and kill me."

Jaycee clenched his fist, "Don't do this, Tripp."

Tripp lifted the K-SPARK strap over his fizzing, brutalized face. Jaycee jumped forward and pushed him against the wall by his shoulders, 'Stop doing that."

Tile dust coughed down around them as Jaycee slammed Tripp against the wall.

"Damn it, *listen* to me," Jaycee whispered. "You're an Androgyne, right?"

"Yes," Tripp's voice developed a jarring and somewhat inhuman tone since the blast to his head, "I am."

"No one cares, my friend. And why should they? What was it you told me when I found out I was, too?"

"No, don't—"

"—You're a *man*, aren't you?" Jaycee thumped him against the wall, shattering the cracks apart.

"Yes," Tripp muttered through his tears, "I am a man."

Jaycee slapped the good side of Tripp's face, "Don't you *dare* cry in front of me, Captain."

"I d-don't know what to—"

"—You have memories? A loving family, right?"

"Yes. I do."

"What's your son's name?"

"Ryan," Tripp's pink tears sluiced through his shiny, synthetic skeleton. It trickled down his exposed row of teeth, "At least, I th-think he's my son. I'm not so sure, now."

Jaycee screwed his face at the lump of emotional

technology he kept pinned against the wall.

"Then as far as everyone's concerned, you're a human being. What's the difference?"

Tripp's broken face revealed he was far from human. Both men knew that the reality of their situation was merely - literally, even - skin deep.

"You may be made of reinforced titanium, but you have a healthy set of organs like any other human. And a fully-functioning brain. You have memories."

"I remember *everything*."

"All that anger deep in your gut? Put it to good use. Focus it at those bastards in *there*." Jaycee pointed at the door with his wiry stump and pushed Tripp forwards.

Wool's eyes fluttered. She pressed her elbows to the ground and groaned. "Oh, oh, my head. I must have fallen asleep."

Tripp moved away from the window and offered his hand to Wool, "Get up."

None of them saw the view of the ocean through the window. If they had, they'd have seen the tree slowly re-emerging in the center. This time, the branches resembled limbs rather than branches.

The spinning sun above it ravaged the sky, creating a soft vortex-like shape amongst the silky white clouds.

"What happened?" Wool groaned and held her forehead. The scratches on her face were still fresh, not that she'd noticed.

"We're going to fight the bad guys—" Tripp threw Jaycee off him and grabbed his K-SPARK in both hands.

"—Wh-where's Jelly?"

"We're going to protect her," Tripp pulled the creases out from Wool's crumpled inner-suit, "Stay here and keep an eye on the E-MRI report. It's the safest place for you."

Wool saw half of Tripp's face was missing, "My God, what happened to your face?"

"I fell."

Jaycee burst out laughing at Tripp's crap retort. At least his friend had finally snapped out his depression.

"That's one hell of a staircase," Wool attempted to touch

the broken half of his skull, "It's okay, Tripp. You're human to me. I can't imagine what it must be like discovering you're an Androgyne."

Jaycee shook his head at Wool's fresh naivety, "Better the devil you know, eh?"

"Jaycee, let's go," Tripp walked backwards toward the door and threw Wool a wink with his right eye. A partial success, given his eyebrow had ceased operation, "And I'm sorry for hitting you."

"You hit me?"

"Never mind," Jaycee bounded after Tripp as he walked through the door.

Wool felt the scratch on her cheek, "That explains *that*, then," She turned to the E-MRI image and clicked her finger, "Commence diagnostic report, please."

The abdomen contour glowed a bright pink. "What's *that*?" she whispered, surprised by the image.

"ETA three minutes," advised the machine.

***

Jelly bounded on all fours through the sliding door to Botanix. She slowed down to a cautious crawl, splashing along the three-inch pool of water that had formed from the broken H2O unit.

She lowered her head and lapped away at the water with her tongue.

CRASH-BAM-BAM-SCREECH!

The force field blanketing the broken end of Botanix prevented thousands of Shanta from entering the ship.

Jelly had yet to clock the apocalyptic commotion from outside. She was thirsty, and feeding time came first. Her ears lifted, finally attuned to the chaos that lay fifty feet away.

Bonnie ran into Botanix and clocked the Shanta trying to get in. She slid behind a battered plant and held her Rez-9 at the force field, "Jesus, they're everywhere."

Tor ran in after her and froze solid. "Oh, jeez. *Forget* that." He turned around and made for the door.

"Hey, ass clown," Bonnie pointed her gun at him. He

threw his hands up and gasped.

"Where do you think you're going?"

"Um, I thought I'd—"

BLAM!

She fired a warning shot across his shoulder, "You're not going anywhere. You're staying and fighting."

"I don't have a gun."

"I know. We might need you as a protective umbrella, so stick around. Get over by the H2O unit and quit your whining."

"Okay."

It was either get shot by Bonnie or torn apart by those things outside.

"Yeah, that's right," Bonnie smirked as she watched him run, "Our own little maggot bait to hook the fish."

Jelly lifted her head at the word *fish*. She clamped eyes on the Shanta jumping at the force field and growled.

"Jelly, sweetie?" Bonnie yelled, "What are you doing?"

She pushed herself back on her hind legs and squatted on her knees. "Miew," She lifted her behind, straightened her tail and stood up straight for the first time in her life.

"*Good God*," Tor's jaw dropped at the wondrous sight of Jelly standing up straight like a proper, regular human.

She arched her back and pushed her chest forward. Her arms stretched out sideways. The infinity claws on each hand sprung out like a bladed star.

"Nggggg," she winced and threw her head back, feeling spine adjust and straighten to that of a human. "Uh, uh, uh…"

Tripp and Jaycee stormed into Botanix, ready for war.

"Shhh," Bonnie turned to them and waved them over, "Something's happening to her."

Jaycee clomped over to the opposite wall and sneered at the Shanta. He lifted the mount lever down on the side of his K-SPARK and lowered it to the ground.

"Stand back, people."

The gun's grip folded out in three directions and attached itself to the floor, propping the bulk of the weapon on a tripod. A devastating-looking turret waved its barrel left and right ready to open fire.

"It's armed."

Jelly's hair dropped down the back of her neck. Standing a clear four feet tall, the back of her neck and shoulders suggested she'd formed into a healthy adolescent.

She turned around and faced Tripp, Bonnie, and Jaycee.

"Jelly," Bonnie said, softly. "You're—"

"—I am," she said in her new sultry and husky voice. Only a small semblance of cat remained as the ship hovered a few feet from the grounds, "They like war. Let's give them war."

"Okay, Jelly," Tripp said.

"Then, we go," she finished in her six-year-old girl's voice. He lifted his K-SPARK in both arms, "Do it."

Gracefully, Jelly twisted around and held her palm out. The pain in her stomach bulged a glowing, bright pink color.

She spread her infinity claws out and held her palm to the force field, humming to herself, "Da-da-da-dumm..."

"Wh-what's she doing?" Tor peered out from behind the water unit.

"Shut up," Bonnie snapped.

The ship's thrusters double-powered, lifting the lip of Botanix up from the sandy surface by a few meters.

A pink beam of light waded through the air from Jelly's stomach and sucked into the padding in her palm.

The infinity claws lit up like a sparkler, surrounding a beautiful pink orb of light between her fingers.

"War... *Mage,*" she whispered softly to herself.

WHOOSH!

She threw the ball of light against the force field and cowered, slapping her tail against the ground, "Quack-quack."

"What?" Tripp blurted.

"Ah. Uh, *duck,*" Jelly giggled, correcting herself.

Bonnie, Tripp and Jaycee turned away and crouched as the ball shattered the force field into a thousand sharp pieces.

The stalactite remains stabbed through the first row of Shanta, severing their limbs and impaling their opened, central mouth-slits.

The badly injured Shanta collapsed to the floor, trampled

by the onslaught of hundreds - if not thousands - more.

"Open fire," Tripp began blasting at the swarm of Shanta bouncing across the walls and swinging from the ceiling by their limbs.

BLAM-BLAM-BLAM-BLAMM!

"Get some of that you ugly bastards!

The floor-mounted K-SPARK rotated left and right, firing off sixty rounds per second. The bullets tore through the nearest flurry of Shanta, separating their limbs in a gory torrent of pink liquid.

FLUMP-THRASH!

Tripp sprayed a round of bullets at the Shanta, killing off the Tetris-like build-up of creatures flooding around the plants and walls.

"Tripp, this is Wool," her voice came through his wrist, "Can you read me? Christ, this is urgent."

"What is it Wool? I'm in the middle of a gun-fight."

"Switch to personal headset. This is *amaziant*."

The side of Tripp's burnt ear lit up, transmitting Wool's voice into his head as he fired shots at the oncoming beasts.

Jelly sprinted on all fours over to the H2O unit with Tor and took cover from the battle.

"Hey, Jelly."

She scowled and flipped him her middle infinity claw, "*Hating you*."

"Tor," Tripp shouted between blasts, "Protect Jelly, or I'll blast your head clean off your shoulders like Landaker."

"What?"

"Protect Anderson."

"Tripp?" Wool yelled into his head, "Personal comms, Tripp. Do you read me?"

"Yes, Wool. I read you. Can't it wait?"

"No. It can't."

Tripp joined Bonnie and blasted a Shanta beast away from the ceiling. Its limbs exploded as the inertia of the bullet pushed it back into the others like a bowling ball against a fresh stack of pins.

Bonnie emptied her magazine into the gory crowd. "I'm out," She flung her Rez-9 at the baying aliens and lifted her knee.

"Look at that," Jaycee booted a creature in the face and blasted its mid-section apart. He pointed at the horizon. The black tree had fully regrown to its enormous size - and developed twelve limb-like branches, "Tripp, man. You seeing this?"

"I'm talking to Wool—" he stopped mid-sentence and clapped eyes on the tree, "Oh, God, it's moving."

The ship jolted around and pushed the edge of Botanix against the sand. The hordes of Shanta crashed along the floor. They spilled over one another and tumbled out of the ship..

A few dozen remained inside and continued to attack.

"We're losing altitude. We've hit the ground," Bonnie held her mechanical leg in her arm and fired a burst of bullets from her toes. She raised her left arm to her face, "Manuel, get us out of here."

"Dr. Whitaker. I cannot engage the thrusters."

"What?" Bonnie backed up to the wall and shot an approaching creature in its mouth-slit. It detonated, contributing to the already-gore-soaked floor with its pink blood and liquefied organs.

"Ugh, this is insane," Bonnie looked at Tor, "You keep Jelly safe, you hear me?"

"Tripp?" Wool shouted over the deafening chaos, "Get Jelly out of there *right now*."

A Shanta jumped from the top of the H2O unit and made for Tripp.

"I can't hear you, hold on," Tripp removed the empty magazine from the K-SPARK grip and tossed it at the creature, "'I'm out,' He retrieved his Rez-9 from his belt and aimed it at the monstrosity, "Come and get it, beautiful."

BLAM-BLAM-SCHPLATT!

Five of its limbs splattered in the haze of bullets, pushing what little remained of its body at Tor's feet.

He yelped and stomped on its slit in utter terror, "Ugh, get it away from me."

"Yes, Wool," Tripp said. "What's that? Oh, good."

Jaycee turned to Tripp and raised his eyebrows, "What's up?"

Tripp lowered his gun and turned to Jelly. The news he received was *very* important, "Are you sure?"

Jaycee hopped onto the back of the floor mounted K-SPARK and aimed it at an influx of Shanta creeping over the dead plants, "Bonnie, reload. Get behind me."

"Thanks," she dived behind him and released her dead magazine to the ground. She kicked it away and palmed a fresh magazine into the grip, "Reloading!"

"I understand, Wool." Jelly's cowering reflected in Tripp's glazed eyes. "I'll… *God*… I'll send her back up."

"Tripp, what's going on?" Bonnie held her foot up and blasted three Shanta creatures to smithereens with her leg.

BLAM-BLAM-BLAM-KA-SCHPLATT!

She took out three Shanta in a row with three shots, "Tripp, what's—"

"—Hey, Tor," Tripp barked. "Take Jelly back up to Medix right now."

"What?"

"Do it," Tripp blasted another creature out of the ship.

SCHTAAAMMM! SCHTAAAM!

The one-hundred-foot tree in the middle of the ocean thumped its first limb to the sand, followed by the second. The pink sky swirled around like milk pouring into a freshly-stirred cup of coffee.

"Get her out of here, numbnuts," Tripp barked.

Tor offered Jelly his hand, more than happy to escape battle, "Come with me. Take my hand."

"Hisssss," she scowled at him and swiped her infinity claws at his face.

"Uh, Tripp?" Tor struggled, "I don't think she likes me. She doesn't want to go."

"Jelly, *bad* girl," Bonnie shouted at her, "Go with Tor. He'll take you to Wool. It's for your own safety."

Jelly bushed her tail out in a fit of rage, disobeying a direct order. She bolted out of Botanix, refusing Tor's offer to escort her.

"Damn it, Tor," Bonnie screamed at him, "Go and make

sure she gets to Medix."

"Okay."

He ran through the door and into the corridor after Jelly, "Come back, girl."

Bonnie held her fists up as the approaching Shanta. She roared at them to come closer, "Ever heard of Jitsaku, you ugly critters?"

She punched the first one in the mouth with such force, its bone-like frame cracked in two and released a jellied substance - possibly its brain - to the ground, "That's today's training over with," she said, butting her palms together.

The tree spider-climbed out of the ocean. The sheer size and weight of the monstrosity created a mini tidal wave, clearing some of the Shanta away in seemingly extreme slow motion.

"What did Wool say?" Bonnie asked Tripp.

Jaycee's turret cleared enough of the approaching creatures to enable everyone to reload.

Tripp replaced his Rez-9 with a full magazine and aimed it at the hoard of approaching Shanta.

"Answer me, Tripp," Bonnie took aim at the army of beasts with her K-12 Combat leg-firearm. The tree's ungodly stomps cracked the ground. It creaked the top of its body and squealed into the sky.

Certain death was on the way.

"I only have one mag left," Tripp said, avoiding the question. "Jaycee, you got any fresh?"

"Nah, I'm out. I got like two left, but they're for the turret. It's the only thing keeping these damn space invaders from smothering us."

"Tripp," Bonnie stomped her smoking, mechanical leg to the ground, catching his attention, "Are you gonna answer me?"

Space Opera Beta slammed to the ground. The thrusters died out. The vibrations in the ship came to a halt.

The trio were twenty seconds away from a stampede of Shanta and the unfathomably large God-like antagonist that stormed behind them, wanting to finish off the job once and for all.

"Tripp?"

The Shanta pummeled through the wall and flooded into Botanix in great quantity.

Tripp cocked his K-SPARK and aimed at the first of at least a thousand creatures.

"Get ready guys," Jaycee punched the back of the floor-mounted K-SPARK turret, "It's do or die time."

BLAM-BLAM-BLAMM-MM!

The turret swung left and right, unleashing its final magazine at the swathes of approaching Shanta.

Tripp squeezed his trigger and blasted the first of the creatures to messy, pink pieces.

"What did Wool say?" Bonnie asked. "What's up with Jelly?"

Tripp trained one eye on her and then immediately back to the approaching monsters. He hooked his finger around the trigger, prepared to take a shot at the next creature.

"She's pregnant."

STAR CAT

BOOK THREE: WAR MAGE

ANDREW MACKAY

STAR CAT

BOOK THREE: WAR MAGE

Chapter 1

"We discover, adapt and create.
Acting on our discoveries is all we have.
Let us not regret our indecisions."
Pascal D'Souza
(2056 - 2111)

***

Botanix
Space Opera Beta - Level Three

Dozens of Shanta creatures snaked through the broken Botanix wall. Tripp, Bonnie, and Jaycee lifted their firearms and prepared to blast the creatures to smithereens.

"What did Wool say?" Bonnie turned to Tripp. "What's up with Jelly?"

He hooked his finger around the trigger and prepared to take a shot at an incoming creature, "She's pregnant."

BAM-SPLATCH!

Tripp blasted the Shanta's slit open. The beast exploded, tossing its twelve severed limbs in all directions.

"What?" Bonnie tore her gaze away from the bullet-storm, "Say that again?"

"I said Jelly's pregnant," Tripp shouted over the gunfire.

"God damn it, there's thousands of them," Jaycee thumped the side of his floor-mounted K-SPARK turret. The meter on the side of the barrel displayed a rapidly reducing ammunition level, "Less than five hundred rounds. I figure we have two minutes before we're outnumbered."

BAM-BAM-BAM!

The turret swung back and forth, firing at the swathes of Shanta creatures scuttling along the ground, walls, and ceiling.

Several of the disgusting beasts exploded. Their pink gore splattered the already-desecrated rows of plants.

Jaycees finally processed the revelation, "Wait a minute? Pregnant?"

"That's what Wool said," Tripp flung his empty Rez-9 magazine at the creatures, "That's it, I'm out."

Thousands of Shanta scurried over the sandy horizon towards the ship. Tripp threw his gun at them. They tussled over each other in an attempt to grab it with their talons.

The water dispenser that Tor and Jelly had taken cover behind earlier caught Tripp's attention.

"Jaycee, we need to get out of here but the door might not hold them back. Come and help me."

"You got it."

"I got you covered, go," Bonnie slammed her Cortex K-12 leg into her palms. The end of her boot slid open and released five canon-barreled toes, "Come and get some, you ugly sonofabitches!"

THRAA-TA-AAA-ATT-TT!

The bullets shredded through the limbs of the dozen-strong Shanta. Most slumped to the floor and bled their internal fluids into the five-inch pool of fresh water on the ground.

"I can't hold them off much longer," Bonnie palmed the lever on the side of her leg, "Reloading."

Tripp watched Jaycee grab the sides of the water dispenser, "Do it."

"I am, I am," the great hunk of android wrestled with the unit, "It's heavy."

"So are you."

"Yeah, but I'm not attached to the wall, am I?"

BAM-BAM-BAM-CLICK-CLICK-CLICK…

The mounted K-SPARK turret emptied its final magazine into the hordes of creatures and clicked into nothingness. The oscillator function whirred down to a close.

"That's it, we're outnumbered and outgunned," Tripp shouted at Bonnie.

CLUNK-SCHLAMM!

Jaycee wrenched the water unit from the wall with an almighty crunch, "Got it. Stand back."

A hefty, continuous blast of pure water splashed over Jaycee as he turned around with the unit in his arms, "Go on, get out of here. Now."

Bonnie stomped her Cortex K-12 limb rifle to the floor and darted over to the door, "Let's get outta here."

Tripp took one last look at the hungry creatures. They shrieked and jumped from the white sand and flooded Botanix, "Jaycee?"

He slammed the unit to the ground beside the door and thumped the compartment on the side of his leg, "Yeah?"

"You coming?"

The Botanix door slid open. Bonnie hopped through it and beckoned Tripp to join her, "Come on, quick."

"You want them to spread through Opera Beta like a damn virus?" Jaycee took out a sliver of wire from the cavern in his leg. He wound it around the one hand he had left and attached it to the water unit.

"I'll take my chances on sealing these bastards in here, thanks."

Tripp stepped back through the door, "No, but—"

SCREEEEEEEEEE!

A Shanta extended each of its twelve limbs and used the back four to launch itself at Jaycee.

"Christ, get out of there," Bonnie said.

Jaycee snapped the wire taut and kicked himself away from the unit.

SCHWIPP!

The wire lifted up and juddered to a halt in mid-air.

SCHTING-SCHTING-SCHTANG!

The creature spun its limbs around like a carnival ride and extended its talons. It smashed against the wall in two halves having been dissected by the goo-drenched wire.

"Jeeez," Tripp slammed the panel on the other end of the door, trying to close it, "C'mon, c'mon, close."

"Wait up," Jaycee bounded toward the door as it began to close.

"Let's go, come on," Tripp held his hand through the closing door as Jaycee stomped towards it, "There's another one behind you."

If Jaycee had stopped to look over his shoulder, he'd have seen a fifteen-foot Shanta fan all its limbs out like a giant, fleshy cobweb.

Tripp saw the bicycle-like monstrosity as Jaycee bolted towards the door, "Oh, oh, damn."

Jaycee's palm slammed into Tripp's, "Gotcha."

"Get the hell of here, now."

Tripp yanked Jaycee through the door and slammed the panel on the wall.

The Shanta fanned its limbs out like a cartwheel and rolled toward the door, "Screeeeeeee—"

SCHWIP-SCHA-JUNT!

Jaycee fell to the floor and tugged on the wire. The gossamer-thin strip wound taut. The door slammed down on it, yanking the water unit across the floor. It crashed against the creature's front two limbs, shattering the bones and flesh. The force knocked the cartwheeled vision of death onto its side. It squealed in pain as the rest of the Shanta stampeded over it.

BOOM.

The door slammed shut, providing a fantastic view of the utter chaos behind the window.

BOP-BOP-SLAM!

Bonnie stepped back and held out her hands, "I don't want to be here, anymore."

"You don't say," Tripp offered Jaycee his hand, "Get up, soldier."

Jaycee climbed to his feet and brushed his exo-suit down. He detached the wire from his belt and moved to the window with great curiosity, "What the hell are those things?"

Tripp couldn't provide an explanation, "I have no idea."

Jaycee reached into the compartment in his leg and took out a red dumb bomb. He teased the pin with his thumb, "Do I have your permission to toss this in Botanix and buy us some time?"

"If you do, we lose oxygen—"

"—Are you out of your mind, Healy?" Jaycee stomped his boot to the floor. The arsenal inside his leg compartment rattled around.

"Have you seen the state of Botanix? It's as good as over, anyway."

"But the oxygen?" Bonnie asked. "We're screwed without it."

Jaycee turned to the window once again. The Shanta chewed and ravaged their way through the charcoaled plants and soil and bashed against the door.

"You're forgetting one thing," Jaycee flicked the pin from the dumb bomb. The lights lit up and the device armed itself, "We don't need oxygen. We're Androgynes."

Jaycee grabbed the lip of the door and pulled it across its slider. "Nggggg…"

Biddip-biddip-biddip-beeeep.

"Go to Medix and find Wool. Go, go," Jaycee tossed the live dumb bomb through the ten-inch gap in the door.

Tripp and Bonnie shot off down the walkway.

Jaycee to pushed the door shut. The Shanta backed away from the beeping device rolling around the floor. One of them crouched on its front four limbs. Its top 'arms' bent over and tried to pick it up the rolling grenade.

"Screeeeeeee," another shouted when realizing what the device was.

KA-BLOICK!

The dumb bomb exploded. A torrent of pink gloop splattered up inside of the door's window. Jaycee caught sight of his severed left hand in the window as he tried to flip them the bird. Unfortunately, no hand - no fingers.

"Bon appetite, you ugly bastards."

He turned around and raced up the walkway where Tripp and Bonnie had gone moments earlier.

Chapter 2

Tor sprinted across the level three walkway and pressed his fingertips along the red mark around his neck. The Decapidisc had turned the skin on his neck raw during the time he wore it. The mark resembled a choker. The pain was very real; an unfailing reminder of just how unpopular he was with the Opera Beta crew.

"Where did that damn cat go?"

He scanned the staircase looking for her. The emergency strip lights on the floor provided limited visibility in the darkness.

"Jelly? Where are you?"

His footsteps echoed along the metal gantry as he made his way to the staircase.

No sign of her.

"Miew," came a familiar cry on the descent to level four.

"Jelly?" Tor hollered once again and placed his boot on the top step, "It's okay, I won't hurt you. Where are you?"

Jelly's light whimpers crept up the staircase. Tor gripped the railing and made his descent.

Her continued whining indicated her close proximity.

"Jelly, I know you're here—Whoa!"

He tripped up and tumbled to the halfway turn in the staircase. His shoulder blades slapped against the ground, forcing him onto his side.

He blinked a couple of times and caught sight of Jelly on all fours, snuggled against the fifth step.

"Miew," she cowered.

"You vicious *pussy*," Tor kicked himself back, uneasy at

the sight of Jelly's cat-like face, "What are you looking at me like that for?"

Her ears pricked up. Somehow, she looked more human than she did not ten minutes ago.

"Hisss…"

"Okay, okay," Tor pushed himself to his knees and stood up straight. He held out his arms and took a step forward.

Jelly revealed her incisors. She flapped her tongue and began to purr - this time, not in a friendly way. An intense growl rumbled through her body as she backed on to the next available step, "H-Hate you."

Tor threatened to scoop her up, "I'm not the bad guy, Jelly. I know you think I am, but I'm not."

"Grrr…"

She climbed onto the next step and hissed at him again. Her beautiful, flowing hair fell down her back. She demanded freedom.

"*Grrr…*" she bushed her tail out and slapped it against the step.

"Come on, sweetie—"

Jelly's face pulled back as she roared at him. A scary-looking half-cat, half-girl. Frozen solid with his arms outstretched he finally processed the vision of perversion in front of him.

"What *happened* to you, girl?"

"*Hate* you," Jelly's six-year-old girl's voice croaked as she spoke. She extended her infinity claws and ran them across the step. The screeching noise and was unbearable.

"We have to get you back to Medix," Tor failed to grasp the bizarre nature of having to negotiate that with a *sort of* cat, "Wool says something is happening to you."

"Stay back," Jelly hopped up the next three steps. She entered a shaft of light billowing in from the level three walkway.

Tor clamped eyes on her face. A moment ago she looked like a cat with a human face. Now, in the unmistakable harsh light, the opposite was true. A girl with cat-like features. Her Titanium whiskers fizzed and sparked.

Her ears remained further up the side of her head, unlike

a human's. Her nose had protruded into human form. A strange, pink hue bleached out from under the white sheet she held against her body.

"I go," she meowed, "You stay."

"You want me to stay here? In the staircase?"

"Away from *the gift*."

Tor looked at her belly and swallowed hard, "What is that you're doing?"

Jelly turned around and climbed the six remaining steps. Her tail swished around as she bolted across the walkway.

"No, come back," Tor grabbed the rail and hoisted himself up the steps, "Jelly, *please*. They'll kill me if I lose you."

Jelly scrambled on all-fours along the metal grilles. The walkway shifted around and began to vibrate. She stopped and pressed the side of her body against the wall in protest, "Miew…"

Frightened, she scanned at her surroundings. Her paws vibrated up a storm and shifted along the floor. The movement had nothing to do with her - the ship had come to life.

One by one, the lights in the walkway punched to life. An intense hum rumbled behind the level three walls as its bulbs shone brighter.

Jelly tried to adjust to the commotion by pacing around.

Tor approached her from behind with extreme caution, "Jelly, come on,"

She spun around and howled in his face, "No."

"But, but—"

KERR-RUNCH!

Jelly's forearms shot out in front of her body. Tufts of fur coughed into the air as the skin underneath bulged. The bones within cracked forward and thickened.

"Mee-oowwww…" She struggled in front of an astonished Tor and rolled onto her back.

"Jesus, what's—" Tor couldn't finish his sentence.

Jelly's abdomen pulled out and up. Her first layer of skin pushed out in all directions. The pink glow in her stomach boomed beyond the sound of transforming bone and flesh.

Tor took a step back in shock, "This is *insanity*."

The ship's rumbling and Jelly's pain was too much for him to take.

"Roowwaaarrr…" Jelly kicked herself against the wall and ran her infinity claws across the fur on her stomach.

"Jelly, what's happening to you—"

SPLATCH!

A mound of pink phlegm soared from her mouth and slapped to the ground. Her tongue flapped around her teeth as she caught her breath.

She pounced forward on all fours and bolted down the walkway, much to Tor's amazement.

"Come back."

He gave chase, realizing at once that she could well outrun him.

Tripp and Bonnie approached Medix at speed. During the battle she'd failed to notice that half of the left side of his face was missing.

Bonnie gasped, "What the hell happened to you?"

"Oh this?" He pressed his fingertips along the cavity on his head. His cheekbone was missing from his suicide attempt. Rows of teeth and a solitary fluorescent bulb lighting up the visible interior of his skull shone through his metal skull, "Turns out we're not dissimilar, after all. You and I."

"How did you take the news?"

Tripp stopped and pointed at his ghastly facial wound, "Does this answer your questions?"

Bonnie smirked and shook her head, "Yeah. I know the feeling."

"You don't know *jack* about how I feel," Tripp pushed past her and continued down the walkway, "Keep your patronizing to yourself."

"Actually, Tripp, I do know how you feel."

The ship fired to life as Bonnie caught up to him. She held the wall as the corridor rotated a few degrees like a tumbling bottle of soda.

"What was that?"

Tripp looked at the ceiling just as the lights snapped on.

"We're moving. Manuel must have gotten the thrusters to work."

"Hey, guys. Botanix and its new guests are taken care of," Jaycee arrived at the pair and thumped his fists against the wall, "There's life in the old girl, yet."

"Jaycee?" Tripp asked. "What's the state of Botanix?"

"I'd say it's in a *terrible* state. She's taken a *second* dumb bomb. Only this one was deliberate, unlike Baldron's."

"Yeah, *for now*."

"Well, I'm glad I wasn't in there when the damned thing went off, that's all I'll say."

Tripp made his way to the Medix entrance, "Let's get the hell out of this godforsaken pink piece of crap."

Bonnie clapped her hands together three times, "Amen to that."

Tripp rolled his shoulders. The whirring connectors and bolts in his face shot through his ears, serving as an unwanted reminder of his current state.

"Let's get to Medix. Make sure Wool and Jelly are okay."

"And Tor?" Bonnie asked

Tripp palmed the panel on the wall, forcing the Medix door open, "Hopefully she didn't spend any of her nine lives kicking his ass to kingdom come."

Medix
Space Opera Beta - Level three

Wool ar-Ban stared at her reflection in the window. Way down below, the virus-like array of Shanta scurried across the sand looking for something to kill. She averted her gaze back to the reflection of her face.

Three fresh cat scratches glowed on her cheek.

She'd only recently come-to, temporarily forgetting about her Androgyne nature. The scratch marks served as a stark reminder that she wasn't human. Lifting her earlobe back with her knuckle revealed the Manning/Synapse logo.

Yet another reminder.

She closed her eyes and sobbed. Feeling sorry for herself

wasn't an action she was used to. She knew that most every day of her life there must have been a point when she discovered she was an Androgyne Series Three unit. Every day since her inception she would have accepted it and gone back to sleep.

Or get knocked out by someone, forcing her to shut down.

Each time she'd wake up with the knowledge of her true self erased.

Still, the pervading sense of being abnormal upset her for the umpteenth-thousandth time in her life. The revelation never got easier.

If anything it got a damned sight worse.

"I hate myself," Wool brushed the tears away from her eyes. She focused on her reflection and saw something she despised staring back at her, "I hate you," she screamed at the top of her lungs.

Wool's fists tightened with fury. She scanned the room for something to strike. Her radio was the first victim presenting itself to her, sitting on the desk like an antiquated idiot laughing at her dismay.

"Bastard," Wool scooped it in her hand and threw it at the window. It bounced off the plastic and slammed against the floor, setting off a music track she usually found comfort in; *Cats in the Cradle* by Ugly Kid Joe from the late twentieth century.

The song reminded her of her childhood. Nothing specific, but just a soundtrack of happier times.

The twang of the opening guitar resembled a bunch of meowing cats. She couldn't be bothered to bend over and stop it, and so shifted the device across the floor with her boot.

The song continued to play its first verse as she moved to the window and held out her palm. Her reflection did exactly the same.

"It was all lies," she said to herself, "But they're *my* lies."

All considerations of life and childhood vanished the moment she looked past her teary reflection.

In the distance, a humongous black tree hulked its root

and frame out of the sparkling ocean.

SCHTOMP… SCHTOMP… SCHTOMP.

It slammed its limb-like branches to the shore and waded out of the water.

She raised her eyes with anxiety, "My God. What *is* that?"

The room rocked around each time the tree slammed one of its twelve limbs onto the sand. The surrounding Shanta shifted out of its path. The tree's front four branches extended across the sand and out of view of the window. It seemed to be going for Opera Beta's back-end.

CLANG!

Medix shifted around with every stomp it took - a none-too-subtle indication that the tree had made contact with the vessel.

"Gah," Wool stumbled back and grabbed the frame of Jelly's bed.

She kept her gaze trained on the window. The three suns in the sky bubbled and formed together like an amalgamated ball of pink liquid paint. The rings around it spun faster and faster in all directions like a furious gyroscope.

"What the hell is going on?"

Pink Symphony's horizon wobbled around as the intensity of the room's shaking grew, "We're moving?"

Wool clutched the metal rim of the bed for balance.

The radio slid along the floor. If the casters on each bed weren't locked into place they'd have rolled around and knocked into each other like mad bumper cars at a fairground.

"We *are* moving," Wool clutched her chest and caught her breath, "Thank God."

SWISH.

An enraged Jelly ran into the room on all fours and made an instinctive bee line for Wool, "Mommy."

"Jelly," Wool hopped onto the bed and opened out her arms, "Where have you been?"

The floor shuddered around causing Jelly to slip off track, "Miew."

An exhausted Tor ran into the room and attempted to

catch his breath, "Where are you… you little—"

The shuddering floor pushed him onto his ass.

"Oooph."

"—Hisss," Jelly clung to the bed frame. Wool caught her under her arms. She set her down on her lap and shot Tor a look of thunder, "What are you doing?"

"She tried to run away from me," Tor complained and caught his breath.

"Look at her," Wool turned to the hassled Jelly, "Her heart is racing a mile-a-minute. What did you do to her?"

Tor climbed to his feet and tried to keep his balance. Unable to look at the girl, he turned to the window, "I didn't do any— Whoa!"

He caught sight of the sand dunes lowering through the window.

"Are we… *moving?*"

"Yes, did the commotion not give it away?" Wool stroked Jelly's fine orange hair in an attempt to calm her down, "Seems the thrusters are working, now."

"We're getting out of here," Tor placed his palms on the plastic window and felt a wave of relief roll down his spine, "Thank God."

"Miew," Jelly wriggled for freedom in Wool's arms. She kicked her legs out and exposed her belly.

"It's okay, honey. We're going back home."

A glowing pink orb buried beneath Jelly's stomach fur caught Wool's attention.

" You're going to be a mommy, yourself."

Tor looked at the three suns form a blinding ball of pink and white. The rings continued to spin.

"What's going on up there? In the sky?"

"I don't know, Wool kept her eyes trained on Jelly's belly. The pink orb slid around and pushed the fur aside. It bubbled up and formed two circular edges which tried to break apart.

"Huh?"

"Miew," Jelly clung to Wool's inner-suit sleeve and kicked her legs out. The orb bubbled out into three, smaller oblong-shapes and nestled side by side.

"Tummy. Hurts."

"Jesus Christ," Tor yelped.

Jelly jumped from Wool's arms and bolted under the bed frame for safety.

Tor pointed at Jelly's ass disappearing under the bed, "Wh-what's she d-doing? And why is the sun growing?"

"How should I know?"

Wool jumped to the ground and crouched to her knees. The bed's shadow rolled over Jelly's body as she cowered on all fours. Her orange-black eyes gave her position away. She didn't want anyone to touch her - not least Tor.

"Hey, honey. It's okay," Wool offered Jelly a friendly hand in the hope she wouldn't lash out, "It's me. *Mommy*."

Jelly scrunched her nose and forced her whiskers up and down, "They come."

"Who... *come*?"

"They come," Jelly said with a childlike innocence, "War."

"What's she talking about it?" Tor asked. He knew full well that no one had the correct answer, "War?"

"Protect gift," Jelly flexed her infinity claws and scraped them across the ground, "War. *It comes*."

Wool kept her false smile up for fear of angering the cat, "What do we do, honey?"

"Fight."

"We fight?" Tor snapped. "Fight who?"

"Did someone say fight?" Jaycee's voice boomed from the door, "I'm up for a fight. I think I'll start with knocking your block off, *Rabinovich*."

"Hey-hey," Tor took one step back and held his hands out at Jaycee, "Don't you touch me, you dumb mound of metal."

Jaycee clenched his one good hand and threatened to punch the man, "Where's Anderson?"

"Under the bed. Look."

"Right," Jaycee thumped the bedside desk and used it for balance. His right knee slammed against the ground, putting a dent in the tile.

"Be careful," Wool said. "You and your heavy frame."

"Shhh," Jaycee peered under the bed and waved at Jelly with his severed wrist, "Hey, girl."

"J-Jaycee…" Jelly squinted and refused to move.

"Yes, it's me. Why don't you come out?"

"Scared."

"We're all scared."

He unclasped the side of the desk and pushed his good hand under the bed, "Com here, girl. It's okay."

Jelly didn't want to go anywhere near him. She shook her head and covered her body with her furry, human-like arms, "No. Safe here."

Jaycee climbed to his feet, "She won't come out."

An idea came to him. He opened the compartment on his leg and took out a black smart bomb, "Wait, I got it."

Wool raised her eyebrows, "You're not going to blow her up, are you?"

"Don't be stupid."

He grabbed the bulk of the grenade in his hand swung it upside down. The metal hook and pin at the top of the device jangled back and forth.

"Here, kitty-kitty-kitty," he smiled, dangling the pin in front of her, "Look at the shiny-shiny."

"Miew…" Jelly's cat-like desires got the better of her. She took a swipe at the jangling metal only for Jaycee to pull it away from under the bed.

"Haha, look at her going for it," Jaycee pulled the smart bomb back . He knew Jelly couldn't resist attacking it.

"Be careful, man," Tor said. "What if she yanks the pin—"

SCHWAPP!

Jelly's right infinity claw sliced through the air and hooked through the metal loop. Jaycee yanked it back, but was too late.

CLICK!

"Oh dear."

"Smart bomb armed," came a tinny voice from the hook, along with three flashing lights, "Warning, smart bomb armed."

"Christ almighty," Tor and Wool hopped to the other side of the room in a bid to take cover, "Make it stop."

"Miew," Jelly bolted from under the bed and hopped onto

the desk. She attacked the rumbling grenade in Jaycee's palm.

"Ah, get back," Jaycee thumped the pin back into place. The lights flashed off one by one.

"Smart bomb deactivated," advised the grenade.

Tor and Wool exhaled in utter relief.

"Jelly... play. Toy," she held out her paw and demanded he give her the grenade.

"You want *this*?"

"Jelly wanting."

"No, Anderson. This isn't a toy," Jaycee slid the bomb in his thigh compartment and clamped it shut, "This is for the big boys."

She thumped her chest with pride, "Me. Big cat."

"No," Wool moved to the desk, "You, silly cat."

"You. *Silly*," Jelly smirked.

Wool looked at Jelly with suspicion, "Honey, you're not a big cat. You're very unwell."

Jelly threw her adopted maternal crew member a vacant stare.

"Wh-what are you looking at?" Wool asked with a side order of dumbstruck awe.

"Beta moves," Jelly flicked her ears and clutched the side of the desk. She looked over Wool's shoulder and saw the pink horizon shudder back and forth, "We fly."

Jaycee, Tor, and Wool looked at the window in surprise.

"I don't get it," Jaycee held his breath and saw the ravenous Shanta horde scurrying across the sand from the ocean, "The thrusters aren't on. How are we moving?"

Tor walked through the holographic E-MRI of Jelly's body and pressed his palms against the window. His breath fogged up the plastic as he muttered, "I don't know. It doesn't make any sense."

A sprawling root filled the lower half of the window.

"We're definitely lifting, though—

SCHLAMMMM!

A black branch smacked against the window. Tor jumped out of his shoes with fright, "H-Holy shi—"

SQQQUUEEEAAKKK!

The black substance smeared out into five, thick digits

and tensed against the exterior of the ship.

Jaycee reached for his Rez-9 and pointed it at the window.

"That tree thing. It's taken a hold of us," he waved the others back to the door, "Get away from the window."

Wool grabbed Jelly and set her in her arms, "Don't shoot the window, you'll get us killed."

The room shuddered once again. The force of gravity shifted from the floor and up the back wall.

Tor, Jaycee, and Wool staggered onto the surface of the wall in an attempt to keep upright.

"Mommy?" Jelly tensed her muscles and clung to the woman's inner-suit, "What goes on?"

"I don't know, honey. Just hold on to me."

Tor lost his mind and snapped his fingers, "Manuel?"

No response.

"Damn it," Tor turned to the door. Tripp and Bonnie clung to it as the ship revolved on the spot.

"What's going on?" Tripp screamed from the door frame. He placed his foot on the wall in an attempt to keep up with the gravity subsidence.

Bonnie placed her boot on the door frame and threw her hands in front of her face, "Wool. Is everything locked to the floor?"

"Everything except the utilities," Wool tumbled next to her and slid up the length of the wall. She watched the beds climb away and released Jelly onto the picture of Jamie.

"Friend," Jelly said.

She pawed her way over the picture as the gravitational pull rolled across the ceiling.

The E-MRI holograph continued to revolve in the center of the room.

"Guys, listen up," Tripp barked across the room, "The thrusters aren't on, but we're being moved. We need to get to the control deck—"

CLANG-SCHPLANG-SCHTANG!

Various medicinal items - including scalpels and syringes tipped out from the trays and crashed against the ceiling. Each sheet lifted from its bed and drew into the air like an angry ghost.

"Tripp, I don't know what you have planned," Wool screamed, "But make it quick."

SHUNT… CREAK… GROWLLL!

"What the hell was *that*?" Jaycee applied his weight to the ceiling.

The three suns warbled together like an unholy light bulb of God, "Captain, we could use some guidance here."

Tripp looked around the floor and snapped his fingers, "Manuel?"

Snap-snap. Still no response.

"Something must have happened to him," Tor placed the sole of his left boot on the ceiling and the other on the adjacent wall. The utilities clanged around his boots.

"The comms must be cut. We need to get to control."

"Wool?" Tripp asked.

"Yes?"

Tripp saw Jelly sliding across the ceiling toward the far wall, "Is what you said true? About Jelly?"

Wool pointed at the upside-down E-MRI. Three glowing dots appeared in the abdomen section of the holographic diagram.

"It's right there. What's the state of Botanix?"

"Jaycee took care of them," Tripp said. "Stay here with Jelly and keep the door closed. Bonnie, Jaycee, Tor. Come with me to the control deck."

"How are we supposed to get there when the ship is spinning like a spit roast?" Bonnie asked.

Tripp pushed himself onto the ceiling of the level three walkway, "Improvise."

Chapter 3

USARIC Research & Development Institute
Port D'souza
(Ten miles northeast of Cape Claudius)

USARIC Chief Executive Officer Maar Sheck sat at the head of the conference table.

When he first arrived in the bunker it resembled little more than a makeshift nuclear shelter. Only the common survival tools one would expect to see were present - a large refrigerator and a sectioned-off compartment acting as a makeshift bathroom.

Now, many months later, and upon his insistence, a selection of life's more amenable luxuries were installed.

A plush couch lined the wall. An antiquated one-hundred-inch TV screen installed on the long wall. It reminded him of his younger days.

His right-hand man, Kaoz, stood by the open door as the board members shuffled into the room.

"Quickly, please," a hurried Crain McDormand led them inside. He placed his briefcase on the central table and took a seat next to Maar.

"Is this all of them?"

"Only seven of the twelve could make it," Crain snapped the locks up on his briefcase and removed a bunch of papers.

Maar pressed his hands together and made eyes at each board member. They took their seats around the table.

"Are we quorate, though?"

"Yes. Seven makes it over half."

"Right, I'm starting—"

"—But don't you want to go through—"

"—No," Maar stood up and held his hands at the seven members of the board.

"Good people, I'm very sorry you've been rushed here on short notice. I'd like to apologize for the lack of refreshments and change of venue. Sadly, it is necessary in light of recent events."

"Does anyone know you're down here?" asked an elderly female board member, "We're concerned about you."

"That's very touching. And, no, no one knows I'm here. Not even my family," Maar waved his hand over the table.

A holographic vector of something named Space Opera Charlie zipped to life and rotated on its axis, "And by the way, *no one* can know I am down here."

"Space Opera Charlie?" another board member pointed at the vector. He clutched at the name placard resting on the desk: Samuel Moore.

"Yes, Samuel. We received a communication from commander Tripp Healy on Opera Beta. Captain Daryl Katz and two of his crew had been killed trying to rescue those on Opera Alpha. Healy went on to confirm that they had decoded Saturn Cry with the help of Anderson, the winner of the Star Cat Project. Then, they disappeared."

"We've heard nothing since?" Samuel looked at the others for a reaction, "What's this got to do with Opera Charlie?"

"As major shareholder of USARIC, I seek approval to change the operational remit of Opera Charlie."

The female board member adjusted her lens-less spectacles and rifled through her papers.

"The board approached the select committee to green light the rescue mission. They agreed and confirmed a launch date of August 29th, 2119."

"That's two weeks from now," Samuel said. "Who are the team?"

The female board member read from her paper, "Colin De St Croix, Captain. Joined the American Star Fleet in 2110—"

"Ah. They're not going, anymore," Maar snapped.

"They're not?" Samuel asked. He expected Maar to explain himself but, instead, received a look of disdain.

"What are you looking at me like that for?" Samuel asked.

"I want to change Opera Charlie's task and finish remit."

"You what, now?" Samuel pulled at his collar trying to cool himself down, "You can't just change Opera Charlie's without proper consultation—"

"—Yes I damn well *can*, Samuel," Maar spat and thumped the table. "I've been trapped in this godforsaken bunker for two months. I've been told I can expect to be here for months, maybe even *years*. Don't talk to me about consultation, you imbecile. Look at the damned vector."

The Space Opera Charlie image continued to revolve. An exact replica of Beta and Alpha before her, it contained a control deck, fit room, botanical garden, and medician center. The board noticed its reduced size when held up against its predecessors.

"No N-Vigorate chamber?" Samuel asked. "You're not taking any canaries on board?"

"No. No need," Maar said. "Are you getting the picture, now?"

Samuel spread his fingers and enlarged the entirety of the second level on Opera Charlie; USARIC Weapons & Armory.

"The *whole* of level two is Weapons & Armory?" Samuel swallowed hard and leaned back in his chair, "It's not a rescue mission, is it?"

"No."

"It's a *suicide* mission."

"Not quite."

"What is it if not a suicide mission?"

Maar nodded at Crain, who turned to the board and rose out of his chair.

"After Dimitri Vasilov's assassination, and the expulsion of twenty-three diplomats from US soil, we feel we should exercise damage limitation. I want there to be no doubt before we seek approval from the board for the new motion."

Crain played the recorded video message sent by Opera Beta. Tripp's face fizzed to life above the table.

"Commence playback, please."

Tripp appeared to speak to the members of the board. In reality, it was his recorded message to the lens on the N-Gage control panel.

"This is Tripp Healy, assumed captain of Space Opera Beta. We have lost her captain, Daryl Katz…."

The board watched as the lens caught sight of Saturn and her revolving rings through Opera Beta's windshield.

"Shortly before boarding Space Opera Alpha we deciphered enough of Saturn Cry to ascertain that it was, indeed, sending a distress call. Baldron Landaker and Tor Klyce are in incarceration. Dimitri Vasilov, I hope you can hear this. Maar, I hope you're with him. This has been a deliberate sabotage of our mission. I hope USARIC finds the powers it has to rectify the situation."

Tripp shifted the lens. The board, and Maar and Crain, peered into the holographic video. A beautiful pink shaft of gas stretched out from the middle of Enceladus.

"Is that what they found?" Samuel asked.

Crain paused the video and enlarged the image with his fingers. He traced the pink light coming from Enceladus with his fingertip.

"Yes, this is what he was talking about. Resume playback, please."

Tripp's recording played on, "Alpha was destroyed. Most of us made it back, but we seem to have contracted some sort of virus. The same extends to Anderson—"

"Anderson?" Samuel asked.

"The cat," Crain said. "Jelly Anderson. From the UK."

"Ah, right. Yes, of course. The limey cat."

" —Botanix has been compromised," Tripp continued. "I am waiting on Manuel to report back on the severity of the damage. I do not expect it to be positive."

Tripp lifted his head. The light show coming from Enceladus reflected across his pupils. Two pink tears rolled down his cheek, "Oh m-my. Look at it. It's *beautiful…*"

The video paused for a couple of seconds and snapped away, leaving the vector of Charlie rotating above the table. All eyes averted to the image. Most in the room predicted what Maar wanted. It made them nervous.

"So?" Maar finished.

Everyone turned to him, including Crain and Kaoz.

"Let's establish the facts, shall we?" Maar left a pregnant pause and made his way behind each of the seated board members, "Opera Beta found Alpha and destroyed it. It would appear the cat has decoded the distress call. They've all caught some hideous disease. I ask you, members of the board, does it make sense of Opera Charlie to go and rescue them?"

"For the sake of the crew?" Samuel chanced. "Yes, I think—"

"—No," Maar said. "You think *incorrectly*, Samuel. The insurance claims alone will sink us."

"You can't be suggesting we—"

"—Beta is missing and contains the key to Saturn Cry. The crew are running out of oxygen. They'll be dead by the time Charlie reaches them. We can't take the risk of bringing them home. But we can go in there, destroy everything and come back home with the answer."

"You w-want Charlie's remit to go from search and rescue to... search and *destroy*?"

"Indeed I do."

Maar waved his hand over the conference table. The images of three mercenaries appeared above the table - two men and a woman.

"Since news of the compound breach got out, we've seen the value of our stock plummet. We lost nearly half of our subjects."

"This is insanity."

Maar didn't care for the board member's response. He threw Kaoz a signaled wink.

"This is *necessary*," Maar said. "The three crew members before you are the cream of the crop. Highly-trained, merciless killing machines. At the very top of their game. It is these five who will be manning Opera Charlie to get our property back. Namely, Jelly Anderson and the answer to Saturn Cry."

Kaoz cocked his gun and aimed it at the board members.

Crain, who was used to more due diligence, closed his eyes and allowed the inevitable to play out, "God help us all."

"All those in favor of Opera Charlie's remit being changed to search and destroy raise your hands."

No one *dared* move a muscle.

"Okay, let me put this another way," Maar kicked the table in fury, "Those of you who wish to remain alive. Raise your hands, please."

Six board members reluctantly put their hands in the air, leaving Samuel to freak out.

"This is *asinine*," Samuel barked. He couldn't believe his fellow colleagues would bow down to Maar's demands, "This is improper. You can't threaten us like this."

"I think you'll find I can," Maar's eyes crept behind Samuel's shoulders. Kaoz marched a few feet away from the door, "All those in favor of Opera Charlie's change of remit... *keep your hands raised.*"

The board members kept their hands in the air, eager to satisfy Maar and Kaoz.

Samuel refused to relent and screamed at his colleagues, "Are you serious? You're just going to sit there and cave in while he—"

"—He's got a gun, Samuel," the female board member whispered, "Just do it."

"I am *not* going to be bullied into turning a philanthropic endeavor into a wanton act of barbarism."

"No?" Maar gave the man a final chance.

"No."

"How very disappointing. We have six out of seven *ayes* at the moment," Maar said. "Would the ascension of the value of your shares not compel you to vote the way your conscious tells you?"

"No, it would *not.*"

Maar nodded at Kaoz and returned to the chair at the head of the table, "That's a pity."

BLAMMM!

Samuel's chest opened in a hail of blood and fragments of flesh and bone. He slumped to his knees and clutched at his heart, bringing Kaoz's smoking gun to sight a few feet behind him.

The board members gasped in terror and kept their arms in the air.

Samuel slumped face-first to the ground, dead.

"Six for six. A unanimous decision," Maar returned to his chair and folded his arms, "Anyone got a problem with that?"

The board members shook their heads with great enthusiasm.

"Good. You can put your hands down, now."

Crain looked up from the desk and winced at the executed corpse bleeding across the floor. He felt like throwing up as he distributed the papers along to each person around the desk.

"My colleague, Crain, here, would like you to sign these NDAs," Maar said to the board, "If anyone discovers my whereabouts, I will know it was one of you who told them. There will be ramifications for violating these non-disclosure agreements."

The board members could barely keep their hands still as they signed the papers.

"Sign them."

They jumped in their seats as Kaoz hovered over them, "You want me to start executing them one by one, Maar?"

"Kaoz, bad doggy!" Maar joked. "Be nice to our friends."

Each board member signed the document without reading a single word. It was either that or risk getting shot.

"It's unlikely we'll all see each other again, of course," Maar nodded at Crain to collect the papers. The old man did as instructed and collected them up from each person.

"Sorry. Can I just take this, please?"

Maar watched as he moved on to the next board member, "My colleague, Kaoz, will escort you back to your cars. If you're feeling nervous about your association with USARIC, then fair enough. I can't say I'd be surprised."

Kaoz rounded the six board members up and pointed at the door, "Move."

"Yes, okay," they hastened over to the door, hoping not to get killed.

"See you idiots later," Maar rubbed his hands together

and looked at Crain at the other end of the desk, "Good?"

"Good."

"I'm going insane cooped up in here, man," Maar kicked the table.

Crain jumped in his seat with fright, "I know y-you are, Maar."

"You have no idea."

"You *do* realize that you've just contravened every rule in the Infinity Clause, don't you?"

"Yes."

"And rendered the Bering Treaty practically useless?"

"Yes."

"If any of this gets out it might start War World Four."

"It won't get out."

"There are six chances making their way to their cars right now," Crain slammed the signed documents on the desk. The feeling of guilt tugged at his insides.

"Ah, when Charlie returns with the goods and we're celebrated as heroes, I'm sure their stock going up by three points *at least* will dampen the blow."

"Who else knows what's going on? Other than them, and you and me?"

"Just this imbecile," Maar kicked Samuel's bloodied body, "I don't think he's going to open his mouth, though."

"I want you to know something, Maar *Sheck*," Crain backed up to the door, "I knew nothing. Don't you involve me in this. If anyone asks, I'll tell them you put me up to it."

Maar chuckled as he watched Crain exit the room, "Fair enough. Oh, and by the way, can you send some lackey down here to clear this corpse away before it stinks the room up?"

"You're a madman," Crain slammed the door behind him.

***

Kaoz watched each of the six board members climb into the back of their waiting limousines. He held his mouthpiece in his fingertips and watched the first two cars drive off.

"This is Kaoz. Do you read me?"

"I read you," Oxade's voice came through Kaoz's

earpiece, "Have they left yet?"

"Yes, they're leaving R&D, now."

"Good. How did it go?"

"All good. We got a unanimous decision to go and blast Opera Beta into the next multiverse…"

USARIC Headquarters
Cape Claudius, South Texas, USA

"Yes! That's *amaziant,*" Oxade punched the air as he made his way into the animal compound. He clutched the grip on his rifle and held out his glove to the panel on the wall.

"Signatures all down?"

"You know it," Kaoz's voice beamed into his head.

"How did he get them to agree?"

The door to the animal compound slid open. The illuminated control hub loomed in the middle of the room, "I guess you could say it was his persuasive personality."

"Ha. He's got bundles of persuasion, that guy."

"Look, don't play around," Kaoz continued. "Maar wants the team assembled within the hour. Some new recruit is joining you. You're leaving one week ahead of schedule."

"Good. Let's get this show on the road," Oxade reached the central control deck. He made eyes at a tall woman in a lab coat. She pressed her forearm against a plate glass surface turned to Oxade. A bizarre-looking telescopic monocle took place of her right eye. It somehow complemented her bright purple lipstick.

"Nutrene, where are the subjects?"

"Just loading the capture data into the bank. They'll be here any moment now," she looked up at the panel and observed the green light loading across the screen.

"How much damage did the protesters cause?"

"They nearly got everything. If it hadn't have been for the intervention, they'd know everything."

Oxade glanced at the technicians at their computers. They turned away and continued working, hoping to avoid contact.

"Yeah, that's right, you lackeys. Keep crunching those numbers."

SCREECH! WAIL! GRUNT!

A dozen chimpanzees slammed against their cages in the right-hand corner of the compound. Oxade did his best to block out the noise, "Those damn monkeys, man. I swear to God, I dunno why those activists didn't just shoot them all."

"Why don't you put a bullet in the back of their heads?"

The chimpanzees hopped around, snarling and wailing at Oxade as he made his way past their cages.

"Hold on, good buddy," Oxade turned to them and clanged the butt of his shot-gun along the cage bars, further antagonizing the animals, "Hey! You vicious turd bags. Shut the hell up."

Kaoz's chuckles flew through the earpiece, having heard his colleague's malicious taunting.

Oxade arrived at the second of three doors, "Byford?"

"Don't call me by my surname. You're not the boss of me."

"Not true. I'm your new captain, sweetheart."

"Really? We're *on*?"

"Yup. Now, let's get these little critters returned to their cages."

Nutrene's monocle twisted at the console as she hit the green button. The wall by the computers slid into the ground, startling the staff at their workstations.

"Right, good people. Keep back. Let the vehicles in, please."

The wall opened out into the delivery area of the parking lot. Two forklift trucks rolled in on their conveyors. Each carried a metal cage rammed to the brim with captured felines.

Oxade approached the second bay and pulled the door across its sliders, "Offload them here."

The trucks stopped by the main console and lowered their forks to the ground.

SCHWUMP.

"No playing around," Nutrene lifted her left forearm and extended her index finger on her right. The tip of her digit lit up, "Head count, please."

The driver of the first truck hopped out and kicked the cage off the metal grid, "Thirteen in this one, and I think twenty or so distributed in the others."

"Be careful with them," Nutrene counted the cats. She scored the numbers off on her forearm with her fingertip, "So, that's eight… nine… *ten*—" she arrived at the tenth cat. An angry-looking, white Japanese bobtail. They caught each other's gaze.

Oxade moved next to Nutrene and nudged her on the shoulder, "Everything okay?"

"Yes, it's just…" Nutrene couldn't tear her eye away from the ball of white fluff, "That's Suzie Q-Two. One of the finalists in the Star Cat Project."

"So?"

"I didn't realize USARIC was keeping her here. She should have been returned to her owner after it was all over."

"Who cares? Let's get the ugly balls of fluff back in their cages."

Nutrene looked at the driver with suspicion, "Did you make physical contact with any of these felines?"

"No," the driver nodded at Oxade, "When he caught 'em, we just bundled them up."

A dozen lab coated USARIC officials pulled the cages from the first truck and moved them to the second bay.

"Damn it," Nutrene scanned the cages on the second forklift, "I'm only seeing a couple dozen here. Where are the rest?"

"We couldn't find them," Oxade said. "We had ten units out scouring Port D'Souza. This is all we could find—"

"—All you could find? There's at least thirty unaccounted for."

Nutrene's monocle focused on the cats in the second set of cages. Her Heads Up Display scanned each of their faces. The bottom-left corner of her lens displayed the total - *48*.

"So, forty-eight there, and twenty-two in the first set," she recorded the number on her forearm with her lit-up digit, "That's exactly thirty missing subjects."

"They're out in the wild," Oxade said. "They'll never survive on their own. If they don't starve, the freeway will take care of them."

"Are you out of your mind?" Nutrene caught the tardy pace of the workers removing the cages to the second compound, "Hey, get moving. I want them bundled up and stored. *Faster.*"

She returned to the console and pressed her forearm to the glass panel, "These aren't your ordinary, everyday subjects. We need those missing thirty accounted for, dead or alive. Preferably *dead.*"

"Why, what's wrong with them?"

Nutrene closed her eyes and ignored the question outright. The panel absorbed the ink from her forearm and fed it onto the screen, "We're leaving in a week's time."

"So I've heard."

"We need to find the escapees and bring them back."

"Why? What's wrong with them?"

Port D'Souza
South Texas
Somewhere near Interstate 35

An elderly man named Glenn Logan enjoyed a bottle of *Rollneck Kojak* beer on the porch of his bungalow. He'd been drinking for a few hours by now. The effects of the alcohol kicked in a while ago.

The full moon hung in the air along with the stench of hops from his umpteenth bottle of beer.

There weren't many cars at this time of night. The occasional lorry passed by. On the rare occasion an Individimedia GPS failed to work, he'd have lost drivers knock on his door asking for directions to Houston. Or the nearest gas station.

Tonight, something caught his eye in the middle of the road.

"Huh? Wassat?" he tried to focus on the thing fifty feet from his porch, "Is th-that roadkill or somethin'?"

He staggered to his feet and tipped the remainder of the bottle into his mouth. Nary a drop produced, he threw the glass in the direction of the *thing* lying in the middle of the road.

"Gaw, nuthin' but damn roadkill," he burped and wiped the end of his sleeve across his wet lips.

The thing shifted around and slapped its *tail* to the ground.

Little did Glenn know that the animal in the road was an Egyptian Mau. The moon bounced off its pupils and projected a sliver of green light at Glenn.

The Mau whined and continued to slap her tail against the tarmac.

"Hey, you," Glen shouted at her and took hold of the porch railing for balance, "Get off the highway. Y'all gonna get yersel' killed."

"Muuhhh…" Mau murmured as a white light enveloped her face. A pair of headlamps from an approaching car folded over the bump in the road.

"What the hell?" Glenn blinked a few times at the oncoming car, "Oh *Jeez*, no. Hey, you. *Pussycat*, get off the road."

"Grrr…." Mau returned to the surrounding trees and licked her paw.

The headlamps belonged to a purple SUV which sped along the freeway. The driver blared his horn, trying to coax the cat off the road.

Glenn looked left and then right. The Egyptian Mau was ten seconds away from getting mauled by the tires of the SUV.

"Hey, *cat*. Move it."

Mau pressed her front paws to the tarmac and lifted her behind into the air, determined to take the SUV head-on, "Meeooowww…"

BEEEEEEEEP!

The driver slammed on the brakes, throwing the car to a screaming stop inches away from the Mau's nose.

"What the heck is goin' on around here?"

The lone driver kicked his door open and planted his feet on the ground. He looked over the roof his car and spotted Glenn watching the scene from his porch.

"Hey, mister. Is this your cat?"

"Nu-huh", Glenn shook his head in a fit of inebriation, "She ain't mine."

The driver turned to Mau and tried to shift her away with his boot, "Go on, get outta the way, you dirty little *varmint*—"

A cacophony of violent "meows" whirled around the driver's head. They appeared to be coming from the trees.

"Huh?"

One by one, a variety of felines trundled out from behind the trees and made their way onto the road.

Mau extended her claws and scraped them along the road, gearing up to attack.

"Grrrr…"

"What in the hell is going on here?" The driver stood still on the road as the cats swarmed toward him like an angry and fluffy virus, "No, no. Y'all stay away from me, ya hear?"

"Screeeeeeech," The Mau launched into the air with her paws out. She buried her claws through his shirt and clung as hard as she could, kicking and gnashing away at his face.

"Ahh, gerrof me!"

The cats meowed as they swarmed the still-running car. Two white American bobtails bolted into the driver's side. The remainder hopped through the window and swarmed around the interior of the car.

Glenn squeezed his eyes shut in disbelief. He looked at the half-full bottle of beer in his hand, "Jeez, I drink too much."

The driver did his best to fight off the Mau but it was no use. His behind slammed against the car as she ravaged his face, "Roowwaaarrrr!"

VROOM! VROOM!

One of the white Bobtails pressed her front paws on the gas pedal, forcing the car to shunt forward.

"Meow," Mau climbed onto the driver's seat, leaving its previous occupant screaming on the road.

She ran the side of her head along the stick shift, signaling three of her tribe to push it into first gear.

The car jolted forward once again.

"My car. They're taking my damn car," the driver pushed

himself to his knees, "Someone call the cops."

An intense whirlwind of squealing and meowing came from inside the car as it rolled forward.

Mau wrapped her claws around the sticky steering wheel. She meowed at the two white bobtails to apply the gas. Two silver Siamese cats joined them and threw their weight onto the pedal.

The car bolted along the road as Mau held the steering wheel still, "Meeeooow…"

The car picked up speed and threatened to veer off the path. Fur spat into the air as the wind rolled through the opened passenger window.

Trying to stave off the effects of drunkenness, Glenn stepped down his porch and made his way over to the driver, "Jeez, did you see that?"

"Of course I saw them," the driver picked himself off his knees and cupped his bleeding eyes, "Call the police. They've taken my car."

Glenn threw his left arm into the air and pulled his sleeve back. He spoke into his Individimedia ink, "Hello? P-Police?"

The ink swirled around to reveal *STPD - South Texas Police Department.*

"Thank you for contacting the STPD," a friendly voice came from the pinpricks in his wrist, "Your call is important to us. Please wait while we find you an agent."

The purple SUV's rear lights shot off the road and into the fields in the distance.

The driver brushed himself down and pushed Glenn by the shoulder, "Why didn't you stop them?"

"Why didn't *you* s-stop them—?"

"—This is the STPD. How may I direct your call?"

"Ah, I, uh—" Glenn swallowed and waded around on the spot, "P-Police?"

"Yes, caller. This is the STPD connecting on your Individimedia channel."

SCH-PRRAANNGG!

The SUV crashed against a giant tree. A cloud of smoke billowed out from under the battered hood. The left indicator blinked on and off as the cats made their escape.

"Caller?"

Glenn couldn't believe what he was seeing.

He double-took and looked at his forearm, "Uh. You'll never guess what's j-just h-happened. A bunch of cats has c-comm—" he spluttered and tried to keep from laughing, "*Commandeered* a... c-car."

"Very funny, caller," the voice sounded extremely put-out, "Please stop wasting our time. Good evening."

Chapter 4

Pink Symphony

The tree that wasn't a tree had grown in size since its re-emergence from the ocean. Standing one thousand feet in height, it sprouted a second stump and root and now resembled a nightmarish hell of pure *black*.

Its two stumps stormed through the water, carrying Space Opera Beta at the end of one of its twelve branches. It twisted the spacecraft upright in its 'palm'.

Hundreds of thousands of Shanta scurried around the sandy shore hundreds of feet below.

A large number of them crawled over the tree's bark-like stumps. Most of them tumbled back down to the ground. Despite having twelve limbs themselves, they weren't able to climb very far up the root.

The tree hulked its way through the water and headed for the dunes. It arched its mid-section and squealed as the blinding light from the converged three suns blossomed in the pink-black sky.

The rumbling from the celestial event taking place thousands of miles above Pink Symphony forced the grains of sand to shimmy around. If something fantastic had already happened then perhaps the crew had been misinformed, or gotten the wrong end of the stick.

The real *fantastic* event had yet to occur...

The Control Deck
Space Opera Beta – Level One

Tripp led the charge along the revolving walkway. The door to the deck lay on its side in the distance as he, Bonnie, Jaycee, and Tor raced along the wall. The bizarre geography resembled a tumbling carnival ride that threatened to return to normal any moment.

"Guys, make sure you keep your center of gravity," Tripp hopped over three wall pipes like a racehorse.

"What the hell is happening around here?" Bonnie asked.

"I don't know. Hopefully Manuel can give us some answers," Tripp reached the panel on the wall and slammed his palm onto it.

The door slid across and allowed them inside.

They were used to seeing the communication console on the left-hand wall. Due to the imbalance of gravity it was technically on the ground.

Tripp walked over it, careful not to damage the panel, "Tor, get Manuel online."

"Yes, okay," Tor snapped his fingers and tested the environment, "Manuel?"

"Be careful with your weight, Jaycee. Don't tread on anything important," Bonnie tiptoed over the screen and ran to the windshield at the far end of the room.

"It's not easy, you know," Jaycee clomped his way past Tor and looked up at the flight deck - which was now on the wall, "What in the *hell?*"

"A-W-A-K-E," Tor lifted the keyboard and sat next to the panel, "Four, five, seven."

The console whirred to life and attempted to boot up.

"Success," Tor clapped his hands and turned to Tripp at the windshield, "We've got—"

Tor's eyes grew with disbelief at the view from outside.

"Jesus *Christ.*"

"I know. Look," Tripp pointed at the view of Pink Symphony.

The horizon staggered up, down, left and right, due to the

tree's transportation of the vessel. They could see the edge of the universe due to the height they had.

Pink Symphony wasn't a globe as previously thought. It was a *disc* - the quasi-planetary equivalent of a dinner plate. Where the horizon would naturally curve, instead, it simply *ended*.

Thousands of tiny white dots scrambled hundreds of feet below them. The Shanta.

The enlarged sun provided a brilliant light source for the view. Worse, it seemed to be growing by the second.

"Is this heaven?" Jaycee attempted to take in the spectacular view, "How are we moving?"

CREEAAAKK-WOOOOSH

The 'floor' tilted up and around, forcing the communication console to climb up the wall to its regular position.

Tripp, Bonnie, Tor, and Jaycee barrel-rolled down from the wall and hit the ground. They were finally upright once again.

"I think that black tree is carrying us," Tripp turned to Tor for an answer, "Where's Manuel?"

"Waiting for him to boot up," Tor tried to ignore an unusual shifting noise coming from the ceiling, "What do you mean *carrying us?*"

Tripp pointed at the edge of the universe through the windshield, "Look out there, we've—"

CREAK-THWUCK!

A giant Shanta carcass slammed to the ground. Its pink, gloopy remains splattered in all directions.

"Gaahhh," Tripp kicked himself back, scared it would attack him.

"No, no. Wait," Tripp held the others back and approached the gory miasma of flesh and limbs with trepidation, "It's dead."

Everyone turned to face the flight deck. A cylindrical metal disc rolled from under the desk and fell onto its side.

"The Decapidisc?" Tor said in fright, "It's been used."

Jaycee thumped his fists together, "Yeah, I think that one was for your friend."

Tripp looked around for something, "Speaking of Baldron, where is he?"

THWUMP!

Baldron's decapitated android corpse crashed against the ground behind the crew.

Everyone jumped back in fright.

"Damn," Jaycee stepped back onto Baldron's severed head, "That's one *dead* Russkie."

His boot accidentally kicked the severed head toward Tor. The jumbled fusion of synthetic skin and protruding neck wires sparked and fizzed as the football of a head rolled toward Tor's knees.

Tripp stomped his feet to the floor, "Okay, everyone. Just keep calm. They're dead. We know about them. We know what happened."

The console produced a succession of beeps.

Manuel's holograph appeared in the middle of the room, swinging his pages around like a flailing Octopus.

"Duh-duh-duh… ¿Dónde estoy?"

"Huh?" Tor pressed the return key on the keyboard, "Say that again?"

"Estoy confundido. ¿Qué me pasó?"

"Eh?" Bonnie asked, "Is that *Spanish*?"

"He must have taken a serious knock, or something," Tor punched in a command on the keyboard, "Wait. Let me try something."

Manuel flapped his pages like an angry pigeon, "¿Compréndeme? ¿Holaaa?"

"Nah, this is no use," Tor hit a button the keyboard, "Let me try something else."

"¡Oh, por Dios! Es *ridículo*…"

As Manuel spoke, his sentence shifted from Spanish to English.

"… You changed my language, you *morons*," Manuel slowed his speech down and realized the crew understood the latter half of his complaint perfectly well, "Umm, did you hear that last part?"

Everyone nodded, taking great exception to what he'd said.

"Yeah," Tripp said. "We did."

"I apologize."

"You can make amends by telling us what's going out there."

Manuel's shivering covers caused some consternation in the crew, "My scan suggests we are still on Pink Symphony."

Jaycee grabbed Baldron's ankles and dragged him over to the door, "Yeah. We figured that out on our own. What's going on out there?"

Manuel shook himself and floated over to the windshield. He took in the impressive view of the edge of the universe.

"Oh my. Would you look at that?"

"What?" Bonnie rocked up behind him and watched the sun with him, "What's wrong?"

"The entity that's carrying us. It's moving us for a reason."

"It's pulled us away from the Shanta creatures. Where is it taking us?"

Manuel bent his spine and ducked, "Its off the charts. That ball of fire in the sky is going to destroy everything. It's headed straight for us."

"So we're all dead, then?" Tripp asked without a trace of emotion.

"Oh n-no," Manuel freaked out and whizzed over to the comms panel, "Everyone grab hold of something. Now!"

BZZZOOOOWWW!

The power in the control deck snapped off.

"Guuuuh," Manuel vanished into thin air.

"You heard him," Tripp clutched the solid surface of the flight deck, "Grab hold of something and get ready."

Tor dropped the keyboard and grabbed hold of the door, "Ughhh, I don't wanna die."

"Shut up," Bonnie and Jaycee blurted at the man in unison.

The interior of the ship rumbled up a storm. Jaycee and Bonnie held onto each other and hit the deck.

"Gahhhh!"

Baldron's body and the dead Shanta slid across the floor and slammed against the wall.

The ground lifted into the air and pushed the crew towards the ceiling.

Tripp closed his eyes and screamed at the top of his lungs, "Hold on, everyone!"

SCHWAAMM!

The rumbling noise grew louder and louder. Anything that wasn't bolted to the floor sprang from the floor and crashed against the ceiling.

Everyone's legs lifted away from the floor.

The windshield staggered around and threatened to break free from its housing.

Pink Symphony's horizon sparked and elongated, appearing to zoom closer and closer against the roaring ball of white sun against the stars…

***

"What was that noise?" Wool lifted her thumb away from the wall. A thin blue line recorded Jelly's height; three feet and three inches.

Jelly stepped away from the wall and looked at the window, "It's coming," she whined and flicked her ears with concern.

"I can see that," Wool slid her detached nail onto the end of her thumb and joined her, "Stay there, honey. By your bed."

"Mommy, I'm scared."

Wool saw the edge of Pink Symphony rock up and down through Medix's window, "I know. We're all scared,"

SCHTOMP-SCHTOMP…

The ground thundered beneath Wool's feet. She spun around and shouted at Jelly, "Honey, grab hold of the bed."

"Miew," Jelly did as instructed and coiled her tail around the metal head rest, "Mommy, I d-don't want to die."

Wool moved to the door and rolled her left sleeve up fer forearm. She ran her thumb along her Individimedia ink and roared into her wrist, "Tripp? Anyone? Does anybody read me—"

KER-WUMP!

Another blast across the ground sent Wool to her knees. She rolled across the floor and grabbed Jelly's bed with her right hand, keeping her left forearm against her face.

"I don't know where you are, but we could use some help up here."

The lack of response caused Wool and Jelly to tremble with fear as they clutched onto the bed for dear life.

Wool's legs launched into the air as the ground thumped harder and harder.

Just then, a blast of pure white light flooded the entirety of the room.

"My G-God…" Wool's pupils dilated as she witnessed the horizon blast towards the window, "We're g-going to…"

Jelly took a final look at the picture of Jamie on the wall. She gripped the side of her bed to prevent herself from flying off, "I want to go home."

She buried her head in her pillow and squealed. The ferocious shaking became unmanageable. The bed's casters rocked from side to side.

"If anyone can hear me, we're trapped inside Medix," Wool yelled into her wrist as her feet darted to the ceiling. Her entire body fell upwards, pulling her right hand away from the bed frame.

A low-pitched hum shot around the room. Angelic in nature, and with an underlying sense of anger.

"Honey. Hold tight—"

Jelly threw her arm under the bedside rail and squeezed her eyes shut.

Wool's voice slowed to a crashing halt, "Don't… let… go…"

Her last utterance echoed around the room.

The white light bleached through the window and turned the room into a miasma of heavenly wonder.

Chapter 5

Forty-Five Minutes Later...

Jelly felt her nose twitch but couldn't see anything. Her eyes were shut.

The eerie silence didn't help matters.

A horizontal sliver of light crept against her eyeballs as she came to. The Medix interior appeared on its side with the beds stuck to the wall.

A blurred vision of a woman peered into the horizontal line with her hands outstretched. Her voice was muffled, "Are you okay, honey?"

Her thumbs pressed Jelly's ears back, enabling a clarity in her voice, "You look like you've hurt yourself, honey."

Jelly shook her head and tried to throw away the disorientation.

It took a few tries.

The beds on the wall crept back to the ground. Such was Jelly's discombobulation; she'd been lying sideways. The confusion slowly melted away and gave rise to the fact that she'd been knocked unconscious.

"Where am I?" Jelly muttered.

FLUMP.

Jaycee dropped Baldron's carcass onto a bed behind Jelly. The noise made her jump to her feet in fright.

"Right, let's see if we can't make some use of this ex-talking junkyard," Jaycee twisted Baldron's left hand away from his wrist. It screwed around and came free.

Jelly hopped onto her bed and licked her lips, "What's he

doing?"

Jaycee looked up and brushed away the protruding wires from his own forearm.

"Spare parts, pet."

"What?"

"Yeah. Anybody need any?" Jaycee placed the removed hand's wrist at the large screw joint at the end of his forearm. It spun around and locked into place, "Bingo."

He admired his new appendage and squeezed the mechanical fingers in and out.

Wool looked away in disgust, "No, thank you. That wouldn't be any use to me."

"Are you *sure*, Wool?"

"Yes, I'm sure."

He lifted Baldron's severed head away from the neck and pointed at the cheek-bone, "I can fillet some skin to cover your scratch if you like?"

"I said no," Wool strained her vocal chords in protest, "Now, just drop it."

"What's all this shouting?" Manuel fluttered into the room, followed by Tripp, "Is there something seriously amiss?"

Jaycee waved at Tripp with his new hand, "Hey, Healy."

"Hey."

"Like my new toy?"

Tripp approached the bed and analyzed the new hand. It seemed slightly smaller than normal, "Ha. Is that Baldron's?"

"Yeah."

"Bit small, isn't it?"

"Pfft, better than no hand at all," Jaycee pointed at Baldron's face, "We can fix you up with a new cheekbone. Won't take me a few minutes to solder it on?"

Tripp felt his facial cavity and closed his eyes. Since waking up from the event, he'd forgotten - much like Jaycee, and the others - that he wasn't human.

"It never gets easier."

Tripp ran his fingertips through the hole at the side of his face. The tops of the bottom row of his teeth pressed into the fleshy part of his fingers, "But I might take you up on the offer."

"Just let me know when."

Bonnie and Tor walked in and spotted Jelly and Wool by the first bed.

"Thank God, you're okay," Bonnie looked from Jelly to Jaycee and clocked Baldron's corpse on the bed, "Spare parts? A regular junkyard sale, isn't it?"

"You know it," Jaycee smirked and pushed the body onto its side by the shoulder, "We can get you that new battery you need."

"Ugh. Maybe, maybe not," Bonnie stroked Jelly's hair and sniggered at Baldron's frozen face of fear, "Thank God I don't need a new brain."

Everyone sniggered to themselves.

"What?" Bonnie protested.

"Nothing," Tripp snapped his fingers and waved Manuel over, "Okay, listen up. Manuel has some information on what's just happened."

The holographic book opened up and landed three-quarters of the way through its tome, "The giant tree *thing* that we thought was going to kill us turned out to have bought us some time. It was trying to save us, by all accounts."

"Save us?" Jaycee snorted, "From what? A tumble-drier death?"

"It threw us to the other side of Pink Symphony. Away from the Shanta. Bought us some time."

"We could have been killed, Crash landing like that."

"Well, it was either that or be outnumbered," Manuel said. He projected an image of three suns floating together, "Pink Symphony has a heavenly body headed toward it. As you can see here, the three suns converged. It's going to wipe everything out in an instant."

The three suns melded together to form a solitary ball of white light.

"By my calculations, I figure we have around twelve Earth hours until it strikes."

Jelly hopped off the bed and made for the hologram, "I want it."

"No, Jelly," Manuel swung his pages around and whipped the projection up against the ceiling, "It's not a toy."

"Miew," she whined, knowing it was too far away to catch.

Tripp turned to Manuel, "You said something a while ago about one month here equals a period of time back on Earth?"

"That's correct. One hour here equals one month on Earth."

"How long have we been here?"

"A little over twenty hours."

Bonnie ducked her head, "Ugh. Two years?"

"Almost, yes."

Tripp folded his arms, "So, you're saying we have to wait for twelve *more* hours until we're scorched to death?"

"That's if the Shanta doesn't get to us first," Manuel continued. The hologram of the sun changed to a live feed of the Shanta creeping from the ocean to the dunes.

"If Pink Symphony had a north, south, east and west, which it doesn't... but if it did, then the ocean is due west. The dunes lie dead in the middle. The tree threw us to the east side. It tried to save us from certain death. It was successful, in that respect."

"Shame about the apocalypse," Tripp quipped.

"Yeah, that's not the best news I've ever heard," Manuel said.

The image zoomed out into a map of four quadrants against a perfect circle. The far east curvature lit up, indicating their position.

"Pink Symphony is, for all intents and purposes, a *disc*. It has a diameter of one hundred and eighteen miles exactly. The Shanta move quickly. They could be here in less than twelve hours. Before the sun strikes."

"So if the sun doesn't kill us, the Shanta will?" Bonnie thumped the wall and let out a long, exasperated wail, "Ugghh, for God's sake, why? Why are we here?"

Manuel lowered himself to everyone's head height and pulled the projection back between his pages. He turned to Jelly to see her crossed legged by the wall, playing with her claws.

She looked up, "What?"

"Whatever Pink Symphony did to her, we need to make sure she's protected," Manuel said.

"Protected?" Jaycee booted Baldron's head off the bed. It hit the floor and rolled nose-over-skull to a halt in the middle of the room, "Protected from what? Certain death? Are you out of your crazy, Spanish mind?"

"Don't start that again," Tor ducked his head and whimpered to himself.

Manuel tried to calm the giant down and relax everyone's nerves. An unlikely endeavor given the circumstances, "You've heard of the two Fs when it comes to conflict, haven't you?"

"Yeah, fight or flight," Jaycee twisted his new hand around and wiggled the thumb.

"Did you know that there is a third F?"

"No."

"Well, there is," Manuel spun around to the others, "It's the worst F of all."

Bonnie shrugged her shoulders, "French?"

Manuel spun around with despair, "Uh, no? How can you *French* your way in a situation?"

"Come here and I'll show you, you useless tome-stone."

"I'll ignore that," Manuel shrugged off the offense, "No, the third F stands for *Freeze*."

Tripp scrunched his face, "I'm sorry, Manuel. Maybe I hit my head a little *too* hard when we crash-landed her, but... what the hell has this got to do with anything?"

"Ugh, you androids," Manuel spat. "You're so particular, aren't you? What it means, *captain*, is that you can freeze on the spot in the face of adversity. If you do that, you'll get killed."

"You're a bad liar, you know that?" Tripp spat.

Manuel slammed his covers together, "Oh, I'm *not* lying, I can assure you. If you were to run, well, you can't run. Unless you want to fall off the edge of the universe. Are you getting my point, yet?"

"No."

"We've established that you can neither fly nor freeze. Both will get you killed. So, which *F* does that leave?" Manuel asked.

"Fight," Jaycee said.

"Exactly. Your only available course of action. Are you all ready for war? Or do you want to fall on your knees and beg for mercy?" Manuel shifted to the window and aligned his pages to the sandy ground, "Because I can assure you, those Shanta things out there haven't shown very much of *that* so far."

Jaycee clamped the buckles on his exo-suit together, "He's right, you know."

Tripp kept his eyes fixed on Manuel, "So we fight?"

"Damn right we fight," Manuel realized something peculiar about what he'd just said, "Hmm, that rhymes. I must remember that."

"Miew," Jelly snuggled up to Wool. The pink glow from inside her belly sluiced around her infinity claws.

Tripp approached the bed and made eye contact with Wool. She seemed upset and very protective of the half-cat child resting against her bosom.

"We need to protect whatever is inside Jelly."

Bonnie kicked herself away from the wall. Tor stood up straight and brushed himself down. Jaycee collected Baldron's head from the floor and dislocated the jawbone.

The three of them stood together in solidarity.

"What do you want us to do, Tripp?" Bonnie asked.

"Taking no chances, and certainly no prisoners. We're all war ready," he pointed to Jelly, "But our little war *mage*, here, is not. We have about twelve hours to make sure she is."

Jaycee and Bonnie fist-bumped each other.

"Leave it with us," Jaycee 'fist-bumped' Tor's face a bit harder than necessary.

"Oww."

"We'll toughen her up."

"Good," Tripp looked at Baldron's body before making his way out of Medix, "Bring what's left of the dead Russian with you. I think I'll—"

"—Which one?" Jaycee joked as he looked from Baldron

to Tor.

"Hey," Tor protested.

Tripp tapped his destroyed cheek bone, "I'll take you up on that face transplant offer. I can't walk around looking like a comic book villain for much longer. It'll scare our guests."

"You got it."

Jaycee thwacked Tor on the back and grabbed him by the scruff of his neck, "Come with me, nitwit. We'll make use out of you, yet."

"Gerrof me."

He booted Tor out of Medix and turned to Jelly, "See you in a while, Anderson."

"Meow," she giggled and dug her claws into Wool's sleeve.

Bonnie held her hand out at Jelly, "Wanna kick some ass, sweetie?"

"Meow."

Kick or lick - it was all the same to this gnarly *half-cat*...

3'5"
The Fit Room

Bonnie moved through the dozen speed cycles and treadmills and headed for a crash mat at the end of the room.

"We'll make a killer out of you, yet. Follow me."

Jelly sprinted after her, fascinated by the way her new jeans rode up her thighs, "What are these called?"

"I told you already, they're called jeans," Bonnie turned around and looked at her, "They belong to my son. It's the closest fit we had."

"Why did you take your son's jeans into space?"

"It reminds me of him. I like to hold them every now and again. Please look after them," Bonnie dug her heel onto a red spot at the edge of the dark blue mat. The ceiling slid apart and dropped a rugged punching bag which swung back and forth over the mat.

Bonnie grabbed it and gave it a hug, "You like this?"

"Miew," Jelly sniffed the scent on her new denim and looked up at the bundle of horsehair hanging in front of her.

She clapped eyes on the USARIC logo plastered over its surface and revealed her fangs, "Let's *kill* it."

"You know Jitsaku, huh?"

"They made me do it at the Star Cat Trials," Jelly socked the punch bag with her fist, "They made me kill Bisoubisou."

Jelly recoiled in pain which made Bonnie chuckle with affection, "Aww. Not quite ready to punch, huh?"

"Miew."

Bonnie rolled up her sleeve up her forearm and thumbed her Individimedia ink. It swashed around her synthetic skin and formed a giant play button at her wrist.

"I find it helps to train with music," Bonnie spoke into her arm, "Start play-list. *Fight Music.*"

Nazareth's *Hair of the Dog* played through the pinpricks in her wrist, "There, that's more like it. Now we'll see who's the sonofabitch."

"Son… of… a… *bitch,*" Jelly mouthed, banking the phrase in her mind.

"Okay, in Jitsaku terminology, this is known as *taking out the trash*," Bonnie rolled her shoulders and held up her fists.

"Taking out the trash," Jelly repeated, somewhat confused.

Bonnie trained her eyes on the bag and prepared to deliver a vicious blow, "Okay, girl. Watch me very carefully…"

Over in Medix, Tripp, Tor, and Jaycee observed a bloodied, severed talon from the dead Shanta laying on a bed.

Manuel threw his beam across its shiny surface and projected the results onto a three-dimensional image via the E-MRI scan.

He floated over to the crew, "Just finalizing the data to check for things I consider to be *abnormal.*"

Jaycee turned to Tor and smirked, "He doesn't mean *you.*"

"What?" Tor asked, failing to get the joke.

Tripp found the remark hilarious. He covered his mouth in a futile attempt to stop himself laughing.

"What are you laughing at?" Tor asked.

"I'm not, I'm sorry," Tor cleared his throat, but simply

couldn't stop from laughing, "I don't—Shut up," He nudged Jaycee on the shoulder. The big fellow turned away and tried to suppress his laughter.

So, too, did Manuel, "Ahem, I'm sorry."

"Even the damn computer is laughing at me," Tor complained, "Right, that's enough, I'm going to Pure Genius to get ready. Where I'm *welcome*."

Jaycee shouted after him through his sudden fit of laughter, "Hey, remember. Put your Decapidisc on. I'll be coming up to check soon."

"Yeah, whatever," Tor slammed the door shut behind him.

Manuel and the two men burst out laughing, "Oh, *my*. That was funny."

"I can't breathe," Tripp gasped through his chuckles.

Manuel cleared his throat and straightened his covers, "Okay. Can we concentrate, now, on the task at hand?"

"Yes, yes. Of course," Tripp swallowed his churlish giggles and pointed at the Shanta talon on the holograph, "Benign bacteria?"

"Probably a coincidence," Manuel said. "A Dodecahydrate, of sorts. Shares a lot of properties with chrome."

"Chrome?" Tripp struggled to comprehend the data.

Manuel pointed his back cover at the results, "Yes. Some of the elements closely resemble potassium sulfate. As far as comparable elements go, that's where it ends. It's absolutely unique, otherwise."

Jaycee thumped the sword-like talon's surface and failed to produce so much as a dent in it.

"Impenetrable, too," Manuel pointed out the obvious.

Tripp pointed to the second image on the E-MRI. A cluster of colored digital blobs, "What about the pink stuff?"

"The blood?" Manuel shook his body around, "Don't even get me started on *that*. The make-up is entirely alien. A thorough Ames test recorded high levels of carcinogens."

The chart displayed an array of red values and numbers.

"So Pink Symphony is *cancer*?"

"In its current form, it's far worse. Way more aggressive,"

Manuel said. "The cell counts dial down. It's more like an immune deficiency. Some evolutionary mix-up."

"Great," Jaycee kicked the bed, "And we've *all* got it?"

Manuel protested, "It's not my fault, nor the bed's. Don't shoot the messenger."

"Symphonium," Tripp stepped away from the talon. "If it needs a name and we have to report back to USARIC, we're *not* calling it Pink Symphony."

"Why not?" Manuel asked. "That's *its* own interpretation of itself. Besides, it hasn't affected any of you Series Three units. *Yet.*"

Manuel's flippant remark caused Tripp to burst with anger.

"I realize that, you *dolt*. But I refuse to call my illness Pink Symphony, okay?"

Jaycee went to hold him back, "Tripp, don't get mad—"

"—I can't go back home and tell my wife the reason I'm wearing a mask and can never breathe the same air as her again is because I'm infected with something called *Pink Symphony*," Tripp threw Jaycee back and stormed out of the room, "It's called *Symphonium*. Manuel, record that name—"

"—But, Captain, I—"

"—Shut the hell up and do it," Tripp felt behind his ear and exited the room in a huff.

Jaycee looked at the floor in bewilderment, "Pfft, dude. *Have a cow*, much?"

THWACK!

Bonnie jumped in the air and scissor-kicked the punch bag against the ceiling.

"Wow," Jelly marveled at her friend's strength. The bag swung back into Bonnie's arms.

"Okay, Anderson. You ready to tear it up?"

"Meow," she flapped her tail and made her way onto the mat, "*Me* wanna kill it—"

In Pure Genius, Tor circled around Jelly, who sat crossed-legged in the middle of the cube. He slid his fingertips over the surface of his Decapidisc.

"What's that around your neck?" she asked.

"Never mind that. Jaycee put it on me while I train you. I'm the communications officer and you have to do what I say—"

"—Ohh, I know what it is. It cuts your head off."

"Look, I'm in charge, here," Tor fumed. "Now, try that again. It's not *me wanna kill it*, as you said. Incorrectly. It's *I want to kill it*. Use the correct first person singular pronoun, please."

"*I* ... want to kill?"

"Very good," Tor clapped his hands together. Twenty panels on the adjacent wall lit up. All but one displayed a variety of adjectives.

Big - Small - Drunk - Sad - Fast - Mage - Elated - Drown

Jelly licked her lips and pressed her claws against the tile underneath her legs. She began to read them aloud, "Big... Small—"

"—No, no. I don't want you to read them. I want you to tell me which one is the *noun*."

"Noun," Jelly repeated. "Like a *thing* word?"

"That's right, like a thing word. Take a look."

She scanned each of the words and landed on the sixth one. She turned to him and tried her luck, "Mage?"

"Well done, yes."

"That's *me*," Jelly clapped her hand-paws together. The ends of her infinity claws clinked together, reminding Tor of just how screwed he was if he ever got into a fight with her. He cleared his throat and snapped his fingers at the tile.

The word *Mage* expanded, followed by a blank box.

"Can you give me the definitive definition of the word *mage*, please?"

"It is a girl God. Girl good with magic."

"I guess that's accurate enough. Good work."

"Ha ha," Jelly swished her tail in triumph.

"Right, let's try something a little more advanced..."

4'2"

The Fit Room
Four hours later

"This is quite advanced," Bonnie walked around the punch bag and traced her gloved fingers around the canvas, "Jitsaku is all about harnessing your oppressor's anger and using it against them. You think you can do that?"

"I don't care about my oppressor," Jelly swiped at the bag and flung her infinity claws out, "I care about *me*. What does oppressor mean?"

"It means the bad guy, sweetie."

"Not liking bad guys."

"You don't like the bad guys, you mean," Bonnie said. "Didn't Tor teach you anything?"

"Tor is a bad guy. He tried to kill us. Not wanting."

JAB-JAB-SWUNCH!

Jelly smashed the bag with all her might. It flew past Bonnie's face, lifting the ends of her hair over her neck, "Whoa!"

"Sonofabitch," Jelly muttered and thwacked the bag once again, this time with her right foot, "Come and get it."

Bonnie gasped. "Jelly! Where did you hear *that* word?"

"*It?*"

"No! The S-word."

"Sonofabitch?" Jelly said with a cute nonchalance.

"Don't repeat it, Jelly!"

"You said it earlier when we started."

"Did I?"

"Yes."

"Oh," Bonnie failed to recollect the incident. She shrugged and allowed her authority to remain intact, "Well, whatever. Just do as I do, not as I say."

"Huh?"

"No, wait—" Bonnie corrected herself and thought over the phrase, "Do as I say, *and* as I do."

"Me confused."

Bonnie exhaled and closed her eyes, "Just don't say that word again, okay? No swears, please."

"Jaycee and Tripp say rude words. One time, I heard

Jaycee call someone a mother—"

"—Right," Tor held his Decapidisc in anger, "Let's get this straight once and for all. Where and *when* to use cuss words."

A variety of colorful curse words appeared on the panels inside Pure Genius.

"Okay," Jelly leaned back on her elbows and started up at the bank of tiles. She clapped eyes on an eight-letter word she'd not seen before, "Tor?"

"Yes, Jelly?"

"What does dick… *head* mean?"

The tile containing the offending word flashed as soon as the utterance left her mouth.

"Oh, uh," he struggled with the literal explanation, "It's, uh, a stupid person? A bad word."

"Like a bad guy?" Jelly added with stern curiosity. Tor breathed a sigh of relief, thankful that he didn't have to explain why boys and girls were different.

"Yes, yes, exactly. Like a bad guy."

A cheeky grin crept along her face. She eyed him with salacious menace and pointed her infinity claw at his face, "Dickhead."

"What?"

"You're a *dickhead*," she said. "A bad guy. And I know what a dick is."

"That's not funny," Tor pointed to a four letter word beginning with "F" on the next tile, "Okay, smart-ass. If you're so clever, do you know what that word means?"

She turned to it and took a deep breath, "I know how to say it but Bonnie and mommy said I shouldn't."

"Good, I'm glad mommy said that."

"Also, she said that's what you can do to yourself if you go anywhere near her again."

Tor punched the wall in anger, "God damn it."

"Umm, you swore, *Tor*," she laughed at his anguish, "I'm going to tell."

"Please don't—"

4'7"

Medix
Two hours later

"—Please don't knock the cups off, honey," Wool watched Jelly press her chin against the surface of the table, "I mean it. Try to resist."

Jelly looked at the five empty cups perched in a row. Her paws twitched, wanting to strike each one.

Wool tested the cat's obedience, "Do *not* touch those cups. Remember what you did during the Star Cat Trials—"

"Miew," the very thought of the needlessly violent competition made her thrash the first cup off the edge and onto the floor.

"I didn't think you'd be able to hold *that* in," Wool said. "But you need to learn to obey orders, honey."

"I wanna knock 'em all off."

"Think of them as fingers," Wool said. "If that was me hanging off the side of the building, I like to think you'd help me back up."

"Mmm, no. My instinct wants me to knock them off. Make them fall."

"Ignore your instincts, honey. Just *look* at them. Exercise some mercy. It's a valuable tool to master."

"Miew," Jelly's snorts of derision fogged up the side of the plastic cups, "No, no… don't…" she whispered to herself, "Resist…"

"Don't do it, Jelly."

"Uhhh," she growled and clenched her fists, "No, it's no use."

Jelly tore into the four cups.

SCHWIP-SCHWIP-SCHWAAP. Clunk.

The final cup spun around on the floor, providing the perfect denouement to her failure of the task.

"Sorry."

"Why did you do that?"

"Because I wanted to. Rule number one. I get to do what I want, *when* I want."

"I see Tor's classes are working," Wool spat with sarcasm. She picked the cups from the floor and returned them to the edge of the desk, one by one.

"Mommy. Don't make me do it again."

"You're going to keep doing it until you learn to resist."

"But I *want* to," Jelly huffed and stood up straight. She seemed taller than just a few hours ago. No longer a six-year-old, she resembled a half-cat adolescent of around thirteen years of age.

Wool covered her mouth with shock, "Jelly?"

"Ugh, what is it now?"

"You've… *grown*."

"Yeah, *so?*" she complained like a typical teenager would.

Wool pointed at Jelly's buds pushing through the chest area of her shirt, "And not just in height, either."

"Mommy," Jelly covered her chest with her furry arm, "Are you looking at me?"

"Okay, that's enough. Over to the wall, please. I want to record your height again."

"Don't tell me what to do," Jelly stormed over to the wall, "I'm only going because you give me food. Remember *that, bitch*."

"Jelly," Wool barked in shock, following her to the wall, "Don't ever say that—"

"—Don't ever say I'm a damn Androgyne," Tripp rubbed his face, looking at himself in the mirror, "Every time I wake up, I feel great. And then something reminds me."

The Rest and Recuperation room provided quiet solace during the crew's preparation for impending doom.

"I swear to God, I cannot go on like this."

The cavity in his head had been patched up using Baldron's synthetic skin. He may have looked like a million dollars, but deep down inside he felt a million *Lira*.

He decided one, simple action could be undertaken to make him happy, "Don't let me regret this. I never want to feel this way again."

He removed his thumb cuticle and squeezed it in his right hand. The sharp, curved nail heated up and sparked.

"Let's test those pain receptors," Tripp angled his head in the mirror and placed the sharp end of his white-hot thumbnail at the logo on his skin.

The heat scorched through the Manning/Synapse logo, burning through to his connecting neck rod.

"Nggggg…. G-God…"

The flap of synthetic skin containing the logo peeled away from his neck. He held out his arm and turned the logo to the mirror.

"How do we like me, now?" Tripp winced in the mirror, "Manning/Synapse… *no more.*"

He dropped the flap of skin down the drain and hit the rinse panel.

SWISSSHHHH!

It gurgled down the drain, never to be seen again.

"Ignorance is bliss—"

5'1"

USARIC - Weapons & Armory
Two hours later

"—but weapons are more blissful," Jaycee unclipped a semi-automatic rifle from the wall and presented it to Jelly, "I'm not sure you've got the muscle strength to be able to hold this."

She held out her paws, "Let me try. I like guns."

"Be careful. It's loaded," Jaycee pushed it into her chest. She caught it and felt the weight.

"I will."

"The D-REZ semi-auto. Three round burst. You can flip the lever on the side down for single shot, or up for continuous."

"Okay," she fumbled with the gun in an attempt to get used to its weight.

"It's light, easy to use and gets the job done. That's why I like it."

Her infinity claws didn't get in the way as she gripped the gun in both hands. Jaycee lifted the nozzle away from his chest, "Don't ever point your gun at the people you're working with."

"Sorry."

Jaycee thumped the cabinet. A slit formed on the wall, producing a plastic handle, "Stand back, girl."

He yanked a blast sheet out. The USARIC logo stretched out across its surface. He pointed at its circular target and bullseye, "Now, see that little notch at the end of the gun?"

She closed one eye and looked down the sight, "Yeah?"

"Match it up to the red dot in the middle of the circle."

She did as instructed. Jaycee turned to her and raised his eyebrows. "Jesus, Jelly. You've *grown*."

"Everyone's been saying that. I'm a big girl, now," she said. "Can I shoot it?"

"Yes, wait a second. I'll just take a few steps back—"

THRAA-AA-ATT!

The first bullet hit the red dot. The rest snaked their way up the blast sheet and popped a hole in the middle of the "A' of USARIC.

"—Whoa, Jelly," Jaycee picked himself up from the floor and shook his head. "Never, *ever* shoot until I tell you it's okay."

"But you said 'yes'?"

"I know I did, but I didn't mean to fire."

Jelly thumped the side lever down and took aim at the blast sheet once again, "Well, you should be more careful next time—"

"—You should be more careful next time," Bonnie grabbed hold of the punching bag as Jelly waved the pain away from her claw, "You can't just keep punching over and over again. I don't care how angry you are."

Jelly squinted at Bonnie with evil in her eyes, "I was taking out the trash. *Bonnie.*"

"Don't look at me in that tone of voice, young lady. You're not getting so big that I can't kick your furry little behind all over this place, you know."

"I can do what I like," Jelly growled and licked her infinity claws. She spat the liquid on her tongue at the USARIC logo on the mat.

"Ugh," she winced, "Tastes like zinc."

"Never lick your wounds, sweetie. It doesn't suit you."

"Force of habit," Jelly said. "And, strange things happen when I try to clean myself."

"What do you mean?" Bonnie asked.

"Mommy said I have to use the bathroom like everyone else."

"Wool said that? Because you can't fit in your tray, anymore?"

"It's too small," Jelly tapped the side of the bag with her paws, "I have to stand in that stupid spraying water like humans do to clean myself."

"It's not stupid, sweetie. It's a shower," Bonnie let go of the bag and took a few steps back, "It's how we clean ourselves."

Jelly struck the bag with her claws, bursting the skin. A tuft of horsehair poked out.

"It's disgusting," she said. "It's more hygienic to use your own saliva and rub yourself down."

Bonnie giggled and pointed at Jelly's paws, "Concentrate, sweetie. Remember, keep your left paw up, and wait for them to strike. One-two, duck, and upper-cut. Use your claws."

"One-two," Jelly jabbed her left paw forward, "back, and upper cut," she finished with a swish to the bag's mid-section.

"If you ever find yourself without a weapon, you'll need to take them off-guard."

Jelly sneered at the bag, "Come and get me, bad guy. Step forward—"

5'4"

Medix

Three hours later

Wool ran her detached thumbnail across the wall above Jelly's head. She looked up at her 'mommy's' elbow.

"Okay, step forward, honey," Wool rocked to her heels and took a step back. A white light raced down the wall and hit the floor. It recorded the distance - five feet and four inches.

"In the past twelve hours you've gained two feet," Wool looked at her forearm and spoke into her wrist, "Time check, please."

The three black lines bent around and formed the current time on her skin - *20:00.*

"It's dinner time," Wool looked at Jelly, "You're nearly as tall as I am."

"How tall are you, mommy?"

"Five foot six."

Jelly extended her infinity claws and moved them from her own forehead to Wool's.

"We're nearly the same height."

"That's what I just said." Wool experienced a sense of impending dread she'd never felt before. Standing in front of her was someone she'd grown to love. Quite literally. Adjusting to Jelly's new height, the unthinkable crept through Wool's mind.

She was smarter, now, but her instincts and attitude remained the same.

Could Jelly be trusted? Who's to say she wouldn't turn on her crew? The ramifications of Jelly's progress - or evolution - were too terrifying to comprehend. None of this was lost on Wool.

"Honey?"

"Yes, mommy?"

"Would you ever hurt me?"

Jelly thought about her answer for a moment. Each second that trundled by perturbed Wool even more. Surely the cat should have said yes in an instant. The delay in answering was too much to bear.

"B-Because, y-you know I'd never—"

"—You're scared, mommy."

Jelly hung her paws by her side and took some offense, "Don't be scared."

"I j-just need to be able to trust you, honey. We all d-do."

"Why are you st-stuttering?" Jelly clenched her fists, thinking the woman was making fun of her.

"I'm n-not."

"Y-Yes, you are," Jelly turned her back on Wool and made for the door, "Feeding time. Are you c-coming?"

"Yes."

Rest & Recuperation
Space Opera Beta - Level Two

Jaycee, Tripp, Bonnie, and Wool sat around the central mess hall table eating their stewed dinner from paper plates.

Cups of fresh water and a large, half-full jug occupied a place in the middle of the table.

Dinah Washington's *What A Diff'rence A Day Makes* provided the perfect background soundtrack for their dining.

"I miss the taste of *real* food," Wool held her hair back as she leaned in to slurp the stew on her spoon, "What is this, anyway?"

"I think it's essentially some sort of beef," Tripp took a bite and chewed it around, "Mmm, not bad actually."

All eyes turned to Jelly at the head of the table, struggling with her spoon. Anyone who hadn't met her would swear she was eighteen-years-old by this point.

"How are you getting on, Jelly? Gotten used to the spoon, yet?"

"My claws are getting in the way," she complained and dropped the spoon on the floor. "I don't like cutlery."

Jaycee chuckled to himself, "Ha. Well, you can always—"

Jelly pressed her chin to the plate and licked at the chunk of jellied chicken pâté."

"Or you *could* do that, instead."

Wool lifted the jug and poured herself a cup of water, "Leave her alone, Jaycee. She's had a rough day."

"Miew," Jelly's ears pricked up at Wool's cup at the edge of the table. Bonnie watched the girl's infinity claws expand.

"Jelly, what are you--"

"—Meow."

SWISH-SWIPE!

She knocked the cup of water off the table. The water splashed across the floor.

"Oh, now look what you've done," Wool huffed and tore a piece of towel from the middle of the table, "You know, you should really clean this up."

"No, I shouldn't, mommy. *You* should," Jelly swung her

head left and right, satisfied at having carried out her instinctive objective.

Tor walked into the room and placed his right hand on his hip, "Hey, Jaycee?"

"Huh?" The big man turned to look at him, "What's up, *comrade*?"

Tor pointed to the hunk of metal around his neck, "I did what you asked. I taught her as much English as I could. It went well. Now can you *please* take this damn device off?"

Jaycee lifted his gloved Baldron-hand and threatened to hit the activate button, "How do you want me to retrieve it?"

"How do you think?" Tor whined.

"Either way suits me. Your head attached or detached, your call."

The rest of the crew giggled to themselves - all except Wool, who didn't find the taunting especially funny, "Jaycee. Come on, leave him alone."

"Attached, *please*," Tor made his way over to the free chair and reached for a piping hot tray of stew.

"Suit yourself," Jaycee hit the second button. Tor's Decapidisc beeped and unbuckled, folding out into a backwards "E" shape.

Tor caught it in his hands and slammed it to the table, "Thank God that's off me. I never wanna wear that again."

Jaycee shoveled a spoonful of food into his mouth, "Then don't be a twit, and you won't."

Jelly's ears flicked out. She looked at Jaycee, "Mommy says you shouldn't speak with your mouth full."

"Mmm," he covered his mouth and spoke through his food, "She's right. Sorry."

"That's okay."

A moment of respite fell across the room as everyone ate their dinner. No one spoke for once. Dinah Washington's dulcet tones soothed their ears as they continued to eat.

It was maybe the second time since Opera Beta left Cape Claudius nearly three years ago that they enjoyed each other's company. They'd been through so much together, after all.

Tripp grabbed his cup of water and held it up, "I'd like to

propose a toast."

"Toast?" Jelly licked her lips, "Like hot bread? I wanna try toast."

"No, it's not that kind of toast, honey," Wool lifted her cup with the others.

Jelly didn't have a cup to lift - just a saucer of milk next to her plate of jellied chicken.

Tor felt like he couldn't join in given his history.

"That's right, Russian," Jaycee said. "Keep your cup of water on the table."

"I will," Tor threw a clump of stew into his mouth and turned away.

"To Space Opera Beta," Tripp said.

"To Space Opera Beta," everyone chimed.

"And to Daryl Katz and Haloo Ess. Gone, but never, *ever* forgotten."

"To Katz and Ess," Bonnie, Jaycee, Wool, and Tripp said before taking a gulp of water.

They slammed their cups to the surface of the table and continued eating.

"So, Jelly," Tripp chewed on his food, "There's something I've been wanting to ask you this whole time."

"What?" She lowered her head and nibbled at her chicken.

"Now you can speak, and all. I think I ask for everyone here. Hell, everyone who ever owned a cat. When you were a regular cat, what, uh—"

"—What, uh, what?" Jelly lifted her head and mocked him.

Tripp couldn't get the question out of his mouth. He'd always planned to ask the question of his own pets if the situation ever arose. Of course, it never did. He couldn't formulate the question and quit talking.

Wool had a go in his place, "Honey, I think what Tripp wants to ask is… when you were a real cat, what was it… *like?*"

"What kind of stupid-ass question is *that?*" Jelly snapped.

"Well," Tripp interjected with his second futile effort, "What is it like? Being a cat?"

"Are you seriously asking me that?" Jelly huffed and palmed her plate toward the edge of the table, "Billions of years of evolution in two days and you want to know what being a cat was like?"

The crew were stunned at her outburst.

"Idiots," Jelly continued to lick her chicken.

"Well," Tripp rolled his shoulders and tried to keep his dignity intact, "What do you think about when you're a cat?"

"I dunno," Jelly eyed the others, hoping they wouldn't clock her secret attempt to push the plate over the edge of the table, "Killing smaller things than me. I like to play with them and watch them scream while they die. It makes me feel good."

Jaycee wiped his mouth and took a sip of his water. The answer she'd given crept under his skin.

"Then I bring the bodies home to pay for my food."

"Like a trophy?"

"*Atrophy*? No, my muscles are strong."

"No, a *trophy*. Like a medal. For your owners? To show your appreciation?" Tripp asked.

"Umm, no. The trophy, as you call it, is more like a pat on the head that they've done well."

"Hmm," Tripp poked his food in deep thought, "Did you ever have a mommy and daddy? Siblings?"

"My brothers and sisters can look after themselves. My real *dad* tried to kill us. I hate him. I hope he's dead."

"Oh," Bonnie said. "That's a bit harsh, isn't it?"

"Did your dad abandon you and your family in a cardboard box on the road hoping you'd get killed?" Jelly asked.

Bonnie looked at the others, "Um, no?"

"Hmm," Jelly shrugged her shoulders, "My loyalty is to the people who feed me. And Jamie. I miss Jamie. *Friend.*"

Jaycee wiped his mouth and swallowed the last of his food down, "Ah, yeah. The kid. Heard a lot about him."

"He was your friend, huh?" Bonnie grinned with affection.

"Mommy," Jelly pointed her infinity claw at Wool and then at Bonnie, "Friend."

"Aww, honey. You're my friend, too."

Jelly moved her claw to Tripp, "Friend."

"I'm honored, Jelly. Thank you."

"Yes," Jelly moved her claw Jaycee, "Friend."

"Thanks, Jelly. You're not so bad yourself."

"You're welcome."

Jelly pointed her claw like a gun at Tor, "*Dickhead.*"

"What?"

Everyone burst out laughing.

"*Dickhead,*" Jelly repeated and pretended to shoot him in the face, "*Pow.*"

"Stop saying that," Tor yelled. "I am *not* a dickhead."

"She's spot on, comrade," Jaycee nearly choked with laughter.

Tor buried his head in his hands, lamenting the day he ever set foot on the damned spacecraft. Of all the ridiculous and nasty events that had happened to him, being called a dickhead by a half-cat was the most humiliating.

Jelly scraped her claws along the table as the howls of laughter died down.

"Jamie wasn't *friend*, really. More like *brother*. Actually, he is my brother. I miss him."

"I'm sure he misses you too, honey," Wool threw her a smile of affection.

"Maybe," she yawned as wide as possible. Her fleetingly scary appearance stunned everyone at the table, "I'm tired."

Jaycee leaned over to Tripp and whispered, "I hate it when she does that. She looks so scary. Those teeth and eyes. Brrr."

"I know."

Bonnie set her spoon down on her plate, "What do you miss about being a regular cat, Jelly?"

"Why, am I an irregular cat?"

"You *could* say that," Bonnie giggled. "You're hardly an everyday pet, now, are you?"

Tripp and Jaycee washed down their food with a gulp of water.

"Hmm," Jelly gave the question some thought, "Probably being able to lick my own butt hole—"

SPRAASSHH!

The two men spat out their water upon hearing the answer. Much of it hit the table and Wool's face.

"Ugh, *really?*" She wiped the water from her cheek and flung it to the ground, "That's gross."

"Sorry, Wool," Jaycee cleared his throat, "Say that again, Jelly?"

Jelly ran the side of her arm along the edge of her plate, pushing it even further towards the edge of the table.

"Licking my butt hole. And other parts. I hate taking showers, but I can't reach some areas of my body, anymore."

"That sucks," Jaycee said, "I know if I could do that, you'd be looking at an empty chair right now."

Wool kicked Jaycee's leg under the table, "Jaycee. Don't be disgusting."

"Sorry. It was just a joke. Don't lose your temper."

Tripp stood out of his chair and collected up the dirty paper plates, "We'd better get some rest. This is truly the calm before the storm."

"You got that right," Jaycee cracked his knuckles.

CLICK-CRUCK-SPLATT!

Tripp looked at Jaycee's gloves, "That's one hell of a bad knuckle you had there, Nayall."

"That wasn't me."

Everyone turned to Jelly to see her plate was missing. She stared back at them, refusing to accept any liability. Then, everyone lowered their head under the table - and saw the upturned paper plate bleeding its chicken fusion across the floor.

"Miew," Jelly whined as the heads returned from underneath the table, "It fell."

"Bad girl," Wool snapped at her. "You knocked it off *again.*"

FIZZ-SWISH!

A book-shaped holograph appeared above the table with extreme haste, "Guys, can you hear me?"

"Manuel?" Bonnie stood up, "Yes, we're here."

Manuel scanned the room and flapped his pages together, "*Where* are you?"

"R and R," Tripp said. "What's wrong?"

"They're coming."

"Who are?"

"The Shanta things. They're headed for Botanix at speed."

"ETA?"

"Thirty minutes, maybe less. If you were planning on getting rest, I'm afraid you'll just have to wait till we're all dead."

Jaycee walked away from the table, "Pfft, *charming*. Okay, girls and boys. This is it."

"Where are you going?" Tripp ran after him.

"Weapons and Armory, Healy. Where my specialty lies. I might suggest you do the same," Jaycee turned to the others, "I suggest you *all* do the same."

He lifted his forearm to his mouth and stepped out of the room, "Tor, this is Jaycee. Do you read me?"

"Yes, I read you."

"Meet me at Weapons in two minutes. We're at war," he said, moving off down the corridor.

Tripp turned to the others. They seemed frightened - Wool, in particular.

"I guess this is it, then?"

"The sun didn't get us first?"

"Nope," Tripp backed up to the door, "Wool, take Jelly with you to Medix, please."

Wool shook her head and screwed her face with anger, "No, Tripp," she reached into her belt and pulled out her Rez-9.

"No? Are you defying a direct order—"

"—I'm defying *death*, Tripp. Jelly and I won't waste away like useless mannequins in Medix. We're fighting with you," she said. "Am I right, Jelly?"

Gobsmacked, Tripp and Bonnie turned to Jelly for her reaction.

"Yeah, okay," Jelly said and rose out of her chair, "I'll help you take out the trash."

Bonnie smiled at the remark.

Tripp exhaled and caved in. What other course of action was there, anyway? Everyone would go down in a blaze of glory - *together.*

Chapter 6

USARIC - Weapons & Armory
Space Opera Beta - Level Four

Jaycee scanned the weapons in the armory store, "If we're going to die, then we're going down fighting."

He unlatched three K-SPARK shotguns from the wall and slung two of them over his left shoulder. He passed the third to Tor, "Here, take this."

"Really? You're letting me have a weapon?" Tor thumped the side lever down and armed it.

"Don't make me regret this decision."

Jaycee grabbed the last six dumb bombs from the wall and tipped three of them into Tor's hand.

"I guess we'll need some of these. You have three, so make them count."

Tor's jaw dropped at the man's generosity, "Thanks."

"I'm not finished yet."

Five Rez-9s and a spare D-REZ semi-automatic stared at Jaycee from the wall. He licked his lips and scooped them up in his arms, "Okay, that's it. That's all our inventory."

He grabbed the D-REZ and pushed it into Tor's chest, "This is easier for you to aim with. The magazine is full."

"Okay," he said, slipping the strap around his head.

SCHWUMP!

Jaycee threw the hatch shut. He kissed his fingertips and pressed them against the surface of the door, praying for good fortune, "Thanks for everything."

He stepped away and looked over his shoulder," You

ready to go down in a blaze of glory, *comrade?*"

Tor ran after him. The sheer weight of the weapons slowed him down, "I don't want to die if that's what you mean."

Jaycee palmed the panel on the wall and opened the door. He clipped the five Rez-9s to his belt and snorted, "Funny how we never get a say in what happens to us, isn't it? *Viktor?*"

Botanix
Space Opera Beta - Level Three

Tripp stood amongst the rotten plants and stared at the flat horizon. The edge of Pink Symphony loomed against a blanket of a thousand white stars.

"This is it," he said under his breath, "This is where it all ends."

Bonnie held her Rez-9 in both hands and saw the oncoming horde of Shanta crawling over the dunes, "I figure they'll reach us in five minutes. I'm going to kill every last one of those bastards before they kill me."

"Amen," Tripp patted her on the back, "How's your new battery holding up?"

She reached over her neck and pressed her fingers between her shoulder blades, "Yeah, it's okay. I'm not freaking out too much."

"Good," Tripp turned to Wool and Jelly, who appeared ready for battle, "You guys okay?"

"We'll do our best," Wool said.

Jelly held her D-REZ in both hands and swished her tail around, ready for war, "I am a fighter."

Tripp walked over to Jelly and squatted in front of her, "I'm proud of you, Anderson."

"If Shanta doesn't kill us, the sun will."

Tripp ran the back of his hand over her face, "That's right. You're very smart, you know."

"I know," she licked her lips and pushed her gun into his chest.

Jaycee stormed into Botanix with a range of weapons strapped to his shoulder, "Tripp, catch."

He flung one of his K-SPARKS at Tripp, who caught it in his arms, "Fully loaded?"

"You know it."

Tripp looked at the D-REZ firearm in Tor's hands as he walked in, "I see you trust the Russkie with a gun, now?"

"Yeah," Jaycee thumped the man on the back a little too hard for comfort, "I think he knows that he's way down the pecking order of what's going to kill us."

Bonnie armed her Rez-9 and rolled her shoulders. She widened her eyes at the horizon, "They're coming. Get ready."

Tripp ran in front of crew and addressed them for perhaps the last time. He pointed to Jelly and made sure everyone was listening.

"This is it. We need to protect Anderson as best we can. Every single one of us needs to return fire if we're to stand a chance of surviving. On *no* account are you to leave Opera Beta."

Jelly nodded and pressed her baby bump with her elbow, "Miew."

"Setting turret, stand by," Jaycee held his K-SPARK out at arm's length. The grip on the gun folded out in three directions and shot downward, attaching itself to the floor, "How many of them are there?"

"We're vastly outnumbered, let's put it like that," Tripp said. "When you're down to your last clip, use it on yourself."

"Last *clip?*" Bonnie chewed back her anger at that statement, "How many bullets does it take to kill yourself?"

"You might miss," Tripp said.

Jelly's eyes reverted to the horizon. Something strange took place, "Look, over there."

Everyone turned to see what she was talking about.

"Is it… *moving?*" Jaycee asked.

Wool stepped back against the wall and began to hyperventilate, "I can't do this. I d-don't want to die," she said. The sweat forming over her hand caused the Rez-9 to drop from her hand. She caught it before it hit the floor.

The stars crawled across the black sky at a snail's pace.

Tripp looked at the desecrated plants. The branch ends and leaves lifted toward the horizon. The grains of sand outside the broken wall trailed away and shifted.

Pink Symphony's surface revolved, enabling a strong pull towards the horizon.

Jaycee felt his arms lift in front of his body, "What's happening?"

"Ugh, ugh," Wool's heels skidded across the ground, "Oh God, I'm falling."

"You're not falling!" Tripp scanned Botanix for something to hold on to, "We're spinning. The whole place is spinning."

"Miew," Jelly grabbed hold of a grounded plant tray to stop herself from flying out of the room.

In the distance, the hordes of squealing Shanta scurried even faster in an attempt to fight off the pull.

The disc spun faster... *and faster*.

Bonnie slipped and fell on her behind. The pull of the external force sent her sliding toward the sand, "Help me!"

"Bonnie!" Tripp grabbed hold of a charcoaled plant and aimed his K-SPARK at the horizon, "Grab hold of something—"

SWOOOOSH!

Pink Symphony's spinning grew exponentially as Bonnie unsuccessfully tried to grab at the ground. Her fingertips jumped off each tile as it whizzed under her front.

Jaycee placed himself behind the turret to prevent himself from flying out with her, "Bonnie, grab the wall!"

She rolled over to her back and bent her knees. The broken wall screamed towards her. She held out her hand and grabbed it, swinging out above the sand.

"God damn it," Bonnie opened fire on the approaching Shanta, "Die you vicious scumbags. Die!"

BLAM-BLAM-BLAM!

The thousand-strong Shanta clambered towards Botanix. A giant creature extended all twelve of its limbs and cartwheeled ahead of them.

"Jeeeeeeeeeesus…" Jaycee thumped the mounted K-SPARK turret. It fired off a round at the enormous rolling beast, "Get some of this, you ugly—"

BLAM-BLAM-SCHPLATT!

The barreling Shanta exploded as the bullets tore through its central section. The pink gore splattered to the sand as its body tumbled back into the crowd of beasts.

"Open fire!" Tripp shouted and blasted at the horde, "Keep holding on."

Bonnie's grip on the wall loosened, "Agh. Tripp, Tripp, my hand… I can't hang on…"

"Don't let go," Tripp fired another round of bullets at the creatures. The bullets whizzed past Bonnie and tore into three Shanta, severing their limbs.

They crashed against the floor and swished into the horizon.

"Nggggg," Bonnie grunted and continued firing at the creatures. Her fingertips traced against the wall and threatened to release.

The relentless spinning of the disc wouldn't cease.

Jelly looked at Bonnie and released her grip on the plant tray.

Tripp screamed over the incessant growling of the sun headed in their direction, "Jelly, what are you doing?"

"Need to save Bonnie."

She launched herself toward the broken wall and held out her paws.

SCHTANG-SCHTANG!

Her infinity claws spread out into a star shape as she rocketed over to the helpless Bonnie.

"Jelly, no," she screamed as Jelly's face darted toward her, "Grab hold of something."

"I'm coming," Jelly turned over as she flew and fired off a fully automatic clip at the Shanta.

BLAM-BLAM-BLAM-SPRATCH-CRATCH!

The bullets chewed through an oncoming creature, busting its mid-section open. The pink goo coughed into the air, twisted toward the horizon and blasted toward the stars at the edge of Pink Symphony.

Its carcass tumbled across the sand like a dead bowling ball, knocking the nearest set of beasts onto the ground.

"Bonnie, I'm coming," Jelly squealed and swiped at the woman's shoulder with her right paw, "Grab my hand."

THUMP!

Bonnie's hand slammed into Jelly's right palm. They squeezed together as Bonnie lost her grip on the wall.

Jelly caught the side of the wall with her left claw - but the propulsive force was too severe. It banged away and sent Jelly and Bonnie tumbling out of Botanix and crashing across the sand.

"Jelly! Bonnie!" Wool cried out after them from behind the plants. She fired a shot at the creatures.

GRROOOWWWWLL!

The sun grew larger and larger, throwing a Godly light into Botanix. It blinded Tripp, Jaycee, Tor, and Wool.

"The sun," Tor pointed at the sky, "We're going to die!"

"Kill *everything*," Tripp shouted over the commotion, "Keep firing!"

Botanix reverberations punched Tripp around and slammed his back against the wall, "Gaaah," he screamed and fired a round at a dozen Shanta creatures infiltrating the broken wall.

Bonnie slid across the sand on her back through the stampeding Shanta.

SWIPE-STAB-SCHTOMP!

Dozens of Shanta limbs daggered into the floor on either side of her as she scraped the sand on her trajectory, "Agghhh, help meeee."

A few feet behind her, Jelly spread her claws out to prevent herself from the same fate.

Bonnie tumbled forward, unable to fight Pink Symphony's spin-pull towards the edge of its mass.

"Bonnie," Jelly whelped.

She hopped onto the back of a trailing Shanta and dug her paws into its flesh. Her claws tore out of the Shanta's skin as she launched over to Bonnie.

Pink Symphony's disc tilted diagonally as it spun around. It angled itself like a radar toward the approaching sun.

SHWOOOOOSH!

Bonnie's waist slammed against another creature, pushing her around on her descent towards the edge of Pink Symphony.

Jelly tumbled around and spun to her feet, "You're not going *anywhere*."

The sand kicked up around Bonnie's as she zipped along the sand. The edge of the disc shot towards her feet.

"Oh God…" Bonnie rolled to her side and looked down the length of her body. Any second now, she'd fall off the edge.

SCHWIPP!

Bonnie's ass hit the edge, catapulting her entire body around. She held out her hands and grabbed the edge of the rock-like surface. Her legs slammed against the edge, "Ugghhh," she screamed and made the mistake of looking down - an infinite drop of intergalactic proportions threatened to take her life.

Jelly slid up to the edge and pressed the butt of her paws to the ground. She stared at Bonnie and whined, "I'm not strong enough to pull you up,"

"P-Please, Jelly," Bonnie squealed and tried to hulk her body up to safety, "D-Don't let me fall."

Pink Symphony's spinning slowed down, forcing Bonnie's front to slap against the cliff edge.

A wave of terror blasted across Bonnie's pupils. Frightened beyond belief, she was convinced she'd fall to her death.

Jelly looked down at Bonnie's fingers and licked her lips, "Miew."

She opened her paw and held it a few inches to the side of Bonnie's hand.

"Wh-what are you doing?" Bonnie turned over her shoulder to see the bottomless pit of stars, "P-Please, help me up."

Jelly viewed Bonnie's five fingers as the enemy. She tried

to fight against her instincts - to little avail.

Her paw tapped Bonnie's hand, trying to release her fingers, "Miew…"

"What are you doing?" Bonnie screamed. "Don't, *please*…"

"Meow," Jelly swiped Bonnie's index and middle finger, releasing her grip, "I need to."

"Jesus, Jelly. Please, *no*—"

"—Miew," she took another swipe and tried to knock Bonnie's fingers off the edge.

"Nuh-nuh," Bonnie focused on Jelly's claw sliding under her thumb, "Oh, God. Please—"

"—Miew," Jelly licked her lips and lifted her infinity claw, eying Bonnie dead in the eyes the whole time, "I'm s-sorry…"

"You'll k-kill me," Bonnie's voice croaked as she spoke. She knew she was dead, "Do you want me to d-die?"

Jelly looked up at the scorching sun and widened her mouth. The light reflected off her fangs and into Bonnie's face.

She saw her feet dangling across the stars and then back to Jelly. In a desperate bid to save her own life, she grabbed hold of Jelly's jeans.

No mercy was shown from the cat as Bonnie's fingers slipped helplessly along the denim.

"I d-don't want to d-die…"

Jelly scrunched her face, unable to resist her instinct. She scraped the sand with the side of her paw and pushed Bonnie's two remaining fingers from her jeans.

"Meow."

Bonnie fell away from the edge.

Her face turned to a picture of hell. She clutched the torn fabric in her hands and plummeted from the edge of Pink Symphony and into the infinite blanket of space and time.

"*Sorry*," Jelly licked her face, satisfied that she'd knocked the *things* from the edge.

Bonnie's death yell funneled from her mouth as her body plummeted away, getting smaller and smaller… until she disappeared altogether.

Jelly flicked her ears and watched a tiny, new star form against the black canvas of space like a single drop of spilled, white paint.

Pink Symphony's entire land mass lit up as the sun got closer.

Millions of grains of white sand cascaded to the ground. Jelly turned to face Opera Beta, one hundred feet in the distance.

The Shanta stopped in their tracks and turned to face the girl standing at the edge of Pink Symphony.

"Miew."

"SCREEEEEE!"

They charged at Jelly in unison. Their new distraction would buy her crew members in Opera Beta some time.

Jelly scraped the ends of her infinity claws through the sand and flapped her tail, ready for war, "Let's take out the trash. Come and get some…"

She ran her claws through the sand and prepared to attack, "Die, you ugly scumbags!"

ROOWWAAARRRR!

Two dozen Shanta barreled toward her as she bolted across the sand in their direction.

"Meeee-owwww," Jelly looked above the first two creatures and saw the towering blackened tree stomp its way out of the ocean behind the ship.

BOLT!

Jelly ran into the Shanta. The first one flung its talon out and stabbed it to the ground. Jelly swiveled around and landed to her front paws, narrowly missing its stabbing motion.

"Screeeee," it wailed as her claws tore through its two front limbs, sending it onto its behind.

SWISH-SWIPE!

Jelly darted through the limbs of the others. In the furor they swung their arms out and hit one another in a desperate bid to stop her from reaching the ship.

She planted her hind legs on the ground and lifted herself

off her heels.

A vicious swipe to another Shanta's slit. The claws tore out its lip, forcing it to gargle and choke. She hit the ground and sliced at its standing limbs, sending its vast body crashing to the ground.

"Yuck," Jelly flung the goo from her claws and raced toward the ship.

Jaycee's K-SPARK turret oscillated back and forth, firing at the Shanta. The crew had done a good job of keeping them out of Botanix - but *still* they came.

"There's another," Tripp pointed at the ceiling and shot a crawling creature in its center. The carcass extended its talons and dropped onto a bunch of beasts, below.

SCREEE-SCHLAMM-SCHPLATT!

"Where did they go?" Jaycee asked over the firing bullets.

"I dunno," Tor took aim at a particularly aggressive creature. Standing a clear ten feet tall, it held out all twelve limbs and formed a spider web at the hole in the wall.

It's slit opened up to reveal a disgusting, black tongue.

SCHWIPP-LASH!

"Ugh, that's one ugly beast," Tor aimed his D-REZ at its mid-section, "Eat this."

THRAA-AA-TAT-A-TAT!

Tor emptied his clip at the creature's mouth. The slit exploded in a hail of pink gloop and pinged the limbs away from its center section. The mass of ungodly monster shunted down the sides of the walls and gasped its last.

Jelly ran between its legs and jumped inside Botanix.

"Jelly," Tripp shouted, relieved that she was still alive, "Get in, quick. Against the back wall."

"What do we do now?" Wool asked, taking potshots at the creatures with her Rez-9.

"The sun is coming," Jelly said. "It's going to kill us all."

Jaycee knocked the side of the turret and swung his secondary K-SPARK from his shoulders, "I'm out. Turret is down."

Tripp grew impatient and snapped his fingers, "Keep firing."

A rectangle of holographic light formed in the middle of Botanix, creating the outline of a book - Manuel.

"Did someone ask for me?"

"What? No," Tripp emptied his magazine and palmed a fresh one into his Rez-9, "We're out of ammo. This is my last magazine."

"In that case, do you mind if I step out of the line of fire and let you perish alone?"

"That would be very helpful, Manuel. Thank you."

The book flapped over to the door to Botanix as the others kept shooting at the Shanta.

Jelly raced after Manuel, suddenly fascinated by his contours. She jumped in the air and tried to catch him, "Miew."

"Miss Anderson?" Manuel pressed his pages against the wall by the door, "What are you doing?"

"I want to touch you."

"In the middle of a gunfight?"

"Yes," she spread her claws out and swiped at him, "Meow."

"Uh, Tripp?" Manuel tried to avoid making eye contact with Wool, who looked at him suspiciously.

"Not now, Manuel," Tripp yelled, "Later."

"The cosmic event taking place in the sky isn't technically a sun," Manuel said. "It does not contain the gaseous properties of what we consider to be a heavenly body."

Jaycee stomped over to Manuel and raised his eyebrows, "What is it?"

"Some kind of *portal* is my best guess. If we seal off Botanix and get you into the hyper-sleep pods I'd say you all have a twenty percent chance of surviving whatever is about to happen."

"Twenty?" Tripp took his eyes off the Shanta for a second longer than he should have.

"Screeeee!"

Tripp pointed his gun at the noise whilst looking at Manuel, "I'll take those odds."

BLAM-SCHPLAT!

He yanked the trigger and throated the creature with his

nozzle, blasting its innards across the dead plants.

"Quick," Manuel scanned the panel on the wall and opened the door, "Get to the hyper-sleep chamber. Follow me."

Wool, Jelly, Jaycee, and Tripp took one, final look at the sky. It wasn't pink, anymore. Instead, a huge gulf of white lamped the entire horizon.

SCHTAAAMMMM!

The black root of the tree stomped down, crushing all the Shanta in front of Botanix.

GROOWWLLL...

"Oh *dear*," Wool said. "Let's do what Manuel said. Run, run."

Jelly ran through the opened door. Tripp and Wool followed after her, leaving Jaycee to open his thigh compartment and grab five dumb bombs. He pulled each pin from them and clutched them in his hand, "Come get some."

He bent his elbow out from his chest and threw them among the plants.

"Screeeeeee!" The Shanta squealed in unison, thumping their talons to the tiled ground.

"Adios, amigos," Jaycee kicked the door shut, sealing them inside.

"Jaycee, quick. Let's go!" Wool yelled over her shoulder as she raced down the walkway with the others.

"Yeah, just gimme a minute," he turned to the wall panel and lifted his right boot, "Just sealing the bastards in."

He smashed the panel with all his might and disabled the door mechanism. The Shanta slapped their limbs against the window in a wild, screeching frenzy.

Jaycee rubbed his gloved hands together and held up his middle finger to the window, "Time to go sleepy-byes..."

He turned around and stormed up the walkway.

KA-BOOOOM!

The walkway shuddered as the other side of the window splattered with dark, pink gore. The bombs eviscerated everything that turned oxygen into carbon dioxide within the room.

"I know the feeling, my friends," Jaycee finished as he

turned the corner, "Rest in *pieces*, Botanix."

The Hyper-Sleep Chamber
Space Opera Beta

Manuel shuffled into the room and bent out his pages, "Hyper-sleep. Engage. Pods one through *five*, please."

The glass on the first five of the nine available pods slid open.

Tripp entered the chamber with the others in hot pursuit.

"Five?" Tripp asked. "There's six of us."

"I only count *five*, Tripp?" Manuel offered. "You, Jaycee, Wool, Tor, and Jelly. I strongly advise you disrobe, now, and enter the pods as quickly as you can."

Tripp looked around the pod and watched Jelly hop into the room, "Jelly, where did Bonnie go?"

She arched her back and stood on her two hind feet. Tripp's eyes grew with wonder. She matched his height.

"She fell off the edge of the universe."

"What?" Wool slipped off her inner-suit top and folded it in her arms, "What do you mean?"

Jelly looked down at her jeans. She'd grown into them so much that they'd torn.

"She turned into a star."

"What are you talking about?" Tripp said.

"She's *dead*."

The crew knew it already, but Jelly's innocent delivery of those last two words sucker punched them in their collective gut.

"I knew it," Jaycee removed his exo-suit. His muscled body glinted in the fluorescent light, catching everyone's attention.

Tor looked away and bit his lip. He flung his inner-suit into the slider on the wall, feeling extremely inferior - both mentally and physically, "I can't do this anymore. Whatever that sun thing is out there, I hope it kills us," he climbed into a pod and exhaled. It felt comfortable inside.

"I hope it kills *you*," Jaycee yelled as he climbed into the pod next to his, "Just know I'm right next to you if you try something crappy."

Tor crossed himself and muttered a silent prayer, "Please, let me sleep while it happens."

Jaycee thumped the side of the man's pod, "Shut up, *princess*. Praying won't get you anywhere."

Tor cleared his throat and swallowed back his pink saliva. He noticed a bleeding scratch on the top of his arm from the melee in Botanix, "Oh God, make it stop," he winced.

Manuel hovered over Tor and Jaycee's pod, "Gentlemen, please. Do try to exercise a little decorum?"

"Put us to sleep, Manuel," Jaycee crossed his arms over his pectoral muscles and closed his eyes.

"My pleasure."

Manuel blasted two beams from his pages, forcing the glass fronts to slide into place.

Dressed in her underwear, Wool helped Jelly remove her ridiculously tight jeans, "Honey, we're about to go to sleep for a while. You can't wear these in the pods."

"I know," she clung to Wool for balance, "I hate wearing clothes. How do you spend all day in them?"

"No time to talk now," Wool chucked the jeans over her shoulder and grabbed Jelly's hand. They walked over to the third pod, "Okay, climb in and pretend you're going to bed."

"Nap time?"

Wool smiled and kept an eye on Tripp, "Yes, nap time."

"Please, Miss Anderson. Hurry."

"Okay, *fine*," Jelly let go of Wool's hand and climbed into her pod, "I'm going. Happy now?"

"Immeasurably."

Jelly looked up at Manuel and screwed her face, "I don't like you, you know."

"That's really of no consequence at this precise moment, Miss Anderson. Now, close your eyes."

Manuel shot a beam over Jelly's pod. The hatch slid up and bolted shut, pressing a shaft of gas within the tomb. Jelly closed her eyes and passed out.

"Phew. There, she's done," Manuel spun around and darted over to Tripp, "So, just you and Wool left—Oh."

He caught Wool and Tripp hugging each other. A quiet and solemn embrace. A moment of sanity in an otherwise *insane* situation.

Wool's pink tears wet her cheeks as she spoke, "Hold me."

"I am," Tripp breathed her scent in, "I am. Do you know how long it's been since I've held someone?"

"Too long," Wool kept her grip on his shoulders and moved her face in front of his, "Longer for me than for you, I think."

"I may be married, but that's no guarantee of physical contact."

"Not now, Tripp," Wool looked down and sobbed into his chest. He held her gently in his hands.

"Tripp?" Manuel mouthed, "Hurry up."

"*Wait*," Tripp mouthed back and tilted his head down to Wool, "Hey. It's okay."

He held her face in his hands and looked in her bleary eyes, "We did everything we could. Right?"

She nodded and wiped her messy nose, "Yeah. Yeah, we did."

"It's going to be okay, you know."

Wool chuckled with disdain. She wasn't buying a word of that particular lie.

"No. It's not going to be okay, Tripp. Going to sleep is just going to prolong the misery. That's all it's going to do."

She grabbed his hand and pulled it away from her face, "But that's what I love about you, Tripp."

"What?"

"Your optimism," she pecked him on the cheek and turned to the fourth free pod, "Okay, Manuel. Load me in."

"Certainly."

Tripp soaked up Wool's last words. It's possible he was far too optimistic. But that was the whole point of being a successful captain, wasn't it? He thought as much in his mind.

Tripp lay in the pod and closed his eyes.

"Are you ready?" Manuel asked.

"I'm ready. Seal me in and wake me up if we survive."

"And if we don't?"

Tripp inhaled and exhaled with a degree of peace, "Then leave me alone."

The hatch slid up and released the sleeping gas.

Tripp may or may never see his crew again.

They may not survive the event in the sky. Even if they did, they probably wouldn't get back home. If they did they wouldn't be able to go near anyone. They were contaminated with Symphonium.

The odds got bleaker by the nanosecond. The best thing to do was *not* think about it at all.

After all, there was a sliver of a possibility that all this was stupid a stupid dream.

"Yeah, right. A *dream*," Tripp's final thought steamrollered through his mind before he conked out, "Dream on, Opera Beta."

***

The sun scorched its way across the stars in the sky. The tree stomped forward and threw its branches out at it in a loving embrace.

GRRUUNNT.

The ball of white fire slammed into its root and stem as the branches closed around it. The two shimmied together and became one.

Next to it, the water from the ocean formed a twisting line in the air and sucked through into the duo like a straw.

One by one, the remaining Shanta creatures exploded as a chorus of light blasted through them.

Space Opera Beta sluiced into the harmonious concoction of light and wonder.

Everything went white - an act of God previously unseen by anyone or anything that ever lived...

Chapter 7

Chrome Valley
United Kingdom

"Happy birthday, poppet."

Emily and Tony clapped their hands together and encouraged Jamie to take a deep breath. He blew out all eight candles on his birthday cake.

Emily rubbed his back as Tony slipped out of the front room. She whispered in his ear, "What did you wish for?"

"I can't tell you or it won't come true."

"Hmm," she looked at the frame of the door, along with her son, "Was it something along the lines of *this*?"

Tony stepped out of the way of the huge gift-wrapped birthday present, "Happy birthday, son."

"Oh, wow."

Jamie jumped from the chair and ran over to the flowery wrapping, "Is it what I think it is?"

"It might be," Tony winked.

Jamie pushed his hand through the pink wrapping paper and felt a cold, metal bar, "Oh, wow. *It is.*"

Off came the wrapping paper in one fell swoop. Jamie laid eyes on the gift standing proud in the middle of the room, "Oh, *wow*. I thought you said I couldn't have one?"

"No, no. It's okay," Tony moved over to the gift and retrieved two rubber sticks and ear buds, "See it muffles the sound. You put these in your ears. When you strike the pad it plays in your ears."

Jamie took the buds from Tony's hands and slipped them in his ears. He lifted the stick and thwacked it against the pad.

BOMPH.

"Oww," Jamie yanked the plugs out from his ears.

"Bit too loud, huh?" Tony pointed at the slider on the side of the sticks, "Just turn the volume down."

"Oh. Okay."

The impressive drum kit meant the world to Jamie. He'd all but destroyed his a few of years ago in an attempt to 'find out what made it bang', as he described it. He loved to bash things. Why not create a cheerful tune in the process, he thought.

He felt life was complete now that he had a new drum kit. Tony and Emily were happy for him.

Jolene toddled over to the table and helped herself to some of Jamie's birthday cake. Her hands scooped up some icing. Most of it went over her face rather than in her stomach.

"Jojo," Emily said. "*Please.* Stop doing that."

Jamie giggled to himself as he banged away at the drum.

Da-da-da-dummm…

Jolene, Emily, and Tony couldn't hear what Jamie was playing. He'd heard the piece of music throughout his life. A fan of ancient classical music (as it was known) his mother used to play the likes of Beethoven, Mozart, and Tchaikovsky to him as a very young boy. She didn't seem to bother doing the same with his younger half-sister, Jolene, though. He put it down to a change of influence now that his biological father had passed away.

Jamie smiled at Tony as he continued to whack the drum skin at full pelt. Like his real father, Tony seemed to be fitting in nicely. His mother seemed much happier.

Something was missing, though - a feline keepsake she bestowed on him shortly before his father died. *She*, the gorgeous ball of orange fluff who should not be named, for fear of reminder of what they had done.

Jamie bashed the drum panels. He felt a tingling sensation crawl up his left forearm.

Boom-boom-boom… he continued playing, using the kit's synthesizer rhythm track to keep him in tune.

Beep-beep-beep. The ink on his forearm became visible as his sleeve rode up to the crook of his elbow.

The ink on his forearm swirled around his skin and formed three flashing dots.

An Individimedia call from someone unknown to him.

He looked up from behind the kit and saw Emily spoon feeding his sister. Tony pinched his thumbnail and removed it from his hand. He placed it on the table and snapped his fingers.

The thumbnail projected a holographic news report above the table. A top-down view of Santiago Sibald looking up at the lens, standing by a purple SUV. Its fender hanging from the front, it had hit a tree and the occupants had fled.

Swarms of STPD officers surrounded the scene.

"Earlier reports from a witness who wishes to remain anonymous recounts that the vehicle had been commandeered by a bunch of *cats*?" Santiago looked at his wrist and shook his head, "No. That can't be right—"

Glenn, the witness, appeared in silhouette on the screen. He addressed the interviewee in a state of shock, barely able to form a sentence.

"I-It was w-w-weird," Glenn burped. "Cats everywhere, I tell ya. They made the man s-stop the c-car and then jumped inside an' drove off, yonder."

"You're saying *cats* did this?"

"Yah-yup," the silhouetted figure threw his hands into the air, "Sure as I'm standin' here, my f-friend. One of them was real ugly, like, with a long-ass body and stupid pointy ears. That one acted all dead in the middle of the freeway."

Jamie covered his forearm and, much like Tony was wont to do on most occasions, slipped out of the front room without being seen.

Jamie hopped into his bedroom and jumped onto his bed. He analyzed his wrist and wondered whether he should answer the call or not.

His arm kept buzzing, begging for attention. A final look

at the bedroom door was all he needed. He planted the sole of his boot on it and pushed it shut.

SCHWUMP.

A poster for USARIC's Star Cat Project Finals featuring Bisoubisou, Jelly, and Suzie Q-Two hung on the back of the door. Jamie took a deep breath and smeared the three inked dots along his forearm.

"Hello?" he whispered.

"Is this Jamie Anderson?" a stern-sounding female's voice radiated from the pinpricks in his arm.

"Yes."

"No, it's no good. I can't see you," she said, "Look, I'll--"

"—My mom and dad won't allow me to visualize. I'll get in trouble."

"That's okay. We know what you look like. Listen, there's nothing to be afraid of, okay? We're the good guys."

"What? What do you mean don't be afraid?"

"Hang on," the voice cut off.

Jamie shook his forearm. The ink sprawled over the skin on his forearm and formed the face of a woman's head. Featureless, it moved just enough to suggest the woman was producing a live feed.

"Do you see me?"

"Yes," Jamie folded his legs and pushed himself against the wall, out of view of the door, "Look, I can't talk to you. I'm not supposed to speak to strangers."

"I know about Jelly, Jamie."

"You know about—" Jamie thought twice about his reaction. On the cusp of giving the game away, he decided to change tact, "What about Jelly? What do you want?"

"Don't play dumb with me, Anderson. That Individimedia broadcast Handax sent out. He said Bisoubisou never made it on Opera Beta. If she didn't go, then who did?"

A pang of terror ran down Jamie's spine. He'd been busted, "I don't know what you're talking about—"

"—Shut up, kid."

Jamie swallowed hard and drew the curtains shut, "Okay?"

"Where's Jelly right now?"

"She's, uh," Jamie looked around his bedroom for an excuse. The USARIC poster didn't help. The scattered pictures of his family and Jelly were too distracting. Jamie thought on his feet and lied, "She's at the medician's."

"Really?"

"Yes, she got, uh, cat flu."

"Liar."

"No, I mean it, she's—" Jamie's voice croaked as he began to tear up. He knew he was in trouble.

"—Don't *lie* to me, Jamie. I know those scumbags at USARIC brought you and your mom back and had you hand Jelly over. She's not been seen since. Go on, deny it."

Jamie blubbed, "Please leave me alone—"

"—No, shut up. And don't tell your mom or dad, or anyone, about this call. Do you understand what I've just said?"

"Y-Yes."

"Good," the dark figure tilted its head on Jamie's arm and took on a more affable posture, "Listen, Jamie. We're not the bad guys. I know it's hard to believe right now. We're going to help you."

"Help me?"

"Yes. You want to see Jelly again, don't you?"

Jamie wiped the tears from his eyes. His left wrist's Individimedia panel caught most of the liquid.

"Ugh. What's the squelching noise?"

"Sorry," Jamie sniffed and returned to his forearm.

"Opera Beta went missing. USARIC are sending up a vessel to go and find them. You remember a guy named Handax, right?"

Images of a carry case containing Jelly flooded into Jamie's mind. Before long, a man in his twenties with blue hair came to mind.

"Yes, he gave us Jelly."

"You saw his broadcast, didn't you? Everyone did."

"Yes."

"They set free a bunch of felines at USARIC. Most of them were caught. It's all over the news."

"I know, I saw something just now—"

"—That's not important right now. What *is* important is that you tell the truth. Did Jelly go to Saturn in Bisoubisou's place? Yes or no?"

Jamie closed his eyes and wiped his face. The woman was serious and seemed genuine.

"Yes, she did."

"I knew it," her voice filtered through his wrist, "Thanks for confirming, Jamie—"

"—But we swore we wouldn't tell anyone."

"It's okay. We're not *anyone*. That's all we needed to know. Goodbye."

"Hey, wait," Jamie interrupted, demanding an explanation, "Who are you?"

"It's better that you don't know. If anyone asks and you genuinely don't know, then you and your family are safe," she said. "There's going to come a time soon when people will know Jelly went in Bisoubisou's place. And when that time comes, the media and others are going to hound you for answers. If that happens, USARIC could act, and no one wants that for you."

"Okay."

"You and your family *must* tell the media that you didn't know."

"You mean, like, *lie?*"

"Yes, we mean like *lie.*"

"We?"

"Damn," the woman cleared her throat and lowered her voice, "Jamie, so you know Opera Charlie is launching in the next few days. To go and look for Opera Beta?"

"No."

"Well you do now. Charlie's mission is to destroy Beta. Kill everything. The crew are all sick."

"What do you mean sick?"

"Ugh, I can't explain. One of our team is undercover on the Charlie mission—" the woman paused, hesitantly, "I can't talk. I have to go."

"But wait—"

"You'll hear from us again. Stay sharp, kid."

The head shape on Jamie's forearm stretched into three separate lines. The connection disabled, leaving Jamie on his bed, alone and concerned.

USARIC Training Compound
Cape Claudius, South Texas, USA

A man in his early twenties approached the weapons bench. An selection of firearms lay on the table - the familiar K-SPARK shotgun and Rez-9 among them. A range of grenades and utilities lined its outer edges.

The man clenched his gloved fists. On the side of his arm he clocked the USARIC logo along with his name - *A. Hughes.*

Beyond the bench lay a makeshift walkway, resembling a movie set. He adjusted his visor and flicked the lever down by his ear.

Bzzzzz.

The headgear whirred to life, "Heads Up Display activated," a friendly female voice advised, "Okay, Alex. You have ninety seconds to breach the perimeter and take out all the hostiles. It's up to you which weapon you choose."

The contours of each firearm lit up as he scanned the table. A medium-sized semi-automatic caught his attention, "I'll go with the D-Rez."

"Ah, nice," she said. "Lightweight, versatile. Are you much of a run-and-gun?"

"Not really. I prefer precision."

"Fifty compact rounds per magazine. Slider indicates three-shot burst, then five, and finally outright automatic."

"I'll go with the three," Alex knuckled the lever right up and inspected the side of the firearm. He grabbed a pair of flash grenades and hooked them around his belt.

"Remember. Don't point your gun at the people you work with. Or any of the civilians."

"I don't intend to."

The woman giggled through his headgear, "That's the spirit. Approach the start position, please."

"Understood."

Alex stepped up to the red line on the floor, ready to breach the first building.

"You look kinda cute in this get-up, by the way," the woman said. "Fancy a drink after the show's over?"

"No, thank you," Alex clutched the grip on the gun and scanned the first room, prepared for battle, "Let's do this."

"Record time is ninety point seven seconds."

"I'll do it in eighty-five."

The room's lights snapped on revealing a variety of desks, chairs, a screen, and a table.

"Here we go. Standby."

CLUNK-CLICK-BZZZZ.

"Go, go, go," her voice threatened. "Tango to the right."

A holographic bad guy jumped up from behind the computer desk and aimed his rifle at Alex, who slid across the floor and fired three bullets.

POP-POP-SCHPANG!

Two in the chest, and the final one in the head. The bad guy hit the deck, dead.

"You're on your own, now, Hughes."

"Understood."

Alex rolled onto his side and flipped himself to his feet. The room was eerily empty, "Left wall, secure."

"Watch your six, good buddy."

Alex spun around and blasted another bad guy aiming his weapon at him. He slid across the table as the bad guy opened fire on him.

Sections of the wall burst apart behind Alex as he reached the other side of the table and yanked on the trigger.

BLAM-BLAM-SCHPANG!

The bad guy recoiled from the bullet and smashed against the wall.

"Good going, Hughes," the woman said. "Get out of there. Detonator set to five seconds.

"On it," Alex kicked himself to his feet and made for the door.

"Four... three... two..."

Alex launched himself through the door frame and threw his elbows in front of his face.

"One... and that's *boom time*."

He rolled across the floor and kicked the door shut.

KA-BLAAAAAAAM!

The door contained the blast. Its frame shunted around against the impact. The HUD display showed the timer rocketing forward - 15:09.

"Go, go, go," the woman said into his headset, "You got family at home?"

"Just a girlfriend," Alex pushed himself away from the wall and stepped back, spying the length of the corridor, "Walkway secure."

He paced along the barren corridor. Two doors faced each other on each wall at the end.

"Be careful, Alex," she said. "One of those rooms is full of civilians."

"Got it," Alex turned a dial on the side of his visor. The dimmed image of the walkway turned a fussy yellow, pink and green.

"Switching to thermal imaging," Alex said. He held the D-Rez in both hands and moved forward with stealth.

"You think thermal imaging will help if you discover creatures in space?"

"I'll give it a try," Alex pressed his back to the wall.

Oxade and Nutrene watched Alex work from the viewing gantry twenty feet above the set up.

"Who is this guy, anyway?" Nutrene asked, paying particular attention to the young man's trim physique.

Oxade caught her ogling and knocked her elbow, "Are you checking him out?"

"What? No," she protested under her breath. "It's just that—"

"—Just that you want to give him some extracurricular training, right?"

"Don't talk *lessense*, you dummy," Nutrene felt her shoulder and went beet-red.

Oxade smirked and thumped the railing, "USARIC shipped him over from Minneapolis-Two yesterday. Fresh blood from the American Star Fleet."

"Oh, he's *fresh*, for sure."

Alex unclipped a flash bang grenade from his belt and tossed it into the left-hand room.

BOOM!

A shower of white light exploded through the crack in the door. He pushed into the room with his weapon drawn. Ten holographic actors acting as bad guys and civilians staggered around within his HUD.

"Be careful, Alex. Not all of them are tangos."

The white mist evaporated to reveal two bad guys with guns. Alex swung his firearm around and popped both in the head with great expediency.

"Two down," he turned around and was about to shoot a woman in a red dress. She held up her arms and begged for mercy.

"Please don't shoot."

"Get down."

Alex spotted a man grab the woman from behind. His heads up display formed a red line around the bad guy's body, indicating a fresh target.

The man grabbed the woman in his arms and pushed the barrel of his gun against her temple, "Put the gun down."

"Unhand her and put your arms up."

"That's fifty seconds, Alex," the female voice advised, "Be careful."

Alex held his arms out and focused on the wall. A line of traveling dots projected a recoil off the wall and straight into the side of the man's head.

The man threatened to shoot the hostage, "Put your gun down—"

THRAA-TAT-A-TAT-SCHPLATT!

Alex let out a burst of three bullets. One by one, they ricocheted off the wall and punched through the bad guy's chest, neck and forehead, respectively.

The civilian woman ran across the room and went to hug Alex, "Thank you."

"No time for that now, Alex," Oxade chuckled from the viewing gallery, "Keep moving, my friend."

"Hostile down," the female's voice into Alex's headgear, "Hostage deactivated."

The woman vanished completely, leaving Alex to back himself toward the door, "Area secure."

"Go, go, go."

Alex bolted out of the room and approached the adjacent door. He slapped the lever down on the side of his D-Rez and aimed it skyward.

"Be careful here, Alex. Don't get trigger happy."

"I don't intend to."

The timer on his HUD read 65:15, "Come on, let's do it."

"I'm not stopping you."

BAMMM!

Alex booted the door open and slid across the floor, aiming his gun at the far wall.

A long metal bridge snaked out to a door fifty feet away. His feet and legs lifted away from the bridge floor.

"Not so tough now, are you big guy?" she laughed into his headgear, "Let's see how your firearm works in zero gravity."

"Holy *shi*—"

The circular room rocked to life and revolved around him. Severely disorienting Alex as he clung to the rails. His feet lifted above his head as he aimed his gun at the far door.

"Look at all the pretty stars, Alex," she attempted to put him off, "Can you defend yourself when push comes to shove?"

"What?"

BOP!

A disgusting alien creature thumped him on the back, knocking him across the spinning tube. The lights from the stars swished around, revealing the creature's six eyes. Two skewers shot out from its body and clawed at Alex as he propelled himself from the metal bridge.

SWISH-SWIPE!

Alex took aim at the beast as he hung upside down in the air, "Damn it."

"Don't shoot it, Alex," Oxade yelled from the gallery. "You don't want to blow your hand off."

"I wasn't going to—"

SNAAARRRLLL! SNASSSHH!

The creature hooked its two front arms up and around the railings and pulled taught on its back legs, ready, to launch at Alex.

He looked at his belt and unfastened a wire with a hook at the end, "God damn it, "cmon, c'mon…"

Alex threw the hook at the top railing. The prongs at the end fanned out and clamped to the metal, keeping Alex tethered in the air by the wire.

Oxade nudged Nutrene and pointed at the nearby staircase, "Come on, let's go."

"Okay."

GROWL!

The creature revealed its fangs and gripped the metal, throwing itself back on its haunches.

Alex slid a grenade from his belt and flicked the pin away. It spun across the air, headed for the far door, "Come on, you ugly sack of scum—"

WOOSH!

It flew into the air and made for Alex, who bent his knees against his chest and released the D-Rez into the floating void.

SLAMMM!

His boot kicked away its skewers, forcing it to scream in pain. Alex's fist rammed into the beast's mouth and down its throat. He released the bomb and booted the creature along the bridge, pushing himself to the exit in the process.

"Go on, get out of there," the girl said in his ears.

Biddip-biddip-beep-beeeeeep…

Alex darted through the air and overtook the whizzing grenade pin. The panel on the wall grew larger and larger as he twisted himself into a flying position.

He slammed his glove against the panel as the beep from the crazy creature flat lined.

WOOSH! The door opened into a small, black decompression chamber.

Alex took one, final look at the creature and grabbed the door frame, "Bon voyage, you ugly mother—"

KA-BLAAAAMMMM-MM!

The creature detonated in a thousand, messy pieces as Alex slammed the door shut.

His entire body hit the deck as a cloud of gas thrust from the vents in the wall.

"Decompressing now," the female on the other end of his headgear said. "All good?"

"Yeah, fine," Alex picked himself up from the floor and held his arms out.

SWISH!

The outer door slid open, releasing Alex into the training compound. His HUD recorded a completion time of 87.7.

"Damn it," he flipped his visor up and placed his D-Rez firearm on the table, "Two seconds short of my target."

"But just over two seconds faster than the record, my friend," Oxade applauded with a distinct over-zealousness as he made his way to the table, "Not bad for your first try. Very well done."

"I could have been quicker," Alex removed his helmet to reveal a devastatingly handsome young man with a chiseled jawline and beautiful crystal blue eyes.

Nutrene made the mistake of looking him in the face. She felt her heart flutter, temporarily disabling her ability to speak, "Oh, m-my."

"Hi, I'm Alex."

He offered her his hand to shake. She stared at it for a few seconds, trying to decide if something spectacularly embarrassing might occur if she made contact.

Carefully, she took his hand in hers and melted inside, "I'm, uh, Nutrene. Nutrene Byford."

Alex chuckled and threw her a heart-stopper of a wink. She yanked him forward without warning and ran her hand over his face, much to his surprise.

Her lips pressed against the side of his face, allowing her to whisper something very serious in his ear.

Oxade wasn't surprised by her actions. Nutrene had a way with her colleagues, not least the men.

"All that time dealing with animals," he muttered, "And she's the biggest animal there is."

"I, uh, don't know what to say?"

"Then say nothing. Alex Hughes," she returned the wink and spun around, making damn sure he could see her svelte frame and behind display its perfection.

Oxade sidled up to his new colleague and elbowed him on the arm, "She's something, ain't she?"

"She sure is," Alex blinked.

"She may be a medician. But don't be fooled, my friend," Oxade patted him on the back and walked off, "Just as she saves lives, she takes them away. She's one helluva killing machine."

Chapter 8

A fighter jet opened its landing gears and made its descent toward the air strip.

Oxade, Nutrene, and Alex sat in the back of a white buggy, headed from USARIC's main building.

"So, Minneapolis Two, huh?" Oxade asked over the noise of the engines.

Alex scoured the air field through his shades. The sun burned brightly, adding to the intense heat he felt within his American Star Fleet suit, "That's right, captain."

"How long did you serve?"

"Joined six months ago on the Bering Strait clean-up operation."

"Right," Oxade raised his voice over the noise of the fighter jet touching down on the strip, "Getting rid of the commie bastards from our soil? I hear they're just getting started"

"Something like that," Alex said. "It's going to turn into a real bloodbath, soon."

Nutrene pointed at a spacecraft looming in the distance. Space Opera Charlie. The scaffolding had been removed. The vessel looked ready for action.

"See that?"

"Yes," Alex widened his eyes.

"That's going to be our new home as of next week."

"Opera Charlie?"

"Yup," Nutrene licked her lips and threw him a coquettish smile, "I've heard it gets lonely up in space."

"Aren't there five of us going?"

"That's right, my friend. A reduced service. Skeleton crew, so to speak," Oxade slammed on the back of the driver's seat, "Can't we go any faster? We have a briefing to attend."

"I'm going as fast as I can."

Oxade turned to Alex, "See this idiot? You can't get the staff, these days."

"Why don't you leave him alone?" Alex shouted over the roar of the jet engine, "He's just doing his job."

"If I had my way, all the lackeys would be fitted with Decapidiscs. That'd make them produce a lot faster."

"Decapi—*what?*"

"*Decapidisc,*" Oxade yelled. "The compliance unit. Take your head clean off if you mess around."

"Oh."

USARIC Headquarters
Conference Room

Maar Sheck's holographic representation loomed over the conference table.

Crain McDormand was physically present next to him. His thumbnail sat at the edge of the table, throwing Maar's projection into the room.

"Where are they?"

Crain looked at him apologetically, "Hughes has just finished training. They're on their way."

"What's keeping them?"

"Why, do you have another conference to go to?" Crain smirked with sarcasm.

"Very funny, ass-face," he walked through the conference table and snapped his fingers, "Bring up the recording."

Crain waved his hand over the table. A paused three-dimensional image of Maar stepping out of the back of limousine appeared above the surface.

The door to the conference room opened. Oxade, Nutrene, and Alex walked in and surrounded the table.

"Hello, Maar," Oxade took a seat at the end of the table.

"Oxade Weller and Nutrene Byford, as I live and

breathe," Maar spat with contempt at their tardiness, "Where the hell have you been?"

It wasn't clear which of the two versions of Maar had spoken - was it the paused image, or the transparent one standing in the middle of the table?

"Umm," Oxade clocked the still image, "What's this? Why are you see-through?"

Maar walked through the wooden surface and arrived at the head of the table. He nodded at Crain, "This happened thirty minutes ago. Play the recording."

Crain obliged and clicked his fingers, enabling the playback to proceed. Maar planted his feet on the ground and stepped out of the limousine. Kaoz ushered him toward the entrance to USARIC HQ, "We have the package," he said into his headset.

"Very good, get him inside, quick."

WHOOSH-WHOOSH!

A rocketing noise shot through the air from behind them, "Maar, get down." Kaoz swung his gun around at the front of the limousine.

Before he could open fire, the driver's head exploded, painting the inside of the vehicle a dark red.

"Get down, now," Kaoz shielded himself behind the limousine, looking for the source of the attack. He pressed his microphone to his lips, "This is Kaoz. We are under attack."

"Kaoz," Maar rolled across the ground and looked into blinding sun, "H-Help m-me…"

A dark object whizzed around and blocked the rays from his face., "What i-is that?"

An attack drone buzzed around in the air. It spun its cannons at Maar and blasted him in the chest, killing him instantly.

"Maar," Kaoz pointed his firearm at the drone and shot it out of the air. The hunk of metal crashed to the floor right beside Maar's bleeding body.

A thoroughly befuddled Opera Charlie team stared at the paused image of Maar's dead body.

"But… *how?*" Oxade muttered.

"It wasn't me," Maar walked around the table, unable to contain his anger.

Security officials dragged the decoy body into the reception area and tore the fake skin away from the corpse's face. The man underneath looked nothing like Maar, but was very dead.

"A decoy. His family has been well compensated for their loss."

"Wow. You really can't go anywhere, can you?" Nutrene clocked Crain's thumbnail projecting Maar's image in the room, "Where are you broadcasting from?"

"I'm not telling you that, you stupid woman," Maar stopped in front of his new team and folded his arms. "No one can know my whereabouts. It's for your own safety. Crain, vector scope of Opera Charlie, please."

"Yes, Maar," Crain lifted his hand over the surface of the desk. A vector representation of Space Opera Charlie appeared above the table.

Oxade, Nutrene, and Alex leaned in for a better view.

"I'm happy to report that the board unanimously voted to change Opera Charlie's remit. It is now a search and destroy operation. We've selected the most dedicated and, shall we say, less morally-observant members of USARIC to go to Saturn, find Opera Beta and return our property."

"Your property?" Oxade chuckled to himself.

"Yes, that's right. Our property. We know they decoded Saturn Cry. Anderson helped them."

"Anderson?" Alex kept up the pretense, "Who's that?"

"That dumb animal they took with them," Oxade snapped and turned to Maar, "What's the situation with Opera Beta? Last I heard they went missing?"

"They're still missing. That's why we're sending you up. We know they found Opera Alpha and Zillah's crew. Something seriously awry is going on up there, and I've had just about enough of it. And so have the board, to be perfectly honest, hence their change of heart."

Maar nodded at Crain, who enlarged the top third of the vector scope of Opera Charlie.

"We've scaled down the ship to the bare essentials," Crain

said. "As there are five of you, you'll only need the bare minimum. All search and destroy operations are equipped with the latest technology."

"Five of us?" Oxade looked at Nutrene and Alex, "I only count three?"

"That's right, *five*," Maar said. "Oxade and Alex, can you stand up, please."

"Why?"

"Just do it."

Everyone rose from their chairs and took a step back, confused as to the nature of the instruction.

"So, what do we—"

Oxade's swivel chair spun around. The spider-like metal plate liquefied and formed into one, solid mass.

"What's going on?"

The liquid metal stretched out across the floor. The armrests tilted up and into the air.

Alex's chair performed the same action, only this time, a circular magnetic plate sprung out from its side.

The two melded together and stretched apart like three-day-old chewing gum.

CLUNK-SCHWIPP.

The metallic rope snapped in half, forming two lifelike androids. The fabric from the chair sunk into the metal and pushed out into the shape of a head.

"Wow," Nutrene looked at Oxade for a response. "Is this what I think it is?"

Maar smirked as he moved to the head of the table, "Opera Charlie, meet your fourth and fifth crew members. Poz and Neg Bass."

Poz, the 'male' droid of the duo, stood three-foot-high and looked like an ugly, mini metal beach ball. He tilted his perfectly circular head up at Oxade and blinked his set of peculiar *eyebulbs*.

"Greetings. I am Poz Bass. I will be joining you on Opera Charlie."

"But-but—" Oxade failed to process the marvel of technology standing before him, demanding an introduction, "What *is* this?"

"*This*, as you've seen, is not an inanimate object," Maar said. "Poz and Neg are prototypes of USARIC's latest venture with Manning/Synapse. Death drones. Ruthless killing machines. Now, don't be rude. Shake Poz's hand."

Oxade turned to the droid, this time focusing on his face. A dreadful synthetic skin glistened in the ceiling light. Oxade heard the whirring of Poz's internal mechanism. A very subtle squelching noise followed with every microscopic movement.

"Yeah, put it here," Oxade slammed his palm into Poz's hand. His skin immediately absorbed into the droid's hand.

"Hey, hey, my fingers," Oxade tried to wrench his hand away.

"Ha-ha-ha," Poz released Oxade's hand and trundled over to his counterpart, "I am sorry. I was attempting humor."

Oxade looked at his hand. It was immaculate, as if nothing had happened.

"I f-felt my soul leaving my b-body," Oxade stammered. "What the hell are these things—"

"—We are death drones," explained the pulchritudinous Neg. Affecting a more feminine touch, she slid her arm around Poz and seemed to weld into the side of his body, "Of course, we'd rather have been named something less *killerish*. We are state of the art killing machines, but that's not *all* we are."

SCHLOOOOO—

Neg's entire frame amalgamated into Poz's body, doubling their height as they twinned into each other. Oxade, Alex, and Nutrene were now looking at a fully-formed killing machine. An exo-suit unraveled down their bodies.

"They look like Jaycee, now. Don't they?" Maar smiled at the trio.

STOMP!

The giant droid in the exo-suit stomped forward and spun its hands around, leaning into Oxade's face, "Human?" it asked in its threatening grunt of a voice.

"Y-Yes."

"I thought so," it held out its palm and closed its fingers, forming a blue-hued fist.

THWOCK!

The hulking mercenary punched Oxade in chest, catapulting him across the conference table. Crain moved out of his path as he landed on his ass and whined.

"Oh, for goodness' sake—" Nutrene jumped behind her chair and focused her monocle on Alex, "I'm not going to Saturn with *them*."

"Get up, Oxade," Maar said. "You're the captain. You're meant to be setting an example."

"Y-You c-can't expect us to go on Opera Charlie with *them*?" He climbed to his feet and brushed himself down. The USARIC logo had torn away from its stitches due the violent nature of the punch.

Maar stood behind Oxade and addressed the team, "I think the five of you will get the job done just fine."

SCHLOOOOOOP!

Poz and Neg twisted into each other in a miasma of metal and pulled themselves apart. They trundled to the table like a pair of scary Siamese twins and pointed at the vector scope of Opera Charlie.

"Is this our new home?" they asked in tandem.

"Yes, it is," Maar said.

"We go to Saturn and kill everything."

Maar nodded, "Yes, but bring Anderson, the cat, back with you. Safe and sound."

"What if she doesn't want to come back?"

Maar made eyes at them, "Listen very carefully to me. Oxade is in charge. He's the captain. So, you do as he says."

"Yes," they said.

"Nutrene is the medician. If something happens to any of you, like you're injured or seriously hurt, she can fix you. Right?"

"Right."

"And Alex Hughes is in charge of the weapons on level two. Not that you guys need a gun, of course."

Poz slammed his elbow into his own ribs. His forearm broke out like an accordion to reveal a triple barreled canon, "We have our own guns."

"I know you do," Maar winked at Neg, who pressed her hands together and fluttered her metallic eyebulbs at him,

"Your sister, here, is a lethal little minx, too. I've no doubt you'll be able to complete the job."

"Excuse me, Maar," Alex said. "There's something I don't understand."

"What is it, Hughes?"

"Well, if Poz and Neg are *death drones*, why do you need us humans to go with them? They don't need oxygen. Resources wouldn't deplete as fast?"

Maar sighed and made the mistake of touching Poz on his shiny head. An electric spark frazzled the holographic image momentarily.

"We made a mistake with Opera Beta. They're all Androgyne Series Three, except for Haloo Ess, the botanist and, of course, Anderson herself. We won't be making the same mistake again."

"What's the mistake?"

"Sending Series Three units on a manned mission. They went missing. They reported seventy-two hours' worth of oxygen, not that it matters to the majority of the crew. But they have the answer."

"If I may add, Maar," Crain interjected. "The whole idea of using Androgynes on a manned mission to Saturn was to preserve USARIC's bottom line. A minimal financial outlay."

"What does that mean?" Nutrene asked.

"Quite simply, it was the cheapest option. All we need to know now is what happened to them. Quickly, and quietly."

Alex shook his head and took a final look at Pox and Neg, "So you're sending humans up with the new generation?"

"That's right."

"And you want us to kill everything that moves?"

Maar and Crain nodded with a quiet solemnity.

"You leave in four days' time," Maar waved the Opera Charlie vector image away from the table, "It's a three-year round trip. I suggest you put your affairs in order as soon as possible."

Ten Minutes Later...

The men's bathroom.

Alex splashed cold water on his face. He squeezed his eyes shut and looked at his face in the mirror. A fine USARIC logo imprint loomed in the bottom right-hand corner.

"You look like hell," his reflection moved its lips as he spoke. "A year and a half to Saturn and we might not find anything."

Biddip-biddip…

"Damn it."

He rolled up his sleeve and looked at his forearm. The Individimedia ink sluiced around and from three blinking dots. He took one last look at his face and thumbed the ink to his wrist.

"This is Alex."

"It's me," the voice of a woman came through the pricks in his wrist, "Are you alone?"

"I'm in the bathroom."

"How did the briefing go?"

"Yeah, it went fine," Alex turned to the stalls. Two of the five were locked but he knew he was alone, "Listen, I can't talk right now. I'm still with the crew."

"You're definitely *on*, though? Right?"

"Yes, I'm on—"

CLUNK.

The door to the bathroom opened. Oxade walked up to the floating urinal concourse in the middle of the room.

"Hey, good buddy," he said to Alex. "All set?"

"Yeah, *amaziant*, thanks," Alex pressed his right palm over his left wrist. A muffled question from the woman warbled through his fingers.

"Who you talking to, there?"

"Oh, you know," Alex fake-smirked and made his way over to the hand drier, "Women trouble. She's always calling."

"Ha. Tell me about it," Oxade unzipped his front and proceeded to relieve himself, "Seems you have an admirer. Nutrene's got the hots for you."

"Has she?"

"Don't act like you haven't *not* noticed."

"Hmm," Alex turned to the drier. A bead of sweat formed across his brow and rolled down the side of his face. He spread the pinpricks on his wrist and dipped his left hand into the drier. He couldn't afford Oxade to overhear his call...

Interstate 45
North Texas Border

Grace had the face of an angel. Her long, flowing brunette hair raced down the back of her combat fatigues.

She pushed her finger against her ear and tried to keep herself steady in the passenger seat of the 4x4 as it raced along the uneven ground.

"Siyam, *please*," she said to the driver. "Can you at least *try* to keep us steady?"

"I am, I am," Siyam, the African-American driver, said. He focused on his rear view mirror. "You want us to get pulled over?"

"Sorry, Alex," she returned to the cables streaking out from her wrist, "I didn't hear what you said. Can you say again—"

SWWIIISSSHHHHHHHHH!

A deafening, prolonged thunder rocketed through her ears. The frequency forced her to snap the earpiece from her head and fling it to her lap.

"Jesus Christ!" she screamed. "What's that noise?"

Siyam threw Grace a look of anger as he stepped on the gas, "What's up with him?"

"He said he was in the bathroom, and then this—Ah, my ears feel like they're bleeding," she fumbled for the device and pulled the wire from her wrist.

"Maybe he can't talk?" Siyam said. "If he says he can't talk, then he can't talk."

"No, I need to know he's okay. I need to know the mission is on," she slung the earpiece against her head and spoke into her wrist. "Alex? This is Grace. Do you read me?"

"Yes—" his voice chimed in to a static rumble, "Everything went well, but I can't talk right now."

"Did you pass the training? Please tell me you passed at least."

"Yes, I did," Alex snapped and hushed his voice, "Where are you?"

Grace looked over her shoulder and watched the border control center disappear from view, "We've just passed border control. About five miles from Corsicana."

"What happened?"

"Oh, the usual," Grace said, "Those Nazis at border control practically performed a cavity search on Siyam."

"That figures. Racist scumbags," Alex snorted through her earpiece, "Any news on where the subjects are headed?"

Grace grabbed Siyam's left arm and ran her fingers over the ink.

"Hey, what are you—"

"—Shut up for a minute and keep your eyes on the road. I need to look at something."

She held his arm up and looked at the white ink break apart into thirty separate dots.

"Ten miles south-southwest," Grace said.

The screen on the dashboard of the 4x4 showed thirty flashing dots swarming toward a dotted line, "We know from Moses' absorption effort in the compound that they're chipped. We have their locations on screen."

"Okay."

"I just hope we can find them in time. Alive, ideally."

"Be careful when you get there. USARIC have reprogrammed them. You don't know how they'll react."

Alex pushed through the USARIC reception area and headed for the entrance. An iron bust of Dimitri Vasilov took center stage in the middle of the area.

He glanced at it as he walked into the bright, clear sunshine. The warmth of the sun rays calmed him down despite the noise coming from the launching jets on the airstrip.

"I can't believe this is where Denny took the shot."

"Are you there right now?" Grace asked.

"Yes."

"I made contact with the kid. Jamie."

"Oh, really?" Alex seemed surprised, "You found him?"

"Yeah, there must be a million Jamie Andersons on *Viddy Media*. Struck gold on the hundred and twentieth one. You'd have thought those Brits—"

"—Did he confirm Anderson's involvement with Opera Beta?"

"Yes, he did."

"Good," Alex said with relief, "that tallies with what I heard at the briefing. Both ends covered. That's better than substantiated fact, now."

"Anderson took Bisoubisou's place. She's up there with them."

"I *knew* it," Alex punched the air with excitement. A gaggle of USARIC officials on their smoke break looked over at him in bemusement, "Good work, Grace. That's exactly what we thought."

"I know, right? If Beta's report is correct, then Jelly is the one who decoded Saturn Cry. They're in receipt of the answer. We just have to hope they're alive."

Alex turned away from the spluttering officials and caught the magnificent Space Opera Charlie spacecraft standing proud within its scaffolding in the horizon.

"Five more days, Alex," she whispered from his wrist.

"You got that right."

He took in the sheer enormity of the spacecraft standing in the distance, "Five more days..."

Chapter 9

The Control Deck
Space Opera Beta - Level One

Space Opera Beta hung in the vacuum of space surrounded by zillions of tiny, bright stars. A bright and vibrant Enceladus drifted behind it. The last of its pink light blossomed against the universe's canvas and swallowed in on itself.

Nothing left. The universe was serene.

Saturn's surface took up the majority of the view through the windshield by the flight deck, appearing to oversee the vessel like a maternal juggernaut. Her rings no longer revolved.

The communications panel lay dormant, a giant husk of its former self. The emergency strip lights across the ground provided the only indication of life or action aboard the spacecraft.

The communications console rumbled to life. Its light snapped on. The processor fired up as if it was struggling to awaken from a deathly slumber.

WHIRRR-POP.

A shower of orange sparks blew out from the mainframe. Four sides of a rectangle fizzed a few inches away from it. Its outline stormed through the air and produced a full hologram of a book.

Manuel had awoken.

"Oh, my," he fluttered around and wrestled with the pages between his covers.

FRII-II-ITT.

The sheets shuffled together like a deck of playing cards. He slapped his covers together and fanned every page out like an extended accordion.

"Ah, that's better."

He shifted around to the communications panel, "Ooh, we've left Pink Symphony, I'm happy to report."

The holographic tome opened out and cast a beam of green data light at the communications panel.

Each circuit within the mainframe whirred as they fired up.

"This is Manuel. Autopilot of Space Opera Beta. Open communication channels, ports one through one-zero-fifteen."

The screen on the panel snapped to life.

"Assess current location."

A slew of white text ran up the screen.

"Feeling better, I see."

BEEP.

The screen displayed its update:

USARIC S.O.B. SIT-REP_
Date: September 1st, 2122
Location: Enceladus (orbit)
Engine & Payload: Operational
Thrusters (Auto & Manual): Operational
Communication channels: Open
Distance to Earth (miles): 750m
*Communication incoming_*

"I see you've survived whatever happened to us. I thought we'd never see each other again," Manuel shut his beam off and fluttered up against the screen, "Twenty-one-twenty-two? Did we really skip three years? Feels like it was just yesterday. I guess to us it was, actually. Hmm."

He folded the edge of one of his pages and brushed over

the last entry, "Communication incoming? Run banked communications."

The text bled out into a white flat line. A mountainous waveform sprawled across the screen from the right-hand side.

Static blew from the speakers as the flat line wriggled around. It curved up as Oxade's voice spoke.

"This is Captain Oxade Weller of the rescue vessel Space Opera Charlie. Do you read me?"

Manuel flipped over two pages and copied the waveform across the blank slate, "Keep playing."

"I repeat, this is Captain Oxade Weller of USARIC's Space Opera Charlie *rescue* program. Contacting Opera Beta on a frequency of zero, five, four, niner. Does anyone read me?"

Manuel slapped his pages together with applause.

"Oh, *my*. We're going to be rescued," he pressed his pages back and transmitted a beam back to the panel.

"Speech-to-text."

As Manuel spoke, the panel transcribed his message in white text, "This is *The Manuel*, autopilot of Space Opera Beta. Can confirm connection. Crew are in hyper-sleep. Oxygen conservation in process. Ess-oh-ess. Please confirm bridging instructions. Send."

The text appeared on the screen and then vanished.

"Thank God. How very thoughtful. Good old USARIC, sending a ship to come and take us home."

Hyper-Sleep Arena
Space Opera Beta

The five occupied hyper-sleep pods buzzed to life. Their transparent plastic panels slid open one by one.

Tripp, Wool, Jaycee, Tor, and Jelly lay asleep with peaceful looks on their faces.

Manuel burst to life by the energy tube and slapped his pages together, "Guys, wake up. I have some *amaziant* news."

"Huh?" Tripp was the first to wake up. The others shuffled around and groaned, half awake, "Are we dead?"

"No, quite the contrary," Manuel zoomed over to Tripp and lowered himself to his face, "We're being rescued."

"Rescued?"

"Yes, Opera Charlie is hours away. They are here to rescue us."

Tripp gripped the edge of his pod and jumped to the floor, "That's great—Whoa," he yelped and lost his footing. The disorientation hadn't quite left his body.

"Be careful, Tripp. Take it easy. We don't want you falling over and hurting yourself before our visitors arrive."

"No, you're right. I'll take it *real* slow for a while," he said." Where are we?"

"We are no longer on Pink Symphony. According to the geo-scan we have returned to our solar system, just out of Saturn's orbit."

Tripp closed his eyes and breathed a sigh of relief. He looked over his shoulder and caught Wool and Jaycee open their eyes and yawn. He turned back to Manuel on the verge of crying for joy, "Thank God."

The book took a bow, "It's on my to-do list if we ever meet him. Or her."

"Did we make contact with Charlie?"

"In a manner of speaking."

"What's that meant to mean?"

"They left us a message—"

"—Right, did you send one back—?"

"—I was just going to say… *yes*, I did. They should have received it by now. No response so far, but by the time we return to control I think we can commence bridging procedures."

Tripp stood to his feet and felt his jaw. Baldron's replacement cheek had settled in nicely during the hyper-sleep. He felt like a million bucks once again.

"Good idea. We'll get everyone oriented and ready to disembark."

"Certainly," Manuel threw a beam at each of the pods and pulled the front hatches down, "The question is, what do we do about Opera Beta? We have forty-eight hours left on oxygen and general supplies."

Tripp watched Jaycee and Wool start to wake up.

"We may have to abandon Beta, depending on her state. I'm sure between us all we can make it back to Earth."

"I knew you said *disembark* a few seconds ago," Manuel muttered and ducked his head, "But if you do that, I'll be left on my—"

"—Everyone, can I have your attention?" Tripp ignored Manuel and clapped his hands together. Jelly rolled around in her bed. She didn't want to wake up.

"Ugh, did we get off that godforsaken disc?" Wool muttered.

"Yes, we did. Guys, I have some good news."

"What?" Jaycee asked.

"We're going home."

The crew didn't believe what they'd just heard.

"Are you serious, right now?" Wool asked.

"Yes, I am. I'm going to the control deck with Manuel to make the arrangements. I suggest you do whatever it is you need to do to prepare."

"Comms are back on?" Tor asked, somewhat giddy with excitement, "Can we send messages?"

"Yes," Manuel said. "Comms are fully operational, now."

Tripp walked to the door in just his underwear. Wool snorted and sighed, "Tripp?"

"Yeah?"

"Put your pants on first?"

"Oh," he looked down at his bare stomach and legs, "Yes, good idea."

An anxious Tor stepped out from his pod, "What does this mean for me?"

Tripp approached the slider on the wall, "What do you mean 'what does this mean for you'?"

"Well, if we're going home..." Tor thought out loud, arriving at the obvious before the others had a chance to dish it to him, "I, uh, can't go back home."

"You damn well can and will, *dickhead*," Jaycee planted his bare feet on the ground, grabbed the edge of the pod, and pushed himself upright, "USARIC will deal with you properly."

"Guys, look," Tor said. "No one knows anything. Please, I beg you. Don't say anything. Don't turn me in."

"That's rich coming from *you*," Wool spat with sarcasm, "You're lucky Jaycee didn't switch you off and wear your reproductive organs as a bracelet."

Tor sighed, close to tears. A pathetic sight, aided none by the fact he was standing in his briefs, "Please?"

"It's out of our control now, *good buddy*," Tripp patted the creases on his inner-suit pants, "You made your bed. You sleep in it."

Wool cleared her throat and held her head in her hands, "God, my head is pounding. My guts feel like they've been through a grinder," She held her arm over her bra in a bid to protect her modesty, "Did I hear you correctly?"

"Yes, Wool. We're going home," Tripp tore his eyes away from her chest and slipped the top half of his suit over his head, "Better get ready."

Wool scanned the room. All but one crew member was accounted for, "Where's Bonnie?"

Everyone looked at their feet. They'd remembered what happened and were as stunned as each other that Wool hadn't.

"She didn't make it," Tripp unraveled his inner-suit down his front and slipped on his boots, "Don't you remember?"

Wool stared at the ground and bit her lip, "Yes. I remember now."

Images from the battle on Pink Symphony flooded into her brain. She took a deep breath, puzzled by her feelings on the matter.

One crew member remained unaccounted for.

"Where's Jelly—?"

CRREEEAAAAAKKK.

All eyes averted to the cat's hyper-sleep pod.

CLUNK-CLINK-CLINK-CLINK.

Four Titanium infinity claws rose out from the pod and pressed their way across the ceramic edge.

"Me… *owww…*"

Wool held her chest with amazement, "Jelly, honey?"

Tor, and Jaycee backed up and watched a huge furry arm

lift up from within the chamber.

"That… was a *long* sleep," came a husky voice from within. The infinity claws on her right hand pressed against the adjacent wall of the pod.

"Oh m-my *God…*" Wool took three cautious steps forward and risked invading Jelly's privacy, "Honey?"

"Mommy? Is that you?" came a sultry, female voice of an adult. "Did we die?"

Jaycee and Tor remained still, as did Tripp. Would Wool approach whatever it was inside the pod? If she did, would whatever lay inside freak out and attack her?

"Wool, be careful," Tripp whispered. "She's still a cat, after all."

"It's okay," Wool focused on the pod and crept forward, "Honey? We're not dead. You can come out, now. We're going home."

"Are we?"

"Yes," Wool just about managed to squeeze the word out of her mouth, "Why d-don't you come out from the pod?"

"It wasn't this small when I went in," Jelly whined, "It's shrunk."

She sat up straight and faced the others.

The first thing they noticed was her face. No longer an innocent and sweet adolescent half-cat. Her jawline and whiskers had thickened. The fur on her face had all but fallen away.

The second thing they noticed was her bust. Jelly was well-endowed, by all accounts.

"My tummy's stuck," she growled and lifted her top half out from the unfeasibly tight oblong that contained the rest of her body, "Ah, that's much better."

"Honey, y-you're—" Wool couldn't finish her sentence. Jelly's beautiful tail swished out and slapped against the side of the pod.

"Jesus Christ," Tor said. "How did that pod even contain her?"

Tripp shook his head, taking in Jelly's evolution, "I don't know, I—"

"—Meow," Jelly swung her left hind leg out from the pod

and slammed her heel against the ground, sending a shudder across the ground. Everyone felt it and gasped.

"Just one…. More…"

SCHTOMP.

Her right heel dug into the floor. The muscles in her arms flexed through her fur, "Ngggg…"

She straightened her arms and pushed herself to her feet. Her head almost hit the ceiling.

Tripp, Jaycee, and Tor's eyes tilted up and took in her new size.

Wool started crying at the sight of the girl's back, "Honey…"

Jelly swished her tail. Her long, orange-brown locks fell over her shoulder blades as she looked up at the ceiling.

CRUNCH-CRICK!

She rolled her shoulders and moved her head, cracking the kinks out of her neck and shoulders, "Feels good to be out of there."

Jelly stood seven-and-a-half feet in height. She appeared to be wider in frame, too - the technical equivalent of a somewhat over-sized adult female. Not an ounce of fat anywhere on her.

"Jelly, how are you feeling?" Tripp asked.

Her cat ears twitched. She moved her arms in front of her chest and faced away to preserve her modesty, "I feel *great.*"

Tor looked down at her behind. He followed the swishing of her tail around with his eyes, "B-But but…"

Jelly turned back to them. Her curvaceous frame and trim legs were an astonishing sight to behold.

A truly exquisite vision.

Then, the bulge in her stomach came into view as she completed her turn. She held her claws over her belly.

"That's one helluva *pussy,*" Jaycee muttered. For the first time in his life he felt threatened - scared, even. A much bigger being shared the room with him, now. Anyone with decent vision could see that Jelly could kick the guy around the room and have him for lunch.

"Hey, don't talk about her like that," Wool said. "Look at

her. You think this is what she wanted?"

"I didn't mean *pussy* in a derogatory way. She *is* a cat, after all. I meant a *pussycat*—"

"—Shut up," Jelly roared at the pair with fierce volume, "Both of you."

Tripp stood to attention and gulped at her instruction.

Jelly's chest heaved in and out with anger. She extended her first infinity claw on her right paw and pointed at Jaycee, "You."

"Me?"

"Yeah, you," she said. Her feminine voice was huskier than ever before, "Did you just call me a pussy?"

"No, I d-didn't mean it like—"

"—You want me to show you how cute I am?" Jelly kicked the side of her pod in anger, "Come here and I'll show you how easy I am to pet, you massive, metal turd."

"I'm sorry."

"Good," Jelly stepped forward and loomed over the petrified man, "Then show me my respect. Bow down."

"Wh-what?"

"Show me my respect," she repeated. "Bow down."

Jaycee looked to Tripp for a get-out. Not only was the attempt unsuccessful, it also angered Jelly even further.

"What are you looking at him for?"

"I, uh—"

"—I'm not playing around, Jaycee. Show me my respect and *bow down*."

"Okay, okay," Jaycee held out his arms and fell on one knee, "I'm doing it. I'm sorry—"

"—Don't you *dare* apologize to me, Nayall. Just do as I say."

Jaycee kept his mouth shut and hung his head in front of her. A giant purr erupted in her abdomen as she looked down at him.

"I'm bigger than you, now. Don't ever forget it. Stand up."

He did as instructed and arched his back, wondering what was coming next.

Jelly turned away and made for the door. "By the way,

Jaycee?"

"Yes?"

She nodded at the slider on the wall and pointed to her stomach, "Mind if I borrow one of your exo-suits? Bonnie's kid's jeans are no use to me, anymore."

"No, not at all."

"I don't think the others' inner-suits will fit me."

"I agree," he said, thankful that he was still alive, "You go ahead and take whatever you want."

She made her way through the door, "Thanks, *human*. See you on the control deck."

SWISH-SCHUNT.

The door slid shut, leaving the others beyond dumbfounded. Tripp looked to the others and thought twice about his next sentence.

"Uh, I guess she's in charge now?"

Tor tapped him on the shoulder, "Good luck telling her otherwise, *good buddy*."

***

Jelly stormed along the level three walkway and kept her head down. The protruding bars across the upper sections of the wall threatened to smack her in the face as she moved past them.

A growl whirled inside her stomach. She stopped in her tracks and pressed her claws along at her belly.

"Miew…" she cried. Her knees nearly buckled. She pressed the pads on her palms against them, trying her best to contain the pink, glowing orb within, "God… I feel sick…"

She managed to turn the corner take hold of the staircase railing. The end of her claws scraped against her wrist, slicing off the ends of a few strands of fur.

BLOICK!

Her hips thrust so hard she nearly tumbled backwards down the stairs. She pulled herself forward and slid down a couple of steps. A whimpering came from within her throat as she spluttered and reached the last step.

"Guhhh…" she stretched her mouth wide open, along

with her eyes, "Oh my tummy… ugh…"

She twisted her body around and planted her behind on the top step, accidentally trapping her tail. Her waist tilted forward and released, "Ugghhh..."

Her heels dug into the third step, trying to kick the intense pain away.

"*Oh God*, not now—"

GRUMBLE… GROOOWWWL…

Jelly held her breath. The pain and rumbling in her stomach abated and settled down. She breathed a sigh of relief.

CLANG.

Sparks flicked up from her claws as they scraped against the railing. She hoisted herself back to her feet and stormed up the next set of stairs.

The Control Deck

Space Opera Beta - Level One

Jelly made a beeline for the flight deck.

Manuel paused his work on the communications panel when he saw her enter the room, "Jelly, you're here."

"Yeah," she kept her focus on the flight deck screen as she approached it, "I heard comms are back on. Patch me into N-Gage. Now."

Manuel tilted his covers in confusion, "Oh *my*, you have grown."

She pulled the chair out from under the desk and spun it around, "No," she quipped, "Do you really think so?"

"Yes, I do *think so*. Your height. Your *frame*, if I can call it that?"

"Stop looking at me like some kind of weirdo," Jelly lifted her tail the way female humans hitch their skirts and slumped into the chair, "Patch me into N-Gage. Anderson household, Chrome Valley. Do it now."

"But, we're awaiting rescue—"

"—Hey, Manuel?" she snapped.

"Yes?"

"Do you want me to scratch your eyes out and hump the

sockets?"

"Umm, *no*?"

Puzzled, he fluttered further away from her, "It's just that we're awaiting contact with Opera Charlie to establish—"

"—Aww, God *damn* it," Jelly slammed the flight deck with her claws and spun her chair around, "You're not listening to me. I want you to patch me into N-Gage. Now."

"But I—"

"—Make no mistake, you floating piece of crap. I want to speak to Jamie and tell him I love and miss him. Not that I have to explain my actions to you."

Manuel tried to calm her down.

"Miss Anderson. I'm fully aware that you, like the others, miss your family. But if we connect to Earth it could jeopardize our bridge with Charlie. We must keep the channel free for—"

"—What's the first rule?"

"Uh, I wasn't aware there was a *first* rule, Miss Anderson?"

"Oh, then let me enlighten you. The first rule is I get what I want. Everything that ever was, is, and ever *will* be is mine. All mine. Do you understand what I've just said?"

"Uh, yes?" Manuel lowered himself, hoping not to get swiped by her vicious infinity claws.

"I want to see Jamie. Now patch me in."

"Okay, okay… don't have *kittens*," Manuel said as the color drained from his covers.

"Har-har, very funny," Jelly stopped herself from giggling at Manuel's inspired quip, "Let's see how funny you are when I tear your covers off, comedian."

"Patching you in now. Please be quick."

"I'll take as long as I want, you encyclopedic-*head*."

"Oh, come now, Miss Anderson. That was uncalled for."

Jelly threatened to push herself off the chair and punch the communications panel.

"Shut up and do your job or I'll tear out your pages and Origami them into a baseball bat and smack you around the covers with it."

"*Fine*," Manuel paused in mid-air, enabling the flight deck screen to come to life, "Here we go."

"*Thank* you," Jelly turned to the screen and briefly caught a glimpse of her own face in the glass. She didn't recognize herself at all. The girl who'd battled on Pink Symphony was no longer present. Instead, a beautiful half-cat looked at her. The screen beeped and displayed white text.

N-Gage

Anderson Residence
Chrome Valley, United Kingdom.
Dialing…

"Come on, come on," she spat, impatiently, "Answer, Jamie."

The screen wobbled around and flushed into white static. A shape of a man's face formed within the dots.

Tony, Emily's husband, appeared on screen and looked into the lens, "Hello. Who's this?"

Jelly shook her head and winced at Tony's face, "Who's *this?*"

"Sorry, who are you trying to reach?" Tony said.

"I want to see Jamie."

Tony's face peered against the screen as he tried to ascertain who, exactly, this strange half-cat, half-women was, "Who are you?"

"I want Jamie. Put Jamie on."

"Not until you tell me who you are," Tony looked under the screen and then back at Jelly, "USARIC?"

"My name is Jelly *Anderson*."

Tony raised his eyebrows in amazement, "*You're* J-Jelly Anderson?"

"Yes. Put Jamie on."

"I've heard a lot about you."

"Don't care. I want Jamie."

"He's not here, I'm afraid," Tony whispered. "He's at school."

Jelly's face fell, fueled with anger. She tapped the side of the screen with her claw as if trying to goad a mouse, "No. No, I want Jamie."

"I'm sorry," Tony said. "If you call in a few hours when he's home, I'll let him know you—"

"—I want Jamie," Jelly burst into tears and clenched her fist.

KER-SMASH!

She punched through the screen and smashed the glass, severing the connection. "Agggghhhh!" She took the screen's wires in her paw and tore them out like a bunch of stringy intestines. The force yanked the screen from the desk. It whipped off the deck and crashed to the floor. Sparks and jolts of spent electricity whizzed into the air, underscoring her juvenile-like sobs.

The color came back to Manuel as he whirred back to life, "All done?"

"No," Jelly wept and stomped her feet on the ground in a tantrum, "He wasn't there."

"Oh, I'm sorry—"

"—What's all this shouting?" Tripp walked into the control deck and immediately spotted the wreckage on the floor, "What happened?"

He looked up and saw the torn wires and cables hanging across Jelly's infinity claws, "Jelly?"

"What?"

"Did you do this?"

"Yes. *Bad* screen."

"You can't go around damaging USARIC property like this. They'll dock our wages if there's any damage done."

"So?"

Tripp crouched down and scooped the battered monitor into his arms. The wires streaked from the shattered glass a few meters away in Jelly's claws.

"Jelly. Let go of the wires."

"No."

"Jelly, I'm the captain of this ship. You have to obey me."

She tugged taut on the wires and refused to let go, "*Mine.*"

"No, Jelly. *Not* yours. Let go of the wires. I need to get this screen fixed."

"*Mine,*" Jelly coiled the metal connector at the end of each strand around her wrist. She wrapped each infinity claw around it and tugged it back to her hip, forcing Tripp to walk toward her.

"I'm not going to say it again, you bad girl. This is a direct order. Let go of the wires."

"No," she reached across the taut wires with her other paw and gripped them, pulling him closer still, "It's mine."

"Look at it. It's useless. What do you want a broken screen for?"

"Don't care. It's *mine*."

Tripp dropped the broken device to the floor. Jelly's elbows hit the flight deck due to the lack of pull.

"*Fine*. You want a broken flight screen and a fistful of wires? You got it."

He let go of the cables and turned to Manuel in a huff.

"Update on Charlie, please."

"Miss Anderson used the frequency to call home. I'm afraid if they had attempted to make contact, we would have missed it."

"Why did you let her make the call?"

"She threatened to scratch my eyes out and make love to the sockets—"

"—Hump them, actually," Jelly corrected him.

"That's right. She threatened to remove my eyes and hump the—"

"—You don't even *have* eyes, you dummy," Tripp spat, about ready to explode with anger, "Manuel, you can't let Anderson tell you what to do. She's not in charge—"

"—Pardon my forwardness, Tripp. But didn't you just cave in to her demands seconds ago?"

Tripp watched Manuel indicate the battered screen. He knew the book was right. His dignity begged to differ. An ill-advised retort formed in two seconds and flew out of Tripp's mouth before his brain had a chance to give it the green light.

"That's not the point."

"Miew—" Jelly acted the sweet, innocent pet.

"You shut up, too," Tripp kicked the communications panel in anger, "You've been nothing but trouble since you came back from that... *thing*."

"What thing?"

"After you disappeared on Pink Symphony and went swimming," Tripp yelled. "You've changed, you know that? Nothing but a spoiled little brat. The others are scared of you, now. You're walking all over them. But not me, Anderson. I'm not scared of you."

He stopped screaming and caught his breath. The pause allowed the reality of the situation to flood his mind.

"God *damn* it, I'm trying to talk sense into a *cat*," he muttered. "We must have died. I'm in purgatory, that's the only explanation. I'm an Androgyne. A robot telling off a household cat who's turned into a woman."

"Miew…" Jelly whimpered, apologetically. No English spoken, but the tone said it all. She felt sorry for him.

"What are you saying now?"

"I'm sorry, Tripp."

"Really?"

She shook her head and wagged her tail, "No. Not really. But I know you humans like to be told sorry."

"I should have figured," Tripp sighed and pressed his hands against the comms panel, "Jelly?"

"Yes, *human*?"

"Don't make judgments like that until you have all the facts," he blurted, mourning his entire existence, "Do me a favor?"

"Do I *have* to?"

"No."

"Then I don't want to," She licked her lips and yawned in his face.

"I admire your honesty," he muttered just loud enough to for her to hear.

"I've never lied in my entire life," Jelly dug her tongue into the crook in her gums, "I don't even know how to lie. I know you humans do, though. I've seen it with my own eyeballs."

"With your own *eyes*, Jelly."

"All of them, yes."

"Okay, you won't apologize. I get it. You're a cat. You don't give a rat's ass—"

"—I can catch a rat and give you its ass as a trophy—"

"—No, no," Tripp gave up the ghost and turned to Manuel, "That's not what I—It's a turn of phrase. Means you don't care."

Jelly didn't feel the need to respond. Tripp, once again, was spot on with his assessment - and she wasn't going to correct him. She genuinely *didn't* give a rat's ass about his feelings.

"And to be quite honest I'm starting to know how you feel."

"Miew," she offered, politely.

"Stop talking," Tripp prepared himself for action. Work needed doing, feelings be damned. He snapped his fingers at Manuel.

"Jaycee is at Weapons and Armory. Wool's at Medix. Can we try to establish comms with Charlie once again, please? Provide something of a salutation for their arrival?"

"Certainly, Tripp."

Jelly rose out of her chair, "I need the bathroom."

"Yes, go and get ready. There's a good girl," Tripp lifted the keyboard and hit the return key, "Manuel, I'm going to my quarters to get ready. I've advised the others to do the same. In the meantime, commence connection to Opera Charlie on a frequency of zero, four five, niner—"

SPRIIIIISHHH…

Tripp turned around, slowly, hoping the sound coming from the corner of the control deck wasn't what he feared it would be.

No such luck.

Jelly crouched in the corner and relieved herself all over the floor. He couldn't help but sneer and lament the fate of the universe.

"*Really?*"

Jelly shrugged and continued her business with a 'when you gotta go, you gotta go,' look on her furry adult face.

"Unbelievable," Tripp shook his head in dismay and walked out.

Chapter 10

USARIC Data Point
Space Opera Charlie
Days traveled: 545
Distance to Enceladus: 178,616 miles

The Hyper-Sleep Chamber
Level Five

A low hum crept around the chamber. It dispelled an otherwise perfect silence. The lights snapped on, illuminating the circular quarters.

Three hyper-sleep pods fanned out like a star from the central feeding column.

The first of the three pods shimmied to life. The screen blanketing its occupier slid into its housing.

WHIZ-WHIR.

A pair of eyebulbs blinked, "Captain?" Its squeaky voice woke Oxade from his slumber.

He opened his eyes and immediately squeezed them shut, shifting his body around the pod's foam interior, "Oh, God. My head."

"It'll take some time to get oriented."

Oxade pressed his elbows onto the fabric and lifted the top half of his body upright. Poz Bass, one half of the death drone duo, spun his head around three-hundred-and-sixty-degrees.

"Welcome to the vicinity of Enceladus."

"Are we there?"

"Yes, five-hundred-and-forty-five days of sleep," Poz extended his rope-like arm and thumped the glass case on Nutrene's pod. She didn't react, "Manuel-2 asked us to wake you up for debriefing ahead of the others."

"Okay."

Oxade threw his legs over the side of the pod and placed his bare feet on the ground. Poz forgot that his captain was only wearing a pair of briefs He looked away in shame.

"Hey, it's okay, Poz. We're all guys together," Oxade stood to his feet and gripped the oxygen tube attached to his pod. His balance was all over the place, "This is going to take some getting used to."

"I respect your modesty, Oxade," Poz trundled over to Alex's pod and pressed his 'nose' - which resembled more a mini ventilation shaft - against the screen, "Look at him. Fast asleep."

"What did you and Neg do to pass the time?" Oxade ran his fingertips over his five o'clock shadow as he stared in the mirror.

"We played chess for a while," Poz chirped. "I won, of course."

"Of course," Oxade cleared his throat and opened the slider next to the mirror. His enhanced leather USARIC mercenary jacket floated inside, "I'd expect nothing less."

"Men are much better at games than women, aren't they?"

Oxade threw his arms into the jacket sleeves. The five letters in his name lit up on the outer part of his upper right arm, "Well, technically, you and Neg are *both* sexes," he said as he reached into his pockets.

"Don't patronize me," Poz moved his head away from Alex's pod and watched his captain unfold his gloves, "We are both, yet we are neither."

"You're vicious little bastards," Oxade finished, snapping his gloves onto his hands, "How did you get on with Manuel-2?"

"Oh, she and Pure Genius cheated. Destroyed me in five

moves—"

"—No, *not* in chess, you dummy," Oxade removed a belt from the cupboard and strapped it around his waist, "I mean generally."

"Neg is at the control deck with Manuel-2. They're trying to communicate with Opera Beta."

"I want an update," Oxade fanned his fingers out on both hands and pushed them down his thighs. A tight synthetic material unraveled from his waist, down his thighs, past his knees and secured around his ankles.

"We found what we are looking for. We want to bring you up to speed before the others awake."

Oxade snapped his fingers "Suits me. Is it bad news?"

"I'd say so, yes."

Oxade made the mistake of patting Poz on the back. The metal crept along his glove for a second and fizzed up a mini electrical storm, "Oww."

"It's better that you don't touch me."

"I've been out of action for the best part of two years," Oxade made for the door and took a final glance at Alex and Nutrene's hyper-sleep pods, "I dunno why they bothered with two separate pods."

"What are you implying, Captain?" Poz couldn't process the funny quip.

"Nothing," Oxade returned to the door, "Okay, my messed-up friend. Let's go and see Manuel-2. We'll wake the two lovebirds up after the debrief."

Control Deck
Space Opera Charlie

Opera Charlie's control deck was of similar build and shape as Opera Beta's, only on a smaller scale. The flight panel stood in front of the windshield. It offered a glorious view of Saturn and the surrounding galaxy-scape.

Oxade's acclimation had all but been resolved, "Right, where is he?" he asked Poz, who followed behind.

"They're here, somewhere."

Oxade noticed something unfamiliar and out of place resting against the wall by the communications deck. A five-foot-high slab of metal in the shape of a sword. A five inch slit formed at the top and drew down the surface, "Ah, you're awake."

"Did that weapon just speak to me?"

Poz shook his head and chuckled, "Neg, stop playing around. Show Captain Weller some respect."

"Sorry," the slit crept down the length of the blade and stretched in half. The two shafts of metal formed into Neg's original size and shape - a three-foot droid with blue lights streaking across her 'scalp', "Just calibrating. Preparing for the inevitable."

"Neg, I want you to go to the hyper-sleep quarters and release Hughes and Byford."

"Why do I have to do it?" Neg twisted her head around and bounced up and down on the spot.

"Because I said so. I'm your captain. Are you defying a direct order?"

"No, no, no," she said. "It's just that I get all the crappy jobs."

"Yes. And until Poz perishes, that's how it'll always be. Now, just shut up and do it."

"Yes, Captain,"

She stuck her tongue out at Poz and made her way out of the control deck.

"Honestly," Poz shook his head, "Didn't she read the instruments and articles manual on appropriate conduct?"

"Speaking of which, where's Manuel-2?"

Oxade trained his eyes on Saturn and absorbed her wondrous beauty.

"Manuel-2?" Poz bounded around the room with excitement, "Your captain is here."

A holographic book appeared in the air by the flight panel. A husky feminine voice issued from the pages, "Good whenever-it-is, Oxade. I'm glad you could join us, finally,"

"Manuel-2?"

Oxade walked around the book and took in Manuel-2's

ridiculous thickness. She resembled an encyclopedia more than Opera Beta's paperback autopilot.

"Please, Captain. For the sake of confusion, I'd rather you refer to me as *Manny*," the weighty book slapped its back cover to the floor and fanned out, "We don't have time to waste. Are you ready for the debrief?"

"Yes, show me."

Manny projected a holograph of their current coordinates. Saturn, represented as a giant circle, hung to the right of a flashing Enceladus.

"We entered the vicinity of Saturn forty-eight hours ago. After establishing Enceladus, we noticed a foreign object in its orbit. It wasn't there when we set off, according to the Star Drone reports."

"Do we know what it is?" Oxade moved into the holograph and enlarged the tiny object with his fingers, "This white thing, the resolution is worse than 8k definition. I can barely make it out."

"That white *thing*, as you put it, is Space Opera Beta."

Shocked at the news, Oxade swallowed hard and enlarged the image as far as he could. He flung his arms sideways and walked through its blocky rendition, "It's the shape of a cone. You're right. This must be Opera Beta."

"It *is* Opera Beta, Oxade," Manny said. "Don't question my reports. They are infallible."

"Have you established communication with them?"

"Several times, yes."

"And?"

"No response. I can reasonably deduce from their lack of communication that the crew are all dead, or—"

"—or in hyper-sleep?" Oxade nodded at Poz. "Can you sat-link to Opera Beta and retrieve their autopilot's set of data points? Get some idea of the state they're in?"

"Certainly," Poz rolled over to the communications panel and fired it up, "We don't know the link code, though. It'll be protected."

Oxade reduced the image and made his way over to the control panel, "I find it difficult to believe that their Manuel refuses to talk to ours. They must be dead."

Poz tapped away at the keyboard and looked up at the screen, "Good. Makes our job a lot easier, doesn't it?"

"Yes, it does," Oxade turned to Manny to find her lying on the floor, "Okay, that's enough. Stop lying on the job."

"Yes, Oxade."

"Tell me about Weapons & Armory," Oxade unbuckled the leather on his left sleeve and inspected his forearm's Individimedia panel, "Patch me into Beta's comms frequency."

"Certainly," Manuel beeped and threw a bolt of green light at the glass on the comms panel, temporarily diverting Poz's attention as he worked on the keyboard, "Hey. Ask first."

"Shut up, you ball of technological inferiority," Manny's sultry voice sounded more of a come-on than a put-down.

Poz twisted his cylindrical head around and scowled at the book, "What did you just call me?" His rope-like arm stiffened, forming a serrated edge, and prepared to strike her.

"You heard."

"No. I didn't. Repeat it—"

"—Hey, enough of your *lessense*," Oxade stepped in between them and held out his arms, "Damn it, you're meant to be state-of-the-art technology. Not jumped-up, melodramatic *simple machines*. Okay?"

Poz fought hard to suppress his desire to stab Manny in her chest. Of course, it would have proved to be futile. Knowing Poz's fortune of late, he'd end up walking through her and spearing his own body.

Manny threw a beam from her central pages and made contact with the communications deck, "You may be our captain, Captain. But don't *ever* call me a simple machine again."

Oxade clenched his fists, struggling with the sheer temerity on display by his two colleagues, "Christ alive. You two really do put the *artificial* in artificial intelligence, don't you?"

"He started it," Manny affected a sarcastic huff and

started to extract the data from the comms panel via her beam.

"I did not start it," Poz muttered. "I'll shut you down and use your memory as toilet paper."

"You don't have an ass, you ass."

Oxade threw his left arm forward.

SCHUNT-CLICK.

A Rez-9 firearm slapped into his palm, having traveled up the length of his sleeve.

"I swear to God. If you two don't stop bickering, I'm putting a bullet right in the middle of the deck."

"Okay, fine," Manny said. "I'll look the other way."

Oxade stepped over to Poz, "Suits me. What's the situation with the live link to Beta?"

"Need the pass-code."

"Try A-W-A-K-E-4-5-7," Oxade looked at the transparent password box hanging in front of the deck, "It's what Beta uses to reactivate their antiquated piece of junk autopilot."

"On it," Poz punched away at the keys. He kept a crafty eye on Manny, who had spun around to face the windshield.

BZZZZ.

"Incorrect," Poz said. "Got any other suggestions?"

Oxade slammed the deck, "Sonofa—"

"—There's no need to swear, Captain," Poz said.

"It's my goddamn ship and I'll fricken well swear if I want to, okay?"

"It's beneath you," Poz looked at the empty pass-code box, waiting for an intelligent response.

"Make no mistake, my little ball of death. *You're* beneath me in this particular hierarchy, and don't you ever forget it," Oxade ran his hands through his slicked-back hair and took a deep breath. He needed to calm down and keep his professionalism intact; both for the sake of the crew and his own sanity, "We haven't been here a day and already we're failing."

"Transfer complete," Manny spun around and displayed the text results across the central pages of her book-body.

Oxade tried to read the text but it was far too small,

"What does it say?"

"Last recorded data point suggests that the crew were on seventy-two hours oxygen. According to Beta's second-in-command, Tripp Healy, many of them have fallen *one-hundred-and-eleven*."

"Eh?" Oxade leaned into the text on her page and raised his eyebrows. Manny had mistaken the word 'ill' for a number.

"It says *ill*, you cretin. Not one-hundred-and-eleven."

"I'm sorry, I thought it was numeric—"

"—Captain, I am at a loss for what to type as the password—" Poz announced, before being rudely interrupted.

"—Shut up for a minute," Oxade returned to Manny. "How long ago was the data point recorded?"

"Two years ago. Approximately. Would you like the exact time in days, hours, minutes and seconds—"

"—No, I've heard enough," Oxade went to pat Poz on the back, remembered the intense pain it caused the last time. He pulled his hand away and stared at the vicious-looking lump of technology, "Ah, forget it."

Poz cylinder 'head' revolved as his eyebulbs followed Oxade to the door.

"Did you want something, Captain?"

"Three days of oxygen in two years? No response to our communication attempts? They're definitely all dead. This is going to be the easiest salary we've ever earned," Oxade palmed the panel on the wall and opened the door, "Manny, how long till we can bridge with Beta?"

"Three or four hours."

"Keep establishing contact every ninety seconds. The more they don't respond, the more likely they're dead. We'll get on board, take what we want, kill anything we find, and go home."

Oxade walked out of the control deck, "And try not to tear each other's throats out until I get back, at least."

Poz and Manny scowled at each other.

***

Alex struggled with the jarring effects of his hyper-sleep. He gripped the edge of his pod and suppressed the urge to vomit.

"God, my organs feel like pâté."

Nutrene, on the other hand, was used to the feeling. Alex couldn't understand how she was able to hop to her feet and casually make her way over to the sink.

"Hey, it's perfectly natural to feel like crap," Nutrene said.

She looked into the basin mirror and focused on his trim figure. Dressed only in her USARIC-issued underwear, she licked her lips at the glorious sight, "You should scrunch your toes and walk around for a bit. Try to reorient yourself."

She turned to the corner of the chamber and saw Neg spinning around, calibrating her extended arm.

"Neg, can you get our friend, here, a glass of water?"

"Certainly."

"Yeah," Alex pushed himself to his feet and stumbled forward, "Oh dear, no. No."

"Hey," Nutrene raced over and caught him as he fell to the floor. She hooked her arms under his and lifted him back to his feet, face-to-face.

She looked into his eyes, "Alex, stand up straight. It's the best thing for you."

"It doesn't feel like it," he pushed her back and tried to remain still.

"Muscle fatigue. Quite normal after such a long journey."

Alex moved his hands in front of his body. He took one step forward and wobbled on the spot.

"A bit like learning to walk again," Nutrene watched as he put his other foot forward, "There, you got it."

Neg rolled over to Alex and extended her metal retractor. At the end of it was a glass of water which she offered to Alex, "Drink this. Fresh H2O."

"I know what it is," Alex took the glass from Neg and sniffed around the rim, "Fresh?"

"Yes, Charlie has the latest filtration system installed. Fresher than fresh, actually."

He took a sip. The trickle of water worked its way down his throat and into his stomach. So intense was the sensation that he visualized the liquid revitalizing his body and organs. It made him close his eyes, thankful for the small mercies in life.

Nutrene giggled at his reaction as she opened the cabinet door, "Good?"

"God, yeah," he muttered in ecstasy, "*Damn* good."

"Gotta keep that impressive physique of yours on-point if we're going to do our job."

Alex looked down the length of his body. The fine hairs around his well-defined chest and abdomen seemed to stand on end, almost as if it had been rubbed with a balloon.

"What's that?"

Neg swiveled her cylindrical head and flashed her eyebulbs, "Interference, probably. We're trying to establish contact with Opera Beta."

"We've found Opera Beta?" Nutrene picked out her USARIC inner-suit jacket from the cupboard. She slipped her arms through the sleeves and inspected the lapels around her neck, "That was fast. How long ago?"

"A few hours. She's orbiting Enceladus, but isn't communicating," Neg said.

Alex looked in the mirror above the wash basin and analyzed his face. As expected, he'd grown an impressive amount of facial hair during stasis. Today, he looked like a different person. His hirsute facial rendition in the mirror added a few years.

"I guess we're going to board, anyway," he said.

"Of course we are. Invite or no invite."

Nutrene placed her hand on Alex's shoulder and smiled at him via the mirror, "The beard suits you, you know."

"It's coming straight off once I'm dressed," he moved his eyes to her reflection, "How come you're not feeling groggy after such a long journey, anyway?"

"I'm used to it," she extended a strap in her hands and placed her right, bare foot on the side of the hyper-sleep pod, "Seven visits to IMS. You get used to it."

Alex couldn't help but look at her flagrant exposure of her thigh as she strapped the belt around her waist. She thumbed the hook and enabled the material to crawl across her skin and turn her porcelain-white skin a synthetic black.

Alex averted his eyes to her face, "What were you doing on the International Moon Station?"

"USARIC set up a Medix center there a couple of years ago. A part of their expansion after the success of the Star Cat Project back in twenty-one-eighteen."

She thumped the sole of her foot onto the floor and jogged on the spot, working her new pants down to her shins, "I guess they wanted to keep animals on standby there."

"You *guess*?"

"They never told us their mission aim. Top secret. My job was to tend to the felines and provide updates. And not to ask questions."

"Are you saying there are cats on the moon?"

"Yup," Nutrene unbuckled her left sleeve and revealed a metal rail sewn inside, "Only a couple. They had their ICs installed."

"The infinity claws?"

"You know your acronyms, I'll give you that."

She flung her arm forward. A Rez-9 firearm rolled along the inner sleeve rail and landed comfortably in her palm. She aimed the firearm at Neg, "You. Stay there, I need to calibrate."

"Please do not point your firearm at me, Nutrene. I work with you."

"Shut up, just hold still," she pressed her thumb on the side of the barrel. A rectangular HUD holograph floated above the sight. The surface drew a white line around Neg's bulbous shape. The phrase *death drone* flashed next to it.

"Pow," Nutrene pretended to shoot Neg and finished with a smirk, "Bang on target."

Neg wasn't nearly as impressed.

"Nutrene, do you know that you should never aim a gun at the people you're working with?"

"You're not a person," Nutrene winked at Alex. "Besides,

a Rez-9 charge wouldn't even put a chink in your armor."

The fact surprised Alex.

"It won't?"

"No. Wanna see?" Nutrene aimed her Rez-9 at Neg once again, "Let me show you."

Neg rolled back and beeped in protest, "Please, don't—"

BLAMM!

The charge blasted out of the barrel and flew through the air. It collided with Neg's metallic surface and disintegrated into nothingness. A couple of orange sparks to flew into the air.

"See?"

"That was just rude," Neg huffed and rubbed her head. "Don't do that again."

"*Amaziant*," Alex said. "Poz and Neg are indestructible?"

Nutrene held her left forearm up and allowed the gravity to return her gun to the crook of her elbow.

"Ha, yeah. Trust Manning/Synapse to include *that* in the Death Drone series."

"I don't trust any of their wacky technology as far as I could throw them," Alex made his way to the cupboard and opened the door, "The Series Three units were a good idea, but, like most of USARIC's endeavors, they were flawed."

"Like most humans, I guess. Only we don't freak out and behave like lemmings when we remember who we really are."

Alex pulled out his USARIC jacket and looked at his name on the sleeve, "Beta's full of them."

"Ooooh," Nutrene pursed her lips and nodded her head, impressed, "You figured that out all on your own, did you? The odds are very high that they'll have killed themselves. Save us the trouble, and the ammunition."

Alex slipped the jacket on.

"Why do you think they named the ship *Beta*, and not Bravo?"

Nutrene's eyes grew at Alex's revelation, "Huh. Good point. I thought each iteration was phonetic."

"If that was the case they'd have called her Opera *Bravo*," Alex grabbed the Rez-9 tucked into the left sleeve, "Sending a cat to Saturn with a bunch of messed-up androids? It was a test. Like a bunch of canaries or guinea pigs."

"I never thought of it that way. It makes complete sense. USARIC expected the mission to fail?"

"Did they *really* think sending a cat into space would work? The chances of success were literally millions to one, if that," Alex threw his left arm towards the ground. His Rez-9 slid down the length of his sleeve and landed in his palm, "It's a stupid idea. If it was a movie or a novel no one would believe it."

"Doesn't matter," Nutrene said. "We're here to rectify their stupid mistake."

***

Nutrene and Alex followed Neg as she rolled through the door to the control deck.

Oxade looked up from the communications panel and clapped eyes on Nutrene's mercenary get-up, "Hey."

"Hey."

"Sleep well?"

"Like a baby," she moved the chair from her path and grabbed his hand in hers. They clutched tightly and bumped fists, "How long you been up?"

Oxade checked her over and smiled, "A few hours, now. You look great."

"Oh, I *am* great. You know that," she nodded at Manny, "I heard we found Opera Beta?"

"Yeah, we did. We've just sent a message back to USARIC updating them on our findings."

Oxade caught Alex staring at him. He seemed to be lost in his own world. Oxade remained professional and refrained from causing any undue upset.

"Hey, soldier. You okay?"

"I'm fine. I just want to get this done."

"You seem anxious?" Oxade said. "Having second thoughts about the mission?"

"No."

Alex tugged at his sleeve. A sense of dread thumped against his chest.

Opera Beta edged closer and closer. Soon, Opera Charlie would bridge with them and instigate an intergalactic act of violence and death.

"Is your suit okay?" Oxade asked, knowing full well that it wasn't the merc gear upsetting the man.

"It's Kevlar and Technomex. I'm used to it."

"It'll save your life if we encounter a fight," Oxade waved Manny over to him, "Okay, enough BS. Manny, tell us about Opera Beta?"

Manny opened his covers and landed a quarter of the way through her holographic tome.

Manuel-2
Space Opera Beta (second revision)
Pg 704,111
(exposition dump #99/4g)

Construction of Space Opera Beta *commenced in 2116 at USARIC's Cape Claudius compound. More than one hundred tons in weight, it measures one thousand feet and contains ten levels.*

The name underwent a last minute change in early 2118 before it set off on its voyage to Saturn. Originally known as Space Opera Bravo, *the original team of humans were disbanded and summarily executed shortly after the conclusion of the* Star Cat *Project.*

It was decided by then-chief Dimitri Vasilov and CEO Maar Sheck that the mission would be manned exclusively by Androgyne Series Three units to save on insurance and running costs. In addition, the winner of the Star Cat *Project, Jelly Anderson, joined them.*

Captain Daryl Katz and botanist Haloo Ess were the only human beings on board. Along with Beta's on-board computer, The Manuel, these were the only entities who knew the true nature of their colleagues - the Androgyne Series Three units. It is understood that Katz and Ess did not survive the link with Opera Alpha.

Data secured from her last communication advises that there are six souls on board at this current time.

1: Tripp Healy, formerly first officer. Assumed rank of captain after the death of Daryl Katz. Former ASF (American Star Fleet) commander and communications and liaison specialist.

2: Dr Bonnie Whitaker. USARIC's then-chief scientist. Honorably discharged from ASF. Specialist in martial arts and prototyping.

3: Jaycee Nayall. Head of Weapons & Armory. Five years' service with ASF. Died during service and subsequently reconstituted.

4: Wool ar-Ban. Chief Medician and Medix liaison. Five years' service. Project medician coordinator of the Star Cat Project and caretaker of subject #6.

5: Tor Klyce. Head of communications and specialist in psychoanalysis.

6: Jelly Anderson. Domestic household cat, and runner-up of the Star Cat Project. Joined Opera Beta after the winner, Bisoubisou Gagarin (Russia) reported dead.

"Thanks, Manny," Oxade said.

"You're welcome."

"We don't know much else. What we *do* know is that the stupid cat would have had something called *infinity claws* installed when they reached Saturn's vicinity."

Alex didn't hide his faux-puzzled expression, "ICs. I know *of* them, but I don't know what they actually are?"

"Titanium talons installed in place of her cuticles," Oxade said. "Also, micro-fibre whiskers. Designed to heighten the senses."

Alex jumped in to the explanation. "Right, they're for an extra layer of protection. The claws are like talons. I hear they're fierce."

"Really?" Oxade folded his arms and took a keen interest in Alex's expertize on the subject, "And the whiskers?"

"Anderson would have had a K-13 chip implanted just above her right shoulder so the crew can track her. The whiskers work in conjunction with it. As I say, heighten the senses," Alex lifted his left forearm and pointed at the three inked lines across his skin, "They also act as a rudimentary one-way communication channel, a bit like our *Viddy Media* installations."

"Wow, check out the big brains on Hughes, here,"

Nutrene licked her lips at him, suggestively, "Not just a fit body."

Oxade cleared his throat and grew suspicious, "That's very interesting, Alex."

"Yeah, out of *all* of Beta's crew, Anderson is the one we need to keep an eye on."

"I'm sure she is," Oxade grunted and punched his left arm forward. "There's just one thing I don't quite understand, though."

"What?"

Oxade's Rez-9 flew into his palm, "How do you know so much about Anderson?"

"Huh?"

Alex held his breath and eyed the gun in his captain's hand. 'Idiot,' he thought. He'd opened his big mouth and said too much. In acting dumb, he'd given the game away. The look in Oxade's face said everything. Alex knew that he knew.

The control deck started to close in.

If Alex hadn't been wearing gloves, both he and Nutrene would have seen his fingers covered in sweat.

"I, uh..." Alex didn't expect his voice to crack so blatantly.

Oxade tilted his Rez-9 and ran his thumb on the side lever, arming it, "Come on, explain."

"I, uh, just..."

"You *just* what?"

"I read up about it before we left—"

"—*Lessense*," Oxade lowered his gun and eyeballed Alex with a devilment usually reserved for people who murder family members, "I'm not stupid, you know. Don't think I haven't noticed what's going on."

"Wh-what? N-Nothing's going on—"

"—Then wh-wh-why are you st-st-stuttering like a goddamn f-f-fool?" Oxade mocked with viciousness and aimed his gun at the boy's face, "Answer me, you st-stuttering d-d-dick."

"I j-just..."

"*Answer me.*"

"Oxade," Nutrene screamed in his ear, "Are you out of your mind?"

"If he doesn't answer me, he'll get a Rez-9 charge in *his*," Oxade pulled his index finger back, teasing the trigger, "Hughes?"

Alex licked the dryness from his lips and hyperventilated, "I'm n-not... I'm..."

"Who are you, *Alex Hughes*?" Oxade roared.

"I'm... I'm... Alex—"

His speech slowed to a complete halt.

The ground twisted into the air and punched him square in the face, knocking him flat out.

Chapter 11

Crew Quarters
Space Opera Beta

Tripp sat in front of his N-Gage screen and stared at the eleven-year-old boy on the screen; his son, Rogan. He'd begun to resemble his father. The comparison of their jaw lines and eyes were unmistakable.

Almost five years had passed since Tripp had left home. It had been ninety seconds since he spoke to his son.

Rogan's ears pricked up as Tripp's last sentence rolled into the front room. He turned to the screen.

"We're on a ninety-second delay, which will make talking to each other interesting, won't it? How is school?".

Rogan eventually sighed, "School is okay, Dad. I hate my math teacher. He's very strict. Why haven't you come home, yet?"

Tripp had to wait another ninety seconds for the message to reach him.

Rogan would be a teenager when he returned home. Tripp looked away from the screen and covered his face, refusing to reveal his emotions.

"Why are you crying, dad?"

Tripp wiped the pink liquid from his eyes and cleared his throat, "I'm not crying, son. It's just that I'm so happy to see you. Where's Spooky?"

Rogan leaned into the screen and moved his eyes left and right trying to soak up his father's quarters "Is that your room?"

"Yes," Tripp muttered, "How is everyone?"

"Spooky died, dad," Rogan said, clearly antagonized by the memory of the event, "She got really ill. She really missed you after you left."

"Dead?" Tripp closed his eyes and felt the bottom of his heart crack open, "Oh."

Tripp wiped his face and saw his wife, Samantha, peer into the screen. She raised her eyebrows in shock before she burst into tears, "I thought you were dead."

Finally, a bit of good news to counterbalance the bad. His wife looked healthy and vibrant as she held their son against her chest.

"Why did you think Daddy was dead?"

"Oh God. Tripp," she traced the screen with her fingertip and burst into tears, "Why didn't you send us a message?"

"Aww, mom. Get off me."

"What message? We couldn't send any messages while we were away."

Another ninety, torturous seconds passed by. It allowed both parties to absorb each other's facial reactions. A sense of dread crept into the delayed conversation.

"Tripp, sweetie," Samantha cried into the screen, "I'm *so* sorry."

"What? What do you mean you thought I was *dead?*" Tripp slammed the desk, spilling his tears onto his fists, "I'm not dead. I'm coming home."

"We thought they switched you off. They said they'd try to rebuild you if they ever found Opera Beta."

Tripp ran his fingers under his left earlobe. He prodded his fingertips into his neck, seconds away from tearing his own throat out and ending it all.

"You knew I was an Androgyne?" He muttered through his weeping knowing it'd be *another* ninety seconds until he got confirmation from her, "You knew all along?"

Another man about the same age as Tripp leaned over Samantha. He ran his hands over her shoulder with over-familiarity, "Is this him, sweetie? Not bad-looking for a Series Three unit, is he?"

"*Sweetie?*" Tripp felt the saliva escape from his mouth. His esophagus turned to stone. The walls in his quarters threatened to entomb forever, "Wh-who's *that?*"

Samantha took the man's hand in hers and ran her face along his knuckles, "You can't blame me, Tripp. I didn't know. USARIC told us you didn't make it. They even paid for your funeral."

"They did *what?*" Tripp huffed and yanked on his inner-suit collar, "No, no, no. This can't be happening."

She turned to the man and waved him away as gently as necessary, "Please, not now, Charley."

"Okay, I'll be in the kitchen if you need me," he bent over and picked up a toddler in his arms.

"Who's that?" Tripp gasped.

"Oh, *sweetie,*" Samantha tried to block the lens with her hand.

"No," Tripp slammed the desk in fury, "Who the hell is *that?*"

"That's Tracey, Dad," Rogan said. "My little sister…"

"No-no-no…" Tripp stammered and felt his left arm tighten. A tingling sensation morphed into an agonizing jolt of pain down his left arm. His fingers moved from his ears and scrambled at the surface of his console, "I c-can't," he huffed and slid off his chair.

"Tripp, sweetie?" Samantha leaned into the screen, trying to see where he'd gone.

Everything went black.

***

When I was a little boy all I ever wanted to be was an astronaut.

I used to spend every waking second looking at the stars and the constellations. Before they became USARIC, the Space Agency used to show reports on Individimedia about what they found.

I remember when they found the first flat surface planet in Andromeda Twelve. It was so exciting to me. Imagine, a planet that wasn't like the shape of a giant soccer ball.

A place where, if you traveled far enough, you could fall off the edge of the universe.

My second love was my cat. I don't remember her name because it was so long ago. One day, we had to put her down because she was sick. The medician said she was in a lot of pain and I didn't like it. We never got to see the medician inject her and I liked that I never saw it.

I don't know about other people. When I think of things that happened in the past, I see them as images.

Right now I can see a bright new star in the night sky. It's not far from the Great Bear. You know it. The arrangement of stars that looks like a frying pan with a wonky handle.

I remember my teacher asked me one time, "Tripp, why are you so in love with space?"

I couldn't answer her.

Why do I love space so much? Because out there are billions upon billions of stars. The law of averages says there must be at least a million other lifeforms out there.

There has to be, right?

I don't regret my decision to put my health, family, and friends behind my first, true love.

Does that sound selfish?

The only thing I would have regretted was indecision…

***

Jaycee's thumbnail lay on the floor. It projected an audio waveform in the middle of the Fit Room.

He wiggled his gloved fingers on his right hand, taking an unusual interest in their operation. He lifted his head and looked at the soft padding stretched across the wall.

The USARIC logo stretched across the padded canvas.

He clenched his fist and turned to the projection. As he spoke, the waves rose up and down, recording his voice.

"My name is Jaycee Nayall, USARIC weapons and armory. I hope those in charge can hear what I'm about to say."

THWACK!

Jaycee's fist connected with the 'U' in USARIC. He pulled his arm away and spun his wrist three-hundred-and-sixty degrees, resetting for another hit.

"When I was drafted into the Opera Beta program I

didn't know what I was letting myself in for. If I'd known what I know now, I would never have gone."

Jaycee lifted his fist and threw it against the padding with all his might.

SLAMM!

The plastic flaked out upon impact. The wall shuddered a second later.

"We've made a discovery," Jaycee twisted his hand around and took one step back. The "S" in the logo seemed to laugh and taunt him, "We don't know the full facts, yet. But know this. It's a discovery far beyond anything any of us can comprehend."

SCHLAMMM!

His punched the canvas so hard that it rocked the Fit Room.

"You can't see this," Jaycee moved back once again as the waveform slipped up and down, "But the noises you hear are me taking out my frustration on my employer, USARIC. One punch for every member of my crew that lost their lives. Every husband, wife, son, daughter… who are no longer around because of USARIC and their bottom line."

THWOCK-SCHLAMM!

A furious double-punch, this time to the "A".

"That's for you, Maar Sheck. Two As in your name, and two extra special blows to your face. If you're listening to this, just know that I want answers. And they'd better be *damn good*."

Jaycee pulled his elbow back, ready to strike the "R".

"And this one's for Bonnie Whitaker. My friend and colleague who's no longer around to ask you anything."

Jaycee went to throw his fist at the canvas, when he heard a wallop coming from the other side of the door. He lowered his arm and squinted with confusion.

"Huh?"

He made his way to the door, "Stop recording."

The audio waveform flat-lined and beeped.

"Save message?" asked the holograph.

"Yes, save and send. Now."

***

Jaycee approached the crew quarters and spotted Tripp's door was wide open.

"Hey, Tripp? Are you there?"

He peered inside and saw Tripp unconscious on the floor.

"Jeez," he moved in and clocked Samantha and Rogan on the screen waiting for her husband to return to the screen. They were unaware of what had happened.

"Tripp?" she asked. "Where are you?"

Jaycee leaned into the tiny lens above the screen. The inset picture in the corner of the screen showed his face enveloped the whole square.

"Samantha?"

He crouched to the floor and slid his giant arms underneath Tripp's. It took thirty seconds to lift his passed-out friend up to his feet - and another thirty to set him down on the chair.

"Jaycee," Rogan beamed with delight, "You're alive, too."

"Nayall?" Samantha gasped. "Is that you? Where did Tripp go?"

He removed his right glove and felt Tripp's neck with his fingertips.

"He passed out. Hey, Rogan. Look at you! You've grown into a handsome, young man."

"Yes, it's been years."

"What happened, here?"

The seconds whizzed by as Jaycee adjusted his friend's head against the back of his chair. "Healy? It's okay. I think you passed out."

Samantha held up her hands, shirking responsibility, "I don't know. We were just talking and he vanished."

Jaycee stood up and pointed to Tripp, "He must have fell—" he stopped talking when he saw Charley carry their daughter in his arms.

"Samantha? Who's that behind you?"

Jaycee turned to the unconscious Tripp. Two and two slotted together in Jaycee's mind, "Oh *no*." He turned back to the screen and scowled at Samantha.

"It wasn't my fault, Jaycee. What was I supposed to do?" she sniffed, "The wait was too much."

Jaycee's heart erupted with anger.

Samantha to turned from an exquisite angel into a selfish harridan in Jaycee's eyes. It only took ninety seconds.

"God, I'm so sorry, Jaycee. The news must have broke his heart. But, please, you have to see it from my point of view—"

Jaycee scrunched his face and turned away, happy that the woman wasn't in the room with him.

"*Bitch.*"

"—You spend close to five years without hearing a damn word," she screamed, scaring Rogan from her arms, "And then Viddy Media goes wild with speculation. Tripp and the crew disappears. No oxygen. I'm sorry. I swear to you, Jaycee, we thought you were all dead—"

KER-SMASSSSHHH!

Jaycee's fist flew through the screen. The plastic exploded around his wrist as his elbow went through the frame. Samantha's image frazzled and froze on the spot around his forearm.

He wrenched his arm out and flung the transparent debris away. The noise slapped Tripp out of his slumber.

"Wh-what's g-going on?" Tripp yelped. He shifted in his chair and grabbed the armrests, "What happened?"

Orange sparks and a thick, black smog drifted away from the smashed screen.

"Technical problems."

"What did the screen do to you?"

"Ah," Jaycee walked to the door and did his best to change the conservation, "It looked at me the wrong way. You know my temper. What do you remember?"

Tripp blinked and stood up from the chair, recollecting what had happened, "I, uh, tried to call home. Waited ages for the connection."

"Okay. What else?"

Tripp's face lit up with joy, "I never got to say anything. But I saw my wife and son's face again."

"Did you speak to them, though?"

"No, the connection must have gone down—"

"—You didn't speak to them?" Jaycee reaffirmed, once and for all.

"No. Everything went dark."

Jaycee held Tripp's shoulder and took a deep breath, "Listen, don't try to contact home until we *get* home. Okay?"

"Okay," Tripp looked up at him with dogged, innocent eyes, "Why?"

"You trust me, don't you?"

Tripp pointed at the smashed screen, "Of course I do. But can't I just—"

"—Then just trust me on *this*, Healy. You know your family are alive and healthy. They know you're alive. That's all you need. Promise me you'll drop it."

"Okay? I promise."

"Good," Jaycee walked out of the quarters, leaving a thoroughly confused Tripp - and smoldering N-GAGE screen - in his wake.

Jaycee stormed along the walkway in a fit of rage. He thumped the walls a little too hard, "I swear to God, someone hand me USARIC on a plate and I'll eat them for breakfast."

He tried to calm himself down.

It was no use taking his frustration out on the ship, despite the fact that it belonged to a company that Jaycee perceived to be the enemy.

The USARIC logo angered him further.

Just thinking the Healy family revelation threatened to push him over the edge.

No sooner had Jaycee caught his breath than he heard a retching sound at the far end of the corridor.

BWUCK-BWUCK-KROITCH.

He lifted his head up and tried his luck, "Who's there?"

No response.

The noises stopped. Jaycee knew he wasn't hearing things.

"Ugghhhh," came a very familiar voice, spluttering in pain, "I d-don't feel too well."

The voice waded down the corridor. It sounded like it

belonged to Tor.

"Rabinovich? Is that you?"

Jaycee sprinted around the corner and skidded on his heels. He went for the Rez-9 on his belt, "Christ, Rabinovich. What the hell is wrong with you?"

Tor doubled-over the staircase rail and coughed up some bile.

SPLOT-SPLISH.

The pink liquid splattered against the floor a few levels down.

"Guuuuh," Tor pushed his top half away from the railing and threw his head back, "Must have been the hyper-sleep. I really don't feel too good."

"Come here. Let me look at you," Jaycee held the man's face in his hands, "Show me your eyes."

His thumbs pressed against Tor's forehead and lifted his eyelids up.

Tiny streaks from Tor's bloodshot eyes snaked across the whites of his eyes.

"You're definitely ill. Where were you going?"

"R and R," Tor said. "Get some water. Maybe have a lie down."

"That's a good idea. We need you fit for when Charlie docks with us."

Tor hyperventilated in Jaycee's arms and pushed himself away.

"Th-they're c-coming to t-take us—"

Tor projectile vomited on Jaycee's exo-suit.

"Ugh, that's gross," Jaycee bopped Tor on his shoulders with disgust, "*Really?*"

Tor spat a mound of pink liquid to the floor. He hugged himself and shivered up a storm, "I'm s-sorry, J-Jaycee," he sniggered through his illness, silently happy that he'd taken some form of revenge on the man.

Jaycee didn't spot Tor's semi-delight, putting his puking down to a spell of extreme misfortune.

He scooped up the puke and flung it to the ground, "You know, not many people vomit on me and get away with it."

Jaycee looked at the shuddering man buckled before him.

He ran through the events of the past few days and, for the first time in their relationship, took pity on him.

"I'll look the other way on this," Jaycee cleared his throat and pointed at the staircase, "Be careful you don't fall down the stairs on your way to R and R."

"Yuh-yuh," Tripp nodded and leaned against the railing.

GRUMBLE... BLUCK...

"Ooophhh," Tor bent over and clutched his rumbling stomach, "Th-thanks, Jaycee."

"I'm going to check up on Jelly and Wool. I'd stay near the bathroom if I were you."

"That damn c-cat," Tor grabbed the railing and staggered down the step, almost losing his footing, "She c-can't be t-trusted, you know. She has a k-killer instinct. She's b-bigger than us, n-now."

Jaycee watched as Tor made his awkward and painful descent down the staircase.

He shook his head and moved away, muttering to himself, "The grass ain't always greener, I guess."

Medix
Space Opera Beta - Level Three

Jaycee entered Medix and saw Jelly sitting crossed-legged on her bed. Wool knelt behind her and brushed the cat's hair with the golden comb.

"Yes, Jaycee?" Jelly waited for a reaction. "Are you getting ready to take out the trash?"

"Huh?"

Jelly smiled at him and pulled her head forward as Wool brushed her hair back.

Jaycee gripped the door frame, "Oh, sorry. I didn't realize you two were—"

"—What do you want?"

He covered the vomit marks on his exo-suit chest plate with his gloves.

"Just to tell you that Charlie is about to dock. Tripp wants us all ready to disembark."

Wool watched the teeth of the comb slide through Jelly's

bountiful orange hair. Every knot that burst apart filled her with delight and distanced the stench of bile that had entered the room.

"What's that smell?" Wool asked.

"It's him," Jelly flapped her tail and lifted an infinity claw at Jaycee, "He smells of sick."

"Really?" Wool asked. "Have you been throwing up?"

"No, it wasn't me—"

"—Can you leave us alone for a while, please," Wool returned to Jelly's hair.

"I'll be in control if you need me. Sorry, again," Jaycee stepped into the corridor and let the door to slide shut behind him.

"Bye, Jaycee," Jelly winked at him and wrapped her arms around her bent knees.

SCHWUMP.

The tiniest sound of the comb's teeth racing through Jelly's hair dispelled the otherwise silent atmosphere.

Wool closed her eyes and moved her face closer to Jelly's head. She pressed her nose against the strands and breathed in.

"Mommy? What are you doing?"

"Be quiet a minute, honey," Wool's heart filled with light as Jelly's scent engulfed her lungs.

"Mmm," Wool felt a tingle roll down her spine. She whispered so quietly, she barely heard herself speak, "God… I love you so much. I hope you know that."

Jelly scrunched her face, wondering what was going on behind her. Playful to a fault and still childlike in her naivety, "Are we going home soon?"

Wool waited a second to allow the last moment of wonder to escape her body, "Yes, honey."

"Why do you keep calling me *honey*?" Jelly asked. "Is it because I'm the same color as it?"

"No, hon—uh, Jelly. It's because you're sweet. It's a term of endearment."

"I don't know what that means."

Wool resumed combing Jelly's hair, "Don't worry. Our

friends from USARIC will be here any moment, now. We need to look nice so we can meet them, right?"

She removed the comb and ran her fingers along Jelly's scalp and brushed past her left ear.

"Look at me," Wool whispered.

Jelly purred and tilted her head to the side. Wool's knuckle ran through the fur on her cheek and down under her chin.

"I like it when you do my chin."

The half-cat's wonderful pupils glowed a dark orange. A mesmerizing sensation tumbled around Wool's chest like a pair of sneakers in a washing machine.

"God... look at you, Jelly Anderson," she muttered, utterly confounded by the girl's beauty, "You're so beautiful. I look into your eyes, and all I see is love."

Jelly pulled a face of naive contrition, "I don't know what to say when you say things like that."

"Then don't say anything," Wool pressed her lips on Jelly's forehead, "Don't say a word."

Jelly licked her lips as she received her kiss. She wanted an answer to a question that quickly formed in her head.

"Do you love me, mommy?" Jelly looked up at her with adorable dough-eyes.

"Yes, honey."

"Are you *in* love with me?" Jelly asked without a trace of emotion.

"God, *no*," Wool held her chest, troubled by the question, "Why would you think that?"

"Because when I was with Jamie, his mommy always said how in love with his daddy she was."

"That's not the same thing, honey."

"Why?"

"Being *in* love with someone is..." Wool found the relatively easy distinction difficult to verbalize, "It's not the same."

"Why?"

Wool arrived at the simplest explanation available, "You wouldn't want to have babies with me. Would you?"

Jelly didn't say no. She was over the prospect of sharing a

child with her new mommy. Wool, on the other hand, was seriously hoping Jelly would say *no*.

"Mmm. No, I don't think so."

"Oh, thank God," Wool exhaled and clutched at her heart, "But, uh, you do *love* your chicken pâté, don't you?"

Jelly licked her lips and providing Wool with an inadvertent reminder of just how sharp her fangs were, "Mmm, chicken."

"See?" Wool smiled. "The difference between being *in* love and love?"

Jelly shrugged her shoulders and planted her bare, furry feet on the floor.

"Not really. Sorry."

"Never mind," Wool tossed the comb on the pillow, temporarily disappointed with Jelly's innate ability to learn the essentials but flatly unable to process anything past nuance.

Jelly turned around and held the bulge in her belly, "Do you think Pink Symphony was in love with me?"

"I don't know. What makes you say that?"

The pink glow shimmied through her fur, "Because it gave me a baby."

Wool considered the statement very carefully.

Jelly had a point. No one knew how the pregnancy could have happened, but, the end result was *potentially* an act of having made love.

"That's too strange to even think about, honey. All we know is you went in the water and came back pregnant. God, just saying it out loud sounds crazy."

"I never wanted a baby," Jelly lifted the bottom of the exo-suit up, "But now it's here I've changed my mind. I feel like it belongs to me. Like I have to save it from harm."

"Whatever that is inside you, we must protect it," Wool placed her palms on Jelly's baby bump, "At all costs."

"Did you have a baby? Jelly asked.

"No, sweetie. I wasn't able to have babies."

"Why not?" Jelly asked.

"It's a long story, honey. I'm not able to have babies."

"Why?"

"I don't want to talk about it," Wool ducked her head like

a sad child, "It makes me sad."

Wool's fingertips snaked across Jelly's belly bump. The synthetic skin on the back of her hand cracked apart and spat pink gunk onto her wrist.

"Ugh, you must have nicked me with your claw, honey."

"I didn't."

The pair shared a moment. Both knew deep down inside that something wasn't quite right.

Wool shook her head and pointed at the wall by Jelly's bed, "Let's get a new measurement, honey."

"Okay."

Jelly walked backwards to the wall, "Do you miss Bonnie?"

Her question caught Wool off-guard.

"Press your shoulders against the wall," Wool squeezed the thumb on her left hand as she marched in front of her. "Of course I miss her. Why did you ask me that?"

Jelly pressed her back to the wall and yawned. Her ears and mouth stretched across her face, inadvertently revealing her fangs and bright orange eyes.

Wool would never get over how horrific Jelly's face looked when she yawned.

"I noticed you stopped speaking to Bonnie before we went to war," Jelly asked. "Why?"

"I didn't," Wool dismissed the accusation and clocked Jelly's height, "I didn't feel like talking to anyone."

She looked at the height marks on the wall beside Jelly's leg.

3'3" - 4'6" - 5'4"

The latter recording marked chest-high to Jelly.

"You've grown so quickly over the past day or so," Wool glanced at Jelly's face, "Hold still a moment."

"Why am I growing?" Jelly asked.

"We don't know, honey. It's something to do with the Symphonium."

"Sim... fow... knee... umm..." Jelly repeated.

Wool tiptoed and pressed the fleshy part of her thumb on top of Jelly's head. The sharp curve lit up and scored a line into the wall.

"Height reading, please,"

The mark on the wall threw a beam of soft, white light to the floor and calculated the distance.

"Seven feet exactly," advised the thumbnail.

Wool paced back and took in Jelly's towering height. A sickening idea popped into her mind. One that she felt couldn't be repeated verbally.

"Is everything okay, mommy?"

Wool rubbed her face and tried to halt her emotions, "If you keep growing like this, it's not good."

"Why are you crying?"

"I'm not crying," Wool lied and sniffed away her tears. "Honey, please. You need to stop…"

Jelly didn't know how to respond. She tried for a smile - a wry attempt to make her assumed mother happy once again, "Am I a big girl, now?"

"Yes. You *are*."

Chapter 12

Space Opera Charlie

Alex opened his eyes. He didn't recognize where he was at first. He felt something crawl across the side of his face.

Whatever it was that touched him had an elbow attached to it. Alex ran his tongue across his lips. A thin layer of film had formed over the skin.

"Where am I? What happened?" he whispered.

"You passed out," Nutrene's reassuring tone drifted into his right ear.

He looked up the length of the arm to find the woman smiling at him. Her scary monocle tore his gaze away from her lips.

Alex felt the urge to grab his gun and defend himself, "Jesus, he tried to kill me."

"No. He didn't. Oxade was just making sure you were on-point."

"*On-point?* He accused me of espionage," Alex blurted, still reeling from the effects of escaping execution, "He sure has a funny way of making sure his crew are okay."

Her face crept over his. An undeniable heat rolled across her pupils as she stared into his eyes, "It's okay, now. We're about to board Opera Beta."

"Is it safe?"

"Perfectly."

Without warning she planted her lips on his and kissed him. He didn't fight at first due to the shock. The deeper the kiss, the more he felt the need to push her away.

Alex clamped his hands on her shoulders and extricated himself from the unwanted attention. Nutrene wouldn't stop and hoped Alex would sink into the event and enjoy it. Her palm slapped against his forehead and pinned the back of his head against his pillow.

"Nggg," he struggled and flung his head to the side. His lips yanked several ropes of saliva across his cheek.

"Hey," Nutrene's monocle twisted around and focused on his face. She grabbed his hand and thrust it against her bare midriff, "Don't you want *this*?"

"No," he shoved back and threw his legs over the side of the bed, "Get off me."

Nutrene jumped off the bed and rotated her monocle, "I guess we don't see eye to eye, then."

"Very funny," Alex stood to his feet and brushed himself down, "Anyway, I have a girlfriend."

"Oh yeah?"

"Yeah."

"What's her name?"

"If you must know, it's Grace."

"Ha," Nutrene folded her arms in defiance. She threw her body weight onto her left leg, making *damn* sure her thigh was visible, "You know what they say about women who are named after adjectives, don't you?"

Alex turned away, "It's not an adjective. It's a noun. *Graceful* would be an adject—"

"—Is she better than me?" she interrupted, taking offense at his dismissal and little interest in his ad-hoc English class.

"What is it with you, Nutrene?" Alex stood up and ran his hands through his hair, "Ever since we met you've been making eyes at me—"

"—That was a cheap jab."

She turned away in a huff.

"That's not what I meant, and you *know* it. Don't think I haven't noticed the way you've been looking at me. You're meant to be focusing on the mission."

"We spend all our time killing on behalf of the government," she tried to win him around with a sly wink from her monocle, "Make love, not war. Right?"

"A bit of professionalism might help, here. *Nutrene.*"

"Oxade was right," she snapped. "There's something not quite right about you."

"Really? How so?"

"Just the way you're behaving. You're not like any USARIC merc I've ever met. In touch with your feminine side? Acting like a little fairy, more like."

"You're screwed in the head. And that's the only part of you that's getting screwed if I have anything to do with it."

"Funny *man*, aren't you? *Alex Hughes*," Nutrene bit her lip and decided she couldn't look at him any longer, "You can't blame a red-blooded woman pining for some human contact."

"That's the price you pay for doing USARIC's dirty work," Alex made for the door with a steely determination to get the job done, "Don't lecture me about right and wrong, Nutrene. You don't know what you're up against."

"What's that meant to mean?" she screamed. "I haven't done anything wrong."

"Assault *them*, Nutrene. Don't assault me," Alex finished and left the room.

Primary Airlock
Space Opera Charlie

"No messing around. Just get on board and transmit your findings," Oxade's voice emanated through Poz's head as he rolled toward the airlock on his cylinder.

"I don't intend to mess around, Oxade."

Poz turned down the walkway and saw Neg rolling towards him, "Would you hurry up, please?"

"I'm sorry."

"Not good enough."

The front of Poz's crescent body opened up and produced a cylindrical magnet.

SPIZZZZ…

It rumbled violently and shook the air in front of it, "Come on, we're wasting time, here."

WHIZZ-SCHUNT!

The magnetic force lassoed Neg across the walkway. The side of her body slammed against his magnetic plate. He released her and spun around to the first airlock door.

"Oxade, we're here. Can you open door A?"

"Opening, now," Oxade advised.

The door slid open and allowed the pair into the chamber. "Standby for decompression."

The Control Deck
Space Opera Charlie

Oxade and Manny watched the giant three-dimensional holographic live feed of the airlock. Poz and Neg rolled into the decompression chamber.

The first door slammed shut behind them.

"Manny will attempt communication with Beta's autopilot. The bridge will connect in sixty seconds."

"Understood," Poz said.

"Can you switch to 3-D representation, please."

A black rod crept out from Poz's scalp and fanned out into three prongs. Three transparent beams blasted around the decompression chamber.

Oxade took a few steps back as the live feed developed depth, slinking out into a three-dimensional box.

"Very good, thank you," Oxade hit a button on the console. "Commencing decompression. Standby."

SWWIIISSHHHH.

A blast of white gas flew out of the chamber's walls and engulfed Poz and Neg. The glass-covered pressure inlet dial on the wall spun around.

"Reminds me of the last time you farted," Neg chuckled to herself through the blast.

"I don't fart."

"Guys, knock it off," Oxade said. "Taking you down to zero point five, ay-tee-em," he turned to Manny, "How's the link-up with Beta?"

"The bridging process is nearly complete," Manny shuffled around in the air. A loading bar hung in front of her cover.

Opera Beta and Opera Charlie hung side by side. Beta's white bridge rails extended toward its sister ship's airlock.

CLAMP.

Opera Charlie's bridge end latched on Opera Beta's. The two vessels connected successfully.

"Connection secure," Manny turned to Oxade, "Decompression set."

Oxade stepped into the three-dimensional image, effectively appearing alongside Poz and Neg, "Okay. Listen up. I want an atmosphere reading as soon as you're on board. Second, we need to know who's alive and, more particularly, where Anderson is."

"Understood," Neg said.

"Keep your feed transmitting at all times. Upon connection break, we will wait thirty seconds until advancement."

"Understood," Poz said. "I will keep transmitting. Twenty second responder time."

Oxade stepped out of the image and held out his arm, "Manny, proceed with disembarkation."

"Yes, Captain."

Oxade winked at the pair of bulbous droids, "Good luck, guys."

"We don't need luck," Neg chuckled and turned to the outer airlock door, "Let's go kill us some bad guys."

Primary Airlock
Space Opera Beta

Tripp checked his appearance in the airlock window. Poz and Neg rolled in tandem across the bridge, pausing occasionally to look up at Saturn.

"Thanks so much for coming to save us," Tripp rehearsed his greeting under his breath, "Ugh, no. That sounds wrong."

He stood up straight and affected a more diligent aura.

"Welcome to Opera Beta. I'm the captain. Tripp Healy," he said. "Ugh, whatever."

Manuel appeared a few feet away and clapped his covers

together, "Tripp?"

"Yes, Manuel?"

"You know those old science fiction movies?"

"Yes, what about them?"

"Sometimes the main character discovers something strange and says 'I have a bad feeling about this' to the others."

"Okay," Tripp shrugged his shoulders, "So what?"

"Well, at the risk of sounding trite, I have a *really* bad feeling about this."

"This?" Tripp turned to the droids on the bridge, "They're just canaries, Manuel. They're mostly harmless—"

"—I'm not referring to the two weird-looking *things* on the bridge," Manuel shifted closer to his captain, "It's the humans that concern me."

"What?"

"According to the USARIC database, two of the three are from USARIC's mercenary division."

"So?"

"Why would they send mercs on a rescue mission? A skeleton crew of three, plus two droids?"

"Space is a big, bad place. You know that," Tripp gave some consideration to Manuel's concern, "We've been missing for three years. You can't blame USARIC for exercising some due diligence and taking precautions. Anything could have happened to us. In fact, thinking about it, anything *did* happen to us. Who knows what effects Symphonium will have on them. The moment we get back we'll be quarantined and no doubt farmed out to pharmaceutical companies."

Manuel wasn't convinced.

"It would have been remiss of me not to have mentioned it."

"I know, and thank you," Tripp finished. "You're right to have aired your concern."

The bridge offered a superb view of Saturn. Poz and Neg couldn't help but take in the glorious wonder of the planet.

"She's one huge ball of gas," Poz quipped as he raced

forward toward Opera Beta.

"Very intimidating," Neg attempted to keep up with Poz's pace, "It's scary."

Oxade's voice rattled through their heads, "Hey, cretins. We don't pay you to admire the view."

"You don't *pay* us at all."

"That's not the point. We're on a time limit, here. Get moving."

"*Soh-ree*," Poz spat with sarcasm. He rolled forward and changed his shape into a giant metal ball, "How's about this for *speed?*"

He whizzed along the bridge at speed, creating sparks against both sides of the railings.

"A Newton's cradle ball?" Oxade huffed, none-too-impressed. "Poz, you're not beyond dispensation, you know. I'll active your little nuclear setting and blast your shiny butt into the next multiverse if you're not careful."

"Neg is slowing me down," Poz shifted back to his regular shape and fanned out his cylindrical magnet. He kept his eyebulbs focused on the bridge floor at it whizzed under his frame.

"I am *not* slowing you down," Neg yelped as the magnetic pull made her entire body soar towards Poz.

SWISH-SCHLAMM...

Her curved frame slapped against Poz's, enabling him to carry her the remainder of the way to Opera Beta.

"Stop doing that," she complained.

"Stop crawling like a snail, then," Poz lowered his volume, "We don't want to anger Oxade," he upped his volume and spoke up the length of the bridge, "Advising an ETA of thirty seconds."

"Understood. I'll have Manny access Beta's Manuel and activate the airlock."

"Awaiting Beta's airlock hatch to allow us in."

Poz rolled up to the door and extended two sensors from his neck joint. His spindly rope-like arm retracted into his body, "Look, that must be Beta's captain."

Poz moved to the left and clanged against the bridge

railing as he focused through the window of the outer airlock door. Tripp stared at him from behind the inner airlock hatch window.

"Handsome man," Neg bounced up and down on the spot which caused the bridge to rattle back and forth.

"Don't do that, you'll get us killed," Poz said.

"Sorry, I'm just super excited."

"We're not here to make friends. We're here to get what we need and get out with the minimum of fuss."

SWISHHHH.

The outer airlock door opened, allowing Poz and Neg to roll inside. The door scissored down and sealed them in the chamber.

"Opera Charlie, be advised. We have boarded Beta."

"Good, now find what we need. Remember, keep it friendly."

A blast of white gas enveloped them, bringing the pressure back to a habitable consistency.

"Shh," Poz stared at Tripp's face through the glass shield on the inner door, "He's looking at us."

"He's cute," Neg beeped.

Tripp grabbed the airlock hatch lever and prepared to open the door, "I'm going manual on this."

"Fair enough," Manuel pushed himself back and opened himself out, "When you're ready."

"Here we go," Tripp yanked the lever down forcing the hatch to slide up. He looked at the two futuristic ball-shaped androids in front of him.

"Welcome to Space Opera Beta."

"Hey. I'm Poz. She's Neg."

He rolled past Tripp's thigh and surveyed the dark surroundings, "Nice place you have here."

Neg moved over to Tripp and spun her bulbous 'head', "You must be Tripp Healy?"

"I am. Very nice to meet you," Tripp held out his hand. She looked at it and drew a confused look across her surface, "That's your hand."

"Yes? I know."

"Why are you doing that, Tripp Healy?" Neg asked.

He relaxed the muscles in his palm.

"It's customary to shake hands with friends."

"Oh, we're not your friends," she squealed, softly, "We're here to make sure everything is *as it should be*."

Tripp folded his arms and gave as good as he got, "Did you sue him?"

"Sue who?"

"The moron who installed your charm chip?"

Neg frowned and twisted away from Tripp in defiance, "That's not funny—"

"—Hey, Neg. Check this out," Poz bounded down the corridor and twisted his head one-hundred-and-eighty degrees on his neck, "This spacecraft is *nasty*."

"What do you mean *nasty*—"

"—Tripp Healy," Poz interrupted, "We need to check out the control deck. Our Captain wants a full sit-rep of Opera Beta."

"Uh, sure?"

Tripp frowned at Poz and Neg's faux charm and insistence on making themselves at home, "I can fill you in, if you like?"

"No point," Poz rolled forward and extended his sensors, "Oxade? Do you read me?"

"Yes, Poz. Please advise."

"Atmosphere levels are fit for human consumption. Which is more than can be said for her decor. Oxygen set at twenty-one percent. Gas readings remain steady."

"Good. That suits us just fine," Oxade's voice chirped into Poz and Neg's head.

Tripp grew weary of the behavior of his guests. Worse, he had no idea who Poz was talking to.

"Who are you speaking with—"

"—But I'm also picking up a strange, unknown element," Poz's eyebulbs glowed as he scanned the walls, "Possibly a carcinogen of some description. It's off the charts."

Tripp held out his hand, "I can explain what that is. You see, we've just returned from a place called Pink—"

"—Tripp Healy," Poz rolled to a stop and retracted his

sensors, "How have you and the crew been able to sustain yourselves with such a high toxicity level? I'm surprised your lungs haven't burst."

"Well, technically, we *haven't*. It's complicated. I don't know if you were briefed before you left. Every crew member Beta, bar one, is a Series Three Androgyne."

"Bar one?" Neg asked.

"Jelly Anderson."

"Oh, yeah. That stupid little ball of fluff. I forgot."

"Yes, everyone else is a Series Three unit. I'm one, too."

"You're *one-two*?" Poz spat with confusion, "A previous series I don't know about?"

"No, I didn't mean—"

"—Oh, I *get it*. He means *he's* a series three unit, *as well*," Neg turned to Manuel, who flapped above her head like a drug-addled bird, "Who the hell is *this*?"

Manuel shuffled forward feeling his temper draw to a close, "Hello. I'm Manuel. The autopilot."

"Huh," she snorted with a metallic whiff, "An old model, right?"

"We've been away for five years. I figured USARIC might have made a few updates in the meantime."

"Hah. Well, you'll get to meet Manny soon enough."

"Manny?" Manuel asked and tried to suppress his displeasure at the revelation of his inferiority.

"Manuel-2," Neg squealed. "She doesn't take any crap from anyone. Not least previous models, like you."

Manuel folded his pages, indicating his hurt feelings, "I'm sorry. Have I done something to upset you, Neg?"

"*You*? Upset me?" Neg blew a recording of a raspberry at him, "You're not capable of arousing any emotion in *me*, my friend."

"Oh," Manuel slumped in the air and huffed.

Neg darted along the walkway and caught up with Poz, "They're seriously out of date."

"Yes, and out-of-touch, too. It doesn't make sense. Opera Beta is spectacularly unfit for human habitation. There's a virus of some description present. Nothing I've ever encountered, anyway."

Tripp paced along the walkway and turned to Manuel in confidence, "Have you ever met anyone *so* rude?"

"Which one are you referring to?"

"Either of them," Tripp huffed. "Acting like they own the place."

"Hey, Tripp Healy," Poz reached the staircase and scanned the first step, "*Stairs*? Really?"

"Ah, yes. Problem?"

Poz butted his circular stomach against the first step, "Look at the state of this. For God's sake."

"*Oh, great*," Tripp huffed and shook his head, "The two of you have mastered nuance and sarcasm, but not stairs?"

"Stairs are for idiots."

Tripp ignored the comment, "No problem. We'll just take the elevator."

"Thank God for that," Poz whistled with relief, "I'm surprised you guys know about the invention of *fire*, considering the antiquated nature of this useless spacecraft."

Tripp snorted with sarcasm and went to touch Poz,"I see Manning/Synapse haven't quite mastered applying manners to their new products."

He felt an unusual stinging sensation in his palm a mere inch away from his surface.

"Don't touch me or I'll kill you," Poz beeped with unease.

"I'm sorry? Are you threatening me?"

"I'm not threatening you. It's a fact," Poz said. "If your hand connects with me, you'll be killed. I am a death droid."

Neg swiveled around and hopped on the spot, "We seriously advise you not to touch us. Your skin gets absorbed and... well, let's just say it gets very messy. We don't care. It doesn't affect us. We just melt your carcass and collect the data in your memory. Or your brain, if you're a human. Which you're not. Are you?"

"No, I'm not," Tripp held his hands together, thankful that he hadn't *quite* made physical contact with Poz, "And thanks for the heads up,"

"You're welcome, big boy," Neg tilted her head and flashed her blue eyebulbs, "Although...?"

Tripp stared at her, waiting for the rest of her sentence,

"What?"

"Maybe when we return home, I'll switch my absorption processor off and we can make sweet, sweet love—"

"—Neg," Poz slammed his body against the bottom step in a fit of rage, "What did we agree? You don't flirt with the normal people."

"Hey, don't appendage-block me!"

"Less of it, you dirty metal testicle," Poz spat and swiveled around and tilted his 'head' up at Tripp, "I'm sorry about that, Tripp Healy. Neg took a bit of a knock to her processor when we were put together," he finished with a sarcastic whisper, "Forgot to fit her with a decency chip, if I'm being honest."

"I heard that," Neg spun around and harrumphed.

Tripp cleared his throat and pointed to the elevator, "So, the elevator is over here, guys."

The Control Deck
Space Opera Charlie

Oxade paced back and forth around the three-dimensional holograph live feed. He slipped himself between Poz and Neg and pointed at the sharp end of the ship.

"Show me Beta's control deck," he said. "I want a live display."

"Understood," Poz said.

"And Poz?" Oxade watched a fully kitted-out Alex and Nutrene enter the room and gave them the thumbs up.

"Yes?"

"Confirm the coordinates with their autopilot. Absorb them into your data field, please. I want every black box equivalent of their time away from Earth. Search every nook and cranny. Leave no stone unturned."

"Do you know how long that will take?"

"No," he said, suddenly concerned, "How long?"

"About fifteen minutes."

Oxade breathed a sigh of relief, "Well, that's good. Gives us enough time to take care of business. Now shut up and get working."

He stepped out of the holograph and snapped his fingers, "Hughes."

"Yes, Captain?"

"You and Nutrene will board Opera Beta."

"Understood."

"Poz and Neg are reporting high toxicity levels. You'll have to strap your space skins on and keep a consistent check on your oxygen."

Nutrene watched Tripp and Manuel walk behind Poz and Neg at Beta's communications panel.

"Look at the *state* of Opera Beta," she pointed at the windshield, "It's cracked to all hell. Look."

"The windshield will have sealed itself if it sustained any damage. A failsafe designed to buy the crew some time in the event of a disaster."

"Captain?" Neg's voice flew around the room, "Are you seeing what we're seeing? Look at this."

"Come in, Neg," Oxade stepped back into the holograph, "Can you focus on the points of interest, please?"

"Yes."

Purple light formed around the damaged flight panel.

"The main control unit is devastated," Neg said. "In addition, the communications panel is barely operational. Beta herself is barely operational."

"Neg, make sure Poz absorbs every piece of data available."

"I will."

Oxade turned to Nutrene and Alex, "Okay, that's decided, then. We're using Charlie to get back home. I don't know what happened to Beta, but she's battered beyond salvation. I wouldn't trust her any more than I'd trust you alone with Hughes."

Alex tried not to giggle at Oxade's prescience.

"Did you have to say that?" Nutrene blurted. "That wasn't nice."

"You want nice?" he stormed up to her, face-to-face and held his palm open, "Maybe a physical reminder of who's in charge, here?"

"Are you going to hit me?" Nutrene stared him down,

"Then be a man and *hit me*."

Oxade slapped her across the face. Her chin twisted over her right shoulder as a blotch of red heat formed over her cheek.

"Speak back to me again, Byford. I will leave you on Beta with Poz and Neg so they can detonate with you. Spread your organs around the solar system like some kind of worthless, spinster milkshake. Is that quite clear?"

She looked him in the eyes more determined than ever for blood, "Yes. *Captain.*"

Alex gulped and hoped Oxade wouldn't deal the same talking-to as he did to Nutrene.

His luck had run out.

"What the hell are you looking at, Hughes?"

"Nothing, Captain."

"Hey, *you*. Hughes," Oxade stood in front of the lad and pushed his chin up with his knuckle, "Prove to me you're on-point and on our side."

"Yes, sir."

"You're gonna board Beta, right?"

"Yes," Alex said with anger.

"And you're going to kill those bastards, right?"

"Yes, sir," Alex lied to his face with great vigor, "I'm gonna kill 'em. I'm gonna kill 'em all."

Oxade grinned and thumped him on the shoulder, "That's my boy."

Chapter 13

Medix
Space Opera Beta - Level Three

Jelly sat on the edge of the bed nearest the door. Her original cat-sized trolley was much too small for her by now.

Wool ran the tip of her lit thumb along the wall and recorded Jelly's latest measurement.

"Before we left Pink Symphony you were just over five feet tall," Wool pressed her palm onto her thumbnail and stood to her feet in order to reach the new recorded height above her head. "Now, you're seven feet *and two inches*."

"What's happening to me, mommy?" Jelly whined in her deep and husky adult voice, "Why am I getting bigger?"

Wool shot the cat-woman a wistful look, "I don't know, honey."

"Hey, Jelly. Are you decent?"

She was anything but decent if she'd have been one hundred percent human woman. Her fur provided the modesty she needed, given the circumstances.

"Yeah."

Jaycee walked into Medix carrying a spare exo-suit and laid them on the nearest available bed, "Got you some fresh clothes. It's okay. I'm not looking."

"You can look," Jelly hopped to her feet and swished her tail around.

Jaycee took her advice and took in her enormity, "Jesus Christ on a pogo stick," he stammered and glanced at Wool, "Has she gotten *bigger* in the past few minutes, or what?"

"She won't stop growing," Wool watched Jelly throw the

Kevlar exo-suit over her shoulders. She pulled the cord from the lapel, enabling it to soak around her chest, arms and abdomen.

"I like this," Jelly said with her back facing the other two.

"Does it fit okay?"

"Yeah."

She lifted her right leg and placed her foot on the bed, forming a statuesque right angle which inadvertently revealed her impressive thighs.

Wool held Jaycee back and took a step forward, "Honey? Are you okay?"

"I said I'm fine."

The subtle croaking in her voice indicated otherwise. She tried her best to keep her cries to herself.

Wool turned around and caught a pink tear welling in her eye with her knuckle. She afforded Jelly some privacy and grabbed the exo-suit leggings, "I'll cut a hole open for your tail."

"No, give me it. You don't know where the hole will be, yet," Jelly cleared her throat and grabbed the waistline with her large paws, "Careful, don't touch my claws."

"Okay, okay," Wool joined Jaycee and watched Jelly yank the fabric out into a thin, Kevlar belt. She wrapped it around her hips, accentuating the muscles in her thigh.

Jaycee's hands shook at Jelly's magnificence. He felt a sensation he was rarely used to. Standing before him was a woman who was his equal - or as damn near as could possibly be.

A beautiful, striking creature.

His eyes followed the fabric unravel down, away from her waist and down her thighs to her knees.

Wool cast a wry eye at Jaycee's face. She knew what he was feeling, and didn't approve.

"Jaycee—"

He half-heard her as he ogled Jelly's legs.

"*Jaycee.* You're not serious, are you?"

"Wha—?"

The fabric crept around her shin and soaked into her fur. She looked up in some discomfort and looked at Jaycee.

His eyes traveled from her waist, past her subtle baby bump, past her well-endowed chest - accentuated all the more by the tight top - and, finally, to her neck and face.

Both sets of eyes met quite by accident.

"What are you looking at?" Jelly stomped right foot to the ground and brushed her tail, "Were you *checking me out?*"

"No, no, I—"

"—You *were* checking me out, weren't you?" Jelly hissed at him.

Wool buried her head in her hand, "Oh, God, don't do that. You'll make it worse."

Jaycee's tongue hung out of his mouth. He didn't realize it at first, but short of having a neon love heart strapped to his head, anyone could tell he was smitten.

"I love it when you hiss at me," he said.

BOP.

Jelly booted the bed off its wheels. She spread her claws out and poised to attack the man, "What the *hell* did you just say?"

"Nothing. I didn't mean—"

"—Do you want me to kill you?"

Jaycee looked at his feet and apologized, "No, I didn't mean anything by it."

"God help me," she scowled in pain and clutched her stomach. The pink shimmer of light from her abdomen pounded through the suit, "I think I'm gonna be sick."

She staggered forward and slammed her paw against the wall. A spider web of cracks shot across the wall and coughed out a plume of dust.

"Guuuh," she cowed and doubled-over, trying not to be sick.

Wool's hands shook. The reality of Jelly's predicament had major repercussions for the safety of the ship and its crew.

"Honey, you're getting worse."

Jelly lifted her head and widened her ashen eyes.

"I'm not g-getting worse," she growled, "I'm g-getting *better.*"

She held herself against the wall and exhaled, blowing the

dust from the cracks created by her claws, "Miew," she whined, "My tail. Cut me open."

Wool raced forward and placed her hands on Jelly's hips, "Where? Tell me."

"Right... h-here..." she tapped her infinity claw at the base of her spine, "Where it usually is."

Jaycee's forearm buzzed to life and tore his attention away from the bizarre spectacle. He rolled up his sleeve and thumbed the ink toward his wrist, "This is Jaycee?"

"Jaycee," Tripp's voice came from the pinpricks in his wrist, "This is Tripp."

"I read you, Tripp. Hang on, why are you whispering?"

"We've docked with Charlie. They're performing an audit and getting ready to take us home—"

"—Mee*oowww*," Jelly whined.

"Hold still," Wool ran her hot thumbnail ten inches down the back of Jelly's Kevlar leggings, "Nearly there."

"What's that noise?"

Jaycee lifted his wrist to his mouth, "You're never gonna believe this."

"What?"

"Anderson. She's getting *bigger*. We're trying to fit her with my back-up exo-gear."

Tripp ignored the comment, "Never mind that now. I need you to come and make yourself known to Charlie. They've sent these bizarre little droids on board but the actual crew haven't docked yet. Getting kinda spooked, here, if I'm honest."

"On it," Jaycee palmed the panel on the wall and opened the door, "Gotta love you and leave you, now. We've docked with Charlie and Tripp needs me on the deck."

"What?"

Jelly's tail whipped out of the hole and accidentally slapped Wool across the face.

"Oww," Wool cupped her cheek in her hands, "Jelly!"

"Sorry, mommy."

Jaycee sniggered and shook his head, "I'll leave you two to it. Leave your Individimedia on, Wool. We might need you."

"Ugh," she spat a tuft of fur from her mouth, "*Fine*. Just

get us home, will you?"

Wool patted Jelly's paw away from her shoulder, "*Please*. Be careful with your tail. You're not a little pet anymore."

"I said I was sorry," Jelly began to purr and made a cute face of contrition at her 'mother', "*Sorry*."

Wool squinted at her face and lifted her hand away. Her eyes suggested she was lying.

"You're not sorry, are you?"

"No."

"Well, if there's one thing you've learned then it's to lie convincingly."

"Lying is fun," Jelly chuckled. "I didn't mean a word I said."

Wool stepped through the open door and glanced at the window, "You're getting weirder as well as bigger."

Jelly stepped after her, "Mommy, wait for me."

Wool focused on Saturn's rings and raised her eyebrows, "Huh, that's funny."

"What, mommy?"

"The rings. It looks like Saturn is wearing a Decapidisc," she shook her head and walked out of the room. "Speaking of which, where's Tor?"

Rest & Recuperation
Space Opera Beta - Level Two

A jolly muzak version of *Swan Lake* played in the gents bathroom.

Tor sat in the first of five cubicles with his pants around his ankles. He grabbed the rail with his left hand and clenched his bowels.

"Uggghhh…" his heels squeaked along the tiled floor, "Ohhh, *no*. I think I'm gonna pass out."

It looked as if he'd been swimming - the sweat smothered his face like a wet cloth. The veins in his temple bulged through his skin as he took a deep breath and squeezed once again.

Then, his left forearm beeped.

"Huh?"

The ink swirled around into three, long lines, waiting to be answered: Tripp Healy.

"Ah, God. Not *now…* "

Tor rolled his shoulders, cleared his throat and relaxed his muscles. He squelched the ink to his wrist with his shaking index finger.

"Tripp?"

"Tor?"

"What is it? I'm kinda busy right now," he winced in pain. "Can it wait a couple minutes?"

"Where are you?"

"I'm *busy.*"

Tripp's huffs of displeasure waded from Tor's wrist, "Look, we've docked with Charlie. You're meant to be liaising with them."

"I'm…" Tor groaned through his turmoil, "Not ready, y-yet…"

"Are you in the Fit Room?"

"No," Tor burst into tears and drooled from his mouth, "I'll be there soon. Just w-wait for m-me-*oh-Christ-alive*—"

"—Tor? I didn't catch—"

He swiped the ink away from his wrist and slammed both hands on the sides of the toilet bowl.

BLOICK-CRUNK!

Something beyond evil occurred inside his abdomen. He kicked his feet apart and tore the waistline of his inner-suit legging apart with his ankles.

"Gaoooooowww…," he squeezed his eyes shut and tore the plastic off the toilet seat. A final squeeze of his stomach muscles was all it took.

Tor's eyes bulged out of their sockets. A blood vessel burst in his forehead.

SCH-JUNTT-SPLASH.

Then, an intense wave of relief smothered his very being. He'd released whatever had been causing the turmoil into the bowl.

"Ohhhh," he cried pink tears with insane joy, "Thank *God.*"

He looked at the toilet paper dispenser and found that it

was empty.

"Damn it," He brushed the empty cardboard tube and muttered to himself, "Does no one replenish the facilities anymore?"

Against his better judgment, and with little option to improvise, he removed his left boot, rolled his sock off his foot and held it up for inspection.

"Farewell, my friend."

Thirty-Eight Seconds Later...

Tor dropped the used sock between his legs and into the toilet bowl. He bent over, grabbed his inner-suit pants and pulled them up his legs.

The pain in his back had gone, too, much to his surprise. All in all, a very worthwhile trip to the convenience.

"A comfort break like no other," he smiled with relief and went for the flush. His face fell when he saw the contents of the bowl.

"Eh? What the *hell...*?"

A fleshy arm the size of a toilet brush wriggled around in the water, thrashing for dear life.

SCHWIPP!

A talon swung out from the end and scratched at the porcelain, trying to climb out.

Tor gasped and slammed the toilet seat shut - right on the end of the limb. It squealed and kicked its talon around in pain.

GROWLLL.

Tor buckled over in pain and clutched his stomach, "Ooof," He could feel something wagging from his behind. He squeezed his stomach muscles and put a stop to the commotion.

"Nuuuhh," he squealed, "What's h-happening to m-me?"

CREEAAAKKK!

The material on his right shoulder snapped apart, pushing the skin and joints through the sleeve. "Oh my God. Nooo--"

KEERRAAATTTCH!

His arm burst apart, splattering the cubicle walls with pink goo. The sleeve tore off and slopped to the flooded ground.

"Aggghhhh"

A Shanta limb unfurled from the socket in his shoulder and swished out its talon.

"Sha...sha..." Tor's head shook around. His mouth flung a rope of pink gloop into the air. "Shaaaaantaaaaa—"

Thinking fast on his feet - and then his knees - he lifted the toilet seat up, scooped the dead limb from the water and lifted it in the air.

"Sha... shaaaaan..."

He gargled through his tears and hacksawed at his shoulder with the talon. The large limb squealed and flailed around as he hacksawed the Symphonium-laced talon across his upper forearm.

The razor-sharp edge punctured through the grotesque right Shanta arm.

HACK-HACK-SLASH!

"Ngggggg," he dropped the spent limb to the floor and slammed the toilet lid down on his newly-formed wrist. He planted his boots on the wall and tore himself away from his mutated arm, all the while keeping his weight pressed down on the lid.

"Gaaaaaah," the arm tore away from his shoulder socket and writhed around in pain.

He slammed the lid down, trapping the vicious limb inside the bowl. The sound of talon-on-porcelain scratched and squealed from inside.

"Take th-that, you Shaa-aanta s-scumbag."

SLAMM-GROOWWLLSSCCHHH!

He hit the flush handle, slammed his palm on his right shoulder's stump and kicked the cubicle door open.

The Bridge

Alex and Nutrene pulled themselves along the weightless metal gantry.

Alex spoke into his headgear microphone, "These outer-suits are kinda funky."

Nutrene burst out laughing when she caught sight of his

USARIC-issued helmet skin. The thick, wet protective membrane looked like his face was melting.

"You look like a waxwork that's been left in the sun for five hours," Nutrene said before realizing she must have looked the same.

"Touché, Nutrene."

A rocketing sound occurred above their heads, forcing Saturn's light away from them.

Alex lifted his head to inspect the source of the noise. A giant fireball the size of Enceladus moved towards Saturn at a snail-like pace.

"What's going on up there?"

"Is that Enceladus?" Nutrene's voice came through Alex's headgear.

"It must be."

"What's she doing?"

"How should I know?"

Alex grabbed the bridge railing and yanked himself further along. The front of his boot drifted a couple of inches from the grille, "I don't want to hang around to find out."

Oxade's voice chimed in with disdain, "When you two lovebirds are quite finished enjoying the view, do you think you could get on Beta and take what's ours, please?"

"We are, we are. But we think you should see this," A pang of nerves socked Nutrene in the stomach.

"What is it?"

"Do you have a feed of Saturn and Enceladus?"

"No, but I can get one. Why, what's wrong?"

"The moon. Well, one of them, anyway. It's a fireball, like a raging inferno," Nutrene widened her eyes and took in the scale of the spectacle, "It's *fantastic*."

"Never mind that now. I've advised Beta team that you are en route. Go in, take the data download package from Poz, and get the hell out of there."

"Oh, uh… yes, of course," Nutrene just about managed to tear her eyes away from Enceladus and focus on Opera Beta's outer airlock hatch.

"Nutrene? Come on," Alex waved her over. "Let's go."

"I'm coming…" she took one, final glance at the giant

inferno rocketing towards Saturn.

The Control Deck
Space Opera Beta - Level One

Neg watched Poz retrieve Beta's data from the communications console via his arm extension.

"Seven minutes until data transfer is complete," he advised to anyone listening.

Tripp watched the process take place with Jaycee. The pair were mesmerized by the technology on display.

"So, this is what the future looks like?" Jaycee whispered. "Manning/Synapse ditches the human look and goes with a tin of beans?"

Tor stumbled into the room looking for all the world like a shivering, bag of sweating nerves with post-traumatic stress disorder.

Tripp, Jaycee, Manuel, Poz, Neg, and Jaycee turned around to see who produced the wretched gurgling.

"Tor," Tripp yelled, "Where have you been?"

"S-Something's happening to me, I'm s-sick," he grumbled through his mouthful of saliva, "M-My organs feel so c-c-cold…"

"Who's this?" Poz asked, flippantly.

"Oh, this is Tor Klyce. Our sort of communications officer," Tripp clapped eyes on the sweating man properly, "My God, Klyce. Pull yourself together."

"I'll b-be okay," Tor's doubled-over and almost vomited on the floor.

Poz knocked the swivel chair over to him, "Here, have a seat."

"Th-thanks."

Tor staggered across the control deck and turned around, thumping his behind onto the chair, "Owww."

"What happened to you?" Jaycee reached into his belt, preparing himself to blow the man's head off.

"I'll be okay. I think I've caught some kind of space flu, or something," Tor lied. He needed to keep his mutation a secret from the others, or else he was dead.

"Ah, that explains it," Poz rolled his head around and blink his eyebulbs, "The flu? Whatever it is pervading the atmosphere on this ship has clearly gotten to him."

"What do you mean?" Tripp spat. "*Flu?* Pervaded the atmosphere?"

"Captain Healy, your ship is infected with whatever this pink gas is. If it's even a gas, of course."

"Bleuurrgggghhh…" Tor pressed his only arm to his knee and spat a rope of pink drool to the ground.

Tripp noticed Tor didn't have a right arm now that he'd uncovered the stump, "Holy hell, Tor. Where's your arm?"

"I had to remove it. It malfunctioned."

"Malfunctioned?"

"Where is it now?" Jaycee asked. "Don't lie to me, Russian. Where did you leave it?"

"Why-why d-do you c-care?"

"When Baldron took my hand it fell to the floor and tried to attack him. It ran out of battery and flipped him the bird. You can't leave Androgyne parts lying around—"

"—It's o-okay, I took c-care of it."

"Russian, huh?" Neg tucked the side of her head onto her cylinder 'shoulder' area and scanned Tor's face.

"Wh-what are you looking at?" Tor wiped the drool from his lips and complained to Tor, "Why is she looking at me?"

"I dunno. It's better than her making eyes at me for a change."

Tor spat another mound of pink phlegm to the floor, "You do all realize that there's a giant cat on the loose who's—"

"—Oh. I know you," Neg beamed and cut off Tor's note of caution, "Viktor Rabinovich."

The sick man sat back in his chair, dumbstruck, "How do you know my name?"

"Dummy," Neg giggled in her childlike electronic voice, "Everyone *knows* you. You were assassinated five years ago. But, here you are, alive and well. Tut-tut. Bad man."

"This is *asinine*," Tor tried to jump out of his seat and accost the rude droid, but slumped back to his seat in pain.

"Four minutes remaining till the transfer is complete,"

Poz's head spun around to Neg and Tripp, "Okay, enough bum-fondling from you two, please. I gather we have visitors at the airlock."

"That is correct," Manuel bent his back cover toward the door, "Tripp? Would you like me to meet and greet our guests from Opera Charlie?"

"Yes, and take Jaycee with you."

Jaycee needed someone to take out his frustration on, and so thumped Tor on the back, "Do I look like a doorman?"

Tripp looked him up and down. That Kevlar suit. His large frame, and booming voice.

"Actually, *yes*."

"Fair enough."

"Stop being insubordinate and go with Manuel. Remember who's your Captain, here."

"Fine," He stomped toward the door in a huff and clenched his fist as he walked past Tor.

"N-No, d-don't hit me! I'm sick—"

"—You got that right," Jaycee lifted his fist and threatened to clobber the man.

"No, no, please—"

THWOMP.

Jaycee slammed Tor on the back of his neck with his new 'Baldron hand' and continued to the door, "Landaker says hello, *dickhead*."

Manuel slumped in the air and shook his covers in disapproval, "Jaycee?"

"What?"

"That was unnecessary."

"*You're* unnecessary, my encyclopedic friend," Jaycee palmed the panel on the wall. The door opened and allowed him out, "Are you coming or what?"

"Very well."

As the pair left, Tripp, Poz, and Neg discovered they had front row seats to the unveiling of Tor's breakfast.

"Bloooarrggghhh—"

SCHPLA-AA-TT.

Chunks of spew splattered around his feet. The pink gunk ran across the floor and down the nearest grate.

"Oh, that's just *gross*," the three of them complained. They turned away and pinched their nostrils shut.

Chapter 14

Primary Airlock
Space Opera Beta

Jaycee watched Alex and Nutrene enter Opera Beta's airlock. He tapped the window and held his thumb up at them, "Ready?"

Both of them nodded and held their thumbs up at him.

"Okay," Jaycee said to Manuel, "Let's decompress and get them in."

"Good idea," Manuel said.

"Here we go," Jaycee yanked the level down and eyed the pressure inlet on the wall. The dial spun to the left, indicating the pressure drop.

SPRIIISS.SHHHH!

A cloud of white gas burst around Alex and Nutrene. The inner airlock door flew up and offered the pair onto the ship.

"Hey, team Charlie," Jaycee stood aside and thumped his chest plate, "I'm Jaycee Nayall, Weapons and Armory. This, here, is our autopilot."

"Thank you so much for coming to rescue us," Manuel said.

Alex went to peel off his mask.

"You might want to keep that on, by the way," Jaycee said. "We don't want you getting sick."

"Right," Alex loosened his grip and made his way out of the airlock, "I heard you guys encountered some alien entity. Is it really that bad?"

"Your robot droid *thing* says Beta is thoroughly infected,"

725

Jaycee said.

"Poz and Neg?" Nutrene smirked. "They're a handful, aren't they?"

"They're certainly not on nodding terms with manners, I'll give them that. The virus isn't affecting us Androgynes, but the same can't be said for you humans."

Nutrene exited the inner airlock door. It sliced shut like a guillotine behind her, "Where have you been all this time?"

"I'd rather my Captain fill you in on the details."

"We need to know everyone's coordinates," Alex said. "Where's Anderson?"

"I think she's resting in Medix."

"Medix?"

"Yes, level three."

"Level three?" Alex raised an eyebrow at Nutrene, "Take us to your captain, please. Let's get you guys out of—" he stopped talking and clamped eyes on the floating Manuel, "Are you the autopilot?"

"Indeed I am, yes. I'm Manuel. Very nice to meet you both."

"You too. Where is Captain Tripp Healy?"

"Just this way," Manuel turned around and fluttered up the walkway, "He's at the control deck…"

Tor slammed his left hand on the communications panel and dry-heaved. The sweat on his face turned to a fine jelly. He fell to his knees, seriously worse for wear.

"Guuuh," his mouth began to foam, "Shaaaa…"

Tripp looked over from the flight deck and immediately raced over to him, intending to help the man to his feet, "Jesus, Tor. What's wrong with you?"

"I n-need to t-tell you something."

Tripp hooked his arms under Tor's one remaining armpit and helped him to his feet, "What is it?"

"I'm d-dying."

"Ha. And not for the first time," Poz blurted, concentrating on the up-link from the console.

"Dying?" Tripp analyzed the man's face. His eyes were beyond bloodshot. Snot and fluids poured from his ears and nose, "Look at me."

"Oh-oh *k-kay.*"

Tor's pupils wound around and turned a murky, urine-color.

"My God. Tor, you're *really* sick."

"I've b-been t-trying to t-tell y-you."

SWISH.

"Hey, you two," Jaycee shouted at the pair as he walked into the control deck with Manuel, Alex and Nutrene behind him, "Get a room, for heaven's sake."

Tripp kept Tor upright, "Jaycee, look at him. He needs urgent medical attention."

"Where's Wool?"

"Still at Medix, I think," Jaycee looked at Alex and Nutrene, "Sorry about this, guys. Our Russian traitor, here, is feeling a bit—"

"—Viktor Rabinovich?" Alex eyed Tor with keen interest.

Tor slid behind Tripp, using him as a body shield.

Jaycee went for his Rez-9, "Huh? Tor, what are you—"

Alex threw his left arm out like a Samurai sword.

SCHUNT.

The Rez-9 flew into his palm. He swung his arm to Tor and threatened to shoot him, "Viktor Rabinovich."

"Yes," Tor removed the Rez-9 from Tripp's belt and thrust the barrel against his temple, "Stay back or I'll blow his head off."

A three-way standoff occurred.

Tor held Tripp's gun at his temple. Alex kept his firearm pointed at Tor's forehead.

Jaycee swung his Rez-9 from Alex to Tor, and then back at Alex, "Hey, what's going on?"

Nutrene held out her hands, desperate to put a halt to the forthcoming violence.

"Guys, please? Can we work this out?"

Alex took a step closer to Tor, who hid behind Tripp's body, "You're meant to be dead—"

"—I *am* d-dead," Tor screamed back, "Don't come any closer or I'll blow this bastard's memory banks out all over this place."

"Drop your weapon, Rabinovich," Alex threatened. "Do it."

"What's this about?" Tripp muttered, keeping his arms outstretched.

"Th-that s-sonofabitch Alex Hughes," Tor thumbed the side of the Rez-9 and armed it, "He t-tried to assassinate m-me—"

"—Why?"

"B-Because, h-he works f-for—" Tor grunted and growled. The barrel slipped away from Tripp's temple and launched into the air.

Alex took another step forward and prepared to blast Tor's forehead apart, "Rabinovich, get on your knees—"

SCHPLATTT-GROOWWWWLLL!

Tor's chest catapulted into the air, taking his mechanical body with it. His one remaining arm cracked apart and released a fleshy Shanta limb.

SCHTOMP-CRAACK.

The limb smashed its talon to the ground, shaking everyone across the ground like a tray of marbles.

"Wuh-wuh," Alex ran to the other end of the wall, "What's happening to him?"

Tripp scooped his Rez-9 from the floor and swung it at Tor - or, what little remained of him, "He's changing into one of those things."

"What *things*—?"

SPATCH-CREAK-SLAMM.

Four Shanta limbs burst from Tor's sides and slammed to the floor. The talons dug against the ground and produced a whirlwind of electric sparks. The synthetic skin over his neck pulled apart and tossed his head to the floor.

A messy fusion of creature limbs and Tor's devastated top half staggered toward the door, squealing and growling all the way.

"Get behind something," Nutrene screamed through her mask and dived behind the flight deck.

"Help m-me…" Tor's head hung by a thread of synthetic skin down the back of the Shanta, "I n-need help."

"Open fire."

BAM-BAM-BAM!

Tor's bottom half ran out of the control deck, carrying its six half-formed limbs with it.

"God damn it," Tripp turned to Manuel. "Raise the alarm, now. It's run off into the ship."

"Yes, of course."

ARRROOOOO-GAH!

The control deck dimmed as red lights swiveled around the walls and floor.

Tripp, Alex, Nutrene, and Jaycee bolted through the door after the screaming monstrosity.

AROOOOOO-GAH!

"Emergency," came the recorded voice, "The alarm has been raised. Please be advised. Remain where you are until instructed otherwise. Thank you, and have a nice day."

Poz turned to Neg and bounced on the spot. They were alone at last.

"I dunno why they're bothering trying to kill it. The whole place is gonna be history soon."

"Yeah, yeah, yeah."

Excited, Neg rolled back and opened up her orb-shaped back. A stack of canisters clanged to the floor, "Want me to prime them?"

"If you would be so kind, yes," Poz peeked at his transfer cable, "Sixty seconds and we have the data. We're going back home with Anderson, dead or alive. Preferably *dead.*"

"Aww," Neg squealed over the racket of the alarms, "Why dead?"

"Because the only good pussy is a dead pussy."

"Huh," Neg knocked into the canisters. The green light on top flashed, indicating they were set. Her eyebulbs turned white as she rolled her head up to the windshield, "Oxade, this is Neg Bass."

"Come in, Neg. What the hell is all that fuss I'm hearing on Beta?"

"Oh, they threatened to shoot each other. Nothing to do with us—"

"—They *what?*" Oxade screamed in both Poz and Neg's heads, "What do you mean threatened to shoot each other?"

"Rabinovich is on board Beta, Oxade," Poz said. "He turned into a man-spider thing and ran off. It was horrendous, quite frankly."

"Have you gone insane? Right, that's enough. I'm boarding Beta."

Neg knocked the canisters on the floor and threw a blue beam over them, "Ah, actually, I wouldn't do that."

The Control Deck
Space Opera Charlie

Oxade pulled the weapons cupboard open. He unhooked the D-REZ semi-automatic, extended its shoulder holster and booted the door shut.

"The nukes?" Oxade roared into his headgear and ran out of the deck, "*Please* tell me you planted the nukes?"

"Yes," Poz's voice rumbled into his ear, "They're primed to go."

"Good. You've just saved yourself a messy execution," Oxade snatched a gelatin swab from the wall and raced along the walkway, "I'm boarding Beta and taking care of this. Stay there and wait for me."

SCHLOOP.

He smeared the gelatinous mush around his face as he walked. The compound material stretched across his skin. Pockets of air burst out of his skin. The end result made his face look like it was covered in cellophane.

"Primary airlock, ETA twenty seconds."

"There's really no need to do that, Captain," Poz's voice reached Oxade's helmet headgear, "We'd rather you not leave Charlie unmanned—"

"—I'd rather you not be a useless tin opener but you don't hear me complaining, do you?"

Poz thought about Oxade's retort, "Actually, yes I do—"

"—Shut up and open the damn bridge."

SWISH!

The inner airlock door flew up and offered Oxade into the chamber.

"As you desire, Captain. In your own time."

"Don't patronize me, you mechanical moron."

Level One Stairwell
Space Opera Beta

Tor stumbled down the steps. His swinging, most-severely head clanged against the railings. Its mouth squealed in pain.

Six limbs shot out from his ribcage and pressed against the wall, aiding his decent.

His left leg slammed to the next step and broke apart. The connective flesh slipped away from his metallic femur 'bone' and swiped its talon.

His right leg fell off when it connected with the next step. Another limb burst out through his metallic ball joint. Tor was no longer an Androgyne but a fully-formed Shanta.

Tripp, Jaycee, Alex, and Nutrene reached the top step with their weapons aimed at the half-man, half-Shanta monstrosity, "Tor, stay where you are."

"Screeeeeeeee," the Shanta widened its slit and whipped Tor's head into the air.

SCHOMP-CLOTCH!

It caught Tor's jaw between its teeth and yanked it away from the top of his skull.

"Damn," Alex gasped, "That virus really kicks ass, doesn't it?"

BLAM-BLAM-BLAM!

Tripp and Jaycee opened fire on the creature. It gripped the railings with all twelve limbs and scurried down the next set of steps.

"Get it," Tripp shouted after it and continued down the staircase.

"Screeeeee," The Shanta's two front limbs hit the next step, tripped on something unexpected and crashed against the level two sign on the wall.

"Miew," came a whine of protest from the step.

The Shanta stomped four of its limbs to the floor and the remaining eight against the wall and ceiling and screeched in pain.

Jelly shifted her weight and stood to her feet, "Not again."

SCHTANG-SCHTANG!

She flung out her infinity claws by her sides and prepared to slash the creature.

"Jelly," Jaycee aimed his Rez-9 at the creature, "Get out of the way."

She turned over her shoulder and licked her lips, ready for war, "No."

"I mean it, Jelly."

The Shanta pushed itself from the wall like an octopus and bolted towards Jelly. She pulled her elbows back, ready to swipe at the monstrosity.

"*That's* Anderson?" Alex lowered his gun, trying to take the information in, "But sh-she's…"

"Yeah. Difficult to believe, huh?" Tripp spat. "Would you believe me if I told you she's pregnant, too?"

SWIPE-SWISH-CRACK!

Jelly right-hooked the Shanta, sending it hurtling over the rails between the stairs, "*Meow.*"

WHOOOSH!

The Shanta plummeted between the stairs. Its limbs smashed against the stairs as it tumbled down.

The signage for levels two, three, and four flew past its slit as its screams echoed up the stairwell.

"Jelly, what did you do?" Jaycee barged past her and hopped down the next flight of stairs.

"I killed it," she said and followed him.

Tripp, Alex, and Nutrene ran down after them.

"Are you gonna tell us what that thing is, now?" Nutrene shouted after Tripp and Jaycee as they jumped down to the level three gantry.

"We've called it Symphonium," Tripp explained. "Some sort of messed up evolutionary virus."

Jelly peered over the staircase, "It came from the ocean. It turned the algae into fish. The fish into mammals. The mammals into apes. The apes into humans, and the humans into—"

"—Shaaantaaa," the monstrosity squealed from two floors below. Everyone jumped in their shoes as the volume of its voice rattled their ears.

Jelly pointed at Alex and Nutrene's faces, "Keep those masks on, humans."

"Yes, we will," Alex failed to comprehend the absurdity of his findings.

Jelly wrapped her infinity claws around the staircase railing and bent her knees, preparing to jump the next couple of flights.

"Jelly, what are you doing?" Tripp swung his gun at her.

She shot him a look of pure venom and swished her tail.

"I'm going to kill it *dead*," she squealed, "Go to Medix and get Wool."

"We can't leave you here on the ship. What if you don't make it off?"

"I'll make it off," Jelly's claws sparked up a frenzy, expressing her desire for death, "I'm going to rip Tor's battery out like you should have done days ago. Now, go!"

"But—"

HOP-SWISH!

Jelly swung her legs over the rail and plummeted down the gap in the staircase.

"Meeoooowwwww…" her voice etched further and further away.

"Guys, let's go get Wool."

***

Jelly landed awkwardly paws-first at level five. She rolled onto her side and clutched her baby bump.

"Ughhh," she scrambled to her feet. The Shanta slapped its limbs along the ground, walls and ceiling, pulling itself across the corridor and well away from Jelly.

"Hey, Tor," Jelly screamed after it as she staggered to her feet, "Come back here."

"Screeeeeeee."

Jelly took a deep breath and lowered her head. The glow from within her stomach formed into three, glowing orbs.

She winced as she tried to move forward, "God. *Not now*."

The Shanta reached the door to Pure Genius. With nowhere else to go, it slammed its talons against the door in attempt to open it.

"Hey," Jelly flung her claws out by her hips and growled as she moved toward the cornered beast, "I know that's you in there, Tor."

The Shanta calmed down and turned to her. The talons on each of its twelve limbs swiped out, ready to kill.

"Shaaaaaantaaahh."

Jelly picked up the pace and ran toward it, "Tor, if you're in there, you better get ready to go to hell."

ROOOAAAARRRR!

Jelly jumped into the air and swiped at the creature. She missed and hit the wall.

The Shanta slithered to the side and punched her in face, sending the back of her head against the wall panel, forcing the door open.

SWISH.

"Welcome to Pure Genius," announced a friendly voice as the door opened. "Please be advised that this is a zero gravity environment."

Jelly laughed venomously and removed the back of her head from the broken panel. Shards of shattered plastic nestled in her hair. She leaned forward and grabbed the Shanta's mid-section on her paws.

"Come with me."

Before the Shanta could scream, she tightened her grip and yanked him back into the chamber with her.

The two of them tumbled into the middle of the perfect cuboid as if swimming underwater.

Jelly lifted her leg and booted the Shanta's slit with her knee. Its metal teeth nicked her leggings as it moved away.

She released the creature and kicked it against the wall.

Both Jelly and the beast waded through the air and hit the two opposite sides, lighting up the tiles.

"Pure Genius activated," the voice advised. "Please specify your command."

RROOOOAAARRR!

The Shanta clapped its limbs against the wall and pushed itself forward like an octopus propelling itself from the Ocean bed.

SWISH-SWIPE.

Jelly ducked out of the path of the whizzing talons.

"Oh, no you don't," She pressed her body from the wall and up to the ceiling that contained the door, "Up here. *Woof-woof.*"

The Shanta's twelve limbs stiffened and prepared to dive skyward.

"Come and get some," Jelly squealed and froze solid. She waited for her assailant to spring towards her.

The pair made eye contact, trying to psyche each other out.

"Come on," Jelly screamed, goading the Shanta to attack, "What are you waiting for? Kill me."

The creature screamed and pushed itself away from the ground. It flew through the air and extended its first four limbs and talons.

Jelly gripped the lip of the door and pulled herself up and through the opening.

The sudden presence of gravity pulled her knees to the walkway ground as she leaned over the gap. She opened out her paw and slammed it against the wall panel as the first two limbs struck at her face.

"Agghh," Jelly squealed as the door sliced across the front of her face.

SWISH-SCHA-JUNT!

The door guillotined the Shanta's two front limbs from its body. Its muffled squeals whirled around the fully fired-up supercomputer. Two severed talons clanged to the floor by Jelly's knees.

"Meow," Jelly palmed the window in anger and looked at the trapped creature one last time, "Go to hell, *dickhead.*"

Her tail swished left to right as she turned around and made her way back to the staircase.

The Shanta hung in the middle of Pure Genius with two of its limbs missing. Pink liquid from its severed arms launched into the air and splashed against the tiles like a Jackson Pollock painting.

It knew it was trapped - possibly for good.

Its center slit widened and tried to take in some air.

SCHTAM-SCHTAM-SCHTAM!

It extended all its remaining arms like a multi-pronged star. Three on the ground, three on the ceiling, and two pressed against the left and right wall.

It remained static like a fleshy cobweb, trapped forever inside Pure Genius.

Medix
Space Opera Beta - Level Three

Tripp and Jaycee approached Medix ready to open fire on anything remotely unfamiliar.

Alex and Nutrene watched their six and their weapons up the corridor.

Manuel floated along with them, "Tripp?"

"Not now, Manuel."

"I'm scared, Tripp."

"What do you mean?" Tripp lowered his gun and turned to Jaycee, "I'll go in there and grab Wool. Stay here."

"Okay," Jaycee joined Alex and Nutrene, "Listen up. We're getting our friend and then getting the hell off this ship."

Manuel slotted himself between Tripp and the door to Medix, "Tripp?"

"Can't this wait, Manuel?"

"You're not going to leave without me, are you? You know I can't leave Opera Beta."

"What?" Tripp acted defiant in the face of his autopilot. But the book had a point - he was restrained to the confines of the ship and knew it would never return home.

"Please don't leave me here."

"I'm sure there's a way to transfer you to—"

"—There is not. Tripp. I cannot lie. They have their own autopilot. Almost certainly more advanced than I am."

Tripp couldn't look at the holograph any longer. He didn't have an answer.

"I thought as much," Manuel's front and back cover slumped, resigned to its fate, "I'm going to leave, now."

"I'm sorry, Manuel."

"Yeah," he sighed, "Keep telling yourself that."

WHVOOM.

The book vanished, leaving the door in plain sight.

Tripp glanced at Jaycee, who looked away with a discreet sadness, "You did what you had to do."

"There was no point in lying to him."

Jaycee lowered his gun and nodded, "Stop pontificating. Get Wool. Now."

Tripp entered the room and spotted Wool looking out of the window with a forlorn expression on her face, "I don't know if you heard the alarms, but we need to get out of—"

She sniffed and placed her palm on the plastic window ledge.

"Look, Tripp. Look at Enceladus. It's heading for Saturn"

He joined her at the window. The impossibly large ball of fire left a thick, pink vapor trail as it rocketed away. The vibrations of the window in her palm conveyed the sheer ferocity of the event.

"It's beautiful, isn't it?" she asked.

"Wool, we have to go."

She kept facing the window with her arms folded and refused to move, "I c-can't go."

"Why not?"

He moved next to her and clocked her reflection in the plastic pane. Something about her face wasn't right.

"I can never go home ever again, Tripp."

He applied pressure to her shoulder and tried to comfort her, "Don't be stupid, just—"

A cold sensation on his fingertips made him look down. A Shanta talon crept across his knuckles, stretching from Wool's fleshy arm.

"Oh, no."

A tear rolled down Wool's cheek, "When you leave, close the door and seal me inside. Have Jaycee break the wall panel so I can't get out."

"Wool," Tripp muttered.

"It's okay," she half-laughed and sniffed through her

tears, "It was bound to happen sooner or later. We're mostly human organs, after all. I guess the Symphonium just takes a little longer to work with our synthetic insides."

She turned to him at once. His face fell when he clapped his eyes on hers. She seemed desperate and beyond hope.

"Oh, Wool," Tripp's lip quivered. He looked at her pink, bloodied arm. The skin cracked apart above the elbow. The three cat scratch marks pulsed and revealed a fleshy, white layer.

"Do you have your Rez-9?" she asked.

He offered her his weapon with caution, "Yes, of course. Here."

"No, Tripp. I can't do it."

He pointed at his jaw, "Remember?"

"Yes, I remember," she turned to the window and widened her eyes at the glorious ball of fire, "Say goodbye to the crew for me. Tell them if it was going to be anyone, then I'm glad it was them."

A pink tear rolled down Tripp's cheek as he hooked his index finger around the trigger. He placed the end of it at the back of her head.

Tripp's voice croaked, "Do you want me to tell Jelly—"

"—No. Don't tell her anything," she reached behind her head and gripped the barrel of the gun in her right hand, "In my battery, please."

Her hand dragged the nozzle down across her back and pushed it between her shoulder blades.

"I could just open you and take it out."

"Destroy it. Make sure I'm dead. Shoot it," Wool burst out crying, "Tell Jelly her mommy is sorry."

Tripp sobbed like a helpless child and made sure his reflection didn't give his emotions away.

Wool took a lungful of air and widened her eyes. The light from Saturn filled her pupils, "Whatever is out there, we found it—"

BLAMMM!

Her chest opened out and splattered her insides against the window. Globs of thick, pink goo slid down the plastic, against the view of Saturn and the infernal Enceladus.

Wool crumpled to the floor, dead. Her smashed battery hung out through her ribcage and hit the floor.

Tripp lowered his gun and wiped his face.

"Sleep well, Wool."

Tripp exited Medix and closed the door.

Jaycee, Alex, and Nutrene turned around, expecting to find two crew members.

Tripp lowered his Rez-9 and marched through them, "Wool won't be joining us."

"What? Why not?" Jaycee asked and chased up to Tripp, "Hey, you can't walk off like that."

THUD.

He planted his giant hand on Tripp's shoulder and prevented him from walking, "Answer me."

Tripp grabbed Jaycee by the collar and shunted his back to the wall. A miasma of self-doubt and fury flew through his eyes, "Don't you ever, *ever* touch me like that again."

Jaycee grabbed Tripp's hand and pushed it away from his neck, "You're out of your mind."

"I know I am. We all are."

"Where's Wool?"

Tripp snorted and continued up the walkway, "She's not coming."

"Why?"

"She's dead."

"Dead?"

Alex and Nutrene decided it best to let the two men carry on their conversation a few feet ahead of them.

"Who's Wool?"

"Ah," Nutrene whispered, "My predecessor. Actually my second predecessor, after Katcheena. She was chief medician for USARIC. She oversaw the Star Cat Project back in *one-eighteen.*"

Alex squinted at her, "*That* Wool? Wool ar-Ban? The Iranian?"

"Yeah, you know her?"

"Oh. Uh, no. Just heard about her," Alex cleared his throat and grew nervous, "Dead?"

"You heard the man," she smirked, "Still, her being dead is good practice for all of them soon enough, eh?"

Jaycee pummeled the wall with his fists in anger, "Bastards."

Tripp held out his arms, "Hey, hey, calm down. There's nothing any of us could have done—"

"—You didn't have to execute her, you know," Jaycee spun his wrists around, ready to break something. A protruding pipe knocked against his knee, "God damn it."

He grabbed the pipe in his hands and wrenched it from the wall in a fit of rage. A blast of steam sprayed into the walkway as he swung it above his head and hurled it up the corridor, "I swear to *God* I'm gonna shoot someone."

"Jaycee, no. No more deaths, please," Tripp screamed at him, "Who are you gonna shoot?"

"*Someone.*"

"Let me ask you this, *tough guy*," he prodded Jaycee's exo-suit chest plate with his finger, "What if what you want to shoot is *inside* you? How are you gonna kill it?"

Jaycee slowed his breathing and pushed his captain's finger away, "I guess we'll find out soon enough. If it turned Tor and Wool, who's to say you and I aren't next?"

Chapter 15

Primary Airlock
Space Opera Beta

The inner airlock hatch slid up. Oxade clutched his D-REZ semi-automatic and entered Opera Beta proper.

He pressed his finger to the ear compartment on his gelatin helmet-mask, "Please tell me this piece of crap spacecraft has its control deck on level one."

"It does," Poz's voice came through Oxade's mask, "I advise you take the stairs. We can't trust the elevator on this malfunctioning hunk of junk."

"Pah. Morons can't even get *that* right," he took a look around the meager inner workings of the ship and chuckled to himself, "You're right, though. Opera Beta really *is* a hunk of junk, isn't it?"

"Soon to be *was*, I'll think you'll find."

"Very true. I'll see you in sixty seconds."

Keen to express his disrespect for the ship, Oxade coughed up a wad of phlegm and spat it on the wall.

Neg danced around the nuclear canister's beeps, "Beta gonna blow, Beta gonna blow."

"Will you knock it off, Neg?" Poz eyed the last of the data transfer through his arm, "Any second *now*."

Ba-Beep.

"Data transfer complete," announced the communications console.

"Thank you, kindly," Poz retracted his arm into his body.

Oxade marched into the control deck and stood in the middle of the room. He looked around with disgust, "Ugh, USARIC really broke the mold when they made Beta, didn't they? This is one stinking hellhole, for sure."

"Hello, Oxade."

"Hey, guys. Where are the others?"

"Something very peculiar happened while we were conducting the transfer."

"Did the transfer complete?"

"Yes," Poz blinked his eyebulbs and beeped, "All fifteen brontobytes of it. The thing is, though—"

"—Where is everyone? I told Hughes and Nutrene to keep an eye on them."

"If you'd let me finish," Poz interrupted, "Something untoward occurred right over there, behind you."

Oxade's heels skidded across Tor's vomit patch by the chair, "Whoa," he yelped and gripped the sticky back rest.

"Ugh. What the hell is this?" He flung the pink slime from his glove.

"According to the Manuel's last data point, it's called Symphonium. An evolutionary entity from whichever celestial territory they visited."

"Celestial territory? What are you talking about?"

"The Manuel recording a place name. Pink Symphony. Not much else is known. I would say it certainly accounts for the virus that has pervaded the ship."

Oxade looked at the concoction of drool in his gloved palm and grew anxious, "You said there was something *untoward*?"

"Yes," Neg hopped over to Oxade and beeped, "They all ran off. Tor Klyce turned into a fleshy spider thing and puked on the floor."

"Eurgh," Oxade moved away from the puke on the floor and inspected his heel, "You could have warned me."

"Well, we did *try*."

"They're all Androgynes, bar two. The botanist woman and the Captain," Oxade scowled, "If there was a virus it won't have affected anyone but them."

Poz and Neg watched Oxade wipe the remains of the goo on the communications panel.

"You're wrong, I'm afraid," Manuel's voice sparked up. His book holograph drew along the air and sparked, announcing his arrival.

"Manuel?"

"Yes."

"Where are your crew, Manuel?"

"Do I detect a hint of antagonism in your voice, Captain Weller?"

"No, you don't."

"It's just that the way you're talking indicates that the safety of my crew is not of paramount importance to you."

"Manuel, I capture and kill felines for a living back on Earth," Oxade huffed. "Don't think my remit *doesn't* extend to autopilots. Where is the rest of your crew? In particular, Jelly Anderson?"

"I'm not at liberty to say."

"I am the Captain of Space Opera Charlie, you Spanish-named lamebrain," Oxade lifted his D-REZ firearm at the communications panel, "I therefore outrank, outnumber *and* outgun you. Now, for the *final* time of asking, and presuming you don't want your physical memory to get blown to pieces, where are the others?"

"The others?"

"Yes, the others."

"As in, the crew?" Manuel butterflied around in the hope Oxade wouldn't shoot his physical home. He bought himself some time when he saw a distant figure move in the corridor behind the door.

"Yes, as you say, the *crew*."

"Oh. Level Ten, Engine & Payload," Manuel hoped Oxade would fall for his untruth, "We had trouble with the thrusters and wanted to check."

"Level Ten? Isn't that, like, a fifteen minute journey?"

"Yes, yes," Manuel clapped his covers together, congratulating himself. "I did it. He believed me."

"Who believed *you*?" Oxade fumed as he asked the question.

"Oh, uh, nothing," Manuel faux-cleared his throat, "Sorry, just another communication coming through. I think the crew will be at least thirty minutes."

Poz spun around to Neg and then back to Oxade, "Captain?"

"Yes, Poz?"

"I'm afraid to inform you that this autopilot is lying."

"I am *not* lying," Manuel lied.

"Lessense," Oxade waved Poz away, "Autopilots can't lie. Thanks for all your help, Manuel. We'll be on our way."

Manuel flapped his covers at the canisters, "Excuse me. You've forgotten your nukes."

Oxade made for the door. In doing so, he stepped into Tripp and Jaycee's path, "Oh."

Tripp eyed Oxade with suspicion, "What was that about nukes? Who are you?"

"Oxade Weller, captain of Opera Charlie," He extended his hand to shake, "We're here to rescue you."

Jaycee spotted the D-REZ in Oxade's hand, "You came prepared, I see?"

"Can't take any chances," Oxade turned to the Rez-9 in each of their hands, "And I could say the same about you."

Tripp shook the man's hand a little harder than expected, "Tripp Healy. Captain. We're relieved you managed to make it here to rescue us."

Alex and Nutrene walked into the control deck. They were surprised to see Oxade. He threw them a snarky smile as if to say 'shut up and let me speak.'

They nodded and lowered their guns.

"Your two crew members, here, very helpfully assisted us with tracking down a tango on board our ship."

Oxade nodded at the splattered chair and lifted up his goo-smeared glove, "So I see."

"Don't get any of that stuff on your person, by the way. It's contagious."

Oxade's breath fogged up the inside of his mask, "Contagious?"

"You wouldn't *believe* the journey we've been on," Jaycee said. "We've been to the center of the multiverse. We saw the nucleus of evolution with our own eyes."

"And we rescued *her*," Tripp added.

Oxade took a step away and looked around the control deck, "Am I right in thinking you've made one of the most important discoveries of our lifetime?"

"No," Tripp said. "We've made *the* most important discovery of *all* time."

Oxade grabbed his gun with both hands. He readied himself for action. To the others, it looked as if he was getting comfortable.

Both conclusions were true.

"We have to get back to Earth," Tripp said. "We need to get Jelly home so she can cure us all."

"Cure you?"

"She's pregnant," Tripp said. "We think her litter is the key to life, when it arrives."

Oxade laughed with a degree of venom, "You're not serious, are you?"

"Deadly serious, yes."

"Do you realize how stupid that sounds?"

"Actually, yes. But it's the truth."

"*Lessense*," Oxade lifted his gun at Jaycee and Tripp. They knew something like this was coming. Alex and Nutrene circled around them and pointed their guns at both men's faces.

"Okay, here's what's gonna happen," Oxade said. "You're going to call Anderson and get her to board Charlie. Once she's on, we'll join her and leave you here. Where are Wool ar-Ban, Haloo Ess, Bonnie Whitaker, Tor Klyce, and Baldron Landaker?"

"They're all dead," Tripp held his hands in the air along with Jaycee, "Only Jaycee and me left."

Oxade shouted at Manuel, "Is that true? Are they all dead?"

"No, they're all alive. Tripp is lying to you," Manuel sped up his speech, "They're on their way to come and kill you.

Tripp and Jaycee turned to each other - initially confused, but very quickly tuned in with what Manuel was up to.

"No, Manuel," Tripp yelled, adding to Oxade's confusion.

"They can't know they're all alive."

"I *knew* it, they're not dead," Oxade palmed the lever on the side of his K-SPARK and pointed it at the communications console. He turned to Nutrene and Alex, "Kill them!"

"Tripp, Jaycee - *now*," Manuel screamed and whizzed into the air.

BLAAMMMM!

Oxade fired a shot at the communications desk. Its panels and wiry guts burst out from the wall in a haze of electric sparks. Manuel's holographic book form began to fizzle away as a result of the explosion, "I'm hit."

Nutrene fired a shot at Tripp.

"Get down," Jaycee jumped on his back and pushed him to the ground. The bullet flew out of her Rez-9 and whizzed past Tripp's head, slicing several strands of his hair away from his head.

Jaycee hit the deck with Tripp. He lifted his gun at Oxade and fired a shot.

KER-SPLATCH!

The bullet penetrated the side of Oxade's left shin, pushing him to the ground.

Nutrene buried her gun in Jaycee's face and winked at him, "Nighty-night, big boy."

"Arrrgghhhh."

THRA-AA-TT-A-TT!

Jaycee closed his eyes and felt a splatter of liquid hit his face. No pain followed, much to his amazement.

He opened his eyes to see Alex had shot her in the shoulder.

"Huh?"

He kicked Nutrene onto the floor and offered Jaycee his hand, "Get up."

"Huh?"

Jaycee grabbed his hand and climbed to his feet. Alex turned his gun to Poz and Neg, "You two battery bunnies stay *right* where you are."

Oxade and Nutrene rolled around on the floor. They clutched at their injuries and screamed blue murder.

"You bastard," Oxade climbed to his feet and went for his D-REZ a few feet away from him.

"Ahh, da-da-da," Alex moved with him and rammed the barrel of his firearm into his head, "Hey, scumbag. Make a move and I'll re-carpet this place with your brain matter."

Oxade thumped the floor in anger, "Alex? What do you think you're doing?"

"Stay there," Alex stepped back and grabbed Tripp's hand, "Don't move, so help me God I'll split your skull open with a bullet."

"Alex?" Oxade gasped and lifted himself up by the communications panel, "You traitor."

"You shut up," he yelled back, much to the amazement of Tripp and Jaycee, "You wanna talk about being a traitor?"

Oxade spluttered and removed his glove. He felt the bleeding wound on his shin and pressed the sole of his foot to the floor, "USARIC will find you. They'll execute you."

"I'm counting on it. Now stay there."

"Who are you?" Tripp asked, not quite sure where to point his Rez-9.

"Alex Hughes. I'll explain later. Let's get off this ship."

"Good luck, *traitor*," Poz rolled toward Alex and threatened to make contact, "You'll never escape the blast. Come here for a killing."

Alex pushed Tripp and Jaycee toward the door, "Get back. Don't let it touch you."

"*It?*" Poz barreled forward, "That's a bit rude, isn't it? I'm quite clearly a *he*."

THRAAAAATTT!

Alex fired into the middle of Poz's body, pushing him back. The bullets absorbed into his body, leaving behind an array of minuscule dents.

Poz spun around and rolled into Neg. His body began to absorb into her.

"Hey, you can't do that," Neg complained.

"How long till detonation?" Alex asked. "*How long?*"

"Ten Earth minutes," Poz beeped with joy, "We're all going to die. We're all going to die."

Alex turned to Tripp and Jaycee, "Where's Anderson?"

Tripp shook his head, "She's, uh… I d-don't know?"

"Does she have Viddy Media?"

"Viddy-what?" Jaycee asked.

Alex rolled up his outer-suit sleeve and showed them his black ink, "Viddy Media."

"Is that what they're calling it now?" Tripp blurted. "No, she never had it installed."

"Damn," Alex thought on his feet and swung his D-REZ at Oxade and Nutrene, threatening to blow them to pieces, "Listen, get on Charlie."

"We have no outer-suits left," Jaycee said.

"Doesn't matter. Use the bridge. Don't look at anything, just run. I'll take care of these scumbags."

"Ten minutes? We'll never make it out alive."

"Well, it's either that or we *definitely* die," Alex huffed in haste, "Wanna give it a go?"

"Okay, we'll go," Jaycee said. "And, thanks."

"Yeah, we'll open up a tea shop together later," Alex quipped, "Now, go."

Tripp and Jaycee ran out of the control deck and made their way to the primary airlock.

Alex leaned against the door frame and lowered his gun. He surveyed the battered room and smiled at his Captain, "Hey, Oxade."

"Leave me alone, you treacherous little runt," he slumped into the splattered swivel chair. Resigned to an early death, he leaned back and hung his arms down by his side, "If you're going to kill us, just do it already."

Nutrene rolled around on the floor and clutched her arm. Her cries of anguish didn't stop the conversation between the two men.

"Oh, I will."

"Just tell me one thing, *Hughes*," Oxade said. "How did— Hey, Nutrene, can you stop your screaming, woman?"

"He shot me in the d-damn shoulder."

A smart bomb grenade tumbled across the ground and knocked the side her hand.

"I don't care. Just quit your whining, I can't hear myself *hear myself*," Oxade yelped.

"You were saying?" Alex asked.

"Yeah. H-How did you get in? To USARIC?"

"It's a long story, my friend," Alex stepped over to Nutrene and snatched the smart bomb from her clutches, "Give me that."

"Ugghhh, and to think I had the hots for you."

"In your dreams, grandma," Alex snorted and returned to the door. He set the grenade down by the wall in the corridor.

"PAAC?" Oxade asked. "You're part of that stupid animal cruelty pack of inbred imbeciles?"

"Nah, they're long gone, now. We're a new breed, I guess you could say."

"Like a revolution?"

"More like an *evolution*," Alex snorted through his mask, "A plan five years in the making. If you thought USARIC were ruthless killers, you should check *us* out."

Oxade shook his head. "Why, Alex? Why all this?"

Alex stepped out through the door and gripped the frame in his hand, "Because USARIC is a hell-sucking, mega-conglomerate behemoth that needs taking down. We can't have whatever Opera Beta and Anderson discovered falling into their hands, now. Can we?"

"You're so dead."

Alex gripped the door and pulled it across it slider, "You first."

SCHLAMMM!

He took several steps back and aimed his D-REZ at the panel.

THRAATATATT-SCH-PACKKK!

He fired a semi-automatic burst of bullets at the panel, shutting the door down and sealing the bad guys in.

Alex's parting shot - a swift flip of the bird through the window - provided the icing on the cake.

Alex sprinted along the gantry and looked for the staircase. He lifted his left forearm to his face and pressed the ink on his skin to his wrist, "Tripp? This is Alex, do you read me?"

Tripp's voice came from his wrist, "Yes, I read you. We're

at the Primary Airlock, now. We, uh, found *something*."

"What?"

"Get down here, quick. We're going to need your help."

"I'm on my way…" he cut the connection off and ran into the depths of the walkway.

The smart bomb outside the control deck remained perfectly still - for a few seconds.

Then, it came to life and shifted around.

CLICK-CLANG.

It fell onto its side and rolled toward the door. The outer shell warbled and expanded.

"Nggg…" it's feminine voice squealed. The shell casing liquefied and streaked across the floor, "Ugh, I hate this *so* much…"

The liquid twisted a few inches into the air and formed a cylindrical shape about the size of a beach ball.

A secondary 'head' inflated into a silvery metal. It shook its head and blinked its eyebulbs.

"Ah," Neg bounced against the door, fully-formed, "That's better."

"Neg," Oxade's damp screams came from within the control deck, "Get us out of here."

"I'm way ahead of you," she said and pressed her curved 'chest' against the door.

SCHWIZZ-SCHPAANG!

A metal sphere formed around her frame and spun at speed, twisting the image of the door in front of her, "Poz, get ready."

Poz hopped up and down from the other side of the door and looked through the window, "What? How did you get out there?"

"Just shut up and connect."

Neg's magnetic strength slipped through the door and pulled Poz toward it.

"Hey, what are you—"

"—Saving everyone's life, you numb skull. Get over here, now."

Oxade scooped his D-REZ from the floor and unclipped

the magazine. He reached into his pocket and retrieved a fresh one as he watched Poz's body lasso toward the door. His lower frame swept the detritus and mess out of his path.

"This is *most* embarrassing."

"Just shut up and open the door, nitwit," Oxade palmed the magazine into his gun and turned to Nutrene, "Hey, you."

"What?"

"How's the arm?"

Nutrene picked up her Rez-9 in her bad arm. She focused her monocle on the bleeding wound, "I'll live."

SCHWUNT!

Poz and Neg slammed together on opposite sides of the door. They blinked their eyebulbs at each other.

"Nice to see you again, sweetie," Neg beamed.

"Yeah, whatever. Just help me open this stupid door."

They slid down to the floor together and rolled across the door railings, pulling it open.

CREEEAAAAAKKK!

"Oxade," Neg beeped, "The door is open, as per your request.

"Thanks, guys," Oxade and Nutrene looked at each other through their masks.

"New plan," he gesticulated with his D-REZ, barely able to contain his anger, "I'm going to put a bullet in Alex's brain. And then Jaycee's."

"Good plan."

"And then I'm going to make Anderson watch me remove Tripp's head, turn it upside down and thump it down the neck hole."

"Upside down? I like that," Nutrene snarled, wanting revenge, but kept up the professional pretense, "Oh. As Opera Charlie's medician, do you mind if I perform a live vivisection on that bitch of a cat?"

"Be my guest, but on one condition."

"What's that?" Nutrene licked her lips and walked toward the door.

"Make it as slow and painful as possible. I want to watch the life fade away from her eyes."

"Get in line, sweetie."

"Kill 'em," Oxade yelled and kicked the chair into the damaged communications console on his way out, "Kill 'em all."

Chapter 16

Primary Airlock
Space Opera Beta

"Manuel?" Tripp snapped his fingers as he reached the inner airlock door.

"Y-y-yessss," The book flickered and spasmed in the air, never fully coming to life, "I c-can't—"

"—Manuel, what's wrong?"

"Oxade shot my m-mainframe. I'm d-dying—" Manuel buzzed in and out of the air.

Tripp realized there and then that Manuel was dying in front of his and Jaycee's eyes.

"You're l-leaving Op-p-p-pera B-Beta—"

"—No, no, damn it," Tripp went to grab Manuel. He forgot that the book couldn't be touched, "We can take you with us. Install you on their comms panels."

"N-No. I'm obsolete. It'll never work," Manuel's voiced ground to super-slow motion, "It's over, Tripp."

White sparks zipped away from the book as it took its final curtain call, "I managed it, though, d-didn't I? I l-lied for you."

Tripp half-smiled and held his thumb up to the transparent book, "You did. You bought us time."

"Goodbye, T-Tripp. Jaycee," Manuel's last words screeched to a halt. His image flapped away like a dove toward the ceiling and burst into several thousand digital atoms, never to be seen again.

Jaycee thumped the wall in anger, "Bastards."

"No time to mourn, now. We gotta get off Beta. Open the airlock."

"With pleasure," Jaycee yanked on the lever. The inner airlock door slid up into the ceiling.

"Wait, what about Jelly?" Tripp asked. "Where is she?"

"I dunno—"

SCHTOMP-SCHTOMP-SCHTOMP…

The two men turned to a colossal thumping noise coming from the other end of the walkway.

Jelly Anderson stormed toward them. They flinched with each step she took.

"There you are," Tripp said.

"Where's my mommy?" Jelly looked around, expecting to find Wool with them.

"No time for questions, pet," Tripp stood aside and allowed her in the airlock.

"I'm not going anywhere without my mommy."

Tripp looked over her shoulder, "Jelly, listen. Your *mommy* didn't make—"

He cut his sentence short when he clamped eyes on the wet patch between her legs. A dusty Kevlar panel hung by her knee. The fabric of the leggings were torn apart, "Jelly, did you embarrass yourself again?"

She looked down at her thighs and whined, "Miew."

"Where did that liquid come from?"

"Uh, guys?" Jaycee waved Jelly and Tripp in from the airlock compression chamber.

Jelly reached into the chest compartment at the front of her exo-suit, "Let's get out of here—"

"Oh my God," Tripp gasped.

A tiny, goo-drenched kitten lay shivering on her palm. It meowed with its eyes shut, clinging to Jelly's infinity claws.

Stunned, Tripp and Jaycee looked at Jelly for a reaction.

"My baby," Jelly held the kitten for both men to see, "We have to protect her."

"But-but," Tripp swallowed and went to touch the newborn kitten. His sleeves rolled up the length of his arm, revealing the holes on his wrist.

"This is Alex. Do you read me?"

Tripp moved his wrist to his mouth, "Yes, Alex. We're at the Primary Airlock, now. We, uh, found *something*."

"What?" Alex's voice came from Tripp's IndividiMedia ink.

"Get down here, quick. We're going to need your help."

"I'm on my way."

Jelly cradled the kitten in her arms. The light from the fireball rocketing towards Saturn illuminated its gorgeous, fluffy face.

"It's a she?"

Jelly nodded and purred, "Yes."

Jaycee joined Tripp and tried not to let his emotions override the severity of their situation.

"Jelly, listen. We don't have any outer-suits. We need to cross the bridge to Charlie as quick as we can."

"But we can't breathe in space?" Jelly asked.

"No," Jaycee pointed to the bridge through the window, "You have to exhale. Push all the air out of your lungs and hold until we get there."

Tripp took Jelly's newborn in his hands. The gunk slopped between his fingers, "What are you going to call her?"

"—Tripp, man," Jaycee screamed, "Not now. We need to leave."

He stormed into the airlock compression chamber and waved the pair in with him, "Let's go."

Jelly took the kitten from Tripp as they made their way into the airlock.

He double-took and looked at the door. A pang of déjà vu throttled through his body, "There's something very familiar about all this."

Jaycee grunted, "You *don't* say."

"Guys, wait for me," Alex reached the door and immediately spotted Jelly carrying her kitten. "My God, what happened?"

"She gave birth," Tripp said. "You know how to operate Charlie when we get in, right?"

"Yes," Alex hopped into the airlock and pressed his fingers around his mask, "Where are your outer-suits?"

"We don't have time."

Jelly ran the side of her face against her kitten, "Hey, honey. Don't be scared."

"What about that *thing*?" Alex pointed to the kitten, only for Jelly to take offense.

"She's not a *thing*."

SCHWUMP.

The inner-door slammed down, instigating the start of the decompressions process. A blast of white gas filled the chamber.

"Right," Jaycee grabbed the lever next to the outer-door, "Let's get out of here and go home."

"Wait, let me go first," Alex pushed his way to the front, "Jaycee, when we get there, Manny might not open the door for you. She will for me, though."

"Okay," Jaycee turned over his shoulder, "Everyone ready?"

Tripp nodded, "Jelly, cover the kitten's mouth."

"Okay," she exhaled and stood poised to blast through the door.

"ETA sixty seconds, here we go," Jaycee yanked the lever down.

SWISH!

The door slid up, allowing them onto the bridge. They had expected it to be a silent journey. The white bridge seemed whiter than usual.

GRRROOOOOAAARRRRRR!

Jaycee gripped the shuddering railings and pulled himself forward, "What the hell?"

He squinted at the blinding light coming from Saturn, above. The fiery Enceladus sunk into it, throwing the planet's surface out like an exploded balloon sticking to the stars.

He held his hand over his eyes and ignored it, pulling himself forward.

Alex followed, clocking some of the celestial event as he moved forward, "Jesus Christ. Look at *that*."

His feet drifted across the bridge floor. Saturn's rings

began to gyrate as if wading through a magnificent lump of treacle. The stars pushed aside as the planet's body pounded away like an aggressive boom box.

"What the hell is happening up there?" Alex muttered, wide-eyed at the spectacular light show. He held out his hand for Tripp, "Come on."

Tripp covered his eyes with his left palm. He grabbed Alex's hand with his right.

"Come on, let's go. Quick."

Jelly cradled her daughter in her elbow and protected her with her claws. She used her free hand for balance as she traversed the bridge.

GWAAAARRRR... WVHOOSH...

A shower of light bleached out their surroundings. Saturn seemed to be growing. Jaycee and Alex saw a giant black hole form like a crazy, liquid cartwheel over its surface.

"Go, go, go—" Alex pushed Jaycee along the bridge and gripped the rails, propelling himself after him, "Tripp, come on."

Alex's voice may have fallen on deaf ears in the vacuum of space, but his haste in ushering Jelly and her newborn couldn't be ignored.

"Jelly, *please.*"

She opened her eyes and clutched her baby tighter than ever, "I'm coming."

SWISH!

Oxade ran into the airlock with his K-SPARK and thumped the outer door, "Look at them. They think they can abscond on *our* ship?"

Nutrene held her arm as she stepped inside the chamber with her Rez-9.

Poz and Neg rolled in with them, "Commencing decompression. Standby."

SPRIISHHH!

Jelly turned to face him with her daughter's scruff in her mouth. The kitten hung in against of her chin and thrashed its spindly legs around.

"Hey," Oxade thumped the outer airlock door in an

attempt to catch Jelly's attention, "Get back here and die like a good little pussy."

The decompression stopped as soon as the outer airlock hatch flung open. Oxade kicked himself away from the frame of the door and arrowed behind Jelly.

Alex caught his action just in time and pointed behind her, "Jelly. Behind you."

"What?"

FWUMP!

Oxade bolted across the bridge and socked Jelly in the face. Her jaw opened, releasing her newborn into space, and away from the bridge.

"There's a good *girl*," Oxade shouted under his mask, "Let daddy pass."

"Jeez," Alex placed the sole of his boot on the railing. He pushed himself after the flying kitten as it headed away from the bridge. He just about caught her in his hands.

Jelly massaged her jaw, taken aback by the attack. She flung her claws out at Oxade. Her eyes felt fit to burst in the airless void.

Tripp and Jaycee reached Opera Charlie's outer airlock door. They hadn't seen the commotion - their attention was on Charlie's outer airlock hatch.

"Open up," Tripp said with his last breath, "Now."

A miracle.

Opera Charlie's outer hatch opened up and allowed him and Jaycee inside. They pulled themselves in and immediately felt the pressure inside, as if their bodies were about to burst.

"Get in," Tripp pushed himself against the chamber and turned to Alex. A few blobs of pink liquid streaked across the air from Tripp's tear ducts. He tried to grab a few of them, but missed.

Jaycee moved forward and hit the lever on the wall.

SCHWUNT-SWISSSH!

The outer hatch closed, forcing the chamber to decompress.

Tripp staggered to his knees and took a lungful of oxygen, "Gaaaah."

Jaycee did the same, coughing the infinite void of space from his lungs, "Ugh, I thought my chest was going to explode."

"Jelly," Tripp pushed himself to the window. Alex blocked the view as he carried the kitten in his arms, "They're going to die."

Alex waved his hands, forcing them to open the door. The events on the bridge - Alex barreled toward them, and Jelly preparing to attack Oxade - seemed to play-out in ultra-slow motion.

WHUMP-WHUMP-WHUMP.

Alex thumped the door, "Let us in."

Jaycee stormed over to the inner-door and grabbed the lever.

The door slid up, "Tripp, get in."

"Yeah," he turned around and launched himself into Opera Charlie proper, "Is there anyone else on board?"

"How should I know?" Jaycee stepped after him and yanked the lever down on the inner door wall, "You got your firearm on you?"

Tripp unhooked the Rez-9 from his belt and armed it, "Oh, yeah. We made it, Jaycee."

"We haven't made it, *yet*. We don't know who - or what - is on board Charlie."

"I'll head for the control deck. Try to get us out of here."

"Good idea. I'll make sure Charlie team doesn't get in," Jaycee turned watched Alex thumping the wall yet again, presenting the kitten at the window, "Go, go, go…"

"Okay," Tripp looked around and ran off in the direction he thought would take him to the control deck.

Jaycee hit the second lever, opening the outer airlock door.

Alex pushed the newborn kitten into the airlock and followed her in, giving Jaycee the 'thumbs up' through the window.

His jaw dropped as he turned to the blinding-white bridge. Saturn's rings gyrated faster and faster. A liquid circle formed over its surface. It appeared to sing as it enveloped the two ships with a brilliant white light.

"My *G-God…*"

SCHWUMP.

Alex couldn't believe his eyes. A wondrous event was in full swing. He caught the newborn in his arms as the decompression thundered around them, "What's happening up there?"

Jaycee yanked the second lever down and opened the inner door, "Give me the baby."

Alex bolted through the door and passed the kitten to Jaycee, "Something insane is happening up there."

"I know. We saw it," Jaycee inspected the kitten. She'd bled a little form her facial orifices but was still breathing, "We need to protect Anderson's baby."

"What about Jelly?" Alex pointed at the door.

Oxade and Jelly faced-off in the middle of the bridge. He aimed his gun at her and threatened to shoot, "My name is Oxade Weller. I am the captain of Opera Charlie," he said before realizing Jelly couldn't hear a word. She could see he was speaking through his mask, but little else.

Nutrene sidled past him on the bridge with her Rez-9 drawn. Her monocle rotated and focused on Jelly, "Let me take care of this putrid ball of fluff."

Jelly lowered her claws and huffed. The absence of atmosphere began to crack the fur and skin on her arms. She harnessed the pain and used it to psyche herself up, ready for war.

"It's very pretty out here, isn't it?" Nutrene looked up at the angry blue planet spinning its rings. She pointed her gun at Jelly's heart, "Now surrender. You're a perversion of science."

Jelly whined. Her muscles tensed up as she held her claws out in surrender.

"Good girl," Nutrene laughed through her mask, "Who's a good girl? Yes, *you are*," she pulled herself along the bridge with her free arm, "Come here for a murdering, you fluffy little—"

SCHWUPP!

Nutrene's gun lifted away from her palm and shot up to Saturn's spinning rings, "Huh?"

She grabbed at it - to no success. The gun sped at that bizarre circular formation smothering Saturn's surface.

Nutrene made the mistake of looking up at the spectacle, "Oh, m-my," Her monocle swirled around, focusing on her gun drifting towards the planet, "*It is God*!"

"Meow," Jelly snarled and swiped her claws across Nutrene's face. Her mask burst apart. The lens in her monocle cracked.

The gelatin frontage sucked into her face and blasted three perfect streams of gas towards Saturn, depriving the woman of oxygen.

"H-Help m-me…"

Nutrene let go of the rails. The pull from Saturn yanked her eyeball through her broken monocle, forcing her head away from the bridge. Her chest cracked out and made its way towards the blackened surface of Saturn as she suffocated to death.

"Aaggghhhh…" Nutrene's suit tore open and punched a hole in her torso. Her organs plumed out and stretched away from her body.

"Oh God," Oxade raced forward and kicked himself down to his back. He spun around on his side and watched what little remained of Nutrene fold out.

The bones in her body crunched together and threw her remains at Saturn like a stretched piece of chewing gum.

Jelly's hair began to lift toward the cataclysmic black event on Saturn, "Miew."

She turned around and held onto the bridge railing and yanked herself toward Opera Charlie.

"Oh, God, Nutrene."

He witnessed the bottom half of her body, and legs, stretch over thousands of miles and melt into the fantastic light show above his head. Her monocle elongated as her messy amalgam of bone, flesh and skin snaked toward the angry planet.

Oxade felt his feet drift up and away from the bridge, "Come back here," he screamed, pulling himself toward Jelly.

Poz and Neg peeked out from Opera Beta's outer airlock hatch and scanned the bridge, "Seems stable enough."

"Yes, but what about that black hole?" Neg tilted her eyebulbs directly above their heads.

"We can make it," Poz said. "I don't want to die on this crappy spaceship."

"Okay, let's go," Neg rolled across the bridge at speed, headed toward Oxade and Jelly.

Oxade clung to the bridge and felt his shin bones crack apart, "Oh, oh…"

Jelly spun around and slammed the outer airlock door, "Let me in."

Alex hit the lever on the wall. The hatch flew up and let Jelly into the decompression chamber. She tumbled backwards and hit her tail on the wall, "Mieewww."

Oxade grabbed the outer door edges, trying to fight back the force of the event taking place above them. He looked at the ground and tried for one last push.

"Nyaaarrggghhhhhh…"

WHIZZ…

Neg rolled into the chamber underneath his chest as he pulled forward.

"Hello, Captain."

"Gah, gah,"

Oxade wrenched the top half of his body through the frame of the airlock door.

SCHWUNT-SMASH!

The hatch sliced down on his right foot and severed it from his ankle.

"Gaaooww,"

The compressed air blasted around Jelly, Neg, and Oxade, sealing them in from the bridge.

Jelly caught her breath and held the end of her tail. The pain was sensational and angered her to the core.

Oxade and Neg looked up at her.

"N-Neg…" Oxade looked through the window and saw his severed foot drift through space, headed for Saturn,

"Touch Jelly for me."

"My pleasure," Neg twisted around and rolled forward, threatening to make contact.

Jelly backed up to the inner door, "Stay away from me."

"Come here, girl," Neg slid forward and beeped, "I want to *absorb* you."

Jelly elbowed the inner door behind her, "Alex. Open the hatch."

"Touch her, you useless marble," Oxade shouted at Neg.

"Okay, okay," She rolled further forward, nanoseconds away from making contact.

Jelly gripped the inner hatch, closed her eyes and squealed.

Neg almost made contact with Jelly's knee. Her cylindrical body lifted ten inches into the air and rocketed back toward the outer airlock door.

CLANNNGGG!

Her frame smashed against the bottom of the door like a super-powerful magnet, "What the hell?"

Neg looked around and saw Poz on the other side of the door slowly drifting up toward Saturn's event.

"Neg, Neg," Poz's muffled squeals blasted from the window, "Help me. Don't let me go."

"Ah, ah, ah," Neg slid up the door with Poz, their magnetized surfaces keeping them bound together.

"Don't l-let me go up there, I'm scared."

Jelly and Oxade's watched the magnetic droids share a moment together as Poz's body dragged Neg further up the outer airlock door.

"Work with me, here, Neg," Poz said. "Let me in."

Jelly screamed and clanging her claws against the window, "Alex, open the damn hatch."

Alex kept his grip on the lever and eyed the pressure inlet dial, "I'm waiting for the chamber to reset. C'mon, c'mon, c'mon…"

Biddip-beeeeeeeep.

The lever lit up, indicating the decompression had concluded.

SWISH!

Alex yanked the lever down. The inner airlock hatch flew up. Jelly backward-rolled inside Opera Charlie..

She thumped her claws to the ground and growled at Oxade and Neg.

"Come here, you defiant *cow*," Neg attempted to break away from Poz's magnetic charge from the other side of the outer airlock hatch.

"Alex," Jelly shouted, "Now."

He thumped the lever down.

SLAMM-SCHWUNT!

The inner hatch slammed shut, sealing Neg and Oxade inside the airlock chamber.

Jelly grunted and slapped her tail against the ground. Alex let go of the lever and turned to her, "What d-do we do, now?"

She trained her eyes on the window as she stood to her feet and wiped her mouth with the back of her hand.

"Jelly?" Alex asked in fright.

She pushed him aside and made her way to the yellow pressure inlet dial. She punched through the glass and turned the dial counter-clockwise, raising the pressure.

Screeeeeeeeee… the spindle on the dial daggered to the right, flying up the atmosphere pressure numbers.

"Oh no," Oxade's muffled voice splashed against the window of the inner airlock door. He scrambled to his bleeding stump, realizing what was about to happen, "Please, Anderson. *Don't…*"

Jelly ran her tongue along her bottom lip and scowled at Neg, then at Oxade, imprisoned in her little playground.

"Anderson, p-please," Oxade begged. He pressed his gloved palms to his ears in an attempt to block the pressure increase.

"Let us out of here," Neg threw bolts of electricity out from her body. Each multi-pronged whip of lightning crawled along the four chamber walls, "Don't do it."

"Jelly," Alex placed his hand on top of Jelly's as she held onto the dial, "Don't do this."

Jelly purred and threw his hand off her paw, "They killed

my mommy."

"I know, but *don't do it*. They're trapped. They can't get out. Let USARIC deal with them when we get back."

"They are nothing but vermin to me. Useless, stinking rodents. Look at them," Jelly rolled her shoulders wanting death. Her long, dark orange hair flowed down her back as she turned to watch the execution, "You might want to look away."

"Oh God, don't—" Alex couldn't bear to watch any longer.

Jelly took one last look at Oxade's face. Fissures and blisters cracked across his forehead and exposed facial skin. He shook his head 'no' and pressed his palms together, "You're a *monster*."

"I'm not a monster, Alex," Jelly screwed her face and allowed the anger in her heart to flow up her torso and rocket into her arm. "I'm a *mother*."

SCHWUNT!

"For God's sake, Jelly," Alex grabbed her hand and tried to remove it from the compression lever, "What do you think you're doing—"

"—Don't touch me," Jelly shoved Alex onto his ass. She kept the dial forced to the right and watched the spindle reached its maximum pressure point.

Oxade slumped to his knees and held his neck for dear life. His mask bloated out and crushed into his face. His suit tore into strips. Neg's ball-like surface indented and crushed in on itself, killing her instantly.

THWUMP!

Jelly smashed the dial with her fist, "Can you hear this?"

Neg's body rolled up the inside of the outer door hatch along with Poz. The charge caused the door to crush outward and create an opening into outer space.

"Got it," Poz squealed, hanging from the opening at the bottom of the airlock hatch, "Now, let me in—"

"—No, Poz," Neg screamed, "We'll die—"

SCHLAAAM!

Jelly screamed into the window, "Meow."

The chamber rocked against the intense pressure drop.

A rope of blood daggered from Oxade's mouth as he screamed, "Noooo—"

SCHPLATTTTT!

His body exploded, throwing his insides through the hatch opening. A concoction of destroyed Oxade limbs and organs rocketed towards Saturn.

"*Holy h-hell,*" Alex backed away from Jelly as she watched every second of Oxade and Neg's death, "J-Jelly, y-you're a—"

"*—Killer?*" She turned to face him matter-of-factly and with little emotion.

"Y-Yes"

"That's right. Don't ever forget it."

Alex pressed his hands against the hatch window. He saw Poz and Neg fly with Oxade's remains towards Saturn.

"What have y-you d-done?"

"I took out the trash," She pushed herself away from the door and stormed down the walkway, "Now let's get out of this hellhole."

Alex clambered to his feet and raced after her, "Where are you going?"

"To the control deck," she shouted over her shoulder, "Keep your mask on. I'm still toxic."

"Toxic?"

"I'm carrying Symphonium. Keep your mask on," Jelly turned her walk into a sprint, clanging her claws along the walkway, "Who's got my child?"

"Uh, I gave her to Jaycee."

"I want my baby. Give me my baby."

The Control Deck
Space Opera Charlie - Level One

Jaycee carried Jelly's kitten into the control deck to find Tripp negotiating with Manny. She hung in the air, refusing to budge.

"What's the score?" Jaycee asked.

"She won't listen to me," Tripp turned to Manny, "Look, this is serious."

"Manny?" Jaycee muttered.

"I'm sorry, Tripp. I can only take instructions from a commanding officer or my captain. And they are dead."

"We're *all* dead if you don't enable the thrusters and get us out of here," Tripp tried to little avail.

"Want me to threaten her?" Jaycee passed the kitten to Tripp, "Give it some of the old 'user friendly' approach?"

"I'm afraid that will not work."

Tripp held the messy kitten in his arms and stared at its face. She nestling into his arms and opened her gunky eyelids.

"Look at you, you have no idea what's going on, do you?" He said, looking at his forearm. The blisters on his synthetic skin bubbled and popped, "Are you okay, Jaycee?"

"Yeah, I'm fine. Ruptured a few vessels. Kind of annoyed about discovering I'm not human, but that's nothing that a good sleep won't fix," Jaycee clenched his fist and threatened to punch the console, "Manny. If we die, you're coming with us."

Jelly stormed into the room with Alex, "Where's my baby?"

Tripp looked up at her and smiled, "She's right here, with me."

"Give her to me," Jelly held out her paws. Tripp dropped the tiny ball of fluff into her palms.

Jelly ran the side of her face along its body. The whiskers on her face lit up, along with her daughter's. They fizzed and connected together, calming the kitten down.

She took a deep breath and looked at Tripp.

"Why aren't we moving?"

"The autopilot won't engage the thrusters."

"Take her," Jelly passed her newborn to Tripp and walked up to Manny, "Hey, *you*. Stupid book. Why won't you engage the thrusters?"

"Because it is not in my remit to take orders from strangers."

"Really?" Jelly marched over to the communications console. She knocked Jaycee out of her way and expanded her infinity claws at the screen, "You have five seconds to get us out of here or I'll rip your guts out."

Manny shuffled in the air in an attempt to seem calm, "You can do that if you wish. It won't help."

Alex stepped forward. He knew what had to be done, "Manny?"

"Yes, Alex?"

"Captain Weller was killed on his mission. That makes me the captain, now."

Tripp, Jaycee, and Jelly turned to Alex with relief.

"Captain Weller is dead?" Manny asked.

"Yes, Jelly killed him. And Nutrene, and droids Poz and Neg."

"I see."

"Make no mistake. Anderson is in charge, now, after me. I hereby assign full captain privileges to Anderson in the event of anything happening to me. "

Manny froze in mid-air and drained the color from her book-body.

"You *will* take orders from us as we see fit. Do you understand what I've just said?"

"In that case I await your commands."

"Engage thrusters," Alex said. "Make up a course for Earth, please—"

"—Nggggg," Jelly grunted in agony, inadvertently catching everyone's attention, "It's h-happening again."

Alex's eyes widened as he saw Jelly pushing her second baby out from between her legs, "Jesus."

A gush of transparent liquid fountained down her thighs.

"Stand back. Give her some space," Tripp said.

Opera Charlie rumbled to life as Jelly rolled onto her side. She arched her knee into the air and meowed at the top of her lungs, "My baby… it's c-coming…"

KER-RUUNNNCCCHHH!

The spacecraft shunted around, spilling the crew off their balance, "What's that?" Tripp screamed and clutched at the chair in front of the console.

Opera Charlie's back thrusters lit up and blasted away from Saturn's spectacular light show.

The bridge cracked and broke away from Opera Beta entirely. Huge clumps of white metal daggered out and tossed Opera Beta into a sustained revolution, like a Catherine wheel.

KERCHUNK-BOOM!

The bridge severed itself from both vessels and twirled in the air like a discarded bone.

Saturn's tumultuous ring revolved so fast it threatened to light up the black whirlpool on its surface. The sound it produced was beyond deafening.

BLAST-BLAASSST!

Opera Charlie's thrusters lit up and sent the structure rocketing away from the planetary event literally unfolding behind them.

The nukes in Opera Beta's control deck detonated.

"Cover your faces. Don't look at the window." Jaycee stood in front of the flight deck windshield, "Beta's gonna blow—"

In an intense slowing down of motion, Tripp, Jaycee, Alex, and Jelly turned away from the windshield. Tripp covered the kitten's face with his palm as each of their faces bleached out into a mass of pure white...

KEERRR - WHUD-WHUD-WHUD-WHUDD-DD...

Opera Beta exploded in sections. The sharp-end of the cone rocketed away from the vessel like a bullet. A running detonation devastated its centrifuge, catapulting sections of its shell and insides into space. The middle of the ship rippled and blasted apart, pushing the thruster-end towards Saturn in a haze of destructed glory - enough of a blast to push Opera Charlie away as its thrusters roared into the huge blanket of space...

Jaycee and Tripp picked themselves up from the floor and looked up through the windshield.

Opera Beta and it inhabitants were no more.

A gigantic tear in the fabric of space discharged a shaft of white light that streaked all the way back to Saturn's core.

"She's gone," Tripp muttered, suppressing his emotion.

He didn't dare look away, "They're all—"

"—*Dead*," Jaycee finished the sentence, "All of them."

Tripp double-took and passed the kitten to Alex, who took her into his arms.

"What am I meant to do with her?"

"Guard her with your life," Tripp made for the flight deck, "Manny? Tell me we're moving."

"Hyper-thrusters currently engaged," Manny said. "They've ten percent damage, however."

"Enough to get us back home?"

Manny went quiet.

The silence drew attention to Jelly on the floor kicking her legs and tensing her muscles, "My baby is coming."

"*Another* one?" Tripp ran over to her and held out his arms, "What do you need me to do?"

"Leave me the hell alone," Jelly squealed and clutched the console edge, "Nggggg…"

"Excuse me, Tripp?" Manny sprang to life, "I'm afraid I have some good news and bad news."

"What is it? Give me the good news first."

"The thrusters are engaged at ninety-two percent. We have a better-than-good chance of making it home."

"And the bad news? I mean, apart from Charlie about to acquire a litter of kittens?"

Manny projected a holograph in the middle of the room. Opera Charlie's escape from Saturn had slowed it down, perilously close to being pulled back, "We may not leave Saturn's orbit intact."

"Oh, *great.*"

"Maximum capacity on the thrusters, please," Alex looked at Manny as he comforted the kitten in his arms.

"We can't outrun a black hole, Hughes."

"Is that what that is? A black hole?"

"It resembles one. It's not fully-formed yet. I'll take my chances on outrunning it and not sticking around to find out."

Manny threw a holographic projection of the engine's view of Saturn. It folded out in the middle of the room and showed the giant planet shaking around like a blender at full speed.

"I'll maximize the capability, but there are no guarantees. The force is threatening to pull us back in," Manny said.

"Just do it. Full throttle."

Jelly huffed and puffed. Her belly glowed a hot pink through her exo-suit top. She strained her stomach muscles and kicked her heels against the ground, "Oh, *God...* it's coming, it's coming..."

Tripp, Jaycee, and Alex looked at the holograph footage of Saturn as per the view from the back of the ship.

"If you believe in God, now's the time to pray..." Tripp said, quietly.

The kitten shuffled around in his arms and meowed its first.

Chapter 17

Port Lavaca
South Texas, USA
(Ten miles north of Port D'Souza)

The sun had set.

The only light provided on the road came from the occasional street lamp and the full moon.

An engine from a 4x4 rumbled beside one of many trees by the road.

Grace held her flashlight against the trees in a hunt for the escaped felines, "Here kitty-kitty-kitty. Where are you?"

A rectangular geo-scan hung above her flashlight. Several purple dots beeped as a blue radar swirled around. She held her finger to her ear and spoke into her mouthpiece.

"Siyam, they're here somewhere," she clocked a similar flashlight a few feet away.

"I know, I'm getting the same reading," Siyam responded through her headgear, "Two clicks further."

"I hope they're willing to come with us. I don't get it, they usually respond."

"It's unlike them to stay in packs. Usually they're—"

A rustling coming from a bush by the road stopped him talking. Grace grew nervous, "What was that noise?"

Siyam waved his flashlight around, "By the road. Highway thirty-seven. Move."

The trees seemed to come to life as the pair turned

around and made their way to the road.

A giant gale rustled the branches and blew Grace's hair back across her neck, "Hey, what's that noise?"

WHUDDA-WHUDDA-WHUDDA.

A deafening noise pushed the gale across their faces.

"Chopper. It's one of USARIC's," Siyam kept an eye on the purple blips on the his geo-scan as he ran over to Grace, "Look. Up there."

A fierce-looking black helicopter with tandem rotors hovered over the freeway and blasted its lights onto the road, "This is the United States and Russian Intergalactic Confederation," a male voice announced through its speakers, "Make yourselves known immediately."

Grace turned to Siyam and exhaled, "That's it. We're busted."

He clutched her arm and held her back, "No, wait. I don't *think* they're talking to us."

The helicopter lowered. The blades of grass and dust kicked across the ground.

"I repeat, come out now and await rescue."

Grace tapped Siyam on the shoulder. She'd seen something crawl out of the bush by the stores.

"Look, over there."

"Oh, wow," Siyam gasped as he watch the Egyptian Mau bolt into the middle of the freeway.

Two cars blared their horns and screeched to a halt, narrowly avoiding contact with the cat.

She made herself comfortable in the middle of the road and looked up at the blinding light coming from the helicopter, "Meow."

"Good. Stay where you are," said a USARIC mercenary sitting at the opened door to the helicopter, "Where are the others?"

"Meow," Mau growled and looked at the floor.

"What is she doing?" Grace lowered her flashlight and stepped forward, "I'm going to take her—"

"—Christ's sake, *no.* They'll open fire on us. On *her.*"

"We can't just leave her there," Grace whispered. "They'll take her back."

A chorus of 'meows' snaked through the trees. Several cats emerged and joined their leader on the road.

"That's right, you fluffy idiots," the USARIC mercenary said through his megaphone, "Out you come. Nice and slow."

Another merc pushed forward as the helicopter hovered to the liquor store's parking lot. He produced a mini gun and attached it to the frame of the hatch, "Just tell me when."

"Drivers," the merc said. "Exit your vehicles and make your way to the parking lot, please."

The drivers in each car jumped out and ran under a giant vertical billboard advertising *Rollneck Kojak* beer. A neon image of a bald-headed man blinked underneath its logo.

"Meow," The Egyptian Mau stood up and walked around in a circle, forcing her twenty-nine peers to stop moving. They sat on their haunches, randomly dotted all over the road.

Grace reached into her belt and retrieved her handgun, "They're *not* taking those cats and abusing them."

"Grace, don't. Look at them, we're outnumbered. We're too late. They beat us to it."

"I'll take as many of those bastards out as I can," Grace bit her lip to prevent herself from crying, "I don't c-care if I die."

Siyam grabbed her shoulder and sidled into her, "Well I do. You're no use to any of us *dead*, are you?"

Grace lowered her gun, resigned to defeat.

"You wanna end up like Handax? Like Denny, Moses, and Leif? Then go out there and go down in a blaze of glory. Just know that you don't have our blessing."

She swiped his hand away from her shoulder and fell to her knees, "Let go of me."

The helicopter's landing gear hit the ground, kicking up a giant whirlwind of dust. The armed Mercenary jumped out and swung his machine gun at the Egyptian Mau, "There you are. Stay right there."

He waved his colleague out of the vehicle.

"Get the net. Tell base we've located the rest of them."

SNAAARRRLLLLL!

The Egyptian Mau looked up at the full moon along with her peers.

"Hey, you," the merc shouted over the noise of helicopter's rotors, "Stay where you are."

His colleague hopped out of the helicopter with a giant net in his hands. He unraveled the ends and yanked them taut, "Ready to capture."

The Egyptian Mau wasn't impressed. She stood on all fours and showed the men her ass, and faced her peers. A tiny white spark erupted a few inches to the left of the moon, a billion miles away from Earth.

"Meow," she cried.

All the cats howled with her. They turned to the mercenary as he aimed his gun at the Egyptian Mau.

"What are you doing?" he said with a heart full of fear, "It's weird."

"Meeeeooowww," the Mau growled and scraped her paws on the gravel.

"Oh no… no-no-no…" Siyam eyes widened, "They're *not* going to—"

"—*Jesus Christ*," Grace held her breath.

A standoff occurred between the two men and the thirty cats, "Don't anybody move or I'll blow her damned head off," he shouted, hoping the cats understood English.

They didn't comprehend the instruction but knew a threat when they saw it. Now was the time to act.

"MEEEOOOOOOOOOWWW," All thirty cats shrieked and launched toward the armed mercenary.

"No, get back!" He opened fire on the stampede of felines. A flurry of them trampled over the parked cars and cracked the windscreen as they bounded toward him.

The Egyptian Mau nodded the two white bobtails ahead.

BLAM-BLAM-BLAM!

The mercenary fired at the cats. The ones who didn't get hit bolted towards him.

"Get back you vicious, little shi—"

ROOOWWAAAAARRRR!

"Look! They're gonna kill him."

"There's nothing we can do," Siyam spluttered in amazement, "Keep back."

The Egyptian Mau jumped into the air claws-first and punctured the mercenary's visor. A jut of blood splattered up the inside. She dug her hind legs into his chest and ravaged his face, "Meow!"

Twelve cats ran up his trouser leg and jabbed their claws into his flesh, tearing bits of him apart. He screamed and fell to his knees in agony.

The two USARIC mercenaries ran back into the helicopter, "Get this bird back in the air. They're killing him," shouted one of them to the pilot.

The helicopter blades fired back up.

WHUM-WHUUUM-WHUUUUM...

The Egyptian Mau ran the top of her head against the mercenaries visor, lifted it over his head. His face was a bloodied mess.

She looked into his pupils and licked her lips.

"N-No, p-please," he screamed as she dove into his face claws-first.

The helicopter's gear lifted from the ground - taking ten cats with it. Half of them invaded the passenger seat area and tore the two mercenaries apart.

The other half - all ten of them - hopped into the pilot seat and ripped up the pilot's legs and arms.

Grace ran into the road with her flashlight and watched the helicopter auto-rotate twenty feet in the air.

Large numbers of patrons from the liquor store and surrounding restaurants gathered at the window. Some of them ran out of the building and into the parking lot.

"Get back, get back!" Grace screamed at them, "The chopper's gonna come down!"

A thrashing of meows and human screams came from the spinning USARIC helicopter.

"Get back!" Grace shouted at the others as Siyam ran up behind her.

WHUDDA-WHUDDA-SLIP-CRASH-CRASH-CRASH!

The blades of the back rotors sliced against the *Rollneck*

Kojak sign. Segments of it blasted in all directions, causing an electrical storm. The neon rendition of the bald man burst into flames and crashed against the ground.

The chopper hit the cement. The first rotor's blades stabbed into the side of the vehicle itself, pushing it onto its side.

WHIINNNEEE… KERRR-RASSSHHHH!

A dozen cats hopped out from the helicopter and landed on the road. They dispersed in all directions, howling and squealing at the night sky.

The patrons from the building ran in all directions, screaming. Some of them held their forearms and Viddy Media ink at the scene in an attempt to record what was happening.

"Are you crazy?" Grace shouted at those brave enough to film what was happening, "Get back."

The once-tiny white dot overseeing the event from the night sky fanned out like bubble by another inch.

The helicopter tumbled over and around, slamming the remainder of its blades against the floor. One of them caught the mercenary's legs and severed it from his thigh, "Gaaahh!"

The rest of the cats propelled from the sides of the helicopter and darted across the road, away from danger.

"Get out of there, now," Grace yelled at them.

SLAP-SLAP-SLAP-BAMMM.

The second rotor slowed to a halt. Its blades crunched against the ground.

The mercenaries inside crashed to the ground, unconscious.

Grace and Siyam dared not move any closer for fear of the vehicle going up in flames.

"Quick, we gotta gather up all the cats and get them out of here."

Grace peered forward and noticed something shuffling in the tilted cockpit, "Wait, what's that?"

A paw.

Then a furry arm.

Two flapping ears of an Egyptian Mau.

She clambered over the lip of the door and bolted toward

Grace and Siyam, "Meow."

"Hey, girl," Grace crouched down and held out her arms, "We're here to rescue you. How did you do *that*?"

The Mau lifted her paw and licked her claw. A shiny, white cuticle - made of titanium.

Grace gasped and tried to process what she'd seen, "Oh, wow…" she turned to the other cats to find that they had the same contraption fitted to their paws.

"They're all—"

"—Meeooww," The Mau ran her claws against the ground,

The helicopter's final blade hit the cement.

KA-BLAAAA-AAA-AAAMMM!

It exploded with such force that its charcoaled body launched thirty feet into the air and exploded a second time.

A slab of fiery helicopter slammed down on both cars, bursting their windows.

Grace and Siyam didn't know how to respond. She looked at the Mau in shock.

"Miew."

"Umm," Grace cleared her throat, "Let's get you and your friends out of here. *Right now…*"

Chrome Valley
United Kingdom

Jamie Anderson pulled his rucksack over his shoulders. He crossed the main road that separated Chrome Valley's east and west side.

A swarm of chuckling school children ran past and ignored him.

"Ugh, there's Lame-y Anderson," one of the chubby kids cackled at his excited friends, "His cat lost the competition."

"Yeah," squealed an excited girl, "A giant loser, just like her ugly owner."

"Lame-y Anderson, Lame-y Anderson," all the kids chanted in unison as they ran off around the corner.

"Shut up," he muttered

He knew in his heart of hearts that it was only a matter of

time before he'd become famous. Everyone would know Jelly won. Maybe *then* they'd like him.

Until then he'd continue to be the loner. On one hand, it suited him. He enjoyed the privacy. On the other, having no friends was a lonely prospect.

No one to talk to.

It wasn't long before he turned the same corner near the Waddling Gate cemetery. He and his mother buried his late father there nearly six years ago.

He couldn't bear to look at the black gates, nor the church standing behind it. The very sight alone upset him. Worse, he had to walk past it twice a day to and from school.

Jamie looked at his Viddy Media ink. 8:10 am.

Plenty of time to make the start of school and his first period.

He looked up to see the chubby kid pant and wheeze further up the road, trying to keep up with his friends.

"One day, Raymond," Jamie stopped walking. He muttered and scowled, quietly, "I'll kick your fat arse into the moon."

A screeching of tires came a few feet behind him. He turned around and saw a black van spin onto the road at speed.

"Pfft. *Whatever.*"

He kept his head down and watched each foot pace in front of the other. It was hard for him to *not* notice the engine and wheels slowing down behind him. as he walked along the sidewalk.

The van crawled to a steady three miles per hour.

Jamie looked over his shoulder and squinted at the windshield. Its darkened, limousine effect prevented him from seeing the driver. The reflection of the trees from the cemetery were the only thing visible on the surface of the windshield.

He resumed his journey to school.

The van did the same.

Jamie knew the van was following him.

"Ugh, no," Jamie looked at the cemetery gates and grew

anxious. He could jump the railings and run across the grounds to safety.

The van slammed on its brakes, startling the boy.

He stopped dead in his tracks.

The side door slid open and revealed a person in a black balaclava. She grabbed the lip of the door and held her head out, "Jamie Anderson?"

He kept his mouth shut and chose not to interact with the stranger.

"Ugh, don't mess me around, you little turd," the person said. A feminine voice, to be sure. Judging by her voice and svelte frame she couldn't have been very old, "Are *you* Jamie Anderson?"

"Who's asking?"

"It's him," yelled a masked man from behind the door. Jamie scrunched his face at the woman.

She produced a gun and lay it across her lap, "Jamie?"

"P-Please leave me alone."

"Jamie Anderson?"

"My mom told me never to speak to strangers."

The woman wasn't interested in his excuses. She lifted the gun and traced her finger along the barrel, "I know it's you, but I need to be sure. What's your date of birth?"

He hoped she wouldn't point the gun at him, "March tenth, twenty-one-twelve."

"Yes, it's you all right," she said.

Jamie blinked, frozen on the spot. He didn't dare move a *muscle*, "What do you want?"

The woman shifted her behind across the seat the van and patted the vacant space next to her, "Get in."

Acknowledgments

For K
Also to:
My immediate family.
The CVB Gang Members / ARC Street Team.
Jolene Huber, the real captain of the ship.
Jennifer Long, the "Bonnie" of stalkers.
Adele Embrey, the "Androgyne" of proofing.
The members and admins of 20BooksTo50K.

Extra special thanks to the following authors for all their help. I really appreciate it:
Michael Anderle, Craig Martelle, Jonathan Brazee, Justin Sloan, Martha Carr, Charley R. Case, Amy Duboff, Sarah Noffke, Dominique Mondesir, and JN Chaney.

This book is dedicated to the memory of Mandy Reed. She passed away five days before this book's release.
A devoted mother, an exceptional wit and a loyal and voracious ARC reader.
A "star cat" in every sense and one of my first champions.
I will miss you.

Up next... Star Cat 4, 5, & 6.

Please leave a review at Amazon.

Get Your FREE ebook

The Last Trilogy has Landed.

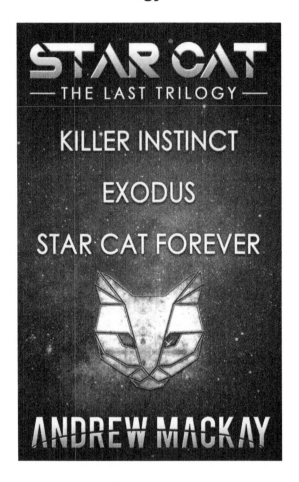

About the author

Andrew Mackay is an author,
screenwriter and film critic. A
former teacher, Andrew
writes in multiple genres:
satire, crime, horror,
romantic thrillers and sci-fi.

His passions include
daydreaming, storytelling, smoking, caffeine, and writing
about himself in the third person.

A word from the author

I hope you enjoyed this book. Please check out my other
books at Amazon and remember to follow me there.

**If you enjoyed the book, please leave a review online at
Amazon US, UK and Goodreads.** Reviews are integral for
authors and I would dearly appreciate it.

I love to engage directly with my readers. Please get in touch
with me - I look forward to hearing from you. **Happy reading!**

Email: andrew@chromevalleybooks.com

NOTE: If you purchased this title at Amazon, then you can
download the e-book version for **FREE** with Kindle
Matchbook. The last pages of the e-book version contains
exclusive author notes and behind-the-scenes material for
each title. It's a real treat for fans, so download it now! ☺